LIFE'S LOTTERY

LIFE'S LOTTERY

KIM NEWMAN

TITAN BOOKS

LIFE'S LOTTERY
Print edition ISBN: 9781781165560
E-book edition ISBN: 9781781165577

Published by Titan Books
A division of Titan Publishing Group Ltd
144 Southwark Street, London SE1 0UP

First edition: April 2014

1 3 5 7 9 10 8 6 4 2

A CIP catalogue record for this title is available from the British Library.

Printed and bound in the United States.

If Napoleon, for Tom Tunney
If Illya, for David Cross

This is the story of a man who always made the wrong choice. He could have had either of two jobs; he picked the dead end. He could have married either of two women; he picked the nag. He could have invested in either of two businesses; he picked the one that went bankrupt. Finally, he decides to abandon his old life, to change his identity and start again. He goes to the airport and finds he can get on either of two flights; he chooses the plane with the engine that explodes over the Atlantic. So, he's in mid-air, in an aeroplane struggling to stay aloft, surrounded by panicking passengers. He goes down on his knees in prayer and begs, 'St Francis, help me!' The Heavens open, and a divine light floods the cabin. An angelic voice asks, 'St Francis *Xavier* or St Francis of *Assisi*?'

DAVE ALLEN
(approx.)

1

My friend, you have a choice. *Of course*, you have a choice. You can go this way or that. You can call heads or tails. You can have coffee or tea.

It's simple.

Except maybe you don't have a choice. Because of matters settled before your father's sperm met your mother's egg, you don't have a choice. You're set on this road. You always call heads. You must have tea.

Maybe that's the choice. To have a choice or not to have a choice. Free will or predestination.

You choose.

Think about it for a while. Use one side of the paper. Leave a wide margin. Don't skip on regardless, though. Really *think*. It's important. It affects everything.

Get back to me when you've made up your mind. When you've chosen.

When you've made your choice, go to 2.

2

This much is certain: you make your first choices before you're born. To kick or not to kick. To turn or not to turn. In the womb, you're already a person.

Determinations are made before you have even rudimentary consciousness. Though you're the size and shape of a comma, each of your cells holds a template. The parameters within which you will grow are set.

You are male. You are white, nondescript Caucasian. Your eyes are hazel. Your hair will be blond in childhood but darken in your teens.

You'll have good teeth, eyes that won't dim until (if) you reach your late fifties, an average-sized penis.

These are the cards you are dealt. You can do little to change them. Nevertheless, you can bet or fold.

Other things are conditional: on diet, exercise regimen, cultural influence. For instance, were you born into certain religious groups or in certain countries, you'd be circumcised in infancy. As it is, you'll keep your foreskin into adulthood. If you're ever circumcised, for medical reasons or upon conversion, it'll be your choice.

You should attain an adult height of five feet eight inches. Even with poor nutrition and a childhood spent in a prison cell (unlikely, but not impossible) you will not be shorter than five five. Only under truly extraordinary circumstances (for example, being raised outside Earth's gravitational pull) will you grow more than half an inch taller than five eight. Sorry. Those are the breaks. Learn to live with them.

It is possible that your mother's pregnancy, by her choice or not, will be terminated before you are born.

In which case, regrettably, you must go to 0.

It was once a doctors' commonplace that 'The first five minutes of life are the most risky'. The saw fell into disuse because wags invariably counter-commented, 'The last five are pretty dodgy too.'

Find a pack of cards. Take a card at random. Replace, shuffle well, draw again. If you get the Queen of Spades twice in a row, you are born dead. Go to 0.

Without knowing it, you've already been lucky. You are born in the Royal Berkshire Hospital in Reading in 1959, to middle-class parents with a comfortable income. In earlier centuries, other countries or different social classes, your survival chance would be a single draw from a pack of cards. In some cases, a draw from only the suit of spades. In others, a draw from the face cards of spades.

Your birthday is 4 October. Your astrological sign, should you care, is Libra. The only non-living sign in the Zodiac. The Scales. There's an amusing irony there, if you're disposed to consider it. Your nationality is British. Cecil Rhodes is alleged to have said that to be born an

Englishman means that you take first prize in the lottery of life.

You are delivered at a quarter to nine in the morning.

'A boy,' your mother is told.

She smiles at you, weakly. Your delivery has not been as traumatic as the twenty-hour ordeal which, three years ago, produced your sister, Laraine. Still, you've demanded all her strength. During birth, your mother thought she was enduring the most extreme physical pain you'll put anyone through in your life. Whether she is right is almost entirely your decision.

Your mother is Louise Frances Marion, born Louise Frances Mason in 1931. After school, she worked in a bank, where she met your father. Since marriage in 1952, she has been a full-time housewife and, latterly, mother. Your father is Harold Collin Marion, born 1923. He served in Burma in the war and is assistant manager of a high-street bank.

Physically, like many boys, you take after your mother. If you let your hair grow and shave your beard, you will at eighteen look much like she did when she married.

Nurses fuss around. The umbilicus is severed and tied. A great deal of mucus discharge is wiped off and tidied away. The afterbirth is disposed of. In 1959, they don't believe in leaving a healthy mess alone.

Somewhere, a wireless is playing, the Light Programme. The first music you hear is 'Smoke Gets in Your Eyes' by The Platters. Your first sight, upside-down, is your exhausted mum, her hazel eyes bright with tears.

All this you will forget.

Once born, you have the power of self-determination. You do not have a complex understanding of the world, but you are born with a tenacious will.

You can choose not to draw the first breath. Or the second. In which case, leave now. Go to 0.

You're still with the programme, as they will say in the 1980s. I'm glad. Nobody likes a quitter.

You're professionally slapped on the bum. You open your lungs and squeak, instinctively sucking in hospital air. Oxygen tickles your alveoli, passes into your blood (you are Type O) and heads for your brain. Congratulations: you are sapient. Your thought processes are already more intricate than those of the cleverest cat that ever lived.

Your dad is allowed in, smelling strongly of Players Navy Cut cigarettes, and you are presented to him. Everyone is thoroughly satisfied with you. You are a cynosure, the object of everyone's attention and approval. Your first smile brings universal delight.

Enjoy it. This may be the last time.

Your parents have had the usual name discussions. Mum wants you to be Rhett or Melanie, after characters in her favourite book, *Gone With the Wind*. If you'd been a girl, Dad would've allowed Melanie, though his choice (for no reason he could articulate) was Morag. But your sister has a slightly recessive R and Dad doesn't want you to be Rhett in case you can only pronounce the name 'Whett'. He puts his foot down and insists you take his mother's maiden name, Keith.

Though your family are only Christmas and Easter C of E, you are Christened. Keith Oliver Marion.

Gifts from historical circumstance and the National Health shower upon you: vaccinations against smallpox, diphtheria and polio. You'll almost certainly not get tuberculosis. You'll be a bottle baby. You'll live in a comparatively warm, clean house. You will not be ignored.

Again, you've been dealt a better hand than many born in other times and places. You live hundreds of years after the plague was driven from Europe, a century after infant mortality was the favoured method of contraception within many English marriages. Barbarian hordes do not descend on Reading in the early 1960s, sweeping from house to house, slaughtering men, enslaving women, tossing babies on spears.

Certain elements of your future are assured. By your parents' standards, you'll be properly fed and clothed. Education to a certain standard is guaranteed. A National Insurance number has been set aside for you. You won't be conscripted into the armed forces. Unless you are declared a lunatic, convicted and imprisoned, or elevated to the monarchy, you will have the right to vote.

From time to time, as you sneer at a plate of spinach or struggle with long division, people – mostly your parents – will tell you that you ought to be grateful. Unless you turn into some sort of saint at an early age, which is about as likely as being made King, you won't be able to give more than a grudging admission that yes, you ought to be grateful. You not having known any other life, 'ought to be' will never translate into 'are'. Don't feel too guilty about it. It's not really a flaw in your character, nor in the collective character of your late baby-boom generation (though your parents, sensibilities shaped by rationing, think it is).

It's the human condition.

Alone in your skull, you can only imagine the outside world. You can never *know*. You can't *truly* experience – though empathy, art and observation offer approximations – what it's like to be someone else living another life. You can only be you. The sooner you get to grips with that, the less mental anguish you'll suffer over the question.

Again, unless you're some sort of saint. Do you want to be a saint? Seriously? Most saints suffer on Earth. Many villains prosper. Remember this. It will inform the decisions you'll be asked to make.

Then again, there are many definitions of 'suffering' and 'prosperity'.

In 1964, your mother has another child, James. He is born with a slight harelip. You are delighted, at least at first. You were afraid you would have another sister, who would gang up with Laraine, whom you think of as 'bossy', against you. A brother, you feel, will reinforce you in the undeclared war with your sister. This is an emotional, not intellectual, perception. As soon as James develops a character, you – and Laraine – grow out of it.

You have many toys. Two teddy bears, Acorn and Big Ted. A wooden fire-engine. A clockwork train. A box of lead soldiers passed down from an uncle. Lego bricks enough to build a Great Wall. Slightly later, spaceships and dinosaurs will invade the toy-box, joining faithfuls whose popularity peaked years before you were born. The toys of your parents' childhoods are still familiar objects to you. Decades later, it might strike you that you were of the last generation to take equal delight in tin spinning tops and plastic Daleks.

You, James and Laraine have books and are told stories. *Teddy Bear Coalman*, *Upside-Down Gonk's Circus*, *Little Noddy Goes to Toyland*. Later, as you start to recognise letters and words, Mum reads *The Lion, the Witch and the Wardrobe* and *Winnie the Pooh* to you. Your sister reads Enid Blyton's Famous Five books, and you are impatient to catch up. Soon, you start on Tintin and Biggles.

You and Laraine learn *The Big Book of Riddles* by heart and madden your parents and other grown-ups by chanting, 'What's big, red and eats rocks?' or, 'Where do policemen live?' until they wearily (and mendaciously) reply, 'I don't know.' Then you scream, 'A big red rock-eater,' or 'Letsbe Avenue,' and collapse in helpless laughter.

Your favourite book, which you read until its covers fall off, is *The Buccaneers Annual*, a collection of illustrated stories about Captain Dan Tempest, an adventurer who has sworn allegiance to the Crown and preys only on Spanish rogues. It also has articles about real-life pirates like Blackbeard and Captain Kidd, with black-and-white pictures (which you colour with crayons) of their exploits and fates. It takes you a while to realise the annual is based on a television series which finished before you were born.

During the pirate craze, you plead with your indulgent parents for model galleons and cannon. You prize Herge's *The Secret of the Unicorn* and *Red Rackham's Treasure* above the other Tintin books. Dad reads a heavily abridged *Treasure Island* to you and helps draw maps on graph paper. The two of you construct an imaginary Caribbean archipelago, pinpointing the location of buried booty on each island. As you grow older, you and your dad won't often have the time or the inclination to share enterprises or interests. Later, if you keep them, the maps will be worth more to you than treasure would have been.

You have a pirate outfit: a hat with the Jolly Roger on the crown, an eyepatch, a plastic cutlass. Your favourite game is boarding the dining-room. Mum worries you'll hurt yourself (and the curtains) swinging from the rigging. Once, you are caught prising up loose floorboards under the bathroom mat. You tell Mum you are looking for treasure. Eyepatch, hat and cutlass are confiscated for a week. You feel like Dan Tempest during his months of unjust confinement in a Tortuga dungeon, and rejoice at the freedom of the high seas when your pirate accoutrements are ceremonially returned to you.

Unlike many of your contemporaries, you do not remember a time when your family did not have a television set. The first Kennedy assassination makes no impression on you, but you vividly remember the first episode of *Doctor Who*, in which two teachers learn that one of their pupils is from another planet and that her white-haired grandfather has a time machine disguised as a police phone box. Possibly, you later discover *Doctor Who* started the weekend Kennedy was shot and wonder how you can remember one but not the other.

In your childhood, Doctor Who is a more important figure than John Kennedy. William Hartnell will regenerate as Patrick Troughton before you learn that Harold Wilson, who has the same name as your dad, and Lyndon Johnson, whom you think of as the regenerated spaceman who was once Kennedy, are the prime minister of Great Britain and president of America. Jon Pertwee, on a new colour TV that is the envy of your schoolfriends, is the Doctor by the time you think you understand the difference between Labour and Tory. Tom Baker is in charge of the TARDIS when you hear Peter Cook on the wireless, explaining that 'In America, they have the Republicans, who are the equivalent of our Conservative Party, and the Democrats, who are the equivalent of our Conservative Party.'

Dad was for Clement Attlee in 1945, but has voted Tory ever since. Nevertheless, he admires Wilson's 'get-up-and-go'. Mum, clinging to politics passed on by her father, has voted Liberal in the last two elections but will vote for Wilson in 1970. You should be old enough to cast a vote in the 1979 election, and may choose between Margaret Thatcher, James Callaghan, David Steel and Screaming Lord Sutch.

A year after James is born, Dad is (finally, according to him) given a managership, of a branch in Sedgwater, a market town in Somerset. The Marion family, which is still the universe to you, moves house. At the time, it seems the end of the world. How will you live without your familiar room, without your friend Gary Black from across the road, without the pirate's cave in the cupboard under the stairs?

Within a week, you feel you've lived in your new home for ever. In the new house, which seems as huge as a mansion, you have your own room. You soon forget you ever had to share with your sister. Laraine, who alternates indulgence and hostility, is old enough to be jubilant at a safe haven free from the invasions of her baby brothers.

The vast back garden becomes a whole island, which you constantly explore. Dad tells you to stay out of the shed where he keeps his tools, frightening you with stories of poisonous spiders lurking in shadowy cobwebs that are spun faster than he can clean them away. Laraine has a horror of spiders, which you don't want to admit you share. The one picture in *The Buccaneers Annual* you can't look at shows Dan Tempest tunnelling out of a dungeon, surprised by compound eyes shining behind a curtain of black web.

Staying well away from the arachnid-haunted shed, you mount a serious surveying expedition, drafting in James as First Mate, and bury a tin of marbles – unpitted glassies, with swirls of colour – in a foot-deep hole, putting a dried bird-skull and a dead shrew on top of the tin before replacing the earth. You draw a map, marking the secret location of the treasure with a big cross. Somehow, despite the map, you never find the tin again. The treasure is lost, maybe for ever.

Dad would like a finned car like the ones in American television programmes, but buys a sensible, made-in-Britain family Austin. He drives into town every day. Your house is on the Achelzoy road, at the edge of Sedgwater, almost in the wild country. Mum learns to drive so she can do the shopping on Saturday mornings.

The family owns a washing-machine (Gran, Mum's mum, still uses a mangle), a fridge, a three-piece suite, an electric oven, a 'hi-fi'. Laraine lobbies for a transistor radio of her own, but you prefer a cabinet-sized valve set, which is put in your bedroom. The living-room contains a thin oval coffee table low enough for you to climb on and repel boarders, the kitchen has formica-topped work surfaces, all cushions and pillows are filled with foam not feathers.

Choices are made for you. Mum decides what to serve at meals, though as an infant you have a choice of whether you eat happily or reject with tears. Dad decides the family will move from Reading to the West Country. Your parents think you and your brother and sister should have separate rooms.

Mum resists her mother's ideas of what children should wear and kits you out for kindergarten in what she describes (in a mocking tone that horrifies Beatle-mad Laraine) as 'fab mod gear': a blue bobble-hat, a tiny duffel coat, yellow wellingtons. Since you can't wear your pirate outfit to kindergarten, you make sure to carry your eyepatch in your pocket, so that you are secretly a buccaneer, if outwardly the image of Paddington Bear.

Disputes between you and your sister, about what to watch on telly or what to call the stray cat that has been accepted into the family, are settled by your parents. (You get your own way about the cat, which is called Phones after the puppet on *Stingray*.) Your parents pick which seaside you go to for your holidays: Falmouth or Scarborough in the '60s, Ibiza or Knossos in the '70s. You are sent to kindergarten, as you will soon be sent to Big School.

For a long time, without thinking about it, you assume you never have a choice. Sometimes you get your own way, sometimes you don't. There's nothing you can actually do about it, no higher court in which to plead your case.

It is possible you'll go through your whole life this way, allowing others to choose for you, following the path of least resistance, unable to decide a preference. If asked 'Heads or tails?' you have a hard time giving an answer. If pressed, you say one or the other, favouring each about evenly. You see no difference between Superman and Batman, Labour and Tory, pease porridge hot and pease porridge cold. Between life and death.

Such people are not rare.

If you are one, **go to 3 and 4 and 5** and all subsequent possibles. But don't get involved. It can't hurt you, but it can't transport you to raptures either.

By the way: if this is you, I'm sorrier than I can say. Believe me, you will die having never really been alive. You riffle through all the possibles but in the end you **go to 0** having been **0** all along.

Still with me, Keith? Good man. You're not yet seven and you've successfully walked a tightrope over a chasm. You've chosen life over death, at least for the moment. And you've resisted the comforts of indifference.

Soon, shockingly, you'll be confronted with a choice. The first of many.

Perhaps it's better not to weigh choices too long. If you consider all sides of the argument over and over before doing anything, you often make a decision after the time for decision has passed and, by default, choose inaction over action. That might be a subtler way of riffling through life, thinking too much instead of not enough. But the end result is, again, a life not lived.

Some choices truly are meaningless, even on a macrocosmic scale. The fate of worlds may rest on whether you have tea or coffee. Equally, nothing at all of consequence can come from a decision to live or die.

Deal with it. Everybody else does. Somehow.

Anyway, here's how it happens.

In September 1966, you have to go to Big School. Some of your friends from kindergarten – Michael Dixon, Barry Mitcham – go at the same time. Laraine has been going to Big School ever since you moved to Sedgwater, but orders you not to hang around her or her friends. Without anyone really telling you, you've got the idea that as a six-year-old boy you aren't supposed to play with girls. Especially older girls.

Ash Grove County Primary School is like Denbeigh Kindergarten, except in a bigger room with more children. Your teacher is Miss Slowley, who takes Class One. In the morning, she asks everyone in turn to stand up and say their name and what their father does.

'Keith Marion,' you say, when your turn comes. 'My dad is a bank manager.'

Shane Bush, whose dad works in the jam factory, laughs. There's a girl in class called Marion Halsted. Shane thinks it's funny that you have a girl's name.

Miss Slowley doesn't think it's funny. She tells Class One you are born with your name and it doesn't mean anything.

'Keith isn't a girl, Shane isn't a bush and I don't always do things slowly. Though sometimes I do.'

'So is Keith sometimes a girl?' Shane asks.

Everyone laughs. You feel bad, hearing the laughter. Close to crying. You feel especially bad because Miss Slowley almost laughs too. You hate Big School. Everyone here laughs at you.

After the whole of Class One has told Miss Slowley their names and everyone except Maxwell Lewis, who says he doesn't know, has told what their dad does, a bell goes, and Miss Slowley says you can all go out in the playground. When the bell goes again, you have to come back to the classroom. Laraine has already told you about this. It is morning break.

In the playground, long-legged and towering Class Six boys play football, using bundled-up jumpers as goal posts. Middle children hang from a climbing-frame, playing 'Off-ground Touch'. You see

Laraine skipping with her friends and think better of talking to her. You don't want to have to tell her Class One laughed at you, anyway.

'Girl,' someone says.

It is Shane. He has others with him. Maxwell Lewis, Paul Mysliwiec, Ivor Barber. And a girl, Mary Yatman, whose dad is a policeman. They are Shane Bush's gang.

'I'm not a girl,' you say.

You don't want to cry but know you might. When you have bad dreams about being chased by scuttling giant spiders, you can wake up crying and Mum will soothe you. If you fall off your tricycle and scrape your knee bloody, you can cry. When your pirate hat was blown overboard while you were on a boat trip at Lyme Regis in the summer, you were inconsolable for days. Mum and Dad got you a new hat (actually, a better one, with a silvery skull-headed pin) but it wasn't the same, and you haven't worn it as much.

You are close to crying now and realise it. If Shane keeps calling you a girl and if his gang join in, there's a danger you will cry.

You can't think ahead at six. You're a *young* six. You don't know that, if you cry now, you'll always be the boy who cried, always be a girl. But instinct – a powerful, not-to-be-underestimated force – tells you crying would be a disastrous thing to do.

You wish you had your lost-and-gone-for-ever hat. Then you could face up to Shane as bravely as Captain Kidd or Blackbeard, or even a lowly privateer like Sir Henry Morgan. Now, you worry that you will snivel like Israel Hands or any other scurvy swab.

'You got a tellyvision?'

This surprises you. It's not the question you expect from Shane. You nod a yes.

'You watch *Man From U.N.C.L.E.*?'

Your bedtime is seven o'clock, but you are allowed, as a special treat, to stay up and watch *The Man From U.N.C.L.E.* on Thursdays. You follow the adventures of the suave American Napoleon Solo and the unsmiling Russian Illya Kuryakin, heroic spies who save the free world every week. Spies are almost as fascinating to you as pirates.

Shane's gang all wear triangular U.N.C.L.E. badges, with the number 11. You wish you had a badge like that.

You nod again. 'Yes.'

'Who do you like?'

You don't know it yet, but you have been asked to make a choice. You're relieved Shane doesn't seem to want to make you cry. But you have a feeling in your tummy that you can't put a word to. As though you might be sick, but not really. You might also do something good, like when your treasure-map drawings got gold stars in kindergarten.

You just don't know.

'Who do you like, girl?' Shane asks again. 'Napoleon Solo or Illya Kuryakin?'

If you like Napoleon Solo, go to 3. If you like Illya Kuryakin, go to 4.

3

'Who do you like, girl?' Shane asks again, 'Napoleon Solo or Illya Kuryakin?'

You think about it. Napoleon Solo has a number 11 on his badge, like Shane's gang. Illya Kuryakin has a number 2.

Maybe that's why you say, 'Napoleon.'

'Do you want to be in our gang?' Shane asks.

Shane Bush's gang gathers around you in a half-circle, accepting you.

'For a girl, you're okay,' Shane says.

'For a bush, so are you,' you reply.

Shane laughs and calls you daft. The gang join in. For the rest of the morning break, you play *Man From U.N.C.L.E.*, shooting THRUSH agents with finger guns, escaping from deadly death-traps, saving the free world.

Big School is all right.

At dinner break, you quietly scrape the horrid custard off your jam roly-poly and give it to Shane, who, unbelievably, likes the vile yellow slime. With two helpings of custard in him, Shane admits you're a good lad.

For six years at Ash Grove, you are in Shane Bush's gang. Ivor moves to a new town in Class Three, but Paul, Max and Mary stay all through primary school. Others join the gang, including Barry Mitcham, whom you knew in kindergarten, and another girl, Vanda

Pritchard. You like Vanda more than Mary, who occasionally hits you when she feels mean. Paul and Max wonder why Shane wants you in the gang; sometimes, they are nasty to you.

When Mary or Paul or Max picks on you, you go crybaby, which makes things worse. Still, you can't help it. Despising your weakness, you work hard to overcome it, proving your bravery to yourself and the gang. Sometimes, you go further than is sensible, taking a fall from the climbing-frame or one of the trees in the copse at the far end of the playground, earning the right to leak a few tears, holding in your impulse to throw a sobbing fit.

Shane is clever but naughty. He gets away with things by being charming, amusing grown-ups enough to avoid punishment for offences which would get you or Max sent to the corner for the rest of the lesson. Later, you understand why Shane prefers Napoleon to Illya: like Robert Vaughn, Shane has something funny to say when he's in trouble, always seems cool-headed, never takes anything seriously; in shorts and a cardy, he gives the impression of being well groomed, though he also takes knocks falling off the climbing-frame.

In Shane's gang, you're Illya Kuryakin. Faithful sidekick, shyer than the hero, more sensitive, never at the centre of things. It doesn't occur to you until Class Six that you're cleverer than Shane but less willing to take a chance. When the class is asked a question, you often don't put up your hand even if you know the answer. Shane always puts up his hand: if he doesn't know the answer, he makes a joke; if he's not right, he can be funny.

You wonder why Paul and Max don't really like you. Once in a while, when the mood takes him, Shane sides with them against you. If the gang plays *Doctor Who*, you have to be the Doctor so the rest can be Daleks, wheeling about the playground with arms stuck out, squawking, 'Exterminate!' This sometimes ends with you crying. Paul and Max, and especially Mary, are contemptuous when you cry, but Shane usually comes out of his mood and sticks up for you.

Shane also sticks up for Mary. There's something not quite right with her. Even teachers notice, though they pretend not to. Shane says Mary is a proper hardnut, and admires her wildness: she's the one who suggests in Class Three that you take slates from the school roof to build your own club house, an escapade which gets you all sent home with notes from Mr Brunt, the headmaster. Shane also tries to calm her down when she gets angry. Mary has rages the way you have crying fits. She loses control. Where you become pathetic, Mary becomes terrifying. It is Shane who makes up her inevitable nickname, Scary Mary.

When Vanda joins the gang – because she's Shane's next-door neighbour – Mary treats her worse than Paul and Max treat you. Shane has to look out for Vanda: if left alone with Mary, she'll be tormented to tears. Mary hates Vanda because she's a girl.

'Why do we have to have girls in the gang?' Mary whines.

Once, off your guard, you say the obvious thing: 'Mary, *you're* a girl. We have you.'

It's the worst beating of your primary-school experience. Mary slaps you until you're crying, then kicks you in the shins, barrels punches into your chest and face. Shane needs Paul's help to haul her off you.

'I'm *not*, I'm *not*, I'm *not*,' she screams at you. 'Say I'm not a girl, Keith! Say I'm *not*!'

You've lost it too and are crying too hard to say anything. Mrs Newcomen, the Class Three teacher, breaks it up.

Next day, Mr Brunt comes to Class Three while Mary is sent off to see someone. Mr Brunt talks to the whole class about Mary, explaining that she has problems and you should try to help her, to understand that she doesn't always mean the things she does. Like Shane and you, and unlike Paul and Max and Vanda, Mary sits on the Top Table. She reads better than you and can do sums faster than anyone in Class Three. She isn't stupid like Timmy Gossett, who is on the Bottom Table and can't get through *Janet and John*, but she has problems. You and Shane look at each other, knowing no grown-up will ever really understand Scary Mary's problems. Sometimes, a monster comes up behind her eyes and everybody had better look after themselves. Even Robert Hackwill of Class Six, the official School Bully, knows better than to pick on her.

After Mr Brunt has talked to you, Mary comes back to class. At break-time, she says she was taken to a lady named Dr Killian, a psychiatrist, who asked her questions about herself and why she gets angry so often. For a while afterwards, Mary doesn't have her monster spells. Eventually, when Vanda has her hair done in Indian plaits, Mary (out of boredom, you suppose) starts tugging them, pulling harder and harder, turning yelps to cries, not stopping until she is stopped. Even when you get to Class Six and start having your eleventh birthdays, Mary's monster comes out from time to time. She isn't as bad as she was: not because the monster has gone away, but because she's got better at hiding it from grown-ups. Likewise, you don't cry so often, but inside are still the same boy who could burst into tears at the slightest prod.

At Ash Grove, you learn to read and do sums. You have a head start on other children, because you already knew your letters and numbers in Class One. You get to the Top Table in Class Two and stay on it all the way up to Class Six. You have Painting, Music and Movement, History, PE, Stories and Sums. You draw better than most, though not as neatly as some of the girls. In Stories, most boys write about football or the war, but you write about pirates (the old craze dims, but the interest is still there), spies, robots, monsters from space and jungle explorers. Teachers indulge your interests, but you sense they'd prefer you to be more normal.

Dad, who fought the Japs in the war, buys you comics and stories about it: you like Biggles and Sergeant Rock, but prefer Doctor Who and Superman. Laraine, who goes to the Girls' Grammar and wears a straw boater and a bottle-green blazer with a badge on the top pocket, moans that you only like horrible things, like robots and pirates, but you discount her opinion because she is only interested in clothes and pop music. Her favourite song is 'White Horses' by Jacky, which drives you mad if you hear it.

Sometimes, Shane Bush's gang expands to take in almost all the school. In Class Four, everyone plays a game called 'Timmy's Germs'. At break-time, someone rubs his hand on Timmy Gossett and then touches someone else, saying, 'Now you've got Timmy's germs.' The victim, choking and coughing, runs around and passes on the deadly touch. Timmy's germs spread rapidly. Everyone falls wriggling on the grass behind the school. Only Timmy is left standing, blinking stupid tears as he walks through the writhing dead.

One day, Timmy Gossett isn't in school and Mr Brunt comes to talk to you all, like he talked about Mary. He says that it's not Timmy's fault he's a bit dirty and that he is very upset about the way you treat him. While Mr Brunt speaks, you feel hotly guilty. But the next day Paul sticks his hand in Timmy's bird's-nest hair, picking up Timmy's germs, and comes after you, to pass them on. Paul slaps you harder than he needs to and says, 'Now, you've got Timmy's germs.'

What do you do?

If you chase Vanda and give her Timmy's germs, go to 109. If you shrug and tell Paul you don't want to play, go to 128.

4

'Who do you like, girl?' Shane asks again, 'Napoleon Solo or Illya Kuryakin?'

You think about it. Illya Kuryakin is small, quiet and blond. Not a leader, and often on his own. He's a bit like you.

Maybe that's why you say, 'Illya.'

Shane Bush's gang gather around you in a half-circle, backing you against a wall.

'We like Napoleon Solo,' Shane says.

'Illya Kuryakin's a girl,' says Mary Yatman.

She steps close and pushes you with both hands. You hit the wall, bumping your head. Hot tears start from your eyes.

'Girl,' sneers Mary. 'He's crying.'

Suddenly, you lose control. You sob, huddled on the ground. Between sobs, you draw in lungfuls of air and let out screams.

The whole world contracts. Children are drawn to you and watch, with interest. A grown-up comes, one of the teachers.

For the rest of the break, you cry and cry and cry. You hate Big School. Hate, hate, hate.

You've lost something before you realised you had a chance to have it.

Respect.

You will cry again, soon and often. You will be a girl.

At dinner break, everyone has to have custard with pudding. It's a school rule, you are told. Rules cannot be compromised. There are no exceptions. All children are treated the same. Custard is mandatory, inescapable, inevitable. No child in the history of Ash Grove County Primary School, stretching back to before the war, has ever got up from the dinner table without having eaten his custard. At home,

Mum already knows better than to serve you custard and she's a far better cook than the Ash Grove dinner ladies. School custard is thick as mud and sickly yellow. Its taste is indescribably vile, like sugared filth, dog's-muck and spinach, sewage in semolina.

Class One queue up first at the cafeteria and are given dinners on trays. You are guided to a table in the dinner hall and sat with Marion Halsted, Ivor Barber, Michael Dixon and Mary Yatman. The first course is sausages and mashed potatoes, which is acceptable. You eat quickly, always aware of the custard cooling and festering on your jam roly-poly. Then, you get up and walk to the tub where you are supposed to scrape out your leftovers – which you are told are given to farmers as pigswill. You think you have escaped.

Poised over the tub, you are caught. Mrs Fudge, the head dinner lady, catches you at the point of disposing of untouched pudding. She sends you back to your table with orders to eat. You sit down and look at the custard, folding your arms in refusal. Your table-mates, even Mary Yatman, almost admire your rebellion. They all shovel down their custard as if it were ice cream. After a while, Mrs Fudge comes over and tells you, as if you didn't know, that you haven't touched your pud. When she insists you have to eat the custard, you cry. When she says your pudding won't be taken away until you eat it, you cry harder.

Your sister, who knows about you and custard, laughs with her friends. Mrs Fudge, who has a hooked nose and orange hair, changes her approach and tells you how wonderful custard is. Children all over the world would be grateful for even the chance to lick a spoon of it. All around, treacherous kids gulp down the dreadful stuff, pretending to like it. You *know* school custard is made of worms and goblin's snot and that it eats away inside at your stomach, destroying your body bit by bit until you turn into custard yourself. The other children have been fooled by Mrs Fudge, who is Evil.

The dinner lady bends low over you and holds a spoon heaped with yellow gloop, waving it in front of your mouth, cooing soothing words like a hypnotist. You calm down, tears drying up. A wicked-witchy smile twitches across Mrs Fudge's lips and she says, 'There now, that's better.' You mop your cheeks with the sleeve of your cardigan. The yellow blob is still there on the spoon in front of your face. You see it move, dripping over the edges of the spoon, spattering on the table-top. Suddenly, Mrs Fudge pinches your nose. You open your mouth instinctively and the spoonful of custard is stabbed against your tongue.

The stuff is inside you. The taste – that horrible, *horrible* taste – is in your mouth, exploding outwards.

You spit the custard back at Mrs Fudge and produce a yell from your stomach and lungs that flows out and threatens to fill the whole dinner hall, rattling cutlery, cracking glasses, bursting eardrums. Mrs Fudge is driven back, wiping her face. All the other children, from Class One up to Class Six, are struck silent. You pause to draw breath, allowing a second or two of silence, then renew the scream, louder and louder.

Mrs Fudge calls Mr Brunt, the headmaster, and Miss Slowley, the Class One teacher. You still scream, trying to purge the custard from your body. You're out of your chair – two curves of plywood bolted to a tubular metal frame – and are on the floor, pounding with hands and feet. Everyone thinks you'll do yourself an injury. Finally, you run down. Your screams become sobs, painful after-burps of the explosion. Miss Slowley helps you up and finds a hankie to wipe your face.

Dinner break is over. Your roly-poly (and custard) is taken away, uneaten, and scraped into the pigswill tub. Everyone, kids and teachers, regards you with a kind of awe. Knowing a screeching beast is caged inside you, they walk carefully as if around an unexploded bomb. You have survived. You've got through dinner break without having to eat your custard. This is a victory.

Next day, as you push away your pud, Mrs Fudge only has to say, 'No more of that nonsense, Keith' to set you off. Cocooned inside your screaming fit, you know you can keep this up all the way through to Class Six in the unimaginably distant Dan Dare future of 1971. After a week, Mum and Mr Brunt hold negotiations behind the scenes and you are excused custard. Mrs Fudge never talks to you again, her world shattered. An exception has been made to the rules that are her life; she'll never forgive Mr Brunt for backing down, or forget you for defying her tyranny. You always knew you could sometimes get your way by crying. Now, you know losing control can frighten even grown-ups.

Your mother calls you 'Nuisance', Miss Slowley calls you 'sensitive', Shane calls you 'mental'. But whatever they call you, you are excused custard.

After a while, you don't even have to explode to get your way. Knowing what you are capable of makes grown-ups and children, even wild creatures like Mary Yatman and Timmy Gossett, wary of you. In Class Three, you have to spend an afternoon with a lady called Dr Killian, the school psychiatrist, talking about your fits. She's the first grown-up to realise that sometimes you don't really lose control, that you pretend. By then, you have proved yourself excellent at reading and drawing and have tried hard with sums. You only go off under extreme provocation. You overhear Mr Brunt telling Mum that Dr Killian thinks you'll grow out of it. You know the doctor is wrong: you haven't changed, you've just got cleverer about holding it in.

You have friends, mostly other children Shane and Mary pick on: Michael, who has a bad stutter, Timmy Gossett, who is the thickest of the Bottom Table thickos, and Vanda Pritchard, who wears glasses. You are all called girls, even Vanda who really is a girl. You say you think Shane and his gang are stupid, though Shane and Mary, who sit on the Top Table with you, are actually almost as clever as you and Michael.

Mary has rages in which she attacks other children, but may well be the cleverest in your class. She is the only person ever to hurt you so much that you are afraid to explode. In Class Two, she comes up and reaches between your legs, squeezing the sac you have only recently learned to call your balls, inflicting unprecedented pain that leaves you in silent agony.

In Class Three, Shane makes up a game called 'Mental Fits'. He taps you on the head at break-time and falls down screaming, imitating the way you used to be, usually laughing too much to do a good job of it. Shane's gang all make a habit of doing this, even Mary. You are almost flattered, though you realise they do it to mock you.

You're in Class Four when it happens. Your ordeal by custard was a long time ago, though Shane and Mary still throw 'Mental Fits' to make fun of you. It's break-time: you've exchanged your *Hornet* comic for the *Fantastic* Barry Mitcham's newsagent dad gets him, Shane and Mary writhe ignored on the grass, Gene Pitney's 'The Man Who Shot Liberty Valance' plays tinnily on a transistor radio. You are called away by someone standing in the copse of trees that is the farthest end of the playground.

'You,' the boy shouts. 'The one they call Mental.'

It's an older boy, in the uniform and blood-red cap of Dr Marling's, the Boys' Grammar. Shane and Mary leave off their 'Mental Fits' and pay attention. Barry runs away, towards the toilets. You all recognise Robert Hackwill, who left Ash Grove last year. He used to be official School Bully.

'Mental,' Robert shouts. 'Come here.'

He *must* think you're mental if he expects you to go.

'Come on. I've got someone you know here.'

Robert is with his only friend, Reg Jessup, who always stands around snickering when Robert hurts another child. You're certainly not going into the copse with Robert and Reg. Even Mary shakes her head at the idea.

'Keith,' squeaks a small voice, 'I'm weeing myself. They won't let me go to the lavvy.'

It is James, your little brother, new to Class One.

'Your brother's a shit. He's no good at all.'

Robert has said one of the Forbidden Words.

'Come and see your brother,' Reg says.

You see Robert and Reg, holding James by his shoulders. James's shorts are dark at the crotch. Wee trickles down his legs. He starts sniffling.

'Everyone heard two shots ring out,' Gene Pitney sings, 'one shot made Liberty fall…'

The bell goes for the end of break. Shane, Mary – even Scary Mary! – and the rest run off, back to the classroom. You don't move.

'C'mon, Mental,' Robert says. 'We're not going to hurt you.'

'Much,' adds Reg, laughing.

If you go to the classroom and get on with your sums, go to 6. If you go to a teacher and tell what's happening, go to 10. If you go into the copse to help James, go to 14.

5

'Dr Cross?'

'That's right. You'll be Susan.'

'Her I'll be.'

'Welcome to our, uh, happy home.'

'It's an honour to be here.'

'Some of our residents don't think that.'

'Of course.'

'This is Marion, by the way.'

'Can he hear us?'

'No reason why not. He's not in a coma.'

'He's asleep?'

'Not quite. Daydreaming, perhaps.'

'I can see the appeal.'

'Me too.'

'Wait a minute. Marion? *The* Marion? Of Marion syndrome?'

'I see you've read up on us. Yes, this is that Marion. Our most, um, notable resident. Excluding staff, of course. Quite a puzzler, our friend. Aren't you?'

'He looks so… well, so…'

'Yes?'

'Ordinary.'

'Quite right. Ordinary.'

6

In 1982, the week after your father's funeral, you are in town, early in a spring evening, going for a drink in the Lime Kiln with your brother.

Laraine has stayed home with Mum, but you both feel the need to get out of the memory-permeated house. James went into the army at sixteen and you haven't seen much of him in the last few years. You remember him as the kid who wet himself when you left him to Robert and Reg; now he's a tattooed squaddie, decorated for valour on the streets of Belfast. You're afraid to ask what 'valour' means. Calmly, without malice, he has said he'd like to be sent to the Falklands. You think he wants a chance to kill an Argie, just to see what it would be like.

The Lime Kiln is full, packed with drinkers whose dads are still alive or have been dead for so long that it doesn't matter. You think about James. Your younger brother seems to have taken on the job of Man of the Family. His eyes didn't water at the funeral, like yours did. He's willing to defend himself, his mates, his family, the country. You know you'd still crawl off to the classroom, shirking your responsibility, losing yourself in the abstractions of arithmetic.

As you force your way through to the bar, a cheer goes up. You wonder why, then remember James is in uniform. There's a drunken wave of patriotism going on in the aftermath of the invasion of the Falkland Islands, a frenzy of kill-the-Argies war-hunger. The barman is Max Lewis, with whom you were at school though he was never a special friend. James orders a couple of pints of bitter. A man claps him on the shoulder and offers to pay for the drinks.

James, flinching from the touch, turns to accept... and freezes. Pressed close to James by the crowd, you sense the tension which draws your brother tight as a bowstring an instant before you recognise the man with the money.

It's Robert Hackwill, grown up.

The Ash Grove School Bully has done well for himself. He wears a sheepskin coat and a trilby hat. His property business is flourishing and he is in line for a council seat. He has a flash car, a Jag. His smile splits the world horizontally in half.

Hackwill repeats his offer.

You look around for Jessup, never far from Hackwill, and spot him in a corner. Reg's smirk is still there, shaped by the fat in his face. He's still a sidekick.

What will James do? It's fifteen years later and Hackwill is off his guard. James thinks he could kill a stranger, and this is someone he hates. You know your brother must be thinking of breaking a glass in the grown-up bully's face.

You remember that day. When James wet himself while being given the worst Chinese burn in history and you ran off. You don't really know what they did to him then, and have tried not to imagine what it must have been like. For the first time, it occurs to you that it probably didn't go much beyond a bit of a shove and a few thumps. Robert and Reg were only twelve, James just six. Until now, you'd imagined infernal tortures and unspeakable atrocities. That night, at home safe, James looked accusations at you. He never told your parents how he came by his bruises, and you didn't speak up either. Telling on Robert Hackwill was an invitation to pain.

You have never talked about it with James. You wonder if it wasn't what led to you and your brother growing apart, living through your teens in a state of armed neutrality. Because you left him to Hackwill, he's never trusted you. He has found in himself the strength to look after himself.

Max puts two pints on the bar. James picks his up carefully, getting a good grip.

You can *see* the pint smashing against Hackwill's smile, glass exploding, blood and froth drenching him.

But James just takes a deep draught and swallows. Hackwill, smile fixed, eyes hardening, repeats his offer, as if James had not heard him over the din. Somehow, the noise of the pub dies down. You know everyone is paying attention.

James does it.

Like a shot-putter, he hefts the half-full glass, drawing it back level with his shoulder, ramming it at Hackwill's eyes. The sunburst of blood and beer and scream stills the whole pub.

A circle clears around James and Hackwill.

James kicks Hackwill in the ribs, over and over, grunting 'Fucker' with each connection. Bones break.

You are on the sidelines, watching. Nobody tries to break up the fight. No, this isn't a fight. This is a beating. A punishment beating, they call it in Northern Ireland.

James picks up a stool: not a balsawood prop from a Western, but a solidly made survivor of rowdy nights in the Lime Kiln. The stool doesn't break, but Hackwill does.

Max is on the phone, talking urgently.

James knows now he is on a deadline. The law will soon be here. He lifts the stool and looks around. His eyes, wild with cold fury, meet yours.

For a moment, you think he's going to batter you. You want to protect your head with your arms. He knows what you're thinking and is disgusted with you. Ever since the copse, he's been disgusted with you.

'Keith, you're as yellow as fucking school custard.'

James sees the one he is looking for: Reg Jessup, trying to make his way to the door. Someone stands in front of him, barring his way.

Everybody remembers their school bully. No one ever forgives.

Jessup is bowled across the pub towards James, a batsman wielding the sturdy stool. Jessup is thwacked across the face, losing teeth, and knocked down. James kneels by him and darts rapid punches into his face, opening old scabs on his knuckles.

The police arrive. Two constables. A bloke younger than James, and Mary Yatman. You knew she'd gone into the police, but have never seen her in uniform.

She hauls James upright. His rage vanished, he allows her to manhandle him. Limp, he gives no resistance as he is hustled out of the door.

Mary frees James into your care without charging him. You have explained – lied – that he has been upset since Dad's death. You claim he's under strain. The real reason Mary lets James off is that she hasn't changed since school. She remembers Robert Hackwill. She was there that day, running away like you. And she admires James, understands in a way you don't what he's just done. As she sees the Marion brothers out of the police station at dawn, she smiles quietly. You remember the Scary Mary smile from Ash Grove; it's all the more chilling for being on the face of a grown woman in uniform.

James is quietly satisfied at a job well done. There's an unbridgeable gulf between you. It's been there ever since the copse. It's too late to do anything about it. Your brother has grown into an unknowable alien, a force of inexplicable, vindictive nature. When you get home, he goes straight to his old room – with soldiers and tanks wallpaper and a life-size commando poster – and sleeps away the day, undisturbed. You can't stop shaking and wish you could still have a crying fit. As ever, you can't tell Mum what has happened.

In the Falklands, James is killed. You aren't told the details, though the family are sent non-committal commendations and a medal. Reading between the lines, it seems James was off on his own somewhere, away from his unit, and picked a fight he couldn't win. The letter his sergeant sends you refers to him as 'a lone wolf', which gives you a stab of guilt. You wonder if you taught him (by example) not to rely on anyone else; if it hadn't been for that, he might not have always chosen to go off by himself, set his own goals, and try to get by without other people.

Two family funerals in six months. At a time when you thought you'd struck out on your own, working in London as a journalist on a magazine called *The Scam*, you are pulled back home. You spend most weekends in Sedgwater, with Mum. It is worst for her, you think. Dad died unexpectedly young, leaving her a fifty-year-old widow; and, though she must have at least considered the possibility of his death as soon as he started seeing active service, James was her youngest.

Laraine is also drawn back to the family home. The oddest side-effect is that she gets back together with her first boyfriend, Sean Rye. He is acting manager of the bank and seems likely to accede to Dad's old job. She is engaged to a bloke you didn't like, but breaks it off and gets engaged to Sean, which surprises you. You always thought he was a bit straight for her.

Mum discovers an interest in antiques through her new boyfriend, Phil Parslowe. They spend weekends tracking down *escritoires* and attending estate sales.

Your presence isn't quite so much needed at home, so you spend more time in London. The Thatcher years grind on and you see victims all around you. *The Scam* runs a lot of investigative pieces. You have a sense of the unfairness of it all. You get angry about James. He stands in for the jobless, the abused, the disenfranchised, the dead.

You go out with a colleague, Clare. She is obsessed with incidences of police brutality against racial minorities and early-1970s pop music. She likes to play Abba while making love.

Mum and Phil get married, which pleases and surprises you. Not least because it gets you off a guilt hook. And then Laraine and Sean.

You split up with Clare and go out with an editor, an American, Anne Nielsen. Her history of family disasters makes you feel normal, but it doesn't last. Anne chucks you and you get back with Clare, on your terms: Bowie, yes; Bay City Rollers, no.

Margaret Thatcher is still in power.

You go on Jobs Not Bombs marches and organise fund-raisers for the miners' strike. Clare lives part-time at the Greenham Common Women's Peace Camp. You write a series of profiles of prominent Thatcherite members of parliament, showing just how much they have benefited financially from legislation the government has passed. You get a few cheerful death threats.

Clare moves all her records and tapes and her stereo down to Greenham Common. You don't know where she plugs it in. She comes back sometimes in the middle of the week, but not often.

You think more and more about James.

You write articles about the sinking of the *Belgrano*, the diplomatic chaos that led to the Falklands conflict, the resignation of Lord Carrington, reports of British war crimes.

Finally, Anne tells you to deal with the thing that really haunts you. She assigns you to write about James. You have to start with the copse. To you, there is an electric line between the copse and the Falklands. In the end, you have to blame yourself as much as anyone or anything else.

When Anne reads the article, she cries. She persuades the editorial collective of *The Scam* to run the piece, and you get quite a lot of attention. You go on the radio and television. You get to debate with Tory MPs.

Clare tells you she's decided on political grounds to become a lesbian. Actually, she's fallen into a sleeping-bag with some rainbow-haired peace bimbo who *likes* Little Jimmy Osmond. Good luck to the both of them. You would try it again with Anne, whom you think you actually love, but there's too much complicated pain in her background. You worry that you would become a grief household. Loss isn't your whole life.

A left-wing publisher offers you a small advance to turn the James article into a book, working in most of your other Falklands pieces.

You aren't sure. The book would be a more permanent record than any number of articles. It would also be good for your career: you can't keep meeting daily deadlines for dwindling fees from struggling, often doomed, periodicals. But it'd take you back to a country you hope you have escaped. It would, in a literal sense, mean you would have to go home.

If you agree to do the book, go to 78. If you turn the offer down, go to 85.

7

In Class Five at Ash Grove Primary School, you're given tests every month. Papers are put in front of you, with lots of questions. Some are hard or easy sums, some ask you to pick out an odd item on a list, some want you to put things in their places. For you, the tests are easy, even fun. You're pleased when you know the answers. Most of you on the Top Table come to enjoy the tests. Mary, who gets even more of the answers than you, asks Mrs Daye, the Class Five teacher, for more tests.

In Class Six, you have tests every week. Dad says you'll soon be given a special test called the Eleven Plus. Which school you go to next year depends on how many questions you get right in your Eleven Plus. If you do as well as you have been doing, you'll go to Dr Marling's Grammar School for Boys. If not, you'll go to Hemphill Secondary Modern. Laraine is in the Girls' Grammar, a separate school from Marling's. At Marling's, you'll have to wear a blazer, a tie and a red cap, and you'll play rugby instead of football. Paul Mysliwiec, of the Middle Table, claims Marling's boys have to do five hours of homework a night. He's glad he won't have to go to Marling's, because he wants to watch telly and play football.

Robert Hackwill, the Ash Grove Bully, goes to Marling's, and is looking forward to old victims arriving so he can resume his reign over them with all the power invested in him by God as a prefect. You hear that Marling's prefects are allowed to cane younger boys and that none of the teachers can stop them. Paul claims Hackwill has already crippled one boy and been let off because he's a prefect, but you don't know if you believe that. Panic-stricken, you tell your dad you don't want to go to Marling's however you do in your tests. Dad is angry and, as he rarely does, shouts at you. Mum explains it's important for your future that you go to the school for clever boys like you.

A good thing about Marling's is that no girls are allowed, but even that strikes you as somehow wrong. You don't like girls, of course, but it'd be strange not to have them around. You realise you quite like Vanda Pritchard. You can talk to her, sometimes. She likes Tintin books too, and has introduced you to school stories, Jennings and Billy Bunter and Chalet School. She doesn't think she'll go to the Girls' Grammar, but Mary – the monster – probably will. Of the Class Six boys, only Shane Bush, Michael Dixon, Stephen Adlard and you are expected to pass the Eleven Plus.

Go on.

8

After the Easter holidays, you turn up at school one day and find the classroom rearranged. A teacher you don't know is in charge of the tests. A rumour runs around. This is the Eleven Plus. The important test. No, not a test. An exam.

Reading over the questions, you realise you could easily answer most of them. That would mean going to Dr Marling's Grammar School for Boys with Shane and Robert Hackwill. Or you could deliberately get quite a few wrong, which would mean going to Hemphill, with Paul and Vanda.

If you fail the Eleven Plus, go to 11. If you pass, go to 16.

9

After the Easter holidays, you turn up at school one day and find the classroom rearranged. A teacher you don't know is in charge of the tests. A rumour runs around. This is the Eleven Plus. The important test. No, not a test. An exam.

Reading over the questions, you realise you could easily answer most of them wrongly. That would mean going to Hemphill Secondary Modern, with Vanda and Paul. Or you could try hard and get many of them right, which would mean going to Marling's with Shane and Robert Hackwill.

If you pass the Eleven Plus, go to 12. If you fail, go to 15.

10

In 1982, the week after your father's funeral, you are in town, early in a spring evening, going for a drink in the Lime Kiln with your brother.

Laraine has stayed home with Mum, but you both feel the need to get out of the memory-permeated house. James went into the army at sixteen and you haven't seen much of him in the last few years. You remember him as the kid who wet himself when you ran to find a teacher and tell on Robert and Reg; now he's coming to the end of his four-year hitch and is talking about getting out. The possibility of being sent to a proper war in the Falklands has shocked him. It's not just about learning to drive a jeep and travelling to exotic places and German brothels, it's about being shot dead on the other side of the world.

The Lime Kiln is full, packed with drinkers whose fathers are still alive or have been dead for so long that it doesn't matter. You and

James have said little about Dad. You think that, as the Man of the Family, you should be able to say something to your brother that will make it easier. Nothing comes to mind.

As you force your way through to the bar, a cheer goes up. You wonder why, then remember James is in uniform. There's a drunken wave of patriotism going on in the aftermath of the invasion of the Falkland Islands, a frenzy of kill-the-Argies war-hunger. The barman is Max Lewis, with whom you were at school though he was never a special friend. James orders a couple of pints of bitter. A man claps him on the shoulder and offers to pay for the drinks.

James, flinching from the touch, turns to accept... and freezes. Pressed close to James by the crowd, you sense the tension which draws your brother tight as a bowstring an instant before you recognise the man with the money.

It's Robert Hackwill, grown up.

The Ash Grove School Bully has done well for himself. He wears a sheepskin coat and a trilby hat. His property business is flourishing and he is in line for a council seat. He has a flash car, a Jag. His smile splits the world horizontally in half.

Hackwill repeats his offer.

You look around for Jessup, never far from Hackwill, and spot him in a corner. Reg's smirk is still there, shaped by the fat in his face. He's still a sidekick.

What will James do? It's fifteen years later and Hackwill is off his guard. James is depressed enough not to give a shit. You know your brother must be thinking of breaking a glass in the grown-up bully's face.

You remember that day. When James wet himself while being given the worst Chinese burn in history and you ran to Mrs Daye, the Class Five teacher, and told on Robert and Reg. She saw the bullies off, ordering them to stay away from the school, and looked after the sobbing James, sending him home for the afternoon. You watched, wishing it hadn't happened, wishing you could have done more.

You have never talked about it with James. Dad commended you for doing the right thing, but you always knew you did it out of cowardice. James needed help *right then*, not to see you running off for a grown-up while he was being tortured. Ever since, James has worked to be self-reliant, self-contained. You realise now that you know very little about the man he has become.

Max puts two pints on the bar. James picks his up carefully, getting a good grip.

You can *see* the pint smashing against Hackwill's smile, glass and beer exploding, blood and froth drenching his whole front.

But James just takes a deep draught and swallows. He drains it.

'Thanks, mate,' he says. 'Now have one on me.'

Hackwill insists on buying the soldier boy another.

You wonder if you were wrong. Maybe James hasn't recognised Hackwill? The bully has obviously forgotten him, one among so many long-ago victims.

Jessup comes to the bar and springs for a round. Your drinks are bought for you too. It is as if you and James were being picked up by a couple of queers, but you know Hackwill and Jessup aren't like that. What they want from you two isn't sex but the association with a potential war hero. You'd prefer it if they were just after your arse. The mateyness of these two blokish men, careering towards middle age while still in their twenties, hits you in the pit of your stomach. You think of the school custard that always made you want to puke.

As the pints go down and your bladder fills, you assume you were wrong. James is friendly with Hackwill, even exchanges names with him. He must have forgotten the whole thing. You've carried the guilt for fifteen years and he's wiped the copse from his mind.

This realisation, combined with the drink, makes you light-headed.

Finally, Hackwill eases off the sturdy bar-stool and mutters about 'pointing Percy at the porcelain'.

'You sure your mate's all right?' James asks Jessup as soon as Hackwill has tottered off. 'He's had one too many. Shouldn't you see if he's okay?'

Bewildered, Jessup agrees and follows Hackwill into the bog.

Lightning-sober, James tells Max not to let anyone use the Gents for five minutes.

'Come on,' he tells you. 'This is for the copse.'

James remembers. He has always remembered.

The barman comes out, on his break, and guards the Gents door as James slips in. You follow.

Hackwill stands at the white wall, urinating loudly. Jessup is wheedling, asking if he's all right, annoying him.

James springs across the room and catches Hackwill with his cock out, shoving him against the wet enamel. He rains blows on Hackwill's head, driving him into the urine-trickling runnel, scattering disinfectant cakes. The smell is strong. James, grunting with each of his well-aimed punches, dances back and forth, jabbing and kicking. Blood trickles in with the piss.

James pauses and looks back. 'You do fat boy, Keith.'

He kicks the whining Hackwill in the side and starts a boot ballet, as if trying to cram the sodden bully into the plug-holes of the urinal.

You look at Jessup, who backs into a stall. You remember the fat face snickering as James wet himself, calling to you.

'It's all right,' you tell him. 'I won't hurt you…'

Relief sweats out of the fat face.

'Much.'

From inside, violent rage erupts. You didn't know that you were still so angry, that you carried the hurt.

You leave Hackwill and Jessup bloodied on the stinking floor of the Gents. Max has lined up fresh, on-the-house pints on the bar. Everybody remembers their school bully. No one ever forgives.

People gather round. You buy them all drinks. You buy a roomful of witnesses. Hackwill and Jessup slink out by a side door.

Drinking your pint, you catch James's eye. As one, you make fists in the air and roar. The Marion brothers are back in business!

In the Falklands, James is severely wounded. He loses his left leg below the knee and is mustered out on a disability allowance. The medal citation commends his 'initiative and conspicuous bravery' in holding a position while someone else went to summon reinforcements. You wonder whether you taught him (by example) that he had to bear the brunt of the attack while others took the problem to a higher authority. James comes home changed but not obviously embittered. He is still self-reliant, even if he has to hobble around on a prosthesis. After a few months, he refuses to use a crutch.

The family regroups around James. With Dad gone and you in London, he becomes the fulcrum. You talk with him every week on the phone, and he updates you on what's happening with Mum –

who has a boyfriend, Phil Parslowe – and Laraine.

Wounds heal. Disabilities are coped with.

It's all been taken out of your hands.

You work as a technical journalist in the daytime but struggle in the evenings with *Freebooter*, a historical novel. You live with Christina Temple, your girlfriend since university. You sell *Freebooter* and are contracted to write two sequels, *Buccaneer* and *Privateer*. You follow your hero, Kenneth Merriam, through a career of piracy from stowaway cabin boy to governor of Jamaica. Once you've used that up, you write about Merriam's ancestors, in *Gallant*, *Galleon* and *Galliass*. You and Christina marry, and have two children, Jasper and Jessamyn. You write about Merriam's descendants in *Crossbones*, *Cutlass* and *Cutthroat*. *Freebooter* is turned into a very unsuccessful film, which nevertheless makes you more money than all your publishing deals combined. You are published in sixteen languages. There is a *Merriam Quarterly*, a fan publication devoted to your books. You take a cruise in an authentic pirate ship for a TV documentary, and try to be good-humoured about seasickness. You write a book about the experience, *Landlubber*.

In February 1998, James wins £6.3 three million on the National Lottery. He buys you a yacht as a birthday present.

The Merriam saga completed, you don't need to write any more novels. Effectively, you retire.

James invests, speculates, develops. Determined not to squander his winnings, he incorporates.

The Marion Group grows. Jasper works for James and becomes a vice-president at twenty-two. James, perhaps because of his leg, never married, though he has been seeing his personal assistant, Kate, for fifteen years. Outsiders sometimes think Jasper is James's son.

You have a seat on the board but can't keep track of James's dealings. You give advice when it is sought but feel cut out of the loop.

This is James's game.

Jasper has come up fast. He's a twenty-first-century man, clued-in to technologies that baffle you, temples shaved to accommodate the decorative plugjacks he wears even though the tech to interface on a brain-level with information nets hasn't been developed and isn't likely to come along in the next few years. James relies on Jasper in communications; he is very obviously Heir Apparent.

You love your son, but – as he nears thirty – you find it hard to *like* him. At school and university, he was erratically brilliant, often depending on you or James to cough up cash to get him out of trouble. He got married young, to Robert Hackwill's daughter Sam of all persons, and made you a grandfather, to little Zazza. Sam has smoothed him somewhat – he had a bit of a stimulants habit at university – but he still likes electronic short-cuts and corner-shaving. James is more tolerant of his foibles than you are.

And you are wealthily irrelevant anyway.

James keeps making speeches about luck and merit. The Marion Group is the first Lottery fortune to last. Most big winners are dead inside six months, used up by hedonism or torn apart by vultures. Their money drains away into the sand. James's win is the seed money of an empire. He always credits you with demonstrating the difference between burying treasure, frittering it away and using it. He has turned his treasure into a treasury.

As the new millennium whooshes on, you face sixty.

Christina, five years younger, asks if you're content. You wish you'd done some things differently and had tried harder in other areas but can't deny that you have been a success.

Then, one spring morning in 2020, your daughter visits you on the latest yacht.

Jessamyn wears living tattoos on her breasts and magenta knee-length shorts. She's had her cheekbones done, ridges of coral implanted around her eyes. It's a look.

'Daddy,' she says, air-kissing you.

Jessamyn has never been as focused as Jasper. Born to wealth, she has pleased herself, not quite making a go of careers as a sound sculptor or an estate agent. Currently unmarried, she is engaged to a woman. Though she's had two husbands, Mandii will be her first wife.

'Jess.'

You're pleased to see her. She was at your Big 60 party, but so was everyone else and you didn't get to talk to her much.

Her smile is serious. You know this is not good news.

'I've had my family area scanned,' she says, tapping her skull. A current fad is specific cat-scans of brain regions. Apparently the walnut-folds can be read like palms. 'I know you always loved Jas more.'

'That's not true, Jess.'

It isn't. Everyone thinks their parents loved their siblings more. You certainly felt yours did.

'No, it's all right. I was a drip as a little girl. What was the word Uncle James used, "sneak"?'

Whenever Jasper committed some naughtiness – which was often – Jess used to run and tell you, the model of public spirit. As you strode off to admonish or punish, Jess's rectitude was replaced by unlovely glee.

'Are you glad I told you?' she would ask.

An impossible question. You needed to know about Jasper but no one likes an informer.

'I'm obliged to sneak again, Daddy.'

'I beg your pardon?'

'It's Jas, as usual. I've known for weeks but not known what to do, who to tell. I thought I'd warn him I knew and he'd make things right and seal the record. But he wouldn't. If you want to know, I'm afraid of what he'd do. You know what he can be like.'

Her tattoos swirl around her nipples like twin dragons, reacting to her minutest skin secretions. They're supposed to match her emotional state.

'He's been transacting in his favour. From the Group, from Uncle Jimmy.'

The dragons' eyes are blood-black.

'I think it's long-term. I know it's major.'

She leans forward and hugs you, miming crying.

'Are you glad I told you, Daddy?'

If you take this to your brother, go to 102. If you take this to your son, go to 116.

11

When your Eleven Plus results come through, your parents think there has been a mistake. But everyone is used to being disappointed in you. Remembering the tantrums you used to have, they always had a nagging feeling that any tests which suggested you were intelligent must be wrong. Everyone could see you were mental. Actually, you haven't pitched a fit since Class Four. After Robert Hackwill dragged you into the copse for the worst Chinese burn in human memory and no one came to help despite custard-level screams, you gave it up.

You are the cleverest pupil in your class at Hemphill, but the lesson you learned in botching your Eleven Plus stays with you. The way to get through is not to scream and shout or show off, but to pretend consistently to be less able than you are. You can't get away with a complete thicko act, like Timmy Gossett (in a special class, even at Hemphill), but keep answers to yourself, let others speak up in class.

Every report you get is a variation on the theme of 'Could do better if he tried'. Academically, you hover just under the top five of your class, conscientiously doing enough to get by, never letting yourself stand out in any way. Your mission is to come through the war without getting your head shot off. That means not shoving your helmet above the parapet.

Your parents – you can see it – give up on you and put their hopes in James. Your brother easily passes his Eleven Plus, but spends only a year at Marling's before comprehensive education comes in. Most teachers realise there's something not quite right about your mediocrity but are too busy with real problem cases like the uncontrollable Tony Bennett or the suicidal Marie-Laure Quilter to give you much thought.

Hemphill is understaffed and overworked. If Dr Marling's is intended to turn out Sedgwater's estate agents and local government inspectors and the Girls' Grammar to furnish them with wives, Hemphill Secondary Modern's job is to grind out leave-school-at-sixteen drones. Hemphill boys who live in town will work at the British Synthetics plant. If they're from outlying villages, they'll work on a farm. The girls work in shops or the jam factory and get married as soon as they can. Many of your schoolmates will have kids of their own before they are twenty.

You still hang around with Barry Mitcham, Paul Mysliwiec and Vanda Pritchard, preserving the remains of your infants' school circle into your teens. With Shane and Mary at grammar schools, you're nudged into the leadership of your gang, though you find it boring always having to think up things to keep your friends amused. The laziness you affect becomes all too real. Vanda becomes something of a nag and Barry makes the odd joke about 'old married couples', which disturbs you. Though you've played kissing games, you aren't Vanda's boyfriend. She develops a serious plague of spots.

One lunch break, Marie-Laure Quilter, who hasn't really tried to kill herself, whatever they say, is hanging around with you for no real reason. Paul, athletic enough to make the junior football side, has brought a couple of his soccer mates, Vince Tunney and Dickie Kell. There's an irritating barking in the air, the constant yapping of a dog that belongs to a pensioner whose garden backs on to the school grounds. Marie-Laure claims it's trying to chew through the fence to get her. You pelt the dog with small stones and are hauled up *en masse* before Mr Taylor, the Head. Marie-Laure and Vanda get the slipper, and the rest of you the belt.

The 'slipper', the 'belt'. None of you – and, more significantly, none of your parents – questions the propriety of corporal punishment in school, administered with instruments as fetishist and symbolic as the top hat or old boot in Monopoly. The Bash Street Kids in the *Beano* usually wind up with throbbing cartoon bums and the frequently televised *Bottoms Up!* features a gowned Jimmy Edwards shouting 'Whacko!' as he humorously thrashes recalcitrants. You've learned from James that it's not true that pupils at Dr Marling's can be beaten by sadistic prefects, but the cane is still used there as an instrument of chastisement. If and when any of you has a twelve-year-old, the idea of ritual child abuse as disciplinary tool will seem as obsolete as public executions or ducking witches. You'll wonder if 'the belt' – three mild lashes administered by the tweedy and unenthusiastic Mr Taylor – could possibly have hurt as much as you remember. Even a hardnut like Dickie Kell is reduced to helpless tears almost before the first lash.

The shared punishment makes you a proper gang. Before, you all drifted around the playground as free agents. Marie-Laure, who has an alcoholic mother, introduces you to smoking. Tension develops between Marie-Laure and Vanda, much like that Mary and Vanda. Mary got her way through violence, terror and cunning, but Marie-Laure prevails by being dependent, clinging and desperate. Vince's great obsession is American comics and he encourages your own budding interest. You hunt around newsagents' together for stray issues of *Batman*, *Doctor Strange* and *The Streak*, and build collections through swapping and delving.

By 1973, Hemphill is falling apart. After next year, it won't even exist. Rumours go round about which of the staff will get the boot. Vanda frightens you all by claiming that at the new school you'll have to do the difficult work her brother Norman does at Marling's. Again, it's repeated that grammar-school kids have five hours' homework every night. You remember the panic spasm that made you botch your Eleven Plus. James does under an hour of homework an evening, but the prospect of giving up television and loitering-and-smoking-in-Denbeigh-Gardens is frighteningly real.

Increasingly, you feel you have no control over your life. You used to have choices. Now, you have a trap. It is slowly closing.

Read 18, go to 23.

12

In the first form at Dr Marling's, you put on a spurt of growth, shooting up six inches. Your parents spend a fortune on new school clothes. Then have to do it again, twice, as your trouser-cuffs rise above your socks. They threaten to put you back in shorts. You say you'll go on hunger strike if they send you to school dressed like an infant. The uniform is okay, except for the blood-red cap, which makes Marling's boys look from a distance as if they've been freshly scalped.

Your long legs make you a runner. The school tries to get you to play fly-half in rugby, but you don't like the idea of twelve larger boys running after you, jumping on top of you. For you, games means track events: sprints, the half-mile, hurdles. Not very athletic at your last school, you discover that if all else fails you can run.

Also, you take to the work. After a week struggling with base eight in mathematics and the lowest slopes of Latin and French, pennies drop. You find that schoolwork, like running, is something you can do, a resource. At the end of the first term, your year takes achievement tests in all subjects; you score in the top five in everything but religious instruction and music. You usually do your homework in under an hour and are in front of the television for *Top of the Pops* or *Softly, Softly: Task Force*. Your parents are delighted by your end-of-term report.

You wonder if you were held back in primary school. Maybe having girls in the class hampered you. You don't see any of the girls from Ash Grove, or any of your friends who failed the Eleven Plus and went to Hemphill. You have a new life.

Suddenly, you are a leader. In the second term, Mr Waller, your form master, makes you form captain. Shane Bush, struggling to keep up in most subjects, is a hanger-on. You are wary of Michael Dixon and his friends, as clever as you but unpredictable, but become closer to Stephen Adlard, whom you barely knew at Ash Grove. Stephen is the neatest boy in the form, tie immaculately tied, homework meticulous. Without a ruler or compass, Stephen can draw perfect straight edges and geometric figures.

In the first year, from 1971 to 1972, cliques and factions coalesce. Kids you knew at Ash Grove you think of by their first names; kids who came from other schools are known to you, as to the masters at Marling's, by their surnames. You, Stephen and Roger Cunningham are the Brainboxes, with Shane as your attendant thicko. Michael Dixon, Amphlett, Martin, Skelly and Yeo are the Forum, clever but useless at games. Trickett, Holmes and Ferguson are the Rugby Hulks. Beale, Pritchard (Vanda's twin brother) and Fewsham are the Trouble-Causers.

In the second year, from 1972 to 1973, you are in a form with Stephen, Cunningham and Michael – you all continue Latin, which two-thirds of your year drop – but Shane is relegated to a thicko stream. You still hang around together at break. Shane brings along Gully Eastment, a new friend from his form. Eastment isn't really a thicko, but mad moments hold him back: if dared, he'll try anything from climbing the outside of the school to setting light to all the magnesium in the chemistry lab. He's the only boy you know well who has been caned, bum striped scarlet by the head, 'Chimp' Quinlan.

You feel yourself draw ahead of the pack, as you usually do towards the end of the half-mile, getting a third wind, finding new strength, new speed. Wally Berry, the games master, calls you 'Streak' and cautions you about pacing yourself. As you run, you always sense others at your heels, gaining fast. Even when you've sprinted well ahead of your closest rival, you sense the shadows of pursuers flickering at your heels.

You run fast because you think you are being chased. You don't like to think about who or what might be chasing you. You just know they are there, relentlessly pounding the gravel, matching your strides.

At the beginning of the third year, in 1973, which you hear will be the last year Marling's exists as a separate school, you draw up a life schedule, carefully writing it out on a sheet of exercise paper. In your future, you'll have two years at Ash Grove Comprehensive, where you will take O Level courses, then two years at Sedgwater College, where you will take A Levels. Then you will read modern languages at Oxford or Cambridge, graduating with a First in 1981. After education, you will get a professional job. Something with a starting salary higher than that your father earns after twenty years with the bank. By 1987, when you are twenty-five, you will be ready to get married, buy a house, and father two children, a boy and a girl, Jonathan and Jennifer. Your wife will also be a professional. You will both have cars. You will continue to run, continue to draw ahead of the shadowmen at your heels. The track ahead of you stretches towards the twenty-first century. At the turn of the century, you'll be forty. You write an essay in English about your fortieth birthday, spent on a day trip to Mars.

Throughout your third and last year at Marling's, you put on speed. Competitors fall exhausted by the side of the track. Even the masters find it a strain to keep up with you.

Sean Rye, Laraine's boyfriend, asks you one evening why you have to keep running.

You don't know, but you just *do*.

'You could always stop,' Sean says, 'take a rest, slow down. You're missing a lot.'

When you ask him to give examples of things you're missing, Sean can't come up with a decent list. But you still wonder if he doesn't have a point.

In your dreams, you run, enveloped by a pack of shadows, losing your footing. You wake up as if you'd really been running, heart pumping, drenched by panic sweat. Often when this happens, you have an itchy erection, sometimes with shameful discharge.

You have known about sex since primary school, when you were given pamphlets explaining the biology. You wonder if Sean and Laraine have slept together, but doubt it. You think your parents have grown out of sex, and Laraine has become a miniature Mum, always perfect and poised, dressed up as if for a party. It's impossible to imagine her putting her tongue in Sean's mouth. Sean works in your father's bank; after his A Levels, he didn't go to university. Mum and Dad like Sean. James says Sean is a pillock and teases Laraine in a disrespectful manner you would never countenance.

Why should you pay attention to what a bank clerk says? Sean is one of your father's slavey young men, with his diamond-shaped ties and wide lapels. How would he know what you're missing?

The whispers of 'Slow down' persist. You think they come from the shadows. They are a trick, a trap. If you slow, you will stumble and fall under the others. Feet will trample over you, imprinting dap-sole patterns on your back, forcing your face into the dirt.

At night, in bed, you take hold of your penis and pump fast, faster, faster. Gully has told you how to toss off. You think of yourself running. Towards your future, your wife, your life. You get faster and faster. You leave the shadows behind.

You have no shame about running.

Each orgasm is a victory. For you, victories come fast and often.

Sean envies you your future. You'll leave him behind. That's why he wants you to slow down: envy. Laraine breaks up with him and goes out with Graham Foulk, an ancient soul of twenty-two who plays the guitar with his own pop group. Mum and Dad like Graham less than Sean. He has long hair and a fuzz of beard and they've heard he is a bad lot, but Laraine says he's sweet really. She starts dressing less like a Sindy doll, more like a flower child. You're sure Laraine has slept with Graham, and is on the pill. He is one of a loose knot of aimless young adults who work sporadically, some on farms in the ring of villages outlying Sedgwater, and are known, even in the mid-1970s, as hippies.

Graham makes you as uncomfortable as he does your parents. Since leaving school, he's done nothing except practise with his group, who have never played anywhere for money, though they do appear at birthday parties and school discos. The summit of his ambition is to have his group, which goes through names the way you go through biros, play at the Glastonbury Festival. Sean, still at the bank, is scornful (perhaps understandably) of Graham and his bunch of wasters, which prompts Graham (quite amusingly) to name his group Graham and the Wasters for a few weeks.

If you slow down, you might become like Graham. As soon as the tiniest fluff sprouts on your chin, you scratch yourself bloody with your father's razor. You shave every day, scraping off dead skin and thin lather. You'll never grow a beard, you vow.

Stephen and Roger look forward to the new school. They are obsessed with the idea of girls. Gully Eastment has already decided to have sex with as many as possible. He claims that though Girls' Grammar girls are tight, Hemphill slags will do anything.

You keep quiet. Girls can wait. You have running to do. The pack are catching up. You have to avoid stitches, wrenched knees, pulled muscles. You notch up more victories.

You read ahead in all your textbooks, getting to lessons before the masters, completing exercises as yet unset. Your parents are called into school and aren't sure whether to be pleased with or worried about you. Mr Quinlan tells your father that if Marling's were not being amalgamated into Ash Grove, he'd have you on an accelerated programme, with a view to preparing you in advance to take Oxford entrance exams in four years' time. But, he shrugs, he is leaving when the school amalgamates, and they'll have to watch you carefully so that you aren't dragged down by the changes. Chimp Quinlan thinks comprehensive education is the work of the Devil.

Your parents wonder about taking you out of Marling's and sending you to a public school. They decide that, quite apart from the money, it's too late. You'd never settle in another school. You ignore all this argument. Whatever the school, you must still run.

Read 18, go to 19.

13

Sometimes, you step off the path, through the cobweb curtain, into the shade. This is where you meet me. This is where I live. Most people step off the path at one time or another. If you press them, they'll tell you their stories. But not willingly. It's private. Between me and them. You'd be surprised how many people you know who've stepped off the path and met me. That, though you don't quite realise it yet, is what's just happened to you. Can you feel the scuttling caress of tiny spider-legs on your hackles? Have you noticed time has changed, slowed to a tortoise-crawl or speeded up to a cheetah-run? The air in your nostrils and the water in your mouth taste different. There's an electric tang, a supple thickness, a kind of a rush. If you come through the shade whole, you'll want to scurry back to the light, back to the path. Most people have an amazing ability to pretend things didn't happen, to wish so fervently that things were otherwise they can make them so, unpicking elements from their past and forgetting them so thoroughly – at least, while they're awake – that they literally have not happened. All of you can affect the warp of the universe, just by wishing. But to wish, you need motivation. What has just happened might be motivation enough. At first, you won't be able to stop thinking about it, asking what has *actually* happened, looking for a comforting 'explanation'. Maybe it was mirrors, maybe you were given drugs, maybe aliens abducted you. Who knows? Maybe you're right. I don't know everything. From time to time, you run into me – sometimes because you get itchy and stray, sometimes by accident. From time to time, I like to catch up with you. I like to catch up with all my friends, Keith. For now, you're shaken. Perhaps you can't believe you're alive and sane. Perhaps you aren't. Whatever the case, you must put the shade behind you. For the moment. We'll meet again. Before you know it, you'll pass through the cobweb curtain and be back. Years may pass between your detours, but when you step off the path again those years will be as seconds. Maybe life is only truly lived in the shade. Well, enough deep thought for the moment. Get on with things. Try to pretend there is no shade. I'll see you soon.

Go on.

14

In 1982, the week after your father's funeral, you are in town, early in a spring evening, going for a drink in the Lime Kiln with your brother.

Laraine has stayed home with Mum, but you both feel the need to get out of the memory-permeated house. James went into the army at sixteen and you haven't seen much of him in the last few years. You remember him as the kid who wet himself while you were being beaten up by Robert and Reg; now he's a Marine, newly promoted to sergeant, trained to kill. It's likely that he will be sent to the Falklands.

The Lime Kiln is full, packed with drinkers whose fathers are still alive or have been dead for so long that it doesn't matter. You and James share a feeling that now you have to be grown-up, that the job of Man of the Family must be split between you. At least James has a direction in life; you're still not sure if you've been making the right decisions. Dad's death, from a cerebral haemorrhage no one was expecting, has made you think. In your mind, you've been going back, reassessing, wondering if you could have chosen better, if you could have changed things.

As you force your way through to the bar, a cheer goes up. You wonder why, then remember James is in uniform. There's a drunken wave of patriotism going on in the aftermath of the invasion of the Falkland Islands, a frenzy of kill-the-Argies war-hunger. The barman is Max Lewis, with whom you were at school though he was never a special friend. James orders a couple of pints of bitter. A man claps him on the shoulder and offers to pay for the drinks.

James, flinching from the touch, turns to accept... and freezes. Pressed close to James by the crowd, you sense the tension which draws your brother tight as a bowstring an instant before you recognise the man with the money.

It's Robert Hackwill, grown up.

The Ash Grove School Bully has done well for himself. He wears a sheepskin coat and a trilby hat. His property business is flourishing and he is in line for a council seat. He has a flash car, a Jag. His smile splits the world horizontally in half.

Hackwill repeats his offer.

You look around for Jessup, never far from Hackwill, and spot him in a corner. Reg's smirk is still there, shaped by the fat in his face. He's still a sidekick.

What will James do? It's fifteen years later and Hackwill is off his guard. James has been trained to kill. You know your brother must be thinking of breaking a glass in the grown-up bully's face.

You remember that day. When James wet himself while being given the worst Chinese burn in history and Robert and Reg, astonished that you had come into the copse to rescue your brother, took great delight in beating you up. They knocked you down and kicked you until your sides were black and blue under your filthy clothes. You never explained your bruises to your parents or a teacher. Telling on Robert Hackwill was an invitation to pain.

You have never talked about it with James. But you've been close ever since, sharing a hidden purpose, a hidden hurt. You've known you could always count on your brother and he on you.

Max puts two pints on the bar. James picks his up carefully, getting a good grip.

You can *see* the pint smashing against Hackwill's smile, glass exploding, blood and froth drenching him.

But James just takes a deep draught of the beer and swallows. Hackwill, smile fixed, eyes hardening, repeats his offer, as if James had not heard him over the din. Somehow, the noise of the pub dies down. You know everyone is paying attention.

'You can fuck right off, Hackwill,' James tells him, verbally slapping the generous grin from his face. 'I'd rather have a drink on General Galtieri than you.'

Hackwill plainly doesn't recognise or remember either of you, the Marion brothers. For a moment, he looks shocked, as though he – the bully – is about to cry. Everyone in the pub notices and laughs a little louder, talks a little more raucously. They are all delighted to see the squaddie see off Robert Bloody Jaguar Hackwill. Everybody remembers their school bully. No one ever forgives.

You clap your arm round James and try to pay for your pints. Max, emboldened, refuses to accept the money and says the drinks are on the house for you both.

Hackwill is still there, smile frozen.

'And Reg,' you shout across the pub, 'you can fuck right off too, fat boy.'

Everybody cheers.

Hackwill and Jessup drink up fast and hurry out. Neither you nor James has to buy a drink all night.

In the Falklands, James, practically on consecutive days, gets close to a Victoria Cross – only this isn't a declared war, so they aren't handing them out – and a dishonourable discharge. On one day, he fights on while cut off from his own unit and brings in three wounded men. Later in the week, he trains a rifle on an officer he claims is about to summarily execute a sixteen-year-old Argie who is surrendering. These actions, officially processed simultaneously, cancel each other out. James has to take an early bath, removed from active duty even before the brief conflict is over. You wonder if you taught him (by example) his have-a-go foolhardiness. This possibly dangerous streak makes him, in a real sense you aren't ashamed of, a hero.

You live in London with Chris, your girlfriend since university. When you got together, you were accused of cradle-snatching but the difference between eighteen and twenty-three is different (legally, apart from anything else) from that between fourteen and nineteen.

You supervise adventure holidays for deprived and not-so-deprived kids. You yomp around Dartmoor or the Highlands of Scotland with spooked inner-city teenagers. The lack of streetlamps at night freaks them. To give the week-long courses shape, you construct them as treasure hunts, burying prizes and giving teams treasure maps full of puzzles to solve. After a few days' resistance, most kids fall in and enjoy using their minds and limbs. When the first 'treasure' is discovered to be a cache of beer, even the most recalcitrant come round.

One day, you'd like to take your treasure hunts overseas, preferably to Tortuga. You've sailed since university and you and Chris get out on the water most weekends. Chris calls you 'Captain Blood' or 'Seaman Staines'; you call her 'Mr Smee' or 'Anne Bonney'. It's not really appropriate to fly the Jolly Roger from a Mirror dinghy, but you do. You name your boat *Hispaniola*, after the one in *Treasure Island*.

You try to spend as little time as possible under roofs.

Chris gets her first degree, in history, and starts postgraduate work on a forgotten Irish turn-of-the-century feminist writer, Katie Reed. She plans to turn her thesis into a biography and is often in Dublin, delving in the records and libraries, while you're out and about, climbing trees and rocks and braving the elements.

You get scars but aren't seriously hurt. You have a few accidents – the odd snapped bone or bruised bonce – but never a fatality. Whenever anyone so much as trips up, you recite your mantra of 'Haven't lost a kid yet.'

Chris falls pregnant but loses the baby. This makes you both think. You decide that, after another six months, you'll either split up or get married.

Meanwhile, James knocks about the world a bit, coming home to Sedgwater to roost every few months. He takes international courier jobs and you twit him about becoming a mercenary or a pirate. He helps out on one or two expeditions into jungles or deserts, and an amateur interest in archaeology leads him to attach himself to the odd dig, where his survival skills and outdoor capabilities come in handy. He even joins you on a few of your rougher adventures.

Chris comments that she could do with a Marine to help her get through those Irish archives. You point out that her heroine would probably have been in favour of assassinating James, which leads her to recount at length Katie Reed's actual position on armed rebellion and her war journalism. Like a lot of your 'disputes', this one ends in bed.

Mum remarries, to a bloke called Phil Parslowe, an antiques dealer. Laraine gets divorced from someone called Fred whom you never liked and floats around, a brittle thirty with a too-frequent sour expression.

The big upheaval in the Marion family is a road-widening scheme. In 1989, Mum receives a compulsory purchase order for the family home. It's an end-of-the-row house, the only one in the street scheduled for demolition. You and James converge on the old home to give support. Phil has got hold of maps and plans and shows you exactly what will be done. The planned extra lane on the Achelzoy road will cut through your living-room and completely demolish the garden.

Will the workmen find those marbles? Phones the cat, in his grave under the forsythia bush, will be disturbed by the spread of the road on which he was tragically run over in 1972.

You can't understand why the road is to be widened on your side. Across the way is a scrap of parkland hardly worth keeping. There was a swing there when you were kids; now it's a hollow where rubbish collects. The council claims it is favouring community resources over individual ones.

You and James agree there's something bent about this. It turns out that behind it all is Robert Hackwill, district councillor, chairman of the Planning Committee. The road-widening is supposed to cope with the extra flow of traffic anticipated when Hackwill Properties finally gets its Discount Development – a major, controversial project – finished.

'He has a long memory,' you say.

'Well, we have too,' James replies.

As part of the on-going re-evaluation of your relationship, Chris insists you have monthly truth-telling sessions. This sounds to you like an infants' kissing game, but it turns out to be her way of admitting to you that on one of her trips to Dublin she has had an affair with another graduate student, someone her own age. It is over, she insists. She says she loves you. You almost wish you had an infidelity to match hers – there have been crush-struck jailbait temptresses on your courses, but you've stayed away from them – but all you can talk about in the sessions is Sedgwater. As you are explaining about James and Hackwill, she bursts into tears. You end up in bed, but you are still not sure which way you'll vote. If anything, the truth-telling has made you less certain how you feel.

James is staying with you in London for a few days. You're going through the action plan. Chris doesn't understand.

'You think this Hackwill is knocking down your mum's house because you wouldn't let him buy you a pint?'

'Essentially, yes,' you say.

James nods.

'That's silly,' she protests.

You and James remember the copse.

And all the other times. All through school, Hackwill was there. After the copse, it was less concerted, but if either of the Marion brothers got a boot in the back or a thump on the head, Hackwill was there.

After primary school, he didn't even do it himself. He had his sidekick Reg Jessup for that, and a coterie of hangers-on: Mack McEwan, Pete Gompers, Shane Bush.

'He was the school bully,' you say.

'And you two were heroes. You stood up to him. Good for you.' Chris is being sarky.

'We just looked out for each other, Chris. Tried not to take any stick.'

'Has it ever occurred to you that you ought to be grateful to him?'

This is hideous heresy. You and James both blurt out, 'What?'

'If you hadn't learned to take care of yourselves, Jimmy'd have been killed in the Falklands, and you'd have broken your neck hauling some kid out of a well. Your bully forced you to become the macho, outdoors, competent, capable Super Marion Brothers you are.'

'Fuck off, Chris,' you say.

'Them's fighting words.'

She biffs you with a cushion. James laughs and she batters him too. By now, you're all a bit drunk.

Weeks dribble away. You're so caught up in appeals and turn-downs on the house – which you still think of as home – that you worry less about Chris and the Marriage thing. James sets up camp in Somerset and sends reports about organised resistance.

However, the M thing starts to grow in your mind. It's not so much the decision that bothers you – though you still aren't sure – but the actual showdown. How are you going to manage it? Who goes first? Is this like scissors-paper-stone, where you count to three and come out with it? If so, then it's fine if you both come out with the same thing. But if there's a split decision, if one of you wants the open road and the other wants to settle down, it could get nasty.

More and more, you want just to carry on – living together, when you're both in London, going out together, thinking maybe about a family when you reach that unimaginable age of thirty (this year, gack!). It's perfectly comfortable and works for both of you, so why change?

Why change anything? You like things as they are.

It's the same with the house. You'll never move back, and Mum and Phil certainly won't have kids to take over the three extra rooms, but you like the idea of the family home being there. It's as if, because the site is preserved, your childhood and adolescence are accessible to you, still there on some level. The marbles are still buried so you're not a proper grown-up. And that's what you want.

Which would be worse? If you voted for a split and Chris wanted to get married? Or the other way round? If you voted for a split and Chris agreed, would you still feel you'd been chucked? If Chris voted for marriage and you agreed, would you feel trapped? Whose idea was this six-month guillotine anyway?

The house goes. Mum caves in and accepts meagre compensation. She and Phil pool their savings and buy a smaller place in Sutton

Mallet, a little way out of town. With the housing boom, they find themselves back on the mortgage hook in their fifties, working harder at Phil's business to make payments. James says they should have fought on but Mum always hated conflicts. Sean Rye, Laraine's old boyfriend, is now bank manager. He eases things a little for Mum, but James reports he's firmly in the Hackwill camp and probably gets a kickback for forcing the deal through.

The house isn't knocked down at once. There's a delay in the road-widening. It sits empty. Windows are broken by kids.

James reports this is Hackwill's real victory. Taking the house and not doing anything with it is worse than knocking it down. He says he is going to take the war to the enemy. Then, he sends you a cutting from the local paper. Robert Hackwill's Jaguar was stolen and driven into a ditch. There's a picture of the councillor looking stern next to the crash site, and a report of his speech against joy-riding thugs. In the picture, you see James leaning against a fence in the background, grinning. A band of hippies, including Graham Foulk, another of Laraine's exes, squats your vacant house. Hackwill condemns the invading wasters.

You'd worry more about James's war but the decision deadline is coming up.

You love Chris. Don't you? And, despite straying, she you?

Think about it.

Which do you decide?

If you decide to vote for marriage, go to 108. If you decide to vote for a split, go to 121.

15

When your Eleven Plus results come through, your parents think there has been a mistake. So does Mr Brunt. After negotiation, to which you are not party, you are called on a Saturday morning for an interview with Mr Brunt and an Exam Person.

None of the other children in your class who has failed is treated this way. You've a feeling you've been found out. The Exam People saw into your mind and knew you were deliberately getting sums wrong or picking the wrong word in a string from which you had to chose the odd one. Shane and Mary passed, and are on their way to Dr Marling's and the Girls' Grammar. Vanda and Paul failed as easily – Paul, whose dad works on a farm, picked 'goat' as the odd one out from 'cow, goat, lion, chicken, pig' – and are going, along with almost everyone else, to Hemphill. Your resolve to go with them, so strong that you picked 'chicken', is taking a battering. Grown-ups are making a fuss, as if this were as important as the custard row.

Your parents seem to think it their right that you to go to Marling's and wear a silly cap, do a hundred hours of homework a week and be keelhauled by prefects. They elaborately do not blame you for your failure. They take you to the school for your interview and keep on at you in the car. 'If they ask you why you want to go to Marling's, say you want to work in the bank,' Dad says. 'Just don't get nervous,' Mum puts in. Mum thinks you panicked under pressure and says it's ridiculous to decide a person's entire life based on how they feel on a random day in early spring when they are eleven. Dad just huffs and insists you say (pretend) you want to work in a bank. That would be a lie. You now think the Exam People can tell when you are lying. When you grow up, you want to walk on the moon like Neil Armstrong.

Your parents sit outside Mr Brunt's office, as if waiting to be punished, and you're sent in. The Exam Person is called Mrs Vreeland, and has glasses that look like plastic bird's-wings with windows in them. Mr Brunt smokes cigarettes throughout the interview, which makes the room stinky. It is Mrs Vreeland who talks to you.

First, she takes out your test paper – you recognise your name neatly printed at the top – and looks it over. You see red ticks and crosses by your answers.

'Cow, goat, lion, chicken, pig,' she says. 'Why is chicken the odd one out?'

You didn't expect to have to explain why you gave an answer.

'Because it's a bird,' you say.

Mrs Vreeland looks at Mr Brunt.

'And what are the others?'

You can't say 'Farm animals', because no one would believe you thought lions were kept for meat or milk.

'Animals,' you say, mumbling.

'Mammals?'

You nod. Mrs Vreeland looks at Mr Blunt again and writes something down.

'You don't like mathematics much, Keith? Sums?'

You shake your head, no.

'What's six away from twelve?'

That's easy. 'Six.'

'Not five?'

You remember that's what you put in the exam. Mrs Vreeland makes another note and puts your exam paper in a folder.

'Are you afraid of anything, Keith?'

Almost everything, you think. Prefects.

'No.'

'We want to help you. You haven't done anything wrong. You aren't being punished.'

You don't say anything.

'Draw me a picture,' she says, giving you paper and a pencil. 'What do you like to draw?'

'Outer space.'

'Draw me an outer space picture. Draw me a grown-up in space.'

As you work on the picture, Mrs Vreeland talks to you, asking who your friends are (Shane and Paul), what you would like for Christmas (a bigger bicycle), if you have brothers and sisters (yes), what you like on television (*Doctor Who*, *Captain Scarlet*).

'Keith, what do you want to be when you grow up?'

If you say you want to work in a bank, read 20 and go to 66. If you say you want to be an astronaut, read 20 and go to 21.

16

At Dr Marling's, you excel in Latin and French. You get bashed about a bit on the rugby pitch but develop a lifelong passion for cricket. You find most schoolwork stimulating and engaging. You make new friends: Mark Amphlett, Roger Cunningham, Gully Eastment. You realise the kids you knew at primary school were put off by the way your mind skips ahead; at Marling's, others can keep up with or outpace you. Everybody hates the uniform and writhes under the tyrannical rule of prefects. You bond for life, as if you'd been through a war together rather than suffered double geography on Thursday afternoon.

'That school's certainly bucked him up,' you overhear Dad saying.

You resent that. The school hasn't changed you. You'd have changed anyway. You're growing up.

You take part in school activities: trips to France, plays, junior cricket fixtures. In your year, you are a star. It makes you a bit uncomfortable, but flamboyant eccentrics like Michael Dixon and Gully draw most of the fire. You're just a regular bloke.

The school puts on *Henry IV, Part 1*. Michael buries himself under cushions and a false beard as Falstaff, but you get all the reviews as Hotspur. You enjoy your death scene and re-enact it whenever you're asked.

Some people think you're a prig. When Stephen Adlard offers you a cigarette in Denbeigh Gardens, you instinctively quote, 'Bobby Moore says, "Smoking is a mugs' game."' You cringe at your self-righteousness but have no desire to suck nicotine death. There's a little pressure on you to be less perfect but you don't feel like anybody's ideal so there's not much you can do.

Maths and physics are as hard for you as for anybody. Your languages skills are a fluke, the way your brain is arranged. You are top in Latin and French, and third or fourth in English, history and art.

At thirteen, it occurs to you that single-sex eduction is a bad thing. By then, Marling's is on a countdown to extinction.

Read 18, go to 24.

17

*B*lit blurt...

Everyone remembers where they were and what they were doing the first time they saw a spider.

You were quite young, in town, on your own, a little out of sorts.

It was nothing you could put your finger on, but you were dissatisfied. It might have been your health. You were coming down with flu. Or it could just have been life, playing its usual tricks. You were frankly in a rut.

You were wishing. Not for what you got – good God, no, never *that* – but for something. A change, of course. A shake-up.

You had always thought of yourself as ordinary. At that moment, as the shade was spreading, you were no longer content with that.

Then, on the Corn Exchange steps, for no reason, you looked up. And saw huge, red compound eyes. A wide face floating in a cloud of black shadow. Extending telegraph-pole legs, thickly bristled with black spines. And nothing was ever the same again.

...blit blurt.

18

Here's what happens in 1974. The tripartite educational system that has obtained in Britain since the war is transforming into a comprehensive system. What this means in Sedgwater is that the three main schools are combined. Dr Marling's Grammar School for Boys, the Girls' Grammar and Hemphill Secondary Modern become Ash Grove Comprehensive. The new school, which is named after your old primary school, is split between the sites that used to house Dr Marling's and Hemphill. The Girls' Grammar buildings become part of Sedgwater College, where you might go if you don't leave school at sixteen, and where Laraine is studying for her A Levels.

As a fourth-year, you are taught on the site that used to be Dr Marling's, though mostly in new, prefab buildings swiftly erected on what used to be the tennis courts, rather than in the old classrooms arranged around the central quadrangle. The most unbelievable thing that happens in the change-over is that the tie you're all forced to wear is designed by overlaying the colours of all three schools to produce a hideous combination of lemon yellow, blood crimson, lime green, violent pink, eggshell blue and dayglo orange. Jason King wouldn't wear one but a whole generation is compelled to hang these psychedelic eyesores round their necks.

You find yourself back with children you haven't seen since infants' school, and are mixed with several lots of kids – notably, the mysterious beauties of the Girls' Grammar – who are entirely new to you. On the first day, Mrs Barringer, the youngish woman freshly appointed as head of the new school, gets up at Assembly and gives a speech. All bets are off, she says, and we're starting anew. You are all capable of leaving behind the dead past and making new lives for yourselves. You don't believe her. You have already found your course, and you are set on it. Nothing can change that.

Go on.

19

In September 1974, you start going to Ash Grove. You really draw ahead of the pack. At first, it's odd. You'd got used to the other runners. Now there are new contestants, from the Girls' Grammar. One or two smart kids from Hemphill, even, nip at the heels of the pack, almost catching up. You don't have to worry about them: they've been hobbled. The girls are more worrying. Mary Yatman, whom you've not seen since infants' school, has subdued her monster and become a blonde calculating-machine. If it ever came down to a race between champions, she'd be put up against you. But you can't ignore Victoria Conyer, who has a bell-like singing voice and a trick memory, or Rowena Douglass, a tiny mouse who threatens to equal your fluency in French and German and is taking Spanish as well.

As you expect, Shane is the first to fall by the side of the track. Without the rigidly enforced discipline of Marling's, he loses his way. His marks decline drastically and no amount of cramming or extra tuition helps. Almost overnight, he slips from the fast stream and finds himself in with a remedial wedge of Hemphill kids, looking to leave school at sixteen. He joins the Trouble-Causers and disrupts many of his lessons. You don't see him much at break, since he's usually off somewhere smoking or hanging around the younger girls he tries to impress with his hardness. The one time you took a serious drag on a cigarette, you coughed your lungs out and swore never to touch one again.

Roger Cunningham soon follows, not quite as disastrously. He is the first of your group to find a steady girlfriend, Rowena. This takes out two runners at the same time: Roger and Rowena slacken and can't prop each other up. Neither will fail, but they aren't threats to you any more. Though still under five feet tall, Rowena sprouts enormous breasts, which become objects of much discussion. Roger sprouts a permanent grin but sometimes it is fixed and humourless. Despite what he says, you think Rowena hasn't let him handle the goods.

You run through your two-year O Level course and score nine passes, none at lower than grade B. Even Mary gets a C in English lit. Shane leaves school and goes to work at the jam factory, assisting the driver of a delivery van. For a while, he is the richest kid you know, with an unimaginable wage packet of £25 a week and the use of the van once he learns to drive. You overcome envy, realising Shane has been sidetracked by the short term. You can put off the gratification of financial independence from your parents for several more years. What is important is to keep running.

After the long, hot summer of 1976, you go on to Sedgwater College, where you don't have to wear a uniform and are required to take only three subjects: French, German, history. You are asked to think harder but this keeps you fresh. It is tougher on your competition than on you. Laraine is at university in East Anglia, reading geography. You know you can do better, and start thinking about Oxford colleges.

Unexpectedly, Victoria Conyer stumbles in the first year at college. Her parents have been training her from infancy, and she revolts. Tired of being clever all her life (she hasn't had many friends at school, suffering the catty envy of all), she decides to be stupid. Graham, who broke up with Laraine when she left for university, starts going out with Victoria and has her sing in his band. Overnight, she exchanges sensible blouses and skirts for greasy leather and ragged jeans. She dyes her hair white and chops it randomly, becoming by default the town's first punk. You knew Graham was a trap, waiting for someone. Now, Victoria is lost. She stays at college but risks expulsion by openly smoking dope in the common room. That seems a hippie thing to do, but she is openly scornful of all things hair-headed, which you see irritates Graham. She keeps pushing the group, currently called Vicky's Vomiteers, to be more 'radical'.

Stephen Adlard, you realise, was never really in the race. You were misled by his neatness, his skill at presentation. Incapable of independent thought, he recycles expected answers in his perfect handwriting, with soullessly ideal diagrams. He will survive, prosper even, but never catch you. A sexless, faceless nobody, he is doomed. If you think about it, you picture him becoming an estate agent or council inspector. Living death in an office, making regular mortgage payments.

You are out in front.

If you ever look around, you're surprised to find your only real competition comes from mad people, Mary Yatman and Gully Eastment. Mary hasn't hurt anyone badly in years but you remember what she was like when her monster was around and leave her alone to get on with it. Gully straggles all over the place – he plays drums in Graham's band and has a fifteen-year-old girlfriend, Bronagh Carey – but keeps revealing unexpected resources. If he lags behind, he puts on a spurt and catches up. He is in trouble with Bronagh's parents for sleeping with her and giving her drugs, but even this doesn't really hold him back. If it weren't for his crazy side, Gully would get ahead of you. But maybe it is only his crazy side that gives him the juice to stay in the race.

In your second year at college – 1977–8 – you decide you haven't been competing in the whole event. Your academic scores are unmatched and you have a shelfload of track trophies, but there are other events in the decathlon. To take home the gold, you need to be a social success.

People don't dislike you, actually; but you make them uncomfortable. At college, the stars are not outstanding academics or athletes but people like Gully or Michael Dixon or even Victoria, the unconventionally clever, setters of fashions, organisers of events. Michael takes over the Students' Union and masterminds parties, revues, discos, concerts. This arena, unfamiliar to you, becomes important.

You know you can catch up.

First, you need a girlfriend. James, two years younger, has been seeing Candy Dixon, Michael's sister. Experimentally, you have got off with two girls: Jacqui Edwardes, who introduced you to tongue-kissing, and Gina, a girl from Wells you haven't seen since. Neither is a serious candidate. You need someone who will complement your strengths, augment your prestige. You consider the question as if you were prime minister of a Balkan state seeking an alliance with a neighbouring principality.

Mary is an obvious, if scary, choice, but you don't want to go out with someone who might get ahead of you. Equally, you can't go with a thicko who would hold you back, like poor Jacqui. Roger and Rowena have been going out for over a year, but argue all the time.

Roger isn't measuring up to Rowena: he smokes drugs with Graham, Gully and Victoria, and Rowena violently disapproves of hippies. That might be an opportunity. Rowena already knows how to be a girlfriend, which would be a clear advantage.

Mary is tall and blonde, with a pretty face and long, slim legs. Her huge eyes are still scary. As far as you know, she has never had a boyfriend. Shane admitted once that he always fancied her but was afraid of what she might do. You find her uncomfortable but attractive. Intelligence is hidden inside her, coiled like a snake, always tensely ready to strike. Rowena is still tiny but shapely. You have thought about her breasts too many times in the dark of night. She has a goofy humour you can't quite follow but which suggests she'd never be boring. Also, you've overheard her tell a friend that if you weren't in such a hurry she might fancy you.

At the end of term, in the run-up to Christmas, the college has a Rag Day. Everyone dresses up in costumes and runs riot, raising money for charity. Michael, still stuttering crazily, is president of the Rag Committee, which consists of his girlfriend, Penny Gaye, and his long-time associates Mickey, Neil and Mark. On the evening of Rag Day, the last day of term, the committee is to put on a show at the college, a mix of comedy sketches and musical acts. Graham's band, this week called Flaming Torture, will top the bill.

You decide, after much internal debate, to ask Mary to go with you to the show and the wild party Michael will hold afterwards at his grandmother's house miles out of town in Achelzoy. Then, you learn Rowena has found out Roger has slept with Victoria and acrimoniously broken up with him. You reconsider your plans. After all, you aren't certain either girl will accept if you ask her to go out with you, and the shame and embarrassment of rejection would be insupportable for someone in your position. You are so used to victory that you cannot bear defeat. You'd not play rather than lose. You sit in your parents' hallway, looking at the telephone. You have numbers for Mary and Rowena written down. You are sweating. You think of Mary's eyes and Rowena's breasts.

Who do you ask to go with you to the show? If Rowena, go to 22. If Mary, go to 26. If you duck out of asking anyone and go alone, go to 30.

20

Your parents look relieved when they see Mr Brunt's face. At the interview, it is agreed that a mistake has been made and that your exam paper should be set aside. For a moment, you wonder whether this is fair: why didn't Paul and Vanda get interviews, with their parents waiting outside the office, to set aside their results?

Mrs Vreeland holds the picture you drew for her, of a bank manager on Mars with a briefcase attached to his space-suit by an air hose. She asks you to go outside and play while she talks with your parents. You do, though there's no one else in school to play with. You walk across the grass towards the copse, bounding slowly under reduced gravity. A Martian monster lives in the copse, so you stay away from it. You've left your ray-gun at home.

On the way home, Dad says you'll be going to Dr Marling's after all. Your mum is so happy she is almost crying. You don't suppose it makes much difference whether you're in a school with Shane or with Paul.

Go on.

21

In the third year at Marling's, the last year it will exist, a group of you are walking through town on a Thursday afternoon. You've just suffered through a geologic age of double geography.

As usual, you put off the moment of getting back for tea. The group aren't your particular friends, just boys who happen to live along the route you take home, through the town centre and out towards the Achelzoy road.

Mickey Yeo has (against regulations) stuffed cap, tie and blazer in his satchel, trying to look as if he goes to a harder school. Stephen Adlard seems about ten in his perfect uniform. Norman Pritchard scurries ahead and darts back all the time, unable to keep to a steady pace.

You hang about Denbeigh Gardens, a rec ground. Younger kids are playing football and Mickey wants to scare them off, sending Norman in as a shock troop. Norman is keen, but you and Stephen aren't so sure.

Stephen asks you a question about homework but you aren't interested. Officially, you are a good pupil, like Stephen. But he's boring. His idea of a good time is drawing a Venn diagram, using all the inks in his multicolour pen. Mickey, clever (too clever) but temperamental, and Norman, a Trouble-Causer, make you a bit uncomfortable. But uncomfortable is better than boring.

You always stop at Denbeigh Gardens, at Mickey's insistence, because a steady file of Girls' Grammar girls pass through at about the time you are there. None of you has ever actually tried to speak to any of these girls, but Mickey and Norman throw each other around in slow motion like stuntmen, trying to attract their attention. Sometimes, the girls giggle.

'*Man Who Shot Liberty Valance*,' Mickey says.

Everyone else stopped playing cowboys in primary school, but with Mickey the re-enactment of fights from films he's seen is less a game than a ritual. When he arranges you into characters from *Shane* or *The Magnificent Seven* and talks you through shoot-outs, insisting you die in order, he's invoking something. He occasionally varies the model, straying from Westerns to war films (*Tobruk*, with you all trundling like tanks, or *The Great Escape*, in which you are Donald Pleasence) and even, once, the assassination attempt on Governor George Wallace. Recently, with 10cc's 'Rubber Bullets' in the charts, Mickey has re-enacted that, with you as Sergeant Baker.

Mickey is Liberty, Lee Marvin. He taunts you, as James Stewart. Norman, as John Wayne, gets to back-shoot him from the shadows. And Stephen is the bald coon who tosses Wayne the rifle he fires at Liberty.

You scrabble in the dirt for the gun you have dropped – a piece of wood – and Norman fires his branch from behind the gardener's shed.

The timing is perfect. Three girls, in straw boaters and bottle-green blazers, come through the latch-gate just as Mickey takes the shot in the back. More elaborately than Lee Marvin, he wheels round, dropping his gun, clutching his wounds. He staggers this way and that, then spread-eagles on the grass, gurgling his last. The girls hurry on, looking down to avoid noticing the mad boy. There's injustice there. Mickey's artistry should be rewarded somehow.

The girls have gone and Mickey is spread out on the grass.

Stephen comes up behind you as you stand over Mickey and nudges you in the back.

'Nothing's too good for the Man Who Shot Liberty Valance,' he says.

You think Stephen has pulled a six-shooter from his satchel and is going to rewrite the script by plugging you in the back, leaving Norman to get off with Vera Miles and live in that half-built desert house with the cactus rose.

Actually, he has a thin pack of cigarettes. Not sweet cigarettes. Players No 6.

Mickey springs back to life and Norman is interested too.

'Give us one, Adlard,' Norman says, barging in.

'Dying for a gasper, I am,' Mickey says.

A dynamic is changing in this group. It should be one of the bad boys offering the cigarettes round. Stephen is the best-behaved boy at Marling's. His homework is always perfect, as if laboured over by a medieval monk; his geography maps are illuminated texts.

Mickey and Norman have fags in their mouths and suck the taste through the filters. Of course, neither has matches.

Stephen is quietly pleased to be prime mover rather than the coon (a word your mum doesn't like you using) throwing John Wayne the rifle. He has a flip-top lighter, metal and shiny. Norman takes it but doesn't know how to use it, so Stephen takes it back. Promoted from coloured help to suave decadent, Stephen plucks a cigarette from the pack, taps it on his hand (like Sean Connery as James Bond), and sticks it jauntily in his mouth. Cupping his hand to shield the flame from the breeze, he flicks the lighter and lights up. He inhales deeply and sends plumes of smoke out of his nostrils.

You couldn't be more impressed if he blew rings.

Stephen holds out the flame and Norman and Mickey light up. Norman gulps down a lungload, coughs and goes greenish. Mickey merely takes a suck, pretends to like the taste and breathes out a cloud.

'Keith?'

Stephen is offering you a cigarette. Your hand goes out, but you hesitate. In adverts in comics, Bobby Moore says, 'Smoking is a mugs' game.'

Norman splutters badly now. Green slime trickles from his nose and tears dribble down his cheeks. Mickey is enjoying the show, smiling in a superior way. He takes another bogus puff.

Stephen raises the pack as if it were a gun.

If you turn down the cigarette, go to 16. If you think you can get away with the fake smoking demonstrated by Mickey, go to 73. If you think you can do better than Norman and smoke properly, like Stephen, go to 19.

22

Rowena says she is coming down with flu and doesn't think she'll be going to Michael's party. She'll be in town for Rag Day, but thinks she ought to get home in the evening.

She coughs into the phone. That makes you think this is a turn-down not a legitimate excuse. Rowena is trying too hard to convince you she's sick.

Maybe she's off men after Roger and needs to be convinced you're not a swine like him. Or maybe you misunderstood her interest in you.

When you put the phone down, she'll call up all her friends and tell them you had the temerity to ask her out, emphasising the ridiculousness of your expectations. Everyone will know.

Score one against the runner.

To get through Rag Day like this, you'll have to wear a mask. Or be invisible.

Or maybe she just has flu. It happens.

'Sorry,' Rowena says.

If you accept the excuse and hang up, go to 30. If you try to use your powers of persuasion to wheedle around Rowena's excuse, go to 28.

23

In September 1974, you start going to Ash Grove. Though on a new site, combining the ivied quadrangle of Marling's with prefab shacks, you still have the Hemphill teachers, the Hemphill classes. You study for Certificate of Secondary Education exams, the thicko versions of the O Levels ex-grammar-school kids are taking. Laraine's O Levels got her into Sedgwater College, from which she'll go on to university. CSEs are a rubber-stamp for cannon fodder in the job market. If anything, the schoolwork is easier than it was at Hemphill, almost insultingly so.

Dickie Kell and Paul Mysliewic work Saturday mornings at the jam factory, hefting boxes. They seem fabulously wealthy, with £10 a week cigarette money. Two more years, they chant, and they can work full time ('go down the Synth'), have money coming in, buy mopeds, move out of their parents' houses – their homes are much smaller than yours, and they have to share rooms – and get on with their lives. They make the last two years of school seem like the remainder of a prison sentence.

Your parents won't let you work at the jam factory, though they don't mind Laraine doing Saturdays as a waitress at Brink's Café. You decide not to speak to them for a month. They don't seem to notice, which shocks you. Somehow, you've become the invisible middle kid. James studies Latin at Ash Grove – on the site which used to be Hemphill – while you're encouraged to take woodwork. Laraine is wondering which university to go to.

You think seriously about British Synthetics. Do you want to work in a factory? Go down the Synth?

At Ash Grove, Shane Bush rejoins your gang. He's struggling with O Levels. He joins Dickie and Paul, counting off the days to release, and is the only one among you with an ambition, to learn to drive and gain command of a delivery van. Three years apart have changed your relationship. Shane is still loud and domineering, but Marling's has convinced him he's thicker than he is. He calls you 'Mental' in public, but asks for advice (even help with schoolwork) when you're alone. You've grown past the age when Shane can get his way with a few cheerful cuffs around the head. You realise you can order him around, a position you sometimes (remembering infants' school) can't resist abusing.

Shane tries to get off with Marie-Laure but she isn't interested. You realise Shane defers to you and Marie-Laure because your parents are, by his standards, rich, which makes you uncomfortable. Vanda's spots clear up and she keeps proposing kissing games, though you've long grown out of them. Marie-Laure kisses with her tongue, which means Vanda has to let boys feel her growing breasts. You all go along with this weird competition between the girls, but Marie-Laure calls a halt when Barry slips a hand into her knickers, and becomes for all practical purposes a nun.

Though three school populations are amalgamated, there's little mixing. You're in lessons with Hemphill kids and hang around with them at breaks. Some kids (Michael Dixon, Mary Yatman) you were at infants' school, even kindergarten, with are around. You don't talk to them unless you have to.

You had expected armed combat with the Marling's boys, but it rarely comes to that. Hemphill lads think grammar schoolies are posh and soft and brainy. Some of them, like Michael, are. As Shane solicits homework help from you, you worry that deep down you're posh and soft and brainy too. More and more, you think about your Eleven Plus. How might things have been if you hadn't failed it? Is the worst thing in the world to be posh and soft and thick? You actually make an effort in some of your classes (English, French) but it's a struggle. It's not the work you have to overcome, it's the sluggishness of your classmates and even the teachers.

You get fed up with Shane, Dickie, Barry, Paul and Vanda. They're so impatient to get out of school and 'on with it' that they keep getting into trouble. You get dragged in with them too often. Dickie has a maniac streak (he threw the first stone at that bloody dog, you remember) and commits an escalating series of acts of vandalism. The prefab classrooms are flimsy and Dickie discovers that he can head-butt cracks in the pasteboard walls, even punch right through them.

It makes sense to distance yourself from your long-time friends, and you spend more time with Vince Tunney and, oddly, Marie-Laure. The three of you are all-round out-of-its, too clever for CSEs, not clever enough for O Levels. You admit to Vince that you find the prospect of life after school terrifying. You don't want to go down the Synth, you've decided. But you don't want to work in a bank or an estate agent's either. You don't want to drag things out by going to college or university. You think of joining the merchant marine and joke about running away to become a pirate.

Vince would like to be a comic-book artist but isn't very good. In the art room, he sees superhero panels drawn by Mickey Yeo, one of the O Level stream, and is forced to recognise how inadequate his own work is. He can never get hands right. Marie-Laure is torn between staying at home – her rich parents are screwed up enough to support her without a second thought – and travelling to India. She's the first person you know who tries marijuana. You and Vince sometimes go to her house in Achelzoy, a village outside town, and loll around her bookless room, getting stoned. Her mum and dad are never home at the same time.

You want time to stop, now. Then you wouldn't have to think about the future, the imminent after-school. Without noticing it, you've become a grown-up. You're sixteen. The fun is over. Vanda and Shane announce their engagement. Paul, Barry and Dickie bunk off school most of the time. Marie-Laure's hands won't stop shaking. Vince endlessly catalogues and rearranges his comics. Ahead of you, a shadowy void gapes. You are sure there are cobwebs stretched invisibly across the path, waiting for you.

At the end of your first year at Ash Grove, your fourth year in secondary school, you have interviews with your class teacher and a careers officer. You worry that the only ambitions you've ever had, to be a pirate or an astronaut, won't impress them.

Mr Bird, your class teacher – you don't have him for any lessons, just for a ten-minute get-together in the morning – looks over your report and asks if you want to shift from maths and French CSE to O Level courses. He thinks you've got a chance of passing.

'You should seriously think about it,' he says.

You don't know. Can you keep up with the more demanding work? And will two O Levels to go with six CSEs mean anything in a year's time, when you pass out into the void?

If you transfer to the O Level stream in two subjects, go to 25. If you stay on the CSE courses, go to 27.

24

In September 1974, you start going to Ash Grove. It's less structured than Marling's, more relaxing, easier to cope with. You study for O Levels now, which means thinking harder. But you enjoy that. You need goals to stretch for. It's the same in cricket, where you constantly try to improve yourself. As an all-rounder, you're distinguished as neither a bowler nor a batsman – though you have a knack for catches when you field – but become captain. Because you see the whole picture, you can best deploy the strengths of your team-mates, compensate for their weaknesses.

The big change is girls. Michael's stutter gets exponentially worse at Ash Grove: it takes him months to get a coherent sentence out in the presence of a girl. Gully and Mickey turn into major leches and obsess over any girl they happen to be in a class with, though they can only actually get off with girls a year or two younger than they are.

You find you like girls, not just in the obvious way. You see how stale your thinking was getting at Marling's, which was all about jumping through hoops and ticking off boxes, and are forced to question all that. You start going out with Victoria Conyer, who is the Girls' Grammar answer to you – smart and on course but with an independent streak. Perhaps you're too similar, because you don't last three months. You see in her a wildness you find a touch frightening. She reminds you of Scary Mary Yatman, who is still around and apparently a reformed personality.

In 1976, you pass eight O Levels, four at grade A. You go on to Sedgwater College to take a two-year A Level course. There, you become president of the Students' Union, with Michael as your deputy. He becomes a small-town impresario, and stages a series of parties and 'entertainments', breaking away from the umbrella of the college to evade censorship.

You go out with Rowena Douglass, also a language specialist. You put off sleeping together for months but both find your parents less disapproving than you'd have thought. Rowena is allowed to stay over at weekends. You are sensible about contraception.

You get your A Levels and go to Manchester University. Ro wants to retake German and opts to put off further education for a year, but comes north to live with you. You get a flat together and feel very grown-up, almost married. She never does go to university, but tops up her qualifications with practical courses at Manchester Poly – secretarial, business, computer-programming.

You get a First Class degree but decline offers of postgrad places. It's 1981 and you want to get out of education into the real world.

You and Ro move down to London and get a bigger flat – part financed by your parents, but you'll pay them back – in Chelsea. She works as a bilingual secretary and you take a temporary job as an international courier and translator. You get to go to every continent, including Antarctica, and discover a knack for setting up and organising business negotiations between many parties. It's like putting together a jigsaw.

Several times, in different foreign cities, you have brief affairs with business contacts. Always, you feel guilty but you don't regret the experience. The women are mostly older, studied in glamour and sexual enthusiasm. They convince you that you're really in love with Ro, rather than just drifting along because you've been together since school.

Dad dies in 1982. The next year, once your mum is out of mourning, you announce you will get married. Without planning it, Ro gets pregnant. Mum, herself engaged, is appalled and delighted that she'll be a granny. Ro blossoms and blooms as she swells. Your sex life has never been better than in the months of her pregnancy.

At the same time, you get capital together to found your own business. You've expedited so much for so many, while going from job to job, that you have more contacts than any of your bosses, and a better reputation in the field. You've picked up some Japanese and are in the forefront of Anglo-Japanese trade links. You've even done a lot of work for the government, though you've never voted for them.

You have a 1984 wedding. Ro gives up work and has twins, Jeremy and Jessica.

You buy your Chelsea flat but start looking for a house out of London. Not in the commuter belt, a real retreat. You have an office in the city and a full staff there, but do most of your work in the field, out of the country. Your wardrobe includes gear appropriate to every climate and social occasion. You own tropical suits and alpaca parkas, and have multiples of dinner jackets in white and black. Ro teases you about dressing like James Bond, and asks if you can have an ejector seat fitted in the BMW.

Finally, you buy a house in Sutton Mallet, near Sedgwater. You return almost as a conquering hero. Your old teachers all want to take credit for you.

You have friends and contacts all over the world but stay in touch with a surprising number of people from Ash Grove. Mark Amphlett founds *The Shape*, a magazine, and becomes a 'style guru'. Michael Dixon is a comedian, TV personality and novelist. Victoria Conyer emerges shrieking from punk and survives as a singer-songwriter. Gully Eastment is another kind of guru, leader of a nomadic tribe of travellers; he goes to jail for his part in a poll-tax riot and is the subject of several television documentaries.

Laraine, a lecturer in history at East Anglia, marries Fred, her university boyfriend. James comes out of the army and starts a security firm. You employ him to run security at conferences whenever there is a possibility of terrorist attack. Councillor Robert Hackwill, your old school bully, is always leaving messages on your answerphone, wheedling support for local schemes.

When the kids start school, Ro comes into the firm. She turns out to have a flair for design, and handles your PR. Victoria poaches her to run her indie record label, which is a surprise but works out amazingly well.

The 1980s are good to you. It's hard not to feel guilty about that. You work closely with a great many business people you feel are no better than crooks but manage to keep your own integrity. You won't work in South Africa, Chile, Indonesia or the Philippines (until Marcos goes). With Michael and Mark, you get involved around the fringes of Live Aid and keep up your charitable work, donating a great deal of free time and expertise to discreet fund-raising and environmental lobbying.

It's possible that you make a difference.

But, as the '80s draw to a close, and you turn thirty, you start thinking.

Isn't everything all just a bit too easy?

The point of a jigsaw is the putting together. Once it's done, you don't frame and admire the picture. You feel you've finished this puzzle. There's a nagging urge to break up the picture into a million pieces and put it back in its box. Then start again.

That's silly.

In many ways, you've only just started. There are the kids. New puzzles, constantly exciting and interesting. You've no real idea what pictures they'll make yet. Work is still stimulating. You and Ro aren't bored with each other.

If the next word in this train of thought is 'But…' go to 169. If the next word is 'And…' go to 274.

25

You call it Year the Second-and-Fifth (of Ash Grove and Hemphill), after James the First (of England) and Sixth (of Scotland). For the first two terms, from September 1975 to Easter 1976, you work hard on your new courses and achieve a middling placing in classes of clever kids.

Your parents are mad keen on the O Level lark. Laraine, who will go to university at the end of the month, is ordered to tell you what a wonderful time she had at Sedgwater College. Previously, toiling in the lower depths of the CSE stream, you were lost. Now, there's the possibility of salvation.

Marie-Laure is jumped to the O Level stream in art and scripture ('religious studies', they call it at Ash Grove). Vince Tunney joins you in maths, which gives you an ally but perhaps holds you back a bit. Reversing the pattern, Shane Bush is only doing English O Level, dropping all his other subjects to CSE.

Now you're all world-weary sixteen-year-olds, former grammar-school kids don't persecute former Hemphill kids. Rowena Douglass, who is with you in French, even makes something of a pet of you, ostentatiously helping you in class. You feel a little patronised but also realise you're out of your depth. You keep up on paper but don't have the confidence to speak in class and have to be painfully drawn out.

The void still gapes. Maybe Sedgwater College is a way of putting it off? But if you have to work full out on an O-for-Ordinary Level course, how could you do at A-for-Advanced Level? The black void extends spider-tendrils.

You are often in a state of suppressed panic.

In the run-up to your exams – mostly CSEs, but those two O Levels loom larger – your parents take you to Sedgwater College for a special interview.

If you pass all your exams – a big if – the college will accept you, studying not for A Levels but for a certificate in business studies. That alone won't get you into a university.

Business studies.

'It's a good grounding,' Dad says. He left school at sixteen to work in the bank. 'It could lead to a position. We always have openings.'

The future is an unimaginable emptiness. You have no conception of what you want from it. But of one thing you are sure. You don't want to work in a fucking bank. You don't want to spend two years on a certificate in business studies. You might as well buy a prat suit, like Laraine's bank clerk ex-boyfriend Sean Rye wears, and bury yourself alive.

You feel yourself falling. Spider-webs of shade cling to you, wrapping you tight.

It's all the worse for the time and effort you've wasted on what turn out to be useless O Levels. You were betrayed. When you were persuaded to take maths and French, you weren't told you needed at least three O Level passes for it to mean anything. You might then have stretched yourself, and gone for history or art or English. It might then have meant something.

But you were conned. You've jumped through hoops – you've been patronised by that big-titted cow Rowena, you've given up hours of free time sweating over a slide-rule – and all for nothing. A big fat zero.

Again, you won't talk to your parents.

You slacken off revising. Oddly, this means you're less worried and more relaxed when you sit the exams, and probably do better than you would have done if you'd been screwing yourself into knots trying to be at your best.

After the exams are done, a German soldier leans over your wounded body and cackles, 'For you, Tommy, ze education iss over.' Whatever results you get, you're not taking business studies. You go home and wait for the darkness to close in.

Go to 29.

26

'Your, uh, *friend's* here,' Mum says. 'She looks very nice,' she whispers. This is embarrassing. Your parents are delighted you have asked Mary out. They don't remember the monster from primary school. Parents have an incredible ability to forget the unforgettable.

Mary lives in Achelzoy, the outlying village where Michael Dixon will throw his party after the show, and she has learned to drive. It seems strange but *she* is calling for *you*, in her mum's Honda Civic.

That she can drive and you can't makes you feel – briefly – like a girl. You've grown up familiar with the rituals of teenage courtship shown in American movies and TV programmes, but things are different in Britain. You suppose you and Mary have a date, but no one at Sedgwater College would call it that. Now you feel as if you are dolled up in a prom dress with a ribbon in your beehive hair, while

Mary idles below in her hot-rod, a pack of cigarettes tucked into the upturned sleeve of her T-shirt and a wad of gum going in her mouth.

Downstairs, Mary waits. She is wearing a yellow dress and an orange overcoat. She has used make-up cleverly, to hide the scariness in her face.

Momentarily, you are certain you have made a mistake. Mary has agreed to go with you to the show and the party as part of her long-planned revenge scheme.

You called her a girl once and she nearly killed you. Now, you've asked her to be your girlfriend and she's going along with it, drawing it out, scheming.

You think of the bucket of pig's blood in *Carrie*.

Mary smiles and makes polite conversation with your mother about college work. Mary says she would like to take a year off after college to work before going on, if she does, to university. She is thinking of working on her uncle's farm.

Dad, hiding behind a newspaper, is stricken. You notice, as usually you don't, that Mary has a yokel burr. You've failed to pick up a Somerset voice but rarely realise how strongly accented your friends are. You imagine Mary driving a tractor, sucking a straw, wearing a smock.

You hurry through the hallway, hustling Mary out of the house. Your parents come to the door to watch you go, beaming with a pride that reddens your face. You mumble promises to be back sometime, though you fully expect not to return until tomorrow. They wave as if you were going to Afghanistan. You want to hit your dad right in the grin.

You struggle with the unfamiliar seatbelt in Mary's car: it doesn't seem to fit together properly, offering two identical catches that refuse to interlock. Mary slides into the driving seat and sits beside you, in the dark. You are sure her X-ray eyes discern the packet of condoms you have got from the machine in the Gents at the Lime Kiln after waiting for twenty minutes in a stall for the place to be empty so no one would see you. It is highly unlikely you'll have any use for them, but you are used to planning for all eventualities.

Mary leans closer to you. To kiss?

A warm, sickly feeling nesdes in your throat. You feel the threat of an erection.

Mary turns on the overhead light.

'Hello, you,' she says.

Are you expected to kiss her?

'Hello, Mary,' you say, almost croaking.

'Your mum don't half go on.'

You *know* your face is scarlet. You mumble that Mary is right. Recently, your parents have been impossible. It must be their time of life.

Mary reaches down and sorts out your seatbelt. You have been trying to fasten yours to hers. You curse yourself for an idiot, knowing what the girl – it's all right to call Mary a girl these days – thinks of you now.

'Well,' Mary says, smiling, 'wagons roll.'

She lets off the handbrake.

It's too late. You are now going out with Mary Yatman, and you have no idea what that means.

Later, with cider inside, you have relaxed. Checking your face in mirrors, you see you are no longer scarlet. You look cool. The black suede jacket was a worthwhile purchase. Some of the other students are in fancy dress, left over from parading round the town centre all day for charity.

The Rag Show is an informal event. Students and hangers-on drift in and out of the college auditorium. Knots of secretive kids drink or smoke, avoiding the lecturers nominally in charge.

You are outside the main building, with Mary. The weather has turned cold. Shallow pools of recent rain turn to gritty ice. The noise of Flaming Torture explodes through the tall windows. All their songs sound alike, and you can only hear Gully's drum-beat and Vic's cut-glass high notes.

Michael Dixon, in a dinner jacket and bow tie, is trying to calm down an irate, shivering neighbour who has turned up in her dressing-gown to complain about after-hours noise. He is talking fast, stuttering all over the show, to distract the woman from Vic's lyrics.

Victoria Conyer is singing a song about strangling the Queen Mother with barbed wire.

Mary thinks it's funny.

'She's got a lovely voice,' she comments.

'She's certainly got the full octave.'

The song ends, with Vic screeching. Dogs in the area must be bursting eardrums.

You still aren't sure about Mary. All through the evening, she's been pretending to be normal. You know all about that. You've been pretending to be normal too. If anyone has questions about you being with Mary, they've kept them to themselves. You've been studiedly casual, occasionally looking at Mary from one side, thinking, 'That's my girlfriend.'

You sort of expected people to come up and congratulate you, to welcome you to the world of coupledom. All that has happened is that Roger has warned you against the wiles of wicked women. He is drifting around drunkenly embittered without Rowena (she stayed at home) and breathing cider on various girls. You think he's got off with Jacqui Edwardes, which wouldn't surprise anyone.

'Are you coming to the party?' Michael asks you both.

'Might as well,' Mary says.

'Top hole,' Michael says.

He is harassed by a hundred things that need organising and explaining. Michael gets off on orchestrating events.

'Gramma's away and there are no neighbours,' Michael says. 'That'll be a relief. No possible complainants.'

Just inside the glass doors of the college hall, Desmond Fewsham lifts a fire extinguisher from its bracket, fending off a desperately drunk Mickey Yeo, who advances under a raised cloak like a punk Dracula. Michael, appalled, knows before it happens that Desmond will let the thing off, squirting foam all over the place. White froth spatters the doors and ghost-faces Mickey.

'Excuse me,' Michael says. 'I zh-zh-zhust have to kill some close friends.'

As he stalks off, Mary laughs. You do too, and find you are holding her hand.

'Glad you came?' you ask.

She doesn't answer, just squeezes your hand. It occurs to you that Mary has never been out with anyone before. She is just as lost as you are.

Maybe that's not so bad.

Mickey, screaming and laughing through his frozen and foamed face, staggers through the double doors like a monster, arms outstretched.

Shadows flit across the car park. You realise how cold it is. Your breath and Mary's frost in the air under the halogen lights.

'Do you remember my monster, Keith?'

You say nothing, pretending. It was a long time ago. You *could* have forgotten.

'My monster remembers you.'

She dances away from you, literally, picking up the beat of Flaming Torture. Harsh shadows make a kabuki mask of her face. Her hair falls over her forehead in a wing. Her lips are red as blood. Her teeth are sharp.

She dances with her shadows. They flicker away from her, spreading like skirts, and fall back into her body, scattered tendrils of her dark.

You wonder if you've drunk too much. Are you going to be sick?

Your head whirls as Mary dances, arms out, fingers beckoning you. With an effort of will, you hold back sickness, swallowing fluid.

You are in control.

You reach and take one of Mary's hands. She pulls you out from between cars and you dance. Her shadow twines around yours.

It is time to drive out to Achelzoy, to Michael's party. Mary lets go of you long enough to get into the driver's seat of the Honda. She opens the passenger door and you get in, bumping your head on the frame.

'Poor thing,' she coos.

She has already reversed out of her parking space, nearly sideswiping a still-foamed Mickey, as you reach for that impossible, unfamiliar seatbelt. Your fingers might as well be sausages as they grope for the catch.

Mary has driven on to the road, face set in concentration. Outside the college is a traffic light. Amber switches to red. As Mary stops, the car interior is filled with a red glow. You are still trying to work the seatbelt.

Her face a glowing red, Mary leans close to you. The engine is in an idling thrum. You smell perfume. Mary's lips are slightly open, her eyes almost closed.

You cannot get the belt to connect.

Party-goers stream across the road in front of the car, ignoring you both. They are whooping drunk.

The moment won't last. Amber will come, then green.
What do you do?

If you insist Mary help you do up the seatbelt, read 35 and go to 37. If you kiss Mary, read 35 and go to 40.

27

You don't tell Mum and Dad you've been offered the chance to take two O Levels. The school gives you a letter for them, which you read and dump. You mumble something about wanting to pass CSEs with good grades rather than fail O Levels, and Mr Bird accepts it. You sense his disappointment but he's busy with too many other crises – Tony Bennett has scandalised the school by assaulting a woodwork teacher with a chisel – to follow up.

You spend more time with Vince and Marie-Laure, getting stoned and worrying. Vince accepts nothingness as his future, and has found out how to sign on for supplementary benefit as soon as school is over. You talk about 'fill-in' jobs, not careers but things you might do to get money.

You make plans to go to festivals, hitching around the country together. You see *Easy Rider* at the Palace Cinema and wonder about saving up to buy motorbikes.

School doesn't take up much time or thought. You're as clever and as qualified as you're ever going to be. A lot of kids in the CSE stream bunk off more or less all the time. You don't go as far as that and turn up to most of your classes. Through habit, as much as anything else. You can do the work without much fuss and bother, so you do.

Tony Bennett goes to approved school. Paul and Dickie idolise him, glorying in their tearaway reputations. They terrorise the more misfit O Level kids, preferably a year younger and a lot smaller than them. They have a collection of stolen ties, and extort dinner tickets from whoever seems easy meat. Once or twice, you go along with them, but the bullying seems childish, a throwback to infants' school. A gang of girls (Vanda is one) harass poor, demented Timmy Gossett, which makes you sick.

Two terms slip by. At Easter 1976, you realise you have only until the summer before school runs out.

You've been in education – from Denbeigh Kindergarten through Ash Grove Primary through Hemphill Secondary Modern to Ash Grove Comprehensive – for all the life you can remember. Soon, that'll be over. If you think about it too much, it stops you sleeping.

Dad takes you aside and a heavy pall of dread falls on you. He asks you about the future, about your plans, your thoughts. You have nothing to say to him. He doesn't notice, and instead goes on about how he left school at sixteen to work in a bank and made something of himself.

You have a heart-clutching certainty he'll make you work in the bank. Laraine's ex-boyfriend Sean started as a tea-maker and minion before ascending to the position of clerk. You'll become a teenage suicide statistic before you wear a prat suit like Sean Rye.

You don't want to work in a fucking bank. You don't want to work in a fucking factory. Let's face it, you don't fucking want to work. You want to be left alone.

You collect a stack of worthless CSEs. Shane gets his wish and goes to work for Hackwill & Son Builders' Supplies, assisting a delivery driver. Paul, Barry and Dickie go down the Synth. It takes them a week to learn to hate the factory the way they hated school. Dickie is fired after a month, for vandalising equipment. Vince talks about the army but doesn't do anything about enlisting. Marie-Laure works for three days as a waitress in Brink's Café but gets sacked for swearing.

You go home and wait for the darkness to close in.

Go to 29.

28

Rowena caves in easily when you promise to look after her and bring along a flask of something to keep her warm inside.

'In that case…'

Was the fuss about flu some sort of test to winnow out anyone who wasn't that keen? Or did she need a few minutes to get used to the idea of you?

Now, she sounds quite keen.

'I'm not wearing any sort of fancy dress,' she says. 'I think it's childish.'

'Me too,' you say, squelching your possible Invisible Man idea.

You think of what you'll look like together. She's a head shorter than you. She'll fit under your arm.

Will she let you kiss her? Or anything more?

Suddenly, you're not sure about this Keith-and-Rowena thing.

She's running through her schedule for the day, suggesting a place to meet first thing in the morning, allowing a few hours to get home in the late afternoon and dress up for the evening.

It's too late now. You're committed.

You feel a tickle in the back of your throat and wonder if you're coming down with something.

If Rowena really has got flu, do you want to snog her? Or breathe in around her?

Do you worry about Rowena's Germs?

Throughout Rag Day, the town centre is clogged with students in costume, accosting passers-by for money. Neil Martin demonstrates the untruth of an old saying by trying to sell hot cakes from the Corn Exchange steps. Desmond Fewsham has found an accordion he can't play and is anti-busking, providing a minute of merciful silence for every 10p given him. A few seconds of tuneless wheezing is enough to solicit a donation. No one is sure which charity Rag Day is supposed to be raising money for, but Michael Dixon, president of the Student Union, assures everyone it's all in a good cause. Mickey Yeo, creeping around in a Dracula cloak with his hair in Johnny Rotten spikes, has voted the Union use the money to send Satanist missionaries to backward Christian countries. Mostly, students take Rag Day as an excuse to loon about.

You meet Rowena at ten o'clock on the Corn Exchange steps. She is bundled up in an orange coat, lower face mummified with a scarf. Her nose is red. She looks like one of Santa's elves.

'Hi,' you say.

Do you kiss? You do not.

Rowena mumbles something.

If she really has got flu, it's good news. She wasn't trying to brush you off, and is interested enough in you to come out in the cold against medical advice.

Roger turns up, dressed as Zorro, cutting Zs in the air with a plastic sword. Rowena hugs you. Surprised, you hug her back. She might as well be wearing an astronaut's suit. You can't feel a girl under all the wrapped-up-warm layers.

You realise she's out with you at least partially to get back at Roger.

Victoria arrives, illegally parking her old Mini van by the Corn Exchange steps. She emerges from her van, decked out in gauzy black rags like Morticia Addams gone punk. For her, this is an everyday look.

Roger ostentatiously tries to kiss her before she can lock the van door. She shudders, driving him away with her spider-web-gloved fingers.

'Give it a rest, Rog,' she snarls.

Rowena presses close to you. Those breasts are between you, albeit an impenetrable thickness of woollies away. Roger looks as though he wants to challenge you to a duel. You feel like a prop in the Roger-and-Rowena double act. Or a trophy.

By the early afternoon, after a considerable amount of under-age drinking in the Lime Kiln, everyone you know is desperately drunk. You brought a flask, filled with whisky from Dad's cocktail cabinet. You and Rowena started nipping at it well before eleven. It's kept you warm and got her drunk.

In the pub, she unwinds the scarf from her face and goes on to brandy. Apart from anything else, you're not sure if you can afford to keep paying for her spirits. This is the 1970s; she ought to buy some of her own. Victoria has steadily refused offers of drinks and got her own in, probably to fend off unattached leches who imagine she's a lot easier than she is. But Rowena is an old-fashioned girl.

She might also not be capable of formulating a sentence as simple as 'Another brandy, please.' As afternoon closing time nears, she might not even be able to stand up. She is singing something that could be 'Wide-Eyed and Legless' or the theme from *Scooby-Doo, Where Are You?*. Her voice, in its current state – abetted by Beecham's Powders, Bell's and brandy – is no match for Victoria's.

Everyone in the pub is appalled and fascinated.

Roger, slunk off in a corner with Jacqui Edwardes, can't stop laughing. His mask keeps going awry. Anyone who gets within reach of Rowena has to avoid her flailing arms. Her drunkenness is so extreme it makes everyone else seem sober and reasonable. And she's your responsibility. Roger is laughing at you.

Victoria, who is at the bar, elegantly drawing on a cigarette in a holder, looks like a goddess through the smoky haze of the pub.

Mary, who is around somewhere, observing, seems like a much better bet. But it's too late.

Rowena interrupts her singing with something between a cough and a burp.

'I'm not sure I feel well,' she says.

People move away from her as if she'd announced she was prone to spontaneous combustion. You're stuck between her and the wall.

She holds her tummy and screws up her face.

'The dam's a-gonna break,' Mickey Yeo announces. 'Head for the hills.'

Mary holds a side-door open and keeps a way clear. Cold air rushes in.

Rowena focuses on the open door and gets up.

Her mind has shut down to the point when it can only deal with the absolute present. She has no memory of where she is and who she's supposed to be with.

You can sit back and let her charge away. You're not really responsible. You gave her Bell's and bought her brandy but didn't hold her nose and pour it down her open throat. She got drunk herself. Even old-fashioned girls have to take the blame.

Rowena, unsteady on her feet, shakes her head. Fluid dribbles from her mouth.

She makes a dash for the door. The whole pub cheers.

If you sit back and wash your hands of Rowena, go to 33. If you go outside to help Rowena, go to 46.

29

In the summer of 1976, you start signing on every week. Queuing is half an hour of misery but it's all you have to do to get a supplementary benefit girocheque for £28. In theory, you're receiving benefit while you look for work. The Job Centre sends you for interviews. The trouble is that you're too clever for real shit jobs and not qualified for anything else. You nearly become a car-park inspector but it turns out you need a driving licence for that. You are even rejected by the

Synth, after scoring outside the parameters on an aptitude test.

Your parents are not delighted.

You hang around with Marie-Laure and Vince and, as soon as he's fired from the Synth, Dickie. You spend mornings in Brink's Café, hoarding cups of coffee until they go cold; you sometimes drink in the Lime Kiln, watching the pennies on halves; and you hitch out to Achelzoy a lot to smoke dope in Marie-Laure's bedroom. A drought in the West Country yellows the fields and bleaches the streets.

You give up shaving but can't grow a proper beard. Marie-Laure takes you and Vince round the charity shops and you dress in oddments. Marie-Laure can make Sally Army leftovers look good, but you and Vince come out like prats in demob suits and trilby hats.

The long, hot summer of 1976 turns to autumn.

Nothing changes. You sign on, cash your giro at the post office, go to Brink's, go to the Lime Kiln, get stoned at Marie-Laure's. The Job Centre catches on sooner than your parents, and stops wasting its time sending you to interviews.

Marie-Laure makes friends with Victoria Conyer, who is at college, and Graham Foulk, another of Laraine's ex-boyfriends, who has been in the sort of life you're living now for several years. In his mid-twenties, he has only ever had casual employment, though he makes some money selling dope.

You spend a lot of time in Graham's bedsit in town. There are always college kids – they have free periods – hanging about. Only Victoria actually seems to notice you and something about her strikes you as scary. When high, she talks, free-associating fantastically. Vince is really impressed, but you suspect she's mad.

Mum and Dad corner you in your room one Sunday and hold a family meeting. They've obviously talked about it beforehand and are serious. They want to hear your ideas and opinions but have made up their minds. They say you've had a nice holiday after school but it's time you did something constructive. You're afraid this means working in the bank, but what it boils down to is that they want to charge you rent, take a third of your giro. You feel stabbed to the heart. Ten pounds a week gone. Your life is over. Then, they say you can earn the rent money back by working for £1 an hour, doing odd jobs around the house and in the garden. Ten hours a week gone. That's worse.

You buckle down and do the weeding, trimming, raking, burning, painting, whatever. But you know you have to leave home. If you get a place like Graham's, you'll be entitled to housing benefit on top of supplementary benefit. You'll be independent of your parents, if not of the Department of Health and Social Security.

You plot and scheme but don't do anything.

One time, Laraine, at home for reading week, catches you alone and has a talk with you. Mum and Dad have probably ordered her to.

'Keith, I can understand you not wanting to be like Sean, but do you have to turn out like *Graham*? If you're choosing career patterns, my ex-boyfriends do not represent the entire spectrum of possibilities.'

Christmas comes and goes. It's 1977.

You do your ten hours a week in the salt mines. It goes up to fifteen hours when Mum decides you should pay a further £5 a week for food and washing. A full half of your giro now has to be earned. If you aren't out of your parents' house by summer, you'll be a full-time slave.

Coffee, halves, dope. Television. Films, in the afternoon when it's cheap. With Vince, comic books. At Marie-Laure's, long-playing records. You haven't read a non-*Doctor Who* book since you left school. You concentrate on distractions, because if you didn't, you'd feel shadow wrapping tightly round you like a living toga, feelers covering your face, the swamp-suck at your limbs pulling you down. It's worse than it was at school.

What will happen to you?

You're seventeen and your life seems set on rails. Nothing will change. Ever.

Coffee, halves, dope.

Television. Actually, television becomes a problem. The programmes are all right but adverts frighten you. The people in them (smiling, prat-suited, shiny people) are obsessed with bank accounts and fridge-freezers and holidays and DIY. Adverts are a window into an unreal world beyond the giro and odd jobs, a world for ever closed to you.

Victoria tells you adverts are propaganda for evil, for bad faith and wrong values. You can tell, she says, because every advert has a black spider in it, hidden like the creatures in those 'How many animals are there in this picture?' puzzles, lurking among the clean machines and clean homes and clean people. If you watch closely enough – usually when you're stoned, perceiving a higher plane of reality – you can see the black spiders, she says. You try, thinking she's mental, but see a scuttling horde at the rear of the frame in a carpet-sale commercial, hairy legs brushing the shagpile.

You don't watch telly for weeks. That means the black spiders come out of the screen and are everywhere, always out of sight. You know it's a metaphor. But that doesn't make them less real.

Vince and Marie-Laure start sleeping together. This makes you a bit more of an outsider. You think they've got together out of boredom. As far as you can remember, Marie-Laure never really liked Vince. You wonder what it is that has bound you and your few friends together for so long. You're mostly fed up with them.

The kids who got jobs seem no better off. Shane comes round Graham's quite a lot to smoke dope, and bunks off his delivery route. His engagement is off and Vanda is seeing Barry Mitcham, who has put on about three stone and seems middle-aged. She is a DHSS clerk but seems no more cheerful than the claimants queuing on the other side of her desk. Dickie and Tony Bennett have been arrested for burglary and are going to grown-up prison.

Victoria talks about the end of the world.

In the autumn, with your eighteenth birthday a few weeks off, you're raking up soggy heaps of fallen leaves when it strikes you that it's all silly.

The movements of your arms and hands and legs as you work the rake are individually silly. You can't figure out how they go together to work the rake. You stop for a moment to think it through.

Are your hands in the best position? Do you need to bend over so much? Your back has a crick from that.

You try to start raking again but get tangled.

You've raked the leaves into a circular pile round your boots as if preparing a bonfire with yourself as the guy. The leaves seem to be climbing your shins.

No, not the leaves.

In the pile are spiders. Millions of them, all concealed under leaves. They crawl up your wellingtons, aspiring to tip over the tops and get to your calves, to wriggle down to your toes.

You black out.

Read 13, and come back here.

* * *

When Mum finds you, there really are insects crawling over your face.
  Something has happened to you.
  Victoria says you are marked out.
  For something?

It's well over a year since you left school.
  And nothing.
  Your CSEs don't count for anything.
  Nothing counts for anything.

'I don't know what's happened,' Vince confides in you. 'Things were going along just like normal, and she just stopped talking to me. It's been going on for over a week. One afternoon, we were chatting on the phone and things were fine. That evening, we all went out and she didn't say a word to me. It was weird, man. The next evening, the same. She won't come to the phone. Nothing.'
  You gather Marie-Laure has chucked Vince but not told him.
  'Face it,' you say. 'She's mad.'
  'Too fucking true, Keith.'

The two people you see most often aren't talking to each other. This cuts your life in thirds – rent-earning chores, comics with Vince, dope with Marie-Laure. You wonder how many more fractions you can take, before each fragment becomes so small as to be not worth pursuing.
  A possibility occurs to you: Marie-Laure.

You're in Marie-Laure's bedroom, mildly stoned. The Beatles' *Double White* is on her hi-fi. The black-and-white telly is on, sound turned down. BBC, so there are no adverts. *Doctor Who*, with that long-scarfed impostor who took over from Jon Pertwee. Marie-Laure won't talk about Vince except to call him 'a drip'. You notice her shakes have come back. You have to roll and light the joints, because her fingers don't work for small tasks like that.
  Marie-Laure has an ideal life. Her dad has moved in with his girlfriend, and her mum, who gets a huge monthly support cheque, ignores her completely. She is pissed more often than her daughter is stoned. Dad would never let Laraine have some bloke in her room

smoking dope. Marie-Laure gets to keep all her giro, though she also has to cook most of her meals. A char does the washing and cleaning.

But Marie-Laure still wants to leave home.

'It's oppressive,' she says, 'like the House of Usher.'

There's a crack in the wall of her bedroom. She has rammed wadded-up shreds of pink tissue paper into it.

You're sure there are spiders in the crack.

A tiny leg extrudes itself, impossibly long, many-jointed. Like a growing hair, it reaches for you.

Inadvertently, you cringe, pressing yourself nearer Marie-Laure. She touches your shoulder, with a shaking hand.

You turn.

If you try to kiss Marie-Laure, go to 32. If you shrink away, go to 31.

30

Throughout Rag Day, the town centre is clogged with students in costume, accosting passers-by for money. Neil Martin demonstrates the untruth of an old saying by trying to sell hot cakes from the Corn Exchange steps. Desmond Fewsham has found an accordion he can't play and is anti-busking, providing a minute of merciful silence for every 10p given him. A few seconds of tuneless wheezing is enough to solicit a donation. No one is sure which charity Rag Day is supposed to be raising money for, but Michael Dixon, president of the Student Union, assures everyone it's all in a good cause. Mickey Yeo, creeping around in a Dracula cloak with his hair in Johnny Rotten spikes, has voted the Union use the money to send Satanist missionaries to backward Christian countries. Mostly, students take Rag Day as an excuse to loon about.

You're in fancy dress. Over a pillowcase with eyeholes, tucked in at the neck, you wear an old trenchcoat and fedora inherited from a deceased great-uncle, thick gloves, and tinted ski goggles. You are supposed to be the Invisible Man.

Probably because no one has ever seen you wear the coat and hat, which have been at the back of your wardrobe since your grandmother passed them on to you, the disguise makes you a genuine man of mystery.

You show up outside the Corn Exchange, which dominates the centre of town, and people pay attention to you.

Not speaking, you wave cheerily and nod your head.

'Who is it?' Michael asks.

'Invisible Man,' says Desmond.

'Then why can we see him?' Roger asks.

'We can't, dolt,' says Desmond.

The disguise is like armour. You decide not to say anything for a while, to see how long you can get away with it. It will be an experiment, discovering what it is like not to be you.

Victoria arrives, illegally parking her old Mini van by the Corn Exchange steps. She emerges, dressed as a ragged Cruella De Vil. Safety pins dot the diaphanous folds of her skirt and cloak. Her black-rooted white hair is teased out in hook-like curls. She wears white-face make-up, with Egyptian designs round her eyes. For her, this is an everyday look.

'Roger,' she says, draping her arms around your shoulders and looking into your reflective goggles. She inclines her head to one side and sticks her red mouth over yours, kissing you through your mask, prodding the tight cloth with her active tongue. You hold her up, gloved hands supporting her ribs, thumbs pressing under her breasts.

The warmth of her body is pressed against you.

'What a great look,' Victoria comments, pulling back. 'Roger, that's so *you*.'

Michael is laughing. Roger looks on, appalled. You smile under your mask, which must be lipsticked, and point at Roger.

Victoria turns, eyes widening. She is astonished, shocked, puzzled and intrigued. This may well be the most emotion you've ever raised in anyone.

'If it's not Roger...'

'We've no idea, Vic,' says Michael.

'Say something,' Victoria suggests.

You shrug, wryly.

'You'll be found out before the day is done,' she says.

Desmond's money runs out and he starts wheezing the squeeze-box, yelling an out-of-tune 'Where Do You Go To My Lovely?' to unbearable chords. Everyone looks through pockets for change and Victoria tosses him a coin to shut up.

'All in a good cause,' Desmond grins.

'It's a shame you didn't dress up as the Inaudible Man,' Michael says.

By early afternoon, after a considerable amount of under-age drinking in the Lime Kiln, everyone you know is desperately drunk. Rowena, loitering around Roger and looking alternately angry and pathetic, is especially stricken, and keeps downing brandy to ward off a sniffly flu. It takes four blokes to haul her upright after she's been epochally sick in an alley. You congratulate yourself on not being here with her. She'd now be your responsibility and you doubt there'd be much romance in wiping off vomit.

You drink through a straw stuck into a tiny hole in your mask, which slows you down. You have also had to drink whatever you're offered, since you don't speak for fear of giving yourself away. You had no idea how vile rum and black really was.

At the table in the beer garden – it's winter cold, but you're all outside anyway – you are still the Mystery Man.

'We can work it out through elimination,' Michael suggests. 'Who isn't here?'

He begins naming your entire male college year, as if calling a register at Marling's, soliciting comments. When a name is mentioned, everyone at the table tries to remember if the person has been seen today and, when a sighting is confirmed, rules him out. Your name doesn't come up, but no one notices it's missing.

Is this all the impression you have made? You have known some of these people since kindergarten. Finally, Desmond mentions he saw you earlier with Mary Yatman. Everyone accepts this and hurries on to the next suspect.

Mary has been on the fringes of everything, not in costume, quietly moving among mortals, not really involved, observing. It's not too late. You could still ask her to the show this evening. No one else will. She's at the other side of the garden, chatting with Neil Martin and someone dressed as a Womble.

You don't think you'd have to be invisible to interest Mary. You'd have to take off the mask to ask her out. The mystery business is getting to be a bore anyway.

'It couldn't be a girl?' Victoria asks.

Everyone laughs.

'You kissed him,' Roger says. 'It, rather.'

She gives the matter some thought.

You've never considered Victoria much. She's one of the Weird Women. Her intelligence and now her style have removed her from your mental list of girls you fancy. Actually, she carries her punk princess persona rather well.

She's not a slag, like Jacqui. But she isn't tight, either. You know she went out with Graham for a while, and has slept with Roger and several others. She is experienced, adult. But not like those girls who already seem married to their boyfriends and are picking out three-piece suites. You don't imagine Victoria thinks about three-piece suites. She firmly believes there won't be a future.

Will she be disappointed when your mask comes off?

'He's not a girl,' she says, having thought it over. She takes your upper arm and squeezes. 'I'd have noticed.'

'You'd recognise him if he took his trousers off,' Roger says.

Victoria picks up her almost untouched glass of cider and deliberately spills it into Roger's lap.

'Fuck,' he shouts.

'Clumsy me,' she admits, hard.

'Temper, temper,' says Michael.

'You need a kick in the cunt,' Roger says to Victoria.

'You'd lose your foot,' she replies, breaking her glass across the side of his head.

She could have blinded him.

You wonder about Victoria. Just how out of control is she? Just how much do you want to sit next to her? By the end of the evening and with a few more drinks or some mix of drugs, that could be your face at the receiving end of a glass or a bottle.

Mary, at least, got over her violent streak years ago.

Michael and Desmond hold Roger down. He isn't badly cut.

'You were out of order, man,' Desmond says.

Roger is in a bad mood, you realise. It must be down to Rowena. In the last few years, you've got used to the tension and attraction and friction running around your peers. It's just fucking adolescence.

Roger pulls a hankie out of his jeans pocket and dabs the trickle on his forehead. He has been lucky.

Mary is leaving the garden, unnoticed by everybody but you. If you get up now, you could still catch her. You could still ask her out.

Suddenly cheerful, Victoria asks you to buy her a drink.

If you stay invisible and buy Victoria a drink, go to 36; if you leave the table, take off the mask and ask Mary to come to the show with you this evening, go to 26.

31

Marie-Laure kisses you. You aren't that interested. But you get together anyway.

She suggests you get a flat together in town, but – now it's a possibility – you aren't sure about moving out. You know Marie-Laure well enough to guess she's not the most practical of girls. At home, you at least eat properly on your mum's cooking and have your washing done.

Once you've slept together, Marie-Laure gets a bit clingy. You're somewhat spooked.

She has 'spells'. She doesn't come out of her room for three days and plays one single – 'Kites', by Simon Dupree and the Big Sound, bought when she was eight – over and over again at full volume.

You get tired of being the dependable one, the sane one, the one who takes care of things. Marie-Laure drinks. With full access to her alky mother's booze cabinet and a lot of time on her hands, it is probably inevitable.

A year dribbles by. The only landmarks are rows. You and Marie-Laure have a lot of them. Once, in a 'spell', she hits you with an ashtray. She's immediately contrite but you finish with her. She telephones. Many times. She screams at your dad.

You live like an emotional turtle, head and limbs pulled in. You try to avoid mad people. You stay at home, watching children's television, listening to records.

Except on signing-on day, you don't get up before noon. The only person outside your family you see regularly is Vanda Pritchard. Behind the DHSS counter, she seems as depressed as the claimants queuing up to present their UB40s.

Your signing-on time is between nine-thirty and ten. One week, you oversleep and are an hour late. Most clerks would give you a hard time, but Vanda sorts it out for you.

She asks you if you want to have a lunch-time drink with her. A lunch-time drink? You are so far out of the mainstream that the concept seems exotic to you. A lunch-time drink.

Why not?

Vanda knows about you. She has access to your social security files, so she knows you're living at home and that you've been passed over by employers. Eighteen months after school, you aren't even going for interviews or wandering miserably around the Job Centre any more.

She doesn't seem much of an advert for employment.

In the Lime Kiln, she tells you long, intricate, involved stories about the politics of her office, and the trials she has with difficult claimants. You know several of them, including Laraine's ex-boyfriend Graham, who moves from squat to squat and has memorised his benefit rights down to the smallest print. He is capable of reciting them very slowly while a needy, irritable queue extends behind him, growing like a monster's tail out the door and into the street.

Your policy has always been to go in, sign on and get out. Make no trouble and you're all right.

Vanda has broken up with Barry Mitcham, who is working in a petrol station. She asks after Marie-Laure. You don't know. She asks after Shane. You don't know.

She buys you several pints and a plate of sandwiches. When her lunch hour is up, she goes back. You arrange non-committally to do this again next week.

Outside the DHSS, there's an awkward moment. Vanda is expecting to be kissed. You oblige. She kisses you back, properly. She hugs you, fiercely. You sense desperation in the fervour of her embrace. She leaves finger-marks on your arms.

You kiss her again and walk away.

If you do see Vanda again next week, go to 34. If you make an excuse and get out of it, go to 150.

32

You kiss Marie-Laure. She doesn't seem that interested. But you get together anyway.

You get a flat over a chip shop. The DHSS reckons you are cohabiting, which you suppose you are, and cut your benefit. It's Vanda's job to write and tell you about it. Signing the letter, she still puts a tiny heart over the 'i' in 'Pritchard'. Marie-Laure's mum gives her odd wedges of cash. You take your washing home to use your mum's machine.

You occasionally do bits of work without declaring income. Stock-taking at the jam factory. Picking up rubbish after the Glastonbury Festival.

Years pass. Margaret Thatcher is elected prime minister. Victoria goes to university, gets a degree in history, and comes back again. Laraine gets married to a bloke called Fred, then divorces. James joins the army. Dad dies. Britain counter-invades the Falklands.

The system changes and you get separate giros for housing benefit and supplementary benefit. You have to have an annual interview with a bored bureaucrat – Rowena Cunningham, whom you remember from school – who knows as well as you that you have no chance of employment.

When you first signed on, you were a school-leaver. Now, you're long-term unemployed. You don't get hassled so much because lots of other people are out of work. In waiting-rooms, you see older men, unemployed since the lay-offs at the Synth, nervous and at sea, unsure how to cope with the boredom and despair. You feel sorry for them.

Your mum remarries, to a younger guy, Phil Parslowe.

Marie-Laure gets pregnant. You work out that the child benefit will come in handy. You have two kids, Josh and Jonquil.

It takes you a few moments to remember what year it is when filling in the date on benefit forms. With each year, the problem gets worse.

You've lived through 1984. Still, you can't believe it's the 1980s.

Vince comes round a lot. You still talk with him about comics but are out of date: he's high on Alan Moore and Frank Miller Jr, while you stick with Stan Lee and Jack Kirby. There's a new Robin, which strikes you as sacrilege. And Doctor Who is a curly-haired pillock in a parti-coloured coat.

You and Vince spend quite a bit of time remembering out loud the names of all the Tracy Brothers or the catch-phrases from *Hector's House* and *Play School*. Marie-Laure always finds something else to do when you're going 'through the round window'.

You never did quite grow a beard, just as Marie-Laure never quite filled out a bra. You eat too many chips and get a bit of a gut. Marie-Laure takes the kids and leaves but comes back after a week. She works part-time in the jam factory. They've laid off full-time, long-standing staff to take on less-qualified people they don't have to pay as much. It's all very well, but when Marie-Laure earns anything, the DSS – reorganised and rechristened – cuts your giro back to almost nothing. With the kids, you can't deny that you're cohabiting.

You smoke dope less, though Graham and Victoria – who live in a squat in Sutton Mallet – still deal in a small way. You've had a headache for years, throbbing slightly, not bad enough to be serious, never clearing up entirely.

It's *ten years* since you left school.

Whenever anyone tells you the '80s are a boom time for the country and that you should be a part of it, you snap, 'Not in this life.'

When you talk with Vince, you discuss either what's happening right now this week – usually hassles with benefit – or minutiae of the years before 1976. You take to running through your old school register and wondering what has happened to everybody you knew.

A lot of them are in the same boat as you. It's just that you climbed on the scrapheap while they tried to get along in the world of work and were thrown there.

The early '70s – which were, of course, the years of the oil crisis, the three-day week, power cuts, strikes, the Ulster troubles, Watergate, flared trousers and the mullet haircut – become an Edenic refuge. Recounting in detail the differences between a Mivvi and a Sky Ray lolly or wondering when blue bags of salt were phased out of crisp packets, you almost transport yourself back in time.

It becomes a project, a game, a pastime.

Vince prompts you, because your memory is more detailed. If you close your eyes and clear your mind, you can banish the writhing black spiders of the present by furnishing a three-dimensional dayglo picture of the world as it was. Pop music you hated at the time – Mud, the Bay City Rollers, the Osmonds – becomes evocative, and Vince haunts jumble sales for scratched albums. He has a complete set of the *Top of the Pops* compilations of chart hit cover versions, with some smiling bird in a dolly mixture dress on the sleeves. You retrieve boxes of stuff from Mum's attic. They turn out to be treasure chests of *Biggies* books, Aurora glow-in-the-dark monster models, Dinky toys (*Goldfinger* Aston-Martin with ejector-seat figure missing), sweet cigarette cards (when did they stop making sweet cigarettes?), board games (Campaign, with Napoleon-hatted General pieces) and comics (Vince's eyes water). For a moment, you feel like a pirate, unearthing long-lost booty.

You're on your knees, scratching at the hard earth of a flower-bed, searching for a tin of marbles. You're wearing a cardboard eyepatch and a pirate hat with a silvery skull-headed pin and a plastic plume.

Then you're back in the flat over the chip shop, listening as Vince tells you how much your April 1969 *Streak* ZC comic is worth, since it marks the first appearance of now-popular arch-enemy Dead Thing.

It was real. You were back there, you were *home*.

The next weekend, when Marie-Laure has taken the kids to see her mum in the hope of gouging a hand-out from the old woman, you repeat the experiment under controlled circumstances.

When you shut your eyes, it is 1990.

In the dark of your head, red-eyed spiders crawl.

You open your eyes, heart pounding. You're lying on your bed, looking at the cracked ceiling. Half your life has come and gone since you left school. You are thirty years old. You have done nothing.

You shut your eyes again, determined. You furnish the dark, imagining your room in Mum and Dad's house. Your room as it was when you were thirteen.

Maths homework. You hate it. You want to get it over with so you can watch Top of the Pops. *A spider crawls on your hand.*

You open your eyes.

It was real. You were there.

Next time, you stay longer, ignoring the spiders. You finish the homework and go downstairs. James and Laraine are in the television room, young again.

Mum washes up in the kitchen. A *Telegraph* is folded up, and you see your Dad.

Alive.

A rush of something makes your eyes water.

Is it love? Or regret?

'What's up, Keith?'

Dad talked to you. You were there.

You made it back. You can go home again. You can, you can, you can.

But how do you want it to be? When did things change? From where do you want to start? And where do you want to end up?

Excited, you make Nescafé and try to think. You're cramped in the flat's tiny kitchen. Josh's scrawled 'drawings' are stuck to the fridge. The place smells of fried food. There's washing-up in the sink. Marie-Laure will nag you about that when she gets back.

Where you were was before Marie-Laure, before the kids. If you go back again, they might not be part of your life. The kids might not be born.

This is what you have. You might complain about the government and the DSS, but you are here by choice. Even in a socialist utopia, you'd be an unemployable layabout who can't support his kids.

It's been eating you bit by bit for years.

But do you really want to leave?

Really?

If you just want things to be better now, go to 87. If you want things back the way they were, go to 89.

33

You're trying to have a conversation with Gully Eastment and his girlfriend, Bronagh Carey. Surprisingly, in the all-bets-off chaos of Rag Day, they seem the most sensible folk around. You and Gully are the only people in your year at college who have been asked by the principal to sit Oxford entrance exams. You've gone along with it, with your parents' support, but Gully is trying to talk you out of it.

'Remember Marling's, Keith? It'll be worse. A single-sex college is like a jail.'

Outside, in an alley, Rowena is being sick. For twenty minutes, she's been puking. Mary keeps coming back with reports. She displays sisterhood with the sick girl, though Rowena was never a special friend. Penny Gaye, Michael's girlfriend, is also helping.

You drink steadily, radiating a nothing-to-do-with-me-mate vibe.

Rowena's heaves are amazingly loud.

'Always know your limit,' you say, sipping another half of cider.

'Too fuckin' true,' says Gully.

You are sophisticates, far removed from the struggling fools all around. You need Gully and he needs you: neither of you has anyone else to pace himself against. If either were to slacken off, the other might also stumble.

Maybe you'll end up at the same university?

Mickey Yeo makes an announcement: 'Dave Tamlyn's chunder-up record has fallen.'

The pub cheers.

A shadow falls over the table. You look up. Victoria stands there, half-full pint glass huge in her delicate hand.

'Hi, Vickie,' you say.

Outside, Rowena pukes again. She vomits with an animal cry. An embarrassment to herself and everyone else. You're well shot of her.

'That doesn't bother you at all, does it?'

You freeze half-way into a shrug and a smile.

Cold beer hits you in the face, dashed into your eyes, soaking your collar, seeping down your chest. You splutter through a noseful of liquid.

You can still hear Rowena.

You want to protest. It really has nothing to do with you. When you come down to it, it's Roger's fault.

Victoria smashes the glass against the side of your head.

The pain is sharp and wet. Gully and Bronagh get out of the way. You feel a warm gush as blood pours down the side of your face. You have splinters in your forehead and cheek.

Victoria has no right. You have stood up.

The bitch glassed you. She could have blinded or killed you. She has crossed a line. She must take the consequences.

Your hands are fists.

There are places you can go from which you can never come

back. Hitting a girl, *any* girl, is one of them.

'You're pathetic, Keith,' Victoria says.

If you hit Victoria, go to 39. If you try to laugh it off and sit down, go to 43.

34

You and Vanda get a flat together in town, above a launderette – which is handy – and, because she has to declare you're cohabiting, your benefit is cut. She gives you pocket money and within a week of your moving in together starts gently to suggest you get a job. Her income supports your idleness and she feels entitled.

Since Vanda is a tease rather than a nag, you allow yourself to be reshaped a little. You admit you were in a rut. You start shaving and get a proper haircut. Vanda buys you shirts and ties. She says you look better when you're smart.

The amazing thing about living together, for you, is the sex. Every evening and all the weekend you spend in the big bed in the flat. You've never made love in a double bed before. It's a major improvement.

Vanda is everything Marie-Laure wasn't. Curvy rather than skinny, open rather than shut, predictable rather than neurotic. She doesn't have mood swings. She doesn't contradict herself. She never hits you with ashtrays.

She says she loves you. In bed, she proves it. She says she enjoys giving fellatio. You suppose you love her. You certainly say so.

Though they weren't sure at first, Mum and Dad come to like Vanda. She can be trusted to carry out their instructions when it comes to you.

Often you overhear your dad's distinctive 'Tell him that…' when Vanda is talking with them on the phone. She then relays the orders of the day.

An opening comes up at the bank.

You still don't want to be a clerk, but Vanda is one so you can't go on about that. Despite the three years of nothing in your life, you'll earn more than she does now the first week you turn up. And three years is a long time to do nothing, to be marking time.

It seems to make sense.

Vanda takes an afternoon off work and joins forces with your mum to help you buy two suits. For the bank. You revolt deep down at the thought of embracing prat-dom.

The bank's policy is theoretically against close relatives working together in a branch but your father has such a straight reputation that he has a special dispensation. And he will not be your direct boss. Sean Rye is still at the bank, as assistant loans adviser. You'll be 'under' him.

Vanda is proud of you in your suit.

It is 1979. Margaret Thatcher is prime minister. It's a new era. You allow yourself to be gentled into the life, to be convinced.

It's not as bad as you thought it would be. The work is easy. Dad arranges that you have two afternoons off a week to take catch-up courses at the college. If you pass exams at the end of the year, you could be promoted within the bank.

You buckle up and knuckle down.

Walking home through town one evening, after your first few weeks in the job, you are passing Brink's Café. Inside, Marie-Laure is having a heated argument with the manager. She pauses in her tirade, sees you through the window, does a goggle-eyed double-take, opens the door and cadges a pound off you to pay for a broken cup.

'Don't go away,' she says.

She has red and grey streaks in her tangle of hair. She's even more jittery than you remember, looking everywhere at once like a paranoid owl, hands always on the move.

She comes back out and looks at you.

'Good God,' she says. 'Arachnoid body-snatchers have struck.'

Over the last year, you've received sporadic silent phone calls. You always assumed it was Marie-Laure. You don't know what to say to her. Her mother sent her away for a time last year. Vanda said her claim was suspended while she was being treated in a private 'hospital'.

'I never really liked you,' she says, spitefully. 'You were always too common.'

'You owe me a pound,' you say.

She kisses you, wriggling her tongue into your mouth.

'There,' she says. 'Even?'

She zig-zags away, ragged blue shawl clutched round her skinny shoulders.

You never forget her eyes.

For the first time, with the job, you have money. You can treat Vanda, buy her things for a change. You enjoy that. You have lunch together every day, in pubs and cafés. You insist on paying, to make up for the last couple of years. Every Friday, you come home with a scarf or a household implement.

She suggests you find a bigger flat, or a cottage. You work out that soon you could afford it.

Vanda has learned to drive and bought a second-hand car, a Ford Cortina. You promise to take lessons as soon as your college course is completed. Again, you're on an exam treadmill. But this time, the results mean something.

You wonder why you ever resisted.

You have two weeks' holiday in the summer. You go camping in Wales. You make love in a tent. You go to quiet pubs, and cuddle in dark corners. You wander round Snowdonia. Nature doesn't care whether you wear a suit. It's just there, magnificent even without you to see it. Alone in the wild with Vanda, you feel calm.

Later, you work out that this is where your first baby was conceived. In a tent pitched by a culvert, water flowing into the mountain as you flow into Vanda.

You get married well before the bump shows. You arrange a mortgage at a preferential rate through the bank and think about buying a cottage in one of the outlying villages. In the end, you get a newly built house in town, anonymous but solid.

Vanda enjoys decorating. Dad gives you DIY tips. Vanda doesn't go back to work after Jason is born. Less than a year later, your son has a sister, Jesse.

Laraine gets married to a bloke called Fred. James joins the army. Sean becomes loans officer. Marie-Laure is institutionalised.

Vanda suggests you have a vasectomy, and you do.

Money begins to get tight.

In 1982, your Dad dies, of a sudden coronary. It's unexpected. Sean Rye is made acting manager. You're worried he'll purge you. You've always thought, deep down, your position was something Dad fixed up.

A week after the funeral, Sean calls you in for an interview. First, he tells you what a great man and a good friend your father was. You've only just begun to see this yourself, and resent the intrusion.

Sean is still wearing a 1975 suit, with wide lapels. He is still a prat. Acting prat.

'Keith,' says Sean, 'I don't mind telling you your dad *was* this branch. I can't replace him, but London have confirmed me in this job.'

Here it comes. You're out.

If Laraine hadn't chucked him for that hippie...

'A lot of customers need a sense of continuity. I know it's absurd, but the name – Mr Marion – means a lot. I'd like you to take over loans.'

A pause.

You're not being fired. You're being promoted.

'I've cleared it with head office,' Sean says. 'They're very enthusiastic.'

'Thank you, Sean,' you say.

'Thank you, *Keith*.'

You worry it will all go away.

The promotion means Vanda doesn't have to go back to work. You approve an extension of your own mortgage and move to a cottage in Sutton Mallet. You lay out on the first new car of your life, a Ford Mondeo.

James comes back from the Falklands. He has been wounded slightly, and leaves the army. Your mum remarries, to a younger man, Phil Parslowe. Jason and Jesse go to playgroup. Laraine gets divorced from that bloke called Fred.

Sean gets married to a woman you were at school with, Rowena Douglass. You and Vanda and Sean and Rowena play badminton together on Thursdays, have barbecues at the weekends in summer.

Though you and Vanda vote Social Democrat, Mrs Thatcher wins a second term. They say it's the Falklands factor.

Your duties at the bank expand. You're required to give investment advice. You and Sean are a bit puzzled by this head office decree. You're mates now. You see that he isn't the prat you thought. Laraine could have done a lot worse; indeed, her marriage to Frightful Fred suggests that she did.

Neither of you has ever invested in anything more venturesome than premium bonds, but everyone is into the stock market these days and your bank wants a slice of its customers' action. Other banks in town have recently established securities desks and you have to compete. You both study the whole thing, and go on week-long courses to get up to speed.

You are surprised Sean is unfaithful to Rowena with women on the courses. Thin, sharp-suited, bright-eyed professionals. You talk it over with him. He says that he doesn't love Ro any less, but that the '80s are about taking opportunities.

'What we learn here makes us better back home.'

You're sort of convinced, but you don't join Sean in his energetic chatting-up in hotel bars.

On the train on the way back from one course, Sean proposes a scheme to make more sense of the investment business. He suggests you each put £2500 into a fund, and have the bank match the £5000 with capital from petty cash. Then, experimentally, you should make investments and see what happens. If you make a go of it, you can pay the bank back and take a bonus out of the profits. If you don't, you pay the bank back and take a loss of part or all of your own investment. After all, it's only £2500.

Two thousand five hundred doesn't sound that *only* to you. And speculating with petty cash goes well beyond the legal grey area into something that could coldly be called embezzlement.

'It'll just be a flutter,' Sean says, 'like the Grand National.'

If you go in with Sean, go to 41. If you back off, go to 47.

35

Achelzoy is miles out of town, across the moor. The road is straight for a stretch, then winds like a snake. Originally, the Somerset levels were marshes. Villages used to be islands: the common 'zoy' in place names is a local contraction of 'zoyland' or 'island'. Roads were navigable waterways. In December, the fields are bare and black. Ditches, called 'rhynes', are deep and water-filled. They separate fields and run either side of the road.

Between you is an atmosphere you can't understand. What has

happened this evening is still sketchy, unconfirmed. You don't know if Mary wants to murder you or marry you. You are excited but hesitant. You really wish you hadn't drunk so much; it's only in the last year that you've looked old enough to get served in pubs, and you downed several pints of cider in the Lime Kiln before you went to the show. It occurs to you that, you don't know how much Mary has drunk.

The road is empty at this time of night. Between villages, the only light comes from the headlamps.

As the road weaves from side to side, Mary drives in the centre, staying on the white line to avoid the curves. Catseyes stare back at you. You aren't sure if this is a good idea.

Mary laughs when you mention it.

Then the Honda loses traction on a slick patch of ice. Up ahead is a right-angle bend.

The car hits the verge and your side lifts up as it slams into a signpost. The windscreen fractures to frost.

Wheels grinding grassy earth and air, the Honda crunches over a bank and its front end falls five feet, crashing through a thin layer of ice.

Mary has driven you into a ditch.

Go on.

36

In the Lime Kiln, Victoria pairs off with you at the bar, keeping up a canny chatter of questions which you punctuate with shrugs and gestures. You see her concentrating, despite the scrumpy she's been drinking and the dope you can smell on her hair. You'd forgotten how clever she was before she made an effort to hide it. The problem of you has piqued her curiosity. She's obviously going to worry at it until she has an answer.

Then, probably, she'll be disappointed.

She's unlikely to make up with Roger; still drips contempt when she talks about Graham; and, though he's obviously smitten, has no interest in Neil.

For now, she's keen on the Invisible Man.

But not – you are certain – on Keith Marion.

The straw-hole in your mask rips. Through it, you can drink from the glass.

'Not a very distinctive tongue,' Victoria comments.

You wiggle it at her. She nips it between her thumb and forefinger, not hard.

'Any solution?' Michael asks, from the other side of the pub.

'Not as yet.'

'Preliminary report?'

She lets your tongue go. 'It's a heterosexual male.'

Michael laughs. Your face goes hot but you smile. No one can see you blush. Behind cloth, you're as cool and suave as you'd like to be. Your blank mask is a screen, and people project what they want on to it.

It really is like being invisible, or a ghost. You've always wondered what people were like when you weren't around. Now you can find out. Are you imagining it, or are people really more relaxed with you invisible? Does your presence, your intense need for achievement, put people on their guard, make them watch themselves?

You've seen Rowena puke until there's nothing more to come up and Victoria break a glass on Roger's head. Surely they wouldn't act like that if you were there?

Or maybe it's just Rag Day.

After time is called, everyone drifts out of the pub and back to the college common room. Most other disguises have come apart and not a few kids are moaning in drunken agony. Roger has got proprietary about Rowena and is helping her stagger down the street. She is either crying uncontrollably or singing 'See My Baby Jive' under her breath. Roger won't let her crawl home to her parents until she's in a fit state.

You've drunk more than you usually do but aren't even slightly giddy. The mask gives you power. Behind it, you can be calculating while everyone else flounders.

Victoria takes your arm and stays close. You are her project.

'Give it up,' Neil tells you. 'It's boring now.'

He is jealous.

'No,' says Victoria. 'Not yet.'

In the common room, people are piled up on the battered chairs. Dreadful coffee brews in an urn. Graham, not a student but always hanging around the college, skins up and passes a joint round a circle of younger kids.

Ancient iron radiators clank, pouring out heat, misting the windows. Outside, it's the Arctic; in the common room, it's subtropical.

Victoria sits you down, takes off your hat and strokes your head through the cloth. She feels bumps like a phrenologist, trying to discern your character in your skull.

'Rip it off him,' someone suggests.

'No,' she announces. 'Then he would have won.'

The afternoon passes in a fug of smoke and coffee. Everyone is trying to purge themselves before the evening, when they'll go to the show at the college auditorium and Michael's party in Achelzoy. This is down-time.

Victoria is sometimes distracted by other conversations but always comes back to you, the Mystery Man.

When it goes quiet, she kisses you again. A proper snog, what they call 'sharing a stick of gum'. Tongues entwined, jaws working, swapped spit. She holds your neck and you hold hers. She's warm even through your gloves.

You aren't the only couple kissing in the room. Neil is disgusted but no one else even notices.

Victoria breaks the kiss and puts a finger on your lips. The cloth around your mouth is damp.

'I don't know you,' she says.

You shrug.

'But I will. Oh yes, Invisible, I will.'

At some point, you have to go to the toilet. When you get up, your brain fuzzes. It's as if movement stirs the alcohol lying heavy in your blood.

You make it out of the common room.

Will Victoria lose interest while you're gone?

Your bladder's need is pressing.

On your way back from the Gents, in a stairwell whose chill contrasts pleasantly with the overheated common room, you pause, leaning on a banister.

What are you doing?

Above you, on a landing, someone stands.

Through the slits in your mask and the goggles over the slits, you only just make out legs in jeans.

It's a girl.

'Keith Marion,' she says.

It's Mary Yatman. Scary Mary.

The brain-fuzz is gone.

'It's nothing you did,' she says, stepping down. 'You haven't given yourself away.'

You make out her huge eyes.

'It's just that you're you, Keith. No getting away from it.'

Suddenly, she darts past you.

Because of your limited field of vision, you have to turn round entirely to see her. It's like trying to train a pair of binoculars on a piece of driftwood far off in a storm-tossed sea. You hear the doors slam on the ground floor but don't see Mary go.

Back in the common room, you assume everyone will now see through you. The disguise will fall apart and you'll be laughed at for a while, then everyone – and Victoria – will move on to something or someone of more interest.

But Mary has gone without telling on you.

The space beside Victoria is still there. She crooks her finger and smiles. You go to her.

You would never have thought it could go this far.

It's nearly midnight and the glass slipper hasn't dropped yet. At the show, you stand near the stage and watched Flaming Torture. Victoria seems to sing every song at you, eyes always on the white of your mask.

Disco strobe light makes neons of white garments. Kids around gasp as your head shines.

Afterwards, you snuggle with Victoria in the back of Desmond's car as he drives out to Achelzoy. She's on a high from performing, a feverish sheen damping her white-face make-up.

Despite the savage attack of her songs, which all seem to be about violent sex, she's almost sweet now in her enthusiastic acceptance of approval. As a little girl she took ballet classes, and she was probably like this when her parents applauded her turn in the school show.

You are kissing again and her hands are inside your trenchcoat, stroking your sides. You cup her breast, feeling warmth through your thick glove.

Occasionally, Victoria pulls back, looks into your goggles, shakes her head as if she can't believe what she's doing, then returns to you with more passion.

You've had an erection for half an hour. You feel as if you'll explode.

Victoria starts gnawing your neck like a vampire, gripping your jugular with gentle teeth, moistening your mask.

Your forehead presses against the cold car window.

A signpost passes by. Desmond has driven past the Sutton Mallet turn-off.

'That's a short cut, isn't it?' says Mickey Yeo, in the front passenger seat.

You know it's not. Sutton Mallet is a dead end.

Victoria's hand, in a fingerless lace glove, slides over your belly and clamps on your cock.

'Let's give it a try,' says Desmond, pulling the wheel over.

If you let Desmond continue down the Sutton Mallet turn-off, go to 42. If you're too preoccupied with Victoria's hand to make a fuss, go to 44.

37

As the car lands in the ditch, your weight is thrown forward awkwardly. The seatbelt, adjusted badly, snaps you back into your seat, suddenly tight across your throat, breaking your neck. You don't have time for a last thought.

Go to 0.

38

The brief pain is so intense it cancels itself out, spot-burning away all memory of the agony. You're left with a slight all-over buzz and a white-out. The pain you've had and lost can't have been worse, more panic-making, than the Tipp-Ex blotch on your recent past. It's like discovering a chunk of your body has been gouged away and lost for ever.

This can't be helping. No matter what they say.

The pain comes again. You try to hold it this time, to keep it in your mind, but it wipes itself out again. The buzz is more extended and you are physically exhausted, incapable of movement. This white patch is longer, larger, spreading cobweb-strands beyond the area where the pain was, obliterating connected lumps of your memory, your mind. A moment ago, you knew what was happening, had the answers to important questions; now you are in a shade, a fuzzy fug, a nothing zone.

Thick ropes of sticky cord bind your wrists and ankles. Your head is held in a helmet of fast-setting stuff. Recovering from the buzz, you find you can arch your body, raising the small of your back from whatever you are bound to. But your head is fixed. Opaque shields are clamped over your eyes, wiry threads of the helmet weaving around them.

You are Keith Marion.

You can cling to that.

Haven't you just died?

Or are you trying to misinterpret? To avoid facing the real? You've been told that before.

The pain comes again.

Briefly, you're not sure: who is Keith Marion?

39

Your knuckles hurt. And you're drunker than you thought. Standing up has made your head fuzzy.

Victoria is still standing but her head is turned round on her neck, almost like Linda Blair's in *The Exorcist*.

The only sounds in the Lime Kiln come from a juke-box burbling 'Nights in White Satin' and Rowena dry-heaving in the alley outside.

You rub your sleeve over your face, wiping your eyes.

You see Victoria's hands hooking into claws. She has sharp, black-painted nails. Her cobweb gloves lack fingertips. She's going to scratch your eyes out.

Her hands come for your face. You reach for her wrists.

The table between you is pulled out of the way.

You and Victoria almost dance.

You see the amazed faces of other people in the pub. Roger, you think, is envious. Gully, of all people, is appalled. Mary's face is shut, concealing excitement. Most of the others haven't been following the plot.

Victoria breaks your hold on her hands and backs off. She isn't going to fight like a girl.

She punches you in the face and pummels your ribs. Your shoes slip on the spilled beer and you lose your balance.

A few folk cheer.

You get a hold on Victoria's neck and force her to her knees. Her stiff, sprayed hair sticks into your face. Now she tries to scratch your hands, to make you let go.

She can't hurt you in this position. But you can't let her go. You are locked in this violent embrace.

Victoria arches her back, trying to throw you off. Her backbone presses into your groin. She is a warm body.

This *can't* be a turn-on for you.

Someone is giving a referee's count. Victoria twists and hisses, like an angry cat. You can't hold her much longer. But if you let her go, she might well kill you.

The bell clangs for time. Even with the distraction, there is a moan of disappointment.

'Break it up,' shouts the barman.

He is coming to stop the fight. You are relieved and wonder if Victoria is.

Rough hands take your arms and pull them away from Victoria's neck.

'Should be ashamed of yourself,' the barman says.

Victoria turns, her face close to you.

'Tonight,' she says, whispering so only you can hear.

'She could have blinded me,' you say. It sounds feeble.

Bronagh has found a towel and gives it to you. As you wipe beer and blood from your face, you see Victoria – with Mary and Neil at the bar – turn and mouth the word 'tonight' at you.

You sit down, uncomfortable with the erection you have sprouted.

What do you think? Is Victoria a promise or a threat? If a promise, read 50 and go to 55. If a threat, read 50 and go to 56.

40

As the car lands in the ditch, your weight is thrown forward awkwardly. You pitch out of your seat – damn fool, you should have taken the trouble with the seatbelt – and thump against the dashboard. Your forehead smacks against the frosted window, shattering it to fragments.

It's not exactly a blackout. You don't lose consciousness, really, but your mind fades. All sensations become fuzzy. You wonder if you haven't broken something major, and this is your brain's way of coping with it. You are uncomfortable but not in pain. Things seem to itch rather than hurt.

Close objects are in focus. Beyond arm's reach, everything is a blur.

The cold seeping into the car makes you stir. The fuzziness goes away and you become sharply aware of your circumstances. Your body is crammed between your seat and the dashboard, but your head is stuck through the broken windshield, which seems to have vanished completely. Your feet and legs are wet and chilled. Water from the ditch is up around your thighs.

You are alone.

Where is Mary?

Tentatively, you push against the dashboard, afraid the buckled car has become a trap. The seat behind you moves back easily, sheared from its bolts. It is not heavy, but you have to brace your back and shrug forcibly to heave the thing off you.

With the seat gone, you can crawl through the windshield-frame. Your palm crunches on a line of jagged crystal still in the frame and you grunt in annoyance and pain.

'Fuck.'

Your own voice sounds impossibly loud. Since the wrench of metal, silence has been marred only by the subtle, steady trickle of water.

You squeeze through the gap and take a careful hold of the car roof, bracing your feet on the sloping bonnet. You're crouched a foot or so above the water, and your lower body is soaked through. Already, icy air is turning your wet trousers into a biting skin.

There is no sign of Mary.

She's a maniac, you think. Her monster never went away, just hid in a deep cave. All these years, it's been waiting for you, waiting to escape. She's turned into Scary Mary again. This time, for good.

That's silly. When Shane Bush racked up his moped, you didn't think he was possessed by Pazuzu. Mary's just a teenage girl who drinks too much and drives like a silly bugger. Being too bloody clever has made her forget how bloody stupid she can be.

Still, where is she?

You climb carefully out of the ditch. You can see almost nothing. The headlights still burn underwater, making ghostly pools of gleam in the ditch. But the moon is covered by cloud. You are between villages, miles from street-lighting or central-heated houses. In the ditch, the headlights hiss out.

You've climbed on to the far bank of the ditch, away from the road. You feel the effort in your knees and arms. You have been cut in a half-dozen places, on your hands and face. Blood flows slowly, either freezing or clotting. You realise your teeth are chattering and think distantly of exposure and hypothermia.

It would be easy to sit down and sleep, wait for dawn and rescue. Even before then, someone must pass by and see where Mary's Honda went into the ditch. There should be many cars going back and forth to and from Michael's party. You can't see your non-luminous watch-face but it can't even be midnight. Which means that it's a long eight hours till light, and it'll get colder before it gets warm. By morning, the car will be ice-locked.

You're worried about Mary. You're not sure, though, whether you fear for her safety or fear her.

You try to call her name, but just croak. You try again, more successfully.

'Mary…'

If it were light, you would probably be able to see the marks of her escape from the car. She's probably staggered off into the field and curled up. She may be hurt more seriously than you. She might have slammed into the steering-wheel, crushing her chest. Was she wearing *her* seatbelt? You think so. When you kissed her, she was held in her seat. You remember the strap against her shoulder.

She let you touch her breast.

Now she's gone.

'Keith.'

You jump, heart knotting.

Looking around, you make her out. She stands by the wonky signpost.

'Mary?'

She doesn't say anything, doesn't move.

'Are you all right?'

A flame flares, brighter than a sunspot. You blink. Mary has a pocket lighter. Odd. You didn't think she smoked. There is so much you don't know about her. Your hand remembers the warmth of her breast. Your face remembers the flick of her tongue.

You were doing well. Until the ditch.

In the flamelight, Mary's face is overexposed, like a bad snapshot. Her eyes are dark holes. Her lips have lost their red.

The signpost reads SUTTON MALLET 1/2 MILE. Beyond Mary is a turn-off, leading to a tiny hamlet. Sutton Mallet is the Somerset equivalent of a ghost town, mostly uninhabited since the '50s, a few broken-down cottages and old barns. But the sign is fresh-painted, proud.

'Come here,' she says.

She's alive. You want to hug her. Perhaps you can rub warmth into each other, tend each other's wounds. Mary doesn't seem hurt, not even scratched. But she might be a jumble of broken bones and ruptured organs.

You step towards her, freeze, and totter at the edge of the ditch. You almost stepped off the bank. You would have fallen into the water.

Mary giggles.

You stagger back, away from the edge.

'Fooled youm,' she says, flicking off the flame.

This is dizzying. As the lighter goes out, shadows spring up and surround Mary. Lightsquiggles writhe on the surfaces of your eyeballs. You still see burn-through where the flame was, a dancing phantom after-light.

For an instant, you thought Mary was not alone. Shadow-spiders stood behind her, closing round her when the light went away. In her darkness, Mary has company. On your side of the ditch, you are alone.

Still, you should go to her.

The ditch is too wide to jump. You could wade it, but that would mean dipping your legs in freezing water, sinking your feet into undisturbed mud and filth. Maybe you could climb across the car, but that doesn't seem a good idea. There are jagged metal edges. In films, crashed cars explode.

Mary might toss her lighter into the car as you are perched on top of it. She could warm herself by the fireball, suck in the smell of you cooking.

'There'm a gate up the way,' Mary says.

Wherever there is a gate, there is a bridge over the ditch, for the cattle to cross.

'Are you sure?'

You don't trust her any more.

'Why'd I lie, Keith?'

Why would she?

She flicks the light, merely for a moment, holding it up. At the blurred edge of your vision there is indeed a gate. On the moor, fields are separated by ditches rather than hedges. Even by day, some of the bridges are hard to see from quite close up, marked only by tufts of long grass growing where planks have been set in concrete lumps.

'Come on.'

Mary is already walking towards the gate. Her boot-heels click on the gritty road.

A car speeds by. You wave your arms but Mary stands aside to let it pass. The driver honks his horn. You shout out for it to stop but are ignored. You think it was Desmond's car, full of kids on their way to the party.

Why didn't Mary flag it down?

The sweep of the headlamps briefly scattered light across the field. Besides the gate, which is nearby, you see a row of tall, thin trees at the far side. The field is empty, but the shadows of the trees waver with the passing carlight, as if beckoning. A small voice of panic shrieks inside.

You walk, keeping parallel with Mary. Just now, you are grateful for the ditch between you.

She sings to herself, cheerfully, 'Nellie the Elephant packed her trunk and said good-bye to the cir-*cussss*.'

Her voice is as clear and high as a six-year-old's. You hadn't known that about Mary. That she could sing. Almost as well as Victoria.

What are the spidery shadows that accompany Mary? Why are you alone?

The gate is only feet away. When you get there, you can swing round it and be on the road. You'll be with Mary and the shadow-spiders, but the next car will stop. You can make sure of that.

'Nearly there,' Mary interrupts her song.

You are already reaching out. Suddenly, there is nothing under your leading foot. This time you tumble, throwing yourself back, and crunch on to the cold earth. A shifting pain stabs you in the side.

'...off she went with a trumpety-trump. Trump, trump, *trump*!'

Just before the gate, the ditch takes a right-angle turn and runs off towards the trees. The gate and the bridge to the road are actually in the next field. Cut off from you.

Again, the ditch is too broad to jump.

Your whole body shivers. The ice has risen from your legs, glaciating your torso and arms. These were your best clothes, too. Your suede jacket is ruined.

'Things have come to a pretty pass,' Mary says, almost singing. She dances in the dark and swings up to sit on the gate, tucking her long legs under her to get balance. She can't be very badly hurt.

'The head of the herd was calling, far far *awayyyy*.'

There must be a bridge into the next field, the field with the gate. But where is it?

'By they trees,' Mary says, answering your unvoiced question. 'I be sure.'

'Shine some light.'

Mary flicks the lighter too slowly. Flame does not catch. Sparks show you her smile, putting nasty lines round her mouth and eyes.

'I can see,' she says. 'By they trees. There'm a stile. If'n youm walk back there, youm can cross over. Then youm can walk back here, and get out.'

She sounds so reasonable.

Should she sound reasonable? Shouldn't she be hysterical? Shouldn't she worry what her parents will say about the car? Shouldn't she be cold and in pain?

'I'll wait,' she says, calmly.

'What did happen to your monster?' you ask. This seems the right time.

'There were no monster. There were just me.'

You know you'll have to do as she suggests: walk to the trees and come back. There's no guarantee that there aren't other ditches. You may have to make your way through right-angles, sometimes walking almost an entire square before you find a bridge.

You would like her to flick on the lighter and hold the flame steady, to give you a point to fix on.

She strikes futile sparks again.

'I'll sing,' she says. 'That way, you'll know I'm still here. Youm can fix on my voice.'

She begins to sing 'Nellie the Elephant' again, ending the discussion. You get up and stumble away from her, concentrating on the ground. You don't want to get too close to the ditch. Sometimes marshy spots spread, setting traps for the unwary foot. These are marked by bursts of longer grass, where the earth is sodden.

The ground crunches under you. Mary is still singing 'Nellie the Elephant' over and over.

Whatever your generation gets into, 'Nellie the Elephant' is buried deep in musical memory. The kids now singing 'I Am an Antichrist' started out with Uncle Mac and *Junior Choice*. 'Nellie' and 'Three Wheels on My Wagon' and 'How Much is That Doggy in the Window?' are imprinted in your chromosomes, as much as 'She Loves You, Yeah Yeah Yeah' and 'Satisfaction' will always mean your childhood, and 'I'm Not in Love' by 10-fucking-cc will be the snog record following 'Hi Ho Silver Lining' at college discos, as much as 'Thus Spake Zarathustra' and 'Ode to Joy' will always mean *2001: A Space Odyssey* and *A Clockwork Orange*. Underneath everything lies 'Nellie the Elephant'.

You are in the dark, well away from the road, stumbling beside a ditch. You can't make out the trees you're heading for, or the gate you want to go back to. Mary's singing is still there, the odd word yelled louder than the rest after she has drawn a breath. Your eyes have not got used to the dark. If anything, you're seeing less. You have only the faintest impression of the ground you are walking on.

You stop for breath. Are you hearing something? Not just 'Nellie the Elephant': something else.

You walk again. Your feet tramp, tramp, *tramp*. There's a disjunction between the feeling in your feet as you lift them up and put them down and the sound they make. The grass is crackly with frost. The earth is hard as iron.

You walk more slowly. The noise is slightly out of sync. You stop, but hear one more footstep than you make.

Not your footstep.

The chill is more than physical cold.

You look up. Even the stars are shrouded by boiling black cloud. You are cut off.

Experimentally, you step backwards. The echo of your step comes before you have completed it.

You are being shadowed.

You walk forwards again, listening carefully. Your noise blots out the other noises. But you can *feel* the shadow. It could be six yards behind you or sixty. It is as if you were undersea, sensing water moving out of the way of the shark-snout pointed at your back. You wade through the air, slowed by settling fear. You cannot afford to panic, scream, throw a fit.

You're walking briskly now. Each breath creates a cloud of wet exhalation which you part as you step forwards. You're jogging, as if limbering up for a race, not running seriously, not even running at all. Jogging to keep warm, to get where you're going sooner.

A tangle of white-coated grass alerts you, and you hurdle a swampy patch. You're running faster now. Mary sings at 78 rpm, gabbling through the song to render it meaningless. You know your shadow is matching your pace.

When you run, you never look behind you. But you know when a competitor is gaining, when he falls back, when he drops by the track. It's as if you have side-mirrors. The clear track ahead shows you signs.

Now there is someone behind you. More than one person, one shadow. A pack of shadows. Shadow-spiders. Running in perfect sync, matching your speed, racing on many thin legs. Maybe bettering your speed, for they are gaining on you.

The field can't be more than two hundred yards across, but seems to have spread. Now you are running full out, fighting the draggy weight of your soaked clothes, arms pumping along with your legs.

You run away from darkness. You run into darkness. The ditch beside you is always there. Mary never gets further away. The trees never get closer.

But the shadow-spiders behind you do.

This is how you have always felt. The screaming six-year-old in you is gaining on the concentrated seventeen-year-old. 'Nellie the Elephant' has lapped 'Satisfaction', drawn past 'Hi Ho Silver Lining' and is neck and neck with 'Anarchy in the UK'. You can't afford to lose it now.

To lose anything.

You clear your mind and run.

The pack are close to you. You realise there are ditches either side of you, that you are running on a narrow strip of field. Beyond the ditches, in the dark, are the other runners, kept to their unlit lanes.

Your heart is close to bursting.

How far must you run? Where will this race end?

Shadow-spiders nip your heels. They are tireless and you are human. They can run until the end of time.

'The head of the herd was calling…'

Where is the finish line?

'Far, far *awayyy*…'

What if there is no finish? What if there is just running? What if you can never definitely win, just run on and on until you must sleep or grow old or die?

The ground beneath is rough, littered with rusty traps. Your ankles are whipped.

'…they met one *night* in the jungle *light*…'

Shadow-spiders are at your elbows.

'…on the Road to Mandalay, *hey*! Nellie the Elephant packed her *trunk* and…'

The song doesn't end. It just comes round again after '*hey*'. Mary still sings. You still run.

You can't think of the miles you must have run. You know this field can't be the size and shape it seems to be. Like the ditch, you took a left turn. You aren't just running on the spot or struggling up a down escalator.

You are getting closer to something. To Someone. As you've guessed, that Someone is Me.

Read 13, and come back here.

You run on and on. You're running beside a ditch. You are ahead of the pack.

Mary singing.

Her voice gets louder.

Up ahead, there is a burst of light.

Mary's flame flickers, reddening her pale face. She is sitting on the gate. Her mouth shapes the words but only an ululation of the tune emerges from her.

You have run there and back again. You are nearly where you started.

Somehow, without turning corners or passing landmarks, you have run round the whole field.

You are still on the other side of the ditch from the gate.

As you slacken, the pack slackens behind you. You fall to your knees at the spot where you started.

The shadow-spiders don't have to come for you. The point has been made.

Without explaining and without pausing in her banshee wail, Mary hops off the bar and unlatches the gate. She drags it open, pulling it out across the road, then pulls it further round, wrenching it through a 180-degree arc, twisting it on its post. The gate is not hinged wood, but rusted tube metal, fixed with frayed rope. It can be pulled in a circle on the fulcrum of its post. She pushes the gate back over the verge, flattening a wedge of grass. It wobbles out over the ditch and hangs in mid-air.

You see what she has done.

You push yourself up from the ground and reach out. The gate hangs just beyond your hands.

'You'll have to jump, jump, *jump*,' she sings.

You jump. Your hands close around cold, dirty metal. The gate wrenches on its post, sagging. Your feet trail in water that is cold beyond cold.

There is an alarming creak as the gatepost rises six inches out of its concrete setting. The gate buckles in several places. Hand over hand, you make your way toward Mary.

She flicks her lighter on and off, assuming different poses between illumination bursts, hanging her head this way and that, putting her free hand in her hair, pouting and smiling.

You are across the ditch. You sink gratefully to your knees.

Mary stops singing.

This is Sutton Mallet. You are alone on the moor, between villages, no cars for miles. Really alone. No shadows, no spiders, no Mary.

You are too tired to scream.

This, you know in an instant, is what will happen. You'll lie by the roadside all night, body temperature falling by the hour, too tired to sleep. In the morning, you'll be found and try to explain. Then they'll find Mary. In the car, her neck broken.

'She must have been killed instantly,' they'll say. 'At least she didn't suffer, poor thing.'

You will never be able to tell what happened after the car went into the ditch.

Eventually, you'll convince yourself you hallucinated it all as you crawled away from the accident. But now, in the cold silence, you know your race was no dream. You know you ran off the path, and from now on you'll be wary in the knowledge that a step can bring you to my home, my shade, my domain.

You think of Mary and can see her in your mind, lolling in the driver's seat, pinned by the steering-wheel embedded in her chest, head hung at an impossible angle, eyes red and empty.

Then, close to your ear, she shouts, '*Hey...*'

The flame bursts, and Mary's face hangs near.

'Nellie the Elephant packed her trunk and said good-bye to the cir-*cusss...*'

If you avoid Mary for the rest of the college year and try never to think of her or this night again, go to 53. If you cling closer to Mary, certain that what you have shared is too important to suppress, go to 57.

41

The experiment is a remarkable success. Within three months, £10,000 has grown to a notional £30,000. You and Sean liquidate a third of your portfolio, pay back the bank's petty cash – a relief, since you've always known just how not legal it was to borrow that – and take out your own initial investments. You leave the rest on the table and cluck over its steady growth. At first, you didn't tell anyone, not even your wives, but now you explain. Ro has money of her own and insists on buying in, which prompts Vanda to scrape together some spare cash and join. You start calling yourself a Syndicate and favour a monthly expensive restaurant meal over your old barbecues.

The ordinary work of the bank seems a bit dull.

You and Sean go on more courses, spend more time on your investments. In London for a course, you buy new suits, very '80s, with sharp angles, thin collars. You get red braces.

You talk about leaving the bank and founding a West Country investment service. Ro is keen but Vanda advises caution. You realise your wife is a little out of her depth.

Sean spends quite a lot of time in London. You have to cover for him at the bank. But the branch almost runs itself. You assume Sean is having a serious affair with one of the women from the courses. He's also getting a lot of information which turns out to be golden. She must be someone well placed in one of the coming firms.

You rely more on Candy Dixon, a school-leaver who is your assistant. She handles the chores you have to neglect to keep up with the investments. You buy her the odd gift (perfume, a bracelet) to keep her sweet, and trust her competence. She has a little crush on you, but you wouldn't do anything about it. You aren't that stupid.

Ro has a small inheritance, which she puts into the Syndicate. Suddenly, the portfolio you share is worth £100,000 and growing.

Sean talks seriously about leaving the bank. You wonder if he's thinking about leaving Ro. If he did, the Syndicate would split. You could all lose out. You think a lot about the money. It can do quite a bit for you. Your DHSS days are dead and gone. You already have BUPA, and are thinking of private eduction for the kids.

'Keith,' Vanda says, interrupting you at your desk at home.

You've been together so long that when you use each other's names, it's usually bad news.

'Vanda,' you say, turning in your swivel chair.

It's late. The kids are in bed. Vanda is wearing her dressing-gown, chewing a strand of her hair.

Despite the vasectomy, you think she's going to tell you she's pregnant. Or that she's leaving you.

'Is Sean playing around?'

'I beg your pardon?'

'Having an affair? Is Sean having an affair?'

Of course, you're sure Ro has asked Vanda to ask you.

'Well?' your wife asks.

Things are spinning.

If you tell Vanda you think Sean is having an affair, go to 49. If you tell Vanda you doubt that Sean is having an affair, go to 58.

42

By the time Desmond has discovered the Sutton Mallet turn-off is a dead end, you don't care any more. Not about Michael's party, not about Desmond and Mickey and the other girls in the car, not about being invisible.

You just want everyone but Victoria to go away.

You have done about as much as you can with mouth on mouth and roving hands under clothes. Now you need space. And privacy.

'I'm going to turn on the lights and look at the map,' Desmond says.

'Fuck off,' Victoria breathes, between kisses.

Light floods the car, hammering your eyes through the goggles. Again, the mask covers your blushes.

Mickey and Desmond are aghast at you and Victoria. You are entwined like Siamese twins. They laugh at you, waking up a girl called Helena.

But you don't care.

'Throw a bucket of water on them,' suggests Mickey, through laughter. 'They'll frighten the horses.'

'Fuck right off,' breathes Victoria.

'Well played, that man,' Desmond says.

'Fuckin' ace,' agrees Mickey.

'Magic,' coos Helena.

Victoria leans across you and unlocks the car door.

'Out,' she says.

'Come on, Vickie, it's miles from anywhere,' Desmond pleads, still laughing.

'Sutton fucking Mallet, man,' says Mickey. 'Arse-end of nowhere.'

'Out,' she repeats, a caressing word.

You back out of the car and stand, mummified in your mask and coat. You feel the cold through your thin trousers. Tiny hooks of ice work into your undone shirt.

Victoria comes out after you and wraps her thin arms round your shoulders. You embrace her, hands on her bottom. You try to pass warmth to each other.

'Drive,' Victoria orders, sideways.

You take off your goggles and pull your mask loose.

It's too late. The door is slammed shut.

You hear Desmond and Mickey laughing as the car pulls away. Its red rear lights move away like insect-eyes and disappear.

'No,' Victoria says, hand on your still-masked face.

You put the goggles back on.

'Sutton Mallet is a ghost town,' she comments, dragging you along down the dark road, towards the shapes of buildings. 'The houses are mostly empty. Graham wanted to squat here in the summer, but I wouldn't let him. It's a strange place.'

You stop and try to look at her in the dark.

'Don't worry,' she says. 'This is a strange night. The rules have changed.'

You ought to wonder what kind of girl takes a man in a mask to a ghost town, obviously intending to sleep with him. But knowing she wants you, you don't think of anything else. For so long, you have thought about sex, imagined it, feared it, hoped for it.

That's all there is. No further questions.

'I know a house,' Victoria says, taking your arm. 'It has furniture. Including a bed.'

You remember the plan you have worked out. You still intend to get married at twenty-five, in seven years' time, and have two children, Jonathan and Jennifer. Until now, you've always had a nebulous image of your wife, a cut-out woman with a ghostly smudge of a face.

You try imagining Victoria's face in the smudge. It doesn't fit. Not with that Pepe le Pew hairstyle and the safety pins.

The Sutton Mallet lane narrows. The hedgerows are taller. Shade closes in, blanketing you. Overhead, the sky is pitch black.

She pulls you by your arm towards a house. She might as well be leading you by your penis.

You stop and kiss, hungry.

In the dark, you are both invisible. You are cold, but you try to find warmth, pressing yourself against Victoria. She feels your cock, hot and hard.

'This way,' she says, leading you towards a house.

Afterwards, you lie in bed with Vic, thinking that everything is different. Springs rake your back through a rotted mattress. You feel more sensitive, more aware, more alive.

Vic strokes your chest and tugs gently at the ragged ends of your hood. All you are wearing now is your mask. Even the goggles are gone.

There is no light. She can't see your eyes.

You aren't the person you were before you put on the mask. That Keith seems an alien, with his running and his stupid plan. As you and Vic fucked, you came to a shuddering stop. You don't run any more, and you have no plan.

Except to make love again.

Your heart beats faster now than when you were having sex. Vic knew what to do with the condom and brought out of you a person you didn't know existed. A confident, persuasive, powerful man.

Not Keith.

The Runner is gone.

Eventually, after more sex, you drift into exhausted semi-sleep, hugging Vic under a makeshift quilt of clothes. You realise your breath frosts invisibly in the dark room. The house is bitterly cold.

Fingers of dawn creep into the room.

Where are you?

In Sutton Mallet. In a bed in Sutton Mallet. Not alone.

You get up, needing a piss, and wrap yourself in your trenchcoat.

The bedroom, at first look, might be in a living house. The wallpaper peels only a little and the dusty windows aren't broken. An empty light-socket dangles overhead, centrepiece of a canopy of cobweb.

What made the people who lived here leave?

You go downstairs to find a place to pee.

They left behind more than just furniture. Plates and cutlery are strewn on the kitchen floor. On each of the stairs is placed a small household object – a plastic comb, a picture frame, a toothbrush. What makes a person leave behind their toothbrush when they move out? The arrangement on the stairs is almost ritualistic.

You think you know what Vic means about strange.

Now you've made love, you each know what the other is thinking. Despite the masks – hers as much as yours – you are one person really.

You go back upstairs.

Vic stretches on the bed, yawning and smiling. A lot of her make-up has gone. Her hair is squashed out of its hooks.

The room is full of light. You're amazingly cold, numbed. Mist has drifted in. You see gooseflesh on Vic's legs and arms. She shivers, a witch rescued from a ducking.

You take off the mask and let her look at you.

'It doesn't matter,' she says.

You kneel on the bed and reach for her.

Now she knows who you are, have things changed?

She hugs you, her body shockingly cold. You rub her up and down, trying to get warmth into her.

'We missed Michael's party,' Vic says.

'Yes.'

'Too bad.'

You both laugh.

Something inside you has gone. Some need, some tension, some impulse.

From now on, you don't need to run.

'You used to frighten me,' Vic says. 'When I was jumping through hoops for Mummy and Daddy, you were always better at it. But I could see what it was doing to you, doing to me. There's a point when you're about fifteen or sixteen when things aren't set, when you really can change. For me, it was early. For you, it was when you put on that mask. You probably think some of the things I've done have been really stupid…'

'No,' you say, wondering if you are lying.

'Shhh. Really stupid. Don't forget I'm still clever, under all the bin-liners. I know what a waster Graham is and how shit my songs are. And Roger! Mistake. I don't regret mistakes. I've got time to make them. So have you.'

She props herself on one elbow and looks at you. You look at her breasts.

'Things change in Sutton Mallet,' she says, running her fingers through your five or six chest-hairs. 'I know you can feel it. The cold, the calm. It's like a time-warp or something. An Outside Zone.'

You touch her breast. She smiles.

Yesterday, it would have been unimaginable that you could touch a girl's breast and not have her hit you.

'Griffin,' she says. 'That was the Invisible Man's name. In the book.'

'I've never read it.'

'I have. I've read most things.'

You don't laugh.

'You don't need any other name. I'll call you Griffin.'

'Fair enough.'

'After all, you're starting again. We're starting again.'

You haven't needed to discuss this. You both knew it, well before you found this bed. Well before, you realise, Vic actually knew who you were.

Only now do *you* realise who you are: Griffin. But who is Griffin. Who will he be?

Griffin and Vic. They are born out of Keith and Victoria, out of the Runner and the Punk Princess. But they are different, completely, inwardly.

In the short term, however, they will have to behave more or less like their old selves. That's your next choice. You and Vic never talk about it, but you know you'll both make the same decision.

Vic could take on the outward elements of the Runner, buckle down to college work, plan for the future, work with you. Or Griffin could reject the plan, join Vic in her skewed revolt, dye his hair, slack off his courses.

If you become more like Victoria, go to 64. If she becomes more like you, go to 77.

43

You mop your face with a wet handkerchief. You aren't bleeding much. Bronagh Carey picks splinters out of your hair. You sit down, trying to control the shakes you are sure everyone notices. Deliberately, you unmake fists.

'Happy now?' you ask Victoria.

Her eyes are narrow.

Rowena is still dry-heaving outside.

Roger is standing by Victoria, holding up his sword. 'That should have been my job,' he protests.

Victoria wheels and looks at him with disgust. 'You're worse than him, you useless prick.'

Roger looks as if he has been slapped.

Time is called. You drift back to college, chatting with Gully. He is playing drums in Flaming Torture tonight, with Victoria.

'Don't mind her,' he says. 'She won't bear a grudge. She tried to ram a drumstick down my throat once.'

It's all been forgotten. Rowena, who has been taken home, and Victoria, who is fending off Neil Martin, have nothing to do with you. No one blames you for anything.

You've been through something. Attitudes have changed.

You realise you no longer have a date for the Rag Show tonight. Rowena is in no state to hold you to your promise. You doubt she'll show herself until well into the New Year.

It's not too late to ask Mary.

'We're going round Graham's,' Gully says, 'until the show. Do you want to come along?'

You assume there'll be a dope session.

Mary, self-contained and by herself, is walking nearby.

'You probably need to mellow out after the harpie attack,' Gully says. 'Come on.'

Mary smiles at you. It's as if you've passed some test.

If you ask Mary to the show, go to 26. If you go with Gully and Bronagh to Graham's, go to 48.

44

'It's a dead end,' you say.

Desmond pulls the handbrake. There's a wrench. The whole car lurches forward and then settles.

Victoria's hand also clutches and relaxes. Instantly, you lose your erection. Desmond and Mickey slowly turn round to look at you. A girl you don't know, Helena, wakes up beside you and Victoria and stares.

Your sentence seems to hang in the car.

'It's a dead end.'

'I know that voice,' Mickey says, grinning, wondering.

'So do I,' says Helena, which is news to you.

Victoria shrinks away.

'Marion,' she says, emphasising your girlie name with a disgust you haven't heard since primary school. 'The runner. Keith Marion.'

Everyone can see through your clothes.

'Never thought you had it in you,' says Mickey.

Victoria has withdrawn, so not an inch of her touches you. The gap between you is cold air. Frost hangs in it.

Inside your disguise, you shrivel. Now would be a good time to be really invisible.

Victoria is in a cold fury. You bridle, resenting her reaction. It isn't as if you have said or done anything to mislead her. She's angry because she didn't guess.

Mickey laughs, in stoned burps. Desmond joins in. They aren't laughing at you. They're laughing at Victoria.

'Well played, that man,' Desmond says.

'Fuckin' ace,' agrees Mickey.

'Magic,' coos Helena.

Victoria leans across you and unlocks the car door.

'Out,' she says.

'Come on, Vickie, it's miles from anywhere,' Desmond pleads, still laughing.

'Sutton fucking Mallet, man,' says Mickey. 'Arse-end of nowhere.'

'Out,' she repeats, a stabbing word.

You back out of the car and stand, mummified in your mask and coat. You feel the cold through your thin trousers. Tiny hooks of ice work into your undone shirt.

'Drive,' Victoria orders.

You take off your goggles and pull your mask loose. It's too late. The door is slammed shut.

You hear Desmond and Mickey laughing as the car pulls away. Its red rear lights move away like insect-eyes and disappear.

By the Sutton Mallet turn-off, you stand in the dark, unmasked. The next car that passes will probably be stuffed with kids going out to Michael's party.

That's not where you want to be.

The cold really starts to bite.

You sit down by the signpost. And wait.

And so on.

45

'Still no response, Dr Cross?'

'No. Nothing.'

'What about the EEG?'

'Oh, there are brainwaves, Susan. Marion is *thinking*.'

'Dreaming?'

'Not much REM. No, I should say our friend here is thinking.'

'What?'

'That's the question. It'd be nice to have a mind-reader, wouldn't it? To peer into that skull.'

'He looks like he's asleep.'

'We shave him, wash him and give him exercise to keep him supple.'

'Might wake up at any moment.'

'Maybe he is awake all the time.'

'You think it's shamming?'

'Not shamming, exactly. But deliberate.'

'What's the background?'

'Just life. Nothing special. Have you ever wanted to curl up and have it all go away?'

'Every day, Doctor.'

'Well, this patient got his wish.'

'If you were Marion, what would you think?'

'I'm not.'

'If you were.'

'I'd plan. Try and work it all out.'

'Maybe that's what Marion's doing in there.'

'I don't think he's a terribly forward-looking chap, Susan. Couldn't be, really.'

'How long has he been like this?'

'A good while.'

'If I had a good rest, I'd think it all through. Every juncture, every possibility, every road taken.'

'Do you think you'd come to a conclusion?'

'I don't think that's the point.'

'No.'

46

Rowena is curled up in a fetal ball, a spreading pool of sick radiating from around her head. You gingerly step round it and kneel down, lifting her up. She writhes in your grip and more vomit falls out of her mouth. She must be almost empty.

This is not what you signed on for when you asked her out.

She tries to say something but is sick again. Then she manages a single word.

'Sorry.'

You tell her it's all right, wondering if you're lying.

It's cold in the alley but Rowena is running a fever. You hold her for warmth. She feebly pokes a hand out and takes yours. Something breaks inside you as she holds your hand.

'Very pretty picture.'

Roger stands in the doorway, looking at you. Zorro's sword dangles from his wrist. His mask is round his neck. He smiles nastily. For a moment, you think you might have to hit him.

Rowena raises her free hand and flashes a V sign at Roger. Disgusted, he goes back into the pub.

Rowena's body racks, but there's nothing to come up. With a handkerchief, you wipe her face. She smiles, tinily.

'I'm not drunk any more,' she says.

You pick tiny scraps of sick out of her hair and flick them away. Greater love hath no man.

Greater love.

It occurs to you that in this moment you have fallen in love with Rowena. Until now, you've just thought of her as a pair of breasts and a threatening mind.

You have to question so many things.

'She can't go home like that,' a clear voice says.

Victoria has come out of the pub, a frayed fairy godmother. She stands over you.

Rowena tries to say she's all right. The words don't come out at all well. Despite her claim, she's still completely sozzled.

'She can sleep it off in the back of the van.'

That's an ideal solution. Presenting Rowena to her parents in this state is not going to make anyone happy in the short or long term.

Victoria's van is by the Corn Exchange, only a short walk from this alley. It might still not be easy to get Rowena to cover the distance.

'Come on, get her on her feet.'

Gently, you pull Rowena up. She clings to you, head against your chest. Somehow, she manages to weigh more than you would think possible.

You are still pondering your own feelings. Your head spins and your heart burns. You have the beginnings of an erection. These might well be the physical symptoms of love as you understand it. If you feel this way about Rowena now, while she's in such a sorry state, you must be serious. Or at least well on the way.

You and Victoria manipulate Rowena out into the open. Rowena is like a two-year-old, tugging in all the wrong ways, a broad smile threatening to turn into tears.

Gully Eastment asks Victoria if she wants to go to Graham's for a dope session before the Rag Show.

She turns him down. 'Duty calls,' she says.

Gully shrugs and catches up with the others.

Victoria opens the back of her van and shifts stuff around inside. She has a guitar and an amp stashed in there. She arranges a sleeping-bag.

'It's snug,' she says.

You help Rowena in, bumping your head on the roof of the van.

'Poor dear,' Rowena says, kissing you where there ought to be a throbbing cartoon bruise rising.

She pulls you into the van with her. It is so cramped that you have to lie down not beside her but half on top of her.

You catch a glimpse of Victoria's raised eyebrow.

The smell of drink on Rowena's breath is very strong. Her eyes aren't focused. She kisses you and you taste the bitterness of vomit on her tongue.

Still she clings to you.

This is not what you imagined. You've always sneered at those little 'Love Is…' cartoons, with their horrible sentiments. But… 'Love Is… Snogging Someone Who's Just Been Sick.'

Rowena takes your hand and slips it into her jumper, guiding it to her breast.

The cold is coming in.

'Goodbye, Victoria,' Rowena says, pointedly.

Victoria doesn't shut the door yet. She is giving you a way out. But not for long.

Rowena's nipple puckers under your palm. You can feel it through her bra. Her tongue flicks at your face.

There might well be rules about getting off with someone so drunk she probably doesn't know who you are. And you could worry that taking further advantage of this situation will imperil your possible future with Rowena.

For the first time, you are interested in a girl and have an opportunity to pursue that interest. And her hands are in your trousers, cold against your buttocks. Rowena clearly wants you to shag her here and now.

But if you do, how will she feel about you in the morning? And, considering how you think you feel, could you live with yourself? Is this the first sexual experience you want to remember for the rest of your life? Under these circumstances, can you even go through with it?

It's not fair, is it? That you should be dumped with a choice like this. You're only a kid, really. How can you be expected to puzzle it through?

It's just that you have to.

Victoria uncertainly starts to shut the door.

If you stay in the van with Rowena, go to 52. If you extricate yourself and leave her to sober up, go to 60.

47

'Your loss, mate,' Sean says.

'I don't think Vanda would –'

'No need to make excuses.'

'It's just…'

'It's all right, pal.'

Nothing ventured, nothing gained. You don't venture. So you don't gain.

As weeks pass, you expect Sean to come back to the subject. Either to gloat good-naturedly about the profit his scheme has yielded, or to admit casually that he's taken a £2500 bath and that you were sensible after all. Then, you'd have a pint and laugh about it.

But Sean backs off a little from you. You and Vanda aren't invited to Sean and Ro's house for several months, though they come to you. Sean spends a lot of time in his office, on the phone.

You just get on with things.

Sean buys a flash car. Not a new car, a second car. A nifty little two-seater MG. Vanda comments that Ro is wearing originals.

You kick yourself a bit. But you've a decent life. Even if your car is three years old and there's a rattling noise under the hood you can't identify, you aren't due for the poorhouse.

The branch wins an award. Suits from head office come down and are photographed with the whole staff.

'You're Harry Marion's son,' says the head suit.

You confirm that you are.

'Jolly good,' the suit says, and passes on.

Long-time customers still telephone the bank and ask to speak with Mr Marion, and are disappointed when Candy Dixon, the new girl, puts them through to you. Each time you have to admit your father is dead, you feel a smidgen of inadequacy. As Sean says, your Dad *was* this branch.

Now Sean is the branch.

Sean wears Italian suits. Very sharp.

Sean asks you to see him in his office. You assume it's about the Shearer loan. You've extended overdraft facilities to Kay Shearer, who runs a small shelving company, and repayments are slow in coming. You understand Shearer isn't doing well. You assume Sean is going to exert gentle pressure, and that you'll have to squeeze Shearer. Instead, Sean tells you he is leaving in two months.

'I'm going to give the City a go,' he says. 'Just thought you should know.'

You don't regret not going in with him.

You don't.

The Shearer loan is a mess. You take a rare Saturday away from home to go through the paper trail again.

Candy comes in to help.

Surprisingly, Vanda is keen on you doing the extra work. With Sean going, she thinks you should draw attention to yourself.

'Keith Marion, manager,' she breathes in your ear.

Shearer's Shelves is tied in with the Discount Development, which Councillor Robert Hackwill is forcing through the Planning Committee. There are a lot of bad vibes about that project.

You are worried the Shearer loan is a dud.

'Keith Marion, dud,' you think.

You ask Candy to bring you the files on the Discount Development. Sean is keeping them up to date.

'Mr Rye has his own office key, Keith.'

You're sure you have keys to every lock in the bank. It's policy. No, Sean has fitted an extra lock on his office door. You wonder why you didn't notice the workman coming in.

'I can open it with a paper-clip,' Candy says.

You're shocked.

'My boyfriend showed me how.'

Before you can protest, Candy has the door open.

'It's a good thing you can trust me,' she says.

It feels wrong, being in Sean's office, even searching for files you know he'd want you to consult. Sean ordered you to keep tabs on the Discount Development in the first place. You compiled most of the documents you want to look at.

You have a key to Sean's filing cabinet. You open it, find the Hackwill file, check the facts you want to check, and put it back.

Something catches your eye. Sean has a personal code for files. They have joke names, USURY, EMBEZZLEMENT, FINAGLING, ARMS DEALS, HARD DRUGS. Sean often raises a laugh by pulling out one of the files, revealing that it contains harmless material.

In between SLUSH FUND and WIDOWS AND ORPHANS (DISPOSSESSION OF) is a file marked HOUSEKEEPING. That sounds legit. But it shouldn't. It should sound crooked. That's the joke.

What do you do?

If you look at the housekeeping file, go to 83. If you shut the cabinet and try to forget about the file, go to 112.

48

Graham lives in a bedsit in the centre of town. It contains a mattress, piles of Michael Moorcock paperbacks, layers of strewn clothing, and, currently, twenty-eight people. Graham either doesn't believe in chairs or has sold off the landlord's furniture for cash. On the walls, he has a map of Middle Earth, a Fabulous Furry Freak Brothers poster and a star chart with the astrological signs highlighted.

'Move over,' Gully Eastment tells Shane Bush, giving him a kick.

Shane, eyes glazed, shifts.

When you stepped into the room, you got an instant headache from the fug of dope smoke. It hangs in a hazy mist, thickening nearer the carpet.

As you sit down in the space Shane has cleared, you feel like coughing. On top of the cider and whisky, you even feel a slight buzz.

Gully eagerly takes a joint from Shane and draws on it, holds the smoke in his lungs, mumbles an obligatory 'Potent brew, my man,' and exhales in Bronagh's face. She licks up the smoke, sucking it in and rebreathing it.

You have no prejudices against drugs. Mum and Dad went on about what a monster Graham was when your sister was going out with him, which made you sympathise with him. Laraine smoked dope for a while, but says she never got much out of it. From what you understand, marijuana is no worse for you than alcohol. But you have never smoked a joint.

Graham rolls a fresh one, sprinkling scraps of black into tobacco laid in a line on several stuck-together Rizla papers.

Gully offers you the joint.

The worst thing in it is the tobacco. That'll kill you quicker than dope or booze. And you don't smoke.

You want to try this stuff. You've had so much craziness today that you might as well go the whole hog.

But your one attempt at smoking was a disaster. You remember Stephen Adlard giving you a cigarette on the rec ground when you were thirteen. You sucked flame to the fag from his match, then drew in a great lungful. You coughed yourself sick and haven't repeated the experiment.

You know you can't get away with keeping the smoke in your mouth. You have to take it into your lungs.

'Have a hit, Keith,' Gully says.

If you take the joint, go to 51. If you turn it down, go to 61.

49

'Yes,' you say. 'I think he is.'

Vanda slides a little down the door-jamb. Her dressing-gown gapes open a little.

'Silly boy,' she says.

'Yes,' you admit.

Vanda is thinking about something. You wonder if you should have lied.

'Ro mustn't know,' Vanda says.

You agree.

'We can't afford to break the Syndicate.'

You're surprised Vanda has thought it through.

'By the way, Keith…'

'Yes?'

'You're not fucking Candy, are you?'

'No.'

'Good.'

She slips out of her dressing-gown. Since she's been going to exercise class, her body is better toned than since before Jason.

You lean back in your swivel chair as she undoes your fly. Her tongue works around your penis.

'Keith,' she says, pausing.

'Yes?'

'We're rich, aren't we?'

You nod. She smiles, licks her lips and bobs her head. You stroke her hair, and can't think of anything but her mouth.

Go to 72.

50

Your bedroom window creaks. Suddenly, torn out of a dream, you are awake.

The room is darker than it should be. Something hangs outside the window, beyond the curtains, blotting out the moon. It could be a man-sized kite.

It is days before Christmas. And you don't believe in Santa Claus.

It is days since Rag Day.

Time has passed, in a blur.

Why is your heart hammering? You've lost the memory of a dream, but have awoken with an erection.

Are you afraid? Or excited?

The window seems to swell inwards, as if a giant breath is gently playing on it, pushing the panes in their beds of putty, bending the wood.

There's a scratching outside.

You get out of bed, flagpole cock stuck out of your pyjama fly, and stand in the dark.

What is outside the window?

You walk to the window, and take hold of the curtains.

Through the weave of the curtains, you sense a white, moon-like circle.

You open the curtains.

The moon has Victoria's face.

Go on.

51

You cough a bit, but can hold it. Things smooth away. You don't feel guilty about Rowena, you aren't angry about Victoria, you aren't uptight about anything.

'Hey,' announces Gully, 'Marion's just turned on.'

The kids applaud. You smile and smoke burps out of your mouth.

'A first-timer,' Graham declares. 'You should have told me. He'll need a special.'

'A special, a special,' the kids chant.

That seems like a good idea. Yes, man, a special. That's what you need.

Graham sees it's you. 'Keith,' he says, 'welcome to enlightenment.'

He asks after Laraine but you can't put enough facts together in your mind to give him an answer.

You hold up the joint. 'Bobby Moore says smoking is a mug's game,' you announce. 'Bubba Moron suss Nosmo King Esau mugwump,' it comes out.

Graham is rolling a special. He fixes a dozen Rizlas together.

'Has to be the size of Errol Flynn's dick,' he explains.

You laugh. That's funny.

A whole packet of tobacco is scattered in a thick line. Then Graham roots in a tea-chest and comes up with a plastic model of Thunderbird 2.

'Calling International Rescue,' he says, popping the central pod. He opens the door and pulls out a lump of something. With a penknife, he scrapes flecks of the lump on to the tobacco.

'Special, special, special,' the kids chant.

The Rizlas are rolled round the fillings, and the ends twist-tied. It looks more like a sausage roll than Errol Flynn's penis.

'Open wide,' Gully says.

You close your eyes and open your eustachian tubes, hearing the roar in your ears.

'Mouth, drongo,' Gully says.

You open your mouth and the special is stuck into it.

'Light the blue touch paper and retire,' says Gully.

Graham flicks his lighter and plays the flame against the end of the special. The twist burns.

You inhale.

An inch of loose tobacco and special mix burns at once. You suck the smoke into your lungs. And hold it.

All through the rest of your time at college and your three years at university, you smoke marijuana regularly. Mostly in sessions with other people, but sometimes at home, alone. It helps you slow down, relax. You think it makes you sharper when you're straight. You feel the time you're stoned is time off from thinking, from achieving. You've always needed that, but now you have it.

You get into the whole dope scene. You let your hair and beard grow. You make your own bong. The walls of your room in a student flat are browned with smoke, carpet ravaged by burn-marks, trodden-in tobacco shreds and other stains. You have a 'Legalise It' badge. You buy grow-lamps and cultivate your own plants in a cupboard.

By your second year, you have a morning joint when you wake up and get through the day with a loose chain, hanging smokes round intervals of taking in tea or beer. You become a connoisseur and can tell where dope comes from at a sniff, like an expert identifying wines.

You have the occasional paranoia spasm. Nothing heavy, but you and your friends all know kids who've been busted, and that makes you think about the police too much, elaborating fantasies about their fiendish schemes to entrap and undo you.

At one point, the big dealer on campus is arrested. In his flat, the pigs find a bundle of cheques, each for £25 – the cost of an ounce in 1979 – and all the signatories are raided over the next week. You've always paid in notes but this still makes you go to ground, finding a neutral pad and staying there until it blows over.

Your throat is dry all the time.

Even your mellows start to feel edgy.

You take another drag on the special.

You need to be further away, where the nagging doubts can't get to you. You realise the dope is just getting you to where you used to start out from.

You try LSD. Lovely. Strange. Delight. It's not like being Keith. It's a three-day holiday from him. You make connections, you become part of them. You discover things about yourself and your furniture.

You trip regularly.

One time, you realise your campus is infested with shadow-parasites. Some people have transparent spider-things clamped round their heads, straw-like suckers implanted in their brains. Those with shadow-spiders are in charge.

Under the sink in your shared bathroom, you find your shadow-spider, waiting for your insight to fade, so it can fasten on you and suck your brain.

As you feel yourself coming down, you scout round your flatmates for another tab of acid. They don't come across and you feel panic as the shadows start to fade. Straight, you won't know who has a parasite and who hasn't. Your own shadow-spider will be invisible, and will come for you.

You have to prolong the trip, spend your whole life outside your head.

But the cupboard is bare.

When you do come down, after a spell as a gibbering maniac under home-made restraint, you opt to slacken off.

You have a couple more trips, but they are in mono and black-and-white. The vividness has faded.

The shadow-spiders are gone.

You miss them.

You take another drag on the special.

As finals loom, you realise you have to catch up. Your grades have been hovering around the acceptable mark but you need a good degree. It hits you that you've burned up the last three years.

You cut down on smoking and kick acid into touch. You lose the long hair and the beard. You ponder your overdraft and wonder how much of that was caused by your – not habit: you haven't been using habit-forming drugs – by your tastes. You're going to need postgraduation funds to get level, or you'll be in debt until the next century.

You hit the books. You're doing economics and business studies. You hit the library. You attend lectures, not only for your own year but for the two years below you, going over ground you have a hazy memory of. You work, restricting stoned periods to a few hours at the weekends.

You get new friends.

Finals are near and you have so much to do. You resent the sleep that takes you away from work.

A friend suggests amphetamines.

A good friend.

You start with a few bennies and manage marathon three-day study fugues. Your brain reconfigures and sorts everything out for you.

You don't need sleep. You need speed.

You start speeding.

This is different. It's not avoiding reality, it's embracing it. You are empowered. The speed jump-starts you, lets you cover three years' work in three months.

Ka-pow! You get an upper second.

Zap! You are recruited by an investment firm.

Whoosh! You zoom out of university, into the 1980s.

You take another drag on the special.

In the City, juggling unimaginable amounts of money, raking off your huge cut, speed seems tame. You shift to cocaine. It's expensive, especially the good stuff you need, but plugs you into the big board.

Your nasal passages scab up.

But you appreciate things. Cars, sex, money.

You get your own silver spoon, like a Beverly Hills tycoon. You keep downstairs coke – cut with everything from baby laxative to chalk – for sluts; upstairs coke – almost pure flake – for clients.

You write off a Ferrari.

It's a blast.

Maybe it's a dependency, a crutch, but whothefuck cares? You could get through a week without coke, you just don't want to. Would most folk be able to get through a week without, say, coffee? Most folk couldn't imagine a whole lifetime stretching ahead of them without the blessed bean, but does that make them dependent on coffee? No fucking way, Hose A.

You turn over the odometer on your bank account. You have a million in the game. Pounds, not dollars.

You snort.

It's all gone.

A big gamble.

You snort.

A dealer wants paying. He carries you for a while.

The money doesn't come back.

You're good for it. Your right nostril prolapses.

You run out of cars, sex, money.

Whappened?

* * *

You take another drag on the special.

In the late '80s, skag is where it's at. Heroin.

Why you ever fucked around with anything else is a mystery.

You inject yourself with liquid joy.

You're an addict, you admit it. It's just a word, not a brand, not a mark of Cain. Everyone's an addict to something. With you, it's smack.

You can explain it.

The shadow-spiders come back. Now, you see them when you're straight. You were wrong about them. They don't become invisible when you change your perceptual relationship with reality. They are literally banished.

While you're up, they can't get you.

You sell stuff left over from the Rush Days. Your early-'80s circle has gone. You try to scrape consultancy gigs but fuck up. All the fucking time, you fuck up. You steal stuff from people. You rob people in the street. You sell yourself to people.

Anything to keep the shadow-spiders away.

You take another drag on the special.

Crack.

It's better than sliced smack.

But it costs.

The shadow-spiders order you to do extreme things. Without a second thought, you obey.

To suck on the glass tit, you kill people.

It's worth it.

People? Who needs 'em?

You don't.

You're not addicted to crack. How could you be? You are a part of crack. You cannot separate yourself from it. You have to get back to it.

It's important.

You take a last drag on the special.

You die.

AIDS. Odee. Murder. Pneumonia. Whatever.

The spiders kill you.

Or maybe you pause somewhere and write a book. A romantic comedy about a smackhead in love with a crackbrain. It's authentic and a best-seller. The movie is a hit. Everyone starts talking like your dialogue. You start a trend, become a role model.

Probably not.

Probably you rot to shit and nobody notices.

Good-bye, dead guy.

You stub out the special.

Everyone looks at you, eager, pleased, anticipating.

You shake your head, almost sad that it's over.

'Great shit, huh, man?' Graham prompts.

'Yes,' you say, 'but I wouldn't want to make a habit of it or anything.'

And so on.

52

It's awkward and unromantic. You're in such a small place that you can't undress. You pull up Rowena's layers of sweaters as she takes off her bra, but that covers most of her face with wool. You can both only get your jeans and underwear down to your knees since you're wearing boots you haven't got the room, inclination or dexterity to get off.

She coaxes you on with breathed sex-talk that sounds fake, as if copied from some porn film. You aren't convinced that she's a slut.

Her stomach and breasts are goosebumped. The inside of the van is hardly protected against the elements. Wind whistles through several apertures. At least the windows are misted up.

You fumble the business of getting the condom on, which feels momentarily as if you've noosed a wire round the head of your penis. You (plural) have to use all four of your hands to angle your erection for penetration.

It doesn't last long.

She bites your chest through your shirt. You're sure she has drawn blood.

Your arse is frozen, especially when you roll against the icy metal of the wheel-housing.

Rowena hugs herself and might be crying.

You pull up your trousers and realise you are still wearing a soiled condom, which is now unpleasantly loose and squishy.

Are you happy yet?

You've imagined this sex business quite a lot. Somehow, though you knew it was ridiculous, you imagined a large bed, a long night of warmth and a champagne breakfast.

Rowena is definitely crying.

You hug her and she thumps you.

Whatever it was, it's broken now.

Rowena twists around and kicks you. It might be accidental but it might not. She definitely isn't drunk now. And neither are you.

'Get out,' she says. 'Please.'

That 'please' is a heart-breaker.

You don't know how to open the van from the inside and have to feel around before you find the handle. You push the doors open and unbend out of the van. You realise you've been steadily bleeding from where you banged your forehead. You have zips and buttons to fasten.

Victoria sits on the Corn Exchange steps, alone, freezing, smoking. She looks at her watch and at you.

'Keith,' she says, 'you're pathetic.'

You have to agree with her.

If you slink home and hide yourself in shame until the New Year, go to 54. If you brazen it out and decide to go on to the Flaming Torture show, go to 63.

53

January 1978. Jubilee year is over.

You don't think about Sutton Mallet. You don't dream.

The first day back in college after the holidays, you see Mary in the common room. You don't make a show of it but find somewhere else to be.

That night is there. Sutton Mallet. Between you.

But it's there *only* between you. If you're apart, it need not have happened. Like a chemical reaction that takes place only if the two components are in proximity.

After a few weeks, you don't even have to think about it. You and

Mary move on different paths, never intersecting. Once, you wonder if she's doing the same thing.

Whatever happened to you, happened to you through her. She was a part of it. Maybe she has finished. Maybe it has finished with you.

Is she... haunted?

It's not an expression you can afford to get comfortable with. You're not *haunted*. You're not obsessed. You've survived, put Sutton Mallet behind you. It need trouble you no more, need not shape your whole life.

To concentrate on avoiding Mary would be to admit the importance of Sutton Mallet. It must come low on your agenda, taken care of but at a constant ticking-over level. You have other things to cope with. Your A Levels this summer. University applications, if you are to stay in eduction. Interviews, for places or – if you want to take time off before university or not go on at all – for jobs.

You still run, though not competitively. College has no organised sport. There is no one to compete with. At weekends, you take long, solitary runs. You go to the empty college site and rack up lap after lap. Running is still an essential.

You've learned to keep your eyes on the course. You stay in lane. You don't tire.

You cut down on wasteful effort. At home, you speak only when necessary to accommodate or negotiate with your parents and siblings. You never venture a comment, never initiate a conversation. You're not sullen, you just don't waste effort.

You read only books for your courses. You rarely watch television or listen to the wireless. You never go to the cinema. You attend college discos because it is expected, but tolerate them as you tolerate your classes. Your eyes are on the track.

Your parents aren't worried about you. Why should they be? There's nothing wrong. You're coping with everything. You're not wearing yourself down with worry, like half your peers. You're not causing the problems Laraine did when she was your age. You're not out all the time, like James. You are exactly what any parent would want.

So why do you detect disappointment? The last time your parents seemed pleased with you was when Mary came to pick you up on Rag Day. Then, they were all secret smiles and suppressed excitement. Later, when you had to have X-rays and Mary's policeman dad came round to get a statement for the insurance, they were less thrilled. But still, there was a sense of admiration. Dad, particularly, was chuckling 'hidden depths' at you through the aftermath of the accident. It occurs to you that your parents find you rather boring. Dad – the *bank manager* – thinks you're dull.

What, you ask rhetorically, does he know? What does anybody know? They weren't there. They don't know what waits at Sutton Mallet.

Neither, of course, do you.

At college, you survive. You're more than adequate in all three of your subjects: French, German and history. Each of your classes has at least two stars, flamboyant geniuses who occupy three-quarters of your lecturers' time and invariably take the lead in discussions. You're not of their number. But they mean your lecturers don't have to think too much about you beyond giving you your usual 65–75 per cent marks.

Between classes, you work in the library or sit in the common room. Everyone is used to you, but no one notices you. You're building invisible armour.

Sutton Mallet can never happen again.

The common room is like an eighteenth-century coffee house. Michael Dixon is the Johnsonian figure, with his cadre – they call themselves the Quorum, for no reason you can understand – of satirists and wits.

Some people really hate the Quorum, deeming them decadent wasters. Others are entertained by them, or envious of their private language, the way they can spin inventions out in chat, tossing them back and forth, elaborating routines.

You have no opinion. Those people don't impinge on you.

One day in the chill of March, you're in the common room, reading up on the Interregnum. Michael presides over a group, lolling about in a quilted smoking-jacket and puffing on a ciggy in a holder, while Neil Martin takes notes and Mark Amphlett concentrates seriously, feeding Michael straight lines. Penny Gaye, Michael's girlfriend, is there, slyly observed by Victoria, who seems removed from their in-group but is included because she is willing to go farther than most. Victoria's velvet dress is held together by safety pins.

This is the year in which everyone has an eighteenth birthday –

yours passed last October, noticed only by your family, who took you out for a restaurant meal and gave you an expensive set of luggage 'for when you go away' – and therefore there will be a crowded social calendar of important birthday parties. Michael plans to hold a major celebration over the Easter holidays, absorbing the birthdays of several lesser lights into his own.

The Quorum run through their guest list.

Your name – alphabetically right in the middle of the roll-call – comes up.

'Keith Marion,' says Neil. You can't help hearing your name and what he says next. For a moment, you think Neil, with whom you've shared classes for five years, doesn't know who you are. Then he says, 'Funny thing about Marion. When he's there, you don't mind him. When he's not, you don't miss him.'

That sums you up and they're on to the next name.

The common room is crowded. Neil might or might not know you're there. But what he said is how everyone feels about you.

You always run in the daylight. As the days get longer in spring, you can run before college.

You run out in the open.

No shadows. No spiders.

As you run, you think about not being minded and not being missed.

It's a distraction. It's not something on the course, not something that affects you really. You don't care about Neil or Michael or Victoria or any of them.

They don't know what you know. Their car didn't pause at the Sutton Mallet turn-off. They don't know what waits in the shadows.

Neither do you. Not really. But…

You run faster, harder. A cloud covers the sun, spreading gloom over the track. You're cold, despite your exertion. The afternoon is getting on, towards sunset.

A spurt of speed comes.

The shadow-spiders are at your heels; as they were that night. The race that got serious at Sutton Mallet is still being run.

How far ahead are you?

* * *

You're coping with the shadow-spiders. On your own: You only have yourself. But something is missing.

You're a non-stick personality, speeding along the track, unencumbered, uninterrupted, unnoticed. Those closest to you, if they think about it, don't know you. You are unexceptional, acceptable, affectless.

If it were not for the shadow-spiders, you might as well be running on the spot.

The shadow-spiders are pacing you now. You aren't ahead. They're on either side of you. If you stop, they'll surge around you, wrapping you in the dark.

Eventually, you will stop. Everyone gets tired, everyone gets old, everyone slows. You are not exempt.

You go to Michael's party. It's an open invite.

It's the Easter weekend, and the party is at Michael's grandmother's house in Achelzoy. By going, completing the interrupted journey, you think you can get beyond Sutton Mallet in your mind, surge away from the shadows, leave them behind.

You cycle out to Achelzoy by an elaborate route that means you don't pass the Sutton Mallet turn-off. You wonder if that is a mistake.

The party starts in the afternoon and is due to last a full twenty-four hours. Nothing less than a record-breaker is good enough for Michael. So you get out to Achelzoy in daylight. You might have chanced the Sutton Mallet route. But you didn't.

When you arrive, Michael is getting a barbecue started. Already, dozens of kids are around. A crowd big enough to get lost in.

A circle of drug-smokers is closeted in a converted coal shed, the Somerset equivalent of an American Indian sweat lodge. Neil and Desmond fiddle with the stereo speakers, trying to fix them up in trees.

Penny Gaye dispenses her fruit punch from an open kitchen window. You get a paper cup full of crimson liquid, with chunks of fruit floating in it. You sip the sweet stuff, nostrils stinging from unidentified liquor.

You are calm, a zen warrior.

Mary isn't here. There will be no shadow-spiders.

Rowena Douglass talks to you. Her chatter is tiresome but gives you a thrill of power. She is more interested in you than you are in her. That could be useful. She notices you when you're there, and misses you when you're not.

'Are you a Martian?' she asks.

You have to pay attention to that.

It's an effort to pretend. You used to have the trick. It was part of the system that kept you on the track, like a cow-catcher ploughing obstacles out of the way.

You pretend not to understand.

'What is it, Keith? You're so...'

Rowena, thank God, is seventeen years old. She hasn't been into the shade. She hasn't got the mental reach or the vocabulary to comprehend what reality is. Mary might, but she *is* the shade. And Victoria, you sense, would know but not care. Poor blind Rowena, not stupid but not aware, can't even think of what you are so...

You construct a smile.

At once, you realise you have become the shade. It is your strength. You have run through night and into the dawn. In you, the darkness grows. A comforting, empowering, warm dark.

Nothing you can do will rid you of the dark.

But what will you make of it?

Rowena ladles you some more punch. You didn't realise you'd finished your first cup.

You work on the smile. You can make it good enough to pass.

Rowena is transparent, shifting from side to side to put her chest on show, looking up at you without trying to seem eager, coaxing out of you sentences upon which she can hang.

You can bring her into the shade. Probably, she will come whether you want her to or not. Tonight, at this party, you can have her. But afterwards, do you stay with her? Or move on, always running? It's getting dark already.

You finish your punch again. A natural gap comes in Rowena's chatter. She draws breath. You fill the gap by kissing her. She responds.

If you take Rowena as a steady girlfriend, go to 67. If you get the business of losing your virginity out of the way with her but refuse to repeat the experiment, go to 74.

54

Your parents don't ask why you've come home hours earlier than expected and choose to spend the evening of the big party at home. While walking back from town, you got soaked when it started to drizzle.

You remember Victoria's verdict.

You can't help feeling you really are pathetic.

You come down with a severe cold, which means you spend most of the next week – including Christmas Day – in bed, eating your meals on a tray, sniffling into tissues, feeling sorry for yourself.

This gives you time to think.

Looking on the bright side, you're now an adult, fully initiated into the mysteries of sex. That's a difficult interpretation, but just about possible.

Rowena is upset not with you but with herself. It's Roger's fault. Sometime in the New Year, you should give Roger a right belting.

You are running a fever. You think a lot about Rowena.

Yes, you realise, you're in love with Rowena Douglass.

That makes you feel better. You can still make things right between you. It will be a project for 1978. If you can win Rowena round, you will be a whole person.

Until now, you've just been going through the motions, an exam-passing zombie. All that isn't worth much if you can't have Rowena.

And you can have Rowena.

After all, you already have. Right? Right.

You put off telephoning Rowena until after your cold has receded. It's a good idea to give her time to get over her hysteria, over her anger with Roger, over whatever it was that made her throw you out of Victoria's van.

Between Christmas and New Year, you decide to call. The 27th seems a good date, one holiday over, the other not started. You can ask Rowena out on New Year's Eve.

This time, you'll be alone with her, not surrounded by distracting people. You're sure now that the problem with Rag Day was Roger and Victoria and Gully and the others.

On the morning of the 27th, you look at the telephone. You have

Rowena's number memorised, though you've only dialled it the once, to ask her out last time.

What if she's still upset?

Your heart pounds as if you'd run a half-mile. This is silly. You're only going to make a phone call, not invade France. And you've already slept with Rowena – if you can call it sleeping – so there's nothing really to be nervous about. You're in there. Well in there. You're Rowena's only option. If she makes it up with you, she can redeem her embarrassing public behaviour on Rag Day.

Yes, it's time to phone.

Laraine, home from university, gets in the way. She asks you if you're going to use the phone. You aren't able to tell her and she makes a call to her boyfriend, some bloke called Fred she's been seeing in Norwich.

Your sister and her boyfriend chat and giggle. Hearing only Laraine's half of the conversation, as you pretend to read the holiday double issue of the *Radio Times*, you imagine Fred's suave, coaxing words. Laraine is thoroughly charmed, but also completely relaxed.

That's what you want to be like.

Your cold has gone, but you still feel as if you're in a fever. All these years, you've listened to songs go on about 'heartache' and 'love-sickness'. You assumed 'tender' meant 'gentle', not 'easy to hurt'.

But – it's incredible – you really do feel sick.

This has got to stop. You have to talk to Rowena, coax and purr and smooth. You have to get things settled. When she's your official girlfriend, you can relax.

The cow is driving you mad. There's nothing to stop her calling you. Unless Victoria has poisoned her mind against you. Or Roger has been creeping around, trying to get back in with her.

Roger really needs a belting.

After what seems like hours, Laraine coos farewells and hangs up. Happy, she sits down on the sofa, and runs her hands through her long hair.

Is she in love with Fred? Probably.

You want her to go away now, so you can call Rowena. You don't want to have this conversation with your sister eavesdropping. It's too important.

You put the magazine down.

'I'm still bloated from Christmas dinner,' Laraine says.

She looks thin to you.

'I'm starting a diet in January. My New Year resolution. When the leftovers run out.'

You have nothing to say. If this doesn't turn into a conversation, she'll go away.

'Keith, do you want a cup of tea?'

'No, thank you, Laraine.'

'I think I'll have one. Are Mum and Dad around?'

They're in the garden. If you tell her, she'll have to go out and ask them if they want tea. Will that give you long enough to make the call?

'They're in the garden.'

Laraine gets up – victory! – and looks out of the window. Your parents are seeing to things neglected over the holiday. Janies helps, raking dead leaves blown from the compost heap.

'I'll make a tea run, then. Sure you don't want one?'

Actually, your throat is completely dry, desert sands swarm over your tongue. But you have made a statement and don't want to retract it.

'No, thank you, Laraine.'

'There are still mince pies left.'

'That's okay.'

Fuck off, Laraine. Go out into the garden. Leave me alone.

'Looks chilly. Do I need a coat?'

Inside, you scream.

Laraine wraps a shawl round her shoulders and goes out into the garden.

Freedom.

You are on the phone within a second. You have the receiver to your ear.

Your finger stabs the first digit of Rowena's number.

Don't think about it. Dial.

You dial the number.

You hear the ringing at the other end. It's not too late to hang up, write this off as a mistake. Maybe you should have this conversation face to face.

The telephone rings.

One of Rowena's parents will probably answer – you don't know if she has brothers or sisters – and you'll have to ask them to fetch her. Has she told them about you? Almost certainly not. You haven't told your family about her.

This is the era of the secret life.

The telephone still rings.

It's been a long while. How big is Rowena's house? If she were in the attic and the phone by the front door, would it take her this long to answer?

You start counting rings. Twenty more and you'll assume nobody's home.

More rings.

'Calling someone?' Laraine asks, returning from the garden.

No, I'm scraping the wax out of my ears with the receiver.

'Uh-huh.'

She goes into the kitchen.

You've lost count. Twenty rings must have passed. Just to be sure, you start again.

Twenty rings.

The Douglass house, no matter how huge, must be empty and cold. They've gone out for the day, visiting grandparents, or just to get away from leftovers and Christmas telly.

Give it a little more time.

Finally, heart heavy, brow sweaty, you hang up.

In the afternoon, you try again. Still no answer. Everybody ought to buy those machines Jim Rockford has that record a message. Or maybe not. You don't think you could put what you need to say in words that could be taped and played back in evidence against you.

'Sure you're over your cold?' Mum asks. 'You still look peaky.'

You shrug that you are fine.

You go to bed early but can't sleep. You run through Rag Day in your mind, over and over again, playing it out as it happened. Then you imagine variations: what would have happened if you had made an effort to stop Rowena drinking so much, or had left her alone in Victoria's van despite her clumsy come-on, or had punched Roger for being a bastard, or had gone to the show in the evening and made an effort, or...

Might-have-beens haunt you.

The comics you used to read as a kid often ran might-have-been tales, 'imaginary stories' – it only now hits you what a tautology that is – in which Bruce Wayne's parents aren't killed or Krypton doesn't explode or Clark Kent marries Lois Lane. All 'imaginary stories' end with the heroes manipulated into the lives they lead in the 'real stories' – with Bruce Wayne becoming Batman anyway or Kal-El as the Superman of Krypton or Clark and Lois being super together.

No matter how the plot changed, the character was the same.

No matter what happened, you'd still be you.

'Keith, you're pathetic,' Victoria said.

She's right. You've discovered too late that you can really love, but you're the kind of person no one could love back. What you did in the van proves it.

You're a bastard. You're the one who needs a right belting.

If you'd been a gentleman and left Rowena to sleep it off, you'd have scored about a thousand points. Instead, everyone is going to know what a swine you are. When you go back to college, it'll be a living hell.

Two more terms, university applications, a bunch of exams, and then it's over. You can leave Sedgwater, like Laraine, and start all over again.

In the meantime, you'll have to deal with yourself.

Shamefully, you remember Rowena in the van. In your recall, the scene is longer, almost romantic. You remember the feel of her breasts, the taste of her kisses

bitter, with vomit

That doesn't work.

Tomorrow, you'll try telephoning again.

'Good morning, Mrs Douglass. This is Keith Marion. May I speak to Rowena, please?'

Negotiations in the background.

Last time you phoned, to ask Rowena out on Rag Day, you were handed over instantly.

More fuss. Seconds tick off, marked by punching thumps from your heart.

'She's out, I'm afraid, Keith. Do you want to leave a message?'

She's not out. It's a brush-off.

Mrs Douglass is being civil to you, so Rowena can't have told her about the van.

'Just ask her to phone me,' you say, giving her your number.

'I'll tell her,' Mrs Douglass says. 'Happy New Year.'

She hangs up. You listen to the whine of the dead line.

You made a mistake. Many mistakes. You should have said you'd call back. Then, maybe, one time, Rowena would pick up and you could talk to her, persuade her of your sincerity, work on her hurt feelings.

She'll never take the initiative, never call you.

She was home. She had her mother lie to you. That's despicable. You'd never ask your parents to lie for you.

They must know *something*. But Mrs Douglass was cheery, polite. She wished you Happy New Year.

Maybe the negotiation was Mrs Douglass asking someone if Rowena was home and being told she wasn't. Rowena's Dad could have been in the room.

You thought you heard a girl's voice. Rowena could have a sister. She could. Roberta, Rosalind, Rosemary…

Mrs Douglass will pass on the message. Rowena will call you. She will.

Then things will be all right.

Days pass. It's 1978. Your nerves are stretched tight. Rowena doesn't phone. Her mum lost the message. You should call again. No, she was there. She's avoiding you. You're in the Arctic. You stay at home, even when the rest of the family goes out, just in case. Rowena doesn't phone. You have to call again and yet you can't. You can't bear this much longer. You're sure you're losing weight. You certainly haven't had a good night's sleep since you were ill and dosed up on Lemsip.

You wonder if you should write to Rowena: a long, detailed, romantic letter. That might work on her. You could explain without interruption. But she might show it to her friends, to Victoria, to anyone. You'd be walking around bleeding and naked for half a year, with everyone knowing about you, laughing.

Actually, if you think about it, all the people you know at college are your age. They're all going through this to a greater or lesser extent. It's adolescence. A fucking nightmare.

But it's worse for you than for anyone else.

It's never been worse for anyone ever in history.

* * *

The holidays crawl by like a glacier. You should be thinking about the future. This is the year you leave college, and – you have assumed until now – go to university. You have UCCA forms and interviews to cope with. And your A levels. You are on the fast track to exams.

But you can think only of Rowena. Ro. Her friends call her Ro. Roger calls her Ro.

You've had sex with her. That must mean something. You'll always have it between you. Even if she never speaks to you again.

You dread going back to college and you can't wait for it. This limbo will be over, but maybe hell will replace it.

Finally, the day before you go back, you give in and call Rowena again. This time, her father tells you she's out. You tell him you'll see her in college.

Not if she sees you first, you imagine him saying.

He just hangs up.

You feel as if you've been stabbed. With a serrated blade that's worked back and forth in the wound, grinding your ribs, bursting your heart.

You can't go on like this.

The night before you go back to college, your parents and Laraine and James are out, taking Laraine to a restaurant because she's going away again to East Anglia tomorrow. You have cried off. You say you want to get an early night for tomorrow.

You dial Rowena's number. After two rings, the phone is picked up.

You stumble over your long-planned sentence.

'Is Ro-wena there?' you ask, before anyone has said anything.

You hear breathing at the other end of the line. Then it cuts off.

You call again. Engaged.

Again. Still engaged.

It was her. You're sure.

The house is empty. All the lights are off.

You realise you are crying. Not just leaking tears, but body-racking sobs.

How can you face college tomorrow?

She'll be there. In all her loveliness, her unassailable, unreachable beauty. Having glimpsed paradise, you've been cast out into the dark regions, there to dwell for all time, your torments all the worse because you have known sweetness.

It's insupportable. You can't take any more.

You cry yourself out. Every muscle in your body aches.

You go upstairs, into the bathroom, and are sick into the toilet. In the dark, you void your stomach. The last of the turkey.

You flush the toilet and wash your face.

You pull the light-cord and look at yourself in the mirrored front of the bathroom cabinet. You are empty. You see yourself as nothing.

Perhaps over your shoulder there is something, a shadow at the window. You turn round.

All that is left in you is fear.

Your own stare fascinates you in the mirror. You know, suddenly, what's behind the reflective glass.

This doesn't have to go on. There's no reason.

The shadows have invaded the room. It's brightly lit, but that makes the darks more concentrated.

And the worst dark is in you.

Your hand goes out to touch the cool mirror, fingertips resting against the handle of the cabinet.

The dark rises up.

If you let the dark surround you and open the cabinet, go to 84. If you overcome the shadow and go to bed, go to 65.

55

You open the window and Victoria tumbles into your arms. She is lithe, in black and white. She wears knee-high black boots, elbow-length black gloves, a hooded black cloak fastened at the neck, and nothing else. Her hair is permed out in a *Bride of Frankenstein* frizz, with an electric-white streak.

She doesn't say anything, but hungrily slips her tongue into your mouth, and delicately clamps her hand on your erection.

You don't wonder how she came to be outside your window.

She pushes you back towards your bed, lays you down and climbs on top of you. Her cloak tents around you both, and she guides your cock into her warm, welcoming slit. She unfastens her cloak and lets it fall behind her. Her slender body shines white like a knife. Moonlight dapples her as she rides you, slowly. You reach up and stroke her small breasts.

Her face is in shadow. She murmurs, throat pulsing.

You want to hurry the building sensation, but she guides you, keeping the pace even, slowing you down.

You always imagined this but never expected it.

Not in your bedroom, with your family asleep in adjacent rooms, with your college textbooks on the shelf, with your outgrown pirate hat in the back of a cupboard, with a Christmas star made by your mum stuck on the door.

You reach up further, feeling Victoria's neck, sliding fingers into her sprayed nest of hair.

Her murmurs get louder. Tiny speckles of red dot her white throat and breasts, drops of blood almost surfacing.

A cooling wind, flowing in through the open window, rushes around your bed.

Your mouth is open. You are at the point of climax. Warm, white, melting, bursting.

Victoria swallows a tiny scream and bends like a bow. You have come almost together.

Her head comes forward, into the shaft of light.

Her face is a blank.

The next morning, your pyjama fly is stiff with dried spunk and your bedroom window is shut behind drawn curtains.

But you can smell her hairspray on your fingers.

This was more than a dream, if less than an experience.

The next night, again, you wake suddenly. Victoria is sitting in your chair. She's dressed all in black again, with jeans and a T-shirt under her cloak. Her hood is up, but her white face is distinct, like a night-light.

'Keith,' she says, 'you're pathetic.'

You sit up in bed.

'You don't think we're real, do you? Women? We don't feel like real people. We don't hurt or exult or break or change. We're just objects of promise, of pleasure. Maybe it's not just women you don't think are real. Maybe it's everyone outside your skull.'

Her face is bone-white, but it's Victoria. Not something else in disguise.

'Last night?' you ask.

'Was that the best you could stretch your mind to? Hammer Films and porn mags?'

She lights a cigarette and sticks it in a holder.

'You'll never let anyone in, will you?'

You are shaken to the depths, but a resolve is being born.

'I'm sorry, Keith. Really, I am. But we'll get on without you. The rest of the world, I mean. If you stay in this room, with your mum making tea and doing the laundry, you'll be safe. No one can hurt you. But you'll be waiting for death.'

'Go away,' you say.

She does.

A pattern has been set.

At university, you're too busy to cultivate a social circle. But you still dream – real dreams, now – of the faceless Victoria. In your second year, you live off-campus, in Brighton. Because you study so hard, you often need to let off steam. You start using prostitutes. There are a great many available in town, especially during the off-season. Your habits are frugal, so you finance weekly women out of your student grant. Orgasm is just a necessity, like eating and bathing; and as easily bought, got over with, and forgotten.

Several women go with you two or three times, but you prefer whores you haven't had before. As soon as you're on the point of becoming a regular, you drop them. You discourage any intimacy beyond sex, always visiting your women in their lodgings, never having them back to your room, rarely giving any name, not answering casual questions. You sense the whores can't make you out – you lose count of the times you are asked, 'Haven't you got a girlfriend?' – but go along with you. That's their job after all.

They are friendly, frumpy, hot-and-cold, overripe, chatty. They are mostly older than you and you wonder how they got to be where they are. Their hair is dyed but with a fraction of natural colour at the roots. They mention absent fathers, boyfriends, husbands, children.

Names: Karen, Sharon, Margie, Ruth, Doll, Ginger, Babs, Debbie. With sex, you get a cup of tea-bag tea. You usually pay £5, in notes – enough to buy two cinema tickets and fish and chips on the way home – for half an hour. Oral sex ('French') costs a tenner, so you rarely demand the service.

Before you have a degree, you are recruited by a bank. Not a high-street bank, like the one your father works for, but a financial institution. You like to keep things neat and move money around, coaxing it into growth. With the job come the trappings of a successful life in the early 1980s: a large flat in west London, a flash but not sporty car, good clothes, fine wines, expense-account lunches, unusual foreign holidays. You don't have girlfriends, fiancées or wives. You have colleagues, bosses and juniors. You don't need friends. You can't afford connections that would make you weak.

You still have whores. Not off the street, but elegant, hard, young callgirls with fashion-model wardrobes and Beverly Hills bodies. You meet them in hotels, scheduling appointments for convenience, consulting your Filofax. They lack the embarrassing sentimental streak of the Brighton women. If they think anything about you, they would never let you know. You find this cooling, comforting.

They are businesslike, glamorous, fire-and-ice, lean, unforthcoming. They are your age and going somewhere. Their bodies are artificially tanned, all over except for the soles of their feet. They have managers, drivers, maids, minders. Names: Judi, Coral, Nina, Suzanne, Julie, Tiger, Opal, Jacqueline. With sex, you get a line of cocaine. You usually pay £100, by cheque drawn on a special account – enough to be worth declaring as an entertainment expense – for half an hour. All night costs a grand, but the expense is not why you rarely exercise the option.

You become a partner in your firm, but stockpile clients and connections against the day, in the late '80s, when you found your own business. You launch very successfully, in the wake of the Big Bang of 1986, which deregulates the market, and buy a house in Esher and a flat in the newly developed London Docklands. You see your girls at the flat. It is deliberately characterless. The nameplate is an alias. The stock-market crash rocks the City, and you lose a considerable number of clients – many flee back to your old firm – haemorrhaging money as if from a cut throat. Despite your manoeuvres, your business goes under. No one tries to prop you up, underwrite you, take you over or buy you out. You've never needed anyone before, so there is no one quixotic enough to assume you need help.

With money tight, as you move from one temporary consultancy to the next, you take to kerb-crawling around King's Cross station. Not callgirls, but whores from the north, from council estates. You pull them into your car and park somewhere dark so they can slip a condom on your penis and suck you off swiftly. Like McDonald's staff, they have only a few set phrases – 'Want a girl?', 'In the car or at a place I know?', 'Thank you, darling' – but you sense hatred in every word.

They are desperate, drab, passionless, unhealthy, lost. They are much younger than you and dying. They have too much eye make-up, to cover the bruises, and pebble-dash needle-marks on their arms. They have pushers, babies, social workers, probation officers. They have no names, but many are black or mixed-race or the British equivalent of Poor White Trash. With sex, you get nothing. You usually pay £20, in hard, heavy pound coins – enough to fill a sock and use as a cosh – for as brief a time as it takes. A blow-job without a condom costs three times as much, which is an extortion you suffer when you think you can afford it.

In the '90s, without the house in Esher, but with the flat in Docklands, you get your business back together. It is absorbed into the Derek Leech Group of Companies, mostly because your flat – from which you operate – is in a block Leech, a multimedia tycoon, has bought and converted. You have learned harsh lessons during your reversal – you have a police record for kerb-crawling and have been obsessive about blood tests – but feel you are fitter than ever to survive the next century.

As an experiment, because you're bored, you refuse to pay a whore after an especially perfunctory blow-job. You hit her, push her out of the car, and drive off. She's a nothing. She doesn't count. Strangely, this retroactively improves your memory of the orgasm.

It's 1994.

This is the first sex you've had without paying for it, since… What was her name?

Victoria. 1976.

And did that happen?

There's a girl in the office called Vickie. She must have been born in the year Victoria came through your bedroom window, and her colouring is different.

You find yourself thinking about her a lot.

You pull her file and find where she lives. She has a flat not far from yours.

One evening, you wait opposite her building. She gets back at about eleven, from the cinema perhaps, with a boyfriend. He stays over. You go home.

The next evening, she gets back at half-past six, straight from the office, alone. You ring her bell, and explain that it's important. She buzzes you up.

You rape her.

Your kerb-crawling conviction tells against you. Otherwise, the judge might have thought this was an office romance gone wrong.

You enter the new century – on 1 January 2000 or 2001, depending on how you read it – in prison.

By the time you are eligible for parole, tough new laws on sex offenders require that you be medicated to suppress your 'urges' and be tagged by the police. Your name, photo and Vickie's shadow-faced account of your crime are broadcast nightly on Cloud 9 cable TV's Crime Channel – owned by Derek Leech, of course – and you are frequently recognised and abused in the streets.

Several times, you are arrested and grilled simply because it has been assumed that you are looking lustfully at a woman or a girl.

You are found low-grade employment. In prison, you have learned computing skills. You do the Century 21 equivalent of addressing envelopes, organising electronic mail-outs for special offers.

Cloud 9's Home Fantasy Channel offers all manner of legal sexual services. No-contact, debit-card exchanges. The women are computer-generated, morphing to suit your tastes as you input desires on a touch-pad.

Because of your medication, exchanges with these virtual whores are unsatisfactory. You go into debt, racking up minute after minute of line-time as you fail, in the terminology, to sustain or achieve.

You lose interest.

In the end, whatever you do, you do alone.

And so on.

56

You open the window and Victoria explodes into your room. She is lithe, in black and white. She wears knee-high black boots, elbow-length black gloves, a hooded black cloak fastened at the neck, and some sort of much-buckled leather corset. Her hair is permed out in a *Bride of Frankenstein* frizz, with an electric-white streak.

She doesn't say anything, but angrily slaps you in your mouth, and viciously clamps her hand on your erection.

You don't wonder how she came to be outside your window.

She shoves you back towards your bed, forces you down and pins you with a spike-heel. Her cloak tents around her and she grinds her heel into your soft, yielding belly. She unfastens her cloak and lets it fall behind her. Her slender body shines black like a whip. Moonlight dapples her as she gouges you, slowly. You reach up and she slaps your hands away.

Her face is in shadow. She growls, throat pulsing.

You want to stop the pain in your stomach, but she stabs at you, spreading the hurt, dragging out the agony.

You always feared this but never expected it.

Not in your bedroom, with your family asleep in adjacent rooms, with your college textbooks on the shelf, with your outgrown pirate hat in the back of a cupboard, with a Christmas star made by your mum stuck on the door.

You struggle, grasping Victoria's neck, sliding fingers into her sprayed nest of hair.

Her growls get louder. Tiny speckles of red dot her white throat and breasts, drops of blood almost surfacing.

A cooling wind, flowing in through the open window, rushes around your bed.

Your mouth is open. You are at the point of screaming. Hot, black, grinding, bursting.

Victoria swallows a tiny cackle and bends like a bow. You have collapsed almost together.

Her head comes forward, into the shaft of light.

Her face is a blank.

The next morning, your pyjama top is stiff with dried blood and your bedroom window is shut behind drawn curtains.

But you can smell her hairspray on your fingers.

This was more than a dream, if less than an experience.

The next night, again, you wake suddenly. Victoria is sitting in your chair. She is dressed all in black again, with jeans and a T-shirt under her cloak. Her hood is up, but her white face is distinct, like a night-light.

'Keith,' she says, 'you're pathetic.'

You sit up in bed.

'You don't think we're real, do you? Women? We don't feel like real people. We don't hurt or exult or break or change. We're just objects of threat, of pain. Maybe it's not just women you don't think are real. Maybe it's everyone outside your skull.'

Her face is bone-white, but it's Victoria. Not something else in disguise.

'Last night?' you ask.

'Was that the worst you could stretch your mind to? Hammer Films and porn mags?'

She lights a cigarette and sticks it in a holder.

'You'll never let anyone in, will you?'

You are shaken to the depths, but a resolve is being born.

'I'm sorry, Keith. Really, I am. But we'll get on without you. The rest of the world, I mean. If you stay in this room, with your mum making tea and doing the laundry, you'll be safe. You can only hurt yourself. But you'll be waiting for death.'

'Go away,' you say.

She does.

A pattern has been set.

At university, you're too busy to cultivate a social circle. But you still dream – real dreams, now – of the faceless Victoria. In your second year, you live off-campus, in Brighton. Because you study so hard, you often need to let off steam. You take to drinking quite a bit. When you drink, restraint evaporates and your temper lets loose. You frequently get into fights which you eventually lose. You pick arguments with groups of men, older and harder, men who naturally dislike students. There are lots of pubs in Brighton. You get banned from quite a few of them, but you are nondescript and often barmen don't connect your sober self with the violent drunk.

To supplement your meagre student's grant, you occasionally mug people. Late at night, on the sea front or in the Lanes, you find someone drunker than you are, thump them a time or two on the head, and snatch their cash, their watch, their wallet. Sometimes, you wrestle off rings. You strike fast, hit hard and get away quick. You are never picked up by the police and none of your assaults gets more than the barest report in the *Evening Argus.* You start out by just using your fists, but your knuckles get badly bruised so you experiment with a coin-filled sock before settling on brass knuckles.

As your violence becomes more commercially oriented, you drink less. You take classes in martial arts and boxing, though you're always expelled before you complete a course, for overstepping the mark and really hurting someone. Sometimes, to teach you a lesson, the instructor gives you a public beating to pay you back. You win a few amateur bouts and spectacularly lose one, and realise you're too smart to rely on this as a way of making a living. But you will keep it up.

Before you have a degree, you are recruited by a bank. Not a high-street bank, like the one your father works for, but a financial institution. You like to take control and wrestle money around, forcing it into growth. With the job come the trappings of a successful life in the early 1980s: a large flat in west London, a flash but not sporty car, good clothes, fine wines, expense-account lunches, unusual foreign holidays. You get 'engaged' several times, always ending the relationship well before you give in to the need to hit your 'fiancée'. You work well in the firm, but you need a life outside it.

At your gym, you take up kick-boxing and repeatedly thrash junior executives and financial consultants. Once or twice, you put friendly opponents in hospital. You go through the formalities of apologising, but they'll always remember you in the frenzy of the clinch. Strangely, this is good for you in your job, giving you an underground rep that helps you close deals and see off rivals. You still mug people, not for the money but for the night thrill. You are extremely cautious, always operating well off your home ground and selecting victims who are too drunk and disoriented to remember much.

You become a partner in your firm, but stockpile clients and connections against the day, in the late '80s, when you found your own business. You launch very successfully, in the wake of the Big Bang of 1986, which deregulates the market, and buy a house in Esher and a flat in the newly developed London Docklands. It has its own gym, and you sometimes invite people back for 'a bit of a punch-up'. The stock-market crash rocks the City, and you lose a considerable number of clients – many flee back to your old firm – haemorrhaging money as if from a cut throat. Despite your manoeuvres, your business goes under. No one tries to prop you up, underwrite you, take you over or buy you out. Everyone knows about your tendencies and too many remember specific instances. No one is inclined to give you any help.

With money tight, as you move from one temporary consultancy to the next, you take to serious mugging. You specialise in foreigners – Arabs or Japanese – and work around the West End hotels. You learn how to convert jewellery, traveller's cheques, top-of-the-line watches and calculators into cash. But these efficient, brutal encounters don't take up all the slack. You need to receive as well as give, so you hire women and men to provide the service. Often, you pay them off with merchandise lifted from your victims. Not many of these professionals will deal with you more than once, because you like to break the rules and fight back.

In the '90s, without the house in Esher, but with the flat in Docklands, you get your business back together. It is absorbed into the Derek Leech Group of Companies, mostly because your flat – from which you operate – is in a block Leech, a multimedia tycoon, has bought and converted. You have learned some harsh lessons during your reversal – you have a police record for aggravated assault – but feel you are fitter than ever to survive the next century.

As an experiment, because you're bored, you throttle a dominatrix to within a breath of dying. But she's more cunning than you gave her credit for and shivs you with a sharpened nail-file, scraping your ribs.

She's a person. She counts. Strangely, this retroactively improves your memory of the encounter.

It's 1994.

This is the first partner you've had who understands you, since... What was her name?

Victoria. 1976.

And did that happen?

There's a girl in the office called Vickie. She must have been born in the year Victoria came through your bedroom window, and her colouring is different.

You find yourself thinking about her a lot.

You pull her file and find where she lives. She has a flat not far from yours.

One evening, you wait opposite her building. She gets back at about eleven, from the cinema perhaps, with a boyfriend. He stays over. You go home.

The next evening, she gets back at half-past six, straight from the office, alone. You ring her bell, and explain that it's important. She buzzes you up.

You kill her.

Your assault conviction tells against you. Otherwise, the judge might have thought this was an office feud gone wrong.

You enter the new century – on 1 January 2000 or 2001, depending on how you read it – in prison.

By the time you are eligible for parole, tough new laws on violent offenders require that you be medicated to suppress your 'urges' and be tagged by the police. Your name, photo and Vickie's mum's shadow-faced account of your crime are broadcast nightly on Cloud 9 cable TV's Crime Channel – owned by Derek Leech, of course – and you are frequently recognised and abused in the streets.

Several times, you are arrested and grilled simply because it has been assumed that you are on the point of exploding into violence against a woman or child.

You are found low-grade employment. In prison, you have learned computing skills. You do the Century 21 equivalent of addressing envelopes, organising electronic mail-outs for special offers.

Cloud 9's Home Fantasy Channel offers all manner of legal experiential services. No-contact, debit-card exchanges. The fighters are computer-generated, morphing to suit your needs as you input specs on a touch-pad.

Because of your medication, your bouts with these virtual opponents are unsatisfactory. You go into debt, racking up minute after minute of line-time as you fail, in the terminology, to damage or be damaged.

You lose interest.

In the end, whatever you do, you do alone.

And so on.

57

Between Christmas and New Year, you cycle out to the Sutton Mallet turn-off. Mary's car has been hauled away. You know if Laraine wrote off Dad's Austin, he'd take a cat o' nine tails to her. But Mary's parents, according to her, are so grateful she (and you) isn't permanently hurt that they've walked on eggshells about the subject. Her policeman father is apparently cooking evidence to put in his insurance claim.

The only person to ask whether either of you'd been drinking before getting in the Honda is James. He looks at you with a new respect since your supposed brush with death. He means the crash, of course. You haven't talked to anyone about what happened afterwards.

Come to that, you don't really know yourself.

At night, though, you often think, despite yourself, about the shadow-spiders. You don't know it yet, but you're thinking of me. Coming towards me. You've disturbed the extremities of a web, and feel the tiny vibrations.

Soon, you'll be used to the idea of me. Of someone like me.

The road is empty, traffic fallen off to nothing in the lull between the holidays. You can see tyre marks grinding through the verge where the car went into the ditch. The Sutton Mallet signpost has been replaced by a temporary one. You doubt anyone has had cause to take the turn-off since the sign was knocked over.

The field on the other side of the ditch is unexceptional. Wetland stretches dully to the horizon. You can't even see Glastonbury Tor –

which is in the other direction – and this is a landscape bereft of magic.

The sky is blue-grey cloud. It might drizzle.

Nothing in the air suggests the shadow-spiders. No sense of the beyond, just a familiar Sunday afternoon-in-winter gloom. Turkey leftovers for dinner, family slumped in front of a Bond film on telly. Christmas isn't what it used to be: you're jaded, occasionally stirred to nostalgia for pirate ships and pre-dawn raids on Santa's stockings.

You lean your bike against the sign and look around.

Though you're cold, even after the exertion of cycling four miles, you're not chilled. The shade has passed. This is not a frightening place.

And yet…

Mary arrives. She has walked.

'Hello, you,' she says.

You shrug.

Since the accident, you haven't said much. There just isn't much worth saying.

Mary slips close to you, hugs you, thin arms around your chest, frosted breath against your mouth. Non-committally, you hold her.

She breaks the embrace and kneels by the verge, looking at the tracks, like a detective searching for clues. She whistles.

'We might be ghosts, Keith.'

She is wrapped up in a violent yellow-green cagoule. Sensible, not stylish.

'For the rest of our lives, we'll always know.'

'Know what?' you ask.

'That we've been touched. That we're special.'

You know what she means. Since Sutton Mallet, everything has seemed clear. You know what value to set upon everything you've done. You are changed and you will change.

You won't stop running – probably, you can't – but you will run with a purpose now.

Mary straightens up and crosses the road. She stands by the temporary sign, then starts walking down the turn-off. It's paved but, by comparison with the smooth tarmac of the Achelzoy road, might as well be beaten earth. Muddy snail-tracks like wheel-ruts show where tractors pass. She stops and beckons. You follow her, wheeling your bike down the path. You catch up.

'Not many left in Sutton Mallet,' she comments. 'There are houses empty, waiting to be claimed. Graham wanted to squat one back in the summer, but Victoria talked him out of it. She said it was a strange place.'

The hamlet is around you. It's like any of a dozen others in Somerset. On the outside.

'I know a house,' Mary says, taking your arm. 'With furniture and all. With a bed.'

You know what you are going to do. Have sex. You and Mary. You have thought of it, on and off, mostly on, for six years. This is not what you have ever imagined.

You remember the plan you have worked out. You still intend to get married at twenty-five, in seven years' time, and have two children, Jonathan and Jennifer. Until now, you've always had a nebulous image of your wife, a cut-out woman with a ghostly smudge of a face.

You try imagining Mary's face in the smudge. It doesn't fit. Not with those scary eyes.

Mary's cold hand is under your shirt at the back, fingers pressed to your spine.

You stop and kiss, hungry.

You are both ghosts. You need a house to haunt.

The Sutton Mallet lane narrows. The hedgerows are taller. Shade closes in, insinuating itself around you. Overhead, the sky is bone-white now.

You are cold but try to find warmth, pressing yourself against Mary. She must feel your penis, hot and hard. Should you slip your hands into her clothes?

'Come on,' she says, leading you towards a house.

Afterwards, you lie in bed with Mary, thinking that you don't feel much different. Springs rake your back through a rotted mattress. You are huddled together under a makeshift quilt of clothes.

You see the red marks on Mary's legs. The weals she got clambering out of the car.

You had thought this moment might be when you were finally able to ease off, to slow down. Maybe this was when you could stop running?

Your heart beats faster now than when you were having sex. Neither of you disgraced yourself, as far as you know, and the mechanics of the condom were dealt with, but the act itself was less important than what it meant.

Keith and Mary, Mary and Keith.

You were in this together.

In what?

This.

A bed in Sutton Mallet.

The bedroom, at first look, might be in a living house. The wallpaper peels only a little and the dusty windows aren't broken. An empty light-socket dangles overhead, centrepiece of a canopy of cobweb.

What made the people who lived here leave?

They left behind more than just furniture. Plates and cutlery are strewn on the kitchen floor. On each of the stairs is placed a small household object – a plastic comb, a picture frame, a toothbrush. What makes a person leave behind their toothbrush when they move out? The arrangement on the stairs is almost ritualistic.

You think you know what Victoria meant about strange.

Mary isn't asleep, though you expected her to nod off. Mary is thinking unreadable thoughts, her skull two skin-layers away from your sternum.

You had believed, without ever articulating the belief, that sex triggered a latent telepathic ability. That it took you completely out of yourself and into someone else, and opened you to them.

But Mary is as much a stranger now as when you first saw her back in Ash Grove Primary.

While you were making love, you were reminded of Mary's monster. You thought you glimpsed it behind her eyes as she bit her lips, hissing impatience.

You hold her breast – because you can, without her hitting you – and try not to notice the shadows growing in the room. These are ordinary shadows.

You are not on the starting-blocks of another race in the dark.

There is blood on the mattress, sticky under your thighs. You were right about Mary. This was her first time. How had she known what to do?

How had you known what to do?

Did you both do it properly?

You think so.

'Do you feel alive now?' you ask.

Mary says nothing.

'We're not ghosts.'

It is dark and you're both dressed. You know you should get home. Since the night of the accident, your parents have fussed about what you do, wanting to have a minute-by-minute run-down of your schedule.

The house, you notice now your sweat has cooled on your skin, is like a fridge, holding in the winter cold. Your breath clouds in the gloom.

'That night,' you say. 'There was something.'

'Yes. In the dark. Of course.'

'You *save* it?'

It's too dark now to see her face. You can't judge her expression. She shakes her head. 'It weren't something you see.'

'Then how do you know it was there?' you ask.

'How you know,' she replies.

You could not have been mistaken but you half hoped she would dispel your certainty, argue that it had all been the drink, the panic, the accident, the hormones, the dark, the hurt.

'Sutton Mallet is special,' she says. 'Victoria was right.'

It's special now, you think.

But what you say is 'It's where the shadows start.'

She understands what you mean.

You take her hand – you've just fucked, but you've never really held hands – and hold tight.

'We'll keep running,' you say, not having to explain. 'Always, we have to run. Now, we run together. But do we run into the shadows, or out of?'

If out of, go to 70. If into, go to 80.

58

'I doubt it,' you say. 'It'd be a pretty bloody stupid thing to do.'

Vanda leans against the door-jamb. She wraps her dressing-gown tight.

'Haven't you noticed? Sean can be pretty bloody stupid.'

'He's not doing so badly.'

Vanda is thinking about something. You wonder if you should have lied.

'Ro thinks he is. Having an affair.'

You have nothing to say.

'We can't afford to break the Syndicate.'

You're surprised Vanda has thought it through.

'By the way, Keith…'

'Yes?'

'You're not fucking Candy, are you?'

'Good Lord, no.'

'Just asking.'

She comes to the desk and looks at the figures you have been studying. A strand of her hair falls down over your cheek. She nods, gently, approving.

You slip a hand into her dressing-gown, resting it on her bum. Since she's been going to exercise class, her body is better toned than since before Jason.

She wriggles a little, her code for seeing you off. You take back your hand. 'Keith,' she says, pausing.

'Yes?'

'We're rich, aren't we?'

You nod. She smiles tightly, briefly grips your shoulder, and goes to bed. You savour the after-smell of her hair, and can't think of anything but the money.

Go to 72.

59

*B*lit blurt…

Shadow-spiders have been among us for years, observing humankind, preparing the takeover, spinning webs.

In your town, there are several major Arachnoids, spiders crammed into human-suits. Mrs Fudge, the Ash Grove Primary dinner lady, has fed successive generations with her mind-warping abdominal secretions. School custard, as you always knew, was at once poisonous and addictive. It has stayed in the systems of all children who went to Ash Grove – except you! – and reshaped their perception of the real world, making all but the most blatant signs of the invasion invisible. For a while, when you were alone in seeing the shadow-spiders, you were treated as a madman.

Councillor Robert Hackwill is another Arachnoid. Since school, he has been challenging and testing everyone, drawing up lists of potential rebels for transfer to the extermination webs in Wales. You and your whole family are on the Hackwill death-list. He has been covertly working against you for decades, striking against your relatives, your house, your pets. Many of his associates – like Reg Jessup – aren't even spiders, but human traitors he has lured through his cobweb curtain and promised high positions on the food chain once the takeover is complete.

The shadow-spiders are behind everything bad in your life. You have always known there was a disparity between the way you saw spiders and the way everyone else did. Your parents, even your brother, never understood your terror of spiders when you were a kid. They were impatient with your insistence someone come upstairs with you and turn on all the lights, checking under your bed, before you went to sleep.

You remember Mum telling you, when you moved to the country, that there were no poisonous spiders in Britain, that none of the monsters you glimpsed crawling all around you could do any harm. Dad let the truth slip, though, in warning you away from his shed, telling you that was where the poisonous spiders – the ones that didn't exist in Britain – lived.

To most people, spiders were the tiny dots they showed on TV nature programmes or in books. Only you saw monsters the size of a big man's hand, black heads bristling with red eyes, each filthy pipe-cleaner limb tipped with a venomous barb, complex and never-still mouth like a meat-eating plant.

Now, everyone knows you were right.

Those were the real spiders. The shadow-spiders.

Of course, it's too late.

They're here, and they're taking over.

…blit blurt.

60

You kiss Rowena on the forehead and pull back, getting out of the van, promising to come back.

Her eyes show disappointment, but something else.

'Tonight,' you say. You shut the van door.

Your erection hurts like a bastard. You can't help feeling a complete pillock.

Victoria is astonished. 'Keith, you've just shot up about a thousand points.'

You wish she wouldn't talk about things shooting up. It's a sore point. Not sore, throbbing. You shake your head and lean on the van, bending in the middle to ease the pressure.

'There are rules,' you say, instantly regretting it. You sound a pompous ass.

'Not many blokes recognise that,' says Victoria. She's impressed. 'In this town, I'd have said there were approximately no blokes who could have backed off from a sure thing like that poor soused baby.'

You don't want to explain. It means too much to you.

Victoria kisses you chastely. It's still torture.

'Let's go to Brink's Café. I'll buy you some coffee. Call it a reward.'

This feels grown-up.

In Brink's, the nearest thing the town has to a hang-out, you drink weak black coffee and eat a Danish pastry. In the strip-lit, orange-wood environment, Victoria looks like a grown-up rather than an alien.

She still dresses like a freak but you remember how clever she is. You talk about the next year. When you all finish college. You've been asked to take the Oxford entrance exam, which your parents think is a great opportunity. Now you talk about it, you aren't so sure. You're surprised to learn that Victoria, for all her punk tearaway carrying-on, still plans to go to university, to get away from Sedgwater. Just because she dresses the way she wants and hangs around with people her parents can't stand doesn't mean she wants to throw everything away. She's well aware of the shortcomings of the kind of waster hippie life Graham lives.

'He wanted us to squat a house in Sutton Mallet,' she says. 'No hot water, no electric light. One day, he'll wake up and realise the summer of '67 is over.'

Though you keep up with the chat, you're thinking about Rowena. You're worried about her and still not sure what the evening will be like.

'She'll be fine,' Victoria says, mind-reading. 'Just isn't used to it, poor lamb.'

'I don't know about her,' you say. 'I don't know if she's really interested in me or just wants to get back at Roger.'

This is the first time you've ever told anyone about feelings like this. You always thought it would give other people too much power over you if they knew what you really felt.

'Roger needs a bottle in the face,' Victoria says.

You are embarrassed. You forgot that Rowena chucked Roger because of Victoria.

'Don't mind about that,' she says. 'I never said I was sensible or sincere. I'm just a mad slut, remember.'

'No you're not.'

'No, you're right. I'm not. Thank you for noticing.'

You start talking about the Rag Show this evening. Michael Dixon and his clique have arranged it. They will be performing comic sketches, and Victoria's band, Flaming Torture, will top the bill.

'What kind of a name is Flaming Torture?'

'It's an episode of a *Flash Gordon* serial we saw one morning at Graham's when we were stoned. It won't last.'

You both laugh.

You feel relaxed but a lot stronger. No matter what happens with Rowena, something as interesting – and maybe a lot rarer – is developing with Victoria. You think she might be turning into your friend.

At the show, you're insulated by noise. This has been an out-of-time day. All bets are off but everything you do seems to have counted on a deeper level than you yet understand. It's as if someone is watching you, keeping a score. Victoria said you'd gone up a thousand points. You have a mild anxiety that you might wipe out the bonus with one wrong move, that you could still crawl out of today as a big loser.

You bop about non-committally in the crowd as Flaming Torture perform. You think Victoria is looking at you as she sings, but with the lights in her eyes she probably can't make out individual faces in the writhing mass of kids.

It occurs to you that, though Flaming Torture is well beyond your usual listening habits, Victoria might be quite good. No matter how she abuses it, her voice works.

You stop thinking, and dance.

Strobe lights make neon strips of white shirt collars and cuffs. Neil Martin, wearing a sheet like a pantomime ghost, shines like a real apparition.

The-music washes your brain.

When the show is over, kids pour out into the car park. Victoria, still in her stage gear, offers you a lift out to Michael Dixon's party at Achelzoy.

You accept.

I'm sorry, was I assuming too much? Of course, you have a choice. You can refuse Victoria's offer, go home, watch some television with Flaming Torture still ringing in your ears, and get an early night.

Interested?

I thought not. You see, sometimes you're on rails. There's no junction. You run on smoothly. You can go off the rails, of course, but there must be something really wrong with you if that's your choice.

And, despite what you're learning about yourself, there's nothing wrong with you. Your default setting is ordinary, typical, usual. Which is not to say that there are spaces in your life labyrinth that aren't deeply shadowed or brightly lit.

Come on. Get into Victoria's Mini van.

What happens next is interesting. Believe me.

You don't need to talk. You watch the red rear lights of Desmond Fewsham's car, which is packed full of kids on their way to the party. Victoria is driving just you. The back of the van is full of Flaming Torture's equipment. The instruments of Torture, you realise.

When you first got in, you darted a look over your shoulder as you did up the seatbelt.

Victoria laughed. 'She's not still there.'

You were sort of relieved.

'Ro just needed a rest,' she said.

Victoria takes a turn-off. Desmond isn't ahead now.

'Short cut,' she says.

The van bumps a little, over pot-holes. This isn't a well-kept road. It might have wheel-ruts.

'Via where?' you ask.

'Sutton Mallet.'

The van stalls.

'Shit,' Victoria says.

You both get out of the van. Featherbreath steams round Victoria's mouth and nostrils. It is cold and dark. There are buildings around but none of them is lit up.

'They're empty,' she says. 'Last summer, Graham wanted to squat one of them. I talked him out of it. I told him I had a strange feeling about the place.'

'You mentioned it earlier.'

The dark façades are unsettling.

'I knew winter would come. It's all very well hanging out in a derelict house in August, but getting through the cold without hot water or electric light or proper heating is different.'

'What now? Is there a Spectrum Pursuit Vehicle stashed in one of the barns?'

She laughs, musically. That's an expression you've heard, but never heard demonstrated.

'No, Graham left some gear in one of the houses. I think there are tools.'

She takes your arm and drags you towards a dark house.

Her touch is warm. You think of hugging her for the heat.

But you don't.

Victoria unlatches a door and steps into a house. You follow her. At least you are out of the wind.

She flicks her cigarette lighter. You're in a kitchen. Plates and cutlery are strewn on the floor. There are cobwebs and shadows.

'Stay here,' she says. 'The stuff is upstairs. I'll be back in a sec.'

She leaves you.

There is a little moonlight, but not much. Your eyes hold the after-image of Victoria's lighter flame.

In the dark, you have time to think. Why doesn't Victoria have a tool-kit in the van? Is she the sort who knows how to fix a broken-down car with a few wrench-twists and a pair of nylons?

She said she'd be back in a sec.

A sec has passed. Several of them.

You're cold and in the dark. Things had been going well. Throughout the day, you'd felt things improving. But now you're off the map, in Sutton Mallet. It's nowhere, a Sargasso where people are sidetracked, becalmed, marooned, forgotten.

You try to listen for small noises. Victoria should be searching, blundering into things, swearing.

Your ears are still ringing.

Nothing is happening. Nothing is going to happen.

Your are in Nothing. You are become Nothing.

There is a noise, now. No, a sound. It might be the wind, whistling through the many broken windows in the house. But it's more musical, an ululation, a single voice beckoning, a siren's seduction.

It must be Victoria. But it doesn't sound like her.

Are you afraid? Or are you excited?

Your toes are ice-bitten and you are hugging yourself against the cold. The dark is all around you, and something in the house is wailing.

You leave the kitchen. You are in a hallway. At one end are the stairs, at the other is an open door.

The sound, louder now, is coming from upstairs. There's also a faint light, flickering, a suggestion of warmth. Is that a giggle? Victoria, if she's upstairs, is not alone. The singing might be in harmony, two or more voices.

You could just leave. You could make it to the main road and hitch a lift to Achelzoy or to town. There will be cars going back and forth all night. People you know.

Or do you go upstairs?

If you choose the door, go to 62. If you choose the stairs, go to 68.

61

Saturday, 14 February 1998. In the back of your Land Rover, Roy Canning is apoplectic. In the passenger seat, Rowena clucks and tuts. You drive on to the travellers' site over a cattle grid and through marshy fields. The caravans are drawn into a circle, like wagons in a Western. You understand these people live more like Indians than pioneers. Some of their structures are teepee-like.

'Think of the filth,' blusters Roy.

As chair of the Sutton Mallet Residents' Committee, you are in charge of the negotiations. But Roy Canning was the first to get a bee in his bonnet about the site and he has been nagging at every opportunity.

These people personally offend Roy on some level you don't understand. You'd be happier with the lot of them resited in someone else's backyard and assume there's a fair amount of drug-taking and loud music going on, but it's not an affront to your very existence.

'We should take a flame-thrower to this field.'

'Look at the babies,' Ro says, as if you were visiting a wildlife park. 'They're so dirty. Poor things.'

Your wife invited herself along out of curiosity. Roy is so vehement about the site that she just wants to have a good look at it. You doubt Ro will be helpful.

Mary Yatman is at the gate, by her police car. In her uniform, she still looks nineteen.

Unlike you and Ro. During your marriage, you have become frankly haggard. At thirty-eight, you're almost completely grey. Ro has blown up like a balloon. She has trouble with the seatbelt in the Land-Rover. It won't stretch over her tummy.

You park and get out. You have to help Ro squeeze out of the door and step down into the field.

Mary greets you. 'Rowena, I didn't know you were pregnant again,' she says.

'I'm not.'

This isn't the first time someone has made that mistake. You wonder if Mary did it deliberately.

'How's the bank?' Mary asks you. 'Tried to rob it lately?'

Whenever she sees you, Mary jokes that you should rob your own bank so she can catch you and get a promotion. She wants to be out of uniform.

Suddenly, you want Mary out of uniform too.

'Ugh!' Rowena has stepped in a mudpatch.

'Revoltin',' Roy says, automatically.

If everyone who left mud in their fields was driven off the land, there wouldn't be any farmers in Somerset.

'Who are we talking with?' you ask, businesslike.

'They claim to be a collective and don't believe in leaders as such. However, they've elected a couple of spokespeople who are empowered to negotiate.'

'Negotiate!' Roy bursts out. 'Appeasement don't work.'

'Calm down, Roy,' you say.

This isn't going to be easy.

'This is them now,' Mary announces.

A small procession advances, making Roy hide behind Ro. In the lead are a couple of small children, faces painted like pantomime savages, dressed in adult-sized cardigans cinched in to become robe-like garments. They have flowers for you, the first few feeble snowdrops.

'For peace,' an urchin says, presenting a snowdrop to Ro.

Ro takes the flower. 'What a sweet little girl.'

'I'm not a girl,' the kid says.

'Oh.'

You catch a sideways look from Mary. She has never liked Ro, you remember.

As you have done many times, you wonder if you shouldn't have asked Mary out in 1977. If you had, you might now be married to a slender blonde in a trim uniform. Not a blubber-bag who ran out of things to say ten years ago and has been repeating herself ever since.

Roads not taken…

'Blessed be,' announces a tall man with a long beard and a staff. He has a sheepskin waistcoat dotted with CND and animal-rights badges. He smells faintly musky, but not unpleasant. He looks a lot more like a man of the land than Roy Canning, a set-aside farmer who wears a suit. The traveller spokesman sticks out a knotty hand.

'This is –' begins Mary.

'I know,' you say, taking his hand. 'Hello, Gully.'

Gully Eastment looks at you, wondering.

For a moment, you think he won't recognise you. That would be an embarrassment: if he had registered in your memory, but you hadn't lodged in his. Maybe his past is full up, insignificant people cleaned out of his mental attic.

'It's the Straight Man,' he says.

He called you that for a while, at college. You've forgotten how you got the nickname.

'Keith Marion,' you say.

Gully lets go of your hand. He grins, amused by some memory. Now you're worried he remembers things about you that you've forgotten.

'This is Rowena, my wife. Rowena Douglass, as was.'

Gully plainly doesn't recognise her. And no wonder. The girl she once was is completely buried in her inflated new body. Gully looks her over – do you detect a trace of sympathy for you in his ironic glance? – and kisses her hand.

'I remember you,' he says, eventually. 'You were sick.'

She laughs, setting her chins in motion:

You've lost the place. This means nothing to you.

'Fancy you remembering that,' she says. 'Rag Day 1977, wasn't it?'

'How could anyone forget?' Gully says.

Now you remember. Rowena being sick in an alley. You trying to ignore her. Your first date. The warning you should have taken. She still can't handle booze.

'So, the Straight Man got together with the Lady Lush to make babies.'

'We have two children,' she admits. 'Jeffrey and Jasmine.'

'Love to you,' Gully says, embracing Ro.

He has to bend down a little and his long arms squeeze her almost spherical torso, lifting rolls of anorak-covered flesh as he embraces her. Ro flutters in his grip, cheeks blotching red, head bobbing like a car toy.

'Roy, this is Gully Eastment,' you say. 'We were at school together, as you've probably gathered. All of us.' You include Mary.

'I was there when Rowena was sick,' Mary admits.

'Oh come now, I was a child,' Ro says, fed up with this.

Roy is livid. He's fifteen years older than you all. He seems to regard your previous association with Gully as treason. Suddenly, he thinks of you all as comrades in crime.

'Straight Man, come to the meeting-lodge.'

Gully lets go of Ro and leads you into the centre of the camp.

The lodge is a well-made windowless hut. You have to bend a little to get in through the door, which is covered by a nailed sheet of clear polythene and, inside, a hanging curtain of beads. The low space is lit by candles. Thick rugs are laid over bare earth. There are no chairs, only cushions. On the walls are tapestries and children's paintings.

'No chairs, I'm afraid.'

The wood is impregnated with the smell of marijuana.

You realise what this reminds you of: Graham the hippie's bedsit.

You were there only once. Rag Day 1977. The day Ro was so sick. The day you first went out with your future wife. A significant moment in your past.

Gully offered you a joint.

'I don't smoke,' you said, 'tobacco.'

Gully found that hilarious, and repeated it in an accent like Bela Lugosi saying, 'I nevair dreenk… wine!' All the people crammed into Graham's bedsit picked it up in their strange, stoned communion and chanted it between choking outbursts of laughter.

That was when Graham started calling you Straight Man.

You've forgotten how to sit cross-legged on a cushion, and get your knees mixed up as you squat. Ro is in an even worse state and has to be helped down on to the cushions, lowered like a hippo being given a bath.

Roy bangs his head on the ceiling and squats uncomfortably, unwilling to let his arse be fouled by contact with filthy hippie cushions. Mary slips off her uniform shoes and does a perfect lotus, her black-tights-clad feet neatly tucked into her skirted lap.

'Welcome, friends,' says Gully.

He sits by a gigantic affair of glass tubes and bowls. The bong is not in use, which is probably a mercy for Roy's heart.

'Are they here?' says a voice.

'Yes, my love.'

A pile of cushions moves, as if there were a land-bound squid under it. They part and a woman erupts from them, long arms – tattooed and hung with bangles – snaking out first. She manages to be elegant in her writhing as she slides to Gully's side and sits by him.

'Is this a reunion?' she says.

It's Victoria Conyer.

Her ears, nose, eyebrow and lip are pierced with rings. She wears a black singlet, cut low on her chest to show flame-coloured tattoos on her breasts. Her black hair is down to her waist, and shot through with a white streak.

'How's your head, Straight Man?'

You touch the spot on your forehead where she once broke a glass. You have no scar.

Gully and Mary understand this. Ro, who was after all too busy being sick to notice, doesn't. Roy thinks he is in the enemy's camp and that cannibals will take him at any moment.

'My head's fine,' you say.

'Are you sure?' Victoria asks. 'Your aura's almost violet, as if you'd not purged in months.'

'This'm all very cosy, but…'

'This is Mr Canning, VC,' Gully says, kissing her on the cheek. 'He writes us the letters.'

'The formal ones or the anonymous ones?'

'Both, I should think.'

Canning splutters.

'If you're going to send heavy legal letters and cut-out-from-newspaper-headlines death threats, you shouldn't use identical envelopes and type the addresses on the same machine,' Gully explains. 'We may be "drug-addled vermin" but we're not stupid.'

'Naughty Mr Canning,' says Victoria – VC? – wagging a long finger at him. She has a silver skull ring with red jewel eyes that wink at you.

'Youm scum,' Roy says, viciously. 'How dare you?'

'We don't threaten your kids,' Gully says.

'Youm sell they drugs.'

'Grass and E, maybe, if they nag us enough – you didn't hear that, Mary – but no smack, no crack, nothing deadly.'

Mary is impassive, impartial. She's set this meeting up, but is an observer.

'So you admit it,' Roy snarls.

Gully works his eyebrows.

Victoria starts rolling a cigarette. No, a joint.

'I think we can have this lot cleared off, then,' Roy continues. 'WPC Yatman, make your arrest.'

Victoria lights up and passes the joint to Mary. She takes a polite little toke and gives it to Ro.

'Think of it as a peace pipe,' Gully says.

Roy's eyeballs are on the point of leaving his skull.

'Thank you very much,' says Ro. She mimes a draught and exhales through her nostrils.

Gully takes in a deep drag. He feints, as if to hand the joint to you.

'Of course,' he says. 'You don't smoke… tobacco.'

He looks into your eyes, smiling, and holds the smoking joint out to Roy.

Roy slaps it out of Gully's hand.

'Youm to clear off the land,' he says.

'And go where? There are people like you everywhere. The council wants us here, well out of town. And there's something *about* Sutton Mallet, don't you think? Something old, something primal.'

'How much do you want?'

'Roy,' you say, 'I don't think this is called for.'

'Come off it, Keith. They'll shift if'n we pay up. It's the old game. Well, how bleddy much?'

'We won't take Danegeld.'

Your head is spinning. Passive smoking, you suppose. You see faces whirling past you. Mary is wearing her Girls' Grammar uniform, green blazer and a straw boater. Gully's beard has gone and he has shrunk inches, become a gangly teenager. Victoria is a punk Morticia Addams, unpierced, untattooed. And Ro is tiny, large-breasted, slim-waisted. Your head aches.

How did you get here from there?

Ro giggles and falls over into the cushions. From one toke? She still can't take anything.

Veins throb in Roy's face.

'Come on,' he says. 'Let's get out of here.'

VC fills her mouth with dope-smoke and french-kisses Mary. Gully strokes their heads, undoing Mary's hairpins and detaching her uniform hat. Both women eventually choke and splutter, and happily snuggle against Gully.

'I nevair smoke… *tobaacco!*'

VC and Mary laugh. Ro rolls over and squirrels towards him, reaching out. He puts the joint in her hand.

'Keith,' nags Roy. He has stood up, bent over to avoid the low ceiling, and is by the door.

'Goodbye, Straight Man,' says Gully, a little sadly, but with a cruel mockery too.

Should you leave Ro?

Why not?

Mary and VC have their hands inside Gully's sheepskin, and are nuzzling his beard. Ro, lying on her back, sucks the joint to ashes.

Everything you ever wanted, this man has.

You don't hate him. You need him. You need someone to show that it was possible. He got here from there. That means you could have too.

That you didn't was your choice.

Roy takes your arm and pulls you out of the lodge.

You see Ro crawling on to Gully's lap. Then the bead curtain falls and the polythene flap drops.

You are out in the field, in the cold.

'Degenerate filth,' Roy declares. 'Let's get away from here. Back to the sane world.'

House, job, kids, DIY, Residents' Committee, five weeks' holiday.

Is this a life, or a trap?

'Yes,' you say, 'let's.'

And so on.

62

You chose the door!

What kind of a man are you?

A situation pregnant with promise, mystery, danger, wonder. And you chose to go home?

Go on, fuck off out of it. I'm not interested in you any more. You might as well join a monastery or the army, or develop an all-consuming interest in *Star Trek* or real ale.

I can't believe you chose the door.

Don't you remember when you were in infants' school, and you had a craze for piracy? You drew treasure maps and wore a pirate hat with a skull-and-crossbones badge. You had a plastic cutlass, and you were always being told off for scaling the curtains as if they were rigging.

What happened to that?

At six, you were ready for adventure. You'd have waded through blood for treasure and glory. You'd have keelhauled landlubbers and made mutineers walk the plank.

And now a little *a cappella* is making you scarper.

It's not too late. You can hesitate as you cross the threshold, your ear caught by something indefinable in that ululation. Your resolve quickened by the memory of Edward 'Blackbeard' Teach, you turn and walk back into the house, taking whatever comes.

In which case, go to 68.

You're still here? You're still walking out of the door. You fucking chicken. You yellow-livered wimp.

I'm disgusted.

Deep down, underneath it all, you're nothing. You're not worth bothering with.

You'll have something like a life. It'll drift past quickly. Things will happen.

Things won't. You meet people, lose touch. You grow up, get a job, get married, have kids, grow old, die. And serves you right.

And so on.

Maybe you'll be haunted by the road not taken.

No, if you leave the house in Sutton Mallet, it's not a choice or a circumstance. It's a fundamental lack in you. There was nothing there for you. There's nothing here for you.

I'm even a little sorry for you.

You won't even dream of the mystery. You won't even think of what might have waited upstairs.

If you were to argue that you left the house because you would rather have the mystery in your life than know the answers, I might respect you. That, I might understand. Then, the rest of your life might be subtly illuminated by that one moment, which would come to seem all-important.

You have chosen not to go upstairs because you want the upstairs always to be a promise, a threat, a potential.

But I'm not buying it.

That's a rationalisation.

You're just a fucking chicken.

Go on, fuck off.

Go to… who cares where you go to.

63

You roll up at the college auditorium and everyone knows what you did.

'Well played, that man,' says Desmond Fewsham.

'Fuckin' ace,' agrees Mickey Yeo.

'Magic,' coos a girl called Helena you've never noticed before.

Mickey, who's always steered clear of you on the grounds that you're a stuck-up git, escorts you through the crowds, and into the theatre. On the stage, Michael Dixon and Penny Gaye are performing some sort of magic act. Mickey finds you a seat.

'Nothing's too good for the Man Who Shagged Rowena Douglass,' he says.

It's a line from a film. You can't place it.

Blokes shake you by the hand, clap you on the back, offer you drinks. Girls don't approach but loiter nearby, giggling. You feel better about yourself.

Rowena isn't around. Or Roger. And Victoria must be backstage, dressing up.

Desmond matily sits in the seat behind you and leans forward. He wants to ask about Rowena's tits.

'When she lies back, do they stand up or slip into her armpits?'

You try to answer.

Some of the show is quite funny. A lot of it is cleverer than it is funny. Bits are just stupid.

You've never understood the kids who call themselves the Quorum. They seem to be running on different rails from real people.

Michael produces a rat out of his hat and there's a black-out, ending the magic act.

The Quorum – Michael, Mickey, Mark Amphlett and Neil Martin – do this sort of thing a lot. Dress up and play, put on shows, put out magazines. They've got this strange ability to get other kids to follow them like lemmings.

The curtains open on a bare stage.

Neil comes out and tries to sell the last of his hot cakes.

People wander past him, some in the fancy dress they were wearing earlier. Some people have swapped costumes, and are dressed the way other people were dressed earlier.

Michael has the accordion, and is doing Desmond's anti-busking act. Desmond laughs.

The people on stage walk back and forth like sped-up silent film characters. They mime drinking and stagger around.

You realise this is a re-run of the day. The Quorum have put everything everyone did on stage. Much of the looning-about is precise.

Looking at the brightly lit crowd, you wonder if anyone is playing you.

Since you just wore jeans and a jumper, you're hard to dress up as. But Mark is kitted out boringly; earlier, he was in a sharp suit with a skinny jazzman's tie. Yes, Mark is playing you.

Mickey, a pair of footballs down his chest, wig askew on his head, lipstick over half his face, lies down on the stage and mimes being extremely sick. He is doing Rowena.

Desmond laughs like a drain. You're not sure how funny this is.

Penny, in a long black shawl, is Victoria, fluttering around dramatically. Stephen Adlard wears a Zorro mask, as Roger.

Mickey is sick for a long time, milking the laughs. He heaves and writhes as if undergoing shock therapy. The others stand around, appalled.

Penny and Mark pick him up. One of his breasts has slipped to his stomach. He hangs limp and knock-kneed.

Mickey drapes himself round Mark, licking his face with a foot-long tongue. Mark Grouchos his eyebrows and mimes a lecherous response.

Desmond is killing himself.

You've gone cold. Somewhere, this stopped being funny.

You look around, uncomfortable. Everyone is laughing. Except, at the back of the auditorium, standing by the door, still looking deathly sick, Rowena.

Your heart is a stone.

Mickey and Mark climb on to a divan and mime ridiculous sex. They wriggle out of several layers of underwear they are wearing over their own clothes.

Rowena dashes out. Doors bang behind her.

You're trapped in the middle of a row. People all round are applauding.

Penny, as Victoria, takes a magician's assistant bow. Mickey and Mark are still at it, grinding away like steam engines.

Michael plays an accompaniment on the accordion.

At the back of the stage, face spotlit but body in darkness, Stephen

Adlard stands, eyes staring through his Zorro mask. Somehow, his glare conveys hatred.

Did that happen? Was Roger watching you and Rowena in the van? You've no way of knowing.

Mickey mock-faints from exhaustion and his footballs roll up to his chin. Mark staggers off him, face disfigured by a big grin.

The audience applauds.

The actors take bows. The audience whistles and stamps. The actors bow to each other. The applause continues. The actors make that 'for the orchestra' gesture and point at you. The applause goes wild.

'Stand up, man,' urges Desmond.

Regretting it, you rise, slowly. You're showered with applause. Long-stemmed roses are thrown at you. Penny winks and blows you a kiss.

Mickey shouts, 'Take me, big boy, take me!'

Stephen carves a Z in the air with Roger's sword.

The ovation extends.

You feel as if you're in the middle of a lynch mob. One wrong move and they'll turn on you. In the seventeenth century, sheep-stealers were hanged on the Corn Exchange. You might be carried down there and strung up.

The applause slowly dies as you extricate yourself from the row. People insist on shaking your hand as you squash past them. Helena kisses you, wriggly little tongue pressed into your mouth. You make it to the aisle just as Flaming Torture come on stage and take up their instruments.

'This first song's for someone special,' Victoria shrills through a microphone. 'He'll know who he is.'

A clash of guitar chords rocks the auditorium. Your teeth are set on edge.

Victoria sings a song called 'You're a Bastard!'.

You back towards the exit doors.

The audience joins in the chorus. It's not hard to learn: 'Bastard! Bastard! Bastard! Bastard! Lower than vermin, filthier than shit! Do us all a favour, fuck off, you bastard git!'

As she sings, shrieking every word, Victoria stabs the air with her accusing finger, pointing directly at you.

So does everyone else.

'Bastard! Bastard! Bastard! Bastard!'

Two hundred angry forefingers stab at you.

You barge through the exit doors, barrel down a corridor, and shove out into the night.

'Bastard! Bastard! Bastard! Bastard!'

A few people mill around in the college car park. In one of the cars, a couple are snogging violently. Someone sits on the front steps, holding his head, smelling of cider, an empty litre bottle beside him.

How do you feel about this? Celebrity?

The cider-drinker – it's Shane Bush, still hanging about, crashing a college event – looks up at you, smiles blearily, and shoots you a thumbs-up. Then he goes back to holding his head and moaning.

Where did Rowena go?

'Shane, have you seen…?'

Shane points towards the side of the building, the path to the playing-field.

'Thanks.'

You walk quickly. It's cold. You want to settle this. It's already out of hand.

'Bastard! Bastard! Bastard! Bastard!'

The playing-field is dark. No windows spill light out on to it. There's supposed to be a lamp but it's been broken. You feel your way along the edge of the building.

You might be able to hear sniffles.

'Rowena?' you ask.

You can hear sniffles.

'Ro?' You want to apologise, make it right. You don't know how.

Suddenly, there's a spotlight. Shadow figures come at you. You are punched in the stomach, hard, several times.

It's your turn to be sick.

As you spew over your knees, a hand takes your hair. You are pulled upright. You are hit in the face.

'Bastard! Bastard! Bastard! Bastard!'

'Roger, stop,' you say.

But it's not Roger. He's there, still in his mask and hat, with a tiny, huddled Rowena. They have the searchlight torch that blinded you.

You are knocked down and kicked in the ribs.

Her face expressionless, her movements precise, Mary Yatman

beats you up. She is a force of nature, equalising things. This has nothing to do with her monster.

You sense justice.

If you spread yourself wide and take your punishment, go to 69. If you curl up in a ball and try to protect yourself, go to 76.

64

Tuesday, 24 February 1998. You don't like to be away from Sutton Mallet for more than a few hours but sometimes have no choice. There are still meetings you have to take in London. Because Vic can't handle some things – many things – herself, you have to. Despite everything, including the way you dress, you've become a suit.

When you drive home from Sedgwater Halt, it's well after dark. You're familiar enough with the route to do it on autopilot, swerving to avoid the permanent pot-holes.

You've had a couple of hours in a first-class railway seat to think over the label's requests. The indie outfit Vic was signed with during the period of her creative output has been absorbed into the corporate colossus that is Derek Leech International. Oddly, they've become easier to deal with. The new execs don't try to wheedle around you with we-woz-all-punks-togevva mateyness and why-are-you-being-such-a-breadhead-man? guilt-trippery. Their contracts may be sinister and loaded with trap clauses, but at least they live up to them. The hand-to-mouth, fuck-the-majors boyos systematically robbed Vic of royalties for years.

There's an offer on the table to buy up the Vic Conyer catalogue for a pretty unimaginable lump sum. Heather Wilde, Leech's sharp-suited hatchet-woman, tells you DLI are better placed to take advantage of the resource than you are, much less Vic. After all, it is unlikely that she'll be producing new material. You dutifully protest, but Heather Wilde knows as well as you that the studio in Sutton Mallet is cobwebby from disuse and that Vic's one album of the '90s was a critical and commercial disaster (you hated it as much as anyone else). DLI's music division already controls several other profitable backlists. In addition to the cash payment, DLI will even pay a (much-reduced) royalty that might well exceed that creeping in under the haphazard current system.

Downstairs, a new band, which Heather Wilde swears is about to break big, wants to do an entire album of Vic Conyer covers. Vic stands to make more from that than she did during her whole performing career (1979–83), not to mention her considerably longer, considerably less successful, recording career (1980–93).

You will have to recommend that Vic sign the deal.

That's going to be the difficult part.

When you walk into the house, Kate – euphemistically Vic's 'assistant' – is in the kitchen, nervously chewing a strand of her hair and looking up at the ceiling as if expecting bloodstains to spread through the plaster. Missy, the dog, cringes in the corner. From the animal's mood, you can tell what the day has been like.

'How's she been?' you ask.

Always, Vic comes first. You and Kate think of her emotional state before your own. If there's room left over in your lives, you have your own problems.

Kate's non-verbal answer – a tiny jump and a sideways look, to make sure you're alone in the kitchen – is more eloquent than her 'Pretty okay'.

Nothing seems broken.

'What did she do all day?' you ask.

'Not much.'

'Did she get out of bed?'

'Oh yes. She watched videos. Fast forward.'

Vic always watches on fast forward. She claims her mind shifted into fast forward when video was invented and that it's the only way she can perceive things.

'She likes children's shows. I've been taping them.'

One thing Vic has never lost is her humour. She can do an impersonation of the Teletubbies on fast forward that always has you in stitches. Sometimes, she shifts into FF for days on end, speaking only in a high-pitched, whining rush, zooming about the house in a jerky, hyperactive blur. She can keep it up longer than you'd think possible.

Kate puts on her duffel coat. Now you're here, she can go home. You've talked about having her live in, which would be more convenient, but, though she's never said as much, she can't bring herself to surrender the last of her life to Vic. She came to you in the first place because of who Vic was – like every teenage girl of the last twenty years, Kate thought Vic was talking directly about her – and her devotion is still based on the music. If she were here round the clock, she wouldn't last.

Before she leaves, Kate hugs you.

'Good night, Griff,' she says.

Then she goes. You are alone in the house. With Vic. Recently, you have started wondering what it would be like to sleep with Kate. It wouldn't be a good idea.

On the worst days, Vic already thinks you and Kate plot against her. Still amazingly perceptive, she'd know if you were having a relationship. She'd interpret it as a threat. She has all sorts of defences against threats.

As you climb the stairs, you remember the long-gone objects – plastic comb, picture frame, toothbrush – once placed on each step. You never did find out what that was all about.

You have the glossy folder Heather Wilde prepared. It won't be any use in an argument. Vic distrusts gloss. So, deep down, do you.

'Vic,' you say, not loud, 'it's me.'

There are no lights on the landing. Above the ground floor, Vic won't have electric lights. You made do with candles until she set fire to her night-dress – her thigh is permanently scarred from that: a rough grey patch on her smooth white skin – and now get by with battery torches and night-lights.

You feel for a switch and flick it. A white plastic clown-head, with very red lips, glows.

'Vic?'

'Griff,' she says.

She has been standing in the doorway of her room. Which you used to share. In the clown-light, she looks as she used to. Only, you know the white streaks in her black hair aren't dye any more. Shadows fill the sharp depressions in her face, under her eyes and cheekbones.

'Don't look at me,' she says.

She steps back into her room, vanishing into blacked-out dark, but doesn't close the door. You are allowed in.

Constructing a smile that's wasted in the dark, you step over her threshold.

Vic not only won't have electric light, but also refuses to heat her room. She mummifies herself in ragged shawls, like some punky Miss Havisham. She still has trunks full of clothes from her stage days – all loose on her stick-thin body – and often dresses up in the gloom, adding layer upon layer.

You feel the cold of the room.

Always, in the cold and dark, you remember the first time you and Vic came to Sutton Mallet.

How did you get here from there?

Of course, you're still physically in the same place. This is where it started, and this – you don't like to admit it, but it's true – is where it will end.

The idea was to reject the notions of success your parents passed on to you. Somehow, that made you both very rich very quickly. Then kicked out the chair from under you.

A noose of expectation tightened round Vic's neck in 1982 and has been throttling her ever since. You have been gripping her round the waist, holding her up.

'Shut the door,' she says.

You obey. There is a flutter and a clunking. A torch-beam shines, making a red mask of Vic's drawn face, and is then directed at the floor. A white circle of light lies on the carpet. You and Vic are shadows, edging round each other.

'We need to talk,' you say. 'Like grown-ups.'

'Don't want to,' she snaps.

'Vic?'

You instantly regret the tiny whine that makes a two syllable word of her name.

'Gri-iff,' she parodies, nasally. She is merciless when she catches weakness.

'Come to me, Vic,' you say. 'Meet me on my level.'

'No,' she replies. 'You come here. Down here.'

She sits on the bed, cross-legged, a lotusing scarecrow. Her elbows are sharp. Her hair is a bird's nest.

'Cut this Howard Hughes shit, Vic.'

She laughs, musically. She deliberately whines and does funny voices, not wanting to use her singing voice, the clear shriek that used to come out of her. It was always the voice that made her Vic Conyer.

Without the voice, the songs weren't that good.

Maybe you had to be a girl to understand?

'Howard Hughes Sings the Blues,' she croons. 'Album title. First track: "Tussle With Russell". Last track: "Nine-Inch Nails".'

She is capable of making up an album's worth of material impromptu and then forgetting it. Vic creates songs the way you blow your nose, then tosses the tissue away with no more intention of coming back to it than you have of revisiting your snot.

Once, you tried rigging up hidden microphones, taping everything on the machines in the studio. She found out and went into her Trappist phase, sub-vocalising the music in her mind, mouthing a song cycle she called 'Vow of Silence'.

'Come down from the space shuttle, Vic.'

'Splash down.'

'Derek Leech has made an offer.'

'He's the Devil, you know.'

'Yes, of course he is. But the Devil always lives up to his contracts. Dr Faustus got the twenty years, remember?'

'Literary reference, Griff. That's cheating. We're not supposed to be clever, remember? That was the point. Being clever is putting your head over the parapet. It doesn't make you happy.'

'Happiness can't buy everything, Vic.'

She has edged back along the bed and now has the board against her back. It's the same bed you found here in 1977: once the mattress was replaced, it turned out to be a surprisingly decent piece of furniture.

You sit on the foot of the bed, stroking the acreage of quilt that separates you.

Vic hugs her torch like a baby, stretching layers of black lace over the light. Spider-web mottles cover her face, like wrinkles. Actually, her skin is too tight to wrinkle.

'Vic?'

She brrrings, impersonating a tone-phone.

'Nobody home,' you say.

'You've reached the brain of the girl who used to be famous. She can't come up to your exalted level of consciousness right now, so leave a message when you hear the primal scream.'

She opens her mouth and fills her lungs. You flinch, knowing the eardrum-assaulting screech she is capable of.

'La,' she sings, a pitch-perfect note, 'la, la, la…'

'Vic, it's Griff,' you say. 'Pick up, would you?'

'La, la, la, la…'

'Oh well. It's Leech's offer. I've been over it. I think it looks good. I think you're protected. I'm advising you to sign.'

'Crrrck! You have been cut off. Replace the receiver and dial again.'

Your knees are on the bed now. You slip off your shoes. It's cold. You'd like to be under the cover. You crouch, like an animal waiting to spring.

'For ever and always,' she says.

You pull up the quilt and dive under, writhing towards her.

'For ever and always?'

Her voice is muffled.

She weighs down the quilt at one end but releases it, slipping her legs under. Your cheek glides past the rough patch on her thigh.

You emerge at her end of the bed. She looks down at you. She will not repeat herself again.

'Always and for ever,' you admit.

She takes hold of you, fiercely.

And so on.

65

On the first day back at college in 1978, you have a morning of 'What did you do over the holidays?' Stephen Adlard even asks you what you got for Christmas. You wonder when presents stopped being the obsessive focus of the holiday. You can't think of anything you did, except wait by the telephone. Rag Day was last year and it's forgotten.

You have a French class with Rowena coming up in the afternoon. She can't avoid seeing you then. You keep an eye out all morning, prowling from library to common room, and hang about in the cafeteria through the lunch period. Ro is a no-show.

Is it deliberate?

Of course it is.

In the cafeteria, you see Victoria, chatting with Michael Dixon and Penny Gaye. Her hair has gone black again but she's wearing red eye-liner that matches her lipstick. She looks like a vampire. She ignores you.

You remember her verdict: *Keith, you're pathetic*. It's hard to argue with.

As you arrive, ten minutes early, in the room where the French class is scheduled, you bump into Stephen again. Is he following you deliberately?

'You look ill. Have you got this flu that's going around? It's murderous.'

'I've had it.'

Mrs Douglass said Ro had the flu. Maybe she's not well enough to come back to college.

That would explain it. You feel almost relieved. You need to sort things out. But not necessarily yet. More time to think, to sort out what to say, would be welcome.

For the first time in your educational career, you haven't done your homework. You were supposed to prepare a translation of the first act of *Les Mains sales* over the holiday, but you didn't. You intend to plead illness.

Flu alone wouldn't have stopped you.

You aren't sick any more. You're just in love.

That's a song title, you remember. You've been thinking more and more in song titles.

Stephen has prepared his translation and typed it up. In its little red folder, it looks ready for publication.

You take your usual chair. The classroom is laid out in a U, as if the lecturer, Mademoiselle Quelou, were being interrogated by a panel of inquisitors. Ro usually sits on the opposite bar of the U, two seats off from facing you directly. Mary Yatman has taken her place, next to Ro's empty chair. Other chairs fill up.

Stephen is still talking but you don't listen.

The lecturer comes into the room and takes her chair. She wishes you all 'Bon après-midi'. The class isn't full yet. It's not due to start for a few minutes.

Mademoiselle, who can't be more than three years older than her pupils, takes off her coat and gets the register out of her satchel.

Ro appears like a shadow, creeps across the wall, and sits next to Mary.

Your heart hammers. You're sure everyone is staring at you.

Ro has changed her hair. She has a long fringe, which hangs over her eyes. She looks down at her books.

Everyone is here. Mademoiselle takes the register.

You don't pay attention to the class. It takes place around you, but doesn't involve you. You try not to stare at Ro. But you have to.

Can you read her? Is she avoiding looking at you? Or is she casual about it? Does she even remember Rag Day? Did she get your phone messages? You know she does and she did. But she is going to pretend otherwise.

This is torture.

You're not sure about her new hairstyle. She used to have very long hair and wore an Alice band. Now, she has a 1920s-looking bob, like Thoroughly Modern Millie. It makes you look at her face more. You see a sadness in her eyes nobody else notices. Only you understand.

After the class, you're going to have to talk to her. You run through approaches.

Mademoiselle asks you about your homework and you explain you have had flu. You promise to get it done by the beginning of next week. You assume the lecturer will buy the story, since you have such a perfect record. She nods, not happy – suspecting something? – but lets it stand. Stephen presents his translation proudly and Mademoiselle – she doesn't like Stephen, you realise with your new-found powers of understanding – clucks over its neatness.

Then she asks Ro. She hasn't done the work either.

'I had flu,' she says, weakly.

'*Toi aussi*? It's an epidemic. Have you been kissing Keith?'

Ro instantly goes scarlet. You do too.

'Very well. But you two had better have it sorted out by Monday morning.'

Mademoiselle Quelou goes on to other things.

You think it through. Ro will hurry off afterwards. You'll have to chase her, maybe trap her against a wall. What will you say? What can you say?

'Ro, I just want you to know that I love you. I'm sorry, but there it is.'

That would have the advantage of being the truth. But is it too scary? Would any girl think you were a wild-eyed loon? Let alone Ro, who knows the beast you really are. You curse yourself.

How about 'Ro, I know how you must feel. I just want you to know that I'm sorry. I acted like a swine,'

– a comical word, surely? One step away from 'cad' or 'rotter'. How about 'bastard'? It'll have to do –

'I acted like a bastard. I shouldn't have.'

That would understate your feelings, maybe draw her out more. The first would be a blow-it-all-on-one-bet shot. She might fly into your arms or spit in your face. Afterwards, there'd be no going back. The second would be more gradual, would open a path, settle the waters. You'd have a step-by-step chance to win her round.

The lesson ends. Mademoiselle Quelou lets you go.

Ro is the first out of the door. You are second. Down the corridor, by the lockers, you catch up. You tug her sleeve. She turns round, face unreadable.

If you tell her you love her, go to 71. If you apologise for being a bastard, go to 79.

66

Wednesday, 25 February 1998. You arrive at work and find a package on your desk with the morning post. It was posted two days ago, 23-2-98, using five commemorative stamps left over from Christmas. The bank's address has been snipped from a letterhead and cellotaped to the brown paper wrapping. Above the address is hand-printed your job title, 'OVERDRAFT OFFICER'. The package is mummified in an entire roll of tape, a transparent layer sealing in the paper. You wonder if some disgruntled debtor has sent you a dog-turd. You've heard of that sort of thing happening at other branches.

Still, it's unusual for you to receive any sort of package at work and hard not to think of it as a present. The rest of your post-bag consists of letters of explanation, pleas and excuses from the recently-unemployed-and-unlucky-in-job-search, newly-graduated-but-still-out-of-work students, mortgage-holders strangled by the latest wave of negative equity and the just-plain-irresponsible. You're not a hard-hearted man. You'll consider each case fairly, but in all conscience you know when a situation isn't likely to improve. You've more patience with those who despair and confess they can't see any way out of their hole than with those who pretend chipper optimism and promise imminent cash infusions.

You told Kate, the work-experience girl, that all letters from overdraft-holders remind you of Billy Burner's expectations of a postal order. Not only does Kate, who has a pierced nose, not know who Billy Bunter is, but she has not heard of postal orders.

You leave the package until last, then consider the best way into it. Your nails can't get a purchase on the Sellotape to scrape through to the flaps of paper, so you use one blade of the scissors to slice through. Inside is a cardboard box, printed in faded cream and red. It originally contained two tennis balls but looks like something you'd keep around the house for spare screws or batteries. It has a flip-top lid, hinged with fabric tape.

When you rattle the box, small objects roll about inside. There's a dusty brown stain on the underside. You feel faintly sick and don't know why. Maybe you should call Kate in to open the box.

Take the money, open the box. Kate wouldn't understand that either. That quiz show – what was it called? – is ancient.

You put the box down on the desk and look at it. It is not going to contain rolls of stolen cash intended to pay off a debt. It is not going to contain dried canine faeces. And it is not going to contain a lump of plastique wired to an old alarm clock. It certainly won't be a pair of tennis balls.

Should you call Tristram, the manager, out of the office you still think of as your father's? This might be special. Or it might be nothing.

Rot and nonsense.

With your fingertips, you lift the lid.

The first thing you see is a postcard. The Cob at Lyme Regis. You pick it up and turn it over, looking at the message. I HOPE THIS SATISFIES YOU, capital letters say. IT'S NOT A POUND OF FLESH, BUT IT'S A START.

Nestled on a bed of cotton wool are four severed human fingers and a thumb, splayed out to suggest they come from a left hand. A wedding ring is loose on the third finger. The cut ends are greenish grey, like spoiled meat. The skin is a little shrivelled. The nails are black.

'Kate,' you call…

* * *

'You're Keith Marion, aren't you?' the policewoman says. 'We were at school together.'

Mary Yatman is now a detective sergeant. Her blond hair is drawn back from a wide forehead and fastened with a grip at the nape of her neck. She wears a man's sports jacket about a size too big for her and smart jeans. She smells healthy and her face is unlined, clear. Like you, she must be thirty-seven or -eight.

'Didn't you marry Rowena Thingy?'

She holds her hands out in front of her chest, making D-cups. At school, a long time ago, Ro was famous for her breasts.

'Douglass,' you say.

'That's right,' Mary says, hands falling to her lap. 'Douglass. How is she?'

'Very well,' you say, too quickly. 'Older, of course.'

'That happens.'

Mary looks exactly as she did when she was eighteen. You remember her as a monster at primary school, but a quiet girl at college, a bit of a brain.

'Your father used to be manager here. It's all coming back to me now. I suppose you're planning to take over his old job one day?'

Tristram Warwick, the manager, three years younger than you, has spent the last year on training courses. The branch is completely computerised and you can't see him moving out much before retirement. If you are ever offered a promotion, it'll mean moving to another town.

'I have a lot of responsibility where I am.'

'Overdraft Officer,' she says, looking down at her notebook. 'Must make you popular.'

'Sometimes, I *give* people overdrafts. I don't just call in debts.'

'Of course.'

'What about the, uh, fingers?'

'The objects themselves have been sent off to Bristol for tests. Of course, we took prints?'

'And?'

'Sadly, not on record.'

She hands over a photocopied sheet with five black smudges. You look at them, but – of course – they don't mean anything.

'I suppose none of your debtors have come in wearing one mitten and looking pale?'

You wonder if Mary's attitude is entirely appropriate.

'They are clean cuts. Your man seems to have done the digits one at a time, with a cleaver or a hatchet.'

She lays her left hand on the desk to demonstrate, putting out her fingers one by one, making a chopping motion with her right hand.

'It's can't have been easy to ignore the pain long enough to finish the job. You'd think that by the time he got to the thumb, he'd have hurt so much he'd have botched the chop. But the last is as clean as the first. Actually, we don't know the order he did them. Where would you start, this little piggy?' She sticks out her little finger, like a duchess drinking tea. 'Or with Tommy Thumb?'

You don't like the way this is going. You've prepared a list of all overdraft-holders and dug out the files of those who have been especially recalcitrant. You expected the police to follow up that angle.

Obviously, the finger-lopper is one of your overdrafts.

'Of course, he could have got his wife to do the job.'

Wife? Of course, the wedding ring. He is married.

'We thought someone else might have chopped his fingers against his will, but unless they used anaesthetic and straps it's not likely. He didn't move about to avoid the blade. You'd expect that if there were a struggle.'

'Was there anything about the ring?'

'Not expensive, but not cheap. Gold. Probably about fifteen years old. Initials inside, but it's hard to make them out. Some letter to some other letter. Both could be K, B, R or P.'

Since the package came, your own fingers have itched. You remember your bout with repetitive stress injury, which sent phantom pains shooting through your knuckles a few years ago. Your sister, in her early forties, already has the beginnings of arthritis.

'You keep making and unmaking fists,' Mary says.

You take a grip of your left hand and fold the fingers to the palm.

'I've been doing it too,' she admits. 'This is creepy. Have you *any* ideas?'

'It has to be a debtor.'

'We thought so too, but no one obvious has showed up. No one has mysteriously disappeared, or waltzed into St Margaret's claiming to have had a firewood-chopping accident.'

'It's sick.'

'Did anyone puke?'

You nod. Kate was nauseated by the package. Even Tristram looked greenish about the gills.

Mary puts her notebook in her shoulder-bag and gets up to leave. You show her out of your office. In the doorway, you get close and smell the conditioner in her fine hair.

Awkwardly, you shake hands. She has a bone-crushing grip.

'You know, Keith,' she says as she's leaving the bank, 'at college, I really used to fancy you. I expect you didn't even notice I existed.'

As you drive home, your left hand feels as if it's been dipped into a nest of red ants. Your knuckles are being nipped to the bone. Your own wedding ring is a white-hot bolt burning through the skin.

You avoid using the hand, and try not to think about it.

K, B, R or P? Inside your own ring, is scratched 'R to K'. In Ro's, it is 'K to R'.

Ro is in the lounge with a gin and tonic, reading *Country Homes and Gardens* while Jake and Jeanette, your children, watch *Independence Day* on video. The first thing you check is whether Ro has all her fingers, then whether she still has her wedding ring.

You're being silly. The fingers came from a man.

When you were first married, you'd come home from the bank and Ro would ask, 'Have a nice day at the office, dear?' in an ironic spirit of sit-com parody. Now, she just says it automatically.

'Have a nice day at the office, dear?'

You don't really want to answer that, but know you have to talk about it.

'I saw someone we were at college with,' you say. 'Mary Yatman. She's a police person now.'

'Scary Mary?' Ro says, not lifting her eyes from the magazine.

'You do remember her, then?'

'Do I ever? I'm surprised she's a pig. I'd have thought she'd be much more likely to grow up to be a terrorist.'

'You shouldn't call the police "pigs",' Jeanette tells her mother.

'My daughter is a Tory,' Ro laments.

Your wife is wedged into an armchair. In recent years, she has grown outwards at the waist and hips. She dyes her hair reddish and wears too much make-up at home.

'Someone sent me a nasty present.'

* * *

You wake up in the middle of the night with a jolt of pain, as if a nail had been hammered through your left hand. You swallow a yelp of pain.

Ro rolls over, disturbed but not awakened. Her breathing-through-her-nose turns into outright snoring. You imagine the downstroke of a saw, shearing off fingers.

You get up and go downstairs. The house is cold.

Like many of your victims, you're stuck with negative equity and mortgage payments hiked up almost to late-1980s levels. You've had to economise on holidays and new cars. Ro is working mornings as a librarian at the college, but that only covers expenses. Sometimes you feel weighed down by the house, by the family, by the regular payments. From time to time, Ro jokes that you should extend yourself the largest overdraft in the bank's history and relocate the whole family to the Club Whoopee, Rio de Janeiro. When he wants new computer games, Jake always says you should dip your hand in the till and that Tristram would never notice you snaffling a pile of to-be-recycled dirty bills. Even Jeanette suggests using the bank's money to underwrite sure-thing investments. Your whole family want you to become a criminal.

You go into the kitchen and run the cold tap over your aching hand. In the merciless striplighting of your showplace kitchen, white goods gleaming, your fingers look perfectly healthy. You don't have black nails or ragged rotten-meat gashes.

Sitting at your stripped-pine breakfast table, you catch sight of a twisted face reflected in the curved chrome of the orange-juicer. Your mouth and brows are set. You are trying not to scream.

Your hand throbs now, rings of monofilament tightening round fingers and thumb. Where your unknown correspondent mutilated himself, you are in agony.

You slip off your wedding ring for the first time in a decade. You're sure the last time you tried to get it off it wouldn't shift.

R to K.

The letters have been blurred by time and sweat. R and K could both be K, B, R or P.

Your hand convulses into a fist. You squeeze tight, crushing your thumb, trying to wring out the pain. It's possible to knot your hand to half its normal size. That concentrates the agony.

You thump the table. For a moment, one pain cancels out the others.

You get up and punch the fridge–freezer. Your left hook is feeble and you don't even dent the white wall. You punch again, smearing blood on your knuckles.

If you were to rig up the food-processor by stabbing the end of a lolly stick where the lid-tab fits, you could get the blades to spin without having to fix on the safety-lid. Then, you could dip your hand into the circling steel and whisk off the pain, slicing your fingers down to stumps.

'Daddy?'

Jake has come down. He stands in his bare feet on the terracotta tiles, leaning on the wrought-iron pan-stand, rubbing sleep from his eyes. His pyjamas are covered in dinosaurs.

'Did you have a bad dream?' he asks.

'Keith, your friend's here,' Ro calls up.

It's Saturday and you're trying to juggle the household accounts again. The Ford Mondeo is on its last legs and you feel a desperate need for a new car this year. With a new car, the bank might value you enough to offer you Tristram's lousy job.

You come out of your den and stand on the landing.

Mary is downstairs in the hall, discreetly checking her hair in the mirror by the telephone stand. Ro, in her greenfingers smock and stretch-across-blubberbum trousers, is waddling back to the flower-beds in the back garden.

Mary watches Ro's rear manoeuvre through the conservatory. Her eyebrow is raised slightly. You know what she thinks of your wife. Sometimes, you think so too. Fad diets have never worked. It's in the glands.

As she smiles up at you, Mary's face silently says, 'Phew, what a porker.'

'Sergeant Yatman?'

'Please, it's Mary. I've got follow-up stuff to do on your package.'

You feel like the Special Guest Murderer on *Columbo*.

'Come through into the kitchen. The lounge is occupied by kids exploring computer-generated tombs. Excuse my shabby clothes. You should have called ahead.'

'That's quite a nice cardigan. It suits you better than the monkey outfit you have to wear at the bank. Did you inherit that from your dad?'

You make Mary coffee in the cafetière. She has never seen one before and plays with the plunger as it brews. The dents in the fridge seem like clues in neon but she doesn't mention them.

'This is a nice kitchen,' she says, clocking all the gadgets. 'That oven has more dials than the space shuttle.'

'And works about as often, I'm afraid. Ro has fantasies of being Lieutenant Uhura, but we've not been able to hack into the control system yet.'

'Expensive?'

'Obscenely.'

'You haven't been taking things home from the office, have you? Ball-point pens, envelopes, a hundred thousand pounds?'

A spasm racks your left hand, screaming pain up to the elbow. 'Has there been a shortage at the bank?'

'Joke, Keith, joke. It's the weekend. You should be off duty.'

'You aren't.'

'Actually, I'm on my own time. I wanted to see where you lived, see what you made of yourself. What's that thing with the handles and the bicycle seat?'

'It's the Rowena Machine. A rowing-machine; you sit there and get exercise by rowing.'

'Amazing. Does Ro use it every day?'

It was a Christmas present from her parents. She tried to sit in it once and couldn't get up. Out of guilt, you did an hour or so just after the New Year. It's waiting to be relegated to the attic with other white elephants.

'Have there been any developments?'

'In the case of the phantom fingers? No. Bristol have been useless. White man in his thirties or forties. Right-handed. Boring blood type O. Probably not a smoker. Chews his nails.'

Your nails are pressed close to your palm. You've tried to stop nibbling in odd moments and mostly kicked the habit, but when you're alone your fingers sometimes stray to your teeth without you thinking.

Mary stops playing with the cafetière and rummages in her shoulder-bag. She brings out a copy of the fingerprints and smooths it on the table. The black blobs, with their lines and whorls, are meaningless. You wonder if there's a code.

'Of course, we'll never get a match. We've got the fingers and the man we're looking for hasn't.'

'What'll happen to them?'

'I've no idea, Keith. Maybe they'll end up in the Black Museum.'

You really are in intense pain. It must be psychosomatic.

Mary takes out a Magic Marker and pops off the top. She scribbles black on her thumb and looks at her own print, then stabs it on the paper just below the thumb-print. Her smudge is less defined.

'You see, my lines swirl the other way.'

She hands you the felt-tip pen.

'Give it a try.'

You worry that you're being set up. This is how Columbo gets Patrick McGoohan into the gas chamber. Is your thumb-print on a murder weapon sealed in a plastic bag at the police station?

It's hard for you even to hold the Magic Marker against your left thumb. Your face must be screwed up with the pain. You manage to stab ink across the ball and stick it on the paper between Mary's print and the anonymous thumb's.

Mary examines the print.

'That's odd,' she says. 'That's not supposed to happen.'

She gives you the paper. Of the three thumb-prints, two are identical. The odd one out is hers.

Read 13, and then come back here.

The pain has faded. Now you just have strange circles of ache, like invisible rings, at the roots of your fingers and thumb. The skin of your fingers looks distinctly unhealthy, grey and dry, with a greenish undertinge. You have only the echo of feeling in your fingertips. Your left hand feels entirely useless.

Mary has left the impossible piece of paper with you.

You've been thinking. The fingers were not an offering, but an attack. Something has been done to you.

It's like a curse.

You go into the bank on Sunday and go through all the files, considering each of your overdrafts. The bank has called in a few mortgages, especially on small farms in the area. None of the debtors seems the sort to have *supernatural* resources.

No other word will do.

This is not the world you were used to, though it still looks the same, with *Independence Day* on video and a rowing-machine in the kitchen. This is a world where curses work.

As you go through the files, you try not to use your left hand. Before this, you never considered how much you rely on having two hands. Even as a confirmed rightie, you need the less capable hand to hold things open, to give support, to provide balance.

If your left hand drops off, how will you wash your right?

You extend the range of your checking and look through all your correspondence over the last year. Maybe the cause of all this is in an overdraft you *approved.* For someone, a sudden cash injection could lead to disaster.

Nothing.

Ro phones and asks if you'll be coming home for dinner. Her parents are expected.

'I have to sort this out.'

'You should have married that bank.'

'This is not about the bank. It's about me.'

'If you say so, dear.'

Your family are worried about you, but pretending everything is all right. They live in a world where curses don't work and everything has a rational explanation.

Psychosomatic pain.

The dead phone buzzes as you put it down.

The bank is completely empty. You don't have the keys and computer codes to get into the vault, but you could open up the back of the cash machine. It's Kate's job to keep the automated dispenser stocked up with thick wedges of notes. Thousands of pounds.

If you wanted money, you could get it.

Kate would be blamed. You could force the locks, and claim to have found them that way when you came in this morning.

Kate's boyfriend has pierced eyebrows and rides a motorbike. He's probably in with a hippie convoy. Just the sort to pull a silly job and vanish.

You've often fantasised about ways of robbing the bank. Towards the end of his life, Dad admitted he had too. You suspect everyone who works in a bank thinks about robbery, thinks about an inside job. It's just that very few get desperate enough to do anything.

Would you be able to escape Mary? Detective Sergeant Scary Mary? Avon and Somerset's own Mrs Columbo?

You look at your left hand. The palm is pinkly healthy, a little flushed, but the fingers and thumb could have been dipped in grey grease. You move each digit in turn, and find that the last two fingers don't respond. You can make a fist, but can't move your ring and little fingers by themselves. You concentrate, straining to shift the fingers, then snap and bend them down with your other hand. They feel cold and unhealthy, like sausages left too long in the fridge.

Stolen money won't help. Doctors won't help. The police won't help. Psychiatry won't help.

You're under a curse.

You sweep the telephone off your desk and it crashes on to the floor, spilling the receiver, buzzing like an insect. You stamp on it until it is silent and in pieces.

Violence makes you feel a little better.

'There now,' you say. 'I've sacrificed the telephone. Does that satisfy you?'

I HOPE THIS SATISFIES YOU. IT'S NOT A POUND OF FLESH, BUT IT'S A START.

There's a framed picture of Ro and the kids on your desk. The frame is heavy, a present two Christmases ago. Rowena is thinner in the picture, but a bulge is beginning to show all round her face.

You drop the picture on the floor and smash your heel down on to it.

Another sacrifice.

You make no pretence that this is not an inside job. You use your keys to get into the back of the machine. The Saturday shopping rush has depleted the stacks of notes, but there are still fistfuls of cash in the press, clamped like staples inside a stapler.

Without thinking, you use your left hand to shut the machine as you use your right hand to put your keys back into your pocket.

You leave a finger on the handle.

The break doesn't look like a chop-wound; it's as if your hand were a tree grown brittle and your forefinger a snapped-off twig.

A little fluid leaks from the stump.

You make a fist around the emptiness where the finger should be. When you straighten out your hand, the little finger falls off.

There is no pain.

But you feel yourself falling into a chasm. You whirl around the cashiers' area, screaming. Not since primary school have you thrown a fit like this. You're possessed by panic. You have lost it entirely.

Nothing helps. You don't expect screaming to help. It doesn't even make you feel better. You exhaust yourself, flailing about.

No one comes. Sedgwater High Street is empty on Sunday.

You throw scales and stools at the wall. You smash the clocks. You toss bundles of notes in the air and let them flutter around you.

You lose your ring finger.

Drained and sobbing, you curl up on the floor. Eventually, the fit peters out.

You have only your middle finger and your thumb left. You snap them off yourself, to get it over with.

It takes a while to gather all the fingers, which have dropped all over the floor. Your ring finger rolled under a desk. As you find your digits, you sweep up the notes, piling them in a heap in the middle of the floor. You drop the fingers into the nest of cash.

From your own office, you fetch a book of matches. The bank is a no-smoking branch, but you keep matches for the sealing wax you have to use on legal documents.

This is a proper sacrifice. You hope it will put an end to the business.

The money burns easily, but the fingers just shrivel and blacken. You squat cross-legged by the fire, a wilderness man warming himself. A stench wisps up. The cash wriggles into hot ash, metal strips curling like magnesium flares.

As the fire dies, you calm down.

You have no fingers on your left hand. It could have been worse, you think. You could have been sent a severed penis.

The next morning, you stay home from the bank. You will soon suffer the consequences of your sacrifice. The children bustle off to school, and Ro is still angry you missed dinner with her parents. Your family avoid looking at your bundled-up left hand. They've got used to your craze.

You're alone in your house when the postman rings the bell, with another package. A whole sheet of Christmas stamps is pasted to it, crowding out your name and home address. The label still calls you 'OVERDRAFT OFFICER'.

This is bigger than the last one. The box inside could hold a basketball.

It is difficult, with only one set of fingers, to open the parcel. Eventually, steadying the thing with your bandaged hand and sawing with a kitchen knife, you manage it. You lift out unread the covering letter and recognise the face nestled in scrunched-up newspaper. You think, for a moment, you have been sent a mirror.

And so on.

67

Monday, 23 February 1998. If you'd thought it through, you'd have written the note, addressed the parcel and stuck on the stamps before you chopped off your fingers. Since you're right-handed, you should be able to accomplish these minor tasks without using the fingers of your left hand – now unavailable to you – but you'd somehow not reckoned with the pain.

To write the note, for instance, you don't just have to put biro to paper and print the letters. You have to hold the paper in place on the table as you write. You instinctively bring your left hand round and press down, getting blood all over the paper, prompting another yelp. You abandon this first attempt.

The fingers are in the box.

That's done.

But the rest of it. You feel it has to be perfect. The overdraft officer will expect no less, *deserves* no less.

You sit back and try to make the pain go away. It feels as if all the nails of your left hand are being slowly pulled out with hot pincers. Five individual throbs of pain under the nails, lesser aches in all nine knuckles.

That's strange. The parts that hurt aren't connected to you any more. The stumps, which leak quite a lot, aren't painful. The blood is inconvenient. If you continue working on the parcel, you'll get blood over everything and ruin the gesture.

You search the kitchen for something to staunch the flow.

It might have been better just to chop off your whole hand. Then you'd only have one big stump to cope with.

You wrap your left hand with a J Cloth, which soaks at once, then jam a rubber washing-up glove over the mess, rolling it over your wrist like a big pink condom. Air is trapped in the fingers of the glove, which fatten and extend.

It still hurts, but won't bleed on anything else.

You can't afford to think about how you got here.

There was a time, five years ago, when you were out of the shade. You'd almost got to the point when you could stop thinking of yourself as an estate agent and claim to be a property developer. Through a strategic alliance with Councillor Robert Hackwill and McKinnell the Builder, you were in on the ground floor of the Discount Development, an in-town shopping centre that remains half-built on the site of the old Denbeigh Gardens.

You re-mortgaged your own house to buy into the scheme.

For an estate agent, that's the equivalent of violating the drug-dealer's code of 'Never get high on your own supply.' But profit was certain. The deal was done. You were a comer, a master, a power.

Rowena never pushed you, but was happy to come along for the ride. She was still buying things for the house, even the week before she left. The kids, Jamie and Jillian, never wanted for anything. They must be resentful now, cooped up in Rowena's parents' spare room.

The Discount Development turned out to be an inflated promise. Crucial land purchases and planning permissions were not secured. The month after Tony Blair's election victory, Labour Central Office sent a hit squad down to Sedgwater and suspended the local party apparatus. Hackwill was replaced on the council, and seems likely to face criminal charges.

You had not lied to the bank deliberately. But you passed on lies told to you. The prospectus, professionally printed and heavy with detailed figures, remained an impressive piece of work.

It had to be your dad's old bank. And it had to be Sean, Laraine's old boyfriend. You remember Sean, the overdraft officer, as a toadying teenager, telling you to slow down. Now he's clamped to your neck, squeezing, sucking.

You've been told you've been treated generously because of your father's memory. Anyone else would have been foreclosed many months ago.

Is Sean enjoying this? Of course he is.

He never forgave Laraine for chucking him and going off with that hippie. He has hated the whole Marion family ever since. Even at Dad's funeral, he was snickering behind his mask of sham grief.

When Jeffrey Archer made a bad investment and found himself cataclysmically in debt, he whipped up a best-selling novel and with one bound was free. You don't think that's an option open to you. And it's unlikely that you could get away with a John Stonehouse-Reggie Perrin disappearing act.

All you can hope for is to appease the Gods of Money with an offering of flesh. It'll make a nice late valentine for Sean. With love from the Marion family.

I HOPE THIS SATISFIES YOU, you print. IT'S NOT A POUND OF FLESH, BUT IT'S A START.

The floppy-fingered paw you have made of your left hand is expert now at holding things down. You hold the tennis-ball box against the table, three-quarters projecting over the edge, and wind Sellotape round and round, burying the box in a transparent thickness.

Objectively, it's quite a neat job.

How many stamps? Normally, with a small package, you'd go down to the post office and have it weighed, paying only the correct postage. Understandably, you can't be doing with the bother now.

Four first-class stamps. That should do it. The package isn't especially heavy. There are jolly Christmas stamps in the Useful Things drawer. You use six stamps, just to be on the safe side.

You don't want to keep Sean, might-have-been brother-in-law, waiting too long. He's told you he wants this matter settled.

Sean always rubs it in with a few preliminary questions, presuming on his long-ago relationship with your family to ask after Rowena and the kids, after your mother, even after James. The giveaway is that he never, *ever*, asks after Laraine. If the old wound were healed, he'd be able to ask about her. But he avoids the subject, revealing beyond a shadow of a doubt that his hatred is still bleeding and fresh.

Then he comes round to business: the defaulted payments, the overdraft, the interest, the mushrooming debt.

For a long time, you still play the promise game.

You both know the Discount Development is kaput. All the money is gone, the Lord knows where. Maybe it's been sucked into a black hole. Or maybe Hackwill has planned an out-of-town shopping centre at Sutton Mallet.

It'll never come right.

You come out of your house. It's mid-afternoon and other husbands in the street are at work, in offices, on InterCity trains, using mobile phones, making money. Their wives are picking up the kids from school, or on shopping trips to Bristol or London.

People who live in your street would never have shopped at the Discount Development.

There is no one around. Still, you hold your pink-gloved hand under your coat, like Napoleon. Or the mutated scientist in the old version of *The Fly*.

With the package – which rattles slightly – in your right hand, you stride down to the pillar-box on the corner. It stands red and righteous on a triangular patch of green where there's a swing for the kids and a bench for the old folks. Neither is used much.

Your hand still hurts. But you've learned to live with the hurt. Just as you've learned to live with the shade.

The miracle is that you put this off for so long.

All through the 1980s and into the '90s, you accumulated things to protect you. The degree, the start capital, the inside information, the contacts. Rowena, the kids, the first house, the business, the second house, the position, the plans, the cars. The fridge–freezer, the rowing-machine, the wrought-iron pan-stand, the home computer, the coffee table, the holidays in Mustique. This was all a wall, thrown up between you and the shade, between you and Sutton Mallet.

There are vast, malign, spidery forces in the world.

And you are their focus. Their weight has been gathering, ever since you first trespassed on their territory, gradually accumulating, forcing you into your protected corner, pressing you into the hole.

You stand at the pillar-box.

This is your supplication. You have sacrificed. You are all you have left to give up. Rowena and the kids are gone. The business is gone. You don't, in any real sense, own the house or anything else.

If this doesn't work, if the shadow-spiders – and their representative Sean – are not appeased, you will have to give up more of yourself.

How much more can you slice away with your kindling-chopper before you are no longer capable of chopping?

There are deep weals in your kitchen table where the blade bit.

You raise the parcel to the slit. It won't fit. The box is a good inch too wide to jam through. You try it sideways, but that's worse.

The world stops.

Then rescue comes. Postman Pat, whistling merrily like a hold-over from those never-were days of before-the-deluge, coming to empty the box.

'I'll take that for you, sir,' she says.

The uniformed saviour is a Postperson Patricia, blond hair pinned up under her cap.

She opens her sack and you drop the package in, relieved of its burden.

At last, the offering is made.

'You're Keith Marion, aren't you?' the postwoman says. 'We were at school together.'

You focus on the woman's face. She smiles, eyes twinkling like frost at sunrise.

It's Mary Yatman.

'You've changed,' she says.

Should the joke become apparent now? Should you understand how you've got here? Were there points at which you could have changed things? Could this have been put off indefinitely? Could you have kept all the balls in the air, beating off the shadows with your successes?

'Didn't you marry Rowena Thingy?'

You shrug.

Mary seems delighted. You wonder if she is pretending. She has always been part of this. You've never seen her on this route before.

'You know, Keith,' she says, 'at college, I really used to fancy you.'

She kisses you on the cheek, and walks away.

You sit by the pillar-box and watch her go.

It is after dark now. The green is turquoised by the bright streetlamp. Residents petitioned for it, after a child in another part of town was attacked on another, more meagre green. Something is wrong with the lamp, which always flickers as if it were a flame rather than a filament.

Mary is gone, into the shade. Her whistling – 'Nellie the Elephant', still – fades into the night sound. The sacrifice is made. For you, it is over.

There is a great fizzing noise and the light goes away.

And so on.

68

What made the people who lived here leave?

They left behind more than just furniture. On each of the stairs is placed a small household object – a plastic comb, a picture frame, a toothbrush. What makes a person leave behind their toothbrush when they move house? The arrangement on the stairs is almost ritualistic.

You think Victoria meant what she told Graham. Sutton Mallet is strange.

That sound is more unearthly the nearer you get to the top of the stairs. And there's a glow, like luminous fungus or Halloween paint.

You stand on the landing.

'Kei-ei-eith,' a voice trills.

A door hangs ajar. Flickering light outlines it. The call came from beyond it.

You have an impulse to turn and run, to dash downstairs, to get out of the house.

In which case, go to 62.

But you don't. You couldn't. You have to know what's beyond the door. What comes next.

'Kei-ei-ei-ei-eith.'

Your name is repeated.

It's a girl's voice. But it's not Victoria's.

You stand outside the door, your fingertips out, touching the wood.

The tiniest push, and you will see. You will be able to go into the room.

You look to either side.

At the end of the landing, Victoria stands, face white. Is she sad or eager?

You don't ask her what's happening. It's too late for that.

She nods.

You push the door.

The room is dotted with candles. Hundreds of them, all burning like flammable stalagmites, dribbling wax on to floorboards or dusty furniture. They are arranged in a vast mandala-like circle around a mattress.

A naked girl lies on the mattress. It is her voice you have heard. Her body glows with candlelight, curves burnished and almost reflective. She radiates heat.

She half sits, and beckons with her arms and fingers.

It is Rowena.

She is sober now, wantonness a choice not an impulse. She smiles, aware of the silliness of this set-up but also of its beauty, its innocence.

The room is warm. There's a fireplace. Some of the candles float in saucers, firelight reflected in ripples.

You join Rowena on the mattress. She helps you out of your clothes. They seem to fall away without struggle.

You kiss.

And it's magical.

After a very long time, after extensive and varied love-making, the candles begin to wink out, one by one. The fire shrinks to embers, filling the room with a dull red glow.

You and Ro nestle.

This was worth waiting for.

'It took for ever to light all the candles,' Ro says.

You don't want to know. The set-up is irrelevant. You want the effect. The magic.

'But you're worth the effort,' she says, hugging you.

The dawn comes up, filtering gloom-light into the room. The cold creeps back, making you huddle beneath the quilt.

The real world returns.

If you wish hard, work at it unceasingly, make untold sacrifices and ignore the serpents, you can have Sutton Mallet for ever; if you have the strength and the love for that – and you must be certain you have, for failing here leads to unparalleled misery – go to 82. If you accept that imperfection is the lot of all, but feel you can make a life for yourself in which the memory of Sutton Mallet is always a power source for a vein of magic, go to 93. But if you feel the lesson you have learned tonight is about sex rather than love, and wonder if it can be applied with other women, go to 104.

69

You are a bastard. You admit it.

You lie on the gravel path, arms and legs outstretched, eyes open wide. You need this.

Mary kicks you in the side. It hurts, but not as much. You don't cry out. You're almost calm.

She kicks you again.

'No.' A tiny voice. 'Stop.'

Mary kicks you again. You cough up more vomit. You taste blood in your mouth.

'Roger,' says Rowena, 'stop her.'

Mary stands back.

You try to sit up, but can't.

Roger comes over, hands fists. He kneels down and punches you in the chest.

Mary stops him, grabbing his upper arms and wrestling him away from you.

You hurt too much to follow this.

Mary pulls Roger out of the light. You wipe your mouth on your sleeve. You work yourself up on your elbows. The torch, put on the ground, is still shining in your face. It makes a wedge of the grass seem very green.

Gentle hands help you.

You look up at Ro's face. She has tear-tracks, and needs to blow her nose. You have lost the place completely. Ro cradles you, and you go limp.

In the darkness, Roger spits disgust. He frees himself from Mary and looks back at you, eyes bright with unfathomable hatred. Mary, turned away from you, holds a hand out, warding Roger off.

This was all Roger's fault. He turns and stalks off, Zorro cloak swishing.

Again, Ro kisses you. This time, you think, she means it. Your jaw hurts too much for you to kiss back. Aches have set in up and down your ribs.

You raise a hand and put it on Ro's back, feeling the nubs of her vertebrae through her jumper. She smiles at you and you do your best to smile back.

'Sorry,' she whispers.

And so on.

70

Friday, 13 February 1998. You wait for Mary to come back. It's her turn to go into town and get food for the weekend. Your DSS payment ran out earlier in the week, and she will have to score some money from her dad, the sergeant, to get into Sainsbury's.

The house is cold, damp. It's never been warm. You sit upstairs in the bedroom, the only habitable room in the place, swaddled in blankets, watching children's television with the sound turned off. You don't care about the fucking Teletubbies, but the telly is the only light-giving gadget in the room that works. You never got round to finding someone to do the wiring for the regular lights. The only power point you have is used by several major appliances but not the free-standing lamp Gully scrounged from a skip before Christmas. The one time you tried to plug it in, you blew the last fuse and lived without power for days.

You've had the beginnings of a cold since the autumn and sniffle constantly, hawking and swallowing phlegm. Scabby patches have grown around your nostrils and lips. Your feel the cold most of all in your eyes, as if two ice bullets were jammed into your skull. The chill radiates into your head, freezing your brain. You imagine it like a grey cauliflower, sparkling in its refrigerated state, electrical impulses dying inside.

You're wearing every outer garment you possess and most of your underclothes. Though you've been camping out in Sutton Mallet for years, people who see you on your trips into Sedgwater assume you're homeless.

They may be right. This house is not what anyone could think of as a home.

You hear the footsteps coming up.

In your mind, you mark off the stairs by remembering the long-gone objects – plastic comb, picture frame, toothbrush – once placed on each step. You and Mary still use that comb, whenever you remember.

In the dark beyond the coloured blobs of the screen, Mary stands. Two shopping-bags hang from her grip like white plastic scrotums.

'It be nearly dark outside,' she says. 'Get up you lazy tosser. There'm work to be done.'

'It's dark inside,' you say.

Mary drops one bag and throws the other at you. Potatoes thump against your chest and spill in your lap. You look at them and imagine grenades with the pins out.

You could do with the warmth of a good explosion.

'Youm should have got thic fire going,' she says.

'Meant to.'

'Meaning ain't enough.'

'Fuck right off will you, Mare.'

She sneers and lays a hand on your brow. 'Poor lover, had a hard day?'

'Too right.'

What did you do this morning? You can't remember. You think you went outside, at least for a while. Come to that, what did you do earlier this afternoon? You've been wrapped up here for a while, but how long? Did you eat anything for lunch? Fucked if you can remember. You'd have to look in the kitchen, for evidence of food tampered with, more unwashed plates and cutlery. Hunger, like cold, has been with you so long that individual meals don't matter.

'What day is it?' you ask.

Mary shrugs.

You focus on the screen. 'It's Friday,' you say, realising. 'It's five o'clock. It's time for –'

'*Crackerjack*,' Mary completes.

When did they take *Crackerjack* off? When did they bring in all these spastic juvenile presenters? Children's telly used to be full of grown-ups.

'It'll be a long weekend,' you say.

'Did you get me a valentine?' Mary asks.

'What?'

'A valentine. For Sunday.'

'Did you get me one?'

'No.'

'Then why should I get you one?'

'Didn't say you should. Asked if you had.'

'Cards cost money.'

'Youm could have made one. We could still. Make cards. For each other.' Mary is speaking in short sentences, with enthusiastic breaths between, hopping from side to side, hanging her head this way and that.

You know the symptoms.

'Cardboard and paper. Scissors and Sellotape. Cellophane and silver paper. Magic Markers.'

Mary likes lists.

'Alphabetical,' you say. A keyword.

Mary stops jerking like a *Thunderbirds* puppet throwing a fit, and freezes in stone, thinking.

Then, she recites, 'And, and, and… Cardboard. Cellophane. Magic Markers. Paper. Scissors. Sellotape. Silver paper.'

You're sure she's got it right. Mary always does the trick. Sometimes it helps her, keeps her from having a turn.

She looks at the television. Beautiful Australians argue. They never used to waste children's TV time on soaps. They were for later, for after bedtime. Why would kids want to watch arguing Aussies?

Last time you mentioned this, Mary had a panic attack. Suddenly, she became very worried about Skippy, the Bush Kangaroo. She didn't know what had happened to him since he was last on and became consumed with a dreadful knowledge that something terrible had befallen him. They turn 'roos into pet-food Down Under. These days, he might be Skippy, the Tin of Discount Doggo Chunks.

Outside, night has come down like a cloud.

The panes of glass in the bedroom windows have long been replaced with squares of cardboard wedged in with plasticine. No dark can creep past.

You switch channels, banishing the Australians. The quality of the picture changes. You can only get BBC2 in black and white.

A man in a suit runs down a corridor, holding a gun. He is wearing a triangular badge.

'*Man From U.N.C.L.E.*,' Mary says.

You turn the sound up, hear the familiar music. You haven't heard it for maybe twenty-five years, but here it is again.

The man in the suit is joined by his blond friend, who wears a black T-shirt. He also has a gun.

'Which did you prefer,' you ask, 'Napoleon or Illya?'

Mary doesn't answer.

You tunnel your concentration, trying to think yourself back to the last time you saw this programme. Before everything dark from the world pressed in on you.

If you can remember perfectly the room in your old house where you watched *The Man From U.N.C.L.E.*, you will be back there again, warm and comforted, with a whole life before you. Each of the children had a special place, declared inviolable after an intense family negotiation. Laraine's was the rocking-chair, where she'd tuck her legs under herself and chew her pigtail, shifting her centre of gravity to work the rockers. James's was the rug nearest the three-bar fire, from where he could look up at the television's dusty grey screen like the apeman looking up at the monolith in *2001*.

And where was yours?

If you can remember, you can **go back to 2**, and things might turn out better. Somewhere along the way, you know, you have stepped off the well-lit path, and strayed into the dark. You have not been welcome in your own world, not for – Lord, how many is it? – years. The best part of two decades has slipped by, as you and Mary huddled in on yourselves like turtles, faces pressed to the mattress, eyes screwed shut, knowing that the spiders in the dark knew where you were. They let you live because living with the knowledge you could be got at any time was worse than any being got could possibly be.

Where was your special place?

Napoleon and Illya are battling men from THRUSH who have torches strapped to their rifles. A beautiful woman in high heels is tied up. Napoleon smiles at the woman. Illya frowns. A villain rants.

A core of warmth inside you begins to grow, to spread. Soon, it will come to you, and you will be back there, in your special place.

Can you go to 2?

Yes, it was –

'April!'

Mary seems to have shouted.

You are confused. You were trying to remember something and it is gone. The core of warmth dwindles and dies. Something goes out inside you for ever.

There's no way back now.

'It's April.'

What is Mary talking about?

'It's February, Mare.'

'April. That's who I liked. Not Napoleon, not Illya, April Dancer. Stefanie Powers. *The Girl From U.N.C.L.E.*'

There is an infinitesimal crackle and the television cuts out. It's not the set, it's the plugboard. A tiny blue flame, the only light in the room, glows where the cord joins the board, and smoke coils.

You hope the flame will grow, but it doesn't.

You and Mary are in the dark.

Neither of you says anything. You don't even try to hold each other any more. You each know you can't comfort the other. You don't even know if you want to.

Deep down, you blame Mary, though you no longer remember quite what you blame her for. Maybe by preferring April Dancer over Napoleon or Illya, and invalidating that question you were asked so long ago – by Shane, wasn't it? – she has upset some cosmic balance and plunged the world into an eternity of darkness.

The dark is perfect, sealed in as much as sealed out. There isn't even a luminous clock-face in the room. You shut your eyes, icy swell of your eyeballs shocking the insides of your eyelids, and there is no difference.

It is as dark inside as out.

And inside there will never be any light. Never.

And so on.

71

'Ro, I just want you to know that I love you. I'm sorry, but...' You don't finish your prepared speech.

Ro stares at you, open-mouthed.

You try to kiss her.

Go to 86.

72

Sean gives his notice to the bank. He gives a three-month warning, partly so they can find a replacement manager, partly so he can perform the delicate surgery of dissociating the Syndicate from the bank. He asks to see all the paperwork, going back to the first £10,000, especially with regard to the loans you've occasionally extended yourselves (including your mortgage, you realise). He says he wants to leave everything neat and tidy for the next administration.

Clearly, he expects you to resign too. For that reason, he does not recommend you take over as manager. And Tristram Warwick comes into your lives.

The Nightmare Tristram.

He's younger than you, and dresses strangely, like one of *The Champions*, a bright orange roll-neck pullover under a check jacket with leather elbow patches, tight gigolo trousers with the fly on the thigh and pointy-toed Italian shoes. He sometimes wears a flat cap; not like a cockney stall-holder, like the Lord of the Manor.

It's nothing to do with how you feel about him, but he's gay. His partner is Kay Shearer, a small businessman whose start-up loan repayments you've been chasing for a while. Shearer's Shelves isn't a huge success.

Tristram Warwick, manager-in-waiting, is to spend three months getting up to speed on the branch. Sean has an easy mateyness with Tristram that you think conceals a vicious battle of wits. They instinctively dislike and distrust each other. Sean's affable complacency riles Tristram. Tristram's methodical, no-short-cuts approach frustrates Sean.

A lot of things have slid over the years. Tristram is especially 'disappointed' with the files Candy has been keeping for you.

'It just doesn't add up,' he keeps saying.

Sean keeps reassuring him, marking off the days till he leaves.

Tristram is always commenting on the expense of Sean's car, clothes, home, holidays. He also notes you aren't short of a bob or two.

'Good investments, my boy,' Sean always says, laying a finger against his nose.

Tristram is never amused.

Sean is leaving, but you'll stay behind. Tristram will pick you over until he gets answers. You start going over the files yourself. Is there anything you should know?

Has Sean been entirely scrupulous? He has 'borrowed' money from the bank, but it has always been officially declared, paid back on time with interest. You only got into this in the first place to improve the service offered to customers.

Many people have benefited from advice you've given. Advice that would have been worthless if you hadn't had the experience you've gained through the Syndicate.

Sean has kept things from the bank, you're sure. He's kept things from Ro, certainly. He still goes to London at least once a week, and receives private calls from a well-spoken woman who is slipping him stock tips.

Has he kept anything from you?

Sean has a big leaving party. It's a supremely awkward occasion. You notice how much Ro is drinking. She tends to be in a huddle with Vanda and, of all people, Kay.

Tristram admires Sean's home, its furnishings. Sean has bought a lot of toys.

Candy keeps bringing you *hors d'oeuvres.*

Sean swans about grandly. He's already had business cards printed. In addition to managing his own portfolio, he'll be offering investment advice and running seminars for people who want to manage their own stocks and shares.

There is a position waiting for you. Something keeps you at the bank.

Before leaving the party, Tristram asks if you could schedule a morning for him next week, to go over the loans department's affairs in detail.

Kay winks at you.

* * *

The party winds down. Ro has to be helped upstairs to be sick and collapses in bed.

Past midnight, you find yourself in Sean's study. You are having large brandies. Vanda is with you, hands clasped round a mug of coffee.

'I should have married your sister,' Sean tells you.

'She's single now,' you mention.

'I can't go on with Ro.'

Vanda's grip tightens on the mug.

'The Syndicate will be fine,' Sean assures you. 'We can buy her out.'

'How?' Vanda asks.

Sean waves a drunken flipper.

'There's more money than she knows.'

'More?' you ask.

'I've been shifting things around, against the eventuality. It's time to make a change.'

'Who is she?' Vanda asks.

'There isn't a "she",' he says.

Vanda's eyes go flinty. She doesn't like being lied to. And no wonder.

'Oh, there used to be a "she". A very "she" Mike "she". But that's over.'

You sip the brandy.

'Look, space kiddettes, when Ro's out, she'll be fine. And we three witches will be set up. I have things perking. Things I've had to keep quiet. Tris the Terrible would have kittens if he knew how I've managed things.'

Your heart goes cold.

'Keith,' Sean says, 'get out of the bank as soon as you can, there's a good chap.'

'What have you done?' Vanda asks.

'I've done very well.'

Your wife shakes her head.

Tristram has questions you can't answer. You're too busy thinking about Sean. He called last night to tell you he was moving out of his house, that he and Ro were separating. He's coming over tonight with papers to sign. Ro isn't leaving the Syndicate, but she's going to sleep in the partnership. It'll be better for her and the kids. Candy fusses around outside your office, picking up on the agitation.

'I still don't understand,' Tristram says. 'Run me through it again, would you?'

'I don't understand what you don't understand.'

You're stalling. There are gaps in the files. Not just Candy-putting-it-in-the-wrong-place gaps, but things-having-been-removed-and-shredded gaps. Tristram looks at the books.

'You know, Keith, I wish you'd arranged your mortgage through a building society.'

This is out of left field.

'My father...'

'The departed Mr Marion, late of this parish. I understand he was eager to set you on course. But we don't operate in the way we did when he was manager. Then, banks were like corner shops or village post offices. We accepted interest payments in chickens. It wasn't fair of him to yoke you to that old system.'

'Does this have anything to do with Shearer's Shelves?'

'No, of course not.'

He's lying. Damn it. Because you refused to extend a loan to his boyfriend, this sleek shark is going to see you hanged. And you don't even know what for.

'I think that's enough for today,' Tristram says. 'I have to make a report. Then we'll talk again.'

He leaves. You want to break something.

That evening, Sean doesn't come round. You get home to find Vanda open-mouthed in front of the television, and the kids squabbling.

On the news, figures are scrolling up and down the screen and a commentator is trying to make sense of it.

'...actually, strange as it may seem, this points fall is greater than that which precipitated the so-called Wall Street Crash of 1929.'

Your ribcage constricts your heart.

'Everything went crash,' Vanda says, dully.

You pick up the phone and begin to dial.

'I've tried. It's off the hook. I got through to Ro. She's drunk.'

'I'll drive over.'

You find Sean didn't even bother to lock the door of his flat. He hasn't been living there long so it's impossible to say whether he's packed up and moved out. There are still kitchen implements and clothes around; but no paperwork. He was using the place as an office, so something must be wrong.

You find the phone buzzing, receiver beside the set. You replace it. It rings at once. You pick up and listen.

'Sean,' a man's voice says, 'thank God I've reached you. How much –'

You hang up and put the phone off the hook again. You are shaking. Without knowing, you know. There isn't a Syndicate any more.

'Sean?'

You turn. Candy stands in the doorway. She is carrying a stuffed suitcase, packed in a hurry. She's surprised to see you. You feel betrayed. You were always the one she fancied.

'Not you too,' you say.

She bursts into tears.

Sean, evidently, is in Morocco. And the bank owns your house. Vanda won't talk to you, but blames herself as much as you. Ro had told her some things she didn't pass on. She had a sense of the extent of Sean's dealings.

Tristram brings a woman to see you in your office.

'Keith,' he says, 'this is DS Yatman.'

'We were at primary school together,' the policewoman says, smiling, extending a hand. 'Scary Mary, remember?'

'That was a long time ago.'

'Wasn't it just?'

'She wants to talk about Sean,' Tristram says.

'Actually, we'd like to talk *to* Sean,' she purrs. 'But that seems out of the question now.'

Tristram hovers. For the first time, you pick up the vibe that he's unnerved too. Scary Mary has got to him.

'If I could talk with Mr Marion in private,' she says.

'Of course.' He beats a retreat.

'Is he queer?' Mary asks. You nod. 'Thought so.'

Mary takes a seat and opens her hands. She still has the clear skin of a child and her blond hair is neatly pinned. The monster has gone from her eyes.

'Well, isn't this a mess?' she says.

You have to agree.

* * *

Sean is caught and brought back. To your relief, his dealings turn out to be bigger than you thought. You don't even get a mention in the local paper for three weeks. First, Councillor Robert Hackwill, who unbeknown to you was a major part of your Syndicate, is indicted on several counts of serious fraud, and it turns out that Sean's little empire wound through Sedgwater like ivy roots, crumbling everything.

You aren't turfed out of your home, though your personal debt escalates as mortgage interest rates get out of control, mostly because Tristram is too busy with the bankruptcy of Shearer's Shelves, on whose board of two directors he happens to sit. Somehow, Sean got to Kay behind Tristram's back and sucked him into the Syndicate, presumably as insurance.

You wonder if Sean was very clever, or if he just let things grow out of hand.

Either way, the town is badly hit.

You move to a flat in town and put the kids in the state school system.

DS Yatman calls personally to tell you that you won't be prosecuted.

You are relieved.

She stands in your tiny kitchen like a slim blonde ghost, looking around at all the new fittings. It's cheap, but fresh.

Vanda comes in.

The two women remember each other.

'This is –' you say.

'I know,' they both cut in, and laugh.

Vanda is still afraid of Scary Mary.

'Some good has come of all this,' the policewoman says. 'I'm back in your lives now.' That hangs in the air. 'Vanda, make me some Cupa Soup would you?'

You are astonished. Vanda, amazingly, looks into the cupboards.

'We only have tinned.'

'Needs must,' Mary says.

Vanda turns on a hot-plate. The ring glows.

'I put in a good word,' Mary says. 'Probably saved you a lot of trouble.'

Vanda opens the can of Heinz tomato soup and pours it into a pan.

'Not everybody is so lucky, Keith.'

The soup begins to simmer.

'To have such a good friend.'

Mary smiles.

Vanda is still shaking when you go to bed. She won't let you hold her. The new bed is narrower than the one you had at the house in Sutton Mallet, and the walls close in on you like a torture device.

'You know what might have worked?' Vanda says.

You don't.

'*Murder.*'

You think about it.

Go to 94.

73

You're not even forty. This can't be happening.

'What if I stopped smoking? Just quit cold? I can do it.'

The doctor shakes his head.

'I'm afraid it's too far advanced for that, Mr Marion. I think you should see the counsellor.'

This is the worst time to have a coughing jag. You think you feel the barb-tipped limbs of the tarantula in your chest as you're racked over. Black matter surges in your throat, tearing tissue.

You try to remember when there was no pain.

How many cigarettes? Since the first? Laid end to end, would they reach to Saturn? Alpha Centauri?

Your lungs are full of brick chips.

The doctor is embarrassed. Anyone else would thump you on the back, trying to dislodge the blockage. But he knows. He's seen the X-rays.

You have a wife, children, a job.

You were going to buy a boat kit and make it up in the space over the garage, get it on the water at Lyme Regis next spring.

There won't be a next spring.

Forty a day. Forty fucking death injections a day.

You are going to 0. If you accept the judgement, and apologise for

misusing the gift you have been given, go to 88. If you refuse to recognise your responsibility, go to 96. Whatever, in the end, very soon, go to 0.

74

Tuesday, 24 February 1998. She is up at four o'clock, to do her rounds. You know a lot about her life, her routine. She must know very little about you. Your house is not on any route she works, so she doesn't even know whatever can be deduced about you from your daily post.

Mary Yatman. Scary Mary. She grew up to become a postman. Postwoman? She is not married, but lives with a man called Geoff Starkey, another postman. Postperson? They have a child, a little boy called Will.

You can't quite fit together the Scary Mary of Sutton Mallet and the mum in uniform. You've gone to lengths to keep up to date with her. Your local government contacts have been able to secure copies of files.

It's an unexceptional record. Mary has done nothing in her adult life that would seem to connect with the monster she used to harbour inside. Also, it seems strange she should be in such an ordinary job. She left college with three A Levels; she could have had a university place, could have followed her dad into the police force. And she had the shade. She should have made something of herself.

As you have.

Since you took control, you've become a Secret Master. You own three local councillors, a magistrate and entire planning departments. You have your MP's private telephone numbers and have arranged his Caribbean holidays. You've shaped the growth of Sedgwater for the last fifteen years, deciding which districts would develop and which atrophy. You've rearranged everything, so that it revolves around you. And you're loved for it. You're always on the front page of the *Herald*. You're thought of as a 'good bloke'. Local businessman, local success. You've built a swimming-pool for the town. You've brought in new business.

You're still young. And you've taken care of almost everything. All the scores are settled. All the bodies are buried. All the debts are paid.

Except Scary Mary.

* * *

Today, you're up at the same time as she is. This is not unusual. You like to get a head start on the day's work. Two or three free hours to think, before everyone else gets to their desk, gives you an advantage.

You walk through the empty town centre.

It is as dark as midnight. You can walk unnoticed but driving might call attention to you. Even now, there are people about who might recognise you. A lone police car patrols. Timmy Gossett, who sleeps rough on the Corn Exchange steps, mumbles under a cocoon of newspapers.

You like being out in the dark. The shade is your friend.

It'll still be dark when Mary finishes her morning deliveries. She'll come home, see to Will's breakfast and get him off to playgroup, then sleep the morning away.

You walk through the estate. All houses here look the same, but you know which one is Mary's. You have done dry runs several times.

You know where she lives.

It occurs to you that you've arranged things to the point where you could walk into Mary's home on Saturday morning with a shotgun and blast her to pieces without suffering any consequences. To this town, you are indispensable. Without you, Sedgwater's prosperity – hard won in the 1980s, hard to maintain in the '90s – would shatter. You have a licence to do anything you might want to.

No, not want to. Need to.

This is not petty, this is not revenge. This is a necessity. A last stitch in the pattern.

Mary was at Sutton Mallet. She's the only one who knows, who might understand. You can gull and charm the whole town, but Mary would never be carried along.

It's possible she's been harbouring her secret knowledge all these years, waiting for the moment to strike, to pick apart all you have made of yourself. That would explain why she didn't go away to university, why she took a subsistence job, why she stays close.

You're excited by the thought. Having an opponent is a thrill. It's comforting to think of Scary Mary, disguised as Postperson Patricia, waiting for her moment, thwarted by your cunning and resourcefulness. When she's out of the way, will you miss her? Will you miss even the possibility of her?

She might have been a partner.

You have no partners. You have and have had lovers, employees, associates, allies. But no partners.

Soon after Sutton Mallet, you realised you had a power. The ice in you could be cloaked. You could make people like you, want your approval, want to make things easy for you.

Rowena Douglass was the first. Only the first.

As a teenager, you fucked her and dumped her. That established a pattern. You've been fucking and dumping ever since. When Hackwill, the councillor who secured planning permissions for the Discount Development, got too greedy, started thinking of himself as your partner, you dumped him.

And he was fucked.

The miracle part was that the dumpees could never hurt you. Rowena, married to Roger Cunningham, still sends you a sincere Christmas card and is hopefully flirtatious at receptions. Hackwill had a strange turn, and accrued to himself the blame for several reversals, freeing you to pursue the Development unencumbered by his obvious crookedness.

You never fucked Mary. And so you never dumped her.

She is a might-have-been.

You find shadows and watch. Pre-dawn blue spreads.

Mary, on a bicycle, arrives home. Geoff, a solid man fifteen years older than her, is at the door, with little Will. He has waited for her to come back so he can go to work. You wonder if Mary will kiss him, but she doesn't.

Geoff walks off and Mary goes inside with Will.

You count to one hundred.

Then walk up to the house and knock smartly.

The door opens and you see an empty hallway. It's cramped, unlike yours. Clothes hang over bannisters. You look down. Will has opened up.

'Mum says, "What do you want, mister?"'

You had expected Mary to answer the door. But you are not thrown off balance.

'To see your mummy, Will.'

'She's changing.'

Of course. She wouldn't want to take Will to playgroup while wearing her uniform.

'Do you want to see my dinosaurs?'

Will has the Scary Mary eyes you remember from infants' school. Has he got her explosive temperament?

You nod, and let Will lead you into the front room. It is tiny, filled with too-large furniture. You live alone but have four times the space these three people are crammed into.

There's no mess in your home.

The table is covered in breakfast things. Plastic dinosaurs are arranged between the cereal packets and milk cartons. Will has them fight for you.

If you had made Mary your partner, this might have been your son.

A strange thought, one for which you had not planned. Does it change your mind? If you tell Will you can't wait, and leave Mary alone, hurrying from the house before she gets down, go to 81. If you decide your strange thought is an irrelevance, and should not sway you from a course decided years earlier and successfully stuck to ever since, go to 91.

75

'It's a very elaborate construct, Dr Cross.'

'It would have to be, Susan. To be worth escaping into.'

'All these variants. What is it, a fantasy life or multiple personality disorder?'

'Strictly speaking, it can't be MPD. To Marion, all these lives are real and valid and *simultaneous*. They all come with worlds. You can note recurrences and confusions. All these mad women and treacherous men.'

'That's a man's multiverse.'

'Of course. That's the primal split, the juncture between Marion and the maze.'

'What happened to her, Doctor?'

'You can look at the file. Marion Keith seems to have been unexceptional. It was a lot of little things, building up. She was married, twice.'

'That'll do it.'

'Not married, are you, Susan?'

'No.'

'I think Marion felt she wasn't appreciated. That the world wasn't arranged for her benefit, that men had a much easier time of it.'

'So she decided to be a man?'

'Marion has constructed a male self, an equivalent man if you like, and tried to live through the life she might have had. The lives she might have had, rather.'

'Poor dear.'

'It doesn't make her very happy. Or him. Keith. It doesn't often work out.'

'Most lives don't.'

'I wouldn't say that, Susan.'

'You wouldn't, Dr Cross. You're a man.'

'I think that's unfair.'

'I think that's the point.'

'Touché.'

76

You aren't a bastard. This isn't your fault.

You lie on the gravel path, arms and legs curled up, eyes tight shut. You don't need this.

Mary kicks you in the side. It hurts, worse than before. You cry out. You are almost frenzied.

She kicks you again.

'Yes.' A tiny voice. 'Go on.'

Mary kicks you again. You cough up more vomit. You taste blood in your mouth.

'Roger,' says Rowena, 'help her.'

Mary stands back.

You try to shrink more, but can't.

Roger comes over, hands fists. He kneels down and punches you in the back.

Mary helps him, grabbing your upper arms and wrestling you open, so he can get in his shots.

You hurt too much to follow this.

Mary and Roger stand in the dark. You wipe your mouth on your sleeve. You work yourself up on your elbows. The torch, put on the ground, is still shining in your face. It makes a wedge of the grass seem very green.

Hard hands grasp you. You look up at Ro's face. She has tear-tracks, and needs to blow her nose. You have lost the place completely. Ro throttles you, and you struggle.

In the darkness, Roger spits disgust. He walks past Mary and looks back at you, eyes bright with unfathomable pity. Mary, turned away from you, holds a hand out, beckoning Roger back.

This was all your fault. He turns and stalks off, Zorro cloak swishing.

Again, Ro strangles you. This time, you think, she means it. Your jaw hurts too much for you to fight back. Aches have set in up and down your ribs.

You raise a hand and flop it against Ro's back, feeling the nubs of her vertebrae through her jumper. She grimaces at you and you do your best to grimace back.

'Bastard,' she whispers.

And so on.

77

Tuesday, 24 February 1998. The evening starts with you trying to park your car in the space where hers already is. You've driven out to Sutton Mallet on autopilot and go through the pre-set moves, swerving to avoid the permanent pot-holes. Kay has to stop you totalling both vehicles by cramming them into the same space.

You stall, your headlamps spotlighting Vic's new car, and laugh. Kay is genuinely rattled.

'It's only to be expected, love,' you tell him. 'I parked here for over ten years.'

He huffs a little.

Stupid faggot, you think.

He spent twenty minutes in the off-licence in town, picking out a chilled bottle of something you know Vic will think is cheesewater. It's not worth the argument.

This is only disguised as a dinner party anyway. You still have divorce business to do and it's dragged on too long. Last time you were on the point of sorting everything out, some broker in Amsterdam shot himself and you had to cope with an evening's worth of clients calling up on your mobiles in a stupid panic. Vic ended up making cups of coffee and rattling off stats for you to drop into repetitious calming conversations.

That was the last time you stayed over at the house. You didn't even get any sleep. You were on the phone or the fax until dawn.

Tonight, you have remembered to forget the mobile.

It doesn't mean much. You and Vic are still partners in business; any clients who call you first – about half of the list – will naturally call her if there is no reply. Neither of you can bear to go along with Kay's suggestion and mute the answerphone.

You both need to be plugged in. All the time.

You reverse a few yards and squeeze the car in beside Vic's. Eerily, she has bought exactly the same model Nissan that you have.

When you get out, it is as if you are seeing double. The only difference is the number-plates. And the fact that Kay is getting out of your car.

The light above the front door is on.

The door opens by the time you're at the step. Vic, wearing a backless black dress you remember, kisses you – not too passionately, not too formally, just right – and you peel off your overcoat, hanging it on the usual hook.

Missy, the dog, jumps up at you, remembering your smell. Vic and Kay look at each other. They met first – he came to her for advice on restructuring his string of shelving unit outlets – and had already established their relationship before you got involved.

Kay presents the bottle. Vic perfectly fakes delight.

'Come through, and meet the Man and the Minx.'

'I need to get a pee first.'

As you climb the stairs, you remember the long-gone objects – plastic comb, picture frame, toothbrush – once placed on each step. You never did find out what that was all about. Without bothering to turn on the landing or bathroom lights, you move easily about. Someone –

Rory? – has left the toilet seat up; after peeing, you put it down.

When you come downstairs again, Vic takes your arm and steers you into the dining-room.

Rory, whom you've met before, stands up and smiles. He's fifteen years older than you and Vic, with a full beard and a crushing grip.

'Griffin,' he says. 'Good to see you.'

You deftly avoid shaking his hand by occupying yours in straightening a picture.

'This is Kay,' you explain.

Rory and Kay look at each other. There is no etiquette for the situation.

'So we're the people they hooked up with when they broke up,' Kay says. 'What do you think?'

'Griffin hooked up with you before we broke up,' Vic footnotes. 'Might have had something to do with it.' She digs you in the ribs.

'Kay,' Rory says, 'this is, uh, Kate.'

Kate is Rory's daughter. She's in her late teens, pretty, nervous. To her, adult life must seem like an embarrassing soap opera she's forced to watch.

Kate and Kay look at each other. You wonder if either will curtsey.

'What do you think of the hair?' Vic asks.

You had noticed it at once.

'No more racing stripe,' she explains.

The dye is even, darkening her white streaks to match her natural colour. She looks barely five years older than Kate. Kay's age.

'Takes years off you,' you say.

'Bingo,' she says, looking at Rory.

'I liked the white,' he admits, sheepishly.

Rory, playing host, gets drinks for everybody. Only Kay and Kate pick his wine. You and Rory have French beers. Vic says she has to keep sober and retreats to the kitchen. The rest of you sit at the table. You realise as soon as you've sat down that you're in the place where Rory expected to sit, and shift over. He's allergic to seafood and has an alternate starter in place of the langoustines. You are opposite Kate, who is next to Kay.

Kay and Kate. Kate and Kay. They look a bit alike.

'They could be twins,' Vic comments, emerging with Rory's avocado salad, 'don't you think?'

Kate and Kay both cover mild annoyance. Kay doesn't look particularly faggoty. Then again, neither do you.

Vic sits down, next to you.

'Get stuck in,' she says.

You and she start eating at the same time. The others are a beat or so behind you.

'You were right about Leatherhead,' you say.

'Did you doubt it?' she answers.

'Not really. Sometimes, you just have to go through with it anyway.'

'Like the thing we did that time.'

'Just like that.'

'What do you do, Kay?' Rory asks.

'I have a chain of shelving shops.'

'Oh.'

'It's not boring at all,' Vic says. 'Kay has a whole new approach to franchising. It's applicable to all kinds of retail specialities. We've been thinking of cloning his systems and sub-licensing.'

'Heather Wilde called you,' you say.

'She thinks Derek will commit.'

You knew that.

'Yippee,' you say, crunching the last crustacean.

'Did you just make a lot of money?' Rory asks.

'Very probably,' Vic says, dabbing her lips with a napkin. 'And so did Kay.'

'I feel left out.' Rory is a painter.

'Rory's a painter,' Vic tells Kay.

'What style?' he asks.

'House,' Rory says.

Kay laughs.

'No, really,' Rory admits. 'I trained as an architect, but since the divorce I've been at the sharp end of the business. Brush and bucket.'

'We could use you at the new place,' you say.

'I can offer a discount.'

'You'll do no such thing,' Vic cuts in. 'Griffin can pay full whack. I want a birthday present next year.'

Vic's birthday is 6 January. She shares it with Sherlock Holmes. Last month, you bought her a pair of antique silver earrings with an eye motif. You knew she'd love them to pieces.

'When we divorce, will you go to the sharp end?' Vic asks you.

'I live at the sharp end.'

She laughs. No one else does.

'Kay,' she says, dragooning him, 'will you help me bring in the main course. It's bangers and mash.'

You know this means expensive herb-ridden sausages and some elaborate variation on creamed potato. But Kay will think of school dinners.

'For afters, it's custard.'

You cringe and laugh. No one else understands.

'Actually, it's sorbet. And fruit.'

Vic drags Kay to the kitchen.

Rory ums and smiles. Kate can't stop looking at you. Maybe you should swish your wrist, to make them feel better.

'My wife left me because I went bankrupt,' Rory says. Vic told you that months ago but the man is clearly trying to be honest with you, to reveal enough of himself to compete with all the things you and Vic know about each other.

'Really? Vic slung me out because I went queer.'

Kay returns, with two plates, which he gives to Kate and Rory.

'No,' Vic says, 'Griffin's a guest. Serve him before Rory.'

Kay switches plates round. Vic sets down plates for Rory and Kay, and darts back to get her own – which has half as much food on it as anyone else's.

'Shouldn't you have become a lesbian,' Kate says, boldly, 'to even things up?'

'Been there –' Vic says.

'– done that,' you complete.

'At university, we did everything,' Vic explains. 'It was mandatory.'

'It wasn't mandatory that you shag that dreadful diesel dike Scratch.'

'Her real name was Serena. She's married now.'

'So are we.'

'To each other.'

Kate has had several glasses of Kay's wine. 'Griffin, did you just, um, wake up gay one morning, or… what?'

Kay looks at you, holding his fork like a dagger. You find your current mouthful needs to be chewed thoroughly.

'No, go on, Griffin,' Vic says, laying a hand on your arm. 'It's interesting.'

'Did you ever fancy anyone at school that you didn't really like?'

You're remembering Scary Mary. Kate, with a more recent and freshly wounded history, blushes ferociously.

'I scent a story,' Vic says. 'We'll have it later.'

'Don't torture the girl, Bitch Queen,' you coo. 'It's a bit like that. Not that I don't like Kay. It's just that, well, I wasn't supposed to *fancy* him. He had all the wrong bits. But, after a while, you don't think of that.'

Kay is almost as scarlet as Kate. Rory cuts a sausage up into very tiny pieces.

'It doesn't mean I don't like Vic.'

'It does mean we probably shouldn't be married, though.'

'Mum and Dad don't talk to each other,' Kate says.

'Please,' Rory interrupts.

'But you don't,' says Kate. 'Not like this. Civilised.'

'This isn't civil,' says Kay, crossing his knife and fork on a clean plate. 'This is savage.'

'We're jungle cats, you know,' Vic tells Kate. 'Predators. It's how we live. We see things and we take them down. Then drag them back to the lair to be rent apart.'

You growl and meow.

Kate laughs. She has a chance of understanding.

'Rory,' says Kay, deliberately, 'would you like to fuck?'

Rory splutters. You and Vic laugh. Kay's face is hard, furious.

'Don't be threatened, dear Kay,' Vic says. 'Griffin is yours, to have and to hole. I give up all claim to this man. It's just that we can't unpick our past, divvy up our memories the way we went through the record collection.'

'I took your *Never Mind the Bollocks* by mistake,' you admit.

'And left *A Day in Marineville*. We'll exchange them at Checkpoint Charlie.'

Rory, Kay and Kate are either too young or too old to understand why either of those records is significant. You and Vic will always share that.

'Why do I always feel I'm billed under the title in the *Vic and Griffin Show*?'

'You've got a spin-off series,' Vic says, soothing. '*Kay's Korners*.'

'No.' Having thought of it, you can't not say it. '*On the Shelf*.'

Kate laughs along with Vic and you.

Vic offers you a basket with apples, pears and bananas. 'Fruit?'

'We like to call ourselves queer these days.'

She howls with laughter. 'I should have served faggots.'

You howl back.

The room seems to be dark. The others are in shadow.

'For ever and always,' she says.

You are laughing too hard to answer.

'For ever and always?'

Her fingers spider up and down your arm.

You control your laughter.

She looks up at you. She will not repeat herself again.

'Always and for ever,' you admit.

She takes hold of you, fiercely.

And so on.

78

You sub-let your London flat and go back to Sedgwater. You think it'll take six months to do the book. At first, you move into the family home – which Mum shares with Phil – and stay in your old room. It has been anonymously redecorated and filled with discreet antiques. You've no idea where your pirate hat and 1970s *NME* run have gone, but also find the resonance of the whole house is changed.

James isn't here.

Mum keeps black-bordered portraits of James (in uniform) and Dad, along with Phil's first wife, Lillian (cancer in her thirties), among photographs of the living. There's a strange one of you and Clare at a demo, holding a placard, silently shouting, 'Maggie Maggie Maggie, Out Out Out!' Laraine and Sean on their wedding day.

You want to talk to Mum about James for the book but she doesn't like to. You should push but it'll hurt. Of course, it has to hurt. You're quite willing to accept your own pain as part of the process. You owe James a great deal of pain. But you aren't sure about anybody else's.

You're not sure if Mum wants you to write about James.

Sources inside the armed forces have got you general stuff on the

Falklands, and even specific detail about James. You know how many times he was shot, precisely the damage done him. He was badly wounded but died of exposure.

You remember leaving him in the copse.

It would be easy to blame Rob Hackwill, but he was a force of nature back then. It was *your* failure, your cowardice. Still, Hackwill needs to be looked at. He's a part of it. He'd have brought charges about the pub incident if James hadn't been about to ship out for the Falklands. He's now a district councillor – Labour, not Tory – and becoming a big wheel in town. Sean knows him quite well, since the bank is involved in local transactions and projects. He says Hackwill isn't such a bad bloke. You think bullies never change.

Laraine is quieter now, not just settled into married life but almost cowed. She's become thin and pale, impossibly beautiful. Having lost one sibling, you pay attention to the other.

Sean is matey. You can see how he *manages* at the bank. He smooths the way. A man like Hackwill would find him useful. As manager, your dad was like a father to the customers, stern but helpful. Sean is a best mate, less judgemental, less serious. If you were in financial deep shit, you'd find it easier dealing with Sean but know deep down that Dad would have done more to help you out. Sean looks after himself first, the bank second and customers a distant third.

Sedgwater is changing in the mid-'80s. An enclave of town becomes prosperous, as funds are channelled in for developments in leisure and consumer areas. But British Synthetics lays off factory-floor staff and is investigated by environmental agencies. Hackwill and Sean are on the up but others slide.

As a journo, you've been trained. You see cracks. Not just in the town, in dodgy deals, get-rich-quick schemes and council backhanders, but in the people. Sean smiles just a little too easily, is a bit too free with handshakes and shoulder-grips.

Laraine seems more fragile. Sometimes, she bruises.

You rent a room in town, over a launderette, and keep it spartan. A bed, a desk, a chair, the things you need to write the book. A typewriter, stationery, notebooks. You put the desk against a wall without a window and cover the wall with photos, clippings, maps.

Some family things, some general, fixing the background.

Hackwill will not give you an interview. No surprise there.

You talk to men and women in their twenties, three or so years younger than you. James's school contemporaries, not yours. If you remember them at all, it's as kids, living remembrances of a childishness you were desperately trying to outgrow. Stick-thin shadow-people are now grown up and filled out; they seem more vivid, more real, than people your own age.

Girls – brats become beauties – tell you how much they fancied James. Or were afraid of him, which doesn't compute. Young men remember him as a good bloke. But Sean says Hackwill is a good bloke. You wonder what James was like at school. You know he learned to look after himself, but did he keep the terror at bay by making victims of others?

Candy Dixon, whom you remember as James's girlfriend, also refuses to give you an interview. She tries to tell you why over the phone, but can't.

WPC Yatman admits the Lime Kiln incident wasn't the first time James was brought in for questioning and released without charge. While you were away at university, running occupations to protest at cuts in overseas student quotas, James was turning into a serious brawler. Not a drunken scrap-picker, but a purposeful master of violence.

In the Falklands, did James kill anyone?

From the reports you have, you aren't sure. It seems almost certain, though. Commendations all stress his 'courage under fire'. That means returning fire. With killing accuracy.

You drink in the Lime Kiln and see people who've been out of your life for six years, from college and school. The kids who didn't go to university or came back immediately afterwards. They don't seem to have noticed that you've been away.

Are you back for good?

You make long, rambling phone calls. Mostly to Anne, because Clare is in a bender well away from phones.

The book, strangely, is coming together.

Anne says you aren't writing about your brother. You're writing about yourself.

Your advance runs low. But you have some money, left by your father and yours on your twenty-fifth birthday. You can take as long as you like.

You can get it right.

Eventually, you arrange to sit down with your sister. You've never really confided in each other, but she's the other corner of the triangle you had with James.

And she wants to talk. She has wanted to talk with you ever since you came back. Reticent though Mum is, Laraine wants to be forthcoming.

Since her marriage, Laraine hasn't worked. She and Sean live out of town, in a house in Sutton Mallet, a hamlet on a turn-off from the Achelzoy road.

You drive out in your patched-together VW. The battered Beetle seems an intruder in the converted barn that serves as Sean's garage.

Laraine welcomes you into her perfect home. It was once a farmhouse, and lay abandoned for years, but has been completely overhauled. The house smells of new paint and good wood.

As Laraine makes you tea, you realise what the place reminds you of.

'Do you remember?'

'That TV play.'

'*The Exorcism.*'

'About the city couple who buy an old farmhouse, and are haunted by the family who once starved to death there.'

That programme went out in 1972, on a Sunday night. Unusually, you and Laraine – everyone else was out – were in the house alone, and watched it together, terrified. It's stayed with you ever since. Now you realise it was supposed to be making a political point – with amazing foresight, at that – but at the time, you took it as just a ghost story.

Neither of you wanted to go upstairs in the dark. You were thirteen and Laraine fifteen. You both slept downstairs, huddled together on the sofa under blankets, still under the spell of the spookshow.

Afterwards, when the sun came up, the fear went away. You were both ashamed at your funk and never mentioned sleeping on the sofa to Mum and Dad or James, though you did tell them about *The Exorcism.* You wonder if you've never talked about that night because you remember the shampoo smell of your sister's hair and the warmth of her thin body in a way that seems now even more transgressive than it did then.

'We slept together,' Laraine says, 'on the sofa. God, that was a long time ago.'

'Half my life,' you admit. 'More than half. Not quite half yours.'

'Thanks for reminding me how decrepit I am.'

Laraine sets out the tea on the Habitat kitchen table with all the formal elegance of a Japanese geisha. You observe her precise movements.

'Are you dyeing your hair?'

She admits it.

'It looks good.'

'Sean doesn't like it.'

'So?'

'Yeah, so?'

You take your mugs of Earl Grey and go into the front room. It is all blond-wood and TV and stereo equipment. Sean has a Betamax. The sofas and chairs are chrome tubes with overstuffed floral-pattern cushions.

You and Laraine sink into sofas.

'What happened to us?' you ask.

Laraine is jittery, afraid to speak.

'It's not just James, is it? There's something else. For both of us.'

Laraine puts her mug down on a glass slab supported by three black spheres, a coffee table disguised as an alien artefact. It leaves a ring. She moves the mug on to the latest *Vogue* and rubs the ring with her sleeve, then tuts over the wrinkled circle eaten into the pouting face on the magazine cover.

You see she is crying.

'Do you remember...' she begins.

'Yes?'

'Do you remember Dad ever hitting Mum?'

The question comes out of nowhere. There were frequent nagging arguments between your parents, some stretching over years, but no blazing rows. You know James's sudden violence came from somewhere, but think that was your fault not your parents'.

'I shouldn't have said anything,' Laraine says.

You riffle through your whole memory of Mum and Dad. Were there clues? Did you miss something vital, an unseen explosion? Have you been so wrapped up in yourself that you've failed to pay attention to the rest of your family, to the rest of the world?

'Only, they say women marry their dads. And Sean *is* Dad's successor at the bank.'

Laraine is talking about her own marriage.

'Sean hits you?'

'Not often. And not hard. Only when I've been bad.'

'"Been bad?" Larry, you're not ten years old. How can you be "bad"?'

'Little things. Distracting him. He's under a lot of pressure.'

'He hits you.'

She nods.

'The bastard, I'll –'

'No, don't. Keith, I shouldn't have said anything.' Now, she's afraid.

'You have to leave.'

'It's not like that. Really, it's not.'

For once, you wish Clare were here. She'd have Laraine in a shelter for battered women within an hour, bring a civil prosecution against Sean before sunset, have him castrated by a gang of biker diesel dikes by the end of the week. And hum 'Super Trooper' all the while.

'Larry, there are rules. Hitting women is against them. If a man does that, he loses all rights. He doesn't have to be considered.'

'You see everything as simple, Keith.'

'This is simple. Unless it's stopped, it gets worse.'

You take Laraine in your arms and hold her. She is racked with sobs, soaking your collar with tears. You smell her shampoo – still the same? – and hug her tight. As she cries, you stroke up and down her back. You kiss her temple. The smell gets in your nose. The clean smell.

You feel a flicker of desire: shameful, embarrassing, noticeable. Laraine pushes you back but not away. She looks into your eyes. She has stopped crying.

This is serious.

If you kiss your sister on the mouth, go to 101. If you break the embrace and stand up, go to 115.

79

'Ro, I know how you must feel. I just want you to know that I'm sorry. I acted like a bastard. I...'

You don't finish your prepared speech.

Ro stares at you, open-mouthed.

You try to hug her.

Go to 86.

80

Friday, 13 February 1998. You get home first, just after six. It's already dark but you've resisted turning on the headlamps during the short drive from town. It's unlikely you'd ever run into anyone on the Sutton Mallet turn-off. You drive into the former barn that serves as a garage and park neatly in your space. You get out and feel a slight tingle. It's not the cold, it's the night. Your Fiat clicks as you activate the central locking.

You stand in the garage. Rusted ploughs are fixed to the walls and the place still smells of hay. Though the farmhouse you live in has been converted, you try to preserve the feel of its former function. To you, this is a working environment, not only because you grow your own vegetables and make your own wine. You look up at the low ceiling you had installed in the barn soon after you moved in, making an above-garage work-room you call the Batcave.

Up there, everything is perfectly ordered, each tool in its place, any questionable products stashed out of sight. For your projects, you often need quite esoteric materials. Two padlocks fasten the trapdoor. You and Mary have keys, kept about you at all times. To get into the Batcave, you must each open a lock. Your marriage is about mutual consent, co-operation, agreement.

You can get to the house from the garage, through the kitchen door. But you like the ceremony of going round to your front door and opening up. In your pocket, you have keys for the house, keys for the car, keys for the Batcave, keys for the bank, keys for the locked cabinets in the house and the Batcave, a key for the bank vault (Tristram, the deputy manager, has the other). You don't need to look to know which is which. You can tell by the feel. The front-door key is the biggest, heaviest, longest. Old, cold metal.

There are four homes in Sutton Mallet now, all converted farmhouses. Two are owned by people who live in London and only appear at the weekends. One of those has been neglected for nine months, since its owner suffered a reversal and has had to put it on the block to finance a desperate stock deal. No takers at the moment.

You don't have much use for people who think of the world in terms of money and what it can buy. You see them coming into the bank, always hoping to get ahead with what they haven't got. You and Mary know there are more important ways of keeping the score. Ways that matter.

The bank is behind you, as sealed off in your mind as its locked vault. When you left your office at five-thirty, you repressed all details of any business you were working on. At nine-thirty on Monday morning, it will all be in your mind, clear and ready.

The weekend is sacred. For personal projects.

You strip off your suit as you go upstairs, remembering the long-gone objects – plastic comb, picture frame, toothbrush – once placed on each step. It is a game between you and your wife. Sometimes, when each thinks the other is off guard, you quiz each other. Neither has ever caught the other out.

In the recently fitted master bathroom, you take a shower. Outside, it's crisply cold. You let hot water pour on to your chest, down your legs, into your eyes. You lobster yourself, scalding away your weekday skin.

While you're showering, Mary comes home. She comes into the bathroom, having collected your clothes, and disassembles her uniform with precise movements as if stripping and cleaning a gun. When the blue shell of WPC Yatman – she keeps her maiden name in the week – is hung up on its frame, she undoes her hair and combs it out.

You finish your shower and towel yourself.

'You look like a fire hydrant,' she comments.

You smile. She has said that before.

'I was out at the travellers' site today,' she says.

Like you, Mary normally lets her weekday work lie inactive at the weekend. But the travellers are weekend work too. Maybe more so than week work. They are your current project.

'Canning has lodged a fresh battery of complaints. Hygiene, mostly. And noise nuisance. Oh, and drugs. It's always drugs.'

You take this on board.

You've been following the story. The district council, forced by law to make provision for travellers, has sited a small number of them in a field near Achelzoy. The travellers' spokesperson is Gully Eastment, who was at school with you. He calls himself 'Gulliver' now, which makes for predictable headlines about 'Gulliver's Travellers' in the *Sedgwater Herald*. He has become some sort of guru. The locals, led by Roy Canning, a farmer who is friendly with Mary's parents, are campaigning vigorously to have them removed.

The Achelzoy travellers aren't Romany, but so-called New Age Travellers: refugees from the cities, unmarried mums on social security, filth-locked crusties with dogs on strings, care-in-the-community headcases, spare-change supplicants. Canning blames them for all the evils of the world, from falling property values to spoiled milk.

He is wrong.

All the evils in the world flow from quite different sources.

'I saw Eastment.'

'Does he remember you?'

'He remembers Scary Mary.' Your wife is quite proud of her old nickname.

'He was a misfit,' you say. 'Too clever to keep quiet.'

'He hasn't changed.'

'No one does.'

'No.'

Mary sits at her dressing-table. She pulls back her hair and ties it in a knot, then begins applying her make-up. A black base with green stripes.

You get into your weekend clothes. Jeans that have been ground in dirt and flogged against stone walls. A dark, loose shirt. Heavy work-boots. A greatcoat, leaking at the shoulders, with most of its buttons gone. A wig: long, straggly black hair, held in place by a Rambo band.

Mary's weekend outfit is similar. Her afghan coat is brown and ancient enough to disappear in the dark. She wears a black balaclava that fits perfectly round the camouflage mask she has made of her face. Only her large eyes, clear and strong, show a light.

'I love you,' you say.

Kissing her, you taste make-up. She hooks her hands into the stringy scraggle of your wig.

'I love you too,' she says back.

Then you go downstairs and outside, creeping out of the house into the dark. No one is around to see you cut across the fields. No moon shows through the cloud. This is your favourite type of night.

Saturday morning. Valentine's Day. You have bought each other large, manufactured cards, the same as last year and all the years before.

As you slob around the house, Roy Canning calls by. Not recognising the concept of off-duty, he thinks of Mary as his personal policewoman. Mary makes him instant coffee – you keep the real stuff for yourselves – and listens to his complaints.

'They'm animals, Mary, girl. Last night were worst yet.'

'But you don't know it was the travellers.'

'Who else could it be?' you put in.

'Animals. When I got up this morning, it were the first thing I saw… what they did. Animals. I tell 'ee. They'm got to be shifted.'

'You should make an official charge.'

'That's what I's doing.'

'Mary's off for the weekend, Roy,' you point out evenly, good-humoured. 'You should see Inspector Draper, in town. Maybe he'll stage a dawn raid.'

'If I'd caught 'en, Keith… I don't know what I'd have done.' He shakes his head, mulling over the hurt.

'For God's sake,' you purr, 'don't say anything Mary might have to remember in court.'

Mary smiles. Roy, shocked, calms himself.

If he ever thought about it, Roy would realise he doesn't like you. But he won't think about it. It doesn't matter anyway. Apart from Mary, people only ever know your weekday self. The one that doesn't count.

You can't help smiling at the thought. If Roy doesn't like the weekday Keith, what would he think of the weekend Keith? It is a temptation. You'd like to show yourself to someone sometime. The circumstances would have to be right. You'd have to choose carefully, someone who'd never be in a position to tell.

'It'd be nothing personal,' you say. 'But the law is the law.'

'They don't recognise laws of God or man,' Roy says. 'They should be shot, like sheep-worriers.'

While Roy talks to you, Mary makes him another cup of coffee. After she spoons in the Nescafé, she hawks quietly and spits on to the brown powder, then pours in hot water and milk.

'It's two sugars, isn't it?'

Saturday evening. After dark, Saturdays have been just between the two of you since before you were married. This is the real time, when your marriage – your partnership – is at its most intense, at its most pure. This is the time when you and Mary can really work on your special projects.

Some projects, you have been working on for many years. Some are thought of, executed and over within the space of an afternoon and evening. Sometimes, you have a plan which you stick to rigorously; sometimes, you act on impulse, improvising giddily. Sometimes, personal feelings are involved, carried over from the weekday world, allowing you to correct imbalances, to pay back debtors beyond the reach of bank or law. Sometimes, you pursue a project mechanically, to see how far you can take something without the impetus of conviction, just to see what happens. On occasion, to preserve your edge, you act against your own interests, pursuing a project though it inconveniences people you're fond of.

You're not a monster: you do genuinely like some people. Though you remember Eastment as a rival and a disturbing loose cannon at school, you rather admire him now. He has sacrificed comfort for a principle you could never embrace. It's because you can feel empathy for some and antipathy for others that your weekend work is so satisfying, offering such a rich variety of emotional stimuli.

At first, you were appeasing the shadow-spiders. Gradually, over the years, you have become the darkness. You and Mary have grown together, passionately. You used to plot and plan, arguing over methods and campaigns. Now you know instinctively what to do, where to push, how to manipulate. When to strike, and when to refrain from striking.

Every project reaches a point where it can continue without you. If people are nudged to a certain point, inertia carries them on. Some people are heavier or lighter than you expect, but you're both patient, adaptable, good-humoured.

Tonight, alive in the dark, you cross the fields again, making your way from Sutton Mallet to Achelzoy. You know all the rhynes and fords from years of study.

You and Mary.

Your weekday selves are perfectly placed to know things, to see cracks that can be worked into chasms. But only your weekend selves count.

You've known the travellers would be a project ever since Mary heard Robert Hackwill, chairman of the council, was scouting around for a community well outside his ward which might host unwelcome visitors. You and Mary have felt little thrills as the players – Hackwill, Canning, Eastment, Draper – moved into their places, each with his attendant followers. It was almost as if they were under your influence, even before you devoted any time to the project.

Sometimes, you have to do very little.

The travellers' site is away from the main road – Hackwill was careful it couldn't be seen from the highway – and fairly exposed. It's little more than a circle of battered caravans. The scents of chemical toilets and incense waft on the sharp winter breeze. As you creep nearer the field, you see the flicker of fires through thin hedge. Music throbs, loud enough to shake fillings. Lights are strung up in the circle, making a pyramid of illumination on the dark quilt of the moor.

Mary stands up. You follow suit.

You are the dark. You can't be seen.

From her Friday recce, Mary knows exactly where the generator is. The caravans have electricity. Some have portable TVs and microwave ovens. All the kids sleep under electric blankets.

You take the crowbar out of your backpack.

Sunday morning. As always, you lounge with the papers spread out over the big bed. There's never anything interesting to read and you often whine about it, but Mary looks at interior decoration articles and you dutifully trudge through the sport section. You listen together to the omnibus edition of *The Archers*.

Throughout your life, you have only ever listened to the radio (as opposed to having it on in the background) on Sundays. *Two-Way Family Favourites* and *Round the Home* and *The Clitheroe Kid*. *Down Your Way* and *Sing Something Simple* and *Gardeners' Question Time*.

This is your idea of British heritage. The culture that binds you to your society. The telly never goes on until well after the God slot.

You were in bed just after dawn. At the weekends, you need less sleep. Often, you and Mary make love in the small hours of Sunday, after getting back from an excursion. It's your private time, after you have served your project of the moment.

When you were first married, while your projects were mainly around the house, you used to have Sunday lunch with your parents or, more often, Mary's. That seems to have fallen by the wayside. You don't really miss the heavy food, the smell of cooking cabbage, the ritual conversations, Mary's dad's story about seeing a flying saucer while cycling his beat, Mary's little cousin Beth's horse drawings.

The weekends are just for you and Mary. That's as it should be.

Sunday afternoon. You work up in the Batcave. The materials for your projects have to be assembled carefully, so they can't be traced or if they can not back to you. Many special items have to be made more or less from scratch. You and Mary have taught yourself skills. Not every task can be accomplished with something as simple as last night's crowbar.

On a hot-plate, Mary cooks up a mixture of horse manure – supplied by Beth's pony and supposedly for the vegetable garden – and glue, stirring in liquid to get the proper texture. You've both contributed your own shit to the mixture, just for luck. The smell is vile, so you have the extractor fan on full blast. For your part, you've been collecting milk bottles – not so easy to find in these days of cartons – and making tight-fitting stoppers. You don't want any leakage.

As you work, you play tapes of Andrew Lloyd-Webber musicals, singing along to favourite tracks.

Carefully, you half-fill the bottles with the mixture you call Sticky Shit and top up with a layer of pink paraffin. Then you get them stoppered and lay them down next to the elderflower wine.

'What's that smell?' someone asks.

'Tomato preserve,' says Mary. 'I think this year's batch is off.'

You have a visitor, Inspector Draper. Mary's boss, you suppose. You both like and feel sorry for him. Many of your projects seem to give him grief, quite incidental to your intentions. Mary tries to make up for it by looking after him on the job. Whenever interesting ingestible drugs are confiscated, she takes a pinch and crumbles it into his PG Tips.

Draper has found you in the garden, enjoying the dusk. You have locked up the Batcave.

'What brings you out this way?' you ask.

Draper nods towards Achelzoy.

'Roy Canning and the travellers?' you hazard.

'You must be psychic, Keith.'

'Not really. It's all anybody talks about round here these days. Roy was over yesterday. I suppose you're following up on his complaint.'

'Which one?'

'The latest.'

'It's gone a bit beyond complaints. Canning's apparently been playing silly buggers. Fancies himself as a commando.'

Mary looks concerned.

'He's not in any trouble, is he? Yesterday, he was wound up tight. Making all kinds of accusations and threats.'

'He must have accomplices.'

'Has Eastment called you in?' you ask Draper. 'That's a turn-up. A hippie calling the "pigs"!'

Draper snorts. 'Eastment's in hospital.'

'Sounds like a range war,' you comment, ironically. 'Wild West stuff.'

'I'm sick of being sheriff in this town,' Draper says.

Mary hugs him. 'Don't worry. We love you. Would you like a jar of the tomato goo?'

Sunday evening. After Draper has gone, without knowing why, you both can't stop giggling.

As it gets dark, you don't turn on the lights in the house. You and Mary sit on your sofa in your lounge, holding each other, as much a couple as the day you were married. The shadows grow inside, seeping across the floor and up the walls, boxing in the last squares of light and cutting them down to slivers then wiping them out. You will always be a team.

You and Mary. And the dark.

And so on.

81

You pause in the shade, which suddenly seems bristling with threat, and look back. Will comes to the door, leading Mary. Her hair is undone and she is buttoning a cardigan. Mildly impatient, she looks out of the door but doesn't see you. You press yourself into the shrinking dark.

She looks around, humouring her son. Clearly, she doesn't believe in the man who came to the door. She can't have heard your knock.

She takes Will inside, and shuts the door.

You straighten and step out of the shade. For the first time, you're unsure of yourself. This is way off your patch. People dressed like you do not wander around this estate and expect to walk away with their watches and credit cards.

Until now, you thought of yourself as a predator. Now you are a victim.

Older kids, who should be in school, cluster behind a windbreak garage wall, lighting up cigarettes. People are all around, going to work.

The night is almost gone.

You wander away, without purpose. It is as if the day has been called off and you are free. You have no appointments, no commitments.

The last thing that seems clear in your mind is something absurd, trivial and long-gone. The seatbelt in Mary's dad's car, and the trouble you had with it.

That would be 197when? Rag Day?

Jubilee year. 1977.

The day you went to Sutton Mallet.

Later that morning, you drive out to Sutton Mallet. The turn-off is still there. The road is paved now. There are a few more houses, new homes for commuters.

You park the car and get out.

It's cold, but clear. You feel nothing. There's nothing unexceptional or strange about this place.

Is this what made you run?

You find the field. The one where you ran, where you were chased. It's just a field, grass crisp where the frost has not gone.

You shout at the shadow-spiders. 'Come out, come and get me.' Nothing.

For the first time, you feel free. You thought you might be afraid, but you aren't. You almost feel excited.

There are things you want to change. Things you want to get out of, patterns you want to break.

Fear will come, you know. But so will other things.

You can do anything. The future is yours, to make of what you will.

You walk away from Sutton Mallet.

And so on.

82

These are not dreams. These things really happen.

But one misstep, and you lose everything.

You and Ro become explorers, of your own love. You stay in the house in Sutton Mallet, on the mattress surrounded by candles, and you make love. With infinite variety, you explore the possibilities of expressing feelings through flesh. You become parts of each other, always striving to make the whole function better as a manifestation of your shared pleasure. You grow together.

You don't need food, clothes, jobs, educations.

The moment extends, for ever.

You don't age or tire or have children or change your minds.

Your bodies are impressed with the rhythms of your movements. You tick over, sometimes exploding into frenzied writhings, sometimes lapping gently.

Eternally, you hear the song of the flesh.

You and Ro become pirates, really you do. You convert a luxury yacht into an assault craft and prey on those evil-doers who use international waters to avoid justice. You rescue slaves, defy drug-smugglers, persecute polluting industrialists, intercept fleeing deposed dictators. You fly the Jolly Roger. Rowena is, literally, your First Mate.

You accumulate, spend and bury treasure. You make love on

tropical beaches at sundown. You duel with villains and always win. You evade the authorities with style.

Eternally, you hear the song of the sea.

You and Ro become explorers, of your love. You stay in the house in Sutton Mallet, and find your communion has become general, has opened up a channel to the divine. You worship through each other. You begin to understand, to map the hidden workings of the universe. You each become part of the whole, never surrendering your selves but opening up to the myriad others. You evolve together.

You don't need.

The moment extends, for ever.

You age, tire, have children, change your minds.

Others join you, venerate you both for your insights, revere you for your humility. You refuse to be set upon pedestals and find joy in working the fields as much as in roaming the universe.

Eternally, you hear the song of the soul.

You and Ro go to university, get jobs, get married, have children, grow old and die.

At each stage, your life is perfect.

You are as content as parents as you are as lovers, as colleagues, as grandparents.

You are unobtrusive, so people don't envy you. And yet you are loved beyond the circle of your immediate family.

Eternally, you hear the song of the world.

Go to 99.

83

You're amazed Sean has got away with it. He has founded a financial empire, diversifying into paper companies notionally owned by Ro, almost entirely on monies 'borrowed' from the bank. He has approved loans – which is supposed to be your job – to Ro at extremely favourable terms. He's paying the loans back and you work out he'll leave the bank just as he gets square. He'll have a clear profit, acquired through – in effect – gambling with the bank's customers' money. He's not an idiot, though. If left alone, he'll be out of it and nobody any the wiser. No one will care about a loan paid back promptly. He's broken the law, but hasn't actually stolen anything.

Then, on some flimsies, you find your signature. It's not even a forgery. It's just your name, written by someone else.

Not Sean. You know his handwriting. Ro? Maybe. Are you culpable? No, you're a victim.

'Is there anything wrong?' Candy asks.

And you're a chump. Sean has been laughing at you.

'Could you get me some tea, dear?'

'Yes, Keith.'

You look over HOUSEKEEPING again. There's no doubt. Sean has been a party to fraud, and instituted a policy of embezzlement. Dad would have been heartbroken.

If you report Sean to the police, go to 114. If you put the file away and try to forget all about it, go to 125. If you go to Sean to talk about it, go to 135.

84

If you think about this, you won't do it. You're just playing with the idea. You don't mean it.

You're blowing it up.

You open the cabinet, expecting to see a gaping dark void beyond the mirror. Instead, there are shelves. The medicine half of the cabinet: sticking plasters, bandages, insect-bite ointment, aspirin, *Mum's sleeping pills*, indigestion tablets, milk of magnesia, haemorrhoid ointment. The toiletries half: scented soap, shampoo, *Dad's razor-blades*, fresh flannel, toothpaste, bubble bath.

How to do it?

You're here. You will do it. No going back now.

Ro will be sorry. She'll understand.

It's the only way you can show how you really feel.

You aren't a heartless bastard. You feel things deeply. Too deeply.

The bathroom, as well-lit as a lunatic's high-security cell, is full of shadows. They press in around you.

They aren't unfriendly. They are here to make it easy.
You reach into the cabinet.

If you take the pills, go to 90. If you take the razor-blade, go to 95.

85

The Scam collapses in 1991, owing a lot of people – including you – a lot of money. There's a great deal of acrimony in the collective. You find yourself in a tiny splinter faction, supporting Anne. She travels into nervous-breakdown country. No amount of restructuring or refinancing helps. Debt sinks the dream.

You work as a researcher for independent television, doing a stint as a fact-finder for *Survival Kit*, a street-level consumer programme. You still freelance for *The Guardian* and the *Statesman*. You self-publish pamphlets.

You write exposés of the privatisation programme, showing just how fat cats benefit from the selling-off of public utilities. Your thesis is that the Tory government enthusiastically embraces the Marxist notion of redistribution of wealth, but chooses to redistribute upwards from the broad base of the poor. The few become enormously rich at the expense of the many. You win an award for your investigative work and a token MP has to resign. Nevertheless, privatisation continues like a juggernaut.

You're one of the first to refer in print to the Community Charge as a 'poll tax'. It is still brought in. You refuse to pay yours. You go on marches. You take photographs at a big demo that turns into a riot as police and anarchist groups spoil for a fight in Trafalgar Square. You write about what it's like being on the receiving end of a cavalry charge.

Margaret Thatcher falls from power but John Major wins the next election. All things considered, you hate him more. She was Medusa-cum-Hitler, he's a bureaucrat with an independent nuclear deterrent.

After the death of John Smith and the rise of Tony Blair, you fume at the Labour Party's abandonment of socialism. You hate Blair more than Major. After all, Major wasn't supposed to be on your side. In a whirl of PR and glitz and spin-doctoring and focus groups and public-school hangers-on, New Labour conceals its acceptance of the baton of authoritarianism. The people are cut out of the system.

Democracy has obviously failed. You consider non-electoral activities.

Clare and her girlfriend Maisie get their indie record label together, trading on a resurgence of interest in the bubblegum pop they stayed faithful to all these years. Indirectly, they are responsible for the Spice Girls. You feel the need to join a travellers' convoy.

Your group is harassed by the police, lackeys of the entrenched interests who want to deny you access to the common land of England. Rumours go round that the army will be sent after you. Remembering James, you do your best to organise a militia in the convoy. You work out an early-warning system alerting you to hostile approaches and try to get the more able men and women together as a defence force.

Your fellow travellers find this a bit heavy and don't respond well to the imposition of discipline. A woman called Syreeta condemns you for reverting to patriarchalism and you are expelled.

You are a collective of one.

Why don't others notice they are being ruled by Evil? Why don't your fellow victims respond to your wake-up calls, your attempts to get a resistance together?

You can't work in television any longer. There are too many controlling interests. In the end, the media is wholly owned by monsters like Rupert Murdoch or – your new *bête noire* – Derek Leech. Demon demagogues atop their monolithic corporations are systematically destroying oppositional access to air-time.

But new media develop. A lightweight camcorder allows you to take moving snapshots of the underside of the glorious new society. The Internet lets you get round octopus tentacles of oppression to tell some of the truth. You no longer care about your own voice, you just want to get through to people.

You still follow the links between top politicians – New Labour as much as Old Tory – and big business, observing the way the law of the land is restructured or ignored to the benefit of the powerful. You become increasingly concerned with cultural issues, with the way a thinking, feeling society is being polluted by an invasion of heartless, bread-and-circuses trash.

No publisher is willing to take *Keeping Tabs*, the book you write about the pernicious influence of Murdoch's *Sun* and Leech's *Comet*.

The takeover is complete. The rebels have been rounded up, bought off, disappeared, seduced to the Dark Side of the Force or ridiculed out of the game. It is as if giant spiders from outer space have taken over the world, and now expect to be worshipped for sucking the life out of billions of souls.

You follow the way the media are spreading thin. More and more TV channels fill with less and less content. Soaps and quizzes and porn fill the frequencies, flooding out towards Alpha Centauri, an expanding sphere of mindwashing drivel filling the universe, a poisonous gift for other civilisations. TV and cable and satellite bosses talk about increased choice and the information revolution, but all they deliver is sex and violence and shopping.

Worst of all is the frenzy of greed, hopelessness and tack that surrounds the National Lottery. From the first you hear of it, you are the implacable enemy of this tax on hope, on stupidity, on futility. It's an aesthetic and a moral atrocity, dangling the promise of unimaginable wealth before demoralised and desensitised masses. Tony Blair calls it 'the People's Lottery', which makes you furious. It's not something for the people, it's something done to them. With deliberate malice and deep-seated evil intent.

You make a documentary about impoverished persistent Lottery players, *Losers*. No television station will take it. They claim problems with securing clips rights to *National Lottery Live* from the BBC, and cite the low technical standard of your interview footage. You know you've been silenced. You transcribe *Losers* and post it on your web page. You get a lot of hits but are mail-bombed with criticism. You recognise an orchestrated campaign.

The Lottery has become the engine of oppression. It sucks in huge amounts, which remain unaccounted-for, and distracts the slaves. It keeps the Tories in power far beyond their sell-by date, and makes sure the New Labour government is business as usual for the vampire filth who really run the country.

It poisons all it touches.

You make a follow-up documentary, *Winners*. Case histories of Lottery millionaires are, if anything, sadder than those of the losers. Ordinary people, sold a dream, learn how worthless money really is. You despair at the lack of imagination the winners show. Quite apart from broken families, death threats, descents into addiction or madness and the high suicide rate, the winners are blighted by a poverty of mind that has been deliberately inculcated in them and which no amount of money will ever relieve.

If you had a million pounds, you'd make it *work*. You'd go on the attack.

You're arrested for harassment of big winners and the new law on stalking – rushed through parliament in Blair's first month in office – means you get six months' jail time. The zombie press refers to you as a 'dangerous obsessive' with an 'unhealthy fixation' on Lottery winners. You are tagged as 'the Lottery Stalker'. You state your case clearly whenever you're caught by the media, but are always edited to seem like Lee Harvey Oswald. Of course, he was innocent too.

Released from jail, you're required to have counselling. You're not disturbed. You calmly state your position. In group therapy, you're abused by genuine neurotics. Mad people all play the Lottery, it turns out. Why aren't you surprised?

You open files on the presenters, past and present. Anthea Turner, Dale Winton, Bob Monkhouse, Carol Smillie. Teeth agleam in studio lights, they are obviously part of the problem. They are the spangled attendants of the people-grinding machines, high priests and priestesses of the sacrifice. Each week, twice, the wheels spin, the numbers come up, and countless bloody, beating hearts are ripped out of chests, displayed with a smile for the cameras. And Mystic Meg. If she's really clairvoyant, why can't she see you coming?

One day, the black ball will come up.

On the Internet, you learn about home-made explosives. You compare and contrast the Oklahoma City bomb with the World Trade Center bomb. You go back over all your IRA coverage and dig as far back as the French Resistance. You're amazed at how easy it is if you just work hard. A combination of DIY and cookery, and a little expensive quarry pilferage, should do the trick.

You always watch the Lottery on Saturday and the new mid-week draw on Wednesday. You have to keep tabs on the enemy.

Can't anyone else see the spiders scuttling in the shadows of the studio? Every week, the celebrities who join in the draw add themselves to a list of saddo sell-outs. Some betrayals are worse than others.

You tell your counsellor you think you see a way through your obsession. You're willing to call it that. She is pleased for you.

You're still a trained investigative journalist. You know how to circumvent security arrangements and get into a studio. You can plan ahead.

You assemble your device on a Saturday evening. The television is on in the room. Ignoring *Simon Mayo's Confessions*, you flatten a lump of gelignite into a doughy sheet with a kitchen roller. After sprinkling on a layer of ball-bearing shards and one-inch nails, you make a jumbo-size Swiss roll which will fit into two paint-cans taped mouth to mouth. This is sweaty work. You concentrate furiously. If you don't, there will be problems.

As the Lottery itself comes on, you fix the timer. You want the bomb to detonate just as the numbers are drawn, when the most people are tuned in. Now, you embed terminals in one end of the roll and fix the battery-powered arming device. With pliers, you attach the wires.

Mystic Meg witters generally about this week's winners, making non-specific predictions that still manage to be wrong in every essential. Something flickers across the harridan fraud's face. Has she seen something? Something real? You hope so. The moment passes. After a hesitation, Mystic Meg is back on the waffle.

You look down at the bomb. Where were you? The red wire or the blue wire? Which should you attach next?

Why are you sweating?

Which?

If the red wire, go to 119. If the blue wire, go to 132.

86

She looks around for the cameras, disbelieving you, thinking this is another cruel joke. You feel stabbed.

She throws her arms round your neck, and kisses you, warmly, passionately. Your stone heart dissolves.

* * *

She pulls her arm back, makes a fist, and slams it into your chin. It doesn't hurt much, physically.

She finds her voice and screams, 'Fuck off, you bastard!' You are staggered by the volume.

She says, 'I guess I've been a bitch as much as you've been a bastard. Let's start again from scratch. My name is Rowena.' You think it over and say, 'And I'm Keith.'

She takes your hand, looks you in the eye, and says, 'No, Keith, *I'm* sorry. What happened was my fault. I'm back with Roger.' You want to die.

She hugs you desperately and whispers in your ear, 'Oh, Keith, I've been so worried. I think I'm pregnant.' You don't know what to feel.

She looks through you with eyes like lasers and says, 'You're a monster, Marion.' You are left frozen.

She whispers close to your cheek, 'I can't stop thinking about you, Keith. Please hold me.' You have an erection.

She says, 'Let's be grown-up, Keith. We were both drunk. It won't happen again.' Your hopes die.

She starts crying, sobbing on your shoulder, clutching you ravenously. You can't bring yourself to put your arms round her. You wonder what it was you saw in her.

She tells you she is entering a convent. She has vowed to atone for her sins. She advises you to pray for forgiveness.

She says, 'Do you like my new hairstyle?' You tell the truth and she says, 'Oh well, it'll grow out.' You laugh. You both laugh.

She drops to her knees in the college corridor, students passing all the time, and unzips your fly, fishing out your penis, and wrapping her mouth round it. You look up at the ceiling.

She takes a small-calibre pistol out of her satchel and presses its barrel against your forehead. Smiling like the Mona Lisa, she pulls the trigger.

She smiles and dissolves. You realise you're talking to Mary Yatman. How could you have made such a mistake? 'Rowena?' she says. 'You haven't heard? She killed herself. On New Year's Eve.'

But you were staring at her all through French class.

She looks incredulous and says, 'Do you really *like* me, Keith? After everything? You're a tragic case.' You shrug.

She tears the skin under her chin and peels off her face. Through the glistening red mucus, you recognise that all along Rowena Douglass has been…

She puts a hand on your chest. You can't tell if she's warding you off or pulling her to you. You can't read her expression. You don't know how she feels.

You only know how you feel.

You take it from there.

And so on.

87

It happens in an instant. It doesn't so much hurt as wear you out, as if you'd fast-forwarded through three hours of running after a bus. There's a lurch, and an instant hangover, which instantly vanishes, leaving your brain fogged with the memory of throbbing fuzziness only fractionally different from the sensation itself.

The house is huge. You feel like hugging the walls, afraid of stepping out into the middle of the floor. You don't see how such vast ceilings can be supported.

You aren't quite you. You're smoothly shaved, with well-cut hair. You're heavier, but less flabby. Bending your arms, you feel unfamiliar sheaths of sleek muscle. You aren't Arnie, but you've certainly kept in shape.

One ear is pierced.

Your clothes – jeans and a sweatshirt – were clean-washed when you put them on. Your trainers must have cost £100 each.

Your mouth tastes different. You can't find any cigarettes anywhere, which perhaps explains that.

What have you done?

Who are you?

You are in a kitchen the size of the *Titanic's* ballroom. A copy of *The Independent* lies on an acre of polished table. It's dated 19 November 1990. Today. John Major is prime minister. Tonight's TV listings are familiar. The world hasn't changed radically, just you.

And your life.

From the evidence available in the house, you try to find things out. An envelope confirms that you're Keith Marion, and reveals that you live in Sutton Mallet.

That tips you off.

This is the house Victoria and Graham are squatting…

…*were squatting, in the other world…*

It's your house. You explore. Upstairs, there's a bedroom which you share with your wife. Marie-Laure? You're not sure. There are two rooms that obviously belong to children, a girl and a boy. Jonquil and Josh? The toys don't seem to jibe with the characters you know.

You find a photograph album, a leather-bound volume with perfectly mounted, professionally shot images. You could mistake it for an issue of *Vogue* or a travel brochure, because there are any number of moody black-and-white shots of beautiful people (including, you are shocked to note, you) or parrot-coloured pictures of exotic foreign locales.

You see yourself transformed, comfortable and casual in an unimaginable colour-supplement world that is now yours. And you see, over and over again, your wife and children.

At first, you think the kids are Josh and Jonquil, with more expensive clothes and better haircuts. But this brother and sister are twins, and mixed in with the familiar features of your own kids are other shapes and expressions.

You wonder if you've given these semi-strangers the names you know. You rather hope you haven't.

Your wife is another person. Strangely, she's familiar. Paging backwards, from the elegant and full-figured woman of recent shots, you feel you are peeling away veils and will find an answer. When you get back about seven years, the face is recognisable.

Rowena Cunningham. No, that was a married name. At school she was Rowena Douglass.

Great Shades of Elvis!

You married Rowena Douglass. Of the enormous breasts and tiny voice. Here, she's Rowena Marion.

What do you call her? Honey? Darling? Ro? Wena? Row-Boat?

You can't find Marie-Laure in any photographs.

But who is this Keith Marion? What does he *do*? How did he get to be so rich? And can you – an impostor – keep doing it?

There's an obvious office, with a computer and many locked filing cabinets. The piles of print-outs and other documents don't tell you much, except that your business is international. Your passport, which you find in a desk drawer, is blotched throughout with stamps from dozens of countries.

There are even documents in Japanese. Or Chinese.

If your fortune depends on language skills you don't have in your current incarnation, you are stuffed.

Maybe you can bluff it. Or maybe there's a way out.

If you try to be the new Keith, go to 105. If you fake amnesia, go to 173.

88

Later, when you get home, you put *The Man Who Shot Liberty Valance* into the video. It was a present from Jon, your son, two birthdays back, but you've never watched it. You mentioned once that it was your favourite film when you were his age, and you bought him his favourite film, *Indiana Jones and the Temple of Doom*, for the Christmas before.

When the theme music comes on, you're faintly surprised. For years, you've remembered the Gene Pitney song as being from the film. Now you realise it came out afterwards, inspired by the story.

In the beginning, John Wayne is already dead. In a plain wooden box, forgotten by the town. You know what really killed the Duke.

The Big C.

You aren't sure whether you're coughing or crying.

What is it about this film?

You picked it off the shelf on automatic pilot. You don't really want to watch anything. With what you know, can you afford to spend time on anything trivial?

John Wayne and James Stewart must have been in their fifties when they made the film. Older than you are now. Wayne's gut and Stewart's neck are middle-aged. Even Vera Miles looks almost matronly. But the characters they play are supposed to be young, like Lee Marvin's Liberty Valance.

Why didn't you ever notice that when you were a kid?

Wayne shoots Liberty Valance but Stewart gets the credit and goes on to become a famous politician. Wayne burns his house down and drinks himself to death, getting only a cactus rose on his coffin.

It's a bitter, sad story. Being a hero is a waste of time, the film says. The world belongs to lawyers in aprons who will become stuffy senators.

For the first time since you had the News, you wonder what will happen afterwards. To Ro, to Jon and Jenny, to the bank? Without you, what will become of them?

Without you, do they count, do they exist?

Perhaps with your death – yes, you will die, you can think the word, you have to – the whole world will pack up? Like when a film has finished shooting, they'll come in and take the scenery down, pay off the actors, promise to get together sometime, have a wrap party?

Around your coffin. With a cactus rose plumped on it.

'Nothing's too good for the Man Who Shot Liberty Valance.'

And nothing's what he gets.

Three months. That's it. All you get. There's a lot of pain and indignity and awkwardness and legal stuff, but you don't need to hear that from me. You can imagine. You have to imagine. Is it fair? Is anything?

Rowena suggests joining one of the mass lawsuits being brought against tobacco companies, but you can't say it's not your own fault. Every one of those cigarettes you put in your mouth yourself. It was your mouth that sucked. It's your lungs that are dying on you.

Still, you make the best of it. You are strangely calm. There were problems at work, problems at home. Not any more. You don't even have the worry of not knowing.

Quietly, inevitably, surrounded by your family, letting your grip relax, you go to 0.

89

You find yourself humming the theme for *Top Cat* and fixating on a world of giants, where the ceilings are further away. As you shrink back into your past, your present-day self recedes. You are tempted to let it go, but wonder whether the point isn't to take some of what you are now back to what you were then.

If you hang on, go to 100. If you let go, go to 277.

90

The bottle of sleeping pills is almost full. Mum got a new prescription filled before Christmas. The recommended dose is one tablet per day. A warning says, 'Keep Out of the Hands of Children'.

You might still be a child. Despite everything, you've never been an adult.

You twist the top off.

It's early yet. Mum and Dad won't be home for hours. You have time.

You are serious. You have no doubts.

You take the toothbrushes out of the toothmug. You put four toothbrushes (Mum's, Dad's, Laraine's, James's) in the cabinet, and throw the last one (yours) into the waste-bin under the sink.

You fill the mug with water.

You cram all the pills into your mouth. They taste like chalk, with a bitter undertang.

You take a swig of the water and swallow.

It takes several mouthfuls. But you get them all down. You aren't sick.

You try to think of Ro and can't remember her face.

'Keith, you're pathetic.'

It was Victoria. It was what she said that hurt most. You set about

274   KIM NEWMAN

it wrongly. You should have tried to explain yourself to her.

She was the difficult one. But she might, in the end, have understood.

Your stomach aches, as if you've eaten a dozen unripe apples. You slowly drink another mug of water.

The shadows blot your whole vision now. Your body is very heavy. You sit on the toilet, weighed down by your limbs. Your head lolls.

Black bands close in around your head.

Go to 0.

91

You leave Mary's house quietly, locking up behind you with her keys – which you later throw away – and wiping your feet on the doormat.

A pattern is complete. You are unassailable, now. The last person who could have stood up to you is neutralised.

You wonder if you are disappointed. When it came down to it, Scary Mary was no opponent. Her monster was long gone. The life she had made for herself weakened her, reduced her from the fearsome creature she might have been.

Now, Mary has been fucked and dumped.

Rowena, oddly, is the person to tell you. She telephones, as she does from time to time on the pretext of getting you involved in one of her charities, and asks if you remember Mary Yatman from school.

'Scary Mary?'

The line goes quiet. Then she tells you.

It is hard not to laugh but you manage it.

You offer a reward and make solemn pronouncements.

Geoff Starkey gets the blame, as you knew he would. He has a history of drinking, and you've arranged a social worker's report to mark him down as a hazard to his son. Will is taken into care and anything he might say about the Man Who Was Interested in Dinosaurs is disregarded. That was the breakthrough. Realising that what Will might say didn't count.

Sedgwater expands, as you have planned, spreading along the main roads, absorbing several former villages. Sutton Mallet becomes a residential district. You buy property there. You even consider living there.

You marry, have children. You diversify, from property into information, from the concrete into the abstract. The new millennium comes and seems to belong to you, to people like you. You win awards, honours. You almost become famous.

In the years that pass after Mary, you realise you are not unique. Others have been to Sutton Mallet and learned what you learned. Some recognise your strength and offer themselves as disciples. You despise most of them, but are pleased.

You have everything anyone could want. And you keep it for a long time.

But in the end, you are fucked.

And dumped.

What he said didn't count but what he knew stayed with him.

A quarter of the way into the new century, in a Sutton Mallet you could never have predicted, you are found; and found out.

Will Yatman still has his mother's eyes.

And it's hard not to feel he has inherited his mother's monster.

At the end, as you look up from your bloodied bed at Mary Yatman's beautiful eyes staring out of a hard man's face, you wonder if you won after all. Maybe the shadow-spiders were just using you, as you used so many others, fucking you.

And dumping you.

He has to tell you who he is, but you knew right away.

'I didn't always like your mother,' you say.

He ends you before you can complete the sentence.

Go to 0.

92

*B*lit blurt…

All the lives fall away, like scales from your eyes.

This is the here and now.

You're running across wasteland, on a cold day. Your lungs hurt, and you have to be careful of your footing. You can't afford a twisted ankle.

Because of the shadow-spiders.

You have no past, no future.

The only thing in your mind is the shadow-spiders.

If pressed, you wouldn't know your name; if you were married, whether you had a living family.

You don't know where you are.

But the shadow-spiders are after you.

Ranging from about the bodyweight of a large cat to biology-defying monsters the size of the Albert Hall, the shadow-spiders are after you.

They scuttle with alarming speed.

You are in the open. You have been sighted.

This is your place. They are the intruders.

You pick up and put down your feet. You draw in and let out your breath.

That's all.

…blit blurt.

93

Friday, 13 February 1998. You get home first, just after six. It's already dark and the exterior light above the garage door has come on. You drive into the former barn that serves as a garage and park neatly in your space. You get out and feel a slight tingle. It's not the cold, it's the night. Your Fiat clicks as you activate central locking, a turtle making itself cosy.

You stand in your garage, enjoying the quiet moment. A sense of belonging. Then you go indoors, through the kitchen door as usual. A present is propped up on the table, with a card. It is not a valentine, but an end-of-the-week present; you and Ro have been exchanging them for sixteen years, never repeating, never spending more than five pounds. This week, you've got her a Hercules fridge magnet. You wonder what she's got you.

Ro is a teacher, at your old school. Ash Grove is a well-respected Comprehensive now. Your own children, Joel and Jacintha – who are out at the Youth Theatre tonight – go there. Ro teaches French, German and English, and coaches netball. She keeps in touch with many of her former pupils and the corkboard in the kitchen is plastered with postcards. Her first pupils have school-age kids of their own.

There are four homes in Sutton Mallet now, all converted farmhouses. Two are owned by people who live in London and only appear at the weekends. One of those has been neglected for nine months, since its owner suffered a reversal and has had to put it on the block to finance a desperate stock deal. There are no takers at the moment.

You feel sorry for people who think of the world in terms of money and what it can buy. You have seen them coming into the bank, always steering into choppy waters. You and Ro know there are more important ways of keeping the score. Ways that matter.

The bank is behind you, as sealed off in your mind as its locked vaults. When you left your office at five-thirty, you blanked out all details of any business you were working on. At nine-thirty on Monday morning, it will all be in your mind, clear and ready.

The weekend is sacred. It is for personal projects.

You strip off your suit as you go upstairs, remembering the long-gone objects – plastic comb, picture frame, toothbrush – once placed on each step. It is a game between you and your wife. Sometimes, when each thinks the other is off guard, you will quiz each other. Neither has ever caught the other out.

In the recently fitted master bathroom, you take a shower. Outside, it's crisply cold. You let hot water pour on to your chest, down your legs, into your eyes. You lobster yourself, scalding away your weekday skin.

While you are showering, Ro comes home. She comes into the bathroom, having followed your clothes, and removes her suit with easy movements, as if giving birth to her nude self. When the outer coating of Miss Douglass – she keeps her maiden name in the week – is pooled on the floor, she undoes her hair and combs it out.

You finish your shower and towel yourself.

Together, you go to your bedroom. Your tradition now is that you share the task of lighting all the candles. When that's done, you cuddle, and ease into making love. You can still surprise each other. Underlying your union is something beyond the physical. But sex is still at the centre of it.

You both owe Victoria Conyer a great debt.

With the kids out for the evening, you enjoy yourselves.

Then, in the candlelight, you glow.

Go to 99.

94

The day after Sean hands in his notice, he introduces Tristram Warwick to you. He is to take over as manager and will be around for the next three months to learn the ropes.

At once, you know Tristram is a threat to you. He will find you out. He will bring down the Syndicate.

He has the power to take everything away from you.

You check the street. No one is near enough to be a witness. You press the buzzer and the entryphone hums incomprehensibly.

'Tristram,' you say, 'it's Keith Marion.'

The door buzzes open. You step into the hallway, followed by Vanda. You exchange a look with your wife.

Tristram has a flat at the top of a modern building, in a decent part of town. Once confirmed in his job, he'll probably buy a house.

He won't be confirmed in his job. He will be found. Dead.

You go upstairs.

You're let into the flat by someone you know, Kay Shearer, of Shearer's Shelves.

'God,' he says shrilly, 'I hope you're not still chasing those bloody repayments.'

Kay wears a tracksuit, as if about to go jogging.

Tristram steps out into the hallway. He wears a towelcloth robe. His hair is wet. He rubs his eyes with a hand-towel.

'What is it, love?' he asks Kay.

Then he sees you and Vanda.

'Marion,' he says.

'This is my wife, Vanda,' you say.

'What do you want?'

'To save us all a lot of trouble.'

You made up a noose from nylon washing line. You take it out of your pocket and let it out a little.

Kay understands first and tries to bolt.

You planned for Tristram to be not alone. It's Vanda's department. Kay slams into her, sliding himself on to the new-bought Sabatier knife, mouth opening in a big circle.

You get the noose over Tristram's head and yank it tight. You remembered the nautical knots you studied as a child during your pirate craze. The line tightens around Tristram's neck. His face goes purple.

Vanda pulls out the knife and finds a point on Kay's chest to thrust, slipping the blade between ribs, into the heart.

Tristram flops like a doll.

They are both dead.

Excellent.

Fine. You aren't being investigated at work. No one is picking through your files, gathering evidence. Your mortgage isn't being inspected by an intelligence vast, cool and unsympathetic.

But Sean and Ro are still breaking up. That crisis continues.

What to do?

Ro has to go. The Syndicate needs Sean.

You and Vanda tell Sean. He agrees.

You hire Candy as a babysitter and Sean and Ro send their kids over to your house. Candy will have her hands full with four little terrors. But you need them all out of the way.

You hold a Syndicate meeting and encourage Ro to get drunk. The three of you hold back, and watch her get insensible. The idea is that she will have an accident while driving over to pick up the kids.

You drive out in both your cars, Sean with Ro lolling in the passenger seat. You stop by the Sutton Mallet turn-off and get out. It's an awkward struggle getting the feebly resisting Ro into the driver's seat and belted in, but Vanda coaxes her.

It's well past midnight. No one drives by.

Sean lets off the handbrake and the three of you heave on his car, pitching it over the verge into the shallow ditch. Ro burbles in childish delight as the water seeps around her ankles. Sean opens the passenger door and climbs in next to her, easing himself into the seat. He holds Ro's hand and smiles at her. She has no idea what is happening.

Vanda finds a large stone and smashes the windshield. It dents and shatters.

Sean has Ro bend forwards over the wheel, getting some slack into her seatbelt, stretching it tight over her neck. Then he yanks her head hard.

The idea is to snap her neck on the belt. Ro yelps and laughs. Sean didn't tug hard enough.

You wade into the ditch, soaking yourself up to the knees, and reach into the car. You grab Ro's head, seeing the panic in her eyes, and *pull*. You feel her neckbones straining.

Vanda gets in on the act, forcing Ro's head from the other side. The seatbelt is throttling her.

You both wrench. There is a snap. And Ro is dead.

You leave Vanda standing by the road and Sean in the car next to his dead wife, then drive home to call the police.

The Syndicate is preserved.

Sean is sobered after the 'accident' – the autopsy reveals how unfit to drive Ro was – and you take more and more charge of the business.

The pressure is off. But there's still the Crash.

Somehow, you forgot about that. You knew the problems Tristram and Ro would cause, but did not understand that the Crash was not warded off by your efforts.

When it happens, you get over to Sean's place before he can skip out.

He is still in the family home.

'Keith, Vanda...'

You surprise him packing.

The two of you drag him downstairs into his basement DIY room. You clamp his hands between vices and apply power drills to his legs.

He tells you where the money is. You make holes in his head.

You and Vanda are covered in Sean's blood when you get upstairs. You think you can recover the money. Sean has involved so many people in the Syndicate that it will be assumed that he was the victim of a professional assassin.

As you walk into Sean's hallway, the front door opens.

Candy steps in, with Sean and Ro's kids, Megan and Liza.

You don't hesitate. Vanda takes the kids. You take Candy.

You drag them down to the DIY room and finish the job.

Detective Sergeant Yatman remembers you both from school.

She used to be Scary Mary.

Vanda makes coffee as the policewoman comments on how nice your kitchen is. She has come to ask about what happened at Sean's house. They have a suspect, she says. You know she means Councillor Hackwill. He's crooked as a corkscrew. Everyone who went to school a few years behind him remembers his violent streak.

Mary drinks the coffee Vanda has made. She finishes the pleasantries and starts asking questions. You try to answer.

Mary coughs. You politely ask if she is all right. Mary coughs again and bends double. She is sick, bringing up blood with her vomit.

Vanda washes out the coffee pot.

Mary lies on the floor, bending shut like a pocket-knife. She is leaking from several holes. After a while, Mary stops jerking.

'Serves her right,' Vanda says.

Read 13, and come back here.

There are more police, more bank officials, more investors, more auditors. You can't kill them all.

You know Vanda is looking for a way out.

Before she can turn you in, you resolve to deal with her. But she is ahead of you. You get up early one morning and find her half of the bed empty. You pull on a dressing-gown and visit her in the kitchen, a claw hammer behind your back.

She smiles. Your bare feet are in a pool of water.

The toaster lies on its side on the floor. Its wires have been wrenched out and lie in the water.

You raise the hammer. Vanda flicks a switch.

Go to 103.

95

This is going to make a mess.

You don't take the blade out of the razor Dad is using. You take a fresh pack, one of those little plastic dispensers.

It's best if you're in the bath. The warm water will sweep you away without pain.

You put the plug in and let the taps run. Steam covers the windows and the mirror. You are no longer looking at yourself.

You take off your clothes, letting them fall where they may, and sit in the bath. It's too hot, but you let it pass. Your body goes lobster red.

You are supposed to punish yourself, after all.

You slide a blade out of the dispenser and cut your fingers getting the paper off the shiny sliver of sharpness. Drops of blood splash into the bathwater and disperse in red threads.

Where to cut?

If you had an old-fashioned Sweeney Todd straight razor, you suppose you'd have a chance of opening your throat. That would be the best thing: sure and certain and swift.

But the Wilkinson's Sword blade is barely two inches long and thinner than a wafer-thin mint. You couldn't even find your femoral artery – it's in your thigh somewhere – to puncture it. So, it's the wrists then.

Both of them?

You'll have to do one and see if you're in any state to finish the job.

You look at your left wrist. You see the blue line of the vein. Easy. Just slice across it.

You hope Ro won't be too upset. This isn't really about her. It's about you.

Keith, this is *your* suicide.

The thin sliver is pressed between your right thumb and forefinger. It is sticky with blood from your minor cuts.

You look at your vein. Do you draw a line across you wrist? Or do you cut in at the wrist and carve down, following the vein?

Across? Or down?

If across, go to 97. If down, go to 98.

96

The hardest part is remembering the name. You lie awake beside Rowena after she has silently cried herself to sleep, remembering his face, his voice, his habits. He was the neat boy. Not inspired, but neat. Full marks for anything that involved copying out presentably.

Which was most things. Probably still is.

Mickey Yeo, who wrote and drew comic books for a while, and Norman Pritchard, who went to jail when they caught him in the front seat of a car with a hundred car keys on a chain, still bob about vividly in your recollection. You remember Norman firing the branch at Mickey, and Mickey hamming up his

death

Liberty Valance act.

Who was the boy who gave you your first cigarette? The one you sucked on, trying to understand the appeal. You must have smoked a dozen fags over two or three years before you learned how to take the smoke into your lungs

that's the killer

but it was that first one that started it.

Without Neat Boy, you'd be alive.

Finally, you decide to do it by elimination. You can still remember the class register. You heard it every day for years. Like the Lord's Prayer, it's written into your memory for ever.

Adlard, Allen, Banner...

Adlard, Stephen. He was the first in the register. That's what marked him out. First alphabetically, he had to be first in presentation.

You don't know what happened to him. Neat boys don't do memorable things, not like Mickey or Norman. Neat boys don't go to Beverly Hills or Strangeways.

Your chest is like concrete, anchoring you to the bed. You are tired of the pain, the constant tiny tearing of Velcro fishhooks inside you.

Stephen Adlard.

He's in the local telephone book. He lives about three miles away, at a nondescript address, 96 Raleigh Road.

You have his number. Should you call? What would you say? What are you going to say?

You remember his sardonic posture, offering

death

the Players packet, daring you to take your first drag, to begin your protracted assisted suicide. You remember Adlard's head cocked to one side, not egging you on, knowing you had no choice. If you hesitated you'd be the prig, the softie, the good boy. And he'd be hard like Mickey and Norman. He'd be with them, attracting the girls' attention. Bobby Moore said smoking was a mug's game, but you had no choice, you had to be a mug or an outcast. You'd be the bald coon – yes, you called black people coons when you were thirteen, you did, you did – in the shadows, whose name nobody could remember. Adlard knew what he was doing when he

began murdering you

made cigarettes available to you.

It was 1973. You were kids; nothing counted yet. Was Ro one of the girls who'd just walked past? No, that would have been too neat. But she was at the Girls' Grammar then. You might even have seen her. Within a year, at Ash Grove, you'd be sitting behind her in French, wondering about her as you wondered about all the girls, not knowing, as you wouldn't know for years, that she'd become your wife, the mother of your children.

Back then, Jon and Jenny weren't.

as you won't be

That first cigarette couldn't be the most important decision of your life. No, that was whether to ask Rowena or Victoria to the Rag Day party. Or whether to go to university after college or take the job your dad arranged at the bank. Or what to call the kids.

But you can remember it. Like you can remember your first kiss. God, Vanda Pritchard, Norman's twin sister. Or the first time you had sex. With Rowena who, apart from Jacqui Edwardes that one time at college when you'd had an argument with Ro, is the only woman you've ever slept with

or ever will

and now you wonder if you should have tried harder, when desire was still important to you, to make love with more girls, women.

Denbeigh Gardens, long gone under the Discount Development. *Man Who Shot Liberty Valance.* Mickey Yeo, Norman Pritchard

and Stephen mr fucking death's neat blue-eyed boy adlard

It's a weekend. Adlard will probably be home.

You stand at the end of Raleigh Road, thinking you should be able to identify Adlard's house by its neatness. But you can't. None of the semi-detacheds – large, spacious, 1930s homes: the Death Cunt must be doing well for himself – is more precisely perfect than the next.

You come to Number 96. It should be Number 13, or Number

666. There's a girl's bicycle on the lawn, its yellow bum-shaped seat scuffed. The grass could do with cutting. Neat Boy is slipping.

If you had a shotgun, this would be easier. The most lethal implement in your possession is a small hatchet, for kindling. No, you're wrong. The most lethal substance in your possession

apart from fucking fags

is in the petrol tank of your car.

You could walk through town with a full plastic jerry-can, you suppose. People would assume you'd run out somewhere and were going back to your car. But people don't run out of petrol in towns. Too many garages.

So you've rescued empty plastic screw-top bottles – milk, lemonade, Coke, the bigger the better – from the rubbish and filled them. These you have put in a suitcase and dragged through the streets.

You would have driven, but you're low on fuel since you siphoned it out. Your hands still stink from the messy business of pouring and the sleeves of your sports jacket are soaked. Your wrists feel as if ten-ton weights are fixed to them. The case got heavier and heavier as you hauled it along your own personal *via dolorosa*.

You've had to stop every few yards to have a cough

because you're a fucking walking dead man

and a rest.

You're in so much pain you know you won't enjoy this. But it has to be done. There has to be an answer.

Should you ring the doorbell?

Adlard might be out. Then you'd have to wait.

No. If he'd gone out, he'd have seen that untidy bicycle besmirching his lawn. Neat Boy would have tidied it up, put it in some bicycle-shaped spot, battened it down as tight as a cat's arsehole. Neat Boy probably numbered, weighed and sorted into alphabetical order his bowel movements.

You hump the sloshing suitcase across the lawn. The bottom leaks. One of the bottles must have been cracked.

Too late to worry about that.

It's nearly over.

You don't think of your wife and children. You think of Neat Boy. And the killing concrete in your chest, clogging all the passages, spider-leg tendrils of pain winding throughout your whole body.

You get the case up on the doorstep and have a coughing fit. It must be louder than ringing any bell could possibly be. You thump the wall and hawk. Black stuff, with bloody chunks in it, comes up. That's lung tissue, that is. That's disease in a basket, death on a stick.

The world is going to end. For you. No. For everyone. Without you, nothing counts. Before then, though, scales can be adjusted.

You stand on a porch, looking at a panel door. There's an ornamental knocker and a functional bell. Frosted glass side-panels, with etched naked fat babies playing musical instruments. A sunrise-pattern semi-circular fanlight, segmented like an orange, each segment a different-coloured glass. Slumped over your suitcase, you must look like a demented door-to-door salesman.

death of same

You brought the hatchet just in case. After the spasms have subsided, you chop at the door, by the chest-height lock. The hatchet embeds itself. As you pull it out, the door opens inwards.

Neat Boy looks at you through an adult mask, an absurd wisp of blond moustache gummed to his lip. He is thinning on top. He wears only a towel. You can't help noticing he has an erection.

'Good God, no!' he gasps.

Hatchet in one hand, dragging the case with the other, you lurch at him, pushing him aside, and stagger into his hallway. The weight of the case has an independent impetus, and dredges an occasional table from the wall, scattering a telephone and an answerphone, smashing a pot-plant.

'We can be reasonable,' Adlard says.

You have interrupted something, but don't care. Neat Boy didn't just interrupt you. He ended you.

will end you

'It's unconventional, Mr Pelham. But Aimée is over sixteen. She…'

A chubby girl stands at the top of the stairs, a sheet wrapped around her, held to her chest.

'That's not my father,' she screams.

Adlard lays a hand on your shoulder.

Coughing, dribbling blood, you whirl round, hatchet outstretched. Adlard gets out of the way, losing his towel. Through pain, you focus on your case, which lies flat and leaking a few feet away, at the foot of the stairs.

You chop down, rupturing the case, and chop again, aiming for the clasps. You wrench the case open and chop at the bottles. They roll and rupture and squirt. You lose the hatchet.

'Petrol,' the girl shouts.

You empty the bottles on the floor, on the stairs, on yourself, on the walls. It gets in your eyes. You don't think you're breathing any more. You're so clogged up you're just going to stop.

Soon.

Then, the bottles emptied and strewn about Neat Boy's hallway, messing it up beyond repair, you turn and look for Adlard. Naked, appalled, not understanding, he stares at you. You want him to recognise you, to remember. You try to explain.

But you can't talk, you can only choke.

You take Stephen Adlard by his skinny shoulders and pull him to you. Hugging tight, you fall on to your case, empty and broken plastic bottles beneath you. Adlard struggles but your grip is fixed, iron.

He was the one who used to have the light. Now it's you.

You get Neat Boy in a neck-lock and probe in your pocket for the disposable lighter. You took a fresh one from the kitchen drawer.

Adlard's heels skid on his petrol-sodden carpet. He is not impressing his girlfriend now. His neatness means nothing

this close to death

his crimes are about to come home.

Your thumb scrabbles on the lighter.

The girl screams.

You toss the lighter, like John Wayne hurling the lamp to burn down his life after Jimmy Stewart has taken the credit for shooting Liberty Valance and stolen away Vera Miles.

You hear the fire before you feel the heat. It starts as warmth, then becomes biting pain, nipping through even the bled-out aches in your chest.

The whole world is screaming.

A rivulet of fire runs up the stairs, towards the yelling girl's naked feet. You smell Neat Boy's cooking meat. You can't relax your hold on him.

Something caves in inside you.

Go to 0.

97

There's a tiny sting as the edge of the blade slips in. You instinctively put your hand under water. The heat covers the sting. A flower of blood blooms in the bath. It's very pretty.

Are you sure about this?

You cut. Another flower.

Sure you're sure.

Further. A big, gulping, blossoming rose explodes from your wrist.

That's it. The vein cut.

You drop the blade. You're too weak to do the other wrist. You feel you're draining.

The bathwater is mostly red. It laps at your body, leaving a red-wine-dreg bath-ring on your white skin.

It doesn't hurt.

You pull the plug with your toes, but turn the taps back on with your left hand, keeping your bleeding right wrist under the water all the time.

Water flows. You lie back in the warm and let it flow.

You can't remember why you're doing this.

Blood slips slowly towards the plughole, swirls in the mini-maelstrom, and slides away.

You don't pass out. You look at the ceiling light fixture.

The water has drained from under you.

Hot and cold water pours on to your ankles, scalding and chilling.

You're bleeding less. The end must be near. You must be empty.

No time for regrets.

Should you have written a note? No. This will be a mystery. Everyone will blame themselves: Ro, Victoria, your parents, your lecturers, everyone. They should have seen it coming.

Your ankles really do hurt. You shift them out of the way, and sit up.

You've stopped bleeding.

Your right ankle is scalded badly. It hurts like a bastard.

You must have no blood left at all, eight pints gone. Your heart thumps, trying to propel smidgens through collapsed arteries and veins.

You do feel weak.

You don't get up. Your ankle throbs. The running taps sound like waterfalls. You are very cold, chilled from the water, your lobster-boiled skin cooling fast.

You lie there for a long time.

You don't die.

You did it the wrong way. Serious suicides cut down. Just-a-plea-for-help bogus self-murder feebs cut across.

You could get up and tidy things away.

No, you've lost too much blood. You don't have the control.

You hear, distantly, your family coming back home, bustling through the front door.

Who'll be first for the bathroom?

There's no way of explaining this as an accident. They'll know what you've tried to do. It'll change the way they think of you. Doctors will be called. You'll be taken to hospital. Then the police, maybe. Psychiatrists, certainly.

You'll be a freak celebrity specimen. The Boy Who Tried to Kill Himself.

This is indeed what happens. As you predicted, everyone blames themselves. Your parents are distraught and keep apologising to you in different ways. They argue quietly when they think you can't hear, blaming each other. This gets increasingly bitter and, after twenty-five years, they break up, ripping apart your family. In hospital, you are visited by Victoria and Rowena, but have no explanation for them and don't know how to accept their apologies. Relatives and friends visit, all cheery. Even your lecturers. Everyone walks on eggshells around you. It gets irritating. You wish someone would give you a hard time, tell you off, shout at you. Even Victoria is conciliatory, which disappoints you. She ought to be the one to scream and shred your pose. You sense the power your act has given you, the enormous hold your weakness gives you over others. You hate yourself for it but it becomes the keynote of your life. You'll always be the Boy Who Tried to Kill Himself. No matter what you do, everyone will always remember.

Maybe you go to university and word gets out there, lending you a certain neurotic glamour. Maybe you take months off college and miss your A Levels, becoming an oddly healthy invalid, hanging around at home as if you were retired, holding audiences with supplicants. Everyone wants you to forgive them. Since you have shown yourself too precious for the world, maybe you are looked after by everyone. Cotton wool is wrapped round you and you don't interact with the world. You don't leave home, but your home leaves you when your parents split. You're still clever. You can catch up in schoolwork. You can get on with your life. With your first family gone, you can get another – you could ask Ro or Victoria or any one of a dozen others to marry you, and they would through love or guilt or fear of what you'll do if they don't or a belief that they alone can save you. And you'll always be the dominant partner, because you've proved what you'll do, how awful you can make it for people, if you're not allowed to have your way.

You live a long life. If others get fed up with you, they have to keep it to themselves. You can have children and extend your powers over them too. Even grandchildren will be wary of you. Whispered tales of the Boy Who Tried to Kill Himself will pass down in your family. You never explain, never tell why. Within months, you don't remember anyway.

When, finally, you are dying, of natural causes, you don't recognise the shadows around your bed. There are too many people in the way, people who genuinely love you because they have no choice, pushing the darkness back out of the family circle.

You ask a grandson if he likes imaginary stories and he doesn't know what you mean. He is a grown-up. He has lived with your legendary potential for self-murder all his life. From whispered family rumour to calmly repeated and much-embroidered anecdote, he has known about this.

You have to tell someone at the end.

That you didn't mean it.

But you don't.

Go to 0.

98

There's a vicious sting as the edge of the blade rips in. You yelp with pain. Blood dribbles. You drop the razor-blade. Blood squirts. You try to staunch it with your hand.

What the fuck are you doing?

You stand up in the bath. Blood pouring out of you.

You don't want this.

That bitch Rowena has no right.

So she didn't phone you back. Tough fucking luck. Big fucking deal.

You just wanted to apologise, to make her feel better, and she's nearly murdered you.

No. That's not fair.

She's locked in her own Roger-and-Victoria-and-Rowena misery and just let you in for a while. She didn't understand what you could have done for her. She thought you were disposable.

She was thinking like a bloke. Fuck 'em and dump 'em.

You grip your wounded wrist hard. The blood makes the grip slippery.

Your feet are boiling. You step out of the bath and sit naked on the toilet.

You've come back from a trip into the shadows.

You have no idea how you could have let it get so out of hand. How you could have thought yourself into such a hole.

There's a horrible possibility that Ro is in her bathroom doing exactly the same thing, but she's thinking about Roger not you.

What a fucking mess!

Make that a literal mess. There's a bath speckled with blood. And a used razor-blade. And you're still bleeding like a pig.

The bathroom cabinet is still open.

You open your hand and look at the cut. It's tiny, not deep, but it's bleeding profusely.

Before you can put on a jumbo-sized plaster and think up an excuse you have to wash the wound. You pull the bathplug and stick your wrist under the cold tap. Blood pours out, washes away. You worry that you may die after all.

You came close. Now you're thinking, you remember that cutting down is the not-a-plea-for-help-actual-attempt-at-self-slaughter method.

You are an idiot.

Your wrist is clean. Blood is still welling. You dab with a dry flannel. You have to blot the water before you can use the plaster.

Ready.

Only now you have, one-handed, to get a plaster out of its paper packet and peel off the backing. You do it, using your left hand as a last resort, but now there's blood all over your wrist, chest, the sink and – God, you can't clean it – the bathmat.

You wipe the blood away and put the plaster on skewed. It soaks through at once.

You expect it to be washed away.

You are angry with yourself. This would be a stupid way to die.

You look at yourself in the mirror. The shadows are gone.

'Fuck you,' you tell yourself. 'You're the pillock of the century.'

Then, with difficulty, you clean the bathroom. You've ruined a flannel, but you can bin it and no one will notice. The coin-sized blood-spots on the bathmat have faded. They resist scrubbing, but they look like spilled oil or something.

By the time your parents are back, you've tidied everything, got dressed and are watching *Blood From the Mummy's Tomb* on BBC2. You can look at severed bleeding hands without feeling queasy. It's just a film.

'I thought you wanted to get your head down early,' Mum says.

'I changed my mind,' you admit.

For weeks, you walk around with a sense of your own power. You've been to the worst place in the world and have come back. You are invulnerable. You see Rowena at college and she is obviously not comfortable around you, but you remain civil, distantly amiable. By Easter, she has apologised for her behaviour and you have told her it was all right and said that you were just worried about her. She confirms Rag Day was all about her and Roger. You just got in the way. You hug her and become her friend. Maybe more than that. But maybe not. It doesn't matter. It can't hurt you any more.

You are more relaxed with your family and your peers. You discover talents beyond those programmed into you. You are surprised to find that people like you. Even stranger, you like them. That was more difficult than loving. And you explore your ability to love too, not just in connection with sex but in your other relationships. A distance you have always felt, between you and other people, between you and yourself, fades like the tiny scar on your wrist.

Only you know about the night in the bathroom.

Eventually, years later, you will tell someone. In return for their deepest, darkest secret, you will explain.

She won't quite believe you, but she will love you.

Even if she's Rowena.

There are still shadows in your life. There's no escaping from that. But there is so much else.

And so on.

99

Finally, you understand.

The struggle is not over. But you realise that the struggle is what keeps you alive. It is the light you love and the dark you fear, wrapped together.

You are not alone.

'I know what love is, Keith. Love is us.'

It is possible. It can be done.

You love and are loved. You have the respect of your peers, and the admiration of society.

You can be rich *and* happy.

You truly live your life, swimming along in the mad, glorious, fascinating, ever-changing torrent.

'You know, Keith, sometimes I think I'd like to be like you. But you're one of a kind. When they made you, they broke the mould.'

'A good job too,' you say, pleased.

You are a success as a son, a lover, a husband, a father. Your work is satisfying, challenging, remunerative, important. Your home is an endless, absorbing, rewarding project.

'Thank you, Dad. Thank you for *everything*.'

You have friends who don't envy you your luck. You are a part of many groups, always close to the centre. You are admired, not piously. Your advice is sought, listened to, often acted on. If you're not there, people wish you were.

'Keith, no one will ever know what this means to me. But I won't forget.'

* * *

You leave the world a better place than it was when you found it. And you are remembered.

Your children carry on.

In the light, you understand everything.

'You always knew, Keith. I never had to do anything. This was just what you expected.'

And so on.

100

But where do you want to be? What do you want to change?

If you want to be a child again, go to 107. If you want to be a teenager, go to 111.

101

You've had sex with your sister. On a cosmic scale, this is not reckoned a good thing.

You can't even blame raging, blazing hormones. An irresistible, blinding lust didn't fall on the both of you like an epileptic fit. It just happened.

It was slow, awkward, gentle. You'd like to think it was a hypnotic spell. But it was what you both wanted to do. And did.

Now, in the bed Laraine usually shares with Sean, as afternoon wears on and your sister dozes, you feel calm – oh God, *satisfied*? – and wait for the shame bomb to explode.

It doesn't.

You felt bad (if also a little smug) about making love with Clare one lunchtime and Anne in the evening. You don't like to think about the time at university when you, nineteen, had screaming sex with Chrissie, only fourteen.

This isn't like that.

Of course, you're afraid. If anyone finds out, you'll both enter a world of trouble. You're not sure about the legal situation, but incest (bad word) is definitely against the law. You have some idea you can be jailed for it. At the least, you'll suffer personal and professional ruin and have to go through mandatory counselling with all the – other? – sex offenders. Then again, fucking Chrissie was illegal.

Laraine is a reasonable, adult, thinking person. Unlike Chrissie, who was a kid on amphetamines. Are you an adult? Are you responsible? Are you proud of yourself? Would it be so terrible to answer 'yes'?

Laraine wakes and slips her arms round you. She must be having the same agonies you are.

Mustn't she?

'Sean will be home soon,' she says.

Being found like this by Sean would be a catastrophe.

You sit up in bed. Your clothes are neatly folded on a chair.

'How do you feel?' you ask.

Stupid question.

Laraine is serene. With this intimacy, her earlier jitteriness is gone. 'At least now I've done something worth being hit for.'

You get up and dress, self-conscious that your sister is seeing you naked.

Laraine stretches out under the duvet. 'You go downstairs, Keith. I'll have a shower. Stay for supper, why don't you?'

'Is that a good idea?'

'We left the Good Idea Country a while back.'

You potter about the kitchen as your sister showers. It's surreally familiar, being left alone in the home of someone you've just slept with. As usual, you want to make tea and don't know in which cupboards the cups and tea things are kept or how the kettle works.

You note how differently other people arrange their kitchens. Laraine and Sean keep their cutlery drawer segmented into knives, forks and spoons, in that order, heads pointing into the drawer, with teaspoons horizontally below them. You just dump your cutlery in anyhow. Cups hang from hooks in size order, like a crocodile of schoolchildren.

This is a distraction.

You look out of the window. Darkness begins to fall on the moor.

Sutton Mallet was almost abandoned when you were growing up. It had a reputation as a haunted place. Sometimes, braver kids – James among them – would play in the derelict houses, but you never did. Now it's a neat little community with central heating.

The only thing haunting it is guilt.

Yours. And, you assume, Laraine's. But are you guilty mostly because you *don't* feel so guilty about something the world has always told you that you ought to? What's so wrong about non-coercive incest? It's not as if you're going to have mutant babies.

Laraine comes down, dressed up a little, as if to go out, and made up carefully. She looks like you in drag. Feminised, but with your basic face. Was your attraction a function of narcissism?

You don't know whether to touch or hug or what. Again, this isn't that different from your experience with women you aren't related to.

You've been together. Now what?

'Here's Sean now,' Laraine says.

You see his car easing powerfully into the garage. You gulp hot tea.

Sean comes out of the garage, smiling like a good bloke.

Laraine is tense. But, from what she said earlier, she would have been anyway. Coming-home time, after a rough day at the bank, is when Sean is most likely to use his fists.

You are here to protect her.

Sean comes into the house.

'Hello Keith,' he says, dumping his car and door keys in the bowl on the phone table in the hall. 'I didn't know you'd be here.'

You'd thought Sean might instantly sniff out what has happened between you and Laraine and fly into a Mr Hyde rage, laying into you both with the poker. But, of course, one of the positive things about unthinkable acts is that few people think of them until they have to.

'Stay for dinner?' Sean asks.

If you stay, go to 106. If you make an excuse and leave, go to 117.

102

James is delighted to see you. It's years since you visited the Marion Group Building.

Your younger brother still looks trim. Compensating for his missing leg means he has taken care of the rest of himself. Your hair is white but his is only just grey.

'I don't have so much to do here these days,' James says. 'You should come by more often.'

James's office staff are pleased to meet you.

'Place runs itself, you know,' James says.

He isn't going to like being told what happens when he lets the place run itself.

'Can we talk in private?' you say.

James is instantly alert. He knows you well enough not to protest or make a fuss. Between you, you know what's serious.

You sit in a hoverchair, while James gloves through the system, powering up search bugs. This is Jasper's world, but James knows enough tech to penetrate the system. What gives Jasper away is that he has ice-protected data areas which should be open if they were legit.

James takes it worse than you. A single tear leaks from his eye. He is heart-sick at the betrayal.

You feel ashamed for Jasper.

When Jasper was a child, it was always Uncle James who gave him the systems he wanted as presents. Always Uncle James who processed.

When James is sure Jessamyn was right – you didn't ask how she found out, but your guess is she was an early collaborator with her brother but had a falling-out with him – he overrides all systems with his own vocode and shuts down, locking Jasper out.

'He'll get round that,' he says.

You wait in the office, with your brother. James seems older now than you. Screens iris but James accepts no calls.

'He'll come here,' he says.

Jasper does.

James runs through the severance package and gives generous terms. Waivers are drawn up ready for Jasper's blood-spot on the DNA type box.

James doesn't ask why.

You feel you have to accompany Jasper out of the building.

'It was a clever play, Dad,' he says. 'But it crashed. There'll be others.'

Your son doesn't understand.

You stay in the lobby and watch Jasper, thin and defiant, even a little smug, as he stalks toward his car. He's young. He'll be back. Even with an Embezzler Jacket, he can get a position high on the totem pole in any corp. What's in his head is worth more than he can possibly skim and skam.

You stay behind.

And think about what has been lost. And what is left.

And so on.

103

You are shocked out of your reverie.

Vanda says, 'We wouldn't be here, if only…'

You're shaking. 'It wouldn't work,' you say. 'Murder.'

Damn.

Then you have to deal with the mess. You can't stay on top of it. You are pulled under.

And so on.

104

'You once told me there were rules,' Vic says.

'There are,' you reply. 'Well, there's one.'

She laughs. Despite everything, she still likes you.

Women like you. You can make them like you. You're good at that. If you weren't, you wouldn't be who you are.

It's past midnight. The 4th of October, 1999. You've just turned forty. You and Vic are back in your flat, drinking coffee with Jack Daniel's in it.

You work for money. Literally: your employer is a nebulous investment business. Money gives you orders and money is your reward.

You suppose you are good at your job, just as you are good at women. But it doesn't interest you.

Vic is a poet.

You have never slept together.

You wonder why. At forty, she's more attractive than she was as a teenager. A bit old for you at your current rate. But still. Her few, almost imperceptible, lines suit her. Even the white streak in her hair is striking.

You get close to her on the sofa, wondering, for the thousandth time.

She laughs and holds up her hands, forefingers like Van Helsing's crucifix. 'Back,' she says.

You snarl playfully, as if showing fangs.

'It's been over twenty years. Don't you ever give up?'

'Never,' you declare, proudly.

Back in 1977, Victoria had seemed your obvious next target. After Rowena, she was there, waiting. If she'd melted then, perhaps your subsequent life would have been different. What you have with Vic is vastly different from all the things you have had with all the others.

Disappointed with Victoria, you went back to Rowena.

But she got tiresome. She was more interested in the world beyond the bed, and wanted to cart you about on her arm like a trophy.

For you, the world has always been the bed.

Vic puts a cigarette in her holder.

'Got a match?' she asks.

'Not since Errol Flynn died,' you say.

She laughs, shaking her head. 'You really are a fucking monster.'

'Good choice of adjective.'

If you put your hand on her breast, she'd pop. You know she would. After all these years.

But you hesitate.

Once you dispensed with Ro, you found there were many opportunities available. Of course, like every other just-broken-up Sedgwater teenager in 1978, the first thing you did was shag Jacqui Edwardes. It was practically mandatory, a tradition like the Queen's telegram on your hundredth birthday. Then, widening the field a little, you fucked Mary Yatman – whose eager, desperate, dangerous coils were surprisingly hard to escape – and fell into bed with Shane Bush's ex-fiancée, Vanda Pritchard.

After that, just to prove you could and to test your mettle, you specialised in taking women away from other people. You borrowed Bronagh Carey from Gully, if only for a weekend, and made a successful assault on Penny Gaye, Michael Dixon's girlfriend. You got together one afternoon with Michael's sister, Candy, who was supposed to be going out with your brother, James, but turned out – painfully and messily – to be *virgo intacta*. Michael asked you if you planned on screwing his mother next, and you seriously thought about it.

Your first older woman turned out to be Mademoiselle Quelou, your college French teacher. Then Phyllis, your father's assistant at the bank.

Then Michael's mum.

You worked through the register of your college class.

There was Marie-Laure Quilter, the neurotic with the rich mother and the stringy hair. Marion Halsted, the week after her wedding to Gerry Trickett.

That wasn't even finished when you went away to university, to experience that Golden Age of Shagging, 1978–81. You were never obsessive about remembering names. There was Tina Temple, though, the wild little girl. Clare, with her bloody Abba records.

It isn't the chase for you, it's the act.

Fucking. Screwing. Shagging. Making love. Sex.

It's what you're best at and it's what you need to do most.

'Do you still see any of them?'

'Who?' you ask.

Vic prods you. 'You know. The shag-hags.'

You think about it. 'Not really.'

'I'm not surprised.'

You missed out on Vic, but you had her sister Lesley. After university, when you came back to town.

And all the girls in your office. Kate. They've all been called Kate. Even if they were named Bella or Marcia, you called them 'Kate'. Most of them found that charming.

You've practised charm quite a bit.

Once, to see what it was like, you fucked a guy, Kay Shearer, a young businessman. The build-up was surprisingly familiar, just like charming a woman.

And the aftermath was the same. As soon as he got clingy, you cut him off.

To prove to yourself that you could, you spent one Christmas working on Laraine, your own sister.

You didn't think you'd go through with it when you got her to the point where she was willing, but you did.

It wasn't any more complicated than most of your entanglements. And you got out of it unscathed, dumping her for Samantha, Councillor Hackwill's teenage daughter.

It's a point of pride to you that you don't wreck lives. You aren't some sort of sexual serial killer. You just like to fuck.

And you make it easy for the fuckees. You withdraw smoothly. You don't leave a barb.

'If I were to ask you to marry me,' you ask Vic, 'would you have sex with me?'

'What is that? Your last resort?'

You're hurt. On some level, you mean it.

After all, she is the *only* woman. She's practically the only one left.

That's not what you mean, though. She's the only one you can talk to. The only one who is still here.

Even Laraine, who has moved to Canada with her second husband, hasn't sent you a birthday card.

At least, you haven't fucked any sheep or corpses. Though, you admit, there's still time.

You've had sex with girls as young as twelve and women as old as sixty-three. You've had sex with beautiful women and ugly ones, and the whole range in between. You've shagged girlfriends, sisters, wives, mothers. Waitresses, secretaries, nuns, politicians, soldiers, dancers, executives, doctors, nurses. Every nationality, every racial group, every body type.

You've let the rest of your life coast, doing only as much as is necessary to keep it going, to free your time and energy for the pursuit of sex.

It's not an obsession.

No, it's a vocation.

You slug back the last of the coffee, feeling that Jack buzz in your forebrain.

Vic is curled up on the sofa, knees tucked in, a delectably taut length of thigh exposed.

You've been here before. Many times. It's been a twenty-year flirtation.

She wouldn't still be here if she weren't interested.

'Why are you still my friend?' you ask.

'Because one day you'll wake up, dear. You'll remember about those rules.'

'I was being a coward, an idiot.'

She smiles, adorably, and a wave of hair falls over her face. 'Maybe, and maybe not.'

It's like a stealth bomber locking on to a target. The whole world fades into black and white, and the woman glows in natural swirls of neon radiating from her vagina. You follow the spiral.

You don't lie, you don't promise, you don't exaggerate. Except for comic effect.

While you are with a woman – or a group of two or three women – you are genuinely wrapped up with her, with her life and personality. Your own sense of self fades and you wrap around her concerns, her interests, her quirks.

It's not conscious. It's not a trick. You're not a chameleon. What you are is a lover.

You lay a hand on her thigh, and stroke.

'Vic…'

She seems amused, a little drunk, exhausted.

The neon is swirling.

But she's different.

It's possible your vocation is actually a search. For the one. And she's been here all along. You won't tell her you'd be faithful to her. She wouldn't believe it. That's not true. Deep down, she'd know you were telling the truth, but she wouldn't believe you were capable of fidelity, of rededicating your enormous energies to her alone.

But you would.

'Vic, marry me.'

There's a pause. A long pause.

You have an erection. Vic is the loveliest of all women, an anemone of neon spider-legs wrapping round you, pulling you to her. You want to make love with her now. And for ever.

She pushes you away.

'Here's the deal,' Vic says, at last. 'Think it over carefully. I'll have sex with you. Here and now. All night, if you can manage it. But then I'll never see you again, never speak to you, nothing.'

She'll have sex with you! Your erection is a compass point.

She loosens the scarf round her neck.

'Now,' she says. 'Do you want to have me?'

If yes, go to 110. If no, go to 120.

105

You prowl the house, memorising objects and distances, trying to pick up clues. Eventually, you fall asleep on the living-room couch, in front of a giant television silently tuned to the news.

You're woken up by two children jumping on you.

'Daddy! Daddy!'

You hug kids you don't know. Whose *names* you don't know.

They chatter at you, about 'Grandma' and 'Mummy'. Their voices are posh, unaccented, angelic.

As soon as you open your mouth, they'll know you aren't their dad. You cannot do this.

A strange woman takes off an expensive coat, shaking out her hair. Not a stranger. Rowena, grown up. Poised in the doorway, she is heart-stoppingly beautiful. But you never liked her. She was patronising at school. Then she got a job hassling you about your dole.

Do you have a good marriage? Or are you as fed up with her as you were with Marie-Laure?

You cling to the kids, for protection.

'J and J,' Rowena says, 'let Dad breathe, now.'

J and J? Josh and Jonquil? Surely, the names were Marie-Laure's ideas.

The kids obediently clamber off. You stand up. Rowena presents her face to be kissed.

You experiment with a cheek-peck of the kind you rarely bestow on Marie-Laure, but are encouraged by the press of your wife's body to move to her mouth, to taste apricot lipstick, and slip in some tongue. Breasts press against your chest and a new scent brushes your nose.

This is amazing!

'Mum sends her love,' Rowena says. 'She's picking things up.'

'The kids make a mess?' you ask.

'No, silly,' she says, shoving you away. 'After Dad.'

Click. Rowena's mother has just been widowed. Or her husband has walked out. Did you ever meet Mr and Mrs Douglass? Weren't they customers at Dad's bank?

The children have rushed upstairs.

'Mum gave them a new game. I think it'll only run on your computer, but Jeremy wants to try it on his PC.'

Jeremy? Gag! You've got a son called Jeremy!

'I told J and J you'd help them get it running later. I hope you don't mind.'

You wouldn't know where the On switch was.

'We'll see,' you say, non-committally.

You are a genius.

Jeremy, you instantly twig, is a know-it-all. *LifeBuilder*, the new game, won't run on his PC, so he's dragged you and his sister – Jessica! – into your study and turned the computer on, then keyed in some commands.

You see you can play this cleverly.

'Show me you can do it on your own,' you tell Jeremy – your son – 'as if I didn't know anything.'

Jeremy likes the game. You deliberately mismanage sitting in the chair, and adopt a Goofy expression.

Jeremy and Jessica correct you. Jessica rearranges your features like plasticine. Jeremy swings the chair round until you're facing the screen.

The children want to get *LifeBuilder* running, but you first have them show you other things. Of course, seven-year-olds can't run a business. But they can tell you what the business is. You pretend to think you're a dustman and scan the screen for files relating to bin-liners and Christmas boxes. Jeremy gets tired of the game before Jessica, but still explains to you what some of the oddly codenamed files on your computer actually relate to.

You're a genius, but you're in trouble.

Keith Marion – you – is some sort of international trade negotiator. Fluent in French, German, Spanish, Japanese and, probably, fucking Klingon. He has deals going in countries whose capital cities you can't even name.

As the children start *LifeBuilder*, you sit back and worry.

The game is weird. The player has to furnish a house and allot time, money and effort to puzzles relating to work, spouse, children, hobbies and sleep. If the balance is wrong, the player goes bankrupt or has a nervous breakdown. It's a bizarre thing to put a child through. And it's what you're now going to have to do. Without knowing the commands or the rules.

After the twins are in bed and you've eaten the best-cooked meal you've had since you left home – Rowena keeps apologising for not being as good a cook as you, promising another impossible hoop to jump through in the near future – you snuggle on the sofa with your slightly tipsy wife, initiating clumsy foreplay which must be as familiar to her as it is strange to you. Can you go through with this? Won't she notice if her husband is suddenly making love to her as if it were the first time, either awkwardly or explosively? And will that be a disappointment or a revelation?

You are overwhelmed by desire.

You and Rowena – Ro, you call her, which slips by unremarked and is probably right – make love on the sofa, then go upstairs and do it again in a canopied bed.

She doesn't remark on the strangeness of this. That suggests the other Keith has had a far more satisfying sex life than you. When was the last time you and Marie-Laure got it together? Weeks ago.

Lulled together, not quite asleep, you play the card you've been saving.

'I've decided to slow down,' you say, 'to take things easy, spend more time with you and the kids. I don't want to miss out by obsessing over the business.'

This is a set speech from *LifeBuilder*.

Ro stiffens in your embrace. You worry she has played the game too and recognises the line. Then she relaxes.

'I love you,' she says.

'And I love you,' you reply, wondering if you mean it.

* * *

As weeks go by, you pick stuff up. Things bleed into your mind, including scraps of Japanese and memories of this life. You got here by being able to remember, but that faculty is clouding. Life in the flat with Marie-Laure seems distant, a phantom. You tell yourself *that* was the dream and this is the way it was always supposed to be.

You get through meetings and discover resources. You find your Idiot Act versatile, working on adults as well as children. People think you get them to tell you things you already know as a way of forcing them to think them through for themselves.

You work out who your friends are.

The biggest surprise is Victoria, whom you now have to think of as VC. Here, she's a successful pop singer, not a near-crusty drop-out. Your family – Mum, Phil, James, Laraine – are the same people, but think a lot more of you.

Otherwise, no one from your old life is here. After all, there weren't many people.

You wonder if you should try to discover what happened to Marie-Laure without you. You even ask Rowena if she remembers Marie-Laure from school, but she doesn't.

Piecing it together, you see you diverged from the old Keith by passing the Eleven Plus. Now, new memories overlay the old like cobweb curtains. They grow thicker. Soon, the Keith who did nothing will be buried.

That thought makes you panic a little.

One night, you are all – as a family – watching TV, the Donald Sutherland version of *Invasion of the Body Snatchers*. This Keith, who has spent less of his life watching the box, has never seen it before.

Screen characters seem insane when they claim close friends and relatives have 'changed'. They look and act the same, but are somehow 'different'.

During one of these scenes, Jessica looks at you with a sudden cold stare. The moment passes but it stabs you. Your daughter doesn't put it into words and may not even formulate it as a thought, but on some buried level she *knows*.

Game over?

* * *

Nothing like that ever happens again. If anything, you're the one who feels your family are strange. You have inherited love for Ro and J and J, but they seem pretend people. They have joys and darks, but are somehow less real than the family you occasionally dream of.

One day, fingers flying over the keyboard, you systematically delete every file on the hard disk and wipe the back-ups. You seriously damage the business.

'What were you thinking of?' Ro asks.

You get over the problem, piecing it all together, but it means long hours of panic.

You think of other things that can be broken.

But not reassembled.

You play with this life until it falls apart.

It was a good game while it lasted.

And so on.

106

Over supper, Sean chatters about a breakthrough with the Discount Development. It's a municipal project Hackwill is masterminding, a big investment which will make several people – including Hackwill, and maybe even Sean – a lot of money. It sounds dodgy: if you weren't preoccupied, you might consider researching it for an article. Your previous pieces have tended to concentrate on corrupt Tories, but you personally hate Robert Hackwill more than any Conservative politician except Margaret Thatcher.

At first, you let Sean rattle on. Then you get paranoid and worry Sean will twig that there's something amiss. You and Laraine, thinking as one, start smiling brightly and asking questions. Your sister is your mirror. You realise you're both overdoing it, eyes a little too gosh-wow, fascination with finance a little too pat. Sean is so wrapped up with the intricacies of the planning that he doesn't notice. But he will, in the end.

You have a blazing need. You want to make love with Laraine again. She feels the same way.

Sean talks about cross-collateralising loans. He sprinkles his technical talk with 'and you should find this interesting, Keith' and 'by the way, Laraine'. Every time he uses one of your names, it's like a tiny bullet in your heart.

You take Laraine's hand under the table. Her grip is as fierce as yours.

You both nod and smile and question.

Sean displays for you. You'd like to stick a meat-fork in his heart and fuck your sister/his wife on the dining-table before his cooling eyes.

Is this madness? Or just love?

'Very nice, darling,' Sean comments as the last of the home-made ice cream disappears into his fattening face. 'Would you make us coffee?'

Laraine lets your hand go and meekly gets up.

Is this how Sean treats her? Like a waitress or a maid. No 'Wonderful dinner, honey-lamb. I'll make the coffee and take care of the washing up.' No 'Don't stir yourself further, dear heart. I can look after myself.'

Sean is a cunt.

As Laraine makes coffee in the kitchen, Sean escorts you from the dining-room to the living-room. He wants to show you the gadgets attached to his 'home entertainment system'. He always has to be the first to buy something. He plays *Genesis*, and twiddles the knobs to make the music come from different corners of the room.

Laraine brings in coffee on a tray.

You and Sean sit on the sofa – where this afternoon you and Laraine oralled each other before going upstairs – and Laraine pours out coffee from the pot.

Sean sighs with the satisfied smile of a man whose world is revolving perfectly.

Laraine perches on a low chair, coffee cup on her knee, a strand escaping from her tied-back hair. When she bends forward to take a lump of brown sugar from the bowl, her neckline flops a little.

You catch Sean looking down the top of Laraine's dress. It surprises you that a married man will still try to sneak a glance at his wife's breasts.

What a bastard.

After his second cup of coffee, Sean goes upstairs for a piss. While he's out of the room, you french-kiss Laraine, intensely, briefly, passionately. As you tongue each other, you cup her warm breast in one hand.

You break apart at the sound of the flush.

Sean comes down and says, 'More coffee, darling.'

It's not an offer. It's a request. Laraine goes back to the kitchen. Sean sprawls on the sofa, almost as if drunk – though he only had a bottle of beer with the meal – and looks up at the low ceiling. He is proud of his directional lights, installed round the edges of the room so people don't bump their heads on fixtures hanging from beams.

In the old fireplace – the sixteenth-century heart of a house knocked down and rebuilt many times over the years – Laraine has set a wood fire. Your attention is drawn to the brass poker hanging next to the wood-tongs from hooks set into the stone. You remember your vision of Sean wielding the poker.

You are, for a moment, afraid. Not of what Sean will do, but of what you might do. And Laraine.

She comes back with more fucking coffee.

You'd like to see her pour it scalding into Sean's lap, boiling his cock. Or dash it into his face, burning out his blasted eyes.

You are quivering.

At the end of the evening, you leave.

'Come back soon,' Sean says at the door, conventionally.

'Yes, Keith,' adds Laraine, with an intensity her husband misses, 'do.'

You shake Sean's hand and kiss your sister's cheek.

As you get into your car, the porch light goes off. You sit in the Beetle, engine not yet on, and try not to think of anything.

Will you go back?

If you continue the affair with Laraine, go to 113. If you resolve that this will never happen again, go to 122.

107

You'd forgotten so much and here it is.

James runs around like a dervish and Laraine sighs at her brothers' 'immaturity'. You've discovered your pirate's chest, and the scraps of home-made maps are genuine treasures.

Dad is alive, striding about the house like a giant, booming comments, distantly affectionate. Mum is younger than you remember, scarcely older than Marie-Laure, disturbingly pretty with her '60s helmet of blond Lulu hair.

It's like having Christmas again.

Of course, everyone thinks you're gone potty. Every minute affords fresh rediscovery. Objects taken for granted seem magically evocative: here's a vacuum cleaner you think of as an antique, there are your Tintin books shelved in order of preference. Even your pyjamas knot you up inside with nostalgia.

But, of course, nostalgia is a yearning for something you can't have. This is a past you can have, over and over again. You wouldn't change anything.

You find yourself see-sawing between now and then. The then end of the see-saw is heavily weighted.

You wonder if you could stay in the past.

If you try to stay in your childhood, go to 177. If you let yourself drift back to the present, go to 192.

108

Within six weeks of your marriage, Chris is pregnant again. With twins, Joseph and Juanita. You buy a bigger flat in a less salubrious area. In 1989, house prices in London are insane. The game plan is to move back to Somerset, at least somewhere in the country, before the kids are school-age. You are a PE teacher in the kind of school you don't want your kids to have to go to. Chris gradually gets back to work on Katie Reed between feeds and nappies and mother stuff.

James sends you cuttings from the *Sedgwater Herald.*

Hackwill's house is broken into. Several times. Hackwill's new car goes the way of the old one. Hackwill's friends – old ones from school, new ones from his businesses – have skulls and crossbones sprayed on their front door. Hackwill's wife gets funny phone calls.

Every time Hackwill gets his picture in the paper – about every week – you see James in the background, often cropped just to an ear or an arm.

You're working too hard to worry about James and Hackwill. Obviously, it's got personal.

It's not just the work, the rearrangements, the sacrifices. It's the twins. All that guff about parenthood. It's true. J and J are a constant delight, even when screaming and shitting. You're besotted with them. You never make an equation in your mind between having the twins and not having adventures. Parenthood is a huge, draining, rewarding adventure.

Katie Reed – who campaigned for birth control and called motherhood tyranny – is less of a presence in your home. Chris has decreed your lives should not end with the coming of J and J, but they absorb so much attention, so much enthusiasm. You look at your children and think, 'We made them.' You have never been happier. You finally think of yourself as a grown-up. You discover maturity by crawling around gurgling wordless love at these wonderful arrivals.

Mum phones to say James is in hospital. He was set on in the street by two men in balaclavas with cricket bats. All very professional.

You want to go down to Somerset at once.

But…

You look at the babies and know they need you here, now.

You try to phone James in hospital but can't get through. It's Hackwill. You know it is. And you are out of it.

James gets out of hospital. Mum reports that he'll be all right once he's got used to the crutches. Your brother talks with you only briefly.

'It's all down to me, Keith,' he says. 'I'll make sure your family is out of it.'

'Don't do anything stupid,' you say, knowing how stupid that sounds.

'I won't,' he says. 'I'll do something effective.'

The next cutting you receive reports a fire at Hackwill's home. In a picture, Hackwill surveys the damage, with his wife, Helen. James is in the crowd. An upper room has exploded, making a black hole in the mock-Tudor eaves. The fire took hold in Hackwill's gunroom and detonated a cache of shotgun shells. Samantha, the councillor's small daughter, is in hospital, eardrums damaged by the explosion. Her room was next to the fire.

You tell Chris you're worried about James.

Juanita has an infection. You lose a couple of nights to real worry, listening to her breathe through a fistful of phlegm. You contemplate losing everything. Juanita's chest clears up.

A petrol bomb is thrown into Phil Parslowe's shop, destroying his entire stock, shutting down his business. There's some insurance but not enough. The bank won't help and insists Phil and Mum keep up mortgage payments on the house in Sutton Mallet. You can't believe Sean is treating his old boss's wife, his almost-mother-in-law, like this. But Sean, as James says, is Hackwill's fuckbuddy.

Interest rates hike again. You have to take extra classes to meet your own mortgage. Chris has to do proofreading and indexing jobs for her academic publishers, who have long since given up expecting the promised delivery of *Katie Reed*, and the twins wring every extra ounce of energy out of you. Life is divided between drudgery and bliss; the latter earned only by an excess of the former.

Reg Jessup is beaten 'within an inch of his life' and dumped on the Corn Exchange steps. Hackwill vows the culprit will be caught and claims rampant lawlessness in Sedgwater will be wiped out. 'There's a new sheriff in town,' he claims, 'and outlaws are drinking in the Last Chance Saloon.'

Joseph gets an ear infection and you think you'll die. It clears up. You know joy.

One night, late, your telephone rings.

'Keith Marion?' The voice is male, flat, neutral.

'Yes.'

'Control your family. Or lose members of it.'

Click. Hang-up.

The ringing has woken one of the twins, who wakes the other. Chris, bleary and scraggle-haired, clamps one to each breast – a lovely sight – and gives herself to them.

You are awake, cold and terrified.

Control your family

James.

or lose members of it.

The twins.

'What is it, love?' your wife asks.

'Trouble,' you say.

You can go to it or wait for it to come to you.

Reg Jessup dies.

If you go to Somerset to protect your family, go to 118. If you stay in London to protect your family, go to 127.

109

In 1982, the week after your father's funeral, you're in Sedgwater, hurrying to the Lime Kiln. You've arranged to meet friends you haven't seen in a while. The country is about to go to war over the Falklands. From the Corn Exchange steps, a shaggy, outsize young man harangues passers-by. You slow down and recognise Timmy Gossett, but don't know whether he's drunk or, in the playground expression, 'mental'. He wears a green army-surplus coat two sizes too small for him and thick-lensed NHS specs fixed at one corner with masking-tape. The knees of his jeans hang at least six inches lower than his actual knees. He is shouting, 'Fuck the Argies.' You know he won't remember you, but a tiny worm of guilt has burrowed in your heart ever since Paul made you play 'Timmy's Germs'. Sometimes it's quiet for five or six years; sometimes it's active enough to lose you a night's sleep to a fretful, gnawing pain. When you were nine, you picked up a sense of Sin. Now, as Timmy lurches towards you, you want to try to set things right. But saying sorry will never be enough. You also know it truly wasn't your fault. Timmy never realised you had a choice, may not even have noticed you passing on the germs to Vanda. You were never a ringleader in 'Timmy's Germs', just one of the followers. You only went along with it, like all the good Germans in the war. Now Timmy grabs your shoulders and you smell his breath. What has he been drinking, shoe polish? 'Fuck the Argies,' he shouts. 'Fuck the Argies!' Timmy falls over, tripping on something invisible. You have backed against the bank your father used to manage. Timmy, screaming his mantra so that you can't make out the words any more, crawls away, leaving a foamy spittle trail on the pavement. Timmy's germs.

Read 7, and go to 8.

110

A wonderful night ends.

Vic's face is wet with happy tears.

You are pleased with yourself. You think you have persuaded her to stay. But she goes.

For a week, you don't think of other women. You pass up certain scores. You think only of Vic.

But she leaves town.

For ever.

After a month, it really starts constricting.

To prove to yourself that it doesn't matter, you start pulling again. Even more frenzied than before, you are bolder, harsher, wilder.

Mostly, you fuck girls. Teenagers. Clever girls, a bit neurotic, impatient with boys their own age, hot ice in bed.

You like people to see you with the girls. You hope it will get back to her.

Out of bed, your girls seem to talk a foreign language. They listen to music you don't know, they have a different culture. Sometimes, they indulge your oldie ways, as if you were a grandfather.

But in bed, you are the savage master.

Years pass. Not a man who knows you doesn't, on some level, envy you. Every time, a new temp or student observer succumbs to you, colleagues groan with admiration and jealousy.

You see Vic on television, sometimes, or read pieces about her in *The Independent*. For a poet, she has become quite famous. She writes a novel, *Neon Spiral*. You read it, certain it's about you, but can't connect with the world of her fictional characters. It makes you angry that you should impinge so little on her that you don't even figure as a trace element in the world of her imagination.

But there are still girls. And you are still on course.

You slow down and settle for lengthy, overlapping liaisons. For the first time, the girls – young enough to be your daughters, but still in their thirties – seem like mistresses. You enter into a sort of domesticity with several, but eventually they move on.

There are always other prospects.

You read that Vic has married a television producer. You see pictures of their ideal home and messy kids in *Hello!* magazine. You think her husband looks a bit like you. You feel superior to him. You had her first. The next bloke just had her last.

She keeps her promise and never gets in touch with you.

You actually get married. Three times. You even remember their names: Emma, Marietta, Aisla. Three-quarters of the women you have slept with have had names ending in 'a'.

You don't suffer for your lifestyle. You don't get herpes or AIDS or any other venereal disease. No jealous husband or boyfriend or angry father comes after you with a pitchfork or a shotgun.

None of them gets pregnant. That probably means you're infertile. You don't like the thought of that. But there it is.

You wonder if Vic's son is yours. No, the dates don't work. Not by years.

Of course, your physical capabilities diminish. But you never fail. You take a less fiery approach, but can compensate for the occasional limpness of your penis with dexterous fingers and an expert tongue.

You can always satisfy your girls. And yourself.

So what's wrong? Why do you feel you've made a mistake you would give anything to unpick?

I'm sorry, Keith. There's nowhere to go from here. Except, eventually…

Go to 0.

111

The heat tells you at once that this is the summer of 1976. In your life, the first major lull. You were just out of school, on the dole, not yet seeing Marie-Laure, doing odd jobs for your parents, hanging around, drifting.

If you'd had any gumption, you'd have founded punk. But you didn't.

You're sitting outside Brink's Café, alone, reading an *Amazon Queen* comic. A Mediterranean sun shines down and Somerset folk walk by in short-sleeved shirts and floppy hats, transformed by a quirk of the weather.

You'd forgotten the physical weight of the heat.

Also, you'd not noticed the gradual softening of your body. Here you are without a gut bulge. You feel almost strong. You're young, sixteen. You absorb strength with the heat.

Despite what the Sex Pistols will say, you know there's going to be a future, even if it will belong to Margaret Thatcher, Sean Rye, Ayatollah Khomeini, Rob Hackwill.

Maybe you can change that.

You don't think you could get it together to assassinate Thatcher. Besides, you're not sure taking her out of history wouldn't leave space for someone worse.

Don't think about the world. Think about Keith Marion.

You're going nowhere in this town. But maybe that can be changed.

If you stay in Sedgwater, go to 178. If you leave, go to 180.

112

By 1997, you've forgotten the filing cabinet. Of course, you remember Sean's spectacular rise in the world of investment; and even more spectacular crash. Tristram Warwick, Sean's successor as bank manager, still makes jokes about going ballistic.

The bank is a different animal now. The staff has been down-sized by replacing almost all the cashiers with machines. Tris and Candy run practically everything, abetted by a computer whizz called Kate who isn't yet twenty. The sort of advice your father used to give is downloaded from head office. Rather than talk to clients to get a sense of what they really mean when they apply for a small business loan or a mortgage, you have them fill in a detailed form which is analysed to a strict grid. People don't really come into it.

Your duties now include stuffing the cash machines. You even make the tea two times out of three. You aren't that old but feel like an anachronism.

At home, you've been through several struggles. Vanda admitted during a row four years ago that she had an affair with Sean. The knowledge always hangs between you. Actually, you get along as well as most old married couples.

Jason and Jesse are sullen teenagers with bursts of brightness. Your son spends all his time building universes on his computer – when not complaining you don't give him enough pocket money to upgrade tech to keep pace with his friends – and your daughter is a fashion-plate who wants to have her nipples pierced before she even needs a bra. They're both at Ash Grove, which seems a much better school these days than it was when you were there.

The house has subsidence problems that drain any money put aside against a new car or a holiday or clothes for Jesse or software for Jason. It's been three years since you decorated.

You've been at the bank too long to be fired. Staff has been cut back well beyond the bone. But you're not going anywhere. Tris has a job for life. If he were struck by divine lightning, the obvious choice to replace him would be Candy. And Kate probably comes after her, even if she wears a nose-stud.

You and Vanda have put on a stone every three years since your marriage. All your shirts are tight across the gut, with missing buttons. And Vanda stretches side-seams whenever she puts on jeans. You feel like a set of those wobble-bottom toys that bounce back when knocked over. But you don't know if you could bounce back and you aren't sure you'd want to.

You find yourself watching a lot of television. *Baywatch*, *Noel's House Party*, *Gladiators*, *EastEnders*, *The X-Files*, *One Foot in the Grave*, *Star Trek: The Next Generation*.

Vanda would like a satellite dish, but money is tight. Jason would like a whole new computer. He claims he's working on the heuristic equivalent of a bone-shaker bicycle in the jet age. Jesse wants a pink leather catsuit. She's decided at twelve that her role models in life are the *Avengers* girls.

There's severe damp in the kitchen. The car is choking.

Tris goes to Venice and Morocco for his holidays, Candy and her partner have a villa in Tuscany, and Kate is always zooming off to Florida and Macao. Two years ago, you took the ferry and did a weekend in French supermarkets.

You watch television and you want things. Cars. Clothes. Gadgets. Homes. Laughs. Women.

It's more than want. It's *need*.

Gradually, the dull throb of need grows to become an all-consuming agony. The defining emotion of your middle age is covetousness.

When you dream out loud, you always preface your aspirations with 'When I win the lottery'.

Since the National Lottery started, you've been playing.

Every week, you're sure you'll win.

Every week, your hopes are dashed.

Jesse, who has a mind for numbers and odds, keeps a running tally of expenses and income on the Lottery. You do win £10 from time to time, even £100 once, but that's not winning.

A million pounds. That's winning.

Eight million pounds roll-over jackpot. That's winning properly.

When you win the Lottery, you will be able to have everything. This you know with fierce, zealous certainty.

You believe in the Lottery because you have to.

Anthea Turner is your high priestess. Mystic Meg is a conduit to heaven. They speak to you from the screen. Dale Winton, Bob Monkhouse, Carol Smillie. They are your friends. You will win.

It is a matter of time. When you are without sin, you will win. You will receive your reward here on Earth.

People say you're more likely to inherit a vast sum of money from a hitherto-unknown millionaire relative or even to find a suitcase full of unmarked notes thrown into the garden than you are to win the National Lottery. It is more probable that a jumbo jet will crash into your house or a spider of ice will close its legs round your heart than it is that the animated Hand of God will sprinkle stardust on your head.

You are a mug. Like all the other mugs.

But you have a sinking house and a swelling gut and a wavering job and a drifting family, and you *need.*

The *need* is everything.

It's Jesse's job to divine the numbers. You don't play the same combinations every week.

You are the spiritual side. Jesse handles the logic. Jason even develops a program to help you.

The odds are long.
But you have faith.

For the first thousand years in the bottle, the genie vowed the man who let him out would be richly rewarded for his charity. For the next thousand, he swore the man who let him out would be tortured beyond endurance for waiting so long. That's roughly how you feel. Love, reverence and veneration of the presenters of the Lottery and the celebrities who pick the balls turn into resentment, hatred and distrust.

Each week, they rob you of your right.

Their sparkly smiles and cobweb-spun hair and spangly dresses and indecent trousers and nervous shuffles and plugged books-films-albums-shows are all a decaying dazzle, increasingly failing to disguise the Evil.

They are against you. You will never win. They conspire in their tinsel lairs. They are so far above you.

But these are dark thoughts you must banish. Your win must be earned. You try again to love the Lottery.

Each week, you play. Each week.

In all likelihood, this is the rest of your life. There should be an And so on here.

Jason and Jesse grow up and leave. You get early retirement. You get a coronary. You die.

Go to 0.

And each week, you have played the Lottery.

You are a dead mug.

However…

Take a pack of cards, remove the Jokers, *shuffle well,* and deal four hands of thirteen cards each.

If you have dealt perfect individual suits of hearts, clubs, spades and diamonds…

…and if the one-eyed jacks jump out of their suits and squirt cider in your ears…

…go to 168.

113

Apart from the other thing (the i-word), you've never had an affair with a married woman before. One of the advantages of the freelance life is that it leaves daytimes open for sexual pursuit. Laraine can't do mornings because a char comes in to clean the house, but her housewife afternoons are usually unspoken-for. How do people with regular jobs handle adultery? Lies about weekend conferences and evening meetings?

By concentrating on scheduling mechanics when you're not actually in bed, you and Laraine manage to avoid dealing with the i-word issue. It never quite fades from your mind but the fact that your lover – mistress? – is also your sister starts to seem less important. For the first time, you're in sync with Laraine, caught up in her world.

She will have to leave Sean.

You knew it as soon as she said he hit her. She's slowly catching up with you.

In bed, she tells you about her marriage from the inside. Your body is rigid with anger as she calmly recounts the details of her husband's rages, pinches and slaps that became punches and knocks.

He has progressed from fists to that old public-school special, the bar of soap wrapped in a towel like a rupee in a thuggee scarf. You wonder if Sean picked it up from his good-bloke mate Councillor Hackwill. He calls the soap-and-towel flail his 'bitch-buster'.

Somewhere, you opened a door. Now you're frightened, excited and angered by what you see. There's another door ahead; an even more extreme one. You're on the path to that other door.

Laraine tells you that when Sean is in a real state – the financing of the Discount Development is coming apart at the seams – he comes home, goes to the bathroom to get the soap and towel, then stalks the house singing nonsense lyrics to the *Ghostbusters* theme, with the chorus 'Who you gonna call? Bitch-*buster!*' Then, he beats Laraine bloody and rapes her.

You open the door.

'Larry, we're going to have to kill him.'

'Yes.'

You hug, naked but chaste. You're joined in this purpose.

* * *

This is not your field. James would just have brought a gun home from work and shot Sean in the head. No fuss, no frills. End of story. Then, admittedly, it'd have been up to you to sort out the mess.

You sit in the kitchen with your sister, over Nescafé and bourbon biscuits, and talk about murdering her husband.

Actually, it's not so much the murder itself that's the problem. It's what to do with the body. If you dispose of it so that it's never found, the story is that Sean has upped and run away. If you make a play of finding it, the story has to be that someone else killed him.

Which of these stories works for you?

If you opt for the hide-the-body plan, go to 126. If you favour the someone-else-as-murderer scheme, go to 134.

114

It's very unpleasant. You have to go through the story over and over. For Tristram Warwick, the acting manager. For Inspector Draper and WPC Yatman. For many lawyers. For the press. In court.

There are always sticky patches. You have to admit Sean proposed you be his partner, and told you he was going to part-finance his investments with 'petty cash'. The business about Candy's paper-clip locksmith skills always sounds suspicious.

Warwick thinks you should have whistle-blown on Sean as soon as he made his proposal. You can't explain why you didn't.

It's worst for Vanda. She and Ro are best friends. Ro, Sean's co-defendant, has a sort of breakdown. She takes to phoning your house, alternately apologising to and abusing whoever answers the phone. Sometimes, it's the kids.

You have to have the number changed. But you can't move house. Sean and Ro are arrested but not remanded to prison. As non-violent criminals, they get bail easily and walk around free.

Sean avoids you but Ro tries to come over. She pleads with Vanda.

You don't know if your wife thinks you've done the right thing. If you'd gone in with Sean, you'd all be rich and nobody would be charged with anything.

Sean keeps maintaining he would have paid back every penny.

It's the forged signatures that convict him. He never says who forged them.

Sean gets three years and will be eligible for parole in nine months. Ro gets a suspended sentence.

There's an enormous fuss but the crimes aren't thought to be very serious. Who was hurt?

Sean liquidates his empire and pays back the bank. When he gets out of jail, he'll still be wealthy. Some of the bank's customers try to sue him privately, alleging his profits should be theirs since he effectively roped them in on investments.

You come out of it with the beginnings of an ulcer.

At the bank, under Warwick's managership, everything you do is checked three times. The things that are remembered are a) you were told what Sean was going to do before he did it and didn't make a noise, and b) you broke into the manager's office for some suspect reason and rooted through the files.

The office is restructured. You are no longer in charge of loans but act in an advisory capacity, which means you don't get to approve or write out cheques. Three days a week, you have to serve behind the counter.

Warwick sometimes asks you to make tea. The Shearer loan is extended, though Kay Shearer has cost the bank more than Sean Rye. Tristram Warwick turns out to be a close friend of Mr Shearer.

Vanda complains about the car.

Sean gets out of jail and moves to London, where he buys a huge house. He sells his story to the *Daily Comet*, and becomes a wide-boy icon of the late '80s. Each time the market crashes, he is the pundit called to discuss the implications on television. He publishes a run of best-selling 'how to' guides to the market, explaining that the small-investing David can often best the corporate Goliath. In a *Hello!* magazine feature in the '90s, you see Sean at home with his new wife, a nineteen-year-old model with lips the size of a doughnut, relaxing and grinning.

Interest rates really put the squeeze on you, and Warwick rigidly enforces a policy of non-favouritism. After the Sean affair, no employee is ever going to get the better of the bank. You keep the house only by struggling, with Vanda going back to work at the DSS.

Your ulcers grow, eating away at your gut.

Only once does Vanda say what she really thinks: 'Why did you have to blow the whistle?'

If she doesn't understand, you can't explain.

'Sean would have looked out for his friends,' she says.

You grapple with what your wife is trying to tell you. Your stomach burns.

Candy is promoted over you. Assistant manager. She's taken courses, and is up to speed in the new world of computer and telephone banking. A kindly woman, she does as much as she can to help you out, often making you look better.

Your salary barely keeps place with inflation. Each morning, you fill the cash machines. Millions of pounds run through your fingers every month. You remember Dad's old fantasies of robbing the bank. And laugh, sadly.

You get middle-aged. Your kids leave home, get married, have kids. You're offered early retirement. You are a martyr to your stomach. As a retirement present, Candy – the manager – pays off the last of your mortgage. Vanda can quit work too. You get old. Your stomach gets worse. You sell the house, buy a smaller cottage.

Tristram Warwick gets AIDS and dies. Sean is on his fourth marriage and third Channel 5 series. Candy has a baby with her partner, the old paper-clip rogue. Ro is in a rest-home abroad. The bank is mostly virtual, customers jacking in or slotting cards in walls. No one seems to work there.

Operations don't help. You assume your ulcers will kill you. But they don't. Angina does.

Go to 0.

115

You can't believe you have such impulses. Even if you don't act on them, their existence is disturbing. You were talking about rules, inflexible rules. Men who break them lose rights.

You try to act as if you were Laraine's father, not her brother, not… not whatever else you might be, not a man. You stand up, give her your hankie, and stride about the room, making declamatory statements.

You say you'll sort Sean out.

That terrifies Laraine. 'No, you've got to go. If you say anything, it'll be worse for me. Worse than you can imagine.'

It's late in the afternoon.

If you stay and confront Sean, go to 143. If you go and leave Laraine, go to 156.

116

'Dad, this is a surprise.'

Jasper is sat back in his hoverchair, gloved up and doing the invisible origami that replaced keystrokes and the mousepad a decade ago. He's careful with his gestures. An involuntary turning away from the task at hand could compromise whatever info-manipulation he's engineering.

There are wall-size clips of Sam and Zazza, huge-eyed and smiling on a three-second loop. It's a typical veep office, full of toys.

Jasper ungloves, leaving them hanging in the air. 'What can I do you for, man?'

You're ramrod-straight, coolly furious. 'Your sister's been to see me.'

'She's still going to marry that girlchik?'

'She told me what you've been doing.'

If Jasper tries to bluff it out, you'll slap him.

'What do you mean, Dad?'

You slap him. His hoverchair, set on minimal floor-grab, slides across the tiles. 'You know what I mean.'

He slams the chairlock and stands. 'Dipping into the till, I expect.'

You nod.

'It's tagged "black salary" in the trade. All the plug-heads do it. It's expected. It's our perk for processing so much more than our owners.'

'You mean your uncle.'

Jasper shrugs. 'I did it for you, man. Why should he run the family? You're older. You were rich first. And you earned it. He picked the numbers. Random mutation. A freak. I'm merely shifting control of the family back to our branch of the tree.'

'Call him. Tell him what you've done.'

Now Jasper looks afraid. 'Dad, it's a delicate time. It could ruin me. Us. Uncle Jimmy too. Take one bit out and the info-wall crumbles.'

'Call James.'

Jasper gulps. His eyes are wide. 'Dad, help me.'

Your heart freezes.

'Think of Zazza.'

If you help your son, go to 123. If you refuse, go to 136.

117

You get the fuck out of there.

Driving away from Sutton Mallet, it all hits you. You just manage to pull over in a lay-by as the wave breaks. It's an intensely physical reaction, as strong as orgasm. You shake for a full five minutes, teeth chattering, skin icy. You think you'll be sick, but you aren't.

You have to leave. The situation, the town, the country. You have to get out. Or very bad things will come down.

Shadow-spiders crawl all over you. Their venom paralyses you, calming the shivers. You have never been more afraid.

You don't even go back to town to pick up your things. You drive away from everything. You have to go first to your London flat – nobody is home, thank the Lord – and pick up documents. You have to be able to get your money. You need your passport.

Then you get off the map.

You never find out the rest of the story. You try never even to think of the story.

And so on.

118

You take unpaid leave of absence and order Chris to take the twins and stay with her parents.

'You're insane,' she says. 'We'll lose the flat.'

Better that than the twins, you think.

'I love you,' she says, kissing you.'

You get on the InterCity 125 for Bristol at seven in the morning. Chris stands on the platform at Paddington and watches you go.

From Bristol, you get the local train.

It rattles south-west. You find yourself humming 'The Man Who Shot Liberty Valance'.

You're the only one to get off at Sedgwater Halt. The train whoops as it leaves. Tumbleweed-like bundles of rubbish are dragged along the track in its wake.

Across the track, you see a welcoming committee. James is waiting for you. He leans on a stick and is wearing a combat jacket. You cross the track and embrace him.

With James are a couple of hippies, Graham Foulk and Gully Eastment. Graham wears a long, ragged coat and a patched leather, wide-brimmed hat. Gully is in pink dungarees, war tattoos on his bare arms, bars of coloured paint on his forehead and cheeks.

'They're with us, Pilgrim,' James says.

You accept it.

Blackbirds, startled by the train, resettle comfortably on the Sedgwater Halt sign.

The four of you walk through town, slowly, like *The Wild Bunch*. Actually, you walk slowly because of James's leg. You don't need to say anything.

Hackwill's influence is everywhere. A council election is coming up. Hackwill posters are plastered over all the boarded-up small businesses shut down to make way for his Discount Development. More than a few of the posters are defaced, distorting Hackwill's bland face with a monstrous snarl and glowing red eyes.

You walk down the middle of Main Street, which has been pedestrianised. Eyes follow you. Some loafers get off the street, scurrying for their phones. The manager of the Wimpy Bar spits at your trailing shadows, and James stares him down, driving him back inside with a look and a laugh.

You wonder what the hell you're doing. This is Somerset in 1989, not Shinbone a hundred years earlier.

But the situation's the same. Varmints and claim-jumpers and rustlers are running the town; and a man's got to do something about that, a man's got to take a stand to protect his family and future, a man's got to kick five kinds of shit out of the scumbag who picked on him at school.

A Mini van is parked by the Corn Exchange. A Morticia Addams lookalike leans on it, smoking a cigarette in a holder.

'This is Victoria,' James says.

Victoria extends her knuckles to be held. 'Charmed,' she says. 'I remember you from college.'

Victoria Conyer. She turns out to be Gully's girlfriend.

Everyone in the group has a grudge against Hackwill. He's been cracking down on hippies, moving on squatters and travellers, clearing the town for his investments. James gave Graham the keys to your old house, so he could move his people in.

'Hackwill's holed up in the council offices, Pilgrim,' James tells you. 'He's got his hired people. You'll know some of them. Shane Bush, Dickie Kell, Mary Yatman, Pete Gompers. Oh, and Sean Rye's in tight with him. They've been robbing the town blind together.'

'There isn't any Discount Development,' says Victoria. 'It's all a con. Money sucked out of the community and salted away.'

She opens up the back of her van and James hands out guns.

'Army surplus,' he explains. 'Careful, that's loaded.'

You're given a heavy automatic and a lightweight sub-machine-gun. James shows you how to cock them for fire. The two hippies and Victoria have obviously been practising.

Passers-by hurry on, pretending not to notice. It is close to twelve, and the sun is overhead.

'Jimmy,' you protest.

Your thought dies. You see determination in your brother's eyes.

You think of the threat to J and J. You'll do anything to protect your own. You chamber a round in the automatic and stick it in your coat pocket.

'By the way,' James says, 'they have guns too.'

Guns make everything different. The town looks like a movie set. You can see it from above, looking down on your little group. Disciplined extras move out of the way, clearing a path between the Corn Exchange and the council offices.

You can't think beyond the end titles.

You still hear Gene Pitney singing 'Liberty Valance'.

'It's our town,' James says. 'Let's make a difference.'

The five of you walk, guns in hands. Now, people hastily get out of your way.

Hackwill knows you're coming.

You stand at the entrance to the council car park. It's after midday, sun glinting off windshields. Employees trickle out of a block-like modern building. The plate-glass and pastel pasteboard offices were built two years ago to replace the Victorian town hall. Hackwill Developments handled all the contracts, of course. Walls are already patched white where they've been rained on too frequently.

Graham unslings an assault rifle and walks up to a chained-off parking-space. A new Jaguar shines. Graham rakes the car with fire, shattering windows, bursting tyres, putting fist-sized holes in the bodywork. Some people scream. There's a rush to get out of the car park. This will be a long lunch hour. Gully fires over the heads of fleeing office workers.

'Save it for when it counts,' James snaps at him.

Gully salutes and a red hole replaces his right eye. He stands, wavering, for a moment, and collapses, pole-axed.

You all duck, taking cover behind cars. You can't see which window the shot came from.

The Jaguar explodes. Someone has taken out the petrol tank. You feel a wash of warmth and are slammed by the blast. A loose car door flips up in the air, turns over several times, and thunks down like a karate chop on the roof of a Volvo.

James stands up, like a stiff target at a firing-range, and looses a burst of fire at the front of the building. Plate glass shatters and hails on to the grass verge, sparkling in the sunlight. James drops down again. Shots slam the air where he was standing.

It's a stand-off. They can't get out. But you can't go in. And your side is one down.

James pulls a grenade out of his jacket, takes the pin out, counts to five, and lobs it through a smashed first-floor window. There's a *crump* and an orange burst of flame, blasting out more windows.

Someone inside screams. And stops. One all.

Graham and Victoria are gathered round.

'On three,' James says. 'One...'

You think of Chris.

'Two...'

The twins.

'Three...'

You all make a run for the main entrance. James stumbles on his stiff leg. You grab his arm, hauling him along. Bullets fly around you. You crash through the doors and spill into the pastel-tone reception area. It's deserted, the desk unmanned.

Hackwill posters and announcements of council events are pinned to a corkboard. A row of uncomfortable school-surplus chairs are for waiting complainants. You flop down on them, still on a rush, breathing heavily, fringe damp with fear-sweat. Victoria has a gash on her arm from flying glass. None of you has been shot.

The indicator shows the lift is coming down from the third floor.

James makes a snap decision. 'It's a bluff. Cover the stairs.'

Graham takes aim at the double doors to the stairwell. Someone comes through and Graham shoots him in the chest, careering him backwards like a burst jellyfish. It is Pete Gompers. Captain of the rugby team at Dr Marling's. Bastard.

The lift doors open. It's empty. James unpins a couple of grenades, drops them into the lift, reaches in to stab the fourth-floor button, and stands back, letting the doors close. The lift goes up.

The explosion shudders the whole building. A dusting of plaster falls, speckling you all. A striplight falls, in sparks.

'That has to hurt,' you say.

Graham turns to say something and gasps. There is a red line round his throat, under his beard. Someone small has whipped up behind him, from behind the reception desk, and looped cheesewire around his neck.

It's a blonde woman, in a police uniform. Mary Yatman. You remember her. Scary Mary. Besides the cheesewire, she has a ladylike pistol, a length of silencer stuck to the barrel. She angles it against Graham's head.

Graham's arms stick out like a blind zombie's, hands contorting. A pulse of blood dribbles from the wire around his neck. You all level guns at Mary, but Graham is in the way.

She backs through the doors, taking care not to trip over Pete. Graham is dragged with her, gurgling nastily. She pushes him at arm's length as she goes through the door, leaving him behind. She lets the cheesewire go. Graham draws a breath. His face bursts outward. The bitch has shot him in the back of the head.

Enraged, you crash through the doors after Mary. James and Victoria are with you. You all three fire upwards, filling the stairwell with lead. The gun-discharge stink you've read about but never experienced gets into your nose. Firing in an enclosed area assaults your eardrums with a ringing that might well last the rest of your life.

Mary has scampered upstairs, out of the way.

Fire alarms are going off.

It hits you that you have yet to kill anybody. Besides possession of unlicensed weapons, the worst you can be charged with is vandalising council property.

You don't want to widow Chris and orphan the twins.

Alarm bells still ring.

James looks upwards, at the stairs. Robert Hackwill is still in the building somewhere.

'Come on,' he says.

If you go up, go to 130. If you get out, go to 145.

119

You attach the red wire. A tiny sizzle. A shock, like static electricity, in your fingertips.

'Oh dear,' you say.

Everything disappears, in a rush.

Go to 0.

120

'I couldn't live without you,' you say. 'Sorry.'

'Nothing to be sorry about,' Vic replies, hugging you.

'There's hope yet,' you say, almost as a question.

Vic gets her fingers into your hair and fluffs. 'There's hope,' she says, tenderly.

You think you both have the same hope.

And so on.

121

You get to go first.

'I don't think we should get married.'

'You think we should split up.'

'I didn't say that.'

'These are your fucking rules, Keith.'

Are they?

'Then we should split up.'

'Fine,' she says.

'What were you going to vote for?'

A pause. A tiny smile. 'To split up.'

'Were you?' Relief. You can get away clean.

'I don't know.'

A plunge to doom. 'What do you mean?'

She swallows a sniffle. 'I was waiting to hear your vote.'

'You hadn't made up your mind?'

She doesn't cry. 'No.'

'I don't want to split up, Chris.'

'You want to get married?'

'No. Not yet.'

'When?'

'I don't know.'

You leave it at that. And you leave.

Feeling bloody rotten, you bolt for home. Only it's not there, at least not for you.

You drive down to Sedgwater and are almost in your old street when you remember the family house is gone. You turn round to drive out to Sutton Mallet.

You think of the Sutton Mallet house as Phil's place. It only has one spare bedroom and James is camped there. You end up on the settee downstairs.

Phil gets up at six to do an hour's run. He always wakes you up by clattering through the room with a cheery 'Don't mind me, keep sawing wood.'

At this point in your life, you want your old room.

Chris goes to Portugal for a sabbatical. You feel an aching loss, all the time. However, it's going to get worse. You know that when you hear Chris is seeing someone else, you will shatter. And that's only a matter of time.

James suggests you should organise an all-girls orienteering week in the Peak District and shag as many of the clients as possible. That way, you'd even get paid. Advice like that doesn't help.

You keep tripping over your spilled guts, tracking through them in scummy slippers.

This is the worst bust-up of your life.

You were with Chris eleven years. Longer than Mum has known Phil, longer than Laraine's marriage to that bloke called Fred. Over one-third of your life. When you got together, there was a Labour government, Tom Baker was *Doctor Who* and Tom Robinson was gay.

Now, it's the future. It's nearly the 1990s. Is there a place for you in this cold, Chris-free, rootless world? It is as if Arachnoid invaders have taken over. You were so wrapped up in Chris that you didn't notice. Now the blinkers are gone, and the shadow-spiders are everywhere, spinning webs.

You want to die. You want everybody to die.

Oh, and happy birthday. You're thirty.

Sometimes, late at night, you phone the flat – you agreed you should be the one to move out – and listen to Chris's answerphone message, saying cheerfully that she's on holiday and thoughtfully giving a number where you can be reached now you're not living here any more. You don't know if these calls help, but you're certainly ashamed enough of them to be extremely furtive about the whole deal.

Fuck. Fuck. Fuck.

You're an idiot. Of Timmy Gossett proportions. That's what you and James used to say at school. Timmy was the school's poor, touched boy. You'd change places with him.

You voted to split.

What's so wrong with marriage? Laraine's been in and out of one. Besides, you only had to get engaged, which is like going to DefCon 3. Happens all the time without leading to World War Three.

Aaaaaarrrgghh!

* * *

James, between jobs, has a hobby. He's preparing a dossier on Robert Hackwill. He has ordered documents about matters that are on public record and collected statements from various people in town. Being dispossessed from the family home is an affront he's not going to forget.

It turns out he's the one who gave Graham the keys, so the hippies could squat. If the road-widening is legit, the council will have to shift them first.

James is not going to let this drop.

One night, you and he go drinking in town and end up staggering back to your old house. It's not quite automatic, because you know who lives there now. You're still feeling at sea and think maybe you need to visit an old home port.

From the outside, you can't tell much has changed. The front garden is neatly kept. The power was cut off but someone has hooked up a connection to get it back on.

The front door could do with a lick of paint. Since Dad died, jobs like that have tended to slip. It's not that he ever did them, but it was his job to order you or James to do it, or get a workman in.

You tell yourself you won't cry.

Vic, Graham's girlfriend, lets you in. She's more Goth than hippie. A pleasant marijuana-and-dye perfume hangs around her long, lank black hair. She wears a lot of ragged black lace and carries a paraffin lamp: there's no electricity in the hallway.

She escorts you through your old home, like a housekeeper bringing ghosts back into the family circle.

The power is on only in the living-room, where about a dozen people between the ages of fourteen and fifty huddle, some in sleeping-bags, in the uncertain light of two flickering standard lamps. Extension cords snake off into the garden through the conservatory, which is full of the sort of pot plants your dad wouldn't have grown. A cloud of dope-smoke hangs at chest height. You cough as you walk into it.

The furniture you knew is gone, and only a few tip-rescuee chairs and an unsprung sofa have been hauled in. The wallpaper is a Marion family legacy. You're distressed to see untreated damp patches and a few deep gouges. Someone is working on a mural that begins at the bottom of one wall and hasn't climbed far. Naked children in a forest, stalked by red-eyed spider-wolves. Not very comforting.

You're offered a joint and take a toke. That's a first. You've never smoked dope in this house, in this room. James huddles with Graham, negotiating. You sit down, cross-legged. About half the squatters are people you know, from school, college or just around town. Gully Eastment, Vince Tunney, Neil Martin, Jacqui Edwardes. Other faces, older or younger, are new.

These aren't hippies in the sense you knew, the '60s hang-overs who chose to drop out; plenty of these people have been thrown out, washed out or squeezed out. They're smoking dope not to get high but to get level.

Gully, once genius-level clever, introduces you around, appending a thumbnail hard-luck story to each name. Lost jobs, broken homes, withdrawn benefits.

You are sitting next to Marie-Laure, a jittery woman with dirty blond rat-tails and panda-circles under her eyes. She remembers you from her two years at comprehensive, but you have no idea who she might have been; just another of the Hemphill kids. She has a severe facial bruise, which she claims was inflicted at a poll tax demo. She's interested in you. Not a good idea. You see needle-tracks, admittedly old, around her inner elbow. And you're not ready: the post-Chris era hasn't dawned.

Sitting up all night in your old front room, you listen to recitals of grievance. These people hate Margaret Thatcher as much as Robert Hackwill – who is, after all, a Labour councillor. Maggie and Robbo are two faces of the changing, cusp-of-the-'90s world that has taken away everything they had a right to expect, and pushed them into this dark place, then cobwebbed them over so they can never come back.

James lists Hackwill's profit schemes and has figures about lost jobs, withdrawn facilities and quality-of-life downshifts. A tiny faction are getting rich and happy, while everyone else is on a slope to the mud.

You've never heard it laid out so clearly. You didn't notice it happening. As part of the Keith-and-Chris experience, you were blinkered. Because you were happy, you didn't understand. Now you do.

You don't know if you can stand it.

* * *

At five in the morning, the room full of grey light and cold haze, James's lecture is illustrated.

There is a knock at the door.

You're jolted from foggy half-sleep. A few people mumble and groan. You find your head is in Marie-Laure's lap.

There is repeated knocking.

Graham stands, sleeping-bag falling away from his thin body like a dropped sack. He wears only a Snoopy T-shirt; from the waist down, he is hairily naked.

The front door is smashed in. There is efficient noise as people swarm into the hall.

Marie-Laure, frightened, clings to you, which means you can't get up. James is alert, Marine-ready to kill.

Uniformed men come into the room. And women. A blonde constable reads aloud from some document. A notice to quit. Policemen root through everything. Searching for drugs?

'What's this shit, Yatman?' Graham asks.

The policewoman is Mary Yatman. You remember her as a monster at school.

'You knew this was coming, Graham. Now get some trousers on.'

'Where will we go?' asks a waif.

'Where you came from, dear. Now hurry up. You've got five minutes to get your shit together – at least, the legal shit – then most of you will be free to go.'

James sizes up WPC Yatman. Another rogue for his gallery.

'There should be a road through here,' Yatman says. 'So honest folk can go to work and get home. It's selfish of you to be in the way.'

'Work and home aren't concepts we've had much opportunity to get our heads round,' says Gully.

You are lumped in with the rest and jostled a bit as everyone is herded out of the front door. The door itself is broken in half and thrown into the garden.

Graham carries his standard lamp, extension cord wound round it. Vic has a heavy suitcase, full of paperbacks. Others tote plastic bags of clothes. The squatters are like disaster victims, clinging to pathetic debris from former lives.

'To make sure you don't crawl back,' Yatman explains.

You wonder what she's talking about.

Then the upstairs windows are broken. A couple of marijuana plants in earthenware pots thump down on to the pavement. The pots break and the plants are trampled. The police rampage inside, trashing the house, making it uninhabitable.

Lights go on in the neighbours' houses.

Mrs Dunphy, who has lived next door since you moved in, peers through a crack in the curtains and clucks approval. She catches sight of you among the squatters, looks a bit ashamed, and retreats.

The police have brought axes and sledgehammers, which you didn't think were the standard accoutrements of the Dixon of Dock Green-style bobby on the beat. It's community policing with just a touch of Attila the Hun. With the frenzied attack of born vandals, uniformed men destroy your home.

Mary Yatman watches. Like Hackwill with his playground gang, she doesn't have to do anything, just tell people what to do. She's an unusual sort of WPC. With a certain smug satisfaction, to show that she appreciates the irony, she whistles 'Tomorrow Belongs to Me'.

A policeman comes out, a little girl under his arm. She is howling. The pig, grinning like a goon, says he found her hiding in a cupboard. He holds her arm, dangling her above the pavement.

Gully steps forward to take the child. Another constable smashes his knee with a truncheon. He goes down, biting on pain.

Good God, you realise, this is the future. British police acting like storm-troopers. All resistance crushed. Refugees on the streets.

...the morning will come when the world is mine...

1990. Year of the Bastard.

You march against the poll tax. You sign petitions. You become active, on behalf of travellers, of prosecuted poll tax refuseniks, of the dispossessed. It's a despairing rearguard action, bitterly fought. You never think you'll win. Even when Thatcher resigns, the euphoria lasts only until you realise this means the Tories are electable again and will continue in power for more years.

You don't exactly have much faith in the Loyal Opposition. Rob Hackwill becomes a rose-wearing New Labour Enterprise hero.

You and James go into business together. You charge executives very high fees for week-long assault and survival courses. Your literature claims the wilderness experience creates bonding within teams and inculcates skills as useful in the boardroom as on the battlefield.

Actually, you just enjoy shouting at suits. You get a little thrill in your gut every time a manicured vice-president of marketing plunges thirty feet into ice-cold shit. You especially enjoy the pit-fights – 'Two men enter, one man leaves,' you chant, copping from *Mad Max Beyond Thunderdome* – in which a couple of sales reps are tossed naked into a ten-foot-deep hole and the one who gets out on his own has the loser's rations for the next three days.

Between you, you and James fuck every woman who takes one of your courses. You work especially hard at it if she's in a relationship with someone else on the course. There's nothing like demonstrating your superiority in the wilderness to pull the fanny. It makes you feel like Tarzan.

When you're not on a course, you live in Achelzoy with Marie-Laure. It turns out that she's rich. You even grow to quite like her.

When Chris invites you to her wedding – to Danny, her just-divorced PhD supervisor – you get very drunk and wake up to find Marie-Laure crying because she says you hit her. You hug her and love her and make it up.

But you wonder what happened to you. Was it the country or your ex-girlfriend? How did you become what you are?

'At last,' James cackles, reverentially putting the letter on his desk. 'Hackwill.' It's September 1997. For three years, you've been sending fliers to the council, offering cut-price deals for Survival Weeks, carefully not including your names. 'He's signed up his whole crew.'

'All the council?' you ask.

'No, just his gang. Reg Jessup, Ben McKinnell, Sean Rye, Tristram Warwick, Shane Bush, Kay Shearer. And, to keep it sweet, Mary Yatman.'

Reg, Hackwill's old sidekick, is another councillor, depended on to second motions; McKinnell is a building contractor who lands a suspicious number of council jobs; Sean, Laraine's ex-boyfriend, has your dad's old job at the bank; Warwick is Hackwill Properties' chief accountant; Shane is Hackwill's driver (and bodyguard?); Shearer is a small businessman, a pilot fish to Hackwill's shark; and Mary Yatman, retired from the police, has been rewarded for services rendered with a job as security manager.

'I'd like to see that lot in a steel cage.'

James laughs. 'You will, boyo.'

You visualise Hackwill taking a slow-motion fall into the shit-dunk. And smile.

'Life would really be complete,' you say, 'if we could get Mrs Fudge, our primary-school dinner lady, along for the ride too. That would just about clean the board.'

James thinks about it.

'But wait,' he says, sincerely. 'Isn't petty personal revenge degrading and ultimately futile? Shouldn't we forgive, forget, get on with our lives unencumbered by resentments that have eaten us up, poisoned our every waking moment? Should we turn Hackwill's application down and prove we've outgrown childish grudges and sadistic vindictiveness?'

If you agree with James, go to 124. If not, go to 133.

122

The next day, while Sean is at work, you phone your sister. You don't trust yourself – or her – to have this conversation face to face. You're worried you'll lose control, find yourself utterly entangled.

'Rye residence,' she answers, as Sean must force her to.

What do you call her? Darling?

'Larry, it's Keith.'

Quiet. You hear the radio in the background at her end. Something by Duran Duran.

'Yesterday was one-off madness,' you say.

'Yes.' Dull, flat, accepting. An answer.

'Larry, I love you.' You've never said that to anyone in your family. They have had to take it on trust.

'Thank you.'

'But I can't *love* you.' Why does this feel wrong?

'I'll see you soon, Keith.'

'Yes. You will. Of course. Always.'

She hangs up first.

Now what?

You sit at your desk and look at the clippings and photos on the wall.

Laraine is speckled everywhere: with you and James in an awkward posed portrait that shows her trying to seem grown-up next to you children; on her own as a teenager with too much eye make-up and an Alice band; at her wedding (with that bastard); with Mum, at funerals.

Your hand falls on the neat stack of typed pages.

Your book is dead in your heart. The point was to tell the truth. About James, and what led him to a lonely, cold death on the other side of the world. And about the rest of you. Now there's a secret that can never be told. It changes everything.

You worry that if you finished the book, you'd give yourself away. A skilled detective could read it and deduce what you and Laraine had done, following clues unconsciously left throughout the text. Or, worse, you'd be so successful in excluding the one thing you didn't want on the record that the book would be empty, worthless, impersonal. That'd be another betrayal, another spasm of treacherous cowardice, invalidating your last chance. The last chance to rush into the copse to help James.

You feed a sheet of paper into your typewriter.

Once, you type, *I fucked a fourteen-year-old. who was drugged out of her mind and didn't know what she was doing.*

There, that's honest. Not pretty, but it establishes your *bona fides*.

You shift carriage-return and indent, for a new paragraph.

Yesterday, I made love with my sister.

Typing it out has given you a half-erection.

You pull out the sheet of paper and read it. You tear it up, and sort out the pieces with words on them. Those, you eat. You scoop the rest into the waste-bin by the desk.

This is not going to be something you can deal with easily.

You go back to London, book abandoned. You tell Anne it went too deep and that you were worried about upsetting your mother. You let Anne think you've discovered things about James that would distress Mum – which is at least partially true, though it didn't stop you digging deeper – and that you've closed the book because of that. She buys it, but only because you hold back enough about James to let her know you're not telling the whole truth.

Wheels within wheels. But you got into this.

You get back to work. To avoid thinking about Laraine, you dig up other painful things. You write burning, angry, insightful pieces. Your reputation grows.

If you can't resolve the Laraine thing, you can deal with the other insanities in your life.

Chrissie.

Her parents were lecturers. You haven't seen her since 1980. Your first thought is that she probably continued her drugged-up fuckpig career arc and is on the streets of Brighton or London, screwed up on smack, turning tricks for violent businessmen. You weren't the first student to fuck her and you certainly weren't the last.

You think about her. At the time, you just thought about your dick and her body.

You nurture the guilt and shame.

You remember the afternoon. Her vagina was small and you only managed penetration with not a little pain for the both of you. When you were ready again, after half an hour and a couple of pills, you buggered her. That's not something you've tried again. You remember it as consensual but at this late date you're sadly sure that's just a rationalisation. You think of Chrissie's face screwed up. In your memory, she's younger than fourteen. She looks ten, six, three.

You can't do anything for James. And Laraine is off-limits. Which leaves Chrissie.

You look up your student diary, which has a blunt, self-satisfied five-line account of the afternoon. At least you thought to write down the thing you're most ashamed of forgetting, her full name. Christina Zoe Temple. You draft and redraft a full, honest version. Your first attempt reads like a letter to a porno magazine, so you rework it more clinically, more emotionally. You write about pain. This feels a lot like flagellation.

At the library, you set out to track her down. They have phone books for the whole country. Her parents are still listed in the Brighton Area directory. The sensible first move would be to call them. But that might lead to a conversation you don't want to have. Not now, not ever; never.

She'd be twenty-one now. Maybe twenty-two. You imagine her in a ragged school uniform, on a street corner, walking over with an affected strut to a car, bending down to barter with a greasy driver. Eyes dead, body wasted.

You look at her parents' number again. Your phone call would certainly intervene in a ghastly situation. What if she's dead? Overdosed in a squat? Or fucked and killed and dumped?

But it's the only way. You have to call them.

You look up the page. There's a separate listing above Chrissie's parents, for 'Temple, C. Z.'. An address in Rottingdean.

You make the call. A young-womanly voice chirrups that Chris and Danny are out but you can leave a message. So she's living with a boyfriend. Or else it's Dani and she's sharing with a girl. If it's a Dani, that might be the voice on the machine. You can't remember anything distinctive about Chrissie's voice – you didn't know her very long – and, thinking about it, probably wouldn't recognise her in the street. She had dyed hair, punky purple. That might be gone now. Her sparse pubic hair was blond.

Later, you call again. Danny – a man – answers.

'I'm a friend of Chrissie's,' you say. 'From a while ago.'

'Chrissie?' Danny hasn't heard the name; he thinks of her as Chris.

You almost say you knew her at university. But, of course, she wasn't at university. She was at school when she bothered to go.

'She's teaching today, I'm afraid.'

Teaching?

'Were you on her first degree course?' Danny asks.

'No, I just knew her.'

'I don't think she's ever mentioned your name.'

Danny sounds older than you, obviously educated. And this Chris, with at least one degree behind her, working (?) for another, hardly seems a credible extrapolation from jailbait fuckpig. But it has to be the same girl. A weird cloud dissipates. You don't have to feel guilty about Chrissie's imaginary death or degradation.

'Should I say you called?'

You make up a story about being only briefly in the country. You'll be off to Ethiopia again tomorrow but Danny is to say 'Hi'. Your guess is that his Chris won't remember your name among the others – though you suspect adding 'Just say I was the one who sodomised her in 1980' would jog her memory – and they'll have a laugh together trying to work out who you were.

When you hang up, you know your 'Fuckpig' article won't happen. But you feel better about it.

You're able to admit not everything is your fault. You aren't spreading moral cancer or a dreadful curse or Timmy's Germs to everyone you touch. James and Laraine and Dad and Sean and Hackwill and Anne and Clare aren't what they are or in the states they're in just because of you. A knot unties inside you.

You wonder what Chrissie looks like now. What Chris looks like. Slim and blonde and cool and together. Not deadmeat.

You call Anne and arrange for her to come over to dinner. You want to tell her about your discovery. You'll even tell her about Laraine. She'll understand – her family are weird too, weirder than yours.

Then the phone rings. It's Mum. Laraine is in hospital. Sean put her there. He's missing. The police are after him. Mum is completely shell-shocked.

Your entryphone buzzes. Still listening to Mum, you stab the button to let the caller in. Anne has made it over quickly, you think, between your mother's halting sentences.

You try to be soothing.

Your door opens and hands clamp round your neck. You drop the phone.

Mum's voice gets tiny. 'Keith, Keith, this line's gone...'

You are on the floor, with a knee in your back. Your lungs burn. You can't breathe easily.

A tiny flame of calm lights in you. Danny – whoever he is – will never know your talk with him cleared so much from your mental attic that you can die if not happy or content, at least free from a guilt that threatened to blot out everything wonderful in your life.

Sean shouts at you but rushing seas of blood obscure his words.

Obviously, in a moment of calm counter-cruelty or shrieked self-defence, Laraine has told him.

Poor fool, you think. What a waste.

Go to 0.

123

'Thank you, Dad. Thank you, thank you, thank you. You won't rue this, I pledge.' Jasper is all over you.

It was Zazza's eyes that convinced you.

'I can set this right,' Jasper says. 'You'll see. Come, let me show you.'

He sits you in his hoverchair. 'Glove yourself,' he says.

You slide your hands into the gloves.

The screen comes alive, projecting holo-columns.

'Sit tight, now.'

Jasper fiddles with a waferboard. 'There,' he says.

Pain floods in through your fingers, reaching for your heart. You are shot back into the chair.

'Dad, Dad, Dad!'

You can't say anything. The pain-waves run through you.

Jasper is at the door, summoning help. 'Malfunction,' he cries.

A woman comes in and looks at you. Her hand comes toward your face. 'Don't touch him,' Jasper says.

The program completes, with one last jolt.

You see Zazza's eyes, open with love. And Jasper's, half-closed with a shame he can't afford.

You don't want to leave. But you have to.

Go to 0.

124

'Yes,' you say. 'I've never thought of it like that, but you're right. It's been years since the copse. We should let it go. We can make lives for ourselves without Hackwill. We can grow, reach the light, put it all behind us.'

A pause.

'You've got to be fucking kidding,' James says.

'Yes,' you agree.

'We're going to *demolish* the bastard, boyo.'

'You said a fucking mouthful.'

You and James slap hands in the air.

Go to 163.

125

There's a big do for Sean's leaving. A hotel ballroom is hired and a lot of people show up. You spend the first hour of the evening on the door, checking invitations and taking coats, then Candy takes over from you.

Sean is already tipsy. He weaves through the crowd, pressing flesh with town dignitaries and bank people. Tristram Warwick, the new manager, stands to one side, a prince about to return from exile. Councillor Hackwill and the mayor beam like proud parents. They'll miss Sean and his easy way with smoothing the finance of civic schemes.

Ro, in a revealing but unflattering evening dress, is extremely drunk. You know Vanda is here but can't see where. You run into Kay Shearer, who has adopted an attitude of superior arrogance to his outstanding debt. He offers you a good deal on some Swedish shelving units.

You haven't checked but assume Sean has taken care of his own debts. The bank has been repaid and he is leaving in the clear, taking his HOUSEKEEPING file with him. He'll have his fortune, and only you know how he got it.

You still wonder who forged those signatures.

Hackwill signals for quiet. Speech-making time. The mayor gets up on the bandstand and makes bad jokes about Sean having embezzled a million and having a first-class air ticket to Rio de Janeiro in his inside pocket.

As you listen, Ro sidles up close to you, cleavage wobbling. 'Poor Keith,' she says, and kisses you.

Sean starts paying the mayor back with jokes about municipal corruption.

Ro snogs you properly, gin-tasting tongue invading your mouth. Shocked, you fight her off. She smiles, lipstick smeared, and staggers back.

Sean finishes his speech. Warwick, face like a mask, leads the applause. Then he hands over the leaving present you have collected for and bought, a state-of-the-art pocket calculator.

'To help me with my sums, I suppose,' Sean says.

He hugs Warwick, who looks as if he'd rather be shot.

'Now,' says Sean, 'as I prepare to leave you all. I'd like to thank the one person who's helped me most at the bank. The person who has literally prevented me from ending up in jail…'

Polite laughter. Your stomach roils.

'…and who has made my parting so bittersweet.'

You don't know if you can go through with it. Getting the present was bad enough. Getting up in public and making a speech about how wonderful Sean is will make you knot up inside and die.

Sean holds out his hand in your direction, and says, 'Come up here and let the people see you.'

You involuntarily move. You know you'll have to go through with it.

And Sean says, 'Candy.'

Candy is pulled past you and up to the dais.

'She'll manage this branch one day,' Sean says, eyes locked with Warwick's.

Candy blushes and stumbles through a few words. Sean gets an arm round her shoulders and lets his hand slide down her back to her bum.

'Now, let's party,' Sean shouts.

Later, when you're both much drunker, you have a brief conversation – your last – with Sean.

'Still hear from your sister?' he asks.

'Laraine's getting married again.'

'Worst shag in town, your sister. Of course, you wouldn't know that.'

Sean is whirled away into the crowd.

You look for Vanda and can't find her.

You wake up with a dead head.

'Where's Mummy?' Jason asks.

Your mouth and nose seem to be stuffed with packaging. Behind your eyes, pain radiates.

Your son looks at you. You are alone in bed.

'Where's Mummy?' Jason asks, again.

'I don't know. In the garden?'

Jason shakes his head and runs away.

You sit up. You got your shoes and jacket off, but are still in your gamey formal shirt and trousers.

At least that bastard Sean is gone. Good luck to him with his investments. Now you don't have to worry about what you know.

You go to the bathroom, where you take off your clothes and have a long shower. The water helps ease your hangover, but you still feel like one of the walking dead.

You stand at the sink and look at yourself in the mirror. You look like a prat. You are a prat. Your mouth still feels congealed. You reach for your toothbrush and pluck it from its holder.

Then you freeze. You have a four-brush holder. You hold your toothbrush, and Jason and Jesse's well-used junior brushes are there. But a toothbrush is missing: Vanda's.

You slide back the mirror-front of the bathroom cabinet. Your shaving gear is there but there's empty space where Vanda keeps her tampons.

Without wrapping a towel round your middle, you go back to your bedroom and open the wardrobe. All Vanda's clothes are gone.

'Daddy's in the nude,' Jesse says, giggling.

Jason and Jesse are at the doorway.

You're trying to put things together. Your head is breaking open.

'Mummy left a letter,' Jason says, holding out the envelope.

'I've known for months,' Ro says. 'I don't know how you could not have.'

Your head still doesn't work.

'Don't worry. It won't last. None of them do.'

'I wouldn't take her back,' you say, meaning it.

'Yes, you will, Keith. You shouldn't, but you will. You're like that.'

You feel such a *fool*.

Ro is right. After six months, during which time you hear of Sean's meteoric rise in the City, Vanda comes back. She stands on your doorstep, with her new hairstyle and expensive dress. You hold out your arms.

Then you remember what you said.

If you let Vanda in, go to 129. If you throw Vanda out, go to 131.

126

'I'm staying with my sister,' you tell Mary Yatman.

'Of course,' the policewoman says.

She has taken down Laraine's statement. The story is that she has waited four days, assuming Sean would come back, before reporting him missing.

'There's nothing to be worried about yet,' Mary says.

'We hadn't had a row,' Laraine insists.

You've decided she'll maintain the happy-marriage façade until the search gets intense. Then, she'll let slip some of the truth. It'll make Sean seem more unstable.

'Husbands usually show up,' Mary says. 'Worse luck.'

She obviously thinks Sean is shacked up in Brighton with a teenage girl.

Four days ago, you used Sean's credit card to buy a railway ticket to Gatwick. Not at Sedgwater Halt but in Bristol, where the counter clerk couldn't possibly recognise you as someone who isn't Sean Rye. Thank God for his bank manager's scrawl of an easily forged signature. Sean's car is parked in the forecourt of Bristol Temple Meads station, presumably collecting tickets under the windshield wipers. The police should connect the car with the missing person but if they don't you'll give them a hint when Sean's credit-card statement comes through.

You show Mary out of the house, leaving Laraine in the kitchen.

'Mary,' you say, as you step outside. 'Do you think he's done a Reggie Perrin?'

Mary shrugs. 'I couldn't say yet. Most people come back.'

You need to phrase this to throw suspicion on Sean and away from you.

'There's something about the bank,' you say. 'He's been secretive. Strange. Something about some development deal.'

Mary nods, once. Good. She's up to speed on whatever dodgy business Sean and Hackwill are doing.

She puts a hand on your arm. 'Look after your sister.'

'I will. Thank you.'

She lets you go and walks towards her car.

As she opens her car door, she turns back, like Lieutenant Columbo about to ask 'Just one more thing'.

'I was sorry to hear about your brother.'

You don't know what to say.

'He did things that had to be done,' Mary says.

'It's a family tradition.'

You're an idiot! Who do you think you are, bandying ironic little hints with the cops.

Mary drives away. Laraine comes up behind and hugs you. You turn and kiss her, deeply.

You and Laraine cuddle on the sofa in front of a comforting fire. The poker – cleaned and undented – hangs from its hook.

Sean is in the garden, deep under the compost heap.

How do city folks without gardens manage murder?

You considered going out on the moors and burying him there. But two of you hauling an inert third over wetlands at dead of night would have been a nerve-stretching risk, and dawn would show the excavated patch, no matter how you tried to match the sod.

The compost heap is at the end of the garden, against a high wall, where you could work out of sight of nosy neighbours. Between you, you dug a hole four foot deep in three hours. You put Sean in and filled it up. Because it's supposed to be a heap, the extra earth displaced by the body wasn't a problem.

If you dug up all England, how many murdered corpses would you find? People would rather believe in a runaway husband than a murdered one.

Mary isn't going to come back with a spade.

You and Laraine aren't sleeping together as much. You'd thought the absence of Sean would give you the opportunity to fuck day and night, but it hasn't worked out like that. Again, you've been surprised by the ordinariness of the affair. You've got past the frenzy-of-sex stage and are settling a bit, maybe even cooling off. You'd thought incest would keep you together. It was the extra element making an affair into a lifelong relationship. Of course, you already had a lifelong relationship with Laraine. You're even a little disappointed: breaking every law and taboo your society has to offer hasn't given your relationship a staying power beyond that of every other fling-cum-thing you've ever had.

You bring it up. 'We're not as close as we were,' you say.

'What did you think, Keith? That we'd get *married*?'

The contempt and disgust Laraine puts into the word are a shock.

Laraine has what she really wanted: Sean dead, her free. Where do you fit in?

You have the sort of petty rows you once had with Clare. Laraine, having known you since birth, has more ammunition.

Every nag begins 'You always did...'

...make lousy coffee... forget to clean the bath... dream too much.

Laraine withdraws into herself, besieged by ghosts. She says she sometimes thinks she hears Sean in the next room, humming the *Ghostbusters* theme.

It's natural. She's used to the idea of him in the house. You had the same thing when Clare moved out, and Clare is not under a compost heap with a dent in her brainpan.

Mary comes back every few days. Sean's car is found. And they track his credit card, which hasn't been used since he bought his ticket.

'If he's left the country, he isn't using his own passport,' Mary explains. 'But that's possible.'

'Is there money missing?'

'I can't say.'

You're relying on the dodginess of the Discount Development to cover for you.

'One thing bothers me,' Mary says. 'Why did he use his credit card for the train? If he bought a plane ticket, he must have used cash.'

'You have to give your name when you buy a plane ticket. If he has a fake passport, it won't match his credit card.'

'Sure. But if he had the cash for an air ticket, why not buy the train ticket out of it?'

God, this is just like *Columbo*.

'You think Gatwick was a feint?' you say. 'That he's still in the country?'

Mary nods.

Now is the time. 'Mary, I don't know if I should say anything, but... well, Larry has told me Sean wasn't what he seemed. He used to... get violent with her.'

Mary thinks.

You've made a mistake. She's remembering James. He got violent too.

'Bastard,' Mary says.

She approved of James battering Hackwill. Rough justice. Would she approve of you and Laraine killing Sean? That's going down a very strange route.

'If a man did that to me,' she says, 'I'd kill him.'

If you want to take Mary into your confidence, go to 141. If you try to throw Mary off the track, go to 152.

127

You call in sick, claiming flu. You can manage this only for a few days before you'll need to see a doctor or risk losing income you can't afford to sacrifice.

Reg Jessup is dead.

Hackwill pays back in kind.

Control your family. Or lose members of it.

You get a heavy wrench from the car toolkit and keep it on a hook by the door, hidden behind the coat-rack.

You can't ask the police for protection. That would mean explaining why you need it. And why you didn't shop James as soon as you knew he'd gone outside the law to continue his war with your old school bully.

You can't even ask James. He has to be in Somerset, in case Hackwill goes for Mum or Phil.

This should be between Hackwill's gang and the Marion brothers. But it isn't. It's spread out. To J and J, the copse would seem as remote as the burning of the Alexandria Library. Even Chris doesn't get it. And you never told Mum about Rob Hackwill at the time. It didn't do to snitch to mums.

Laraine gets in touch, a bit hysterical. She's had the same phone call. She lives alone, in Bristol. You tell her to go on holiday. She protests that she has a job and a cat.

How did you all get anchored like this? Jobs, mortgages, family, pets. They've made you vulnerable. They've given you a last ditch to defend.

You'd send Chris and the twins to her parents' in Brighton, but how do you know Hackwill isn't having you watched? You could be ready in the flat with the wrench while Hackwill's balaclava boys are calling on Chris's parents.

This was private. How did it get to this?

After three days, you have to go back to work. You tell Chris – who still doesn't take it seriously – not to let anyone in while you're gone, and give her instruction in the use of the wrench.

Driving back from school, you're certain you'll find the flat door open and your family gone. As you get stuck in a traffic jam, the worry becomes a certainty.

Chris is making tea. The twins are simultaneously asleep.

You're so relieved that you cry. Then, taking advantage of a rare moment of peace, you make love with your wife.

This can't go on.

Being cold about it, the best thing would be if Hackwill killed one of your family and then James killed him. It would be over.

And you'd still have a family. Most of one.

You remember *Sophie's Choice*. It's Chris's favourite book and movie, but you've never understood it until now. Which would you let go to save the others? Chris for the twins? One twin for the other? Which?

First, you could do without Phil. You barely even know him. Then, agonisingly, it would have to be Laraine. Then Mum. Then – God, you can't be thinking this – your wife.

No, this is all wrong. First, you'd die yourself. To save everyone. That's right.

You need James alive to avenge you, to end the cycle.

If James were to kill Hackwill now, before Hackwill strikes at you, would that be best? Why do you have to stick to this move-and-counter-move deal? This isn't chess.

Yes, James should kill Robert Hackwill.

You're a PE teacher, not Michael Corleone. How did you get to this? You take to hugging your wife often.

Finally, they come. Three of them. Balaclava helmets. Professional home-invaders, like the police or soldiers.

You are home in the evening.

'It's about your brother, sir,' says a voice on the entryphone.

You think it's the police and, with relief, buzz them in.

You make it to the wrench, but have to drop it. You had a blunt instrument ready, but they bring guns.

Chris is on the sofa, hugging the twins. They have no idea what's happening but pick up on their parents' fear and grizzle. Chris desperately tries to keep them calm. You are in an armchair.

Three guns – pistols, barrels extended by silencers – play around the room. The leader of the men takes off his balaclava. Your heart dies. If you're allowed to see his face, you aren't expected to live.

'Hello, Keith.'

It's Shane Bush. One of Hackwill's old mates.

'We'm a long way from Ash Grove, ain't we?'

You barely knew him. He was just a thug. Now, he's a killer.

'Sorry about this, but local gov'ment be a good job. Lot o' opportunities these days.'

'Shane,' you say. 'This is my wife, Christina, and my babies, Joseph and Juanita. I beg you, don't hurt them. They aren't part of this.'

'Hwaa-neeta,' Shane laughs. 'Bleddy daft name.'

By telling him the names, you hope to reach him, to make them seem real to him, to make it harder to kill them. It obviously hasn't worked. Are Shane and his friends on drugs?

They're people too. It can't be easy. They must have screwed themselves up to this.

'You don't want to hurt babies,' you say.

You look at the eyes of the others. If you break their solidarity with Shane, you've a chance. They'll all be guilty. One of the three might have qualms, or be afraid of getting roped in with the others.

'Yurr, Shane,' says one. 'Her with the teats. Can I fuck her?'

You try to stand up. Shane puts a bullet in the wall behind you. The silenced shot is a *thwick* sound. You freeze. Chris is crying. Juanita, screech a little higher than Joseph's, starts up, loud.

Shane is impatient. 'Your kid brother's a bloody sight harder than you, Keith.'

Of course he is, you think. He doesn't have anyone to lose. Not like you do.

Another balaclava comes off. Not the rapist wannabe, but the smallest of the three. Long blond hair falls out of a bun. It's a woman. Her cold eyes are familiar but you don't know the face.

'Don't kill my babies,' Chris implores the woman.

It doesn't get through. The woman looks disgusted with Chris and revolted by the twins.

'Quiet them down,' she says.

'Mary,' says Shane, almost whining, 'you said I could do the talking.'

'You're a fuckhead, Shane. Always have been.'

A name dredges up. Mary Yatman.

She sees you recognise her. 'Yes, that's right, Keith. It's an Ash Grove reunion.'

She was a little monster as a kid. Obviously, she's grown up to be a big monster.

'Reg Jessup is dead, Keith,' says Mary. 'Your boy did it. Trained to kill in the Marines. Give him a medal, eh? But that means we have to pay back and take it to the next level. Like Space Invaders. You kill one of us, we kill all of you.'

All?

'Be a waste to kill teats,' says the wannabe rapist.

'Shut up, Grebo,' Mary says. 'Or I'll shoot you in the balls and let you bleed.'

Mary holds her gun casually. Shane and Grebo – ? – hang on to theirs as if they were their dicks. Mary lets her wrist flop, but you know she's more comfortable with the firearm, probably better with it.

She wipes a strand of hair from her face.

'Here's the deal, Keith. Death is going to happen in this room. Soon. Either we kill you, or we kill wife and two-point-four. It's your choice. Think about it.'

She begins to whistle the theme to *Top of the Form*.

You look at Chris's wide, horrified eyes. You look at the twins, flesh of your flesh, your genetic future. You try to conceive of a world without you in it.

Mary finishes whistling.

'It's make-your-mind-up time,' she says. 'So?'

If you say 'Me', go to 139. If you say 'Them', go to 153.

128

In 1982, the week after your father's funeral, you're in Sedgwater, hurrying to the Lime Kiln. You've arranged to meet friends you haven't seen in a while. The country is about to go to war over the

Falklands. From the Corn Exchange steps, a shaggy, outsize young man harangues passers-by. You quicken your step and hurry on past him, eyes down. You spend the evening arguing about the Falklands War. For the first time since Dad died, you feel the numbness wearing off. You get heavily into an argument, pointing out that Galtieri wouldn't have invaded in the first place if Thatcher's defence cuts hadn't pulled the fleet out of the South Atlantic and practically run up a flag on Goose Green saying, 'Invade, why don't you? We wouldn't mind.' Warmed up by beer and argument, you all go for a curry afterwards. You pass the ranting loony again, but are so deep in criticising Paul Mysliwiec's patriotic trigger-happiness you don't even notice him.

Read 7, and go to 9.

129

Vanda never says she's sorry. She resents you for being weak enough to take her back. You tell her it's for the children, but she knows you're lying.

One night, two months after she comes back, she tells you the worst thing. 'I forged your signatures.'

You had guessed.

'Aren't you going to explode?'

You shake your head. You don't want her to see your tears.

'Keith,' your wife says, 'you're *pathetic*.'

You are promoted to assistant manager. Proudly, you tell Vanda.

'Warwick's only approved the promotion because you're no threat to his job.'

Since she came back, Vanda communicates only in isolated sentences, sharp and calculated as a boxer's jabs.

She won't make love with you. You can't remember the last time she did, before she went away. You didn't notice at the time that your love-making had become infrequent, but it must have.

She is good with the kids.

It's not much of a comfort, but you hear Sean is almost wiped out on Black Monday by the stock-market crash of 1986. He has to scrabble around for a job in the ruins of the City, his dreams ashes. Vanda is quietly exultant. She hates him because he threw her over for a skinny teenager.

You congratulate yourself on not getting into Sean's schemes. If you had, you'd now be the one who got wiped out.

The recession affects you, though. Escalating mortgage payments start to bite badly. The preferential package offered to bank employees turns out to be nastily structured. Hidden penalties come into force and snap like man-traps.

Warwick orders you to get tougher on customers who default on loans. And to sign up those who don't to pension plans and all manner of insurance, taking advantage of the general panic to bind customers to ever-heavier regular payments.

It's hard. You understand each and every sad story you hear. Lost jobs, negative equity, evaporated savings, the recession, split families. You feel you've lived through all the tragedies.

That's what it's like. Vanda at home with her icepick insults. Warwick at work with his overseer's whip.

But people like you. Candy, who you think might feel a little sorry for you, takes care to be kind. And your customers, especially those in trouble, appreciate the consideration.

The world divides. People with power over you treat you with casual contempt, but people over whom you have power are genuinely fond of you.

You wonder who you are. You feel hollow, defined only by the contempt or indulgence of others. You yourself have ceased to matter.

Sean, you hear, has tried to kill himself; but botched the job. So he's worse off than you.

If you'd done something, he'd be better off. You'd all be better off.

And so on.

130

James, despite his leg, takes the lead. After all, he's been in battle before. He's the only one who knows what to expect.

You and Victoria follow.

You're feeling hyper. You've seen death and it's terrifying, but you've rarely felt so alive. You can taste life. It's almost sexual. And almost pure, like your feelings for your children. You're doing the right thing. No compromises. You might not live past sunset, but you'll have made a difference.

You make it to the fourth floor. Smoke is all around, filling the stairwell. James moves into Hackwill's open-plan office suite, firing rounds.

You follow him, keeping an eye out. There are monsters here.

James kicks away a desk. Someone in a suit is curled up, snivelling, trouser-crotch stained. He puts up shaking hands and can't get out a coherent sentence. It's Sean.

James cocks his gun, but doesn't fire.

Sean squirrels out of the way, back towards the stairwell. As he passes, he pulls out a knife and sticks it into Victoria's leg. Running at a crouch, he tries to get to the door. You shoot him in the back of the head.

Without thinking, without making a conscious choice, you have killed. You are a killer. You can't afford to think about that now.

Victoria extracts the blade from her leg and throws it away. Sean has stuck her in a muscle. Her leg seems to contract. She's obviously in a lot of pain. Bastard Sean.

Mary steps out of a store-room, arms wide. She has her gun but it isn't pointed at any of you.

'We have to talk,' she says.

James nods.

'The place is on fire. Unless we stop this, we'll all die.'

The smoke is thick, stinging your eyes. Victoria coughs badly.

'So?' says James.

'I don't want to die,' Mary says.

'Should have thought of that when you threw in with Hackwill.'

'You weren't hiring then,' she says.

The strangest thing about this is Mary's uniform. It's not an outfit you associate with guns.

A door at the other side of the open space bursts and flames run in.

'Hackwill's in there.' Mary nods towards the store-room. 'You can have him.'

'She killed Graham,' Victoria protests, through pain.

James is focused. This is about Hackwill.

'And you killed Gompers,' James says.

Mary beckons to him.

The fire is spreading. Air pours in through the shattered windows, feeding the flames.

'You bitch,' someone shouts, exploding out of the store-room. Mary shoots him in the heart. He falls. It is Shane Bush, a long way from Ash Grove playground.

'Come out, Hackwill,' says James.

The councillor does, hands up. 'I surrender,' he says.

James laughs and chambers a bullet.

'Get on with it,' says Mary.

This isn't battle. This is murder.

Do you say anything?

If you protest, go to 138. If you let James continue, go to 164.

131

As Vanda walks away, leaving her suitcases on the doorstep, you know she's silently sobbing. There's no place for her anywhere in the world.

You harden your heart.

You have to.

Within a year, you're married again. Candy turns out to be a super mum to Jason and Jesse, and you have a daughter together. You want to call her Janet, but she insists on Kim.

You become assistant manager. Candy tells you Tristram Warwick is afraid of you.

'It's your dad. Customers still ask for Mr Marion and he thinks they mean you. He's self-conscious about being an outsider. Probably because he's gay.'

You are surprised. You didn't know Tristram was gay.

'Keith, you're so sweet,' Candy says. 'You're like someone from the fifties.'

'I was born in the fifties.'

'I wasn't.'

'I know.'

You've had to live with cradle-snatching jokes. Actually, you're only twenty-eight to Candy's twenty-one.

'It's that you still know all the customers' kids names and their aches and pains. You treat the bank as if it were a corner shop. Tristram can't understand that. He's like Sean, really, juggling money and reporting to head office, squeezing the pound. He knows the depositors count, but also that they'll never like him the way they like you.'

She kisses you. Since Kim was born, you've made love at every opportunity. Jason and Jesse make jokes about you being 'at it again'.

You don't care.

Sean was wiped out on Black Monday by the stock-market crash in 1986. Vanda is working in the DSS, and since the divorce has been seeing Ben McKinnell, a builder. You genuinely hope both of them can put their lives back together.

As the slump begins to bite, you become more important. Warwick's schemes to modernise the bank take a back seat as you have to extend help to those struggling with the recession. You discover his boyfriend is Kay Shearer, whom you manage to save from bankruptcy with a last-minute restructuring.

At the bank, they call you 'Dr Kildare'. When cases seem terminal, you find a way to save the patient. Customers save their homes or businesses in consultation with you. Because of Kay, Warwick keeps head office out of it.

You can do some good.

When you hear Sean has killed himself, you get drunk. Candy finds you downstairs after midnight, openly crying. She takes you in her arms and strokes you.

'I could have done something,' you say.

'No you couldn't. Sean was responsible.'

'I stood by. I could have stopped him.'

'Whatever you did would have had the same upshot. It wasn't your fault, darling.'

She gentles you out of despondency. You make love slowly on the rug. Candy conceives again and you call your new daughter Suzanne.

* * *

Eventually, you are made manager. In Sedgwater, you are someone. Mum tells you that Dad would have been proud of you.

And so on.

132

You attach the blue wire. 'There,' you say. 'Done.'

Soon, they'll pay. The Lottery fuckheads. All of them.

But wait, what about the innocent people? The studio audience, the technicians, the passers-by? The presenter, the celebrities? Mystic Meg? Bob Monkhouse? Are they dupes or monsters?

Sometimes, dupes have to be sacrificed.

If you can live with the sacrifice, go to 144. If you abandon the project, go to 157.

133

James thinks about what he has just said. You see he is on a knife-edge.

'Nahhhhhh,' he concludes, chuckling.

'Hackwill is going down,' you say. 'Down, down, down.'

You and James slap hands in the air.

Go to 163.

134

Sean and Laraine are invited to a reception at Councillor Hackwill's home. You get to tag along. You assume the host won't be too pleased to see you, since the last time you got together he wound up with stitches. Laraine has been before and seen something you want to borrow. Hackwill is proud of his collection of shotguns and makes great play of taking business associates shooting in spring and summer.

Once you've done away with Sean, you'll be tempted to have

Hackwill blow his own head off in an accident– You cut that thought there. Murderers get caught because they get stupid, let murder take over from motive. The way to get away with it is to set a target, hit it, and retire undefeated from the homicide game.

At the door of Hackwill's graft-funded mansion on Cliveden Rise (Sedgwater's Snob Row), Helen, Hackwill's wife, greets the guests. Laraine introduces you: it's clear 'my brother Keith' doesn't ring any bells with Mrs H.

Hackwill's smile freezes a bit when you come into the room, but political instincts kick in. He comes over to pump your hand sympathetically and tells you he was sorry to hear about your brother. You suspect Hackwill threw a party when James was killed.

Before you can be smarmed silly, Hackwill is called away by the ever-sidekicking Reg Jessup. The councillor makes an excuse about business, then has Reg drag Sean into another room. They proceed to have a hushed but embarrassing argument. Helen talks loudly to cover the row.

You and Laraine slip away from the party. She knows where to go.

In the hall, you overhear a snatch of argument.

'The shortfall has to be filled,' Hackwill says.

'I'm not Old Man Marion,' Sean replies. 'The bank needs to be coaxed.'

You'll be doing the town a favour.

Laraine tugs you upstairs, to the gunroom. It's not even locked. The councillor is a megalomaniacal pillock. Rows of weapons are racked in display cases. Directional lights bring up the metal shine of the killing instruments.

'Penis substitutes,' Laraine declares.

Hackwill brings guests here sometimes – which means you have to be quick now – to pose as a Bond villain, elegant and sophisticated, worldly and filthy rich. You pick a gun at random. A double-barrelled shotgun. The case is locked, but Laraine opens it with a hairpin. It must be illegal to store deadly weapons this sloppily.

The gun (you have no idea of the make and model) is lighter than you expect. You break it in the middle to check that it isn't loaded. Even Hackwill isn't that stupid. Laraine locks the case again. The gap isn't too noticeable.

'Bullets,' you say.

'Shells,' she corrects.

She pulls out a drawer and takes out a pack of shotgun shells, like a brick of disposable lighters wrapped in blue paper.

'Are these the right bore?' she asks.

You can't afford to be wrong, so – though seconds tick and sweat trickles – you tear one corner of the pack open and slip out a cartridge. It fits perfectly in the breech. You take it out again and put it in your pocket.

There are bars on the window – a rare sensible precaution – so you have to find another room.

Laraine has the shells. You have the gun. You turn out the lights and leave.

The landing light comes on. Hackwill is bringing people upstairs.

'I've a new Purdey,' he says. 'Beautiful lines.'

You only know a Purdey is a gun because it was the name of Joanna Lumley's character in *The New Avengers*.

You silently open a door and pull Laraine into a dark room. Hackwill drones on about guns, anticipating the vermin-blasting season.

Your eyes get used to the dark. You're in a small bedroom at the back of the house, a baby's room, with a dangling Postman Pat mobile. Someone small is asleep in a crib. Hackwill and Helen have an eighteen-month-old daughter, Samantha.

You open a window and look down at the garden. A fan of light spills from french windows, but beyond is a stretch of shadowed lawn. Laraine breaks the gun again, to make sure you've taken the shell out, and drops it out of the window. It thumps, and lies in the shadows.

Samantha wakes up and gurgles. You freeze. The gurgle becomes a whine, the whine threatens to become a scream. You look at Laraine, willing her to do something. She shrugs. The incipient scream starts coming.

You both stand over the crib, cooing. The scream stops and down-shifts to something like a gurgle but with the occasional sniff-verging-on-a-sob.

'Pick her up,' Laraine whispers.

You can hear Hackwill and his guests in the next room. Voices are raised, Sean's among them. They must have come upstairs to continue the argument out loud, away from the others.

You pick up the small baby-bundle and cuddle it. Her. Thank God, she's not wet.

There's a sharp slap from the next room.

'Just get the money, Rye,' Hackwill says.

Wouldn't it be wonderful if Hackwill lost it, hauled out one of his prized guns and shot Sean dead?

The world doesn't work like that.

Tiny hands pull at the lapels of your jacket. It's as if Samantha were frisking you.

'Present,' she says, a perfectly formed word. She's been taught acquisitiveness before she can walk. She presses your hankie pocket. There's something there, a hard cylinder. 'Gimme,' she says.

You fish it out and give it to her.

'Present,' she says, satisfied, clutching it in tenacious little fingers.

Laraine gasps.

You put Samantha back in the crib. The baby sticks the shell in her mouth and starts gumming the metal end.

It's not going to go off.

Samantha makes a tastes-bad face and throws the cartridge away. You scoop it out of the crib. Luckily, the baby's vocabulary isn't developed enough for her to give anything like a credible account of this incident.

You sneak out and go downstairs. Laraine returns to the party and you creep out the front door. You feel your way round to the garden, find the shotgun, and nip back to Sean's car. Laraine has left the boot unlocked and there's a cloth inside to wrap the gun. You put the shells beside it, rearrange things to conceal the murder weapon, then lock the boot.

The hard part seems over.

A little giddy, you go back to the party and one drink gets you pretty drunk. You're satisfied that Hackwill and Sean are skulking around glaring at each other, and concentrate on enjoying yourself. To rub it in, you flirt with Helen and suggest charades. You give a distracted Sean 'How to Steal a Diamond in Six Un-Easy Lessons', and watch him make an ass of himself. After a few more drinks, you can't stop laughing. Laraine gets quite embarrassed, but it's not as if you were married.

* * *

The difficult thing is managing it when Hackwill doesn't have an alibi. If you make an effort to lure him out of the way, he'll know you've framed him. He might not be believed but you want not to be involved at all.

You have to be ready to kill Sean at a moment's notice, depending on Hackwill's movements.

This means an agony of waiting. Over the days – weeks – your nerves stretch.

Sean gets antsy about the way you spend all your evenings hanging around his house, not least (you suspect) because it cuts into his bitch-busting. The loaded shotgun is in the larder, hidden behind the ironing-board. As Laraine says, Sean is never going to look there.

Laraine's biggest sacrifice, which she bitterly resents, is that she has to let the char go and do all the vacuuming and ironing herself. That ought to carry a mandatory death sentence in itself, she claims.

Finally, while you're all watching *Top of the Pops*, you get a break. Sean receives a telephone call that makes him uncomfortable.

'Keith,' he says, after hanging up, 'I'm going to have to ask you to leave.'

'I'm sorry,' you say.

'Rob's coming over. Business. Confidential.'

Bingo.

'Do you want me to go too, dear?' Laraine asks.

He shakes his head. 'No.' He is sweating.

Excellent. If ever there was a credible murder set-up, this is it. Sean and Hackwill are like actors in your play.

'When will he be here, dear?'

'Five, ten minutes... Keith, *please*.'

'Of course,' you say. 'I understand.'

'You're a mate.'

If he's at most ten minutes away, Hackwill must be on the road now.

'I'll put on the kettle,' Laraine says. 'Will Councillor Hackwill be bringing anyone?'

'No. Just Rob.'

Perfect. No witnesses. No alibi.

You make a fuss of finding your coat and gloves. Laraine sees you to the door and gives you the gun, which she has fetched. You drape your coat over it.

Sean fusses and frets inside.

This would have been an uncomfortable meeting for him. He'd probably rather be shot in the face than meet Hackwill tonight. You're doing him a favour.

On the doorstep, Laraine kisses you. Since you've been plotting, the affair has been less intense physically, but you're obviously more intimately and deeply involved than before.

'It'll be over soon,' you say.

Has Hackwill taken the Sutton Mallet turn-off yet?

You think you hear his car coming. You smile, to encourage Laraine.

You break the shotgun in your gloved hands and check. It's loaded. It's been thoroughly cleaned, which means Hackwill's prints aren't on it either. You hope that's misleadingly suspicious in itself.

You and Laraine stand well away from the porch.

'Sean,' Laraine shouts, loud enough to get her husband's attention, 'there's a problem with Keith's car.'

He comes to the door, grumbling.

Can you do this?

You bring up the shotgun.

If you blast the bastard, go to 147. If you hesitate, go to 151.

135

Sean makes no pretence of being angry that you've pried into his files. That irritates you a little: he assumes you're the sort of person who habitually sneaks and spies and looks into other people's business.

You've visited him in his office and laid out everything you know he's done. You've kept the flimsies with your 'signature'.

Sean has two more weeks at the bank. You can see he's thinking, looking at you as a problem he has to solve. What is he capable of? Why is it that you are the one who feels uneasy?

'I suppose you want something.'

You really haven't considered that.

Could you report him? He's your friend. And there would be a scandal that would hurt the bank. Dad wouldn't have liked that.

But what do you want?

If you try to persuade Sean to give himself up, go to 137. If you try to force Sean to pay you off, go to 140.

136

'Dad, you have to,' Jasper pleads.

'Not this way. Not at James's expense.'

'I'm your son.'

'James is family.'

He looks as if his toys have been taken away.

'You'll come out alive. No mind-jail time. And Zazza will be looked after. Sam too. But I can't let you abuse and betray James. He's been betrayed enough.'

Jasper is impatient, disgusted. He has no idea what you mean.

'Put things right,' you say. 'Put the credit back where it should be. And resign. Retire early. I'll seed you in any business you like up to a hundred K. But that's it.'

Jasper is used to dictating terms not being forced to them. He has acquired power without learning to be tough. His survival has been based on what he knows, on tricks he can pull off. Without James behind him, and you, he wouldn't be in this office.

He is in a sulk, being forced to a corner.

Finally, he goes through with it.

You stand over him, watching him as you once watched him do unwanted homework properly or rake up garden leaves. He could be wiping the mainframe for all you know but is just scared enough – of James finding out – to do a decent job of reparation. When it's over, he's empty.

For the rest of your life, you're going to have a sorrow you can never share with James, with Christina, with anyone. There will always be Jasper. The taste is bitter. But Jasper isn't everything.

And so on.

137

'Sean, you have to tell someone what you've done.'

'Who do you suggest? The police?'

'Warwick.'

'Warwick!'

'He can help you.'

'He'll love that.'

'Sean, you can't go on like this.'

'Actually, Keith, I think I can. In two weeks' time, I'll make the last repayment. Nobody will be any the wiser. When I leave this office, I'll take my *private* files with me. Nobody will get hurt.'

'But it's wrong. Legally, morally. You've abused trust. The bank's trust. Our customers' trust. My trust.'

'Keith…'

'Dad trusted you, Sean. You wouldn't be here without him.'

'Neither would you. He made us take you on. You and your bloody CSEs.'

'That's irrelevant.'

'No it's not, it's a hippopotamus.'

'You won't do anything?'

'Keith, not everyone wants to spend his life in some provincial bank branch. We used to call your father "Captain Mainwaring". Being manager here isn't all there is.'

'What'll you do?'

'That's not the question. What will you do?'

'…'

'Well?'

'I don't know.'

'So, Keith, it's make-your-mind-up time.'

You have to talk to someone. If Tristram, go to 142. If Vanda, go to 146.

138

'You can't,' you tell James. 'It'd be murder. It'd make you like *him*.'

James's gun wavers.

'You're right,' he says.

'*Mary*,' Hackwill shouts.

She levels her gun and neatly shoots James in the head, swivels, levels again, and shoots Victoria.

'Pity about Shane,' Hackwill says.

Blit blurt.

Hackwill's face is changing. It becomes liquid, bloats, whitens. For a moment, you see him as a middle-aged woman: Mrs Fudge, the Ash Grove dinner lady. So he was behind that too, the ordeal of custard. Hackwill has always been the monster in your life.

Mrs Fudge's red eyes grow, become compound. The Hackwill-cum-Fudge head loses all semblance of humanity. Black bristles swarm all round the egg-shaped mass. A ruff of spider-legs sprouts from his neck. It was an Arachnoid. All along.

Mary's gun is aimed at you.

'Finish it,' the shadow-spider says, with Hackwill's bark.

You hear the shot that kills you.

Go to 0.

139

'Me,' you say, mouth dry.

'Pardon?' Mary asks.

You clear your throat. 'Me.'

Mary is surprised. She can't understand anyone who'd volunteer for death.

'I'm sorry,' you say.

'What for?' Mary snaps.

'That you don't get it. I'm sorry for you.'

'Bloody cheek,' she says, and shoots you in the knee.

Agony explodes. Chris screams, the twins screech.

'Promise me,' you say through tears.

Mary is almost sad. She can't promise. Chris knows their names and has seen their faces.

'Spare the children,' you say. 'Kill her, but spare the children.' Your heart is a stone.

Grebo moans disappointment. 'I want to *fuck*.'

Mary thumps him in the face with the butt of her gun.

'You're harder than your brother,' Mary says. 'Much.'

'Give me your word. Kill Chris, but not the twins.'

'Want me to adopt them?'

'No, just make sure they're found. Make an anonymous call.'

Chris has stopped crying. She's scared speechless, but you know your wife agrees with you.

'Okay,' Mary says. 'I respect you.'

You try to remember Mary as a little girl, as a teenager. You knew her so little. Will she honour her word? She seems stranger even than you expected. Shane and Grebo are the mindless thugs you thought Hackwill would send. Mary is incalculable. Can she kill babies?

Mary points her gun at Chris's forehead. Your wife's eyes are expectant, eager, hopeful.

If you trust Mary not to kill the twins, go to 181. If you don't, go to 194.

140

'What do you want?' Sean asks. 'Money.'

It occurs to you that Sean could arrange things so that when he leaves, you – not Tristram Warwick – become manager.

Or you could go for a pay-off now, and more later.

If you ask for money, go to 155. If you ask to be made manager, go to 165.

141

'If a man did that to me,' Mary says. 'I'd kill him.'

Funny you should say that...

You catch the laugh before it escapes, but Mary spots the smirk.

'I thought so,' she says.

Your heart throbs.

You're in the kitchen with Mary. She looks at you, a cat-smile playing around her lips. You remember the monster she used to be.

Laraine comes in. She's been shopping, in town.

'Good afternoon, Mrs Rye,' Mary says, warmly.

'Constable Yatman,' your sister acknowledges, dumping bags on the kitchen table.

'There's no news,' you say.

Mary looks at Laraine's back. Your sister sorts out tins for the cupboard and perishables for the fridge.

'I don't think we need to bother you any more,' Mary says. She gets up and puts on her uniform cap. 'I don't think it's coming home.'

Laraine is struck by the expression and turns.

'Goodbye, Laraine,' Mary says, and leaves.

You ought to be relieved. But there's still Laraine. You and she haven't slept together in days. Since you moved into the house, you've been in the guest bedroom except for sex. Even with Sean gone, it seemed foolish to sleep together in the master bedroom.

Sean is fading as a ghost. But another is taking his place.

You think about James. You came back home to write about James. That project is long abandoned, but you were getting somewhere. You were close to an understanding of your brother, of the strengths that helped him get by, but which also finally got him killed.

James did things on his own.

He would have understood that murder was best managed by a single person. Two people who kill together can never rest easy, because each knows there's someone in the world who knows what they've done.

How can you trust someone with a secret like that? How can you know anyone well enough to know they'll never tell? You almost told Mary. You think she knows. That scene could easily have played out very differently.

You realise you'll leave this house soon, go back to London, get on with your life. Leaving Laraine behind; with Sean under the compost heap. She already thinks she's haunted. How long will it take, if she's left alone, for her to hear a voice calling her, begging to be dug up, to be freed from mulch?

She's close to the edge – she wouldn't have slept with you in the first place if it weren't for that – so she could all too easily succumb to some fugue of guilt. What if she cracks open, spilling it all? Then you'd get sucked into the morass.

Even if she gets over it, what? A few years go by. How long will it be before her marriage is declared void by virtue of desertion or notional widowhood? She's an attractive woman. She'll meet someone. She has a knack of falling for the wrong man. And she's open, good-natured, trusting. That's how she gets into these situations.

She'll tell him.

You try to picture the man she'll tell. It could be anyone. How can you predict what he'll be like, how he'll take the news, what he'll do?

If he's someone like Sean, who sees other people's weaknesses as business opportunities, you could find yourself being blackmailed, squeezed by someone who taunts you with your nastiest secrets. Or if he's someone like Dad, with an inflexible morality, he'll get through the horror and work on Laraine, easing her towards confession. Her psychological healing will be at the cost of your freedom. You see yourself years from now, hauled out of your unimaginable future life to face charges. There is no statute of limitations on what you have done.

You are cold with fear. You imagine James shaking his head. He'd have gone it alone. He did. It got him killed.

What about the best-case scenario? Laraine's man, the man she tells, loves and forgives her. You have a ghastly feeling he'll have more trouble with the incest than the murder, but he's strong inside, confident of his own feelings, and he'll want to protect Laraine. Still, he won't care about you. He'll see you as the instigator of everything, forcing your sister into sex against her will, then coercing her to murder. Maybe he'll try to arrange some deal whereby Laraine is treated lightly by the law if she gives evidence against you. You trust your sister enough to know she'll resist, that she'll insist she was an equal partner, if not the dominant one, in everything, but this *man*, Mr Unknown, won't believe her. He'll love her, so he'll blame you. And you'll take the fall.

James quotes from Charlie Chan. 'Murder is like potato chip. Cannot stop at "just one".'

You sit up in bed, heart pounding.

If you follow James's reasoning, go to 148. If you resist the thought, go to 158.

142

You arrange to meet Tristram Warwick outside the office, at a pub out of town, in Achelzoy.

Your guts feel stretched like a drumskin.

Shortly after dark, you make your excuses to Vanda and drive out to Achelzoy.

Just before the Sutton Mallet turn-off, you start wondering about the car following you. This isn't a busy road and you're driving slowly, concentrating.

Why doesn't he overtake? Is it Sean? In the dark, you see only headlamps.

On impulse, you take the Sutton Mallet turn-off. It's just a dead end leading to a tiny hamlet. The other car also takes the turn. As you proceed over the pitted road, your stomach troubles you. This is fear.

Eventually, there's nowhere to go. Past the hamlet's few houses, there's a triangular space where cars can turn round. You manage that and are facing the other car head-on.

The road is too narrow for two cars to pass. You're trapped. You've trapped yourself. The buildings around are dark. No one to see or hear or help. You want to be sick.

The headlamps get nearer, like tiger's eyes. It's Sean's MG.

You turn off your own car lights and unbuckle your seatbelt. There are two people in Sean's car. You guess one is Sean, but you can't make out the other.

What will Sean do?

The MG rolls close to your car. Its lights die, but the engine still purrs.

You open your door. Sean gets out of his car. You make out his suit rippling in the dark. He has something in his hands. A gun?

You get out of your car. In the cold of the night, you are calm. You don't shake and shiver. But your insides are water.

Sean walks towards you. He's carrying an iron crowbar.

Just before he hits you, you turn your head, trying to see who is in the passenger seat of Sean's car. It's a woman. Not Ro.

You die not knowing who it was.

Go to 0.

143

You get Laraine calmed, by ordering her to make more tea. When you phrase wishes as commands, Laraine buckles to. That gives a frightening picture of life with Sean.

At six on the dot, the smiling bank manager comes home.

Is he just a little disturbed that you're here?

He shakes your hand and grasps your shoulder, invites you to stay for dinner, rabbits on about the Discount Development. There's been a breakthrough. He's on an up now: happy hysteria. You see the slightest dip would affect him, plunge him into the depths, turn his sweaty open hands into hard, heavy fists.

'Sean,' you say, getting his attention. 'I'm only going to say this once. Don't ever hit my sister again.'

He mimes astonishment, tries to get his eyes to twinkle merrily, and makes as if to deny it.

You throw hot tea in his face.

'Not ever,' you repeat.

You imagine James standing at one shoulder and Dad at the other. All the force of the Marion men is in you, channelled against the pathetic Sean Rye.

'Of course, Keith,' he assures you. 'I'd never hit Larry. I love and cherish her.'

He is telling the truth. As he sees it.

Driving away from Sutton Mallet, you still feel the dead with you. Dad is in the back seat, quiet. James is next to you, finally beside you.

'I was wrong,' he says. 'You've changed since the copse. You can take care of things.'

It won't last. Sean's resolve.

'He'll forget. He'll hit her. He can't help himself, the bastard.'

'Then we'll have to deal with him.'

You know you can deal with Sean as James dealt with Hackwill. You know you'll have to. You're even looking forward to it.

And so on.

144

You sit in the audience. The device is in a hold-all under the stage. It's always been your intention to be here. You wouldn't ask Bob Monkhouse to make a sacrifice you weren't willing to make yourself.

A troop of Girl Guides dance to Abba.

In addition to their music interests, Clare and Maisie have a string of music and clothing outlets, Dancing Queen. They have ridden kitsch, nostalgia and cool, and triumphed. So it can be done. The world is not completely against people.

The Girl Guides all have awkward smiles or stern frowns. Their bodies work perfectly but they don't know what to do with their faces. Knowing they are on television discombobulates them. Their faces are shown on the huge monitors up above the stage, grainily enlarged and sweating through make-up.

Do they deserve to die? Just because they bought into the lie fed to so many, the lie that the Lottery will make them happy, that being on television is the apex of all human life.

Three minutes to go. Enough time for Mystic Meg, shrouded in smoke, to make predictions and the guest, singer-songwriter VC Conyer, to begin the draw. Enough time to evacuate the studio.

If you sit tight, go to 154. If you cry out, go to 167.

145

'People have been killed, James,' you say. 'That's enough.'

Your brother looks at you as if you were shit.

'I have to think of my family,' you say.

'I *am* your family,' James snarls.

He starts stumping up the stairs. Victoria looks at you, neutrally, and follows him.

You drop your guns and leave the building.

As you get outside, to be welcomed by the police and the fire brigade, you hear gunfire from inside.

'What the fuck happened here?' asks a detective.

You can't say.

Another explosion on the fourth floor rains debris into the car park. Uniformed men scurry out of the way.

There are armed officers, with rifles that seem feeble next to the monster you were using. The detective, Inspector Draper, gathers the men together. He orders them in. At a trot, they go through the doors.

You're crying. There's a lot more gunfire. Then a signal whistle and the firemen go in. Hoses spurt. Foam mushrooms.

Draper keeps an eye on you.

After twenty minutes, the fire is under control. They start bringing bodies out, faces uncovered.

First out is Shane Bush. Then some bloke you don't know. Then Victoria, pale and still alive, hands buried in a huge stomach wound. She dies in the car park, before they can lift her into an ambulance. You keep wiping away tears.

Television cameras arrive. You overhear comments about a 'Wild West gun battle in sleepy Somerset'.

A fireman brings James out. Your brother is dead. Shot about a million times. You howl.

Then, through smoke and foam, Robert Hackwill staggers out, supported by WPC Mary Yatman. He raises his hand in victory. Bystanders applaud him.

Red rage explodes in you.

If you try to kill Hackwill, go to 149. If you tear your hair and pound the ground, go to 159.

146

After the kids are in bed, you tell Vanda the whole thing, from Sean's initial offer through his obvious success to what you discovered in the HOUSEKEEPING file and your conversation with him. Halfway through the story, she digs out a packet of cigarettes – she's supposed to have given up – and starts chain-smoking. She hurries you through the whole thing, rarely even asking, 'What did you do then?' or needing a clarification. At the end of it, you feel relieved of a burden but Vanda appears weighed down. You don't understand.

'What should I do?' you ask.

'I'm thinking.'

Vanda drags on her cigarette, nasty little sucks that unnerve you.

Finally, she comes to a decision. 'Keith, go outside into the garden and look at the moon.'

'Pardon?'

'Just do it. I'll make the call.'

'I don't understand.'

'You can't be expected to blow the whistle, not in your state. I'll arrange everything.'

This is what you wanted. You've passed the baton and it's out of your hands. As you let yourself out of the kitchen door, Vanda is on the phone.

There's no moon tonight. You stand in the dark, thinking. Through the kitchen window, you see Vanda as she makes her call.

You always knew she was stronger than you. It's not that you're weak. You just need her. *Together*, you're strong.

Thinking about it, you realise your marriage keeps you on track. You didn't go in with Sean in the first place because of Vanda and the kids. You couldn't jeopardise your family.

If Sean and Ro had a marriage like yours, perhaps they wouldn't be in the state they're in.

You sit on the swing you built for the kids. For the first time in weeks, you feel calm. The right thing has been done.

Vanda finishes her call. She comes to the kitchen door. You turn on the swing seat. Her face is in shadow but she's outlined by the light in the house.

'It's taken care of,' she says. 'Sit tight.'

'What did the police say?'

A pause.

'Someone is coming over,' she says.

'Fine.'

'Just think it through. What you're going to say. I'll put the kettle on.'

'I love you,' you say.

You can't see Vanda's face. But you know what's there.

'Oh, Keith,' she replies, stepping out into the garden. She puts a hand on your shoulder and squeezes.

'I feel so much better,' you say, 'now it's decided. Now it's set.'

'Poor old Keith.'

'It was ripping me up, knowing what I know, not knowing what to do.'

'I understand.'

Vanda fusses in the kitchen. You swing back and forth, long legs dragging on the lawn.

You hear a car drawing up outside the house. Vanda answers the door before the bell can be rung.

You are calm, ready. You know what to say.

Vanda escorts someone through the house, out to the garden. You get off the swing and stand up. You straighten your jacket, brushing invisible dirt off the lapels.

You turn and put out your hand. And an iron bar smashes across your cheek. Pain explodes in one side of your skull and your neck is wrenched.

You are on your knees.

The iron bar smashes again. Sideways, you see Vanda watching, smoking, looking away. Someone stands over you, raising the killing bar.

It comes down.

Go to 0.

147

The noise is incredible. The gun – which you've never fired before – slams against your shoulder like a rubber bullet. A double circle of shot the size of two dinner plates splatters Sean's head against the door. He's driven back into the house and goes down. There's no doubt he's dead.

You don't have time to think. Headlights are coming.

Laraine tugs your lapel to get your attention and taps her chin, as if she wants to be kissed.

You swipe her with the stock of the gun. You hit harder than you intended. It has to seem real. She staggers and falls. You're afraid you've snapped her neck and ruined it. But she's alive. She's not even unconscious, though an angry black bruise is rising on half her jaw.

You kiss her and slip away into the darkness, towards the moor.

Hackwill's car is in the drive.

Lights are going on in the few other houses in Sutton Mallet. The shot has been heard.

You bend low and scoot along by the hedgerow, towards the Achelzoy road. You can't afford to be too far off. Your story – feeble as it sounds – is that you went for a walk on your own after dark. The strength of it is that you have no obvious motive.

You find a deep bit of ditch and drop the shotgun through the duckweed. It sinks. The rippling weed re-forms over the hole.

You walk, upright, back toward Sutton Mallet. Hackwill's big car cruises by at speed. You're almost run down. You see Hackwill, alone in the car, intent on driving, eyes black holes.

Good, the idiot is running. He must have wanted to be a culprit when he grew up.

You're light-headed now. Everything is paid back. Not only is Laraine free of Mr Bitch-buster but James has been avenged for the copse. It's amazing how murder makes sense.

Back at the house, a nosy neighbour – Roddy Smedley, who used to play commandos with James – has found Laraine, who is rambling and hysterical, and Sean, who is head-deprived and dead. The police have been called.

'It were that Hackwill,' Smedley says. 'He were a bully at school. Bastards don't change.'

You take over with Laraine, hugging her as you wait for the police.

Hackwill isn't quite stupid enough to make a dash for the Channel ports. The next morning, he calls the cops to report his innocent-bystander-on-the-scene version. By then, he's facing charges anyway as collateral damage. The investigators found all sorts of incriminating documents in Sean's study, detailing dodgy deals going back a few years. He might as well have filed it all under HACKWILL'S MURDER MOTIVE.

What you can't believe is that the police don't find the gun. It's not as if you hid it in the Amazon jungle. They get a court order and inventory Hackwill's collection. A weapon of the requisite bore turns up missing. Hackwill does a stone-me-guv-I'm-innocent act.

Mary Yatman does some of the gruntwork, taking statements from you and Laraine, but this is a big-shot CID investigation. It spirals out from murder into civic corruption. There are bankruptcies and reversals as Hackwill's empire falls. The Labour Party forces him to resign or face deselection at the next council elections.

Helen leaves him. He hangs himself in jail. Congrats. You've got away with it. You've got the girl, the gold watch and everything.

You move in with Laraine, to see her through this. Sean turns out to have been almost broke, thanks to his Hackwill involvements. But he was massively insured. Laraine is set for life.

Is this a happy ending?

There's a downside. You live together but have to be careful. Your actual relationship has to be kept a secret between you. No one else must know you sleep together. And you get a lot of attention. The corruption-and-murder story is juicy. Newspapers, television and radio are all over it. The *Comet on Sunday* offers Laraine a big fee for her story. You decide to take the money and she has you write up her version – including the bitch-busting, to blacken Sean's name further – which sets in stone the Hackwill-blasts-Sean story.

Nothing's too good for the man who shot Sean Rye. The BBC makes a drama-documentary, with Lindsay Duncan as Laraine, Bob Peck as Hackwill and James Wilby as Sean. You're in two scenes, played by an actor whose name you can never remember, who is always the best friend in sit-coms.

Reg Jessup goes to jail and sells his own I-was-Hackwill's-minion story to the papers.

The Discount Development is abandoned. Jobs are lost. The economy of Sedgwater takes a killing blow just as the country is coming out of recession into boom.

You wait for a wave of guilt that never comes.

Two years later, kids fishing find the shotgun.

Mary says that dots the last i.

You and Laraine are seeing quite a bit of Mary. She was the one who told you what police press statements actually meant. You never forget how clever she is. You never quite relax around her. Then again, all the way back to primary school, you always found her slightly uncomfortable so she's not going to notice any difference in you.

Your book about James, abandoned for over a year, mutates when you get back to it. You contrast James with Sean. You write up Hackwill as a villain. It becomes a book not just about your family but about the town, the country, the '80s. Hackwill represents much that is dangerous to everyone. It's easy to write and sells surprisingly well. But, of course, it's structured around two big lies and a lot of evasions. It's as if you keep pouring concrete on aspects of your life that can never be examined.

The real story, you worry, would make a better book.

And so it goes on.

You live with Laraine, almost in a marriage. Unmarried siblings, no longer young, kept together by family tragedy. You have sex about as much as Sean and Laraine did when their marriage was rocky, but you remain attracted to and interested in each other.

You actually stay in love.

You write more books, analysing the state of the nation as Thatcherism gives way to Majorism, observing the rise of Tony Blair, the influence of Europe, the end of the Cold War. Your books, which come out every few years, feel like personal reports on the state of the nation as seen from Sutton Mallet, through a veil of family tragedy.

Twenty years after the murder, in a new century, the seconds it took to kill Sean are still central to your life. You still have to think of it every day, and hesitate often, to avoid exposing yourself. You'd thought that after a while you'd come to believe Hackwill shot Sean but you don't.

Sometimes, your hands still shake and your ears still ring.

At a reception in town, to mark the launch of your collected works on CD-ROM, a pretty face catches your eye. You've never been unfaithful to Laraine – you know too much about each other to risk the relationship for trivial distractions – but take an aesthetic interest in girls. You're like a decadent old uncle, hiding sweets in his pockets so that little nieces will perform intimate searches.

The face is not only pretty but vaguely familiar. She must be about twenty, with nose and eyebrow piercings, and a blond buzz-cut. In this future – you think of anything past 1984 as the future – she has quite a conservative look. She's one of the girls your publisher has hired to pour wine and carry canapés.

She looks at you the way you look at her, with interest, and puzzlement. At last, she comes over and talks to you.

'I'm sorry,' she says. 'It's silly, but we shouldn't have to avoid each other.'

Behind her face, you see another: smaller, rounder.

'I'm Sam Kellett,' she says. 'Kellett's my step-dad's name. I was Samantha Hackwill.'

Good Lord! You remember her chewing a shotgun shell.

She thinks she needs to nudge you further. 'My father killed your brother-in-law.'

'It was a long time ago,' you say, conventionally.

'All my life. It's been with me.'

'Feels that way to me too.'

Sam almost gushes. 'I knew you'd understand. Mum doesn't. No one else does. Your book. It was banned in our house but I read it when I was twelve. I'd like you to know it really helped. It made them real to me. Dad, Sean, your sister. Knowing you started out as kids, like everyone else. That no matter how it went wrong, you were all just people, not those actors in that TV film. Just kids who grew up, with all your quarrels and private jokes and messy lives.'

You find your eyes are watering.

Sam Kellett, Samantha Hackwill, the cartridge-biting baby, the damaged-but-struggling-woman, kisses your cheek.

You want to cuddle her, as you did once before. But you don't.

And so on.

148

Fuck subtlety. Mary won't buy another disappearance. She knows Laraine wouldn't be capable of coolly going through the abandoned wife bit before sneaking off to join her embezzling bastard of a husband in the Club Whoopee, Rio de Janeiro.

Suicide she'll swallow.

Before you lose your nerve, you go through with it. You go to the master bedroom and scoop the sleepy Laraine up in your arms.

She resists a little. 'No, Keith,' she says, misinterpreting.

You go out into the hallway, carrying her. You have opened the window first. You throw her out, awkwardly. She nosedives on to crazy-paving.

Of course, she isn't immediately dead. You use a big stone to flatten a section of her skull. Then you call Mary.

As you wait for the police and the ambulance, you think over things to say. 'I should have known. It's hit her hard. Dad, James, Sean. Everybody was leaving.' In the end, you keep it simple, don't venture analysis or opinion. You were woken up by the window being opened and didn't investigate until you heard the impact. No cry. No note.

Mary questions you tactfully.

You want her to think Laraine did it out of guilt but not be able to tell anyone else. She'll feel she alone knows the real truth of Laraine's suicide and be content with that secret knowledge, without needing to probe for any realer real truth.

God, this is complicated.

You stay on in the house in Sutton Mallet. Legally, it passed to Laraine when Sean died and to Mum when Laraine did. But since Sean won't be officially dead for seven years, it's his; and, when seven years are up and Laraine isn't around to inherit, it'll go to his next of kin, whoever the fuck they are.

You seem to have *de facto* inherited the place. You doubt if you'll ever be able to sell it. After all, if it wasn't haunted before it certainly is now.

And could you trust the new owners not to dig up the compost heap?

Of course, you could kill them. By then, the superstitious locals would believe in a curse.

There are other people you could kill; to make sure. Mary, for a start. Hackwill, maybe; he knows too much about Sean, and must be wondering about the Reggie Perrin theory.

Yourself. That would solve it all.

You are dozing in front of Sean's television, on which greenish people have sex in clinical close-up – you found a stash of Swedish-language porn videos in his den – when the doorbell wakes you. As you make your way to the hall, you scratch your chin, realising you haven't shaved for two or three days.

You let Mary in. She's out of uniform, in a summery orange dress with a light fawn raincoat. Her hair is down. She looks like a normal young woman. But you remember Scary Mary from school.

In the living-room, you hastily turn off the video. Mary doesn't even raise an eyebrow at your viewing material. She'll have seen worse.

'You must feel mucky,' she says, looking at the blank screen. 'Let's take a shower.'

You don't follow this.

'Together,' she clarifies.

Mary is, you realise, a pretty girl. Since Laraine, you've been missing the sex. If the cop on the case wants to get wet and naked with you, you're probably off the suspects list.

'I always fancied you at school,' she says, smiling.

You are naked, under the warm rain of the shower. Mary is down to her half-slip. She folds her clothes carefully. You reach out for her. She has turned flirty and teasing, pushing you back under the water jet. You find it slippery underfoot and grasp the chrome handle set into the wall.

Mary takes something from her bag and hides it behind her back. She steps into the shower, underclothes instantly transparent. As you look at her nipples, she takes her handcuffs out from behind her back. Kinky, you think.

She clips one cuff round your left wrist, then – swiftly, purposefully – clamps the other round the chrome handle. You are tethered to the wall.

Mary steps out of the shower and wraps herself in a towel-robe. The water is too hot now. You cringe against the tile wall, your chest and thighs boiled lobster-red. Mary looks at you as if you are an idiot.

'There weren't any clues,' she says. 'I just knew. Like I knew Hackwill deserved what James gave him. And Sean, come to that. But Laraine was wrong.'

You don't protest that you don't know what she's talking about.

Mary looks through the bathroom cabinet. She tuts disgust at Sean's electric razor and puts it back. But she finds the blades for your safety razor and clucks approval.

'I brought my own, just in case. But this is better.'

You try to wrench the bar off the wall, but it's designed to withstand the weight of a falling pensioner.

'Is the water too hot? Can't have that.'

Mary reaches in and turns the heat down. You relax into the warm stream.

'That wasn't a lie about fancying you,' she says, slipping out of her robe. 'But doing Laraine was wrong. It meant we had to come to this.

Why do you think I became a ladypig? I'm not interested in the law. I believe in justice.'

She takes off her half-slip and her panties. She is naked. You try to grab her hair with your right hand but she gets a strong grip on your wrist. You wrestle a little, water falling all around you.

You feel a sting on your wrist, striking up your arm.

Red splashes around your feet. A used razor-blade drops. Water flows over your opened arm, blood-trails mixing in, flowing down into the plughole.

Mary gets out of the shower. She's brought her own towel, which she uses to sponge the blood from her belly. You watch her as, fastidious as a cat, she cleans herself. You've flopped weakly at the bottom of the shower stall, one arm wrenched up above you, the other draining down by your side. You're still conscious but can't do anything.

Mary unlocks the handcuffs, examines your left wrist for chafing, is satisfied, and puts them away. She turns the water to cold and gets dressed. It's like watching a striptease in reverse.

You're too tired and empty to do anything. The long, straight cut, from your wrist almost to your elbow, isn't bleeding so much now. The edges are wrinkled and blueing.

You've been in the shower too long.

Mary sits on the closed toilet and watches you. She won't go before you do.

Go to 0.

149

You push yourself up off the ground and run for Hackwill. He is giving a few words to a TV interviewer, stressing the victory of law and order.

You slam into him, wrenching him away from Mary's shoulder, and hammer him against a car. Your knee connects with his groin, your forehead crunches his nose. You get your hands round his throat and squeeze. People feebly thump your back. You see Hackwill's red eyes bulge. He snarls, teeth glistening like metal.

'Your brother's a little shit,' Hackwill says. 'He's no good at all.'

Your head swims in blood. You and Hackwill are at the end of a funnel that spirals out to take in the universe.

How have you come to this?

A wrong path has been taken. Disputes like this are settled in small claims courts, not in pitched gun battles. Some cowboy movie has superimposed over the real world.

You still try to throttle the bastard, Hackwill.

'Come and see your brother,' Mary shouts, close to your ear. No, not Mary. Reg Jessup.

Reg is supposed to be dead. James killed him.

You are pulled away from Hackwill. He chokes and stands up. He has never looked less human. He's a grown-up, in shorts and a stretched-tight boy's-size cardigan. His face is pure evil.

As you are held by the police, Hackwill hauls your dead brother off a stretcher and shakes him. James's wounds bleed like stigmata.

There are trees in the car park. Reg slips out of them, battered face healing.

Everything is unravelling.

You're going back.

You see Robert and Reg, holding James by his shoulders. James's shorts are dark at the crotch. Wee trickles down his legs. He starts sniffling.

'Everyone heard two shots ring out,' Gene Pitney sings, 'one shot made Liberty fall...'

The bell goes for the end of break. Shane, Mary – even Scary Mary! – and the rest run off, back to the classroom. You don't move.

'C'mon, Mental,' Robert says. 'We're not going to hurt you.'

'Much,' adds Reg, laughing.

If you go to the classroom and get on with your sums, go to 6. If you go to a teacher and tell what's happening, go to 10. If you go into the copse to help James, go to 14.

150

Your fortieth birthday is in 1999. At ten o'clock in the morning, Mum comes into your bedroom, the same room with the same pirate map on the wall, with a tray of tea and biscuits, waking you up. She gives you your present, a new dressing-gown (not wrapped, but in a nice paper bag from British Home Stores). She kisses you and gives you your cards.

One is from her, one is from the char.

Laraine and Jimmy are out of the country. They usually remember to send cards but don't often calculate delivery time correctly, so you have to wait a day or two. Your friend Vince will deliver his card by hand, later.

'The big four o,' Mum says. 'Well, I never.' She clucks and leaves you alone.

You are living at home. In fact, you've never lived anywhere else. Mum cooks and a char comes two days a week to clean the house and do your laundry.

After Dad's death in 1982, Mum thought about remarrying. There was this bloke Phil hanging around, asking her out to antiques fairs and car-boot sales. You thought he was a bit of a pillock and he went away in the end. Dad's insurance, topped up by Mum's own investments and the occasional contribution from your brother and sister, keeps both of you comfortable, though the house occasionally suffers because repairs and maintenance are supposed to be your department and you rarely get it together. Though your benefits were stopped nearly twenty years ago, you still do odd jobs around the house and garden to earn your keep. Mum, at sixty-eight, is spry, but her hip gives her gyp. She can't cope with things as well as she used to. You have to be the man of the family.

Laraine is married for the second time, to Kay Shearer, the discount shelving tycoon, and living in Canada. She has six children, whom you can never keep straight, though Mum can pick them out of a group photograph and rattle off their names and statistics like a football fan listing the goal averages of his team's players. Jimmy is Major James Marion, stationed with the UN peace-keeping forces in some foreign trouble-spot. He has married a Czech girl, Pavla, and they have two sons. Mum worries that he will be shot by insurgents, but he says he mainly does admin work.

Last Christmas, Mum went to Canada to see Laraine and Kay and the children. Laraine paid for a first-class air ticket. She offered to bring you over too but you didn't like the idea of flying. Mum made sure the char popped in to see you were all right, and telephoned on Christmas Day, only she got the time difference muddled and called up after midnight, on Boxing Day.

It occurs to you that Mum gave you a dressing-gown for Christmas too.

You worry about her.

You have never had a job. You haven't had a girlfriend since Marie-Laure Quilter.

You weigh sixteen stone. Your usual outfit is corduroy trousers, slightly split at the crotch, and a baggy pullover that has its frayed areas. You shave every third or fourth day. Your hair gets long until Mum gets fed up with it to cut it for you. You have a bald patch, and don't comb your hair over it; probably because you rarely comb your hair.

You find ways of passing the day.

You sleep in the mornings. You follow Australian soaps. Vince comes by some afternoons with videos. He has a shop in the old Discount Development, selling second-hand comics, records and videos. He only opens in the morning.

You have a lot of little things to do; to prevent you dwelling on the big things.

'It looks lovely,' comments Mum.

You are wearing your Christmas dressing-gown, not your birthday one.

'Just your size.'

She still sometimes calls you a growing boy.

Mum makes you cups of tea every two hours and teases – well, nags – you about getting out more with your friends. Her official version is that you stay at home to look after her, and that she doesn't want you to sacrifice yourself for her.

'You're only young once.'

You were only young once.

You go into town once a week, to help Mum with the supermarket shopping. She gets a taxi back and you loiter, putting off going home. You sit in the Outlet, the fast-food place where Brink's Café used to be, watching the kids hanging out, chattering and moaning. You can't remember ever being like that.

Sometimes, in the street or the Outlet, you see withered faces that remind you who their wearers used to be. Timmy Gossett, the loony who sits on the Corn Exchange steps mumbling, was at primary school with you. Locked in his own mind, he fills you with dread. You always felt sorry for him, and now you fear he feels sorry for you.

Not a day goes by that you don't think about Marie-Laure. She doesn't live in Achelzoy any more. Her mother sold up, and they both moved on. You wonder what she's doing.

Less often, you think of that woman from the DHSS. Her name usually escapes you, but it was Vanda.

Vince brings you a *Doctor Who* video as a birthday present. 'Inferno', with Jon Pertwee. You spend the afternoon watching it together.

Mum asks if Vince will be staying for your birthday dinner. Vince says he has to be off. He's taking evening classes. Tonight, it's sociology. His hobby is evening classes. He has more O Levels than Einstein. Each time he gets one, he picks another course and works on that for a few years.

In the video, Doctor Who slips sideways in time to a parallel world where all his friends – the Brigadier, Liz Shaw of UNIT, Sergeant Benton – are evil.

You and Vince have one of your long conversations, about parallel worlds. They usually turn into arguments, but Vince thinks of a row as a species of performance art.

His contention is that 'Inferno' is a radical departure from the usual parallel-world science fiction story. Most are about societies rather than people, and posit worlds in which Germany won the Second World War or President Kennedy wasn't assassinated or England lost the Cup Final in 1966. The stories demonstrate the effects of these events. When real people, like Winston Churchill or JFK, figure in parallel-world stories, they appear as themselves, and authors suggest how, given their established real-world characters, they'd react in changed circumstances. 'Inferno', in which England is a fascist state, goes further and suggests personality itself is defined by social and political circumstance, that a person's degree of niceness or nastiness is conditioned by the regime under which they live.

You point out that the same thing is done in the *Star Trek* episode in which Spock has a beard and Kirk succeeded to command of the *Enterprise* by assassinating the captain played by Jeffrey Hunter in the pilot.

Vince concedes that is true. 'Think about it, Keith. If the world were different – if Britain had lost the Falklands or Neil Kinnock was elected prime minister – you would be different. Who knows what you'd be?'

You find the idea a bit threatening.

'I'd still be me. Under any circumstances. If we passed through a time-slip tomorrow and woke up in a world where the Vikings had triumphed and Somerset was an outpost of an Icelandic empire, I'd still be Keith and you'd still be Vince.'

'But maybe you'd be Evil Keith. Like the Brigadier with an eyepatch or Spock with a beard. You'd have a helmet with horns.'

'That's a common fallacy. Viking helms didn't have horns.'

'You'd ride out every day in your big Icelandic car, the Volvo Björk, and put Achelzoy to the sword, looting and raping, then come back home in time for tea.'

Sometimes, Vince loses you. You think he's a bit sad.

At the end of 'Inferno', Doctor Who slips back to his proper time and his friends are nice again.

At the end of your birthday – Mum made you your favourite, sausage toad – you go up to your room and put Vince's present with your other videos.

You have the old TV and video in your room. The new home-entertainment system Kay bought Mum is set up downstairs, filling the front room with speakers and screens and decks like the Borg taking over in *Star Trek: The Next Generation*.

You undress and put on your birthday dressing-gown.

You are torn between Nichelle Nichols, Lieutenant Uhura in *Classic Trek*, and Katy Manning, Jo Grant – who took over from Liz Shaw – in *Doctor Who*.

So, you ask yourself, is it a *Doctor Who* day, or a *Star Trek* day?

If *Star Trek*, go to 160. If *Doctor Who*, go to 170.

151

When it comes to it, you hesitate. You can't take it that one step further. You can't kill.

Sean, on the doorstep, stares at you. 'Keith,' he says, astonished.

'Do it,' screeches Laraine.

Now Sean is terrified.

'I'm fucking him, Sean,' Laraine says.

There's anger in Sean's terror. He makes fists.

Headlights in the drive. Hackwill is here.

The gun in your hands is a dead stick. You're a statue. You can't go forward and you can't go back. You begin to unravel.

Laraine takes the gun away from you.

With a snarl, Sean comes for her. The gun goes off and Sean's shoulder dissolves into red mist. She has fired both barrels.

Your eyes are hurt by the flash. Your ears ring like police sirens.

'Fuck,' shouts Hackwill.

'Shells,' Laraine demands.

You bring the packet out of your pocket. Laraine snatches it.

Sean is screaming now, rolling on the drive, one arm dead, lower face splattered with blood. Hackwill is fixed by his car, goggling.

Laraine breaks the gun, shucks the used shells, and jams in fresh ones. She is clumsy but manages it eventually and snaps the gun shut.

'Sorry, Rob,' she says, and shoots Hackwill in the face. Almost in pieces, he lies on his car bonnet, life blasted out of him.

If Laraine had seen Robert Hackwill drag James into the copse, things would have been different. Of course, Laraine seems to be mad.

She can't reload. Her motor skills are deteriorating. She stands over Sean, fumbling with shells. The packet comes apart and shells patter over Sean's kicking legs.

Lights go on next door.

Laraine picks up two shells and, concentrating, gets the gun loaded.

'What do you think, Keith,' she says. 'Me, or him?'

If you say 'You', go to 161. If you say 'Him', go to 174.

152

'If a man did that to me,' Mary says. 'I'd kill him.'

'Sean was one of those men,' you say.

'What do you mean?'

'One of those men people want to kill.'

'People?'

This is it. Play this right and you're home free.

'I probably shouldn't say this, Mary. But there've been calls. Men, asking for Sean, late at night. Not bank-customer voices. Threatening, somehow. And before he left, Sean burned some papers in the grate. Things are chaos at the bank. They sent someone over to go through his files at home.' This is true. 'I think Sean was keeping a lot from us.'

Mary's face is stone. Then it cracks just a little. 'We've found out some things,' she admits. 'Your sister is better off.'

Then she goes.

You want Mary to think Sean is on the run somewhere, pursued by dangerous criminal associates. After a few months, you think it would make sense if his body were to show up in the sea somewhere, identifiable only by dental records.

Laraine doesn't want to dig him up.

You construct stories, strong enough to believe. You see connections between Councillor Hackwill and his shadowy business partners and organised crime. You imagine deals gone wrong at dead of night, with Sean floundering under blows from a thug's blunt instrument as a godfather smokes a cigar.

It makes sense. You try to will Mary into parallel thoughts.

Laraine clings, insisting you take the risk of staying with her at night, sharing the bed where she once slept with the man now lying dead under the compost heap. She uses sex to keep you there, making herself desperately available whenever you want to draw away.

You worry about her. She is under strain. If Sean were found and Persons Unknown took the blame, this would all be over.

You go through Sean's den. There are files on business deals. Most of it is beyond you. You've burned a few, just to back up what you told Mary.

How can you make this more incriminating?

Laraine answers the phone one evening and a deep voice asks for Sean. She gasps and hangs up. Wrong attitude.

You try to believe it. In this world, Sean was taken away by the mob, tortured and killed. You and Laraine are innocent bystanders. Maybe you're in danger. Maybe Sean's killers didn't get what they wanted from him and will be coming after you.

You are authentically worried. You tell Mary the calls are continuing. They do. You take a few yourself. The voices – there are more than one – mean nothing to you.

'Where's the merchandise, Mr Marion?'

That's the calmer, suaver voice. You imagine a '50s face, with a slash of moustache and plenty of hair oil. An astrakhan collar. A cigar.

'Tell Rye he's fucked.'

That's the one you think of as a cross between Arthur Mullard and Moose Malloy. A big bruiser who crushes nuts in his hands and has scars on his face. An ex-wrestler, with tattoos done in jail.

'Where's the merch?'

Laraine is going spare. You're caught between panic and disbelief. Surely, you can't have willed these callers into existence, to back up your story? It has to be a coincidence.

Sean really was crossing gangsters and you took him out of the circuit. Because he's dead, he hasn't made payments or committed crimes. His confederates are getting heavy, assuming he's hiding out. You could be in real danger.

Mary is reassuring. This is too big for one WPC, you think. A disappearance, she can handle. A murder, she could cope with before the CID showed up. A major case against a crime organisation is way out of her fighting weight. But she is still your preferred police contact.

You think you're being followed. Cars keep just out of sight. Unmarked vans are parked wherever you go. You imagine the red dots of laser sights playing over your skull.

While you are away, people break into the house and search. Somehow, Laraine doesn't notice. She's becoming a zombie. In the evenings, she clings to you, too wrung out to speak.

You wonder if this stage of the affair is through.

An anonymous envelope arrives. It contains blown-up photographs, taken through your bedroom window. You and Laraine. Unmistakably fucking.

Laraine goes white and emits a single sob. You look for a note. For a demand. Nothing.

The next call is from Mr Suave. 'There's someone here who'd like to talk to you, Keith.'

Laraine is in the room. You look at her. She'll be no help.

'Keith?' says a small, tired voice.

It's Sean. The world spins.

'Is Mrs Rye with you?' Mr Suave asks.

'Yes.'

'Good. You're unusually close, aren't you?'

You imagine the sneer of contempt tinged with lechery.

'Perhaps you'd put her on, Keith. Our friend would like to talk to her.'

'She's in no state –'

'And neither are you. Not to get between man and wife.'

You hold out the phone and look at Laraine's eyes as she hears the voice.

'Sean?' She can't believe it.

'Yes… no… yes.'

She hangs up. 'They want money. Or they'll kill him.'

You dig up the compost heap. You go down almost to bedrock and find nothing. It's a bad time for Mary to call by.

'Busy work,' you explain. 'Just trying to sort things out.'

'There's a lot of money missing at the bank. And Councillor Hackwill's had a domestic incident with a paper guillotine. Four fingers gone.'

'An accident?'

'That's what he's calling it. Funny thing, though. He claims he was alone, but his secretary says he was in a meeting with two unfamiliar men at the time.'

You are sweaty and filthy, neck-deep in a grave. Mary hunkers down at ground level, looking into the hole.

'Not a good place to plant,' she says. 'The shade from the wall.'

'Buried treasure,' you say. 'I found a pirate map in Sean's desk.'

Mary smiles.

'I don't care what they do to Sean,' Laraine says. 'But they have those pictures.'

Your mind isn't working round this. 'Laraine, they can't do anything to Sean. It's too late, remember?'

'No, they have Sean.' She has been able to wipe her memory.

This is your fantasy, though. You can't impose it on reality.

'It would be best if they killed him. If they showed him the pictures, he'd kill us. Both.'

Laraine is satisfied with the thought. 'If we give them what they want,' she says, 'they'll kill him for us.' She flings her arms round your neck.

'But what do they want?' you say.

'They call it "the merchandise".'

'But what's that?'

You didn't think your story through in enough detail. You wanted to drop hints, to leave gaps to be filled. As a consequence, you've no idea what the people who have Sean mean by 'the merchandise'. It could be money, drugs, gems, postage stamps, a tin of marbles. You search the house over and over again. If Sean can disappear, the merchandise can appear. If the world has shifted to back up your story, that'd be logical. Is a suitcase full of fissionable material hidden in the basement? An ancient Aztec sacrificial idol with a hideous curse on it behind the fireplace? Cap'n Kidd's treasure buried a dozen paces due east of the compost heap?

Laraine spends more and more time in a daze. Her grip on reality is so skewed she is no back-up at all. You have only what you see and feel to go on.

You know the house is being watched. Whoever took the pictures is out there on the wetlands, up a tree pretending to be a bird-watcher. You take to staying out of the sightlines of the windows. Doing as much as you can in the dark.

You receive a package containing four severed human fingers. At first, you think of Hackwill but Laraine recognises Sean's wedding ring. The fingers seem fresh.

You call Mary. She is amiably baffled and says some explanation will come along.

Mr Thug laughs at you down the phone. 'Next time, it's your dick on the chopping block.'

You wake up in the middle of the night, a pillow over your face, pressing down? Is Laraine trying to stifle you? No. You hear her struggling, trying to cry out around a big hand clamped over her mouth.

Your wrist is wrenched and a metal cuff clamped around it. This is an arrest. It's over. You are almost relieved. The pressure is off the pillow. Your nose hurts and you think it might be bleeding.

Laraine sobs.

You expect to be wrestled out of bed. But you aren't. Doors close.

You tug on your cuffed arm. You're tethered to something, perhaps the bed. You brush the pillow off your face. A smell of putrefaction assaults your gummy nostrils. You are handcuffed to something indescribably foul.

Laraine turns on the bedside lamp.

You look at the green mess that was Sean's face.

The hand you are cuffed to has a thumb but no fingers. You work the cuff off the stump and are free, albeit with a dangling charm bracelet.

Sean, as you always knew, is dead. He has been for a while. There are dots on his face you didn't make. Cigarette burns? But the dent in his skull looks as if it was done with a poker.

Laraine sits, useless, in a chair at her dressing-table, head in her hands.

Sean is making a mess on the duvet. You didn't cut off his fingers, so far as you remember.

'Did you see their faces?' you ask. 'There must have been two or more of them.'

She just cries.

What to do with Sean?

There's still the hole where the compost heap was. You've not shovelled it back yet. You order Laraine to help. Meekly, she takes Sean's stinking feet. You carry the body downstairs and out into the garden, then unceremoniously dump him in the hole.

You shovel in a few spades of earth, then see your mistake.

You and Laraine haven't killed Sean. Mr Suave and Mr Thug did that, and dumped the body on you. Why should you cover up their crime? Mary has been following the plot. She saw the fingers. She knows you're innocent. God, you *are* innocent. You didn't do this. You might have dreamed up the people who did, but you are guilt-free.

It's near dawn.

You finish your call to Mary and hang up. The handcuffs clink on your wrist. They make you look guilty but you decide not to try to get them off. They are part of the evidence.

There must be a ton of it.

Mr Thug and Mr Suave. Hackwill's secretary saw them; and so, presumably, did Hackwill. You and Laraine have heard them on the phone. They'll have been seen by others. They must have killed Sean somewhere, which will be scattered with gobbets of forensic evidence. And they must have come by car – didn't you hear an engine when they left? – which someone might have seen.

It is odd that you never saw them. But there was something pressing that pillow to your face.

Mary turns up, not alone. There are several police cars. Inspector Draper, Mary's boss, has been rousted from bed and isn't happy.

'Mr Rye was delivered here and handcuffed to you?' Draper says.

'Yes,' you admit. 'That's about the size of it.'

'So why did you put him in this hole?'

You've stepped off a cliff and are looking down. You were going to haul him out and take him upstairs again.

'Looks like he's been down here a while,' a voice says from the hole. Mary climbs out, knees earthy.

'The fingers,' you say.

Mary shrugs, having no idea what you are talking about.

'Keith Oliver Marion,' Draper says, holding a document, 'I have here a warrant…'

And so on.

153

'Them,' you say.

Chris howls in fury. Mary is surprised.

'You must be some kind of liquid filth,' she says.

Shane tears the twins away from Chris, who claws and bites as Grebo grabs her.

You are a zombie. Moving, but dead inside.

'Do you *really* mean it?' Mary asks.

She admires your decision. It makes you like her.

You think about it.

If you really mean it, go to 166. If you don't, go to 179.

154

Bob Monkhouse makes jokes about VC Conyer's punk princess days, which the somewhat haggard rehab survivor takes in good part. You realise you were at Sedgwater College with the woman, though you can't remember ever speaking with her. Clare was scathing about the singer–songwriter's miserabilism.

An envelope is delivered by Royal Marines who rappel into the studio. Then they go over to the machines, Arthur and Guinevere. The apparatus of oppression.

You know you'll have achieved something.

As the first number is drawn, a wave of heat and sound and light blasts you.

Go to 0.

155

Sean writes you a cheque for £2500. You took the sum out of the air. He tears the cheque out of the book – he's with a rival bank, you note – and holds it out. You take hold of the slip of paper, but he doesn't let go.

'This is the last of it, Keith,' he says, looking you in the eye.

'Of course, Sean.'

He lets go.

During Sean's leaving do, you take him aside and tell him you've thought about it and that he should pay you another £2500.

'Think of it as a retainer.'

'Why does blackmail make people talk like that?'

'I don't understand.'

'Suddenly, you're purring out of the side of your mouth. Like George Sanders.'

'Two and a half grand. Tonight.'

'And that's Bob Hoskins.'

'Fuck you.'

'No, fuck you.'

'Okay. But just pay.' You still have the flimsies. The evidence.

'Later.'

The mayor wants Sean to make a speech. Sean is reluctantly pulled away and puts up with a lot of embarrassing joshing. As you watch, thrilling to the power you have over him, Ro sidles up.

'Watch the bastard squirm,' she says.

Your heart catches. Has Sean told Ro about you?

You are called up to give Sean his leaving present. A bottle of Scotch older than he is. You smile at him. He thanks you, eyes incandescent with rage. This is good for you.

You drink too much and Vanda drives you home in the new car you bought with your 'windfall'. There will be more luxuries from now on. Whatever Sean makes, you will be on a percentage. It's a no-risk investment, with a far better yield than anything he could have sorted out. You have the new cheque in your tuxedo pocket.

Vanda parks the car.

'What is it, darling?' you ask.

'Now,' she says, not to you.

There is a blur. A thin line descends, close to your eyes. Something brushes your nose and chin. A line of pain cuts into your neck. It burns. Someone has a wire noose around your throat.

'Pull, you bastard,' Vanda shouts.

The pain cuts deeper. And ends.

Go to 0.

156

You try to phone Anne but get her answerphone. You'd really like to talk this over with her. This is not your field of expertise. You can't call Mum: she'd be even less able than you to cope.

You go for a pint in the Lime Kiln. It's a slow Wednesday evening. You and Max Lewis spend an hour or so running over mutual friends from school. Neither of you knows what happened to most of them.

You go back to the flat. Your telephone is ringing.

It's not Anne; it's Mum. Laraine is in hospital. Mum says there was an accident, but you know it was Sean.

When you get to Casualty, Sean is in the waiting-room, looking devastated. Mum and Phil are comforting him. You make fists and stride towards Sean. Casualty is a good place to get teeth knocked out.

'Sean,' you say.

Someone bars your path to him. A woman in blue serge. Mary Yatman. 'Keith,' she says. 'There are some questions…'

If you pay attention to Mary, go to 162. If you assault Sean, go to 175.

157

So what are you going to do with this fully armed, home-made bomb? It's rigged to explode if anyone tries to dismantle it. The timer is set for a week from now. If nothing goes wrong, it will go off then.

You think. Should you take it somewhere where it will do no harm? Throw it into a culvert in Snowdonia? How much movement will it take to be jarred into detonation? Would it stand a coach trip to Wales?

You're giggling. It's what you always said about nuclear weapons. When you invent something which has only one function, eventually that function will be fulfilled. Only it's on your living-room table. Your mouth is dry.

The Lottery draw is complete. It's a roll-over week. No big pay-out. Next week, someone is liable to be a major winner.

The bomb is a cylinder, wrapped in brown paper.

You can't move. Literally. Your arms and legs are numb and unresponsive. You're aware you've wet yourself.

The parcel just sits there. How much time has passed? *Match of the Day* has ended. Now, it's a film about American cops.

You can nod your head slightly.

What's special about that parcel? It annoys you. The bloody parcel blocks your view of the telly.

Days pass and you have time to think about your life. That's what television gives you: time to think. You wish that parcel weren't there, though. You sleep and wake, wake and sleep. You get very hungry and very thirsty but that goes away. You are surprised how quickly you get used to it.

You can't quite put together all the pieces. You aren't sure how and why you're here.

You hear clocks ticking in the room.

The answerphone takes messages. Mum and Laraine call up to see how you are. Your counsellor wants to know why you've missed an appointment. And you might have won a holiday home in the Algarve and isn't that wonderful?

Life has fled from your body. Only your mind remains.

It's a cool, calming sensation. They can't get you in your skull. You're still free.

You know things will change when Saturday comes round again.

They do.

Go to 0.

158

Ten years pass. Fifteen. Twenty. It starts to seem like a dream you once had. At first, you think not a day will go by that won't be dominated by thoughts of Laraine and Sean. Your sister's body and your victim's. But, like everything else, it fades. You lose touch with Laraine, hearing of her only through Mum. Only rarely do you remember that she's out there, her secrets festering. She must feel the same about you. She remarries, to a Tom Owen (Mr UN Owen?).

You are married, to Anne, and you have two children, Jared and Joy. You've written books. You've taught courses. You broadcast often. Sean's body is like a piece of grit in your oyster, a piece that doesn't become a pearl. The further away you get in time, the less it matters.

You know joy, sorrow, peace, disturbance. Regular life things.

One day, in your study, you take a phone call.

'You bastard,' a man says. 'You fucking bastard.' He hangs up.

You stab the trace button, but the caller withheld his number.

You sit there, staring at half a leader article on your computer screen, mind wrenched.

You're dragged back. You aren't a respected journalist and public figure, a well-loved husband and father. You're the guy who fucked his own sister and killed her husband with a poker. You're the bastard who buried Sean Rye in the compost heap.

You get another call. 'You'll pay,' the man says.

Because of who you are and what you do, your reaction is to write about it. You've kept diaries, journals and notebooks for most of your life. Naturally, you left some things out, though you've used very private codes to mark exact dates.

The calls continue. The same voice. Hard, threatening, mean.

As soon as you heard the voice, you knew it would all come out. There'll be a protracted torment first, but it will all come out. The most you can do is limit the damage. You have to have your say, to leave the world your version of what happened. No, to leave the world the truth.

You've written about painful things before. Joy died at eighteen, of AIDS. Researching the piece you wrote about it meant you found out things about your daughter's life that you'd rather you didn't know. Then you put them in print, so that everyone knew. Anne threatened to leave if you published, but in the end understood why the piece had to be made public. It didn't make your daughter any less special.

But that was different.

Between taking the taunting, abusive calls, which gradually become more specific – 'It's been a long time, but there are still consequences, fuckface' – you draft and redraft a confession. Where to start? With the murder? With the incest? With Laraine's marriage? With James's death?

It becomes a family history. You hope the murder will be seen in context. It wasn't an aberration, a monstrous moment. It was a natural outgrowth of what had happened. You don't let yourself off the hook – you accept that it was your fault – but you try to understand yourself, to see some meaning, some ray of redemption.

Anne notices you're preoccupied, but she's used to that.

'How long has it been, fuckface? Twenty-five years.'

The calls are almost incoherent. The caller is working himself up. The crunch will come soon.

'And you're the *respectable* Mr Marion.'

'Mr Owen,' you say, 'I know you'll find this difficult to believe, but I accept your judgement.'

'*Owen!*'

You're wrong. It's not Laraine's husband, it's someone else. Someone else knows. Who could Laraine have told? Or maybe...

The caller is laughing hard. 'You don't even remember, do you? Were there so many? So many broken people?'

Maybe Mary Yatman. She knew. You knew she knew. To what

unimaginable person could she have passed the information?

'You'll pay, fuckface.' He hangs up.

You don't bother with the trace now.

The crisis is coming.

You do a final polish on the file of prose you've stopped thinking of as a confession and started to consider a memoir. Then you key in the e-mail addresses of those to whom you need to send it: your agent, of course; the newspaper you mostly work for; your lawyer (who's really going to be surprised); the Avon and Somerset Constabulary (you have to search this address); oh, and Laraine, and (at work) Anne.

You feel calm. You're stronger than the caller. He can't know you'll pre-empt any blackmail attempt, any humiliating shot at tabloid exposure. Soon, you'll have to defend yourself in all sorts of ways. But the memoir will answer all the questions.

The telephone rings. You almost look forward to a final verbal joust with Mr UN Owen.

'Keith Marion?' It's a woman's voice, hesitant, unfamiliar. 'My name's Christina Temple. I need to see you. It's about the calls.'

A confederate of Mr UNO.

'Very well.'

'I'm on the corner. May I come to your home?'

'Yes.'

You'll be face to face. You'll discover how the secret got out. You'll be able to follow the chain.

Before Ms Temple arrives, you send the memoir into e-limbo. It will be scrolling on screens across London and beyond. You feel light-headed, free of it all. The calm will soon end but you are protected from whatever the Temple woman demands. Should she try blackmail, you can laugh at her.

Christina Temple is about forty. Thin, still hesitant, a little twitchy. Of course, she's asked herself into a murderer's home.

'Keith,' she says, on the doorstep, assuming the intimacy of your forename.

'Please come in.'

She shrinks a little in your hallway.

You lead her into the study.

'I have to apologise for Danny,' she says. 'We've been having problems. He's the sort who needs someone to blame.'

UN Owen has a name. Danny.

'It came out in therapy,' she says. 'You weren't the only one, of course. But since your name is always in the papers and your face is on television, you were the one I remembered. Your name, that is.'

Something is nastily wrong here.

'You don't even remember, do you?'

Twenty-five years, Danny said. Not twenty.

You look at your terminal, grey-screened and dead. The memoir is out in the air.

'I used to call myself Chrissie,' Ms Temple says. 'I had purple hair.'

After a while, it comes back. It's funny, but you don't laugh. Christina Temple is still trying to apologise when the police arrive.

And so on.

159

You throw a fit. Your worst since childhood. You hate Hackwill, you hate the world, you hate yourself. You hate James, for dying. You hate Mary, for living. You tear at your face, your clothes, your hair. You batter the tarmac, a nearby car, your legs.

Cameras swing to you. Hackwill staggers over, shouting and pointing at you. Draper gets out handcuffs.

You won't be cuffed. You are twisting and screaming.

The taste of school custard is in your gorge.

Some strange path was taken. Somehow, Shinbone was overlaid on Sedgwater.

Everything unravels.

'…the point of a gun was the only law that Liberty understood…'

Your ears still ring. Hands are laid on you, trying to keep you down. You bite your tongue and froth at the mouth.

You have wet yourself.

'…and when it came to shooting straight and fast, he was mighty good.'

You puke up school custard.

And you hear the question again.

'Who do you like, girl?' Shane asks, 'Napoleon Solo or Illya Kuryakin?'

If you like Napoleon Solo, go to 4. If you like Illya Kuryakin, go to 3.

160

It's a *Star Trek* day.

You slot in 'Mirror, Mirror' – the episode you and Vince were discussing earlier – and fast-forward. Evil Uhura of the parallel universe has a uniform that shows off her bare midriff. You freeze-frame on Nichelle Nichols's taut tummy.

You lie back on your bed, think back to 1973, and toss off.

You can imagine what the rest of your life is like.

And so on.

161

'You,' you say.

It's the only way out. Sean is dying anyway. He must be. You can sell this as Laraine-Goes-Mad.

Laraine nods. 'Of course,' she says, 'you mean "us".'

She gives you one barrel, in the chest. It's like being hit with a sledgehammer. You try to suck air into torn-open lungs.

From the ground, you see Laraine fit the gun barrel under her chin, and work the second trigger with her thumb.

At the blast, you both go.

Go to 0.

162

'Do you have information that might help us understand this accident?' Mary asks.

'Accident?'

'A witness says your sister fell out of a window.'

'Was he home?' You nod at Sean, with contempt.

'No. He was driving home at the time.'

'You're sure?'

Seeing Mary smile slightly, you remember how her mind works.

'I checked that first thing, Keith.'

Mum and Phil have caught something of your attitude to Sean, and move several seats away from him.

'It wasn't an accident,' you say, softly so that only Mary can hear. 'It was an attempt.'

'Did she confide her intention in you?'

'No. God, if I'd have known, I'd never have left her.'

You wouldn't have, would you? There was no hint, was there?

'But she confided in you about other circumstances?'

'He hits her, maybe worse. Can anything be done?'

Mary thinks. 'She won't bring charges?'

'If throwing herself out of a window was easier than facing him, I think not.'

'Neither do I.'

You both look at Sean. He sits glumly, sorry for himself. He hasn't been paying attention to you and Mary.

A doctor tells you Laraine is sedated and won't wake up for hours. She's doing well but her leg is broken in two places.

'We should stay,' says Mum.

'Of course, Lou,' says Phil.

Phil calls your Mum 'Lou'?!

'Perhaps I can give Mr Rye a lift home?' ventures Mary.

'I'll stay too,' says Sean.

'I think it'd be best if I took you home,' Mary insists.

Sean came in the ambulance, so doesn't have his car.

'I really think my place is with Larry.'

'I'd like to see the scene…'

…*of the crime.* The penny drops.

Sean agrees.

'Perhaps you'd like to come too, Keith?' says Mary.

'Yes,' you say.

Sean isn't sure why you're included. But he has too much else to think about to be concerned.

Mary parks the compact police car outside Sean's house. You are in the back seat. Sean sits up front, in the passenger seat next to Mary. An upstairs window is open.

'That's it?' she asks.

Sean bends forward to look out through the windshield.

Before he can say anything, Mary takes his head and rams it against the dashboard. The impact shakes the whole car.

Mary gets out of the car, walks round, and opens the front passenger door. She hauls Sean out. He holds his bleeding forehead. She drags him up the drive like a sack of potatoes. His legs flail, heels scraping crazy-paving. Mary kicks open the kitchen door and drags him inside.

If you sit in the car and wait, go to 172. If you get out and follow Mary, go to 185.

163

You have been at the Marion Compound for two days, preparing. The Compound is in the middle of Snowdonia, half-way up a minor Welsh mountain. It was a bankrupt farm, leased cheaply and recently bought for a song. You've converted sheep-pens into a sleeping hut for the clients. You and James have a cottage as quarters and an office.

It's November. You usually shut down for the winter but this is special. Normally, you provide heating in the pens. You've taken the stove out for the Hackwill party. The weather forecast is for drizzle, a consistent climatic feature in these parts. The slate-grey skies seem cheery to you, pregnant with long-deserved retribution. Cloud boils, ready to rain on Robert Hackwill.

You see the minibus coming, slowing to cope with the gradient. A road winds up from the valley. A long way. You've let it fall into pitted disrepair, and even gouged out a few new pot-holes to give the approach to the Compound that 'Abandon all hope' feeling. On maps, you have the pens and the cottage down as Colditz and Castle Dracula.

Is Hackwill worried now? Has he recognised James? Of course he has. Are the others catching on?

James parks by the pens and lets the Hackwill party out. They unbend and stretch, after several hours in the cramped minibus, groaning and stamping.

'You remember my brother, Keith,' says James.

Hackwill, in an expensive anorak, nods but doesn't smile.

'Good to see you, mate,' says Sean Rye, grinning too widely. He is wearing a violently orange cagoule. 'This is like a reunion.'

Reg Jessup glumly goes along with it.

This is delicious.

Shane Bush stands at the back, hired help rather than executive level, not paid to have an opinion. Mary Yatman, alert, wears a bodystocking, Doc Martens and a padded camouflage jacket. You and James have discussed her: she'll be the dangerous one. The older bloke, heavy in the gut, is Ben McKinnell, a builder who stands to make a mint out of Hackwill's long-gestating Discount Development. Tristram Warwick and Kay Shearer, who you understand are lovers, hang back in matching survival gear; squash-hardened, confident, competent. You'll see how they manage away from the confines of a gym, forced to exert themselves for longer than a lunch break.

'Where are the bogs?' Sean asks.

You point at the mountainside and try not to smile.

'What? No facilities?'

'There's a flush toilet in the cottage,' you tell him.

'Terrif,' he smiles, taking a step towards the tiny stone building.

You stretch out an arm and bar his way. 'You have to earn the right of access.'

'What?'

You see Hackwill and Mary exchange a look. They're catching on too early.

'I'm paying a hundred quid for the week,' says Sean, 'and I can't pee?'

You shrug. Your usual rate is £500 a week.

'Of course you can pee,' James says. 'You just have to use nature's toilet, otherwise known as the Principality of Wales.'

While this has been going on, Shearer has stepped behind the minibus and pissed against the wheel. Sean gets the idea, and hops to it, relieving himself in a gush.

'It's bloody cold,' he says.

'Yes,' you agree.

* * *

You get the Hackwill party bedded down in the pens. There are eight of them, but you provide only seven sleeping bags. Hackwill, instantly leader, arranges a game of potatoes to decide who gets to be cosy. Sean, shaping up as runt of the litter, loses. You sloshed a couple of buckets of water in the pens yesterday so the ground should be nicely damp. Nothing too obvious. Yet.

In Castle Dracula, warmed by the open fire, you and James split a bottle of Jack Daniel's and listen in on the party's chatter. Colditz, of course, is bugged. The low-tech appearance of the Compound is supposed to be deceptive.

Sean, aptly, pisses and moans. McKinnell and Jessup say this isn't what they expected. Warwick and Shearer agree.

Hackwill merely says, 'I know the Marions.'

'This was your idea,' Jessup whines.

'Shut up and sleep, Reg,' says Hackwill, darkly.

You and James laugh.

At four in the morning, when it is still dark as midnight, you and James get up, put on outdoor kit and go outside.

The pens are fitted with a klaxon that blares wake-up-you-fuckers at a million decibels. It also triggers a series of thousand-candle flashbulbs. You throw the switch. Some guests scream loud enough to be heard above the klaxon. They scramble out of Colditz.

A searchlight circle serves as a gathering point.

'Gents, and lady,' you say, 'good morning. Breakfast will soon be served in the luxury lounge. First, however, you have to bring home the bacon.'

James hands out hunting knives, with serrated blades and compasses in the handles. Every guest gets one. By the end of the week, it will be their only friend.

'Out there, somewhere, is your breakfast. Go and get it.'

You swing the searchlight manually, playing light across the mountainside.

Hackwill and Mary set off at a run. The others follow. Sean, predictably, is last. You watch them go.

Dotted around the Compound are eight bowls of cold porridge, swimming in milk, clingfilm-covered to keep scavengers away. One breakfast is heavily dosed with laxative. It will be interesting to see who gets it.

You and James laugh uncontrollably. Shouts and cries come from the darkness.

By dawn, everyone has found a bowl and, overcoming reluctance, scoffed porridge like a good little Goldilocks. McKinnell's guts come to the boil and he squats over a latrine pit, audibly voiding himself. His sufferings sober the others.

The first day's programme is a treasure hunt. The party is split into two teams, given maps, and sent out to bring back Cap'n Kidd's doubloons. The winning team gets a hot meal, access to the toilet and a warm bath. The losers go hungry and make do in the cold.

You appoint Shane and Mary captains and have them pick up sides. Shane goes first and naturally picks his boss, Hackwill. Mary picks Shearer and Shane picks Warwick, splitting the couple neatly. Mary, given a choice between Reg, McKinnell and Sean, picks McKinnell, whose bowels are calming. Hackwill has Shane pick Reg and Sean complains about being picked last. You attach yourself to Mary's team. James will tag along with what's supposed to be Shane's crew but has become Hackwill's command.

'One team gets an hour's head start,' James announces.

'Which one?' Mary asks.

'The one that can remember all the lyrics to the theme song of *Top Cat*. Nominate your singers. Fine, so it's Tristram versus Sean. Start singing, *now*.'

'Top Cat!' James sings, letting the others take it up.

'The most effectual…' Warwick and Sean join in.

'Top Cat!' you and James sing.

'Whose intellectual close friends get to call him T.C.'

Sean stumbles over 'providing it's with dignity', and McKinnell, dreaming of a porcelain toilet with a roof over it, looks hate at him.

Warwick keeps on singing, climaxing with 'yes, he's the chief, he's the king, he's above everything, he's the most tip-top Top Cat!' He looks pleased with himself.

Hackwill, Warwick, Shane and Reg yomp off up the hillside, following their map, which Reg holds upside-down. The map, if read properly, will lead them to two locations, where separate portions of another map are hidden. Combined, these show where the treasure –

a suitcase full of Monopoly money and Bounty bars – is buried. Since they've only had cold porridge in the last twenty-four hours, the sweets are a real treasure. A catch is that at one of the sites they have to pick up a key for the suitcase or forfeit the game. Mary's team have a different map, which also marks the locations of two half-maps, which show where the booty is. There are two keys, but only one case.

Over previous courses, you've learned that the team that loses the *Top Cat* challenge, with an hour to look at the map, usually wins. The other side often hares off desperately and gets lost.

Mary studies, relating the hand-drawn map – which is covered with Jolly Rogers and crossed cutlasses – to visible landmarks.

'Keith,' she says, using your Christian name for the first time, 'what would the position be if I left you all here and searched on my own?'

'You'd concede the hunt. You have to take your trusty shipmates with you.'

She looks at the belly-quivering McKinnell and the nose-dripping Sean. That's what she's afraid of.

She folds the map and puts it in her padded jacket. Then she takes out her hunting knife and examines the blade. 'Sharp?' she asks.

You agree that it is.

She puts the point of the knife at your balls. 'Keith,' she says, 'where's the treasure?'

You look into her eyes and see she means it.

If you tell Mary where the treasure is, go to 171. If you tough it out, go to 184.

164

James shoots Hackwill in the brain. You don't even flinch.

'Now we leave,' Mary says, before Hackwill has hit the floor.

James shoots Hackwill again, in the back of the head – what's left of it – just to make sure. Then he drops the pistol and unslings his machine-gun.

'Dump everything,' he says.

Mary tosses her pistol. You and Victoria throw away your weapons. The flames get nearer. With Hackwill dead, you're thinking ahead again, of ways out of this, of ways back.

James pulls half a dozen grenades out of his jacket and drops them on top of the pile of guns.

'It'll be a mystery,' he says.

'Let's go.'

You help Victoria down the stairs, through eye-assaulting smoke clouds. James and Mary follow. Firemen greet you in the lobby and help you out.

TV cameras and police marksmen mark the boundary the fire brigade have set up. Everyone asks what happened.

It's all down to Mary. She says Hackwill went mad. He had a huge cache of weapons and killed a lot of people. She commends the Marion brothers for trying to save innocents.

You are bewildered. What about all the people who saw you walk through town with guns? The workers who escaped before the firefight? Anyone who remembers James's feud with Hackwill? You look at faces in the crowd.

As Mary talks, people nod and tut. They always knew Robert Hackwill was a wrong 'un. (So why did they keep voting for him?)

'Are you shocked?' a reporter asks.

'Hackwill was a bully at school,' you say, explaining everything.

You walk away, unscathed. You go back to your family, justified.

And so on.

165

At Sean's leaving do, you make a fulsome speech about him. You see Warwick, officially redesignated a consultant by head office, clapping slowly amid the rapid applause. No wonder.

When you hand over Sean's leaving present – a giant-size Filofax – and shake his hand, you feel power pass from him to you. He used his position as manager to get rich. So can you.

You drink a lot but the buzz of power keeps you sober. On the way home, you stop and park.

'Keith, what is it?' your wife asks.

'You forged my signatures.'

Vanda doesn't bother to deny it.

'Sean isn't taking you with him,' you say.

She yelps once, like a dog.

'We've agreed. You'll stay. For the kids. But you're on probation.'

You start up the car again.

To show how tough you're going to be on defaulters, you force Kay Shearer to declare bankruptcy. You've discovered that Shearer and Warwick are lovers. You use that to get Warwick dismissed. He has several times interceded to help Shearer, stepping beyond the bounds.

Head office are impressed. At the bank, they call you 'the Killer'. Mortgage rates are rising, so there are plenty of victims. You target outstanding loans and go after them. You *can* get blood out of a stone.

Shane Bush, whom you remember from school, married some slag when he was eighteen and has three children. They got a mortgage and bought a terraced house in a drab part of town. Shane should have been a council tenant like his parents, but home-ownership was sold to him as a birthright in the early '80s and his dream is only just going sour. He's well behind on his repayments and bridging loans are getting him in deeper.

You foreclose and put the house up for auction. In Vanda's name, you buy the house at a knock-down price, then resell it at a profit within two days.

There are plenty of opportunities like this.

You muscle in on the Discount Development, which is Councillor Robert Hackwill's money-making machine. It's been in the works for years and council money has been lining the pockets of builders and their cronies. You take your cut and Hackwill realises you're a worthwhile partner. He doesn't trust you, of course, but he needs a man who isn't trustworthy.

Candy resigns and goes to work for South-West Gas. You don't understand why she seems to feel sorry for you.

You keep in touch with Sean and even let him invest some of your invisible funds for you. He compliments you on catching him up and you enjoy explaining to him how you have pulled off this or that deal.

He says he might have something big for you eventually.

Vanda drinks a lot and chain-smokes but you keep her in line. You sleep with Bella, Candy's replacement, and Grete, the Danish nanny.

You become sleek, almost chubby. People say you look prosperous.

Money piles up. Sean gets you into the City and you funnel

everything into certain stocks. Sean has inside information and the stocks go through the roof.

WPC Mary Yatman, investigating a break-in at a builder's offices, reads some papers she shouldn't and threatens the Discount Development. Hackwill consults you and you freeze the woman's bank account for a week. Mary backs off and another primary-school grudge is paid off.

'Another notch, Killer,' Hackwill says.

You wonder how long Robert Hackwill can last. He's not a cool hand. He enjoys cruelty too much. He doesn't see the figures.

Keith Marion, manager. The Killer. The City player.

Prosperity balloons.

On Black Monday in 1986, the stock-market crash wipes Sean out. And you. You're seriously in debt to your own bank and there's no documentation to justify it. Your own home is in the mortgage hole for once. The scent of blood in the water brings out the sharks. Mary Yatman comes back, with her boss, Inspector Draper. The bank sends investigators.

Questions are asked. Charges are made. Convictions are secured. A sentence is served.

When you get out, it's the '90s. Vanda and the kids are long gone, and she has remarried. Your mother hasn't visited you often and Laraine and James are overseas. Sean fled the country and is in exile somewhere, living on money probably filched from you.

You get a flat in town. You have to go on the dole.

Vanda's old assistant is your case-worker. Paul Mysliwiec, whom you haven't seen since school, is your probation officer. You're found part-time work in a betting-shop but are not allowed to handle money.

People tend not to remember you: which may be a good thing.

One week, as you are waiting to see Mr Mysliwiec, a demented woman comes into the room and harangues your probation officer's receptionist. It's Marie-Laure Quilter. God knows what she's on probation for. Or if she's found the right office.

She pauses in her rant, and looks at you. She's dressed like a bag lady.

'Do I know you?' she asks.

You shake your head.

'Yes, I do. You're an Arachnoid spy.'

Mr Mysliwiec comes out to see what the fuss is, and hurries you into his inner office. 'Mad bitch,' he says.

You agree.

Years pass. You don't get anywhere.

And so on.

166

'Kill them,' you say.

'Then you kill me, right?' Mary prompts.

She shoots you in the face. As you die, you hear the other *thwicks*.

Go to 0.

167

'There's a bomb,' you shout.

'Sit down, you bastard.'

'Bloody loony.'

'But there's a *bomb*!'

Soldiers rappel down from the ceiling. You try to escape. The Marines are after the Mad Bomber. You.

'Run,' you tell everyone.

Security men wade into the audience. A Girl Guide sobs at her ruined moment in the spotlight.

You run down the aisle towards the stage, towards the machines, towards the bomb. Marines point guns at you but don't fire. You keep shouting about the bomb. You make it up on to the stage. Your face is huge on the monitors.

People shout. Some have taken notice.

'Ladies and gentlemen,' you say, 'if you would proceed to the exits.'

Bob Monkhouse looks annoyed to have a punch-line pre-empted.

Someone somewhere has made a decision. You're a loony but you've been listened to. People are ferried out. There are crushes at the exits. A Marine uses his rifle-butt on someone's grandmother's head. You're not surprised.

Your ears ring and you are blinded by arc-lights.

The monitors show a 'technical problems' logo. It's roll-over week. Millions of dupes must be in agony at the delay, afraid they'll miss the announcement of the winning numbers.

How many more minutes to go? Or is it seconds?

This week, maybe, they'll realise there are no winners in the lottery of life. Not real ones.

VC Conyer, the celeb, is escorted past by minders. Her unfocused eyes meet yours.

'I know you,' she says.

'We were at Sedgwater College at the same time. You never spoke to me.'

'Kenneth, right?'

The stage lifts off and fragments. Din ruptures your ears. Flame flays your skin.

It's over in a flash.

Go to 0.

168

You do everything you've imagined.

You tell Tristram you're leaving the branch. You add that you're putting the money in a rival high street bank.

You buy a new house. You buy a new car. You have holidays. You buy everyone everything.

Money pours down from the skies.

Minders keep the piranha people away, the crawl-out-of-the-woodwork creeps, the con-job merchants, the charity solicitors, the fruitcakes.

You screw around a bit, but get back with Vanda. Money makes you thinner, more ardent. Money lubricates everything. You are convinced that everything has come right.

Or are you?

If you're entirely happy, go to 187. If you still have questions, go to 200.

169

But are you living your life or is it living you? Have you vanished inside your own PR? Are you just the sum of what other people think of you? What do you have that's yours?

Memory.

You're on your knees, scratching at the hard earth of a flower-bed, searching for a tin of marbles. You're wearing a cardboard eyepatch and a pirate hat with a skull-and-crossbones badge and a plastic plume.

Then you're back in the house in Sutton Mallet, listening as Ro tells you VC is going to be on the cover of *Q*.

It was real. You were back there, you were home.

The next weekend, when Ro has taken the kids to see her recently widowed mother in the hope of cheering her up, you repeat the experiment under controlled circumstances.

When you shut your eyes, it is 1990. In the dark of your head, spiders crawl, red-eyed. You open your eyes, heart pounding.

You're lying on your sofa, looking at the distant ceiling. Half your life has come and gone since you last stumbled. You are thirty years old. You have done everything.

You shut your eyes again, determined. You furnish the dark, imagining your room in Mum and Dad's house. Your room as it was when you were thirteen.

Maths homework. You hate it. You want to get it over with so you can watch Top of the Pops. *A spider crawls on your hand.*

You open your eyes.

It was real. You were there.

Next time, you stay longer, ignoring the spiders. You finish the homework and go downstairs. James and Laraine are in the television room, young again.

Mum washes up in the kitchen. A *Daily Telegraph* is folded up, and you see your Dad. Alive. A rush of something makes your eyes water.

It's love. Or is it regret?

'What's up, Keith?'

Dad talked to you. You were there.

You made it back. You can go home again. You can, you can, you can.

But do you want to? When did things begin? From where do you want to start? And where do you want to end up?

Excited, you make yourself espresso and try to think. You're alone in the house's huge kitchen. Jeremy's precocious 'paintings' are stuck to the fridge. The place smells of coffee beans. The dishwasher hums through a cycle. Ro will tease you about the lack of piled-up dirty dishes when she gets back.

Where you were was before Ro, before the kids. If you go back again, they might not be part of your life. The kids might not be born.

This is what you have. You might try modestly to put it all down to luck and being in the right place with the right idea, but you are here by choice. Even in a fascist dystopia, you'd still be a smart cookie with a loving family.

But there are things you'd do differently, aren't there? Some things might make more sense?

If you want things to be different now, go to 183. If you want things back the way they were, go to 189.

170

It's a *Doctor Who* day.

You turn the sound down and put in your tape of 'Carnival of Monsters'. You fast-forward and freeze-frame, making several wrong freezes before you are satisfied.

Finally, you catch Katy Manning centre-screen, wearing jeans rolled up and leather boots.

You lie back on your bed, fix your eyes on the screen, think back to 1973, and

…blit blurt…

are transported at once to a parallel universe.

A warm mouth is wrapped round your erection. You look down. Your stomach is flat. A long sword-scar runs from your thigh to your right nipple, cutting through your chest-pelt.

A head of tousled hair bobs. You slip your hands into it, guiding Jo as she sucks you off. It's her birthday present to you.

Later, when there's time, you'll make lingering love. Just now, as midnight nears, you're on the run.

You climax pleasantly, and Jo swallows.

She stands and hugs you, her head resting on your shoulder.

You look up, through the shattered roof of the bombed-out barn. One of the shadow-saucers floats in front of the moon, spider-limbs dangling.

You draw a bead with your blaster. The invaders are blown from the sky with a single beam.

You and Jo make your way through town, towards the safe house the rebel cadre you command has established in the old Discount Development.

Jo clings to you, gasping at shadows.

By the Corn Exchange, you're shocked to see Timmy Gossett dangling from a noose of piano wire. You cut him down and promise to make the invaders pay. For this one innocent life, a hundred Arachnoids will fizzle in the beam of your blaster.

Travelling, even by night, is risky.

A trap has been set, at the Outlet. Your sixth sense tingles as you scent spider-stink. You tug Jo's arm, pulling her behind a wall.

Just in time. A blinding zap arcs to the spot where you were standing.

You dart out and beam away. Three Arachnoids curl up and crinkle, limbs a-flame.

'Eat death, spider-scum from outer space,' you shout.

Grey cobweb tendrils creep from the Outlet and spread across the road, coating cars and corpses, reaching for you.

Jo passes you the bug bomb. You bite off the celluloid tag, and toss it with remarkable accuracy. Jo comments on your amazing arm. Modestly, you admit you were Somerset's best bowler since Hallam Moseley. Before the invasion.

The bug bomb explodes inside the Outlet. The last Arachnoids pour out, burning like fireworks. You beam-blast them out of their misery.

Finally, a Queen Arachnoid scuttles enormously out of the burning ruin, expanding the doors to get all her limbs through. Her egg sac is distended with a hundred baby shadow-spiders, all clacking their claws and gnashing their venom-injectors, hungry to be born, to pour forth in a black tide of evil.

'Keith,' she coos. 'Remember me?'

It's Marie-Laure, transformed, her pale face peeping out through a balaclava helmet of chitinous carapace. Her skinny white arms stick out ineffectually from a bulbous thorax.

'It doesn't have to be this way,' Marie-Laure says. 'We can rule together.'

'Not in this universe, baby-cakes.'

You blast the Queen to atoms. The screams of her unborn horde rip the air.

Diving behind the wall for cover, as spider-foetuses explode like hand-grenades, spattering the street with burning wet muck, you find Jo has slipped off her soft leather thigh-boots and is wriggling out of her cut-off jeans.

'Take me now, Fearless Leader.'

You know what she means. This time tomorrow, you could both be dead, so why wait?

You unfasten your Apache-head belt buckle.

She takes off her rainbow-pattern wool tank-top and frilly-fronted, round-collared watered silk blouse. Her breasts are enormous.

As she smiles, her cheeks dimple.

On a bed of fur coats, retrieved from a smashed shop window display, you make love. As you come for the third time, Jo's cries rise above the Arachnoids' dying screams.

She is weeping.

'Thank you,' she says. 'Thank you so much.'

At the safe house, Vince is manufacturing the bug bombs. Mum mixes explosives in the tiny kitchen. James, from his wheelchair, pores over maps of the area, looking for weaknesses in the invaders' cobweb castles. Shane, your lieutenant, drills the latest rebel recruits.

As you and Jo come in, everyone turns and applauds.

'We were getting worried, chief,' says Shane.

Mary Yatman, wearing a khaki bikini and camouflage stripes all over her skin, kisses you passionately.

'Thank God you're here,' she says. 'The broadcast said the Spider

Queen had you wrapped and sucked dry.'

You chuck her on the chin, and say, 'That'll be the day.'

You and Jo have an open relationship. Sometimes Mary joins you in bed. It's important for the rebellion.

Mum brings you a mug of tea. 'Well done, Son.'

'I'm sorry about the house, Mum.'

You had to blow up your own home, trapping Spider Colonel Hackwill and his Killer Aphids. It was a significant victory.

'That's all right dear. One day, we'll have another.'

You drink your tea.

Vince explains that the Arachnoids have regrouped, and are operating out of the old DSS building. The files they have there will be of inestimable use to them in tracking down rebels.

'Well, old chum,' you say, 'we'll have to blow those files up. And if a few shadow-spiders get in the way of the blast, that's just too bad.'

Everyone cheers.

A plan is forming in your mind.

'Some day, the Arachnoids will be beaten off,' you say, 'and we'll be free to live and love and laugh again. We'll have homes and jobs and cars and families. A sun will rise over the Somerset levels, and we'll rejoice in the warmth and light. I know things seem black and dark and hairy at times, but we must never give up hope. They'll never understand, those spider brains, that we always hope, we always struggle, we never give up. That's what makes us *us*.'

Everyone cheers.

'Long live Keith,' shouts Shane.

Everyone joins in.

'No,' you say, arms round Jo and Mary. 'Long live the Rebellion!'

And so on.

171

At about midday, you and Mary's team are at the foot of a seventy-foot loose shale incline. Mary has the suitcase, and has discovered that it's locked.

Sean reports that he can see Hackwill's team in the next valley, crawling through thick brush.

'What's up there?' Mary asks, nodding at the slope.

She hasn't put her knife away.

Your hands are cuffed behind your back. Mary's jacket is a right little utility belt, heavy with souvenirs from her law-enforcement career.

You're losing control. For the first time, it occurs to you that the Compound's isolation is not altogether a good idea.

'What's up there?' Mary repeats, knife tapping the air.

'The key,' you admit.

'Mr Bank Manager,' she tells Sean, 'hop up and get the key.'

Sean looks about to protest but doesn't. He wades upwards about a dozen yards, then slips, tumbles and rolls back down again, ripping his cagoule up the back.

McKinnell is behind some rocks, still crapping. It's a wonder there's anything left in his lower bowel. It's possible he's dumping innards as well as faecal matter. James suggested putting ground glass in with the laxative but you overruled him. Perhaps he went behind your back?

Mary looks at Shearer, who doesn't volunteer. She sighs and darts up the hill like a mountain nymph. The key is tied to a bright yellow plastic anchor. Mary snatches it and foot-skis back down, leaving tracks in the crumbly shale.

'Game over,' she says. 'Now, I'd like a bath.'

'If you uncuff me, I'll blow the whistle,' you say. That's the signal that the treasure is found.

Mary looks up at the sky. 'It's early yet. Be a pity to lose Councillor Hackwill an afternoon's exercise.'

You shrug. You can't do much else with the cuffs on. Mary leads you back to the Compound. You can't help feeling you've ceded command. If the course continues as planned, it will only be because Mary lets it. And she's unknowable. Everyone else – even McKinnell, whom you've never met – you can fathom. They will act predictably. But Mary doesn't follow rules, even those of her own character. Whatever that is.

You feel the cold and your shoulders are cramped.

While Mary baths and McKinnell sits on the toilet, Sean tries to be mates with you. He asks after Laraine. You tell him she's married again, to an alcoholic named Owen. He asks after Mum and Phil, but can't remember their names. He reminisces about the way your dad took him under his wing at the bank.

Shearer has been told to make the tea but resents getting a woman's role because he's gay. He uncuffs you and orders you to get busy in the kitchen. Mary's defiance has brought something out in Shearer.

When James gets back, you have to reestablish control.

Mary comes down, wearing your towelling bathrobe, hair in wet spikes. She looks like a little girl dressed up, not dangerous at all.

'Kay,' she tells Shearer, 'you're next for the tub.'

Shearer goes upstairs.

Sean sulks at being passed over. 'I feel filthy,' he says. 'Those pens were vile.'

Mary looks contemptuously at him. 'I don't bank with you,' she says.

'Meaning?'

'I can tell you to fuck right off.'

Sean goes beyond sulky into upset.

At nightfall, Hackwill's team trudges back, cold, hungry and depressed. James asks what happened to the whistle and you signal discreetly towards Mary.

Hackwill is furious that he's lost. He blames Reg for leading them along a blind trail. Of course, he couldn't have won, anyway.

'You smell nice,' Warwick says, moving on Shearer for a cuddle.

'Ugh,' Shearer says. 'You don't.'

You've seen this happen before on courses, between straight couples. It's always good policy to get them on opposing teams and watch relationships – usually based on economic rather than character compatibility – come apart.

Perhaps you should think about fucking Kay Shearer? If he were a woman, you'd definitely be working round to it by now. It's part of the Marion Course strategy. You've been straight all these years but your heart is untouched, especially by Marie-Laure. Shearer looks a bit like Chris.

'The map was inexact,' Reg whines.

You remember the fat boy giggling as James weed himself, as Hackwill gave you the Chinese burn. There's another couple on the verge of crack-up: Hackwill and Reg. They were only friends in the first place because they were both children no one liked. The link between bully and sidekick must involve a lot of contempt.

McKinnell will probably be out of action for days. So you needn't think too much about him.

Shane Bush works for Hackwill. It'll take a while for Shane to get surly, but it'll come. One of the features of your method is that it gets juniors to speak their minds when their bosses try to force them to do stupid things. In the business world, it's theoretically a bad thing for the company if subordinates are too cowed to speak up; but no boss you have ever dropped in a shit-pit has ever taken kindly to being trampled under by his executive secretary.

You set six places at the dinner table and cook a vat of stew. Mary's team sit, waiting to be fed.

'I'm afraid the losers have to go back to Colditz now,' James announces.

It's starting to drizzle outside, and it's dark. Hackwill makes no move. He can smell the stew. You begin doling out the food.

'I can't eat,' says McKinnell.

Hackwill makes a move to replace McKinnell.

'Against rules, I'm afraid,' James says.

'Are you going to stop me?'

'Read the contract, Councillor. If you break rules, you're liable to a ten-thousand-pound fine. For each violation.'

Usually, it's £1000.

Hackwill freezes in a mute fit of cold rage. Mary's team, except McKinnell, tuck into their stew.

'This is really good,' Sean says. 'My compliments to the chef.'

Reg whimpers.

'I'll save you some, love,' Shearer says to Warwick.

Hackwill is outraged. 'Is that against the rules?'

You and James shrug. It is, but you see potential in letting it slide.

'Victors can dispose of spoils as they see fit,' you say.

'Fine,' smiles Hackwill. 'We split the food evenly.'

Sean protects his bowl as if in a rowdy school dinner hall. Hackwill used to extort food from smaller kids, you remember.

'No,' says Mary. 'Councillor Hackwill, you lost. You have to go by that.'

Hackwill's face is purple. What game is Mary playing?

'Rye,' Hackwill demands, 'give me your stew. I'll pay fifty pounds.'

Sean barks laughter. 'Not bloody likely, Robbo.'

'I'll break you, Rye.'

'This was your idea,' Sean reminds him.

'Enough argument,' James says, clapping once. 'Losers, outside. Now.'

Hackwill fumes out, banging the door behind him. Reg, Warwick and Shane follow.

Shane looks back, at Mary. He must have fancied his chances this week. He used to think he was Napoleon Solo, the prat. Now, he's Napoleon No-food.

You finish your meal without conversation.

'Congratulations, winners,' James says.

You hand round cigars. Sean, Shearer and Mary light up. Even McKinnell perks up a bit, thinking things are better.

The next day of the course is the chain-gang game. There's no way Mary can cheat on that. Hackwill's team comes out the winner. The prize this time is that the team can elect one of their number to sleep inside the cottage, in a warm bed.

The election is where the fun starts.

'By the way,' you explain, 'you can't vote for yourself.'

Hackwill sits back, confident. After all, he's won a few elections.

'I vote for Rob,' Reg dutifully toadies.

Warwick gets to vote next. He's sulking because Hackwill called him a 'useless poof' when he took a tumble, dragging the whole team a couple of yards down the mountainside. He thinks it over and votes for Shane.

Hackwill wastes his vote on Reg and looks at Shane. Shane ought to vote for his employer. But coming on this course wasn't his idea and he's fed up. He votes for Reg, bitterly.

Hackwill bristles and looks at Reg.

Reg, momentarily wistful about a warm bed after two nights in Colditz, suggests a recount. James says the decision is final. You know Reg is pleased. And you know Hackwill wants to fire Shane.

The next day, everyone gets up to find that their boots have disappeared. Those who didn't sleep in their socks – Sean, Kay and Reg – lose them too. Your boots are gone too, and so are James's. You assume James is responsible for this especially fiendish bit of cruelty.

You assemble everyone by the minibus to drive them across country to the mud-pit assault course. The engine won't start.

'This is part of it, isn't it?' Warwick says.

James frowns. It's not part of the plan. You look at the engine. Tubes have been pulled out and taken away. It's obvious sabotage.

'So, someone's displaying initiative,' you declare, looking at the other eight people. With the exception of the Zen-serene Mary and the smug-stupid Reg, everyone looks guilty. It hits you that with two teams of four and you and James, there should be nine other people.

'Where's McKinnell?'

'The shits again,' Warwick says.

'Find him,' you order.

No one volunteers to go.

'Shane,' you say, 'you find him.'

Shane still doesn't like taking orders from the snotnose who threw a fit about school custard, but hops to it. He just wants to get off the mountain and look for a new job.

Your mind races. What's going on? Is it James? Has he escalated the revenge programme without consulting you?

Shane comes back.

'You've got to see this, Marion,' he says.

He leads you and James towards the pens. Hackwill strides along after you, trying to keep up. The rest of the pack, like sheep, drift in your wake. Sean hops a little, bare feet on icy ground. Only Mary isn't interested, and when she's alone by the minibus even she shifts herself.

Ben McKinnell is slumped in a hollow in the earth, throat cut. The blood on his chest is frozen and dewy, like a crimson, crystalline Santa beard.

Sean gasps.

Your heart leaps.

Is James surprised?

'How far to civilisation?' Mary asks.

'Two days' walk, maybe three,' you say.

'In Wales? Nothing's two days' walk away.'

'It's up and down mountains. We bought the place because it was the arse-end of nowhere.'

'And you don't have a telephone?'

'No, Mary, we don't,' James says.

You have a mobile and James knows it. You don't contradict him. Everyone else was banned from bringing portable phones. No one speaks up to claim they've broken that rule. This once, the fine might be waived.

'We should walk, then,' Hackwill says. 'To the police.'

'There's a problem,' you say.

Hackwill looks disgusted. 'Come on, out with it.'

'Frostbite. How do your toes feel?'

He looks down at his stockinged feet. His socks are wet and heavy. Your own toes are dead.

'Where are the fucking shoes?' Hackwill asks James.

James shrugs. In that shrug, you realise how deep the shit is. Either you can't trust the only person here you could trust yesterday, or someone else has crippled the lot of you. And someone must have killed McKinnell.

'My feet are freezing,' Sean says, redundantly.

'We couldn't walk for more than an hour without shoes,' Mary says. 'At the end of two days, we'd just have blue stumps at the ends of our legs.'

'We have one pair of boots,' James says.

You've worked that out too. You wonder whose feet are cold enough for the option to be tempting.

'Who has boots?' Hackwill demands.

James points at McKinnell. He has died with his boots on.

If you take the boots yourself, go to 190. If you stand back and let someone else claim them, go to 203.

172

After a pause, Sean flies out of the open window. His arms and legs wave as he falls. He arcs a little, as if thrown with considerable force. You think he's going to crunch down on the windshield but he falls short. He lies face down, like a broken starfish.

Mary comes out of the house.

'Overcome by grief and guilt, in a spasm of self-hatred at his own worthlessness, Mr Rye threw himself…'

Sean groans and tries to get up on his knees. He can't make it. Mary takes his belt and pulls him up, then heaves him over her shoulder in a fireman's lift.

'Finding himself still alive but resolved to end his useless life, Mr Rye dragged himself back into his house, crawled painfully up the stairs and, for the second time, defenestrated himself.'

You stand frozen and Mary carries Sean indoors. You are impressed that she has used the word 'defenestrated' in a spoken sentence.

This time, Sean falls vertically, head first, and his neck goes.

Mary appears at the window. 'Mr Marion and myself stood by helpless,' she shouts.

You look at the leaky bag that used to be Sean.

'By the way,' Mary says, 'welcome home, Keith. Your brother would have been proud of you.'

And so on.

173

The problem you have is that you *can* remember things, so it's difficult to keep your story straight. You're asked hundreds of questions about your life and it's hard to keep answering that you don't know when you do.

Asked the names of your children, you want to say 'Josh and Jonquil' but have to get over the hesitation with a pretence of searching empty memory banks.

Dr Cross makes cryptic notes. You know he knows you're faking. But you also manifestly don't know anything about Keith Marion.

Dr Cross asks you a question in Japanese. You shrug. He makes a note.

'Where did you go to school?'

'Sedgwater,' you answer.

'Which schools?'

'I can't remember.'

'Dr Marling's and Ash Grove?'

'Hemphill and Ash Grove,' you correct, instinctively.

Dr Cross makes a note. You've just shot yourself in the foot.

'I have you down in the records as a Marling's boy,' the doctor says. 'Hum the theme from *Top Cat*.'

'Pardon?'

'The TV cartoon.'

You hum the song.

'Well, something's imprinted on your memory. That's good.'

'I think I'd rather remember my wife's birthday than the *Top Cat* song.'

'I sympathise with you.'

Your family treat you as if you were an alien. Dr Cross puzzles at the case but can't make it out. People seem afraid of you. Rowena is nervous about undressing in front of you, but you start having sex. The children keep forgetting you don't know things. The business is on hold.

You have medical insurance. Dr Cross thinks you're trying to pull off some con, but can't understand why. It turns out you are already rich enough to retire.

You walk on eggshells. You keep making mistakes. But the truth is so far beyond belief no one gets near it.

The problem is that your cover story starts coming true. The more Dr Cross questions you, the easier it is not to know the answers.

When asked your children's names, you answer 'Jeremy and Jessica'. Of course, you knew this even in the first session. The point is the slight hesitation as you dredge up information that should be instinctive. That hesitation is gone, which the doctor approves.

Thinking about it, you can't really recall Josh and Jonquil. They are the phantoms, receding behind the cobweb curtain. The life you are forgetting is your own.

But the new one is still not quite convincing.

You try, once, to undo the trick. You lie in your living-room, shut your eyes, and try to picture in detail the flat you shared with Marie-Laure. You run through Vince's comics, your chipped crockery, Josh's Ninja Turtles, Marie-Laure's blouses.

But the shift doesn't come. And you can't remember *anything* about Jonquil. Bloody silly name.

You're stuck here.

You have to leave. Ro takes it well and you let her have the house, custody and most of the money. It's not really yours, anyway.

You spend some time with Mum. She's still the same, but even here there are subtle, jarring dissonances.

You set out to wander the world, away from the lives of both Keiths.

Here, you can be someone new, someone who owes nothing to any of his past selves.

Born anew at thirty, you look for a life.

And so on.

174

'Him,' you say.

Laraine presses the barrels against Sean's forehead. His eyes are still alive, but he's in too much pain to say anything.

The blast explodes his head like a watermelon.

'Now what?' she asks.

You can't think of a way to sell this.

Hackwill and Sean attacked you and Laraine, and she defended herself with a gun rested from Hackwill. No, not when forensic science will reconstruct her head-blasting of a severely wounded, helpless, harmless Sean.

Hackwill and Sean shot each other. With the same gun? They struggled over it? Hackwill wounded Sean, Sean killed Hackwill... Then who killed Sean? And what about reloading? How could Sean reload without his shoulder?

There must be another story.

Mystery Man blasted Sean and Hackwill, left the gun with Laraine – who isn't wearing gloves and must be leaving fucking fingerprints all over it – and headed off across the moors.

Can you fix up that toad Reg Jessup as Mystery Man? It's not good, but it's something.

What about powder burns? It's too late for Laraine to go and wash her hands. Besides, soap and water won't fool the tests they have these days.

Cars are coming. Flashing blue lights.

How about Laraine went mad and killed Hackwill and Sean? It has the advantage of being fucking true.

Can you write yourself out? You didn't kill anyone. (Though you told Laraine to shoot Sean, which she'll remember.) At worst, you're an accomplice. If you turn queen's evidence, you might get off.

Get off on murder. But incest will come out. Laraine's off the deep end and she'll be a talker.

Without her, you could handle this.

Laraine shoots it out with the cops and goes under in a hail of bullets? No, this isn't Texas. It takes a while for British police to get guns.

'Put the gun down, Mrs Rye,' says a policewoman. It's Mary Yatman.

Laraine is puzzled. She hasn't been thinking. She whirls round, aims the gun at Mary, and pulls the triggers. Mary throws herself forward. The gun clicks. Laraine has dropped the hammer on used shells.

A rugby scrum falls on your sister. If her neck breaks, you're home free. Well, in a position to work up a story. You'll have to say Hackwill brought his gun with him. Somehow, Laraine got it from him.

The police scrum sorts itself out. Laraine is alive and gunless. Mary wipes dirt off her knees and skirt.

The bodies are found. Neighbours are shooed away. Every copper in Somerset is in Sutton Mallet. Handcuffs are clamped on Laraine.

There are ambulances here, too. Lots of flashing lights. The doctors can't do anything for Sean and Hackwill. They look at Laraine's bruises. She gets all the attention.

Beyond the carnival, the moors are dark. You can walk away. Vanish; get amnesia; start a new life somewhere, with no name, no money, no home and no job.

If Laraine talks, you're going to be famous. Still, it's your best bet. You back away, working between police cars.

'Keith,' Mary says. 'At last, someone with sense.'

Your way to the moors is barred. You're part of the carnival. Soon, you'll be the high-wire act.

'Keith, what's the story?'

Your throat is dry. You can't speak.

And so on.

175

You gently push Mum and Phil aside and roughly grab Sean by the lapels. You see fear and surprise in his eyes and enjoy it. You think like James. Mary's job is to stop you. She'll hesitate, but she'll do it. You have to be quick and efficient.

You nut Sean, ramming your forehead against his nose. You break his red-framed yuppie glasses and feel cartilage scrunch against your hard skullbone.

You knee Sean in the goolies, doubling him up; you chop his neck with a double-handed thump, laying him on the floor; you kick him in the ribs, again and again and– Mary lays a hand on your shoulder. You stand back like a boxer pulled out by the referee. Sean hears the count and doesn't try to get up. Blood pools under his face.

'All right, game over,' you tell Mary, raising open hands.

She stands away. You turn and put one last kick into Sean's face. Mary grabs you round the waist and throws you at a chair.

Mum and Phil are appalled. They don't understand.

'Obviously, there's a story here,' Mary says.

'That bastard hurt my sister,' you say. 'Put her in hospital.'

'Are you alleging…?'

'I'm accusing my brother-in-law of criminal assault, or whatever.'

'No,' Mary says.

'You don't understand.'

'You're the one who doesn't understand. There was a witness. Mrs Rye fell or threw herself out of a window. Mr Rye was in his car, on the way home.'

…or *threw herself*…

'He did it.'

'It was an accident, Keith,' says Mum.

You shake your head.

Someone examines Sean, turning him over amid groans.

'I don't care if it was an accident. He did it.'

Mary reads you your rights.

Sean doesn't want to press charges. After a night in a cell without your belt or tie, you are let go.

'We seem to have been here before,' says Mary as she shows you the way out of the police station. 'Why doesn't anyone want to take the Marion boys to court?'

Outside the police station, bright sunshine strikes Mary's blond bun. Her blue eyes seem white.

'We hit people who deserve it?'

She thinks about it. Obviously, she has pieced together the story. Even if Sean and Laraine aren't talking, their attitudes and actions –

not to mention yours – add up to something like the truth.

Mary kisses you.

You didn't sleep much in the cell. And Mary was on night duty, clocking off when she let you out. So you fall asleep after the first, frenzied coupling. You wake in early afternoon, naked in a tangle on the single bed in your room, and get back to it.

She snaps on her handcuffs, running the chain through the slats of the headboard, linking your wrist to hers. Neither of you can get away.

It's not slower or gentler but it lasts longer. When you flag, Mary tugs the chain. She bites you, leaving tooth-patterns on your chest and shoulders.

When it's over, around sunset, your bodies are bruised and throbbing. You feel the pounding of her pelvis against yours for days afterwards.

She finds the cuff key with her toes and pulls it within reach.

'What would you have done if it'd fallen on the floor?' you ask.

'Fucked until the bed fell apart.'

'Fair enough.'

She does her hair up first, then puts on her uniform.

'Was this a police reward?'

She laughs, which she doesn't do often. 'A job well done,' she says.

'Did you…?'

'With James? Yes.'

You bang your head against the board.

'It's not an everyday thing,' she says, buttoning her jacket.

'Scary Mary lives.'

'Believe it, girlie.'

'What about Sean?' you ask.

'If I were married to him, I'd have at his bollocks with a Stanley knife.'

'But you're not. Laraine is.'

She sits at your desk, doing her make-up with a small mirror and compact.

'Sean's in a different ward, so he can't get to her. Her leg will get better and so will his face. For a while, they'll hobble around, not hurting anyone. Sean will be careful. He remembers you're out there. But the scars will heal. And Laraine will make the wrong pud or put the cups in the wrong place and he'll hit her. She won't say anything, because she's afraid for you now, as well as herself. And maybe she's stupid enough to love the bastard. Women are like that. Sean will be apologetic after the first time, beg her to stay, promise not to hurt her again. She'll believe him, because she has too much invested in him not to. Then, on less of an excuse, he'll hit her again, harder this time. Maybe leave a mark. She'll lie about it to anyone who notices. He'll start doing it regularly and she'll start making more excuses for him, blaming herself, coming up with stories of accidents. At that point, Sean will be consumed with disgust for her, probably take to raping her once in a while, to prove the point. Then, someone kills someone.'

You sit up, listening.

'Best-case scenario is the least likely,' Mary continues. 'That's Sean kills himself. After that you have Larry kills Sean. Justice served and a tiny jail term, lots of counselling, lots of sympathy. More likely, though, is Sean kills Larry. It's not much consolation but he'll get arse-raped so often in the nick that anything Larry took from him will seem lightweight. And more likely still, considering last night, is Larry kills herself. Further down the odds, you have various murder-suicide combos. And there's Keith kills Sean, which I wouldn't advise since even I can't really turn you loose after that. Or Total Stranger kills Sean, which you might be tempted to arrange but which I'd also advise against since I'd get a promotion for catching you and your confederate.'

'What about Larry leaves Sean, meets wonderful bloke, lives happily ever after?'

Mary laughs, nastily. 'In your dreams, Keith.'

She slips on her shoes and crawls on to the bed, hovering over you in her slightly gamey uniform. Her hands spider-inch their way up your torso. She dips her head and takes your flaccid, drained penis in her mouth. Her tongue slithers around, coaxing another erection, stretched and painful, ringed with lipstick.

'Something to remember me by,' she says, withdrawing from you and standing up. She lightly swats your dick aside and leaves.

You look at the ceiling.

You refuse to accept the future Mary has laid out. Sometimes, there are happy endings.

And so on.

176

'We have hundreds of cases now, Susan. Of Marion syndrome.'

'No wonder. The last five years haven't been easy on those of us who chose to stick around. When the Spiders came, everyone suffered enough to drive them to fantasise alternate realities.'

'My wife was killed in the invasion.'

'I'm sorry, Dr Cross. I didn't mean to be insensitive.'

'That's all right. I incline to agree with you. The miracle is that there are people who *don't* suffer from Marion syndrome.'

'What is he actually doing? Retreating to some arcadian past? Some bucolic twentieth century?'

'Not quite. It's cleverer than that. The syndrome, I mean. It's almost as if it has a personality of its own, separate from the sufferer. Mind-scans indicate that it's like a voice, whispering, describing, coaxing, even shouting abuse. It takes Marion back over his life, in sometimes minute detail.'

'So he's remembering?'

'Not exactly, though his personal memories are the raw material of the syndrome. When the crisis point came, Marion's mind shot backwards through his life and he surrounded himself with the furniture of his earlier years.'

'I've noticed people prize things that used to be ephemera. Food packaging, newspapers, used envelopes. Anything from before. They become almost talismanic objects. My boyfriend collects unscrambled videodiscs. Of anything.'

'This is a more extreme reaction, but the cause is the same. No matter what one thought of it at the time, a world without the Spiders seems utopian to us now.'

'So Marion is back there?'

'He used up his real life, his throughline, very swiftly. Since then, he's been shuffling, rearranging elements, wandering and wondering.'

'I don't understand.'

'He's living life in multiples. Fragmenting himself, spreading himself thin, sometimes almost to invisibility. And he can't quite keep the Spiders out of it. He's weaving a tapestry of lifelines, crissing and crossing. Some are wish-fulfilments, some are nightmares. Some are achingly real.'

'Good God!'

'What is it, Susan? What's funny?'

'A question occurs, Dr Cross. Objectively, if you had spent the last five years away from all contact with the world, which Keith Marion would you believe in?'

'I don't see what that has to do with it.'

'The Keith Marion who manages a bank in the West Country? The Keith Marion who was chemically castrated after conviction as a sex offender? The Keith Marion who is married to whoever and has whichever children? Or the Keith Marion who became catatonic after battling against Arachnoids from outer space?'

'Well, if you put it like that...'

'The world is a fantasy, Dr Cross. A kid's power fantasy, or an adult's nightmare of loss of control. It's lost all claim to be credible. Marion syndrome is a retreat to something more reasonable, more convincing.'

'Where does that leave us, Susan?'

'Voices in the night.'

177

You drift in joyful reverie from day to day, greeting each moment like an old friend. Dad comments that you dream too much. You aren't like yourself, he says. But, of course, you are. You're more like yourself than you were the first time round. You wonder if it'll be different. If you can change things.

You wonder when you first had a choice, when you'll first come to a juncture where you could have taken another path. This time, will you do better? Should you even try, considering that some tiny change might have vast ripple effects. By not getting together with Marie-Laure, will you fail to have the children who'll rally the surviving Earth people against an invasion of alien spiders in the twenty-first century?

That's silly. It's equally likely or unlikely that by doing something different you'll avert a disaster as cause one.

Do you want things to be different? Do you want to undo Josh and Jonquil's lives, for instance, take them back out of the world by not making love with their mother? Do you want to manipulate reality so that your own life is better in the far-off world of 1990?

Or do you just want to do it all over again, but to pay more attention this time?

* * *

Eventually, the moment comes.

'Who do you like, girl?' Shane asks, 'Napoleon Solo or Illya Kuryakin?'

If you like Napoleon Solo, go to 4. If you like Illya Kuryakin, go to 3.
But this time, *think* about it.

178

Given that you're going to get together anyway, you opt to hurry things up and cut in on Marie-Laure, edging Vince out. Marie-Laure is surprised, but you get round her by showing how sensitive and intuitive you are. It's not difficult. Since you have the memory of living for ten years with the woman this girl will turn into, you have insight into her likes and dislikes and know things about her she won't be able to tell you for years.

Vince, annoyed, drops you both. Fine. He's a deadweight.

Your parents notice how hard you work in the garden and comment on your improved attitude. Dad says there might be something for you at the bank.

A job.

For a moment, from the perspective of fifteen years of unemployment, you're so overwhelmed that you consider accepting it and going into the bank.

No. With what you know, you can do better.

Surprisingly, Marie-Laure chucks you. There's something creepy about you, she says. You're sly and you know *things*.

You resolve to pretend more, to do a better imitation of your younger self; but you can't. You have years of experience, even if of the dullest imaginable life.

So you get together with Victoria, who is at college and putting together a band. You can't play an instrument and can barely hum a tune, but you have a memory of the future.

You 'write' as many 1980s songs as you can remember, poaching from The Clash, The Sex Pistols, Ian Dury, Elvis Costello, Blondie, Tom Robinson, Culture Club, Frankie Goes to Hollywood, Duran Duran. It occurs to you that you're robbing these people of slivers of their minds. You might in the future be able to sue for copyright violation when they independently write songs you have introduced to the world. You suggest styles of clothes for Victoria's band, piecing together something somewhere between late punk and early New Romantic. In the end, you wind up dressing them as pirates.

Victoria sings 'Sex and Drugs and Rock and Roll' at a college disco. It goes down a lot better than 'Relax' or 'Karma Chameleon', probably because it's a song from next year rather than next decade. Actually, it's not quite the same song: you've channelled bits of Ian Dury, but Victoria, who genuinely is talented, has added her own input.

When you sign a contract with Real Records, you phase out your 'song-writing' and encourage Victoria to take over, which she does.

Whenever you feel guilty about what you've done to Ian Dury or Elvis Costello, you remember that the Victoria you knew first time round became a complete waster and moved in with that hairy clod Graham Foulk. Now, she's a passionate, involved, valuable artist. She brings out of you an invention you didn't realise you had. You gradually phase out the borrowed ideas and try to retro-fit an alternative world image for her.

And just maybe you'll prevent Duran Duran from ever happening.

This might work out.

And so on.

179

'Kill them,' you say.

'Then you kill me, right?' Mary prompts.

'Yes,' you admit.

Shane and Grebo have their hands full.

Mary shoots you as you leap at her. You feel a *push* in your shoulder but ignore it. You think of Juanita as you gouge out Mary's eyes with your thumbs. You think of Joseph as you take Mary's gun and shoot Shane in the face.

'No,' says Grebo, yelping as Chris chews his wrist like a ferret.

'Yes,' you contradict.

Chris gets free. You think of her as you shoot Grebo in the balls. Chris scoops up the twins, hugs them.

People are coming. The police. The noise.

You stand over Mary. She isn't screaming. She's patting the floor, looking for a gun. You point her gun at her head.

If you shoot her, go to 182. If you don't, go to 186.

180

In the first torrential rain of the autumn of 1976, you find yourself in a coffee bar in Soho, wondering how much further you can stretch the small sum of money your parents gave you to seek your fortune in London.

An anonymous man sits opposite you.

'Keith Marion,' he says.

I say. For it is I.

Read 13, and come back here.

You're surprised. Not only do I know you, but I know all about you, about where you come from. You can sense this in an instant.

I tell you the name I am using: 'Derek Leech.'

Not many people can do what you have done; and they always have to pay a price. Not necessarily to me, but often to someone like me.

I offer you a position. My terms are favourable, though, as always, there's a catch. 'You have to think about what's important to you.'

So, are you interested?

If you are, go to 195. If you turn me down, go to 197.

181

You sit back, almost relaxed. Mary's gun *thwicks*. Chris snaps back, blood on her forehead, eyes frozen.

'Bleddy waste,' moans Grebo.

Mary slips her gun into her waistband. With gloved hands, she picks up the wrench from the floor. 'This yours?'

You nod.

She whirls, landing a crunching blow on Grebo's head. The man goes down and she hits him again, three times. His legs are kicking, but he's dead.

'Somebody has to take the blame,' she says.

Shane is appalled but frozen. His gun is still on you.

'Congratulations,' Mary said. 'You died fighting for your family. Got a lick in.'

She hands you the bloody wrench and pulls out her gun again. 'Put your dabs on that, please.'

You grip the sticky steel.

'Ta,' Mary says.

'What about James?' you ask. 'And Hackwill?'

And the twins?

'I'm sorry,' she says. 'You'll never know how the story comes out.'

She shoots you.

Go to 0.

182

You finish Mary off, a bullet in her skull.

Armed police officers charge into the flat. Heavy visors, chest-protectors. Things are shouted at you. You spread your arms.

Chris shouts at you, 'Put it down!'

You look along the length of your arm and see Mary's gun in your hand.

You are shouted at again.

You try to let go of the gun, but it's stuck. Hammer-blows hit your chest. You hear explosions, unsilenced *bangs* rather than muffled *thwicks*.

In enormous pain, you're slammed against the wall.

Chris screams.

Go to 0.

183

It happens in an instant. It doesn't so much hurt as wear you out, as if you'd fast-forwarded through three hours of running after a bus. There's a lurch, and an instant hangover, which instantly vanishes, leaving your brain fogged with the memory of throbbing fuzziness only fractionally different from the sensation itself.

You're trapped in a tiny room. You're dragged down on to a ratty couch and lie there.

You're different. There's a bulge of stomach, a thin fungus of beard, and your arms and legs are feeble. It's as if you've spent years in a prison camp on a diet of chips.

A copy of the *TV Times* flops on a ratty magazine rack. It's dated 17 November 1990. This week. John Thaw is Inspector Morse. You hunt through the magazine for a political fact, and infer that the Major government is in power. The world hasn't changed radically, only you have.

And your life. The room is full of stuff. People live here. There's a television, a stereo, a stack of LPs, bright-coloured paperbacks, cheap plastic toys, posters and snapshots Blu-tacked to the walls. The place smells of fried food.

You live here.

The creepiest thing you find, when you force yourself to ignore the gunge in your head and carry out a search, is that among the LPs are albums you can remember buying – *Dark Side of the Moon*, *Diamond Dogs*, *Never Mind the Bollocks* – and even a few jazz and blues albums inherited from Dad – *Ella Sings the Cole Porter Songbook*, *Blues for Night People*. The older discs are not copies of the albums you own, but the records themselves (Dad always printed his name neatly on the label). The sleeves are in worse condition, with shreds of rolling tobacco stuck to them.

The photographs on the wall give parts of the story. You appear as a glum lump, often with a thin blonde woman you don't recognise and two kids who don't look like Jeremy and Jessica but might be their cousins. The only familiar face is VC, who shows up in a few snaps looking like a younger version of the Wicked Witch of the West, all black hair and ratty black shawls. None of her records is in the stack, which makes you wonder how much has happened differently in this life.

You look at your own face, in the snaps and in the mirror. Under flab, pallor and hair, you think you have fewer lines around your eyes and mouth. This face doesn't seem to have been used.

You have a feeling this is the life you'd have had if you hadn't tried.

Whoever you are here, no one will miss you.

If you walk away, go to 191. If you stay, go to 196.

184

'That would be telling,' you say.

She prods, not sharply but enough for you to feel.

'Who would you rather deny a warm bath, me or Councillor Hackwill?'

'I don't have favourites.'

That's true. You remember Mary supervising the smashing-up of your home. And her terrifying monster fits at school. She's earned her place on this course fair and square.

Mary puts her knife away. You swear she'll never get that close again. You count off the minutes and tell Mary when the hour is up.

Near nightfall, Kay Shearer works out how the map fits together. Mary recognises a culvert they trudged through earlier. That's where the treasure is.

They make their way down the valley. In the gathering gloom, you see Hackwill's team ahead, spread out around the culvert, scratching with their hands at the dirt. James is enjoying a cigarette, watching the work.

'They haven't found it yet,' Shearer deduces.

Mary's team rush into the culvert. Shane tackles Sean, bringing him down. They scuffle.

Mary fixes on the spot where the case is buried, under a thin layer of shale. Hackwill is crouched over it. Mary tries to slam Hackwill aside but the councillor leans out of the way. Mary careers on and sprawls.

Hackwill pulls the case out of its shallow grave and holds it up in triumph. He bellows apeman victory. Mary won't let it go easily. She stamps on Hackwill's instep with her heavy boot. Hackwill clouts her with the suitcase. She stops fighting. You know she could take Hackwill but has calculated the long-term effects.

As Mary's team huddles outside, sheltering in Colditz against the soft rain, Hackwill presides pompously over the dinner table, wolfing down extra helpings of stew.

'I had my doubts last night,' he says. 'But I'm beginning to see how this course works. I think we'll all come out of this stronger, better.'

You catch James's eye, and try not to snicker.

'What's up for tomorrow?' Hackwill asks.

'All good things come to those who wait,' you say.

Just before dawn, you assemble the teams. Hackwill's lot, a little smug, are more chipper. Sean and Shearer snipe at each other, and Mary is irritated with them. McKinnell says his bowels are in better shape. You almost hope so, because if not he's going to have a *really* bad day and be *extremely* unpopular.

You get out the gear and start fixing it to the teams, while James explains. 'Today's game is called *I Am a Fugitive from a Chain Gang*. Keith is shackling you together into four-man coffles. Well, one four-man coffle and one three-man/one-lady coffle.'

You fix chains to ankles, allowing about three feet between team-members. 'All you have to do is get to the top of the mountain over there' – he waves at a peak emerging through the dawn haze – 'and find the keys to the shackles.'

'What do we win?' Hackwill asks.

'Each team gets to elect one among their number who can sleep inside Castle Dracula in a warm bed.'

Hackwill grins. He's used to winning elections. Probably used to fixing them. 'Let's go, then,' he says. 'Unless we have to hum the theme to *Wacky Races* first.'

'Not at all,' James says. 'You start level today. One team will be driven to the other side of the mountain. You'll set off at the whistle.'

Hackwill is confident. Mary, shackled to Sean the wimp and McKinnell the potential shitter, is less pleased but a hell of a lot more determined. She'd chew off their legs to win this one.

'There's just one more thing,' James says. 'During the jail-break, you prisoners were heavily tear-gassed and raked with machine-gun fire.'

Hackwill is puzzled.

'One member of each team was blinded,' James says, 'and another badly wounded in the leg.'

You bring out two sleeves and fix one to Shearer's leg and one to Warwick's. They seem light at the moment, but half-way up a mountain will magically turn into a hundredweight of agony.

'You're not going to poke our eyes out,' Hackwill sneers.

James nods.

You have to do this next move simultaneously, because previous team-leaders have fought back. You and James produce eyeless S&M

hoods from your bum-bags and slip them over Hackwill's and Mary's heads. Any pretence that Shane leads his team is forgotten. You get close to Mary and feel her tension but she doesn't resist. Hackwill complains but is cut off by leather. The hoods snap shut at the neck.

'The keys to the hoods are with the keys to the shackles,' you say. 'Your comrades vote on whether you proceed with your mouth-zips opened or closed.'

Hackwill's head bobs up and down. He mmm-mmm-mmms furiously.

Shearer unzips Mary's mouth and she breathes in.

Reluctantly, it seems, Reg lets Hackwill talk.

'This is insane,' he says.

'Yes,' you admit. 'But it's equally insane for both of you.'

James herds Hackwill's human charm bracelet into the minibus and drives off to the other side of the mountain.

Mary and Shearer huddle, making plans, roping Sean and McKinnell in on them. She knows how to delegate to a sighted person, which gives her an advantage. You're sure Hackwill will shout orders and confuse his team-mates.

In her hood and body stocking, she looks like a Batman villainess, sexy in a pervo sort of way. You'd thought the Marion brothers' shag-anything-female policy suspended this once, for the special Hackwill course, but start to reconsider.

James's whistle sounds across the valley.

'You can go now,' you tell the team.

They hobble off, Sean guiding Mary, McKinnell ready to support Shearer when the weight begins to drag. Wishing them well, you sit back to watch the mountain.

Mary's team wins. Her comrades vote that she gets to sleep in Castle Drac. You have a feeling gallantry has less to do with her win than a desire not to wake up with a knife through the scrotum.

You and James sleep in twin beds, leaving the other room – a prize that becomes even more hotly contested towards the end of the course – for lucky winners. It has a cosy four-poster left over from the Compound's days as a dying farm.

You lie awake and think of Mary. You can't help wondering. Would it be clever? She's supposed to suffer like everyone else, but there's nothing to say you can't rip her off for a grudge fuck. You're miles away from the world. The only rules here are the ones you've set.

You have the beginnings of a hard-on. From James's breathing, you can tell he's asleep. Tomorrow, it's the assault course. Mary's tough, but won't win that: she hasn't got the weight. You'd guess Shane was favourite, with Shearer – whose wiry strength and coolness in crisis surprise you – as an outside chance. One of those blokes will be in the four-poster tomorrow. Unless you go queer overnight, that won't be any use to your currently intense sexual urge.

You imagine Mary next door, waiting.

If you go into Mary's bedroom, go to 188. If you go to sleep and try to forget Mary, go to 201.

185

You get out of the car and follow Mary inside.

Sean pleads feebly. 'Keith,' he says. 'Help.'

'What are you doing?' you ask Mary.

'What you should have done.'

You agree. You take Sean's other arm.

'No,' he says.

Mary is soothing to Sean as you take him upstairs.

The three of you squeeze into the room Laraine threw herself out of. It has a low ceiling. There's an old spinning-wheel, like the one in *Rumpelstiltskin*, by the window. This is your sister's special room.

You let go of Sean. He looks indignant.

'Your move, Mr Marion,' Mary says.

'Keith,' Sean pleads.

You have come this far. You push Sean in the chest. He tumbles back against the open window, arms flailing, and bends backwards. The low sill doesn't come up to his knees.

You push him again. He disappears into the dark and crunches on to the driveway.

Cool night air blows against your face.

You turn to Mary.

'I thought you'd just belt him,' she says, open-mouthed.

You've misread her completely.

'I didn't think…' she says.

You look down. Sean is a dark sprawl, a human swastika on crazy-paving.

'Keith, what have you done? I can't cover this up.'

You feel walls closing in.

Mary arrests you.

And so on.

186

Shane is dead. Grebo, who turns out to have been called Dickie Kell, dies. Mary, who turns out to be a *policewoman*, loses her sight in one eye and gets fifteen years in Holloway. Robert Hackwill resigns from Sedgwater District Council and flees the country to escape charges. James is convicted of the murder of Reginald Jessup and gets life imprisonment. Chris has a nervous breakdown and goes through a thinking-of-divorce period but comes back to you. You never talk about it, but you both know now how far you're prepared to go to protect your kids. After the police go away – any knowledge you might have had of James's crimes is discreetly forgotten – you still have the press to contend with. And memories. You have to think of yourself as someone who has killed. But James must have killed in the Falklands. Whole generations who fought in wars killed with no comeback. You killed to save precious lives. You can't afford to think of Shane and Grebo as people. They were Fury, invading your home, threatening your family. You resisted them. You have survived and are tempered. You just get on with it.

And so on.

187

You're happy? With the wife, the kids, the house, the car, the travel, the ease, the luxury, the loot, the life? Is this what you want? What you really really want? Lucky you.

Lucky, lucky, lucky.

And so on.

188

You step silently into Mary's room and are surprised not to be in complete darkness. A night-light burns on a tiny bedside table. The candle is scented and the room smells strange, spicy.

Mary shifts in her sleep, unbound hair twisting on the pillow. She breathes through her nose, sharp little breaths. You wonder whether you should leave. Her eyes open.

Beside the candle on the table is her knife.

She sits up, duvet falling away from her breasts, and snatches up the knife. You back against the closed door.

Mary looks at you and beckons with the knife-point.

You worry that you must have woken James up with the sex. The bedposts creak, the canopy threatens to fall. It's not a grudge fuck, but something stronger, stranger. You've not had such an animal episode since… well, since the first (illegal) time with Chris at university. You thought you'd grown sedate.

At the height of one round, Mary jams the hilt of her knife against your tight rectum, opening you as you open her, prompting a climax that makes you black out for seconds. When you come round, the knife-blade is drawing ice-lines down your chest.

Mary's knife is an extension of her body, a sex organ, a she-penis. It makes her different from any other woman you've been with. She doesn't bite but you're bleeding when the dawn comes up. Mary is damp all over, hair sweat-matted, skin sheened.

This is one you're going to feel for a long time.

'There was something I was supposed to do last night,' Mary says, running her tongue along the knife-edge, 'but I've changed my mind.'

It's the first non-sex thing she's said since you joined her. You're drowsy and don't pick it up.

'It's not you,' she says. 'Not just you. But these last two days have shown me something.'

'What?' you ask.

'Hackwill,' she says. 'He's a loser. I don't want to lose with him.'

'You're on opposite teams.'

'I don't mean this course. I mean everything.'

'What were you supposed to do? For Hackwill?'

'Not "what". "Who".' She taps the knife-point against the pulse in your throat.

'You were supposed to kill me?'

Mary laughs. It's a weirdly girly tinkle. 'You overestimate the importance you have for Councillor Hackwill, Keith. You may have fixated on him for years…'

How did she know that?

'…but you're a long way down his death list.'

She takes the knife away, kisses the dimple it made, and gets out of bed. 'Unless you let me have a shower, I'll cut your eyes out.' Now she seems to be speaking literal truth. Utterly terrifying.

'If you put it that way,' you say, 'go ahead.'

You lie on the bed and watch her gather her bath things. She wraps her knife in her towel.

You still feel her moving against you, a tidal wave in your bones. Fuck, you think.

You assemble everyone outside. Today, they are to be driven over to the assault course. It's an individual event, not a team thing. Its placing is calculated to break up the cliques that have formed on the first two days. There's only one winner.

James looks at you askance, but doesn't pass comment. He must know where you were last night, and what you did. The cottage is stoutly built, but the walls aren't thick enough to be soundproof. And you and Mary made a lot of noise.

Someone is missing.

'Where's Tris?' Shearer asks.

Warwick isn't among the slightly ragged-looking group gathered by the pens. Everyone looks at Shearer.

'He wasn't here first thing,' Shearer says.

'Probably wandered off looking for a place to pee,' Hackwill snaps. 'Flaming faggot.'

Shearer looks as if he's been slapped. If he gets a chance to drop Councillor Hackwill in a shit-pit, he will.

Back home, these people could ignore the things about one another that annoy, irritate or inculcate contempt. Out here, those things are rubbed in faces.

'Homophobic cunt,' Shearer says, evenly.

Now Hackwill looks as if he's been shot.

If there's a fight, it's your policy to let it play out. Sometimes, it's better than tormenting the guests yourselves, letting them have at each other.

Hackwill huffs and puffs and pretends to ignore the remark. He has seen over the last two days how much better Shearer is than he is at the physical stuff. If there's going to be a fight, he'll order Shane to have it.

Warwick doesn't come back.

'Has he given up and tried to walk home?' Sean suggests.

Shearer doesn't like the thought. You can see him thinking, indignantly, 'Without *me*?'

'That'd be very foolish,' you say. 'Walking off at night, in this wet weather. It's two days to the village, and that's if you know the way.'

'In Wales?' Mary says. 'Nothing's two days' walk away.'

'It's up and down mountains. We bought the place because it was the arse-end of nowhere.'

'It looks like Warwick's buggered the schedule for today,' says James. 'We'll give him half an hour to come back, then send out a search party.'

The guests look at each other.

'What'll we do till then?' Sean asks.

'I'm glad you asked,' James says, smiling. 'Push-ups.'

Hackwill snorts.

'Yes, Robbo,' James says. 'Drop and give me a hundred. Or no brekky.'

Shearer and Mary find dry-ish patches and go to it, pounding the ground with practised ease. You're astonished Mary can manage it after her exertions, and are disturbed by the stirrings you have watching her bottom push up and down, her elbows kink and unkink.

'Hungry, Councillor?'

Hackwill grumbles and gives in. He gets down on his knees and lies flat out. Shane, Jessup and McKinnell follow. James does push-ups himself, to pace them, to show off his physical ease. Sean is the last to get down.

It's a special struggle for Jessup and McKinnell, who carry extra stomach weight. Hackwill determinedly raises and lowers himself, not showing weakness. You mustn't underestimate his bully toughness.

You watch James and wonder whether he's doing the exercises to show you up. After a night of Mary, you couldn't do ten push-ups without flopping face down in the dirt.

You had hoped to find an excuse to take a nap in the van while the guests were doing the assault course.

Jessup is the last to finish his hundred.

Warwick hasn't come back.

James hands out Mars bars.

'This is breakfast?' Hackwill asks, red-faced.

'Helps you work, rest and play. There's coffee to come.'

'What about Tris?' Shearer is determined not to be worried, but obviously can't let the absence go.

'Keith,' James says, 'take Kay and Shane and scout around.'

You wonder why James has made you three the party.

Shearer asks questions about the landscape. Shane is sullen, only along on the expedition because Hackwill gave him the nod. Mary as good as told you Hackwill had ordered her to kill someone last night. If she didn't do it, would Shane be second choice hit-person? And does (did) the councillor have anything against Tristram Warwick?

At the lip of a culvert, you find a pair of boots, knotted together by the laces, balled socks shoved into the toes.

'Are these Tristram's?' you ask Shearer.

He looks at the boots and you see something odd – bewilderment? fear? – in his eyes.

'No,' he says, 'they're mine.'

You look down at his feet.

'Yes,' he says. 'I'm wearing them. But these are them too. Look.'

His name is written inside the leather lip in neat biro. That must be a habit from school.

'This is what I do with my socks at night,' Shearer says, pulling out a ball. You compare the tartan pattern with the socks he's wearing: an exact match.

Putting the boots beside his feet shows that they are identical to the ones he is wearing. Every dent, scratch and crease is the same.

'Twilight Zone,' you comment.

'Come here,' says Shane. He is at the edge of the culvert, looking down.

Tristram Warwick lies at the bottom, in an inch or two of water, a rain-swollen trickle. He is face up, mouth and eyes open, dead as a fish. Scattered around him are more boots; eight pairs. You recognise your own among them. And Mary's distinctive Docs.

Read 13, then come back here.

Shearer lets out one cry, a bark of grief.

You slide down to Warwick and check. He is indeed dead. You're more spooked by your own boots, simultaneously on your feet and lying by Warwick.

There are nine pairs of boots too many in the universe. Why not ten?

If you leave Shearer with Warwick and go back to the Compound to confer with James, go to 198. If you stay yourself and send Shearer and Shane back, go to 215.

189

You find yourself humming the theme for *Top Cat* and fixating on a world of giants, where the ceilings are further away. As you shrink back into your past, your present-day self recedes. You are tempted to let it go, but wonder whether the point isn't to take some of what you are now back to what you were then.

If you hang on, go to 202. If you let go, go to 277.

190

'I know the terrain,' you say. 'I'll take the boots and go.'

You can't read James's expression.

'Why you?' blurts Hackwill.

'Because I know I didn't do it.'

'You could be a split personality and not know you did it.'

'Don't be silly.'

Though you're resolved, it's still distasteful. It's up to you to unlace McKinnell's boots. Your cold fingers fumble with the ice-stiff laces. Your breath frosts against McKinnell's open throat.

Everyone stands round in a circle, watching. You tug and get the boots off. Dead man's shoes. Peeling off the socks is worse, more intimate, creepier. You'd wear just the boots but know that, after a couple of hours, your feet would blister. You'd walk on pain.

Sean *ughs* in distaste as you pull on McKinnell's socks.

'Do you have to?' he asks.

You ignore him.

You stock up on chocolate bars and sausage rolls and take a thermos of coffee. Before you go, you want to talk to James. But Hackwill always pushes in, not letting you alone.

'What if you've cooked this up between you?' he says, voice carrying across the valley. 'You could be plotting to kill us all.'

You try to look sadly at Hackwill, but the main reason you want to talk to James is to reassure yourself that this isn't his plan.

'We've never had dealings with McKinnell,' says James. 'Why should we want to kill him?'

That hits home. Hackwill shuts up. Interesting.

'Why should we want to kill any of you?' you say.

Hackwill doesn't bring up the copse. Or the Lime Kiln. Or your house. You almost enjoy his discomfort. But McKinnell's corpse, a tarp thrown over it, brings you down. This is serious.

'What about the phone?' you ask James, when you're alone. You've walked about a hundred yards from Castle Drac.

'There's an opportunity here,' your brother says.

You don't understand.

'One of this crew is a murderer. There's no passing trade up here.'

'I'd thought of that,' you say.

'If anybody else dies, the murderer will take the blame.'

'Meaning?'

'Keith, this is it. We're going to do Hackwill.'

'James, you can't mean it.'

But you can see he does. You'd forgotten that James has killed before. Has had to. To him, it's a natural solution to a problem.

'You didn't kill McKinnell?' you ask.

James looks shocked. 'Of course not.'

You are torn.

'Look,' James says, 'it was probably Hackwill himself. A dodgy deal gone wrong. In that case, Robbo's got a cache of warm shoes and socks somewhere. As soon as you're gone, he can continue his game.'

Back at the Compound, Hackwill and the others stand together, watching you from a distance. What if they're all in it? You'll be leaving James to them.

'Here's the deal,' he says. 'Get over the hill and go to ground. I'll work on Hackwill, hint that we have another car stashed near the old shepherd's hut. He'll bolt for it. Then we'll have him.'

You think about it.

If you agree with James, go to 206. If you argue with James, go to 216.

191

All you take from the flat over the chip shop is an ancient child-sized eyepatch you find pinned to the wall. You lost it years ago, but this Keith hung on to it. The eyepatch predates the point, whenever it was, when your lives split.

This Keith has obviously walked out on his wife and kids – as you have, you think – and so there's no obligation on you to stay. They'll probably be better off without him.

You walk through Sedgwater in the afternoon, finding things the same. Robert Hackwill is up for re-election. Brink's Café is open for business.

Your mother probably still lives here. No, *his* mother, not yours. You aren't him. You have to get that straight.

You walk out of town and hitch a lift. You end up in London. On the streets.

It's November, brutally cold. You don't panhandle – that takes more guts than you think you've got – but take casual, cash-in-hand, sweeping-up and washing-out jobs. A publican, impressed with your attitude, gives you a line on a bedsit. You land a place in a housing co-op and a temporary job as a barman. In the mornings, you re-educate yourself in libraries, catching up on skills you were letting slip. You jog to get in shape, losing gut, building muscle. You spend your first surplus cash on a decent haircut. You keep but trim the beard.

You work on a believable story. You've been in the Far East, were in fact brought up there, and have recently returned. All your documentation is lost. You get a photocopy of your birth certificate from the Reading records office, and use it to get a new passport.

Newspapers keep you up to date on your clients. Without you, some are floundering – which ought to please you but doesn't – and between the lines you see where connections are missing. Deals you have brokered have gone unmade.

All you've brought with you is in your head. But that turns out to be quite a lot.

You sketch out a few financial articles, using inside but unaccountable knowledge, and sell the pieces to *Financial Times*. You call yourself Marion Griffin, perhaps to bury yourself deeper.

After six months, you've gone from bum to barman and from journo to expert. Working out of a tiny flat, you take consultancies. When your knowledge of Japan, specifically your near-fluent Japanese, gets out, you become sought-after.

You can never be as flamboyant as you were, but you can be a behind-the-scenes player, putting things together. You have started over.

When you first start seeing women, you have twinges of guilt. But you feel worse about the thin blonde woman, whose name you don't even know, than about Ro. You've discreetly checked up on Ro, and she's married to Roger Cunningham, whom you vaguely remember from school. The *Sedgwater Herald* didn't even run a news item about this Keith's 'disappearance', which is obscurely depressing.

You start seeing Christina Temple, a lecturer at London University. You move in together but don't marry. You assume the other Keith, who you are legally, was probably married. The issue doesn't arise, anyway.

You begin to command high fees. Nobody ever asks about your qualifications. Your work is mostly talk and you can demonstrate your ability to do it.

It occurs to you that you've recreated a life you performed a miracle to leave. Maybe this has taught you what you really want. Or maybe you'll find yourself, eventually, making another switch.

Maybe.

And so on.

192

Next time Josh and Jonquil are bored, you draw them a treasure map. It's a desert island which topographically mimics Sedgwater. You tell Josh it's in another dimension, where the town is an abandoned settlement in a Sargasso Sea overrun by giant spiders.

'Once, long ago, I buried a treasure,' you tell them. 'When I was your age, I searched but never found it. The lost treasure – it doesn't matter what it was – is still there, but it's not the finding that's important. It's the searching.'

You aren't sure, but you think Josh and Jonquil see you differently for a moment. Not as layabout Dad, part of the furniture, a disappointment to everyone, but as the magical visitor to the Admiral Benbow Inn, opening up a world of wonder and adventure and tragedy and triumph.

You give them the map and send them out to search.

Marie-Laure, who has been watching this, is surprised and pleased. She'd thought she knew everything about you. She was willing to settle for you, you realise.

But you've found something else, which you can share with the children and even with her.

'Let's get married,' you say.

This isn't what she was expecting. 'Pardon?' she says.

'I love you,' you say.

Marie-Laure, under the mannerisms, is beautiful. She has trembled between neurosis and practicality on her own, with no support from you, having to mother you as well as the kids.

Going back has helped you understand that.

'I may not be able to get a job,' you say, 'but I can still make a home, be a father, be your husband.'

Marie-Laure is crying. You embrace her.

After you're married, Marie-Laure tells you her mother will settle £50,000 on you both. She's repeatedly made this offer, pressuring Marie-Laure to marry, but Marie-Laure – your wife – has always held back from telling you. She didn't want to get married simply for financial security, feeling the situation would fall apart. You half feel her mother made the offer in the hope of prodding Marie-Laure into a marriage as disastrous as her own, just so she could say, 'I told you so.' It's like finding buried treasure.

Your trips into the past have reminded you of the spirit you once had and made you wonder how you lost it. As a child, you had no long-term hopes, because being grown-up was as remote as taking a trip to the moon. But you had a home, a family, a sense of the eternal present.

The money enables Marie-Laure to quit her job and study for a degree. You two buy into Vince's comic book and nostalgia shop just as the '60s and '70s retro-industry takes off as big business. It's almost magic.

As the '90s wear on, things get better. Sometimes, considering the state of the country, you feel guilty about it. But while financial comets like Laraine's old boyfriend Sean Rye were streaking upwards in the '80s, you were ploughing along in a rut. Now, Sean and his whole Thatcherite yuppie class are burned out, and your ruts are foundations.

You give up travelling into the past, and travel instead into the future.

And so on.

193

*B*lit blurt...

This was your home. Now, it's a ruin, wisped over by layers and layers of cobweb. You rend the web apart with your hands, only to find another grey veil underneath.

It frightens you that you have so many memories. Irreconcilable memories.

When you think of your wife, too many names and faces come to mind. And the same for your son and daughter. A pixilated, drunken-haze conglomeration of lives seems to be clogging your mind.

What are you looking for? Food? Survivors? A tin of marbles?

There's a movement in the distance, and you look over across the plain of rubble. Black pipe-cleaner legs poke over the horizon as an

Arachnoid crawls up from one of the holes.

You don't think you can stand to look at the spider-face.

The legs strain and the body emerges like a cloud of infested soot. The face is coming.

You feel an electric touch in your mind.

…blit blurt.

194

Ignoring the pain in your knee, you launch yourself out of the chair at Mary. The other two are stooges. They don't count.

You come down hard on Mary's arm. Her gun *thwicks*, kicking up a divot of carpet, lino and floorboard.

You are being battered.

You wrestle for Mary's gun. You get it and fit it into your fist. You fire, dizzyingly certain you'll hit Chris or one of the twins. An orange poke-hole appears in Grebo's gut. He starts yelling – your neighbours must hear.

Mary has Grebo's gun now, held to Chris's ear. 'Drop it,' she says.

You shoot her in the throat.

She shoots Chris in the head.

Shane shoots you in the back.

Mary lies against one wall, gurgling blood, hand pressed to her throat wound. Chris is curled up on the sofa, obviously dead. The twins howl like dogs. Grebo shouts profanity.

You're still crawling, towards the sofa. Shane stands by the sofa, gun aimed at the twins, barrel drifting between Juanita and Joseph.

'Don't,' you say. It's all you can manage. You haven't got a gun or a wrench.

'Don't,' you say.

Shane looks at your children. And can't.

People come. The police. You fade.

Go to 0.

195

What I want of you is quite simple. I want you to keep doing what you have been doing. You can go back to the beginning, to **1**, if you wish. Or re-enter wherever you choose. You'll learn you're not just one Keith, but a legion of Keiths, and that a legion of lives are affected by you, or even depend on you.

You may think of me as an enemy of man.

Not so.

I am fascinated. I am pleased to encounter those truly rare individuals who see beyond the game, who do not constantly succumb to deals and catches.

Believe me.

And, if truth be told, I am disappointed each time I win.

There've been complaints, I know. Altogether too many **Go to 0** outcomes. Premature, sudden **0**s. Statistically, that's unlikely. There are an infinite number of outcomes, and I'm guiding you within only a comparatively narrow band. I haven't let you go down the Synth, for instance. You can venture further on your own, ponder the outcomes between the lines we're treading together.

Most people, in my experience, live **And so on** lives. At some point, sometimes frighteningly early, they fix their futures and just live them out. **And so on.** Often, the **And so on** point comes as suddenly as a **Go to 0**. The difference is that you have to live with it.

Are the **And so on** lines really inescapable? Once you have received that verdict or reward or punishment or revelation, do you really have to stick with it?

Maybe not. Some people never surrender. I like them; though they can be infuriating. Perhaps they should look for satisfaction rather than adventure.

You can crap out now. Go to **300**, maybe. Or **37**. Whatever.

Or you can explore. Make conclusions. Make something of yourself and for yourself.

Don't be afraid.

Just go on.

196

The woman's name is Marie-Laure Quilter. You aren't married but have two children, Josh and Jonquil. You can't help but laugh at your daughter's name, which is the highest possible scoring word in Scrabble. You don't work. You don't seem to do much of anything.

Okay, so you live in a tip. But, hey, there are advantages.

You sit back and take a holiday, coasting through things. It's easier than it ought to be, since you only have one or two friends – VC, here called Victoria, is one, and a loser called Vince – and they're used to you nodding as they talk at you. The same goes for Marie-Laure, who nags a bit but does your washing and cooks for you.

Admittedly, you put off seeing Mum. But that seems to be in character. Doing nothing but pig out on stodge, watch videos, smoke dope and drink beer, you perfect your 'Keith Marion' impersonation. Your kids jump on you a bit and Marie-Laure lets you shag her, but you keep everything low-key. God, this is an easy life.

If you let go and become 'Keith Marion', go to 204. If you resist and remake yourself, go to 237.

197

As you walk away, I am proud of you. Few can resist a sure thing. **Go back to 1.**

It will be different this time.

198

You find Mary in charge. James and Hackwill have driven off in the minibus. This disorients you.

'Warwick is dead,' you say.

Shearer is in glum shock. The others don't believe it.

'Why did they go?' you ask Mary.

'You weren't back. Hackwill demanded to be taken to the village to bring help. James argued but agreed to drive him.'

It's not like James to give in.

'What's this about boots?'

You check Mary's feet. She still has her Docs on. Bovver boots, they used to be called. Skinheads wore them in the early '70s, for aggro, for putting the boot in.

'I can't get my head round that,' you say.

'But Warwick's dead? How?'

'I couldn't tell.'

'*Warwick?*' Mary is as fazed by this as you. You want to hold her hand. Are you allies out of bed?

'Do you have a phone?' she asks.

'James does. A mobile. It's in the bus.'

'No help, then?'

You shake your head.

By nightfall, James and Hackwill haven't come back. The rain gets worse, cranking up from drizzle to downpour, with storm in the offing.

You let the guests into Castle Drac and organise a hot meal. You've been left with the glum, no-initiative losers: Shearer doesn't say anything, Shane never did add much to a group, McKinnell spends most of his time on the bog, Jessup and Sean compete to see who can whine the most.

You realise Hackwill kept his troops in line. Without him, it's all falling apart. Mary is some help but seems softer than you thought, more uncertain, more vulnerable.

The rain assaults the cottage. There are drips everywhere.

'Tomorrow,' you announce, 'if the rain lets up and James isn't back, I'll lead you out of here. It shouldn't come to that. If James isn't back himself, he'll send someone.'

James doesn't know Warwick is dead. Or that the universe is spitting out surplus boots.

'Tonight, we just sit tight.'

'Inside?' Sean asks, eagerly.

You're tempted to enforce course discipline and send them out to Colditz in the rain. A river will be running through the sleeping quarters. You let them stay.

Shearer and McKinnell, psychologically and intestinally upset, get your twin beds. You and Mary take the four-poster, which makes

Shane look glumly angry and almost excites prurient comment from Jessup. The rest settle in chairs downstairs.

Mary lights candles by the bed and you make love. Differently. Last night was fucking. Now, the violence is gone, the desperation in check. You draw each wave out, opening yourselves to each other, coaxing not pounding. Again, you have no parallel with the experience since early Chris.

Of course, it occurs to you that you might not survive the next few days. Warwick is dead, stranger things are happening. Mary might be your last love.

She's got a lock on your heart. It's not just sex, it's emotion. This time, you're not confusing lust and availability with a real connection. You've known this woman since she was a little girl, since you were a child. And yet not before now have you reached each other.

You see the monster in Mary Yatman was a desperate fiction, a protective cover. Like the uniform she wore as a policewoman, like the hardness of her body and mind. Inside, she's confused, reaching, wounded, generous, loving. Just like you.

Lying together, sharing body-warmth, her hair over your face, you try to find a calm centre. The roof rattles, clawed by wind and rain.

You are woken by the door opening. Someone hangs in the frame, holding himself up by hanging on the jamb. He is wet and dripping.

Mary holds up the candle. It's James, face dead white, clothes soaked. He pitches forwards, collapsing.

You and Mary get out of bed. You pull on a dressing-gown and kneel by your brother. Mary crouches naked, balanced like an aborigine, and lifts one of James's eyelids.

You feel his chest. His heart is racing.

'Let's get him on the bed,' Mary says.

You lift him. His arm flops round your shoulder.

'Get his wet clothes off first,' Mary says.

She pulls off his boots and socks. You work from the top. James isn't quite unconscious. He mumbles, wavering on his feet as you help him out of his clothes. When he's naked, you and Mary towel him down. It seems he'll never get dry. Then you push him into bed.

You want to ask him many things, but he conks out.

You and Mary sit in the office – the others haven't been disturbed – over coffee and review the situation.

Outside, the rain is a liquid wind. To go for a walk would be to risk drowning.

James has come back on his own: no Hackwill, no minibus. Something has happened.

Mary is tense but cool. Not so air-headed she doesn't see how serious this is, but not in a panic either. Good girl. You love her outside bed too. How does she feel about you?

'Mary, were you supposed to kill Warwick?'

'No,' she says, not hesitating to answer. 'McKinnell. He wants to back out of the Discount Development. The idea was to scare Warwick into line. He has doubts too. But Warwick would have been next. Having people killed gets to be addictive.'

The woman you love has just admitted she was a hired killer. How does that make you feel? Your guts churn. You're sick at heart. But you surf in a tube of joy.

'I told myself I'd never do it, though I agreed to. I lay there in bed last night, knowing I could do it. If I'd been in Colditz, it'd have been easier. I'd just have had to wait for McKinnell to go out for a shit and follow him. But you came into the room.'

'And changed things?'

She doesn't answer that.

'Shearer might have killed Warwick,' she says. 'They weren't exactly the Happy Homos. Warwick strayed a lot. This week was supposed to bring them together. I think you and James fucked that up. Good plan, by the way. Or it could have been Shane. Hackwill can count on him to do things I might not, if not as well. He's still just a thug. Remember he wanted to be the Man From U.N.C.L.E.? Prat.'

'Any other theories?'

'Yes. You and James. Hackwill sussed as soon as he saw your brother's smiling face that the special rate was a come-on. This was all about you getting your own back. He thinks it's because he took your mum's house away because James showed him up in a pub. But it's the copse.'

'You remember?'

'I remember everything. You and school custard. I thought my monster was an extreme way of getting what I wanted, but I couldn't match your custard fit. Hackwill doesn't like to think back that far. He's gone beyond bullying children. Now, he demands to be loved for what he does. Jessup might remember.'

'He was there too. In the copse.'

'Tell you what, if James killed Warwick – I know it wasn't you because I was clamped round you at the time – let's frame Reggie Jessup. If anyone deserves ten years of solid arse-rape at Her Majesty's pleasure, it's him.'

Mary's softer than you thought. But not that soft.

'It wasn't James,' you say. 'He'd have let me in on it.'

'Like you let him in on you coming to my room?'

Good point. You imagine James lying there, listening to a sonata of shagging, pissed off at the exclusion, wondering how to crank up the game. Could he have got to the point where murder was the answer? He's the only one here who's actually killed anyone before, and he's got the commendations to prove it. How much easier would it be to ice a Hackwill toady than some panicked Argie conscript? Why Warwick? Opportunity. He was the unlucky sap who got up early to take a leak.

No. It feels wrong.

It's more likely to have been Robbo himself. You imagine Warwick making a gay pass at the councillor, to piss off his boyfriend, to attach himself to the power source. You see Hackwill repulsed, personally affronted, taking things into his own hands rather than delegating to Shane or Mary.

Or Shearer. Jealous, enraged, murderous. Or Shane, in an uncontrollable burst of homophobia. Or anyone.

Suicide? Act of God? Extra-dimensional boots showering down on Warwick, trampling him to death?

In the morning, the storm hasn't let up. You can't possibly lead six people through it over treacherous ground to the village.

James is in a deep sleep, shivering under a pile of blankets. McKinnell is locked in the bathroom. Sean demands you get him out of this hellhole and Mary satisfyingly slaps him across the face.

'Well done,' says Hackwill, barging through the door. 'Someone should have done that years ago.'

You are as astonished as anyone else that Hackwill has come back.

You thought he'd be miles away by now, doing his best not to send you any help.

'Where's the minibus?'

'In a valley, upside-down. Where's your fucking brother?'

Mary stands by you as you face Hackwill.

'Bastard hit me with a wrench,' Hackwill announces to the room, displaying a bruise on his forehead. 'Then shoved me and the bus off a cliff. But I'm not easily killed. You're both going to prison for a long time, Marion. I'll see to that.'

Shane has stood up, awaiting orders.

'Yatman, secure this bastard.'

Mary doesn't move.

'Mary,' Hackwill says, voice rising in alarm. 'Do your job.'

'Fuck right off,' she replies. 'I don't work for you any more.'

'He's tried to murder me!'

'Naughty naughty,' Mary says.

Hackwill looks betrayed, not to be taken seriously. 'Bush, hop to it,' he snaps.

Shane steps forward and Mary punches him in the throat, staggering him backwards.

'The problem isn't the alleged attempt on Councillor Hackwill's life,' you say, 'but the actual killing of Tristram Warwick.'

Hackwill doesn't look surprised but he's always Mr Poker-Face.

Mary – the only person you know didn't do it – is with you. Which line of investigation do you pursue? Think about it.

Go to 199.

199

Whom or what do you suspect?

If Hackwill, go to 210. If James, go to 211. If Shearer, go to 212. If Shane, go to 213. If Jessup, go to 214. If Sean, go to 224. If McKinnell, go to 225. If suicide, go to 226. If natural or supernatural phenomenon, go to 227.

200

As Columbo says, there's just one thing more to worry about.

You split the double roll-over jackpot. You took home £6.5 million, but so did someone else. You might have had £13 million, but someone was mimicking your thoughts as they filled in their card. Someone was stealing from your mind.

Someone who has half your money.

The other winner ticked the 'No publicity' box. You find yourself thinking more and more about him; or her. Is their life better? Did they have more to build on? For them, was the money extra fuel for a rocket already cleared for lift-off?

Or have they cracked up?

Who is it?

Who is it?

Out there is someone with £6.5 million that might have been yours if they'd made a random pen-stroke in a different way, if some unknowable synapse in their brain had fired left instead of right.

Do they think of you?

You don't mind publicity. You *want* it. You want people to know you've got what you *deserve*. You let television crews into your new home, to follow your family as you relish your just desserts.

So the other winner knows who you are.

If they get Cloud 9 satellite TV, which followed you around for six months, they know how many luxury cars you own and have written off, which quiz-show presenter you had an affair with, what brand of champagne you filled the swimming-pool with at Jesse's fourteenth birthday party.

Are they obsessed with you? Are they thinking of you as you think of them?

Is it a woman? Is she attractive?

Would you like them?

Were they rich already?

You make inquiries with the Lottery people. Even as a big winner, you don't have a right to know.

The other winners are your peers. Soon there will be a community of Lottery millionaires. A class, even. Maybe a seaside township will be built for them, like the village in *The Prisoner*. A party town, a money town. One long holiday. One long soap. Cloud 9 would love to have the rights.

There are functions for you all. You meet other winners. But not *the* other winner.

Your family don't understand.

You have what you wanted. Why can't you just enjoy it?

'Just let it go,' Vanda tells you.

If you can forget the other winner, go to 205. If you can't, go to 217.

201

You wake up for a moment and see James standing, in his dressing-gown, by the door.

'Go back to sleep,' he says, softly.

You obey.

In a dream, you are married to Marie-Laure but your wife manages never to be in the same place as you. Elements of your life are missing. The situation goes on for years. It's not a nightmare, it's a tragedy.

You are woken up by creaking. Lying awake, with an angry erection, you hear the four-poster in the next room. It's a noisy bed. Through the cottage wall, you hear your brother and Mary Yatman fucking, trying and failing to be quiet about it.

If that's the way it's going to be…

You put a pillow over your head and try to get back to sleep. No luck.

'Harder… deeper… yes.'

Nothing is so guaranteed to make you miserable. You want to knock their heads together and slam them into sleep. Eventually, it starts to get light outside. No let-up from next door. Oh, for a bucket of cold water!

You are wide awake. And still dog-tired. You get up and get dressed, clumping around as noisily as possible. Then you go downstairs and outside, to suck in a breath of icy air.

The cold hits you like a hammer and cuts you like a knife, but cleans you out. In the pre-dawn, the countryside is grey and green and gloomy. You can't tell if the fine droplets of water on your face are thin drizzle or thick mist.

You look at Colditz and almost feel sorry for Hackwill's party.

They must all have been kept awake by seven sets of chattering teeth. The puddles around the pens are ice-cakes.

This morning, you're giving them hot soup for breakfast and taking them to an assault course.

Something stirs in Colditz. A head pokes out, mole-like, and looks around. Hackwill. He gets out and stands up, stretching.

You press yourself against the side of Castle Drac, trying to blend in. You swear the whole building is shaking from sex.

Someone else gets out of the pens. Warwick?

'We can start the minibus,' Hackwill is saying, 'and be in a warm hotel by ten o'clock.'

It's almost funny. They're plotting an escape.

'*Raus! Raus!*' you shout, striding across the grass.

The escape committee are startled. Hackwill is a deal more shocked than Warwick. It's as if you'd caught them fucking, not planning to run away.

'You men haff been tunnelling from A Hut,' you sneer in an Anton Diffring accent. 'Attempted escapees vill be shot.'

Warwick grins nastily and *heils*. Hackwill looks sheepish. There was something else going on but you don't get it.

'Press-ups, vun dozen,' you say. 'Zen hot breakfast.'

For a moment, you think Hackwill will argue, but he gets down on the cold ground and does his twelve. He doesn't even break into a sweat. That might be because it's so cold.

The others crawl out and you pass on the press-ups order. Since Hackwill is finished first, you tell him to make sure the others do their exercises.

As you go back to the cottage, Hackwill is shouting at a writhing Sean. The councillor is a born *kapo*. Collaborating with the guards comes naturally. Bastard.

Shearer wins the assault course. James asks if you'd mind Shearer having the other bed in your room so he and Mary can have the four-poster. That's not how it's supposed to work. But he's your brother.

'Look,' he says, 'if it's a problem, forget it.'

If you let James have his way, go to 223. If you insist on sticking to the rules, go to 236.

202

Where do you want to be? What do you want to change?

If you want to be a child again, go to 207. If you want to be a teenager, go to 209.

203

'I'm paying for this,' Hackwill announces. You realise he means the course, not his sins. 'Reg, get me McKinnell's boots.'

Jessup Muttley-grumbles.

'Do it, Fatty,' Hackwill insists.

Jessup gets down on the ground and wrestles off McKinnell's boots. He doesn't enjoy himself.

Hackwill gets the boots on, stamps around in them, gets his feet settled. Warm feet give him authority. The game-playing is over and the Councillor is back in command.

'You lot stay here,' he orders. 'I'll send back help.'

Jessup whines a bit, like an abandoned dog.

'I can't take you with me, idiot,' Hackwill says.

You all watch as Hackwill walks down into the valley, until well after he is lost in the trees.

'Let's get back to the Compound,' you suggest.

'What about him?' Shearer asks, meaning McKinnell.

'Heave that bit of old tarp over him,' James says. 'He doesn't feel the cold any more.'

You cover McKinnell.

'Let's just hope he doesn't get any company,' you say.

You all sit in the small dining-room of Castle Drac, trying to keep your feet off the uncarpeted stone floor. The fire burns in the grate, but nothing takes the ice out of the slabs.

'What if it was Hackwill?'

Tristram Warwick says it. But you've all been thinking it.

'Perhaps you should have mentioned it at the time,' James says.

'You, Jessup, you're his friend, what do you know?' Warwick shouts in Jessup's face and grabs him by his furry jumper.

'Nothing, Tris. Honest.' Jessup blubbers, a bully's sidekick without the bully around, at the mercy of turning worms.

'We could make him talk,' Shearer says.

Jessup looks aghast.

After a few moments, James steps in. 'We don't do torture here,' he says.

'You could have fooled me,' Shearer snaps.

You and James laugh. Someone's dead but you can still laugh. That's a surprise.

'I don't know anything,' Jessup insists.

Warwick drops him.

'Hackwill might come back,' Warwick says. 'This fat shit could be the inside man.'

'Why would Councillor Hackwill want to kill anyone?' you ask.

Warwick shuts up. But Sean cracks.

'McKinnell was going to pull out of the Discount Development,' Sean says. 'Robert thought he would take the deal apart.'

'Idiot,' Warwick says, and you don't know who he means.

'He was going to use this week to persuade him not to.'

'Well, he won't now,' says James.

'Robbo's not a killer,' Jessup protests.

You and James look at Jessup, sneering.

'If he is, he's gone now,' James says. 'And we sit here like pillocks for a while.'

When will he mention the phone? He's playing his own game, and hasn't roped you in yet.

'Tell them, Tris,' says Shearer.

Warwick's face shuts tight.

'I think we have to assume we know each other well enough for secrets,' Shearer prompts. 'Tris was...'

'I agreed with McKinnell. Robert is overextended. It's time to get out while we can.'

'So that puts you on a hypothetical death list?'

Warwick shrugs at your suggestion.

Outside, it rains hard. This is that proverbial dark and stormy night.

You and James get to keep your beds, Mary is gallantly offered the four-poster, which she declines to share with any of the prospective candidates. Jessup, Sean and Shane wrap themselves in blankets on chairs downstairs.

Warwick and Shearer opt to go back to Colditz. They take knives with them and clearly intend to resist anyone who tries to get at them in the night. You realise that, despite the danger, they intend to take advantage of the privacy of the pens to make love. Maybe it's the danger that makes them so keen. This might be their last chance, the lucky bastards.

If you all die, your last physical contact with a woman was Mary stroking your balls with a knife. Not much to show for thirty-seven years.

Lying on your beds, you and James talk.

'Do you think it was Hackwill?' he asks.

'My first thought was that it was you.'

'I had the same thought about you. But you'd have started with Hackwill, or Fatty.'

'You too,' you say. 'I think it's most likely Hackwill had it done.'

'He had Jessup pull the boots off.'

'He doesn't do things himself.'

'He did in the copse.'

'Long time ago, James.'

'Who?'

'Take your pick?'

'Shane. Hired man. Hard man.'

'What about Mary?' you suggest.

James doesn't answer.

You wake up and it's still dark. Not early-morning dark, but small-hours dark.

You don't know what has woken you.

Slowly, you sit up in bed. The slate roof rattles with rain and wind.

There's a small torch on the bedside table. You cover the end with your hand and turn it on, making your fingers a transparent red, giving you some light.

James's bed is empty.

Someone is talking downstairs, very low.

If you go back to sleep, go to 208. If you investigate, go to 221.

204

The big discovery is the kids. They make J and J seem precious, but there's a lot of Jeremy and Jessica in Josh and Jonquil. With Marie-Laure working at the jam factory, you spend time dropping them off at school and picking them up afterwards. Then comes what you call the 'pre-Mummy' spell, the two hours when you have Josh and Jonquil to yourself before Marie-Laure gets home.

At first you just watch TV with them, but soon you start talking, telling stories about pirates, drawing maps that lead to 'treasure' hidden around the flat. They argue a lot but quarrels usually pass, like storms. Because they share a room, Josh and Jonquil are closer but thornier than Jeremy and Jessica. They understand territoriality.

You want to be the world for your kids. You try to furnish their minds with wonders. After all, as you know, many things are possible.

At weekends, you insist Marie-Laure come along with you and the kids on expeditions. You seek further afield for treasure. You often visit Mum, who is bewilderingly the same in this changed world, and even sometimes see James and Laraine, who are closer to the people you remember than the other Keith was to you.

You don't think of yourself and the other as separate people any more. You're submerged in his life but he's transformed inside.

The kids do better at school now, which you suspect is a side-effect of your interest in them. Marie-Laure is a kindlier, tolerant presence. She must have been fed up with the way things were, but is settling down. She gets a promotion at work and you move out of the flat into a terraced house, where the kids get their own rooms.

You've become a housewife. You're still not the world's greatest cleaning-person but you display an interest in cuisine which affects the family's health and disposition. The first time you cook a meal for the whole family, including Mum, using only ingredients you can afford on this Keith's budget, it is a revelation.

There are struggles and heartbreaks, but there are triumphs and joys.

You live Keith Marion's life. And, mostly, are content.

And so on.

205

After a while, the knot unravels. The question goes away, unanswered. You even find out the other winner's name (a man's, French-sounding) but it doesn't matter any more. Your life is too complex, rich and vibrant for that.

And you know you have a decision coming up.

You first think of it when trying to get insurance for your new home – a mansion next to the managing director of British Synthetics at the top end of Cliveden Rise (Sedgwater's Snob Row) – and are told that actuarial tables done in the States suggest the life expectancy of a big lottery-winner halves the night his number comes up.

Wealth is lovely. But it can kill you. You can shove it up your nose, stuff it into your stomach or smear it on your dick. And you can die.

Quite a few lottery millionaires commit suicide. Lots more kill themselves by excess.

Then again, you have to **go to 0** sometime, and there can't be a better way.

You imagine Dad telling you to spend the money wisely. And some haggard alternate version of yourself telling you to splurge the lot and go out with a bang.

Which voice do you hear?

If you spend wisely, go to 228. If you splurge, go to 241.

206

The shepherd's hut is a roofless box of stones. Too old to demolish, it's useful as a hiding-place for treasure hunts. It affords some cover from the wind but none from the rain.

You eat a Twix and wait, trying not to think about murder.

McKinnell's eyes were frozen. Not just wide with fear, but iced and sparkly. The dripping stalactitic gush from his throat was once warm blood. Someone did that to him. And you and James will do that to Hackwill.

Morning passes. At this time of year, day is a pathetic, drab, brief interval between eras of darkest, coldest, most dreadful night.

This isn't fun any more.

At last, you hear them coming. James talks loudly, to alert you.

Through chinks in the stones, you see James and Hackwill walking towards the hut. Tagging along with them is Jessup. Not part of the plan. But Jessup was there at the beginning, in the copse. It makes sense he should be here at the end.

You unsheathe your knife.

You assume James will do the deed, but you are a part of it, a collaborator, a co-murderer. You have to be ready to do your bit. Perhaps you'll kill Reg.

Their feet are wrapped in bright towels which look like hallucinogenic fungal elephantiasis. Your feet are frozen in scavenged boots. You can imagine what the seeped-through towels feel like.

'Where's this fucking car hid then?' Hackwill demands.

'Over the rim. By the hut.'

'Fuck this for a game of soldiers.' Hackwill strides ahead.

James bends over to get his breath, incidentally blocking Jessup's way. He is sending Hackwill to you. You'll have to do it. Yourself. The messy bit.

Your heart hammers. This isn't what you expected. You grip your knife.

Hackwill is just outside the hut. He turns away from you, looking back at James.

'I can't see it,' he says.

You see the back of his neck. You remember the copse. You stand up.

If you stab Hackwill, go to 219. If you can't do it, go to 232.

207

You're still you, but you're a kid. You're about seven, which would make this 1966. A good year to put a bet on England winning the World Cup. They were sentimental favourites anyway, so you wouldn't get great odds. Thinking about it, you wish you'd paid more attention to sport. You could grow up rich if you remembered a few long-shot winners. Here, in the past, you know a lot of things: election outcomes, wars, investment tips (get into computers – now!), storylines of hit books and movies, chart-topping songs.

Your grown-up mind crams awkwardly into your kid's brain. It's not quite like being your adult self in the body of a child. Sometimes, it's like being a passenger in someone else's body, lurking at the back and watching as kid Keith goes through his routine. There are some things you can let him do.

At school, you find you can't quite do joined-up writing. Your increased vocabulary is noticeable and you sometimes make assumptions that draw attention. You're frustrated at the total control adults have over you.

You would like a cup of coffee, but when, after nagging, Mum lets you have one – very watered-down, you notice – the taste is vile. You still have kid tastebuds.

School custard induces a spasm of horror.

You wonder if you could write *Jaws* or compose 'Goodbye Yellow Brick Road'. If you could, it'd be hard for a seven-year-old to reach a mass audience. And 1966 probably wouldn't embrace those things anyway.

The colours are different back here.

You cry, easily. The world you left for this seems thin and remote.

Are you a kid with a wild imagination?

You catalogue the toys and books in your room. You remember them all. Here are *The Buccaneers Annual* and *Red Rackham's Treasure* – a pristine copy, which you remember as covered with orange scribble and which you make a note to keep away from little James and his crayons. And here is a tin of shiny new marbles. Unchipped and perfect spheres, with intricate coloured swirls. Glassies.

At last, you've found them again. No, this is before you buried them.

You finally believe what you've done and grip the tin in triumph. You have found treasure.

What to do next?

If you bury the tin as you remember doing the first time round, go to 218. If you hang on to the tin and break the cycle, go to 239.

208

You drift back into fearful sleep, haunted by dreams of human-legged, red-eyed spiders. You stand again outside the copse, roots growing from your feet, fixing you in place.

'Mental,' Robert Hackwill shouts, 'come here! Come on. I've got someone you know here.'

'Keith,' squeaks James, 'I'm weeing myself. They won't let me go to the lavvy.'

'Your brother's a little shit. He's no good at all.'

'Come and see your brother,' Reg Jessup says.

You see Robert and Reg, holding James by his shoulders. James's shorts are dark at the crotch. Wee trickles down his legs. He starts sniffling.

'Everyone heard two shots ring out,' Gene Pitney sings, 'one shot made Liberty fall…'

The bell goes for the end of break. The other children run off, back to the classroom.

The dream grips hard. In a few seconds of sleep, years will unfold. You are afraid that if you go into the copse, you will die. And if you die in this dream, you will die in your bed.

'Come on, Mental,' Robert says. 'We're not going to hurt you.'

'Much,' adds Reg, laughing.

It's no longer a dream. It's the real thing.

If you go to the classroom and get on with your sums, go to 6. If you go to a teacher and tell what's happening, go to 10. If you go into the copse to help James, go to 14.

209

Worst-case scenario: you start, as if after a moment of dozing, and find yourself sitting in the assembly room at Ash Grove, looking down at an exam paper. All around, your contemporaries get on with it.

You can speak Japanese. You can estimate the short- and long-term progress of the stock market (c. 1990). You could put a bet on Britain and Argentina going to war in 1982.

But you're looking at a maths O Level exam paper.

This is not what you were expecting.

You remember this exam as a bastard the first time round – you had to revise intensively to get up to speed – and recall you only scraped a Grade C pass.

You've used a calculator for so long you barely remember how to multiply or divide in your head. And the paper is from the 'New Math' period, full of sines and cosines, base eight, fractions and other arcana.

You look around.

You're struck by the impossibly young faces – they must be fifteen or sixteen – and are painfully aware that even the thickos are beavering away.

Your hands are frozen.

You hold a biro but can't bear to sully the white spaces of the paper. Fail this exam and you scramble your whole future. You can't even go back, for you might well find that botching this crucial moment would lead to you becoming a homeless derelict in the '90s rather than a successful businessman.

Fuck fractions.

If you try to complete the exam, go to 249. If you try to get out of here, go to 263.

210

You look round the room and know it has to be Hackwill. If he didn't do it himself, he ordered it done. Now he's trying to fit James for the frame, claiming your brother is the homicidal maniac. You have to take the initiative.

'You wanted Warwick dead,' you say, directly.

'He was my business partner.'

Shearer snorts. A crack in the solid front.

'You don't have partners, Hackwill,' you say. 'You don't have *friends*. You have accomplices and victims.'

'This from the man whose brother tried to kill me.'

'We've only your word on that.'

'All right, Marion. Let's put it to a vote. Who believes James Marion, the sadist who's been rubbing our faces in shit for days, is capable of murder? Show of hands.'

Hackwill raises his hand. Shane and Jessup follow suit. Shearer folds his arms. Sean dithers, then puts up his hand. You look at Mary. She keeps her hand down. Momentarily, you wish she'd vote with Hackwill to keep in with him, get him to lower his guard.

'Four-three,' Hackwill says. 'James, of course, gets no vote.'

'This is ridiculous,' you say.

'What about Ben?' Sean asks.

'Oh *him*,' Hackwill sneers.

In that sneer, you catch something chilling.

'Mary, check on McKinnell would you?'

Read 220, go to 243.

211

This is out of control. You've been trying to put it together in your mind and the only story that makes sense – providing you ignore the boots from beyond – is the one you like least. It means you've been shut out of the family business, but left to clear up the mess.

James killed Warwick, then tried to kill Hackwill. Why couldn't he have fumbled the first shot and scored the second?

'You killed Warwick, you bastard,' you say to Hackwill.

You have to hit this hard. You need the others behind you if you're going to protect James.

'What do you know?' Shearer asks you.

'Warwick wanted to back out of the Discount Development,' Mary puts in. 'Like McKinnell. Hackwill needed them in, or the whole thing goes up in smoke. It's a seven-million-pound boondoggle.'

Shearer is convinced. He stands up and spits in Hackwill's face. Shane hits Shearer. Mary throws Shane. She always could outfight him.

'I'll see you pay,' Shearer sneers at Hackwill.

Hackwill doesn't even bother to deny the accusations. You worry this means he has some proof. He *knows*, of course. James tried to kill him. On his way back, he must have worked it out. The signs have been there all along, proving James was spinning out of control. It was going beyond a joke – poisoned porridge, impossible boots – and someone was bound to die.

James killed Warwick just to frighten Hackwill: a warm-up act for the big finish.

Mary makes a move for the stairs.

'Where are you going?' Hackwill demands.

'The toilet. Do you mind?'

Mary goes upstairs, and comes back down again.

'That was quick,' Jessup says.

Read 220, go to 244.

212

'Kay,' you say, using Shearer's first name for the first time, 'you're not as upset as you were yesterday. Are you getting over it?'

'What do you mean?'

Jessup snorts. 'Keith thinks you're a wife-killer, old fruit,' he explains, delighting in someone bullying someone else as usual. 'Reckons you shoved Trissy in the hole.'

You're disgusted with yourself. You hate the idea of Jessup toadying to you. It puts you on a level with Hackwill.

But who else would have done it? Most murders are committed by immediate family members, and Shearer and Warwick were a family.

'Tris was putting it about all over,' Jessup says, digging in. 'Couldn't get enough arse, they say. You must have hated that.'

Resentment of gays runs deep in Jessup. It occurs to you that the bully's sidekick is almost totally sexless himself. Is there something you're missing here?

'Tris said Robbo could have him.'

'That's enough,' says Hackwill.

'I didn't say you took him up on it. As I recall, you hit him in the face.'

'Sounds like a motive,' says Shearer. 'I've been queer-bashed enough to know the story. You straights get so worked up about the fucking come-on, the smallest let's-get-to-know-each-other look. A lot of breeders think that's an invitation to murder.'

Hackwill looks at Jessup, at the end of a very long rope with his lifelong toady. By sticking it to someone else, Jessup has merely swung the suspicion back on to his master.

'I didn't want Warwick dead,' Hackwill says patiently.

'No,' says Mary, 'you wanted *McKinnell* dead.' That hangs there in the room.

'Tris,' Shearer says, addressing a ghost, 'you were such a *stupid* bastard.'

'Mary,' you say, 'let's have the full house. Get McKinnell.'

She goes upstairs and comes back down.

Read 220, go to 245.

213

It strikes you that yesterday you didn't have to look long before you found Warwick. Shearer and Shane and you. Shane was the one who found the body, as if he knew where it was. Mary said Shane was Hackwill's number-two choice as murderer for hire. He must have done it.

Hackwill has made a mistake. You know Shane. You were at school with him. He's slower than you, always has been, but he was never a thicko, and he's got a sense of himself – he was Napoleon Solo, right? – and must resent being a stooge. He used to talk and joke all the time, but now he has to shut up and listen to Councillor Mastermind dish out the orders and snap the funnies. Once a little tyrant, he's now attached to a big one. But he's put himself in the fall-guy spot, and he might still be clever enough to want to shift.

'You didn't do it, did you?' you say.

Hackwill realises you're talking to him. Everyone else takes a second or two to catch up.

'But you had it done.'

Hackwill doesn't bother to say he doesn't know what you're talking about.

'Who did do it? Jessup? Sean? Mary?' (Hackwill doesn't yet know about you and Mary. Keep him off balance.) 'Shane?' you say, as if it were a ridiculous idea. You see Shane flinch. 'McKinnell?

'You're going to walk away clear from this and let someone else do the time. You're still a cunning bastard. You shouldn't be let off the mountain alive.'

'Your brother had the same idea,' Hackwill says, nastily.

'Where is he?' Jessup asks.

'Upstairs, asleep, recovering from your uncharacteristic face-to-face murder attempt,' you say. 'When you try to do it yourself, you fuck up.'

'Mary, check on the brother,' Hackwill orders. 'And on Ben McKinnell while you're at it.'

Read 220, go to 246.

214

You look around for the weak link. Sean is scared to the point of hysteria. Shearer is silently cried out. Shane positions himself just behind and to the left of Hackwill, ready to be ordered into action.

Sitting down, in front and to the right of Hackwill, is Reggie Jessup. The bully's sidekick, the boy who gets his jollies egging on his bigger pal.

Now you think about it, Jessup is even more contemptible than Hackwill. The councillor will stand up to you, put on a blank face, tough it out. Jessup won't. And you'll bet he knows where the bodies are buried.

'Reg,' you say, 'what's going on?'

Jessup looks startled even to have been noticed. 'Keith?' he asks.

'You always know, Reg. You know everything. You like to sit there smiling to yourself, knowing. You know more about all this than anyone.'

'I don't get your drift.' Jessup smiles, fatly.

Mary has slipped round the room, and stands over Jessup's chair. Suddenly, she leans in and pinches his cheek, not playfully.

'What happened to Warwick?' you ask.

If Jessup knows who did it, if it seems he's going to take the blame, he'll talk.

'You were seen,' you say, 'sneaking out after him. Were you lovers? Secretly, behind Kay's back? Did you quarrel? Was he going to leave you?'

'I'm not queer,' Jessup mumbles.

'You've never been married,' says Mary. 'Never had a girlfriend, so far as I know. At school, they said you were Hackwill's bum-boy.'

The pinch is hurting badly now. Jessup looks to Hackwill for support. 'Who saw me?' he asks.

'You admit it?'

'No.'

'This is silly,' Hackwill says, at last. Not a very strong protest.

'You're on your own now, Reggie,' you say.

It occurs to you that Reg Jessup, past forty, is probably a virgin. There are still people like that. It's almost sad.

Jessup tears his face loose from Mary's grip and bolts upstairs. You follow. He pulls open the bathroom door and drops to his knees to be sick.

'Couldn't you make it to the toilet?' you ask, in disgust.

Then you see that the bathroom is occupied. McKinnell is sitting on the toilet, dead.

Go to 230.

215

Why have you stayed behind? It's not as if Warwick is going anywhere. In too many movies the kids fetch the sheriff back to where they found the corpse, only to find it's been shifted. That doesn't happen in real life.

Then again, this doesn't happen in real life either.

You've identified most of the boots. You know yours and James's, and recognise Mary's Docs and Hackwill's specially-bought-for-the-course top-of-the-range survival boots. You work out which of the others belong to which guest. You think the 'missing' pair are McKinnell's.

You study your own boots and the duplicates on your feet. The pair you aren't wearing seem more like the originals, the real boots.

Water ripples around Warwick. The rain raises the level until it's lapping around the dead man's face.

This culvert is a place of gathering, filtering out things from great natural movements. Things like Warwick. And the boots.

There's a shimmer in the drizzle. Mary appears.

'They sent you,' you say.

She is startled to see you. She is wearing long mittens on her feet.

Suddenly, you know it's not Mary.

Yes, it is. But not the Mary you spent the night with. That Mary has a scarf arranged over bite-marks on her neck. This Mary's throat is bare and unmarked.

She is carrying James's mobile phone. How did she get that?

This Mary is hostile. Her knife comes out. She rushes at you and embeds the blade in your chest, twisting hard. In her eyes as she kills you, you see puzzlement. She's not your Mary; but you aren't her Keith, either.

She tosses the phone down next to the straggle of boots.

As you die, she steps back through the shimmer.

Go to 0.

216

'No,' you say, firmly. 'That'd be insane. Look, you sit tight, keep everybody together, watch them all. I'll go for the police. When you get a chance, phone ahead and say I'm coming. This whole gig is way out of hand.'

'You're right. I'm sorry.'

'That's okay, James. This isn't a normal situation.'

'Good luck.'

James hugs you and walks back to the Compound.

Your feet are loose in McKinnell's big boots. You know your ankles will tense up. It'll be agony by nightfall.

You turn and start walking down into the valley.

Two and a half days later, when you make it to the nearest village, you find that no one has phoned ahead to the police. You have tried not to think about what was happening back at the Marion Compound.

Your feet are numbed and you are as cold as you've ever been. Last night, there was a thunderstorm. You were out in it, wading forward, resisting the impulse to curl up and sleep, to succumb to hypothermia or even drown.

In the village, you collapse.

'We're sending a helicopter,' the Welsh police sergeant says. 'The rescue boys.'

You let yourself sleep.

When you wake up, there's a media circus. A lot of plainclothes police are around. You are dragged into a room and questioned minutely about what happened.

The thing is, you don't know. You realise you're being probed to see how much you know. You catch from a slip of the tongue that McKinnell isn't the only victim. A policeman refers to 'suspicious *deaths*'.

They hammer on and on about James's mobile phone. The one on which he didn't call them. You try to keep your story neutral. You worry that James is in trouble, that he tried on his own to do for Hackwill.

You're asked a lot of questions about the others, and what your relationship with them was.

'Tell me,' the sergeant says, 'this Councillor Hackwill. You'd known him a long time. Did you or your brother have any ill-will towards him?'

If you lie, go to 229. If you tell the truth, go to 242.

217

Finally, you get a break. The *Daily Comet*, the Derek Leech tabloid, runs an exposé of 'Day-Trip Lottery Thieves', foreigners who buy tickets in our Lottery because theirs are restricted, offering far lower pay-outs. Leech is crusading to make it illegal for foreigners to play, claiming it's supposed to be national, not international.

Among the Lottery thieves is the Other Winner: Thierry Lethem, from Brussels. A Belgian.

There's a blurry passport photo in the paper. A bland, anonymous young man. With £6.5 million that should be yours.

If Leech gets his way, Lethem wouldn't be eligible to carve off half your jackpot. He couldn't even buy a fucking scratch-card.

But even if Leech prevails, it's not going to be retroactive. Your money has gone abroad.

You've been cut in half. You feel transparent, a shadow-spider, empty.

You can't enjoy Mustique.
The mansion is a cell.
Your family are ghosts.
Only Lethem is real.
Bastard Belgian.

The *Comet* reports that Lethem, Lotto Snatcher Number One, has been deluged by sackfuls of righteous hate-mail from patriotic Britons. In his 'Derek Leech Talks Straight' editorial, the proprietor says Britain has had enough of the fascist jackboot of Brussels. The country is dying, assets bled away by Eurovampires like Thierry Lethem.

You write Leech a personal letter of thanks, and he responds in kind.

Someone understands.

Read 13, then come back here.

You go to Belgium but Lethem has left the country. He's unmarried – lucky git – and has no children, no living relatives. He is alone in the universe with £6.5 million. He stalks your world like a giant spider, chortling at you, extending cobweb tendrils of power. You know he is plotting against you.

You have only £4 million left. You're getting poor and the Belgian is getting rich.

You pay the Rhodes Investigation Agency, a reputable firm, to track Lethem down. To convince Sally Rhodes, its director, to take the commission, you spin a story about receiving letters threatening your co-winner and having dreadful visions of his spiral into danger. You claim to feel an almost supernatural connection with the Belgian.

That, at least, is not a lie. Sometimes, you *know* what he's doing. You have a scent of perfume and the sense of tropical night, an unfamiliar taste on your tongue or buzz in your nostrils. Soft skin pressed against yours. Warm liquid coursing over you.

You know he has your life.

The Rhodes Agency reports that Thierry Lethem is in the Far East. You thought as much. Thailand, Malaysia, Macao. Some fleshpot where everything is available for a man with £6.5 million.

You ask the agency to look further.

'Mr Marion,' Sally Rhodes says as you step into her office, 'I'm so pleased you could fit me in.'

She smiles easily, deep lines round her mouth. There are pictures of a kid – her son, you suppose – on the desk, and quite a bit of personal clutter. She's wearing a man's pinstripe jacket over dark tartan trousers. You find her attractive.

'Have you any news?' you ask.

She sits you down and buzzes her receptionist to get you coffee. Then she prowls round the room, playing with things as she talks.

'I've had a Far East agency we sub-contract for over here do some digging. They're good people. We're all international these days.' She takes a file out of a cabinet. 'I'm probably talking myself out of a nice little earner, but I thought I should ask you a bit more about your actual *interest* in M. Lethem.'

'How do you mean?' You aren't comfortable.

'Don't feel awkward. I'm not a conventional person. I know people do things for strange reasons and that there are vast unknowables. There's something about your link with Lethem that makes this inquiry out of the ordinary. It occurs to me that, well, there might be something unhealthy in it. For both of you.'

You're sure your face is red.

'I'm a detective,' Sally says. 'I feel a need to find things out. To *know*. Probably neurotic, but there you go. I often wish I didn't know things that I do. But you can't unpick your character like that. My reading is that you're suffering a touch from that disease just now.'

'You've found him,' you say.

Sally does a little shrug, perched on her desk, fanning herself with a file.

'You and Thierry are doing this little dance round the money you both won. All over the world. Maybe you need to meet, to sort out something cosmic. Or maybe you should be kept apart, maybe you'll be fissionable together. You remind me a bit too much of John Wayne in *The Searchers*.'

'He takes the girl home,' you say.

'But he was going to kill her. Frankly, Mr Marion, do you want to kill Thierry Lethem?'

Should you answer honestly? Can you answer honestly? Do you know what you'll do?

'I just need to know,' you say. 'You understand that, Sally, don't you?'

'Sadly,' she smiles, 'yes.'

She hands over the file. You *think*.

If you give the file back, go to 233. If you open the file, go to 260.

218

Solemnly, you inter the tin of marbles. Men have died for lesser treasure. This time, you take careful markings with a tape measure, triangulating between the forsythia bush and Mum's washing-line. You draw a pirate map, with Dad cheerfully helping out – a moment of closeness that prods you near tears – and resolve to dig up the tin next week. That will be the signal that this time you are in control.

But Mum moves the washing line.

You'd forgotten that. It was why you could never find the tin again.

You dig several holes but Dad's patience runs out and he tells you not to do any more damage to the lawn.

That happened too. You remember it all now. The worst thing was not just losing the marbles but not even being able to search for them. You dig one last covert hole and try to put the turf back. Laraine tells on you and you get a smack.

That's a shock. You've never smacked your kids but you were punished whenever you really went beyond the pale. Your shorts and pants are pulled down and you get a stinging but hardly heartfelt smack with your Dad's bare hand.

You cry for hours.

You burn with a sense of injustice.

You've lost something.

Now, where were you?

Paul Mysliwiec sticks his hand in Timmy's bird's-nest hair, picking up Timmy's germs, and comes after you, to pass them on. Paul slaps you harder than he needs to and says, 'Now, you've got Timmy's germs.'

Considering what will happen, what do you do this time?

If you chase Vanda and give her Timmy's germs, go to 109. If you shrug and tell Paul you don't want to play, go to 128.

219

Without a thought, you step out of the hut and slip the blade easily into Hackwill's neck. The blade transfixes him, point appearing through his double chin. You hold him as he dies.

Jessup turns to run, leaving his friend to die. One of his foot-towels comes apart and he yelps. James is on the bastard, stabbing in a frenzy, spreading blood all around. James purges himself of something, finishing off business begun in the copse all those years ago.

Hackwill is dead. You drop him. James finishes with Jessup and gets up. Now what?

'Get on your way,' James says. 'There's still a murderer up here with us.'

There are three now, you think. Unless Hackwill or Jessup killed McKinnell: that'd feel right. You've killed a murderer. Almost in self-defence, rear-approach self-defence.

'I'll dump the refuse,' James says, meaning the bodies.

You don't feel changed. You don't feel like a murderer. You're still just you. It's a mountain. Air is thin. The rules are different.

'Get going,' James says.

You start at a run.

During your long hike, you think of James arranging things for the police. Your story is that you left, spent a day getting lost, and continued to the village. James will sort out the rest of it.

What will he have to do? Will he have to kill anyone else? Some deserve it. You remember Mary Yatman at your old house, turfing out the squatters and trashing the place. Can James kill a woman? Could you? You've killed someone now. The next time might be easier. That frightens you.

As cold rain lashes you and you come to hate the land you're crawling over, you wonder whether you have defied God and are being punished for it. Your fingers and toes have no feeling. You are shivering, sobbing and babbling. Branches batter you. The ground repeatedly trips you up. Your eyes are blurry and you see only ghosts all around.

You must be covered in blood. Not all of it is yours.

It's over, you think. Whatever began in the copse is finished. This hell is just a protraction of it. You'll escape only if you face the consequences, if you tell the truth.

Up ahead, you see lights; the village. Rain tears at your face.

Confession would ease the pain.

You stagger into the village. You know where the police station is. You collapse outside and are carried in. The warmth lulls you. Uniformed men are all around. You have to say something before you pass out.

If you confess, go to 222. If you just blank out, go to 235.

220

'Ben McKinnell's dead,' Mary says. 'Stabbed in the heart.'

'She probably did it herself,' says Jessup.

Mary backhands him, slamming him into his seat.

'Fetch the other Marion bastard,' Hackwill orders Shane. 'It's time this was sorted out.'

Shane goes upstairs, and comes back dragging James, hauled out of sleep and way behind the game.

'Now,' Hackwill demands, 'who's a fucking murderer then?'

'Good question,' you say. 'Perhaps you'd like to answer first.'

Go on.

221

You dress quickly and take your knife out from under your pillow. You haven't time to be afraid.

The cottage has two bedrooms and a bathroom upstairs, two rooms and a kitchen down. You left Shane, Sean and Jessup in the dining-room, but the talk comes from the other room, which you use as an office.

On the landing, you pause outside the other bedroom. You don't hear anything, then catch just the faintest moan. Mary should still be asleep in there. It occurs to you that she may not be alone.

Warwick and Shearer might have prompted someone else to take a chance on Mary. Scary as the prospect is, it certainly occurs to you. Thinking on, you hope James *is* with Mary, or else he's in real trouble.

You go downstairs quietly. Your office door is slightly open. Two men talk in low, breathy voices. Static crackles. That gives it away. You step into the room and turn on the light. Sean turns, startled. The talking fades, in crackles, into the unmistakable sounds of love-making.

'Keith,' Sean blurts, ashamed and indignant.

'Very clever,' you comment.

Sean has found your surveillance system. He's listening to Warwick and Shearer.

One of them gasps and sighs. You've heard women sound like that.

'I was playing detective,' Sean explains.

One of the lovers is vocal, a 'fuck me, fuck me harder' screamer, a 'deeper, faster, *now*' grunter. You think it's Warwick.

'I thought they might talk about us.'

'Yes, Sean, of course you did.'

He is embarrassed. 'I'll switch it off.'

He reaches for the intercom board. The loud lover's cry rises to a peak and chokes off. It doesn't sound like sex.

'You!' shouts Warwick or Shearer. Then a scream. Pain, panic.

You run out of the front door, straight into a wall of horizontal rain that soaks and blinds you. Colditz, thirty feet away, might as well be across an Arctic waste. Your eyes are full of water. You can't see anything.

You take a few steps. Someone is moving near the pens. You aim your torch, but the beam lights only driving water. You struggle on.

Something barrels into you from the side, staggering you. Your torch falls nose-first into mud. You see black legs scissoring round your own. You trip and fall, heavily.

Sean shouts into the rain. Good God, your life depends on Captain Useless!

The person who has knocked you over stands over you, a sexless shadow. Sean is still shouting. The edge of a long coat trails wetly across your face.

If you grab the coat, go to 234. If you lie prone, go to 247.

222

'Councillor Hackwill's dead,' you say. 'I killed him.'

Sleep enfolds you. You can keep James out of it. You'll take the consequences.

For a while, it seems you can pull it off. The trick is not to give details about Jessup, claiming you went into a frenzy after attacking Hackwill.

The trouble is that James moved the bodies. You claim to have killed Hackwill and Jessup by the shepherd's hut and left them. James has tossed them off the mountain, to shatter on rocks five hundred feet below.

You and James are charged. In James's otherwise accurate statement, he claims to have killed Hackwill without you. The police keep asking about McKinnell. You keep saying it wasn't you or James.

'It's a bit thick, isn't it?' says the sergeant. 'A group of ten people, with three murderers?'

All sorts of questions are never answered.

You and James get twenty years apiece. In jail, you both get a lot of fan mail. Some is from local people who knew Hackwill for a bastard, but a lot is from young women who think the killer brothers are sexy. Or youths who think you're well kewl. It's a sick world, you think.

You're with other dangerous prisoners. Not madmen, hard criminals. You have even harder guards. There's no brutality, just deadening fascist control, a sameness of days that dribbles away into a sameness of years. Legislation passes and you're dosed on anti-aggression drugs. Your mind dies, wrapped in cotton wool.

When you get out, you're fifty. The world you enter is the future, the middle of the twenty-first century. It's not like *Thunderbirds* or *Blade Runner*. It's like being a child again, not knowing nine out of ten things adults take for granted.

You see James for the first time since your mother's funeral in 2005. He seems older than you, having had a harder time inside.

A surprising number of people you know are dead. It's not an easy century. There is nothing for you in this new world. Nothing.

And so on.

223

At the evening meal, you drink half a bottle of Jack Daniel's. You're indefinably out of sorts. You feel betrayed by James and Mary; by your brother because he has formed a liaison with one of the victims, by Mary because you feel you passed up a chance with her. Yes, you admit you can't have it both ways.

The losers, exhausted and battered after the assault course, grumble softly. You sense they are bonding together in hatred of you.

With James and Mary split off, you're taking the full force of it.

Outside, it's storming up a swine.

* * *

You lie there half cut, listening to the sonata of shagging from next door.

'Fuck it,' you think.

Kay Shearer lies in the next bed. You only live once. You should at least find out what it's like. You get out of your bed and go over to the twin.

'You're drunk,' Shearer says.

In the dark, his face looks womanish. He could almost be Chris.

'Lucky for you,' you say.

'I've come here to patch things up with Tris.'

'Warwick bangs botty for Britain,' you say. 'He's had half the youth-experience lads in Sedgwater.'

You sit on the bed and touch Shearer's face. You feel tears.

'You're right,' he says.

'Deeper… faster… *yes!*' You giggle at the sound effects.

'Fancy a fuck?' Shearer asks. 'I can't take much more of that' – a nod to the wall – 'without at least tossing off.'

You neither, you think.

You find your hand is in Shearer's soft hair.

If you want to go through with this, go to 248. If you back off, go to 261.

224

'Sean, you cringing bastard,' you snarl, 'why did you kill Warwick? Was he digging too deep into your shenanigans at the bank? Dad always said you were a born till-dipper.'

You lean over Sean, hammering him with questions. 'Answer me, shitface!'

You slap him. He starts blubbing like a kid, protesting his innocence.

Could this weakling kill? Maybe weakness makes murderers, not strength.

(You used to cry a lot, as a child. Remember? Kids like Shane and Robert would pick on you until you threw a Mental fit. How does it feel, growing up to be like them?)

'I didn't do it,' Sean whines.

'Stop it,' says Mary, softly. 'He's broken.'

'I didn't want Tris dead. I'd have voted with him and Ben. I wanted to get us out of the mess.'

You dart a look at Hackwill, who is coldly angry.

'Mary,' you say, 'fetch McKinnell.'

Sean is pathetically grateful. 'That's a fine idea,' he says, through snot and tears. 'Ben will back me up.'

Mary goes upstairs.

'So you, Warwick and McKinnell wanted out of a deal? A Hackwill deal, perhaps? An interesting Development?'

'That's enough,' Hackwill says.

Mary comes downstairs.

'McKinnell's dead,' she says. 'Stabbed in the heart.'

Go to 230.

225

'Let's get McKinnell down here,' you say. 'His trots have been going on too long. I think he's faking, covering something up.'

'Nonsense,' blurts Sean. 'He's been crapping walrus turds.'

'Get him anyway.'

You send Mary upstairs. She comes back down alone. She asks you to come upstairs.

There's no lock on the bathroom door. McKinnell sits, trousers up, on the shut toilet. He is slumped, a gouge-wound in his chest. He's dead.

You look at Mary.

'It wasn't me,' she says. 'I'm off the payroll.'

You look at McKinnell.

'Whoever actually did it,' Mary says, 'I guarantee Hackwill paid for it.'

'We're agreed McKinnell is out of the running for Warwick.'

'It was a real long shot.'

'You're right.'

'Let's go downstairs and put the screws on.'

'Are you sure you want to go through with this?' you ask.

'I hate not knowing answers,' she says.

Go to 230.

226

'What was Warwick's mental state?' you ask, mainly addressing Kay Shearer but including the others. 'Was he depressed?'

'He wouldn't have killed himself,' Shearer says. 'No matter what.'

'There was a matter?'

'They've been quarrelling since we set out,' Sean says, eager to get someone in trouble, even a dead man. 'Not outright rows, just nasty looks and bitten-off bits of bitchy dialogue. Typical gays.'

'So all you breeders have perfect relationships,' Shearer sneers. 'Rowena – yes, your wife, Sean – said she'd fuck me if I were interested. You're too wrapped up in this Discount Development scam to notice.'

'Enough,' says Hackwill, prematurely ending an interesting avenue of argument.

'Why were you arguing?' you ask Shearer.

'Warwick couldn't keep it in his trousers,' Hackwill said. 'A menace to any boy in the office.'

'It wasn't that,' Shearer says. 'It was the same thing as with Rowena and Sean. Tris was in too deep with the fucking Discount Development. Finally, I thought, he was seeing you, Robert, for the crooked shit you are and was going to pull out entirely. But you had Jessup working on him, mean little blackmail stunts: this boy would go to the police, that polaroid would be sent to me. It was only yesterday he'd decided –'

'You decided for him, more like,' says Jessup.

'– to get out. He knew McKinnell was pulling out and he was going to back him up. Our argument, such as it was, was over. It was only then that he died. Not, Keith, much of a suicide scenario.'

'Let's get McKinnell down here to confirm this,' you say.

'That's going to be difficult,' Mary says.

She has slipped upstairs and come back down.

'Ben McKinnell's dead. And unless he stabbed himself in the heart and flushed the knife down the toilet, he didn't commit suicide.'

Go to 230.

227

'You think one of us is a murderer?' Sean asks. 'That's insane.'

'It's crazier than that,' you say.

'The boots,' Shearer says. 'My boots.'

'I have no explanation,' you say. 'But it can't be an elaborate hoax. I mean, it would be so hard to stage. My boots – the duplicates, I mean – have a scratch on them I got tripping on the boot-scraper just before getting into the minibus to come here. Even if someone went to the trouble of getting matches for all our footwear, they'd never have got that. I think the boots are what they call an "apport", objects that appear out of thin air.'

'Supernatural objects?' Mary asks.

'Yes,' you say, reluctantly.

There is a general protest.

'You think Tris was killed by this apport?' Shearer demands.

'I didn't say that.' But it's what you think. A literal act of God. Or of some other extra-human entity or force.

'What's this nonsense?' Hackwill asks.

Jessup explains about the boots.

'And who saw this fabulous apport?' Hackwill asks.

Shane timidly puts up his hand.

'You're telling me my boots have a *doppelgänger*?'

'Everyone's have, Councillor,' you say, 'except McKinnell's.'

'And why wasn't McKinnell included in this cosmic largesse?'

'Maybe the footwear demons couldn't face duplicating the diarrhoea,' says Jessup.

'And where is McKinnell?' Hackwill asks.

'On the bog, Robbo,' says Jessup. 'Where else?'

'Fetch him down.'

Reluctantly, Jessup stirs himself. You all stand and sit in silence while he's away. You look at faces.

'And where's your killer brother?' Hackwill demands.

Jessup comes down, face pale. 'McKinnell's dead,' he says. 'Stabbed.'

Go to 230.

228

You aren't a man of leisure. You don't just employ advisers to invest for you, you take an interest. You build up your holdings, then diversify from stocks and bonds – merely shifting numbers around on a screen – into actual business, into making things, providing services.

You can afford to lose money for a while. You pump cash into the town. You take up the skeleton of Sedgwater's Discount Development, a wasteland ruin since its collapse, and refashion it as an enterprise zone, backing an array of small businesses.

Part of the money is set side for Jason's computer business and Jesse's fashion-design consultancy. They are only seventeen and fifteen, but they will grow into the businesses waiting for them.

You use your money to make more.

You can't just sit idle.

It's harder work than you've ever had to do. Money *doesn't* buy you everything. It can make almost everything easier but it's no substitute for work.

You get over your minor celeb status. You want to be the first Lottery millionaire to be taken seriously.

Your marriage is better than it's ever been. When you apply yourself, Vanda wakes up. She sticks with you.

You have come a long way. But there's still a long way to go.

And so on.

229

'No,' you say. 'We were friends at school.'

The word 'friends' is like a pebble in your mouth. You are so shattered that one more verbal stumble won't stand out in a statement full of them.

'Um,' the sergeant says. 'I think that'll be all for today. The doctor wants to take a look at you.'

You wonder if you've passed.

Read 250, go to 255.

230

A week later, you are interrogated in Llandudno. This has proved too much for the village police. The survivors have been brought to town and are giving their stories.

It's not been easy for you. You've been taken through everything several times. Your first account is so full of lacunae – from your reasons for offering Councillor Hackwill such a substantial discount and operating the course well after the season has ended to who you spend your nights with and Mary's admission to you that she had been hired by Hackwill to kill McKinnell – that the inspector taking your statement won't let you sign it.

Frustratingly, you're kept apart from the others. You especially need to square stories with James and Mary. It must be this bad for them all.

Hackwill can't talk about hiring Mary as a hit woman. And whoever killed McKinnell and/or Warwick will have to adjust their own statement to cover. Unless someone's cracked and told everything.

You decide the best policy is total honesty. You go through everything, telling as much of the truth as you know. The only thing you hold back is Mary's 'confession'. After all, she didn't kill Warwick: you can alibi her for that. But she could have killed McKinnell. She was paid for it. In advance.

To cover for this dishonesty, you vouch that Hackwill alleged James tried to kill him. You are confident – aren't you? – that he was lying. Repeating his lie doesn't hurt James. If anything, it reinforces Hackwill's crookedness.

You don't want to talk about the boots. You mention them but not that you can't believe they were natural things. Police statements do not require apports.

You are very tired.

Between interviews, you wonder about the immediate and long-term future. You suspect your business is in ruins. You can't stop thinking of Mary. If you come out of this together, it'll be worth it. You'd accept the deaths of any number of crooked businessmen; you'd let Robert Hackwill get away with murder; you'd see your business go under. If you and Mary have each other, you're ahead.

When you get back to Sedgwater, you'll have to break up with Marie-Laure. There'll be a fuss about that, but you don't care.

You haven't seen Mary for four days. And it's agony, a heart-stabbing pain.

You write it into the official record. In your police statement, you say that at a certain point during the week you fell in love with Mary Yatman. It's a fact that can be used in evidence, for or against both of you. It makes you feel better.

Finally, the question comes. 'Mr Marion, at any time, did Miss Yatman confide in you that she had been hired to murder Mr McKinnell?'

If you tell the truth, go to 238. If you lie, go to 251.

231

'Can we help him, Dr Cross?'

'Marion is physically stable, Susan.'

'This read-out. All these criss-crossing lines, different colours.'

'Strands of the construct. Lives, if you will.'

'And the colour-bursts before the flatlines?'

'Deaths, mostly. Or stalemates. Sometimes, just a loss of interest.'

'What happens when Marion has only flatlines?'

'At this point, that's not an immediate probability.'

'Come on, Doctor. There are more ends than beginnings. Eventually, Marion will run out of lines.'

'So far, we haven't observed any alternatives in which he becomes immortal. Though quite a few stray into what we might call the fantastic.'

'If they all end, will he wake up?'

'Remember, Susan, he isn't, in any useful sense, asleep.'

'You're interested in seeing how the lines weave, aren't you? More than in upsetting the chessboard. Is there a best-seller in Marion syndrome?'

'That's harsh. I had considered a paper, but we don't yet have the philosophical apparatus to cope with Keith Marion, much less the medical. And given the way things are outside his skull, coping is a more realistic approach than helping. I'm not sure if we should even try to *help*.'

'What are we for, then?'

'Paying him some attention?'

232

You can't do it. Your knife is raised. You only have to step out of the hut and stick it into Hackwill's neck. James will do Reg Jessup. Then you get out of here fast. Whoever killed McKinnell will take the blame.

But your feet won't work. Dead man's boots anchor you.

'It's a fucking wind-up,' Hackwill shouts.

He deserves to die. But you can't kill him.

'Robbo,' Jessup shouts, like a pantomime audience, 'behind you!'

Now, too late, you move. You step out of the hut as Hackwill turns. His hand grips your wrist and you drop the knife.

He has a knife too – you gave it to him, remember? Suddenly its cold blade is under your chin, the flat pressing against your Adam's apple.

'So I was right,' Hackwill says. 'It was you bastards. You were chickenshit at school and you're chickenshit now.'

Jessup scuttles away from James.

Your brother looks at you. It's like the copse. Only this time Hackwill has you and James is looking on. You remember the choices you had.

James doesn't have a choice, doesn't have to think. Knife out, he comes at you in a run.

The knife is taken away from your throat. You feel a warm gush of relief. No, a warm gush of blood. James is close, fury in his eyes. He'll kill Hackwill. But you don't live to see it.

Go to 0.

233

You put the file down on the desk. You did that once before, you remember. Are you pre-programmed for this?

'It's gone, isn't it?'

You look at Sally. You know what she means.

'The need to know?'

You nod.

'I envy you,' she says.

You leave her office, in the clear. You are free.

And so on.

234

You get a grip on the coat and intend never to let go. You open your mouth to yell. Sean must have woken everyone up. Rainwater pours into your throat.

The person you've got hold of bends. You are beyond cold and fear.

Something thuds into your forehead. A knife-point. Weight is exerted, your skull splits. It doesn't hurt. Which shows how serious it is.

Go to 0.

235

When you wake up, the mystery is solved. It was Mary. You always knew she was dangerous. You are commended. If you hadn't gone for help, the rest of you might have died.

Mary confesses. There's something strange there. In detail, she explains how she murdered them all, McKinnell, Hackwill, Jessup. She never says why she did it, and she never says why she confessed. She is found guilty but insane and disappears into a special hospital.

But you killed Hackwill. You know you did.

James doesn't want to talk about it.

While you were yomping to the village, things happened at the Compound. He has picked up fresh scars and wants to dissolve the business. After the publicity, you suppose you wouldn't get many clients anyway. When the Marion brothers offer you a Murder Weekend, they really mean it.

You marry Marie-Laure, get a job as PE teacher at Ash Grove, and have two children, John and Jean.

Mary sits in a cell, not speaking. James emigrates. Mum dies.

In 2014, Sam Hackwill – Robert's daughter – visits you and asks about the murders. She has grown up a nervous wreck, fatherless and out of control. She has screened everything about the case, which is extensive since Mary is the 'sexiest' female murderer since Myra Hindley. Sam's head is stuffed full of the contradictions.

'The how is established,' she says, 'but the why is up in the air.'

By now, you remember it as if you'd seen Mary kill Hackwill and Jessup. You've edited your own mind to fit the official version. Remembering a film from childhood, you print the legend.

'Mr Marion, have you any idea?'

You don't like to disappoint this watery-eyed girl with an open wound for a heart. You know she's had dependency problems. Growing up with Robert Hackwill as a living father might have been worse. She talks as if he were a saint but he must have been a domestic tyrant, a bully in every room of the house of his life.

You shake your head. 'When we were just kids, Mary was wild. Sometimes, she'd explode. I think, deep down, she never got over that. She used to say she had a monster inside her.'

That was in all the texts now. Other people remembered.

'Maybe, sometimes, the monster came out. Your dad just happened to be in the way.'

'If there was only a reason.'

'Maybe at school, your dad dragged her into a copse and hurt her.'

You didn't mean to say that.

Sam thinks about it. She is arguing against the mental image you've given her.

'Robert did do things like that,' you say.

A tear tracks down from Sam's eye, following the line of a coral cheek implant.

'I know,' she says, tinily. 'I didn't want to remember.'

John comes into the room, wanting to ask you about filling in his mandatory work-experience form, and backs out.

You pat Sam's shoulder. She is crying now. She grabs you and you hold her, not the way you once held her father, but from the front, her face against your chest.

'I didn't want to think I was right,' she says. 'I wanted to think he was the man Mum talks about, the good man. But he hurt me. When I was little.'

You've never regretted killing Hackwill less than you do now. But you do regret not knowing the full story. You always will.

Sam Hackwill composes herself, and leaves.

A year later, Mary Yatman is killed in a prison riot. You'll never know now.

And so on.

236

You lie awake in righteous triumph, certain James is lying awake in angry frustration. After a while, you regret your pettiness. Just because James scored and you didn't is no reason to piss on his parade. In the next room, Shearer does a Captain Chainsaw act, snoring mechanically.

You should be tired, but you can't sleep.

The next day, you and James are both groggy, hung-over even. Of the group, only Shearer seems to have had a good night's sleep. Afterwards, you'll always blame your blurry mind and slowed reactions for the accident.

Because James is dead, only you come to court to be found responsible.

James, Shearer, Sean, McKinnell.

By a miracle, Mary survives, though as a paraplegic. She testifies against you. Because of James, your family don't support you.

You aren't sure if you could have helped. Certainly, you could have cut yourself loose from Hackwill's team and tried to crawl down to where James was hanging, the others dangling freely below him, their weight dragging on him. You could have taken the fall with them, probably. But you could also have taken the strain. If one of the others – Mary? Shearer? – had got a grip, you could have clung to the mountain.

But you didn't.

For the rest of your life, you go over and over those few seconds. When you didn't do anything.

You remember the look in James's eyes as his fingers lost hold of the outcrop. It was the copse all over again except that this time, you thought first.

Before the courts, before your family, before Mary, he blamed you. But not before you blamed yourself.

And so on.

237

You smarten yourself up, start jogging home after dropping the kids off at school and while Marie-Laure's out at work. At first, it's murder. Your legs just won't work. Then it gets easier. Marie-Laure comments that you're looking better.

You're bored with vegging out and the circular conversations everyone you know has.

You can speak Japanese. You can broker multi-million-dollar deals. You can organise events. But you can't get a job. And you are anchored by Marie-Laure and the kids and your own past indolence to this life.

You come to despise the old Keith. What a fucking loser!

But you *are* the old Keith.

No matter how much you jog, that jiggling pouch of gut won't go away. And your head never quite clears. The old Keith has polluted it permanently. You find chunks of him surfacing.

Every night, you try to think for a while in Japanese. It becomes harder and harder. But you know how to roll a joint. And Vince's prattle about comics begins to make sense.

This is your hell. You're being punished for daring to question what you had with Ro and J and J.

Your new kids are dullards. All they do is watch telly and whine. You miss Jeremy and Jessica with an ache you never thought possible, even more than you miss Ro; than you miss your whole life.

You can't go back. You try, but it doesn't work.

You have a feeling that the switch only works if two Keiths are trying for it at the same time, and why would the other one – who is presumably living your old life – ever want to come back here?

Bastard.

No, you're the bastard. He's a lucky bastard.

Years pass, crushing you, breaking you.

Eventually, bored, you tell Vince the whole thing. He is fascinated. Alternate realities crop up every week in comics, so he knows all about them. He is surprised by the detail of your story but doesn't take it as real. It's exactly the sad fantasy ('I'm really a princess in exile') a complete lump of a loser like Keith Marion would come up with.

After that, you yourself mostly forget that you weren't always here. Life grinds on.

And so on.

238

'No,' you say. 'Where did you get that from?'

You should just have said 'No'. Asking the question was like admitting that you lied. The policeman takes a note.

'That'll be all, sir,' he says.

He knows you've just lied. He's writing off your whole statement as a lie. And your statement is the only alibi Mary has for Warwick's death. It turns out he was strangled before being thrown into the culvert.

You are let go.

Only at the trial does it come out that it was Reg Jessup who said Mary was hired by Hackwill to murder McKinnell.

Hackwill slips the country, and goes on the run like Lord Lucan. But the smaller fish left behind all go down for various offences. Jessup turns queen's evidence, and trades his inside story – which he also sells to the *Comet on Sunday* for a five-figure sum – for a vastly reduced sentence for some minor crimes.

The complex intricacies of the Discount Development, which turns out to have siphoned millions of pounds of council-tax-payers' money out of Sedgwater, wouldn't be such a sexy story if it weren't for the murders.

Mary is always referred to as a WPC in the press. They run pictures of her in uniform, airbrushing the famous Scary Mary stare – they ask ex-schoolfellows about her and discover the nickname – into something of Countess Dracula proportions.

You visit her in prison, holding her fingers through mesh. Loving her is agony. She tells you to cut her loose but you can't. Marie-Laure will have you back but you can't face that.

You are lucky to escape prosecution as an accomplice. In the end, the lawyers do a deal you aren't a party to, whereby you aren't called. You would have given your testimony, affording Mary an alibi for Warwick, and probably have wound up charged with perjury for telling the truth.

And you couldn't alibi her for McKinnell.

Even you wonder whether she slipped upstairs that morning and stabbed McKinnell. The knife – McKinnell's – was found in the grass near the cottage, thrown into the storm from the bathroom window. If Mary killed Ben McKinnell, it wouldn't stop you loving her.

She is found guilty and gets life. She accepts it and co-operates only dutifully with the appeals.

Hackwill shows up dead in a hotel room in Belize, killed by a teenage girl, a prostitute. You think he's escaped justice and has doomed Mary by dying without saying who he had kill Warwick and McKinnell.

Bastard.

Years pass. The dead, useless weight of absentee love turns your heart to stone. You drive Marie-Laure away without even having to beat her. You stop writing to Mary in prison, visit her only rarely. Any contact at all makes the love flare up like an old wound.

You get back to work. In the aftermath of the scandal, you and James lose control of your business. Sean Rye, of all people, steps in and organises a financial package. You still run the courses, but the bank is your master.

There is no joy in doing what you do. There never is.

When Mary is killed in a prison riot, it freezes you solid. You don't love her any less because she's dead. You still walk and talk but you're dead too. You just wait. You don't believe you'll be reunited with your other half in death. You think you're both gone for ever, into the void.

Occasionally, some Fortean publication brings up the boots. There is magic in the world. Terrible magic, perhaps. So maybe there is something.

Maybe Mary – another Mary who goes with the other Doc Martens? – goes on somewhere. Maybe there are an infinite number of Marys, and infinite Keiths. Maybe this horrible love of yours is satisfied somewhere.

It's no comfort: if you ever believe it, you hate those other Keiths and Marys who are themselves and not you, and even feel contempt at the thought that there might be other Keiths and Marys who don't realise the love that consumes you.

Life grinds on.

And so on.

239

You don't bury the tin. This time, you keep your marbles. You find that funny both as a grown-up and as a kid, but in different ways.

At school, you see faces superimposed over grubby kids', the faces of the adults they will become. You know enough now to stay away from Mary Yatman, and are horrified when Shane Bush's gang pick on poor, dim-witted Timmy Gossett.

After a while, Shane starts picking on you. 'You're mental, you are.'

'And you're going to be a failure as a van-driver.'

'What?'

'Forget it.'

'Yahh, Mental.'

You remember this kind of treatment as crippling but it seems silly. Shane may be bigger than you but you can't take him seriously as a threat, even when he tries to beat you up.

Two days before the event, you tell Shane's gang who will score the goals in the World Cup final. After Bobby Moore's lads have won the cup, you're a hero too.

Shane's gang becomes your gang. Even Mary is impressed.

You're very sparing with the kid-mystic act, partly because your memory of specific events is shaky. You should have memorised a book of general knowledge. You do remember one other snippet of World Cup trivia: the trophy will be stolen, and found by a dog called Pickles.

Your biggest coup is in November, when you foretell William Hartnell's regeneration as Patrick Troughton. You can remember all the actors who play *Doctor Who*. But you find it strange actually to watch, with grown-up critical faculties, the show as it goes out, realising how ropey the sets are and how repetitive the storylines. Surely it got better in colour?

You write a letter to the BBC telling them not to wipe their master tapes of *Doctor Who* because they will reap a fortune in the unimaginable but impending future when retail videos will become a significant ancillary market. You get a patronising letter back, saying your amusing suggestion about the next century has been passed on to the *Doctor Who* production team, even if it is a bit far-fetched for the scientifically credible standards of the programme.

You write to John Lennon and tell him not to move to New York, and, if he does, not to move into that block of flats in *Rosemary's Baby*. After you've posted the letter, you realise *Rosemary's Baby* hasn't been made into a film yet, though you think the book has been published.

Well, you tried.

A lot of things come back to you just too late to be of any use and you dread the process of relearning all the subjects you will take at school when you pass the Eleven Plus – you'll have to be careful not to score too well there since that's a test of skills not knowledge – and go on to Marling's. Christ, you've got three years in uniform at a single-sex prison camp before comprehensive education comes in.

And you're a virgin.

You start saving your pocket money. Eventually, Microsoft is going to be founded and you plan to be a very early investor.

If you don't watch out, you're going to rule the world.

And so on.

240

*B*lit blurt.

'Mr Marion? Keith?'

You look at the man.

'Do you know who I am?' he asks.

You don't. Do you?

'I'm Dr Cross. This is Susan Rodway.'

A nice-looking woman smiles.

'You've been away,' he says.

'Away?' you ask.

'Voyaging, I suppose. Inside yourself.'

'Am I mad?' you ask.

'The term no longer means anything.'

Dr Cross is rather stuffy, pompous. But Susan, who seems also to be a doctor, is warmer.

'You're not alone, Keith,' she says.

'The Spiders?' you ask.

Dr Cross and Susan look at each other.

'You remember the Spiders,' Dr Cross says. 'I suppose that's a good sign. Most Marion syndromers edit them out of their memories.'

'I have a syndrome?'

'Not if you remember the Spiders.'

'No, I have a syndrome named after me.'

'You weren't the first,' Dr Cross says, 'but you were the first to be studied. You've not responded as well to treatment as some, so you're not the first to come out of it.'

'What about the Spiders?'

'Gone,' Susan says. 'Just as they came. We're not sure what they were, really. A large-scale, inexplicable phenomenon.'

'But I didn't dream them?'

'No, there were Spiders.'

'Actually,' Dr Cross says, 'they can't have been Spiders. Arachnid physiology is such that no true spider can attain great size. They have no respiratory or circulatory system which could keep a large body functional, and the increase of mass would render their limbs inoperative.'

'So where did the webs come from?' Susan asks.

You sit up. Your mind is clear; but you have phantom memories.

'Don't worry,' Dr Cross says. 'You'll soon get over the after-effects.'

You can't believe it.

'It's a happy ending,' you say, wondering.

241

Fuck it.

That's your motto. Literally.

You set up Vanda and the kids with trust funds and the house, and move out.

You live in hotels. All your meals are in restaurants. All your beds are temporary; and populated.

* * *

Everything you've heard of, you try. Cocaine, crack, call girls, caffeine, cherry trifle.

You bury yourself in them. You can't spend fast enough.

Somewhere there are two graphs. One line is your life expectancy, the other your bank balance.

You want them to hit zero simultaneously.

Then, fuck it.

Money isn't everything. But it can buy you everything.

You plough through the world. Fucking it.

You live rich. And die broke. Congratulations.

Go to 0.

242

'He was a bully at school,' you say. 'Not that that's any reason to kill him.'

The sergeant catches that. He hasn't said anything about Hackwill being killed.

'I'm not,' you begin, 'sure Hackwill was, uh, the most ethical of businessmen.'

'Um,' the sergeant says. 'I think that'll be all for today. The doctor wants to take a look at you.'

You wonder if you've passed.

Read 250, go to 268.

243

'Your business partners are dying,' you say to Hackwill, hoping to spook Jessup and Sean.

'So are your customers,' Hackwill replies.

'When will this rain end?' Sean asks.

You and Hackwill look at him. He's working on a fright fit.

'Not soon enough to save you,' you say. 'Not if he's determined.'

'Shane,' Hackwill says, 'hit Mr Marion.'

Shane steps forward. Mary trips him. He gets up and backs down.

She always could outfight him.

Hackwill looks betrayed. 'So that's how it is? Strange bedfellows, if you ask me.'

'You're a murderer,' James says, coherent.

Hackwill shrugs in disgust.

'He tried to kill me,' your brother says. 'And he wrecked our quickest way out of here.'

On balance, you believe James. So does everyone else in the room, though you guess Jessup and Shane will stick by Hackwill. Sean is wavering and Shearer is tentatively with you. You have James and Mary.

'When we get back, I'm going to make sure you pay, Hackwill,' you say. 'This is one charge you're not avoiding.'

Hackwill can't be bothered to look you in the eye. You know he's scared. You've got him. You know it was him. No doubts. He killed them both. Maybe he had Shane do it, but he'll be brought to book for it. You see wheels working in his head. His patience is thinning. He senses walls closing in. He'll try something desperate.

'Looks like the rain's letting up,' Sean says, with a pathetic attempt at cheer. 'We can send someone for help.'

Hackwill shakes his head. He won't sit tight at Castle Drac while you or James go for the police. And you're the only ones who know the country.

'Shane,' he says, 'get your coat on.'

'Not a good idea,' you say.

'You'd skip away free and leave us here to freeze,' Hackwill says. 'I've already had to crawl out of a gorge thanks to one of you. We can trust Shane.'

'*You* can trust Shane.'

The only person you could both trust to go to the police is Sean. He'd trip and sprain his ankle. Then, if he didn't die of exposure, get lost and limp back to the Compound bedraggled and useless.

'Why doesn't one of you go with him, then?'

You look at James. He's still shaky from last night, but gives a thumbs-up.

Hackwill has just shot holes in his own story. If James had really tried to kill him, would he let his hired man take a long walk over dangerous ground with him?

It would still be more logical for you to go; but you want to keep an eye on the situation here.

If you go with Shane, go to 256. If you send James with Shane, go to 269. If you veto the suggestion, go to 282.

244

You're thrown. You need to talk with James in private. If he has a plan, you need to know about it. If he's just killing his way through to Hackwill, you must talk it out. Now, he's keeping quiet.

Obviously, you need to help your brother, but how? Join in with his killing spree, no matter what the consequences? Try to talk him out of it, get him to settle for two down? Protect him while he finishes the job? Or stop him before anyone else gets killed?

You have Mary to think about now.

Snap judgement, boy: who is more important to you?

If Mary, go to 254. If James, go to 267.

245

This confuses you. Shearer could have killed Warwick in a lovers' quarrel. But why McKinnell?

'Did he see you do it?' you ask Shearer.

'What?'

'McKinnell. Did he wake up early and see you and Warwick leave Colditz together, then you come back alone? Or did he follow you and see you kill your boyfriend?'

Shearer looks panicked.

'I'm convinced,' says Hackwill, adding his force to yours.

'All of you,' Shearer sneers, 'fucking breeders. That's what it's all about, isn't it? Kill the queers.'

Your certainty wavers.

'Well, you won't have to kill me.' Shearer pushes the door open and sprints across the wet grass, past the pens.

If you chase him, go to 257. If you let him escape, go to 262.

246

Hackwill has a great poker-face but it's working against him. He's so intent on not looking guilty that he's forgotten that McKinnell's murder should at least surprise him.

Wait a minute, he is covering something. Not surprise, exactly. He's pleased. He's pleased McKinnell is dead. That means it wasn't him; but he's benefited.

It was Shane. Sometime earlier this morning.

All along, McKinnell was supposed to die. Mary didn't go through with it, so Hackwill switched to Plan B, heading off into alibi land with James, leaving the Man From B.U.N.G.L.E. behind to do it. He probably doesn't even care if Shane gets caught.

Work on that.

'So that's two dead people who won't be backing out of your dodgy deal,' you say. 'It must be amazingly convenient to have such staff.'

'Whatever you say,' Hackwill replies.

'Looks like the rain's letting up,' Sean says, with a pathetic attempt at cheer. 'We can send someone for help.'

Hackwill shakes his head. He won't sit tight at Castle Drac while you or James go for the police. And you're the only ones who know the country.

'Shane,' he says, 'get your coat on.'

'Not a good idea,' you say.

'You'd skip away free and leave us here to freeze,' Hackwill says. 'I've already had to crawl out of a gorge thanks to one of you. We can trust Shane.'

'*You* can trust Shane.'

The only person you could both trust to go to the police is Sean. He'd trip and sprain his ankle. Then, if he didn't die of exposure, get lost and limp back to the Compound bedraggled and useless.

'Why doesn't one of you go with him, then?'

'There is no way my brother or I would take a walk over a mountain with your hired killer,' you say.

Shane doesn't have a poker-face. He snarls. He hates you. And he'd enjoy killing you.

'You've had my idea,' Hackwill says, 'and shot it down in flames. Now it's your game.'

'Any objections if Mary goes?' you ask. 'We know she can read a map.'

Hackwill thinks about it. He still isn't sure about Mary. He thinks she might be stringing you along. He doesn't know about you and her. He's wrong. Mary is with you. Whatever deal she had with Hackwill is off.

'Very well,' Hackwill says. 'Mary goes.'

You wave at Mary as she walks off, following the path. At least she'll be safe out there.

You and James have to spend the next day and night on your guard. You've agreed you should keep a close watch on Hackwill and Shane. The others – Jessup, Shearer, Sean – aren't a threat. Shane's the killer, the one you need to mark.

When you get back to Castle Drac, James is mateying up to Shane, talking about Ash Grove Primary. He tries to keep the thug away from his boss. No conferring, no messages from the brain to the hand.

'She's off, then?' Sean asks.

You nod.

'I'll be glad to get out of here. No offence, but this has been a fucking awful three days.'

Hackwill and Jessup sit at the table, not talking.

'Where's Shearer?' you ask.

'Gone for a walk.'

You let it go. Unless there's a madman on the mountain out there, Shearer is safe. All the killers are here. It's always possible Shearer, grief-stricken, will kill himself, but frankly you're too exhausted to care.

The people you want to survive this are James and Mary. And you, of course. Mary is safe. You and James can handle yourselves.

You sit down with James and Shane. Hackwill notices and glares across the room.

'Hackwill probably couldn't have killed McKinnell,' you say to James. Shane goes stiff. 'Probably had Mary do it, or Jessup.'

'What about Warwick?' James asks.

'Open book.'

'Shane, you found Warwick. What do you think?'

'You're both mental,' Shane says.

He used to call you 'Mental' at school. You're suddenly angry.

'He could have done that himself,' you say, 'if his hired killer wimped out. His Master's Voice always has to go first, test the waters for Captain Chickenshit.'

Shane's face is beet-red. So that's it. A lucky strike.

'Let me get this straight,' James says, catching on. 'You figure Councillor Rob snapped Warwick's neck and dumped him, because no one would do it for him. Then, making up for earlier yellow-bellied trembling, his hired thug murdered McKinnell, to get back in the boss's good books.'

Shane tries to stand up. You and James hold him down. Hackwill folds his arms and watches.

'He'll let you go down for it all,' you whisper in Shane's ear. 'He'll be sipping pina coladas in Barbados, while you're doing porridge. Providing he lets you live until the trial.'

'Don't bend over in the showers, Shane.'

Shane tries to hit James, but you grip his wrist.

'What's going on?' Hackwill asks.

'Detective work,' you say.

'What's going to happen to me?' Shane asks Hackwill.

Hackwill has no answer.

'You fucker,' Shane says.

Hackwill turns away. You and James sit back.

Have you done enough? Or do you need to push Hackwill and Shane some more?

If you've done enough, read 253 and go to 259. If you push some more, read 253 and go to 264.

247

You see a knife miles above you, flashing in the rain, the last of some blood washing from its blade. You're ready for the end. Then the person standing over you is gone.

Sean and Jessup are there, soaked.

'What happened?' Jessup shouts.

You don't know.

'Where are the others?' you try to say.

Sean picks up your torch. He plays the beam on Colditz. There's a puddle round the entrance. It ripples red with the impacts of raindrops.

You get up and run over. You don't want to make Sean shine the torch into the pens but you do. Two naked men. Cut badly, couldn't possibly be alive. Enough.

Jessup is sick. You and Sean get him back to Castle Drac. Shane stands outside, fully dressed, getting wet.

'The queers are dead,' Jessup says.

Panic has reduced him to schoolboy level. Whatever he thinks, he's been careful never to tag Warwick and Shearer with their sexual preference.

Shane grunts, and you can imagine him thinking 'Good job too', the thug bastard. It could have been him: he could have killed the lovers, knocked you over, got rid of his raincoat, and doubled back to the cottage, waiting to be called for.

The only people it couldn't be are you and Sean. That's bad, if Sean is the only one you can trust. And he could still be in it with whoever. He could have been listening in to make sure the murder went well.

You get inside and wipe your face on a kitchen towel. Your bare feet are blue.

When your face is clean and you've done your best to dry yourself, James and Mary are there too. You're sure they were together. James has been outside to check the bodies and he's wet. Mary's hair is dry, but she could have covered it. The murderer's coat was voluminous and might have had a hood.

You can trust only yourself. And James: even if he's the murderer, he'll count you as an innocent.

You're very cold and very tired. You wish this would go away.

The next day passes in armed neutrality. Everyone sits around Castle Drac as it drizzles outside, keeping a grip on their knives, trying not to nod off. Despite everything, you have a long doze in the afternoon. When you wake up, no one new is dead and your throat isn't cut so things are looking up. Then the sun sets.

James gets a few moments alone with you in the kitchen.

'The phone's gone,' he says.

'Were you with Mary last night?' you ask.

Sean blunders in and James clams up, not confirming or denying.

'Can we get some more tea on?' Sean whines.

'We might have to ration it soon,' James says.

'Surely not. Councillor Hackwill must have got to the village by now. Help will be here in an hour or two.'

'Unless Councillor Hackwill hung around and paid the lovebirds a visit last night,' you suggest.

'Oh,' says Sean, who clearly hasn't thought of that.

'Make tea,' James says. 'We're not short of water after last night. And we've enough PG Tips to survive worldwide eco-catastrophe.'

Sean gets busy.

That night, you sleep in shifts, three of you awake, three asleep. Sean wonders why not two and four, allowing longer uninterrupted sleeps. James asks him which of the others he's sure enough isn't a murderer to share a shift with. Sean takes the point.

Ironically, you could have answered the question. You could pick Sean. Instead, you get Mary and Jessup. Mary doesn't talk; Jessup doesn't do anything else. He monologises about Councillor Hackwill, from where he is right this minute – heroically making it out to bring back help for his old pals – to their lifelong friendship and happy schooldays.

'Do you remember dragging me and James into the copse at Ash Grove?' you ask.

Jessup seems not to.

'I remember that day,' says Mary. 'The end of break-time. You and Rob had James in the copse and weren't letting him go. Keith ran in to rescue him. Bravest thing I've ever seen. He got in trouble for missing the start of lessons.'

'You can't possibly remember that far back,' Jessup says. 'You were just a little girl.'

'I'd have beaten you bloody if you said that to me then. I might still. What I remember most is the shame.'

'What shame, Mary?' you ask.

'You were the girl, Keith. Threw a fit rather than eat school custard. I'd have said you were the biggest chicken in school, yellower than the custard. But when it was your brother, you didn't think, you ran in to protect him.'

'You're making this up,' Jessup whines.

You're glad it's dark in the room. Mary can't see the tears on your face.

'I was ashamed I didn't run into the copse too,' Mary says. 'It wasn't my fight but I wasn't supposed to care about that.'

Can this be the monster? The WPC who turfed out the squatters? The woman with the knife at your balls? How long have you misunderstood Mary? Or have you?

Listen to what she's saying.

'I should have torn the both of you apart. That was *my* school, Reg. You and Rob had gone on. You were coming back to my country. I owned that playground. I was the monster.'

Jessup shuts up, afraid.

'Hackwill's not coming back,' Mary says. 'Is he, Fatty?'

Jessup says nothing.

The next day, the rain stops. You wake up mid-morning, having done the graveyard watch. Jessup snores in the blacked-out room. Mary sleeps curled up like a baby, looking tiny and innocent, not deadly. You still haven't processed the conversation you had while you were awake and the world was shaking.

James and Shane are in the kitchen, inventorying food.

'Where's Sean?' you ask.

'Checking on you,' says James, knowing he isn't.

'The idiot,' you say.

You go to the front door and see the bank manager disappear into the trees. He stumps along awkwardly, feet wrapped in big blue towel-balls.

Mary, bleary, comes into the narrow hall.

'Sean's bolted,' you say.

She shrugs.

'I'll bring him back,' says James.

'Why?' you ask. 'He's not the murderer. He was with me when Warwick and Shearer were killed.'

'Not because of that, because he's a prat. He'll fall over and die.'

'One bank manager fewer,' Mary says, uncaring.

'Our dad was a bank manager,' you snap.

'Sorry,' she says.

If you volunteer to go with James, go to 252. If you stay behind, go to 265.

248

You stroke Shearer's shoulder. You've never felt a man's body like this, the way you've so often been close to women. Shearer, as demonstrated by his winning of the bed, is in great shape, sleek skin over smooth ropes of muscle.

You kiss him. You feel fine stubble on his cheek, but his tongue is just like a woman's. He coughs and breaks the kiss.

'I'm sorry,' he says. 'It's the whiskey.'

Your mouth must taste like a still. You back away, almost offended.

Shearer laughs, not unkindly. 'Look, get some sleep, if you can. If you're into this when you're sober, get back to me. My guess is you won't be.'

Somehow, being turned down by a homosexual doesn't improve your disposition. You dream furiously.

The next day, a full storm is on. James wants to cancel the day's event – an ascent of a cliff-like mountainside in teams – but you're pissed off enough to insist that no weather is going to make sissies out of your boys. You look to the clients for support. They all look as if they'd like a day off. Yellow fuckers. It's as if it were raining school custard.

You rope them all together and drag them out. James, reluctantly, backs you up. He's gone soft now he's got a regular shag, but you think you can drag him back to the schedule. On the face of the mountain, lashed by rain, you'll get back with your brother.

'I really don't think this is a good idea,' whines Sean.

'What do you want to do, Wank Manager?' you say. 'Play tiddly-winks in the warm?'

'Sounds fine to me.'

It takes a long time to struggle through the rain to the scaling cliff. It's a face you know intimately, wet and dry, from dozens of earlier courses.

The teams rope up. James, of course, goes with Mary's gang; which leaves you with Hackwill. It would be easy to snip his rope and let him drop. That would finish this permanently.

If you set out to kill Hackwill, go to 266. If you squash that thought, go to 279.

'I think I've just buggered my future,' moans Roger Cunningham. 'I can forget college.'

Nobody is confident. Then again, in your whole educational career, you can't remember anyone going into or coming out of an exam on a high, feeling they're perfectly prepared or that they got exactly the questions that showed off their skills.

'I didn't do *any* revision,' whines VC.

You are consumed with depression.

It's too deep even for you to be hyped on being this age again, surrounded by these long-gone kids.

But your mind snags on VC. Victoria, she is called here. Having known her between the ages of fourteen and thirty as a contemporary, you have always thought of her as poised, adult, mysterious, other. Here she is as a real kid, a layer of chubbiness over the cheekbones which will eventually make her a beauty.

She's going to be a pop star. She doesn't need a fucking O Level.

Ro trots along and you reflexively prepare to be hugged and comforted. But she goes to Roger. You won't get together for over a year. You'd forgotten she went out with Roger – and whatever happened to him? – before you. You remember fancying her like mad at this age. But this Ro is a little girl. You'd be a real perv to want to go with her.

'It's geography tomorrow,' Victoria laments. 'That'll be worse.'

It probably will. When you got down to it, you could puzzle out most of maths. But geography is about *knowledge* and whatever you learned – about the principal exports of Peru or the Swiss practice of transhumance or how to irrigate the desert – is long faded, buried under detailed but useless facts about the future economies of countries that don't even exist yet. Was Iran called Persia in 1976? Is it too late to apply for O Level Japanese?

You would exchange your foreknowledge of world events for a couple of years' basic education in boring things.

As Roger said, if you don't pass these exams you aren't going to college. Or university. Or anywhere.

And you won't.

Walking out of the hall, you find yourself separated from Roger and

Rowena and Victoria. You are caught in a stream of former Hemphill kids, fresh from their CSE exams. You remember how you all looked down on them as thickos.

'Keith,' says a boy you don't recognise.

'How was it?' asks a thin blonde girl.

You don't know these people. They know you.

Then you know their names, somehow. Vince Tunney and Marie-Laure Quilter.

'We'll soon be out of here,' Vince says.

'Not soon enough,' chimes in Marie-Laure.

You look around for Ro and VC, but they are gone. You're stuck with these people. With another Keith's life.

Go to 29.

250

Hackwill is dead. So is James, and so are most of the others. The survivors are Kay Shearer and Mary Yatman. Sean was alive when the helicopter arrived but died being loaded aboard. Mary has lost a lot of blood and slipped into some sort of catatonia. Medical examination suggests she's been raped. Shearer claims he took off from the Compound when Warwick was found dead, and survived what they're calling a massacre by going to ground in a shepherd's hut. His story is backed up by symptoms of severe exposure; three frostbitten toes have to be amputated. Mary comes back from her personal space voyage and is extensively debriefed by the police, but appears to have selective amnesia, retaining only a few images from the last three years. She thinks she's still a policewoman, and has no recollection of sexual abuse or receiving knife-wounds on her back and thighs. Naturally, Mary and Shearer are the chief suspects. Along with you.

Go on.

251

'Yes,' you say. 'She told me that. She also told me she had no intention of going through with it. I believe her.'

The policeman nods. He believes you. Does that mean he believes Mary?

'I think that's all, sir.'

Hackwill slips the country, and goes on the run like Lord Lucan. It's still officially a mystery but with the financial implosion of the Discount Development, the police seem to read his flight as a cover-all confession.

You and Mary are living together, engaged. James is almost as surprised as Marie-Laure. You spend your days making love and raking over what happened.

Hackwill could easily have killed Warwick, you decide, but McKinnell is a problem. He'd have had to sneak into Castle Drac – not easy with so many of you about in such cramped quarters – and gone up to the bathroom, silently murdered McKinnell, flung the knife through the window, sneaked out again and barged in loudly, announcing his entrance as if it were his return.

It could have been done. That's what all the true-crime paperbacks and TV movies say, with speculative but unconvincing dramatisations of Hackwill's skulking – Iain Scobie's meretricious paperback *Killer Councillor* even has him shin up a drainpipe to get to McKinnell – and elaborate unravelling of the evidence.

No version, from the soberest police account to the most lurid tabloid story, can deal with the boots, so they are left out of the story. Even you and Mary prefer to ignore the boots.

Hackwill shows up dead in a hotel room in Belize, killed by a teenage girl, a prostitute. Most people are satisfied that the story is over.

You and Mary get to live ever after.

Happily? For the most part. You marry, bring Mary into the business, and have two children, Jed and Johanna. Your love for Mary, forged in the crucible of that week, lasts, growing and bending when need be, always with a core of steel.

Eventually, you can let it go; but it always worries Mary. She hates not knowing. She feels Hackwill cheated by dying without explaining. She constructs versions in which all of you, in various combinations, are guilty of either or both of the murders. She even includes you and herself in the stories.

It hurts you to see her grow obsessive. It doesn't put a wedge between you, but it adds a sliver of pain to the constant sunfire of love that binds you.

When Mary gets cancer at forty-seven, you're sure worrying at the mystery killed her. You live out the rest of your life, remembering. And wondering.

And so on.

252

You and James bind your feet, fixing towels with string. It looks absurd, but no one laughs.

'I'm coming with you,' Mary says.

You don't argue.

'Shane, stay and watch Jessup,' James says. 'If he tries to kill you, break his neck and eat him.'

Shane, who has become monosyllabic, grunts.

Mary slips long mittens over her feet. You're concerned they won't be enough.

'Don't worry about me,' she says. 'I used to be a beat copper. I have indestructible feet.'

The three of you set out.

The skies are clear enough to let a strong November sun shine. With the grass wet, stones slick and vegetation dark green, the mountainside is beautiful. The smells are wonderful.

Out of sight of the Compound, it's possible to pretend life is normal. You and James walk with Mary between you. She sings 'Nellie the Elephant'. It's charming but also suggests she's cracked up.

'I see something,' Mary says, launching herself away from you, and plunging lithely into the undergrowth.

You and James look at each other. Has she gone on ahead, or escaped?

You follow, more carefully. It's hard for you to get through thorny gaps still vibrating from Mary's easy passage. Finally, you catch up with her.

She's found Sean. He's dead. Recently: his throat is still bleeding.

'He was alive when I got here,' Mary says. She is leaning over him. 'He said, "Hackwill".'

James looks around, for paths. You look at Mary, for the truth.

'Really,' she insists.

Her knife isn't bloody. She shows it to you. She could have wiped it clean, but you can't see where. Even if she'd used Sean's clothes, you'd see.

'He must have gone this way,' James says.

Like you, your brother wants to think the worst of Councillor Hackwill.

'Let's go,' says Mary.

You follow them.

A stream crosses the path and there's a patch of mud. There are boot-prints in the mud. Hackwill. Mary is innocent, at least of killing Sean. You wonder if you could love her.

James is all for pushing on but Mary holds him back.

'He's dangerous, remember.'

'So are we,' says James.

'You're amateurs,' she says, 'compared to him.'

You have to go on. But carefully.

'We've got him,' you say.

Your advantage, which Mary has just made you think of, is that you've been all over this mountain for the last two years. You know this path.

'This path comes out at a sharp drop. Five hundred feet or more. He'll have to clamber down the slope. He'll be in the open. Vulnerable.'

'He's right,' James says.

Mary leads you.

You come to the end of the path, thick greenery all around, and are at the lip of the fall. It's too much of a slope to be a cliff, but has to be climbed not walked. There's someone a hundred feet down. Hackwill.

'He can't see us,' Mary says. 'He's concentrating.'

The slope gets steeper towards the bottom and there's a fast-running river, swollen by recent rainfall, rushing through a culvert, plunging into caves. Hackwill doesn't realise the way gets more perilous the further down he goes.

'Keith,' says James, hefting a rock, 'what do you want to do?'

If you vote for throwing a rock at Hackwill, go to 258. If you vote for climbing down after him, go to 271.

253

You and James take turns on watch through the night. Your bedroom door is barred.

You're trying to guess Hackwill's next move. As James sits up awake, you can't fall asleep for trying to imagine Hackwill's position.

He's killed with his own hands. He'd do it again if it'd help. If he can kill Shane and put the blame on you and James, he'd have a way out.

You sit up and tell James.

'We should be watching Shane,' you say, 'not just keeping ourselves safe.'

'Hackwill's in the four-poster, next door,' James says. 'The others are all downstairs, in the one room. Except Shearer' – he still hasn't come back. 'Hackwill can't get to Shane without tripping over Jessup and Sean.'

'Jessup'll back him. And Sean's expendable.'

You get out of bed.

Go on.

254

'I'm going to walk to the village and get help,' you say.

Hackwill snorts.

'James will stay behind to look after you.'

Your brother nods.

'I'll take Mary,' you say.

As you walk, you explain what you think has been happening.

'James was a Marine,' you say. 'Physically, only you or Shane could stop him. You're not in the game any more and Shane is thick as a brick. He'll get to Hackwill.'

You take your time about getting to the village. You spend the night in a sleeping bag in a dry-ish spot under the tree canopy, mostly making love.

Back at the cottage, James will be killing. You don't care if he does them all, though Sean and Shearer aren't really involved.

But Hackwill. Fuck him to death, Jessup and Shane too. Lose them. You wouldn't mind. Then it's up to James.

You don't think he'll let himself be caught. The reason for dawdling is to give him escape space. He might make it out of the country. Or he might throw himself into a river and be swept underground. Would your brother do that?

For him, this is personal. It is for you too, but he was the one dragged into the copse, you came along later. He was the prime target.

Once he's got rid of Hackwill, he might have a sense of closure. He might see his job as being to get out of the way, passing everything on to you and Mary.

You imagine him gone, leaving you and Mary to continue together.

When the police get to the Compound, things aren't what you imagined. Shearer is dead, and so is James. Hackwill's story is that James went mad, killed Shearer – as he had already killed Warwick and McKinnell – and Shane had to break his neck to save the others.

You can't imagine Shane killing James in a fair fight. It was the old gang from the copse, Hackwill and Jessup.

Hackwill becomes a hero for surviving. No one worries about the Discount Development. Millions more pour in.

James is buried, remembered as a mad-dog killer.

You and Mary stay together, looking after each other. You marry and have two children, Job and Julienne. But there's always something missing. Not just answers. You can't help feeling you've not earned your ease. At a crucial point, you turned away, looked after yourself. That beating in the copse taught you a lesson. Maybe you should have saved the heroic spurt for when it counted.

Mary has to look after practical things. She eventually resents that. After ten years, you split up. By now, Robert Hackwill is the richest man in the West Country. And Shane Bush is mayor of Sedgwater. You live out your life in mild disappointment. Somehow, without meaning to, you let everybody down.

And so on.

255

The police don't dig deep enough to find out about the copse. But a pubful of witnesses remember you and James telling Hackwill and

Jessup to fuck off just before the Falklands War. And the business with the road-widening scheme (your house still stands, derelict) comes out. In James's office, which the police seal, they find a file of documents relating to Hackwill's extensive dodgy deals.

The business of who killed whom is impenetrable, especially since James and Hackwill were stabbed with the same knife, the one used on Mary.

It is Shearer, you're certain. But the police let him go. You try to get in touch with him but he doesn't want to see you. He is scared of you, which could make him the murderer, or suggest he thinks you're the murderer.

You don't suspect yourself. You're not a split personality, with unaccounted-for memory blackouts during which you might be a homicidal maniac. Besides, you have an alibi: you were walking into the valley. You couldn't have loitered, done the murders, and made it to the village.

Some back-packing amateur Sherlock demonstrates you could have done it. Out of public-spirited bloody-mindedness, he covers the distance between the Compound and the village in a little over a day, with a Cloud 9 TV camera team hovering overhead in a helicopter. Of course, he doesn't do it in a thunderstorm. He doesn't say you did do it, just shows you could have done. After the programme goes out, the police um and ah about trial by satellite television and the lack of concrete evidence against you. They don't bother you any more and pursue other lines of investigation. Despite an extensive search, no vehicle tracks are found, but the police claim to believe someone could have driven up to the Compound, killed everyone, and got away clean.

You get anonymous hate-mail accusing you of murder. Helen Hackwill brings her two children, Samantha and Colin, to look at you, and spits in your face. So she has no doubts. Your business is gone. Mum has a coronary and dies. Marie-Laure can't stand the hassle and flees.

There's an emptiness in you. Not knowing what happened at the Compound eats you up. If you could fold back time, you'd send James for the police. You'd rather have died up that Welsh mountain, if it meant understanding.

But you never find out. You never put it together.

You manage to scrape out some sort of life. Every few years, an Unsolved Mysteries show digs up the mountain massacre and profiles you – triggering another wave of nuisance calls – but nothing is ever settled.

Mary changes her name and disappears.

Shearer commits suicide in 2002. His note reads, 'I didn't do it.' You realise he was persecuted like you.

It has to be one of the dead. Mortally wounded, he killed until he died. But who? Hackwill? James? Shane Bush? Sean the bank manager?

No, that doesn't compute.

You die not knowing.

Go to 0.

256

You kiss Mary goodbye, trusting her to keep a watch on Hackwill, and set out through thin drizzle.

The grass is as wet and thick as kelp. You know this will be a long walk, and you don't exactly have the most exhilarating company.

First, you try to get to Shane by jamming a wedge between him and Hackwill.

'I hope you're not being fitted up, man,' you say. 'You know how Robbo likes to walk away clean, leaving other folk to take the blame. This isn't two years for GBH or a suspended sentence for insider dealing. This is life for murder.'

Shane grunts.

The November sun comes out, casting a cold light over the sodden landscape. It's quite beautiful. The smells are incredible. You wish you were with Mary, to see the world in a new light.

'*Boss Cat*,' Shane says, after hours of quiet. 'It weren't called *Top Cat*.'

'It was in America,' you say. 'The BBC changed the title because of the cat food.'

You're walking up a mountain road. There's a spectacular view coming up. You wonder if Shane will notice.

'Why isn't kids' telly any good these days?' he asks.

'Because you aren't a kid any more?'

'They *Power Rangers*, though. Not like *Thunderbirds*, is it?'

'They're still showing *Thunderbirds*. It gets good ratings.'

'Thirty years' time, they still be showing *Power Rangers*? Fuck no.'

You come round the shoulder of the mountain. You stand almost at a peak. Below you is the valley. You can see the village. It's a clean, lovely sight.

You and Shane stop and look.

'The first time I met you, you asked me about *The Man From U.N.C.L.E.* Then you beat me up.'

Shane smiles. 'Not your life, is it mate?'

He picks you up and throws you off the mountain.

As you tumble, you think of Mary, with an extraordinary mix of love and panic. You'll die, you know that, but will she live? If you're being killed, she probably will be as well.

You're not sure how you feel.

You break your neck on the first bounce, and are dead when your body stops rolling.

Go to 0.

257

You run after Shearer, rain on your face, lungs desperate for air, legs weakening. Shearer, without thinking, outpaces you and pulls ahead. You collapse. Mary picks you up. You didn't realise she had run with you.

You see Shearer stop, turn to look at you. What is he thinking?

You're gasping for breath. Mary holds you up, hugs you and kisses you.

Shearer starts walking away, determined. Then he begins to run, properly. Before, he was just haring off. Now, he knows where he's going.

'He's getting away,' you say.

Mary shakes her head. 'No. He's just leaving.'

There's a lot of confusion about what happened. Kay Shearer is sought for questioning, but never surfaces; you assume he has left the country. No murder charges are ever brought, but Shearer is generally thought to have been the killer.

The police investigation ruins Robert Hackwill. A simple look into Warwick's files discloses monumental fraud, and casts a little doubt over Shearer's guilt.

You and Mary see a lot of each other. And try to forget everything else.

And so on.

258

James lobs the rock. It arcs through the air and bounces off the shale two yards above Hackwill. The councillor looks up. The rock buzzes past his face. A mini-landslide falls around him.

You let go your own rock, which slaps down on Hackwill's back. His cry echoes but is lost in the rushing of the river.

'Come on up, you bastard,' you shout. 'You can't get away.'

Hackwill doesn't move, either to crawl up to you or to scurry down away.

James throws another rock, which thumps against Hackwill's head. He whoops as if he'd just bowled out the captain of the visiting team.

You see a smear of red on Hackwill's face. Then he rolls, over and over. He disappears, over a drop and into the river. His body is never found.

Ten years into the new century, you wake up. You'd dreamed yourself back to the mountain. Vickie shifts beside you, too deeply asleep to be disturbed.

In dreams, you often go back. Minute things occur to you. The experience of those few days has still not been exhausted.

'Mary's knife,' you say, aloud. The words fall flat, not echoing in your familiar bedroom.

Maybe it wasn't hers.

You pick up the bedside phone and thumb-key James's code. This isn't the first time you've done this.

Maybe Mary showed you *Sean's* knife, so naturally it wasn't bloody. Maybe hers was thrown into the bushes, gory to the hilt.

You cut off the call before James can be wakened.

You lie back, convinced you've understood something. But it's just a stray night-thought. You don't want to bother James with it.

His wife isn't as heavy a sleeper as Vickie. She'd be woken by the call too.

Your brother's wife. Mary.

And so on.

259

First, you check the other bedroom. The four-poster is empty. You have a gut-sick feeling. Hackwill has had the whole evening to stew, to think it through. And he's clever.

He must have asked Warwick to come for a walk, 'to talk things over', 'to settle all our problems'. Then killed him. He's a fucking cool hand.

In the dining-room, you find Sean dead. Shane, Jessup and Hackwill are gone.

The next morning, Mary comes back with the police. Hackwill and Jessup, suffering from exposure and shock, come out of hiding. They were in Colditz.

A Welsh copper comments that he wouldn't keep pigs in quarters like that. He clearly thinks you and James are sadistic neo-Nazis.

Shane is dead at the bottom of a cliff. Shearer, also dead, is with him.

Hackwill blurts out a story about being afraid of the mad Marion brothers and gathering his forces to make a run for it. When they found Sean dead, they thought you had killed him and would come for them next.

He was wrong, he says. The real murderer was Kay Shearer. He ambushed them as they were struggling across country, confessing – according to both Jessup and Hackwill – to all the killings in a convenient Bond-villain rant before he and Shane went off the mountain together.

Very neat.

Mary advises you not to make a fuss.

If you let Hackwill's version stand unchallenged, go to 270. If you try to get the truth out, go to 297.

260

Occasionally, you've wondered what was in Sean Rye's HOUSEKEEPING file, the one you put back unexamined. Now that you have that moment again, you act differently.

Inside the file is a report, typed on a sheet of flimsy paper, from someone with an office in Kuala Lumpur.

The words don't make sense. They are in English and fit into sentences. But you can't *understand*.

Thierry Lethem, according to this, has bestowed his money – all £6.5 million – on children's hospitals in Thailand, Vietnam and Singapore. Now he lives in Tibet, in a cave. Not as a monk, but as a hermit. He has left everything behind.

'I don't understand,' you repeat.

'Some people are saints,' Sally Rhodes muses.

'There must be some trick. He's shed his identity to escape.'

'That's exactly what he's done.'

'No. I mean, escape with the money,' you say.

'I don't think so.'

You can't imagine it. You write Sally a cheque and leave.

If you go home, go to 276. If you go to Tibet, go to 281.

261

'I'm not into this,' you mumble, tasting the drink on your tongue. 'I'm...'

Shearer's eyes flash anger. 'Thought you'd wind up the queer, breeder?'

You can't think. You want to deny that.

Shearer has a grip on you, strong hands on the back of your neck. You try to fight but your arms are like wet fish. You protest but Shearer twists you over, face into the mattress. Your open mouth jams against a bedspring.

'Fuck you,' Shearer says.

Your rectum is split open as he rapes you.

It's one of those experiences – first kiss, first sex, first bust-up, first baby, first kill, first dead parent – that ought to change everything.

It does but not the way it should. The shock is that the rest of the world is the same.

It's you who are changed. It's you who are raped.

Shearer fucks you and leaves you on the bed, the bedclothes on the floor. Then he goes to what was your bed and gets a good night's sleep.

You lie there, too hurt to sleep, too worn out to move.

At breakfast, you're locked inside your own skull. It's raining too hard to climb a mountain. James gives everybody the day off. He's feeling generous and you're in no mood to argue with him.

Shearer and Warwick are in full couple mode, sitting together, not needing to talk.

Shearer will tell Warwick, and Warwick will pass it on. Everyone will know. Bastards.

You get on with life but it's as if you were behind a barrier of invisible cotton wool.

When the week's over, you take no joy in sending Hackwill home humbled, or in the deepening of James's attachment to Mary. You don't feel anything about Kay Shearer.

You're not going deaf or blind or losing your sense of taste or smell. You're just distracted.

You don't even think much about the rape.

But you've been dislodged from the world. You see spiders in the shadows. You see things that didn't happen. They all have the same weight.

You've been slivered off from your real self. You are alone and dwindling.

Years pass. You continue as you are, glimpsing impossibilities, not caring about them.

You could avenge yourself.

There are aspects of you which would spend years plotting and executing revenge against Shearer, taking from him everything and everyone he loves, leaving him alive but a human shell. But it seems a fantasy.

Too many possibilities seem like fantasies: you might as well retreat to old dreams of piracy, or imagine yourself battling alien invaders, or living the life of a heartless stud, or solving complex murder mysteries, or travelling through time, or slipping between worlds.

Other yous might do those things. But you're the you who does nothing.

And so on.

262

Three days later, when you're all getting your stories straight for the police, Kay Shearer's body is pulled out of a culvert, where it was washing against some rocks, about to be swept under the earth.

There's an open verdict. It could be accidental, it could be suicide. When he ran out of Castle Drac, Shearer didn't care any more.

Because he's dead, Shearer never has to answer charges for the murders. You and Mary argue about it for the rest of your lives. You think Shearer killed Warwick and McKinnell; she says Hackwill has got away with it.

As far as you know, Hackwill prospers.

You and Mary live together, but don't have children.

Something lasts.

And so on.

263

You're back home in Sutton Mallet. The room hasn't changed. You haven't fouled up your past.

Your heart thumps.

That was worse than any back-at-school, unprepared-for-an-exam nightmare you've ever had.

Ro and the kids come home. They are overwhelmed by how pleased you are to see them, and seem to feel that Daddy has geeked out while they were away. You don't care.

From now on, you don't think about the past much. Just the future.

And so on.

264

First, you check the other bedroom. The four-poster is empty. You have a gut-sick feeling.

You and James spent the whole evening nagging at Shane, and – by extension – Hackwill. Shane was in a sweat about going to jail. He all but confessed the whole deal. Every word sharpened Hackwill.

In the dining-room, you find three bodies. Jessup and Sean stir, sleep interrupted. You check Shane.

'What the fuck?' he says.

'He's alive,' you tell James.

'Hackwill's bolted,' James announces.

'Fucker,' Shane says.

The next morning, Mary comes back with the police. Shane is arrested and confesses to the murder of Ben McKinnell. He denies killing Tristram Warwick.

Searching the mountain, the police find Hackwill dead, with a knife in his heart. You wonder how James managed it. Then they find Shearer, half out of his mind. Kay Shearer killed Robert Hackwill. In revenge.

Shane gets twenty years.

You marry Mary. You have two children, Jerry and Jocelyn.

You turn the Compound back into a farm and make a go of it, selling goat's cheese.

Happy ending?

And so on.

265

James binds his feet, fixing towels with string. It looks absurd, but no one laughs.

'I'm coming with you,' Mary says.

James doesn't argue. Again, you wonder if Mary was with him the night before last.

'Keith, hold the fort,' James says. 'If we don't come back, try smoke signals. Jessup is flammable.'

You look at Shane, wondering if you could fight him off.

Mary slips long mittens over her feet.

'Don't worry about me,' she says. 'I used to be a beat copper. I have indestructible feet.'

James and Mary set out.

Two days later, the police helicopter arrives. You, Shane and Jessup are air-lifted out. It turns out that Mary made it to the village.

You get her story second-hand from the pilot. She and James found Sean dead, throat cut. James and she separated, hoping to trap the killer – they thought it was Shane and were worried about you – and she got lost.

James is missing. So is Hackwill, who never turned up at the village. Police and emergency services swarm over the mountainside. No trace is ever found of either of them.

You feel half your life has been torn away.

Your business collapses, of course. In town, you're not the only one. Without Hackwill, a lot of the local developments are exposed as financial balloons and burst. Even the losses of Sean and McKinnell have ripple effects. The evaporation of Shearer's Shelves with the death of Kay Shearer puts eighteen people out of work.

Mum elaborately doesn't blame you. She knows too well that it's always James who leads you on, gets you in trouble.

Led you on. Got you in trouble. You are sure James is dead.

You think of him and Hackwill like Sherlock Holmes and Professor Moriarty, plunging together over a waterfall, bodies lost in some torrent.

Open verdicts are returned.

Mostly, people assume Hackwill killed McKinnell, Warwick, Shearer and Sean, and that James hunted him down. A minority opinion has it the other way round, with James as the killer of them all.

You don't know.

You take a bottle of Jack Daniel's. You can either drink it, or think some more.

If you drink the Jack, go to 278. If you think, go to 291.

266

This is where you get the bastard. On the cliff, years away from the copse, from the Lime Kiln, from your compulsorily purchased home. This is where Robert Hackwill pays.

You insist you be second in the human chain, with Hackwill ahead, and the others – Shane, Jessup, Warwick – behind you.

Half-way up, there's a shelf. When you and Hackwill are on it, with the others dangling below, you act fast. You shove Hackwill into space and sever the rope. You can claim it was quick thinking, saving the others from being pulled down with him. Hackwill disappears, plunging down along with the still-torrential rain.

It's too thick for anyone to be sure what they saw.

Hackwill kicks the cliff as he falls, tumbling. He plummets head first, bouncing towards the valley. The rain is so thick you can't see bottom. You won't see the bastard hit.

But Hackwill sticks to the cliffside. Something has caught him. His legs are moving.

James, free of Mary's team, is on the shelf beside you. He has rappelled down.

'What happened?' he asks.

'He fell.'

James holds up the cut end of the rope. 'Yeah?'

'He was falling,' you correct yourself. 'I had to cut him loose.'

James looks at you, appalled. 'I can't believe you did what you've done.' He crouches and leans out as far as he can, looking down.

'I'm going down after him,' he says.

'No,' you say, not knowing whom you're afraid for.

If you let James try to rescue Hackwill, go to 272. If you go down yourself, go to 284.

267

Night falls apparently at three in the afternoon. You're all stuck in Castle Drac with a corpse, glaring at each other, split into hostile camps. You have an alliance with James and a liaison with Mary. The others are enemy, with Jessup and Shane sticking by Hackwill.

Shearer is on his own, with neither major faction. And Sean comes on like Switzerland but looks more like Poland. If you all had to agree on someone to sacrifice, Sean would get the vote.

Your frustration builds because you cannot get alone with James to confer. Hackwill has ordered Jessup to mark you both. Whenever it looks as if you'll snatch some time in the kitchen or outside the cottage to talk, Jessup pops up. You still can't read James, or understand why he has done what has been done, but you are with him. When he makes his move, you'll back it up, no matter who gets hurt.

What you feel for Mary is new and exciting and dazzling, but you can't let that blot out the link you've shared with James all his life, instinctive ever since the copse.

If you'd killed Hackwill then, this wouldn't be happening. You wonder if you could have done it, a small boy attacking a bigger bully like Bambi battering Godzilla.

You and James aren't allowed to sleep in the same room: Hackwill decrees you be split up. Until this came up, you had thought you would be sleeping with Mary.

Now, it's an issue.

'This is our place,' you say. 'We make the rules.'

'All that ended with Warwick,' Hackwill says.

Nobody else protests.

'I'm going to be in one of those twin beds,' Hackwill says. 'And one of you will be in the other, where I can keep an eye on him. Which of you will it be?'

If it's you, go to 280. If it's James, go to 293.

268

You are arrested and charged with the murders of Benjamin McKinnell, Tristram Warwick, Shane Bush, Sean Rye, Reginald Jessup, Robert Hackwill and James Marion. Assault and reckless endangerment of Mary Yatman and Kay Shearer are attached seven pages into the document. You're even charged with sexual assault upon Mary Yatman, though her violator either failed to ejaculate or used a condom, so no DNA match is possible.

You have a breakdown and the pre-trial period passes in a drugged blur. Because of this, you never present a coherent defence.

The worst thing is that Mum thinks you killed James.

Though you are present at the trial, which ends with you being found guilty and committed to Broadmoor, you don't fully understand the case against you until the paperback comes out, with its dramatic reconstruction of your rampage, and subsequent determined double-time trek to the village to establish your alibi.

Iain Scobie, hack author of *Mountaintop Massacre*, interviews the sergeant who first took your statement. He claims to have known you did it when you said Hackwill was a bully at school. In your eyes, he saw a lasting hatred that cut through your pose of shock and grief. He thinks you're shamming insanity and should be in prison not a secure mental facility.

You find yourself sharing a rec room with Dennis Nilsen and Peter Sutcliffe. They argue over what to watch on television: Nilsen likes nature programmes, Sutcliffe wants the God slot. You don't care. You resent the fact that good books have been written about both of them, but all you rate is Scobie's fanciful drivel.

The BBC makes a film, *Mountaintop*, with Paul McGann as you and Warren Clarke as Hackwill. It 'explains' the murders with hazy flashbacks to playground tussles and a weirdly homoerotic bit of bullying in the showers. It is trite compared with your memory of the copse.

You hear Kay Shearer has got married (to Victoria Conyer), so you assume his sexual orientation has changed. Mary, who is played by Amanda Donohoe in the TV film, ghost-writes *Survivor's Account*, backing up Scobie's conjectural version with memories excavated through hypnosis. Michael Eaton, screenwriter of *Mountaintop*, points out that Mary's recovered memory includes incidents and lines of dialogue he freely admits to making up 'for dramatic purposes'.

A few years into the new century, Broadmoor – overcrowded with motiveless madmen, all with fashionable nicknames and book-to-TV-movie atrociographies – becomes known for periodic hellish night riots. The authorities see these as a chance to institute an unofficial death sentence, culling the famous names.

Your turn comes.

As you lie, twitching your last, on the rec room floor, something comes to you. The police combed the whole mountain for evidence. But they never found the boots.

For a moment, it seems as if you know where they went wrong, where the cache of now-perished footwear still nestles, but then the life goes out of you.

Go to 0.

269

As James and Shane walk away, you can't help noticing how much broader at the shoulders Shane is than James.

The drizzle is clearing. Within a day, this should be over. If they make it to the village.

Hackwill is smug again, in control. You'll have to watch him carefully over the next twenty-four hours.

The first awkward thing is McKinnell. It seems best to leave him where he is, but that means no one can use the toilet. A day of pissing outside won't be too much of an ordeal.

Warwick is still out there, with the boots.

You'd like to spend the time alone with Mary, but that wouldn't be sensible.

Everyone sits around in Castle Drac. Jessup gets up a game of cards, but you and Shearer duck out of it. You try to read an orienteering magazine but can't concentrate. You keep wondering how far James and Shane have got.

The day crawls by. The sun comes out and shines briefly with wonderful intensity. Then it gets dark.

James and Shane should be on the downslope. The village will be in sight long before they reach it. They'll have to walk most of the night. Towards the end, they'll feel as if they're wearing divers' boots.

Hackwill is the big winner at cards. No surprises there. Jessup lets him win.

Every time you look at the group round the dinner-table, you think 'Murderer' at Hackwill. He has blanked his face completely.

The game winds down.

Rather than get into a face-off, you agree to prepare the evening meal. It would have been your responsibility if the course were continuing.

'Where's Kay?' Sean asks.

You think he went upstairs to lie down. He's still in shock.

'He went out,' Jessup says.

'What?' you ask.

'Hours ago. I thought you knew.'

Hackwill cracks a smile. You aren't keeping this together.

You leave Mary in charge and take a torch outside. It's not full night yet and the stars aren't out. Everything is dark grey-green.

You find Shearer in Colditz, dead. Head at a wrong angle, like Warwick's.

They were all playing cards. It can't have been Hackwill.

James could have dumped Shane and hurried back; or the other way round. Why did you think of James first? He's smart, Shane isn't.

Damn. Damn. Damn.

A scream from Castle Drac. A woman: Mary.

You begin to run. Then you freeze.

If you run to the cottage, go to 273. If you run away from the cottage, go to 286.

270

Mary is right. You are still discovering her, the strength you give each other. She helps you and James through the crisis as your business almost goes under in the burst of appalling publicity. But the notoriety helps in a way. In a sick moment, you think of offering murder weekends at the Compound, site of the Shearer Slayings. That doesn't come off but you realise some of your clients do find taking their survival course on blood-soaked ground adds something to the experience. It's sick, but there it is.

Hackwill gets back to his dealings. You follow the story, almost as a hobby. First, Reg Jessup cracks up and is committed to an expensive asylum. That must be a constant worry to Hackwill. What will Jessup do? Will he ever tell a new story? Will anyone listen?

Though the police buy the Shearer story, their investigation into the murders focuses on Warwick's business interests and, through him, Hackwill's affairs. Folders are passed on to the Fraud Squad.

Hackwill is nipped by the occasional charge.

Mary anonymously sends the Avon and Somerset Constabulary a caseful of documents she happened to have smuggled out of Hackwill Properties.

Helen Hackwill leaves her husband, taking little Samantha and baby Colin with her. Hackwill is forced to resign from the council. The charges pile up. Not murder, but everything else.

Hackwill goes to prison. Not the maximum security hellhole he'd rate as a murderer, but still a prison. His political and business allies desert him as quickly as his wife did. After all, it's not as if anyone *liked* him.

You and Mary marry. You have two children, Jack and Juno.

Things get better.

And so on.

271

You're the best climber, so it's down to you. Hackwill scrabbles away, panicking. If you don't reach him, he'll probably lose his grip and fall into the river. The water will pound him into the centre of the earth.

Your towel-muffled feet feel strange on the rock outcrops. You monkey your way down. James is about twenty feet above and to the left of you, following at his own pace. You can't see Mary.

It's not like her to stand and watch.

'Stay back,' Hackwill shouts.

'Bastard,' you reply.

Hackwill loses his hold and slides a couple of feet, anorak scraping rock. He jams against an outcrop. You reach him. He thumps your leg feebly. You kick him in the face and hurt your swaddled toes. He clings to the ground. The incline is just getting steep. He's trapped.

If you kick Hackwill again, go to 275. If you help him up, go to 285.

272

James makes it. He gets down to Hackwill, at the end of the rope you feed him.

What will happen if he gets back, with Hackwill alive?

He signals that Hackwill is alive but hurt – thumb up, but shaking

– and starts winding the rope around him. You feel the added weight. You brace yourself.

James starts climbing, hauling Hackwill up. Then James loses his footing. The rope saws your hands.

If you grip the rope, go to 289. If you let go, go to 299.

273

You run towards the cottage. Mary is still screaming.

You'll kill anyone who is hurting her. She's the woman you love. All these fucking-around years, the Chris era and the Marie-Laure period, were preparation. This is the real one.

You shoulder right through the door.

Hackwill holds Sean down on the sofa. Jessup stands over them with a knife in his hands, not knowing what to do with it.

Sean is white with fright.

'Do it, Reg, or you're out of the gang,' Hackwill shouts.

Jessup shuts his eyes and stabs. He barely grazes Sean's chest but the bank manager yells. You haven't time to get involved. Coldly, you care a lot less about Sean than about Mary.

More screams come from above.

You run upstairs. In the bedroom, Mary is being raped.

You get instamatic flashes. Mary's wrists cuffed to the bed-posts, her legs scissoring, someone massive covering her. Shane.

Fuck.

James must be dead.

You roar and rush for the bed. You don't make it. You feel a knife slipping into your back. Hackwill.

You die loving Mary and hating Hackwill.

Go to 0.

274

You'd be insane to jeopardise what you've got.

In the '90s, you and Ro have another daughter, Loretta, then adopt

Ion, a Romanian orphan. You specialise in negotiations that bring jobs to communities shattered by the gutting of the British mining industry.

You enter parliament in 1992, as MP for Sedgemoor West. In 1997, in the first Blair cabinet, you're made junior minister for trade. Though fit for survival in the New Labour Party by virtue of your '80s background and PR skills, you have the feeling Tony keeps you around as a socialist conscience. You consistently oppose alliances with media barons like Murdoch and Leech and argue against information monopolies. Power interests you very little, but you see opportunities to rearrange the country, to unpick the reverses of the last twenty years, to revitalise the hope you believe all men and women should have as a birthright.

In 1992, Phil, your stepfather, puts a £10 bet on you becoming prime minister by 2010 and is given 500:1 odds. He lives to collect his £5,000.

You keep fighting. Surprisingly, you often win.

And so on.

275

Your foot satisfyingly swipes Hackwill's head. You've remembered to point your toes and get some swing into it. His gloved hands open. He slithers down, hovers on the lip of the drop, then disappears into the river.

You stand up in triumph. James shouts something at you.

The wicked witch is dead! It's over!

A rock thumps against your head. You pitch forward, senses jarred. Your face scrapes across rock as you follow Hackwill, plunging head first. You're in the air, then in the water.

The icy cold is an all-over electric shock. You are too paralysed to struggle for breath.

Go to 0.

276

It eats at you from inside.

The sainthood of a Belgian.

Numbers on a card make him a martyr, and you…? What is left for you?

You are down below £3 million, then below £2 million. Where is it all going?

You have a slight heart attack. You're treated privately, of course, and offer to pay for a heart transplant.

If it were medically possible, you'd opt for a whole-body transplant. Maybe even a brain-wipe.

You'd like to wake up innocent. And rich.

You're not so rich any more, though.

Maybe you *can't* be innocent and rich.

You're barely even a millionaire any more. Spiders are scuttling closer. What you have just isn't enough, so you start playing the Lottery again.

And so on.

277

Go back to any earlier choice.

If all else fails, go back to 1.

You'll be here again. You've probably been here before.

278

Twenty years later, your body gives out. A bottle of Jack a day, topped up with interesting prescription and non-prescription anti-depressants on the market in the new century, slowly assaults your liver and kidneys. Finally, you're carried away in an epidemic of Beijing flu. You have moments of clarity towards the end but have too much complicated past to put together.

Thinking about it, you loved your mum and dad, and your brother and sister. And Christina, who married an academic. That's something.

But you're sorry.

Go to 0.

279

You can't believe you seriously thought about murder. This whole week is supposed to be punishment, a lesson. What can a dead man learn? If Hackwill died, he'd be out of his misery.

Mary's team, with James's help, is way ahead.

Hackwill, slowed down especially by Jessup, fumes and frets. Tonight, he wants to be in the warm.

You certainly aren't going to try anything with him. You also can't believe you nearly got into bed with Kay Shearer.

This course is dragging things out of you. Things unthought.

You see the outcrop shudder as Hackwill grabs it, and know it'll come free.

Roped to Hackwill are Shane, Warwick, Jessup and you. You try to shout but rain fills your mouth.

James, at the end of Mary's roped-together team, turns to look.

The outcrop detaches itself from the wet cliff. Hackwill bends back at the waist. The weight of his head pulls him into the air.

If Shane hangs on tight, you'll be saved. (It's not your decision. After all this fussing, when a crisis comes your life depends on Shane, on the Man From B.U.N.G.L.E.) Shane panics and makes a grab not for the rock but for Hackwill's legs.

Warwick calls Shane a fuckhead. Hackwill and Shane fall, dragging Warwick and Jessup away. The weight of all four men snaps the rope round your waist as if with a guillotine blade. You're dragged away from the face of the rock.

You see a sky full of rain as you fall.

Go to 0.

280

Hackwill snores lightly in the other bed. Mary is alone in the next room. The others are downstairs. Only Shane's a danger and he's slow. James can handle him easily and have enough left over for Jessup.

It's down to you.

James has killed for this, cleared your way to Hackwill. You sit up in bed, quietly. You lower bare feet to cold floorboards.

You take your pillow and stand over Hackwill. Asleep, he's like anyone else. The eyes you remember from the copse are closed. You hold your pillow over his face.

Can you do this?

If you can, go to 283. If you can't, go to 295.

281

Christ, it's cold. Being rich doesn't keep you warm. No matter how many layers you buy, the cold still gets in, needles of ice scything through every seam, carving into you.

And, God, but Tibet – Nepal? Wherever – is shit. Corruption and poverty and Chinese uniforms, and fucking monks, leeching off everyone. You've spent quarter of a million on this trip (mostly in bribes) and you're still miserable.

The helicopter can't land near Thierry's perch, so you have to crawl up the lower slopes of some mountain with a serial number rather than an English name, roped to a gang of cut-throat guides. Why couldn't the Belgian pick a cave in Snowdonia?

You fight the rock, the snow, the ice, the smell, the hate. Inch by inch, you climb. The air gets thin. The rush of wind is eternal in your ears.

It's not what you've imagined. The hermit hole is not really a cave but a hut-sized house built against the slope. Its roof is a bright orange plastic sheet. Not your idea of spiritual.

Lethem is outside, pottering. At home doing the garden. He must grow his own vegetables.

You tell the head guide – you can't but think of him as a Sherpa – to stay back, and walk across stony ground, wind carving your face even through the fur mask and goggles. You are more tired than you ever have been, but the thinness of the air is giving you a high, almost a rush.

Lethem glances up. Swaddled in furs, he could be a bloody yeti.

You have an ice-axe in one hand, in case you want to kill him.

You look at Lethem. His face is exposed, blue at the lips a bit, weathered on the cheekbones.

You take off your goggles.

If you see an enemy, go to 292. If you see a brother, go to 300.

282

'I don't think that's a good idea,' you say. 'Either we all go or we all stay. Someone will come eventually. We'll be missed.'

'So you'll have time to kill us all,' Hackwill says.

'No,' says Shearer. 'You're the one Tris and Ben were walking out on. You're the one who needed to keep them in line. You did it. Or you had her do it.' He nods at Mary.

'Kay, you have my word –'

'As what? District councillor? Chairman of the Planning Committee? Corrupt bastard? Murdering cunt?' Shearer is on the point of collapse.

Hackwill looks round the room. 'All right,' he says, without conviction, just to shut Shearer up, 'I did it. I fucking killed wimpo Warwick and shit-guts McKinnell and I drove myself into a gorge while leaving James here safe by the road. I'm guilty of every bloody thing you think I am. Happy?'

Shearer calms. You relax a little. It seemed for a while that Shearer and Hackwill would go for each other.

Hackwill takes his knife out of his coat pocket and drives it to the hilt into Sean's eye. The bank manager's face spurts blood and he stiffens against the wall.

'Now *that*,' Hackwill says, 'I admit to.'

Everyone alive in the room is electrified. Hackwill pulls his knife out of Sean's skull as if it were a slightly recalcitrant cork. He stabs Shearer in the heart.

'And *that* too. I did that.'

Shearer looks more surprised than dead.

'Shane, take Mary,' Hackwill snaps. 'She's the only dangerous one.'

Shane, brain on a five-second delay, moves. But Mary is fast. She kicks him in the groin, doubling him over, gets her own knife at his throat, cutting swiftly.

Hackwill grabs Mary by the hair and holds his blade to her neck. He makes her drop her knife.

Shane kicks on the floor.

You are frozen. You haven't done anything.

Jessup is terrified.

'Reg, time to join the homicide club,' Hackwill announces.

Reg blubbers.

'Think about it. If you don't, you're a witness.'

Hackwill holds Mary's head close to his. Her face impassive, she relaxes. The blade smears blood and optic gunk on her neck.

'Why should I care about her?' you ask, trembling.

'Because you're not a murderer, you idiot,' Hackwill says. 'If you were, you'd never have let it get this far. Your brother, however... Reg, do James. Now.'

Jessup rushes across the room. He shuts his eyes and sticks his knife into James's stomach. James yowls in agony and sinks to the floor, hands round the knife-hilt, face twisted.

'That's not a fatal wound,' Hackwill comments. 'Cut his neck open or something.'

James pulls the knife out and drops it. He is doubled up, lap full of blood.

You can't do anything, or Mary will die. She'll probably die anyway – Hackwill must plan for you both to die – but every second gives you another chance.

James is going. Mary's still here. Prioritise.

Jessup picks up his knife with distaste. It's squirmy with blood.

'The neck,' Hackwill says.

With an animal cry, Jessup stabs and slashes at James's head. Blood arcs. James raises his hands from his stomach but is whipped this way and that by the blows.

'That's enough,' Hackwill says.

Jessup is exhausted, drained, bloody and insane.

'Clean yourself up. Congratulations. Now I won't have to kill you too.'

Hackwill looks at Shane on the floor.

'I promised him you,' he whispers to Mary.

She blinks.

Is she signalling you to come on or to go back? To rush Hackwill, or to hold off?

If you rush Hackwill, go to 288. If you let Mary make her move, go to 296.

283

You force the pillow down on to Hackwill's face, feeling his whole body stiffen as he tries to throw you off, and lie on top of him, pinning his limbs with your body, pressing with as much weight as you can manage. It takes minutes that pass like hours.

Eventually, you can relax.

When you strip the bed, you find the knife in Hackwill's hand. The bastard thought he was ready.

You can't wake James without alerting the others. Do you ask Mary for help?

If you ask Mary, go to 287. If you go it alone, go to 290.

284

You clamber towards Hackwill, knowing you'll have to kill him, then climb back.

To what? James is part of James-and-Mary now. The Super Marion Brothers are a bust. You and Marie-Laure are pathetic; she's stopped even complaining when you call her 'Chris'.

You've never done anything right. You can take Hackwill out of this game. And yourself.

Instead of kicking Hackwill out of his perch, you hug him and launch yourself out away from the cliff.

Falling.

Go to 0.

285

You grab Hackwill's collar. James is with you. He lays a hand on the exhausted councillor too.

Two nights outside have worn Hackwill ragged. He seems thinner, older, more battered than the man who left 'to get help'.

Between you, you and James haul Hackwill up the hillside. Mary waits, a rock in her hands.

'You,' Hackwill says, to Mary, 'help me.'

'I resign, sir,' she replies.

Hackwill's face is purple. 'It's too late for that,' he says, reaching for his knife.

Mary sees the attack coming and dives. James punches Hackwill in the stomach. You grab for his knife-hand. The sharp edge passes across your stomach, cutting your padded waistcoat but not your skin. You lose your grip.

James and Hackwill struggle. The old school bully still has fight in him, the bastard. Mary bashes his head with the rock. With a roar, he turns, knife towards her. She backs away. James launches himself at Hackwill's knife-arm, but misjudges and rolls over the edge, getting a grip on an outcropping.

You examine the fluff pouring from your gashed stomach. You aren't yet convinced you aren't hurt.

Hackwill stamps on James's hand. 'Fucking Super Marion Brothers,' he snarls. 'You were always shits.'

James clings on with determination. But you hear the whimpering he made in the copse as he weed himself.

Mary yells like a lioness and smashes the rock into Hackwill's face, obliterating his nose. He grabs her and parks his blade in her chest, twisting viciously.

'Traitor,' he breathes through blood.

Mary, eyes sparking fire, holds Hackwill's anorak with both hands and pitches herself over the edge.

You see Mary and Hackwill in their death embrace. They bounce several times off jagged rocks, then launch into open space, legs waving like a starfish, and fall together into the torrent. You see a pale water-trail that might be Mary's hair, then they're both gone.

'Help,' grunts James, voice cracked.

You pull him up. Whatever it was, it's over. You listen to the roar of the river, pouring into the caves like an ocean emptying into Hell.

When you're asked what really happened, you have no theories.

And so on.

286

You turn away from the cottage and run.

You love Mary, but not enough to die: two nights' fucking doesn't mean that much. As you run through the dark, you pour contempt on yourself. You don't know what's happened to Mary, or to James, and you don't care. You just want to be away from all this. You keep running.

Two days later, you wander into a village. The story is out. Most of them are dead, but Hackwill is alive.

Officially, James takes the blame. He went mad and killed people, until Hackwill took him down. Before he killed Mary, James raped her.

It doesn't matter if you believe it. You almost do. What counts is that you ran. You're congratulated on surviving the massacre, but some say you were your mad brother's accomplice. You turn down all tabloid offers for your story. You wind up the business and stay home, looking inwards.

When it was just a Chinese burn, you ran into the copse; but when it was life or death, you ran away. You hate yourself.

You loved Mary. Those few days gave you a connection to her as important as your lifelong link with James.

And you let them both die.

Hackwill is hailed as a hero. No one dares question his business practices now. He prospers. Through his influence, streets in Sedgwater are named after Jessup, Warwick, Shearer and Shane, the victims of James Marion. You let him get away with it.

Marie-Laure tries to console you. You tell her to fuck off. You tell her you hate her and wish she had died too. You live on for quite a few years, but it eats you up that you ran away.

And so on.

287

Mary helps you get Hackwill out of Castle Drac and into a river. You watch the bundle swirl a little as it is rushed away. The river flows underground. He'll probably never come up again.

Without him, Jessup and Shane are useless. All your problems are over.

Months later, you and Mary tell James what you did.

'That's a damn sight better than my feeble shot,' he says. 'And it didn't cost us a minibus.'

'We're safe,' you say. 'You're safe.'

Hackwill has taken the blame for Warwick and McKinnell.

'One thing bothers me,' you say. 'Why did you kill Warwick and McKinnell?'

'Me?' James is shocked you can think such a thing. '*Me?*'

Your brother stays away from you for a while. After all, you're a murderer and he isn't.

Eventually, he comes round. He realises you killed to protect him. That's what it's all about.

Now all you have to worry about is Mary. Your relationship had better be for ever, because she's the only one outside the family who knows what happened.

After a while, worry frays your nerves. Sleeping next to Mary, you find yourself holding the pillow, remembering Hackwill's body under you.

What to do? What to do?

And so on.

288

You leap across the room. Hackwill's knife cuts through Mary's neck...

in slo-mo, you see skin and flesh part and blood burst, and your heart dies...

and is waiting for you.

You slam against Hackwill's knife, but get your hands round his neck. You feel the blade in your chest, a hard obstruction, and hear your heartbeat. You're going to last long enough to finish him.

You see life die in Hackwill's eyes. He can't believe you've killed him. You roll off the dead councillor and look at the blurry ceiling.

Reg Jessup is going to have to answer for this. You almost laugh.

Your hand flounders, but finds Mary's. With your last strength, you grip her hand. Sticky blood binds your palm to hers. You feel the grip returned.

You both die. In love.

Go to 0.

289

Instinctively, you grip the rope, taking the strain in your arms.

The full weight of James and Hackwill, bulked up by rainwater, drags at you.

The shelf is slippery. You are pulled forward. You are in the air. Below you, rope flapping between you, James and Hackwill tumble.

You see the grey of the ground.

Go to 0.

290

If you get Hackwill outside, you can cart him to a river that flows underground. Throw him in there and the body will never be found. Your story will be that he knocked you out and made a run for it. You'll clout yourself later to back that up.

You wrap him in a duvet cover and toss in his clothes and boots, even his knife. It's a heavy sack – too many municipal free lunches in his gut – but you make it downstairs and out of Castle Drac.

You're wearing pyjamas and the temperature is down around zero. At least it's not raining.

You hump Hackwill along the grass, hauling him towards the pens. You muffle your sobs of exertion. The bundle is heavy, awkward. You're leaving a dragging track that will be obvious in the daytime.

A light goes on in the cottage. You haul harder and the duvet cover splits. A white hand sticks out. Is it clutching the grass, anchoring you?

People come out of Castle Drac, running towards you.

Someone tackles you and hammers you to the ground. A torch shines. James is on top of you. He looks surprised.

'I thought you were dead,' he says.

'No,' Mary comments. 'That's Hackwill.'

Oh God, you've fucked this up.

'What were you thinking of?' James asks.

You have no answer.

'I can't help you now,' James says.

And so on.

291

You visit Mary in hospital. Suffering from exposure and shock, she has lapsed into semi-coma. Stuck full of tubes, she looks like a little girl in a true-life TV movie. Her doctor, knowing what you went through with her, lets you in to watch her for a while. He thinks it might help.

You work out how it might have been. Mary worked for Hackwill, even when she was a policewoman. When she vandalised your home, she was under his orders. Shane was hired beef, just for show. Mary, who used to be a monster, was the effective one, the wetwork specialist.

'Did you, Mary?' you ask.

Her respirator goes up and down. Her cardiogram beeps.

'McKinnell would have been easy. Too wrapped up in gut-ache to hear anyone coming behind him, with a knife.'

You see Mary creeping, ready.

'Then Hackwill craps out, gets himself an alibi, and leaves his little helper behind to finish the job. You distract James with your kisses, fuck him until he's in a deep sleep, then go out and kill Warwick and Shearer, knock me over, get back into Castle Drac to be around when James wakes up. You're great in bed and he trusts you, the idiot. Then, it gets hazy.'

Her face doesn't move.

'Somehow, you get turned round. I think it was when I told Jessup about the copse. All the resentment you felt about being

Hackwill's creature bubbled up. You went rogue. Hackwill was out there somewhere, pretending to be lost, nice warm boots on his feet, snacking off emergency rations. You traipsed after Sean, caught up with him, killed him. Collateral damage. You didn't have to, didn't want to, but by then killing seemed easy. Certainly, you found and killed Hackwill. And James.'

The last, you're not sure of. Hackwill could have killed James, before himself being killed by Mary. James could even still be out there, a Welsh Tarzan living off berries and leaves. At the end, confused by it all, Mary could have felt mercy for James. Couldn't she?

You reach into the nest of tubes and take hold.

If you pull, go to 294. If you let Mary alone, go to 298.

292

'Thief,' you say.

For a moment, you wonder if he can understand English. *Voleur.* That's the word.

'You are him,' Lethem says. 'The other winner.'

You knew he knew you were coming.

He rushes at you – to attack? to embrace? – and you fumble, dropping your ice-axe. You collide, thumping together through layers of fur. You roll through the snow, clinging tight to each other. Snow packs round you, wrapping you in an ice grip. A giant ball grows round you.

Your fortunes are one. Your matched halves mesh.

People run after you.

Rocks tear at your furs but can't reach you. You have become a two-scoop snowball. Together, you roll over a precipice.

In each other's arms, you plunge from the top of the world.

Go to 0.

293

You and Mary lie awake in the four-poster. Tonight, you haven't made love. You're too concerned with thinking about the next room.

James and Hackwill are in there. Will one try to kill the other?

James has already tried to kill Hackwill, so Hackwill knows the danger and might plan a pre-emptive strike.

Mary strokes your chest, understanding.

'I hope he gets it right this time,' you murmur.

'What?'

'Killing Hackwill. Enough of this fucking around with Warwick and McKinnell. James has to go for the bull.'

Mary props herself up on her elbow. 'James didn't kill McKinnell. That was my job.'

Your heart clutches.

'I didn't do it, lover. It was probably Shane.'

'Then James *isn't* a killer?'

Mary looks at you, her face curtained by her hair: you can't see her eyes.

Damn. How could you have thought such a thing?

You get out of bed and go on to the landing. The other bedroom door is open. Hackwill and Shane stand over a bed, pressing a pillow down.

Hackwill sees you. 'Fuck being quiet,' he says.

Shane falls on you, knife sliding between your ribs. As you die, you regret thinking what you did of James. You don't wonder whether Mary will be all right.

Go to 0.

294

You wake up in prison, not sure what you were dreaming. Now Mary's dead, your conclusions are tenuous. Hackwill killed them all except Mary. You killed her.

While you were away (in a fugue of babbling, apparently) you've become a famous case for all the wrong reasons. The assumption is that you mercy-killed your catatonic friend. What you went through together – you must have been in love? – was a bond that brought you to Mary's bedside, intent on freeing her from her functioning but empty shell.

You are too bewildered to argue. In a precedent-setting verdict, you get a suspended sentence. Marie-Laure leaves you, certain you betrayed her with Mary. How she managed to miss realising you'd fucked every other woman you took on a course (but not Mary) is beyond you.

For the rest of your life, whenever you pick up the phone and the other party hangs up, you're certain it was James. Or Hackwill.

Or Mary. You don't think she's dead. She can't die. She's Death Herself.

In the Arthur C. Clarkeian year of 2001, you receive an e-bomb from a militant anti-euthanasia group. Your computer terminal blows apart, riddling you with glass, plastic and wire shrapnel.

You don't linger.

Go to 0.

295

You aren't your brother. Your arms won't work. The pillow hovers.

Hackwill's eyes flutter open. 'Mental,' he sneers.

A point prods up through the duvet. Hackwill has been sleeping knife in hand. The blade catches you in the soft of your belly, under your ribs. Hackwill twists the knife.

The pain is like nothing you've ever felt. You scream and try to raise yourself off the knife.

People crowd into the room. Mary, Shane, James, the rest.

You're dying in mind-blotting pain.

'He tried to kill me,' Hackwill says.

'I believe you,' says Mary, taking his neck and twisting.

Hackwill dies before you do, but that's no consolation. James and Mary hold you, getting your blood all over their dressing-gowns and hands.

You make it through a century of pain until sunrise.

Go to 0.

296

'I should thank you, Mental,' Hackwill says. 'You and your brother will be remembered as the murderers. Warwick and McKinnell can't wreck the development deal. The others are out of the way, collateral damage. Rye was wavering. He'd probably have wimped out with Warwick.'

'What about him?' you say, nodding at Jessup, who is a quivering wreck.

'I don't think he'll make it till help comes. I'll be with him when he dies, though. Friends for life, that's us.'

Hackwill is enjoying this. You can't believe it but he's doing that stupid Bond-villain thing of explaining it all before killing the hero.

That makes you a hero. Then again, as he pointed out, he's a murderer and you're not. Mary, though. She killed Shane. She'll do it.

Does this change how you feel about her?

'And you really were trying to kill me,' Hackwill says.

You're too tired to argue about it.

'Very clever. Get me up here. Have an accident. I almost admire that. But your brother got impatient.'

You suppose you realised hours ago that James really did push Hackwill into a culvert in the minibus. You're sad that your brother should be dragged down to Hackwill's level. You wonder if going to Mary made James do it.

'And all because of that stupid house of yours, and that stupid pint. If your brother had just had a drink on me, we wouldn't be here knee-deep in dead people.'

'It wasn't the pint, you stupid fucker,' Mary says. 'It was the copse.'

Mary's hand closes on his balls. You have hold of his wrist and wrench it back. Mary twists. She gets his knife. She doesn't go into frenzy, like Jessup. She is calm, detached, meticulous. She takes five minutes to kill Hackwill.

Watching that kills something else. Your love.

Hackwill gets the blame for everything. Jessup gives a lengthy confession. Hackwill becomes a bogeyman to rival Nilsen or Fred West. Iain Scobie's book *Hackwill: The Will to Hack*, filmed with Alan Rickman as Hackwill, makes him a Manson or Rasputin figure, influencing Shane and Jessup to crimes. His ordinary financial motivations are played down so he can be seen as some kind of monster superman.

You have nightmares for ever. Hackwill doesn't haunt you and you rarely dwell on James's ghastly death. What you remember is Mary killing Hackwill. She knows what she has done. You become formal strangers, meeting only when it's a legal obligation.

You marry Marie-Laure, but it doesn't last. Only the nightmares last.

And so on.

297

You can't let it lie. Hackwill's a multiple murderer. Besides, he was your school bully. Calmly, you and James set out the whole story. The big surprise is that James admits to trying to kill Hackwill in the minibus. His honesty makes the police take you seriously. Then Hackwill accuses you both of attempted murder. The police think again, wondering whether Kay Shearer acted alone. They can understand why he killed Tristram Warwick, but not the others.

James gets five years.

You are grilled off and on for weeks. Nothing sticks, except reckless endangerment. Your business is shut down and investigated.

Everyone who ever twisted their ankle on a course sues you. One day, you wake up and Mary's gone. You hope she's hunting Hackwill. But Robert Hackwill gets richer; serves as mayor of Sedgwater; wins Businessman of the Year awards; exults in the grand opening of the Discount Development, grinning in photographs with Tony Blair and the Spice Girls.

You are sidelined. The worst thing is that you know the whole truth but no one will believe you.

James is killed in a prison riot.

You bitterly marry Marie-Laure.

You make things worse for yourself.

And so on.

298

Mary's body lives on but her mind has flown. You feel you've a lot in common with her. You feel yourself sinking. Sometimes, you don't talk for days.

Then Marie-Laure tells you she's pregnant. It's like a rope lowered into a well. You take hold of the fact and haul yourself up. You rebuild a life. You have a son, Jan, then a daughter, Josie. You get on with it.

In dreams, though, you are back in the copse. Only, it's not at Ash Grove Primary but up a mountain in Wales.

Hackwill, Mary, James. They keep beckoning, outstretched hands gloved with boots which bob like comical hand-puppets. There are others with them, in the cobwebbed shadows.

You always wake up before you go into the copse. If you can, you wake your wife and make love with a desperate urgency, an embracing of life.

You spend the rest of your life running from the dream-copse.

And so on.

299

For the rest of your life, you wish you'd gripped the rope tightly. It burns your hands as it passes through them, even through gloves.

You can't hear screams in the rain.

Everyone will say you couldn't have held them up. You'd just have been pulled down to death with them.

It's no comfort.

And so on.

300

You stay in the hut with Thierry. Apart from Tibet, England, family, friends. You don't love them any the less but you do not trouble them.

Your world shrinks to Thierry, the hut, the garden. The money is gone. It means nothing. You wish it well and hope it does some good.

You work and eat and sleep. Every mouthful of food, every moment of comfort, every second of warmth, has to be earned.

At last, you live honestly, with love, with bravery, with joy. Always, you are grateful to your brother for making the path, for understanding first. You are amazed at his generosity in welcoming you.

Alone among the legions of men and women, you understand.

You are truly fortunate.

Only now do you understand this.

Only here do you feel, of all the possible paths you could have taken, that you have really won the Lottery.

Life's Lottery.

ANNOTATIONS

In the early 2000s, I prepared these annotations for an abortive US ebook publication of the novel – they were intended mostly to help Americans with specific British references, so British readers can now chortle at being told things every fule kno. I also include a few notes about the links between *Life's Lottery* and my other books.

KIM NEWMAN

2014

2

The Light Programme
In 1959, BBC Radio broadcast three main channels within the United Kingdom: the Home Service, the Light Programme and the Third Programme. The Light Programme eventually became the channels that are now Radio One and Radio Two, the BBC's pop music stations. The Third Programme became Radio Three, which puts out serious music.

C of E
Church of England. While the American Constitution insists on a separation between church and state, the United Kingdom has no written constitution and the ritual and legal apparatus of the state is inextricably bound up with the Anglican Church. The reason this hasn't led to anything like the Inquisition or witch-burning in the last few hundred years is that Anglicanism has become the mildest, most decaffeinated church on the block. The C of E certainly asserts far less influence on the country – for instance, in terms of pushing through laws or criticising government sponsorship of the arts – than the religious right does in the United States. When I was asked at school to state my religion and I claimed 'agnostic', I was aptly told 'that's C of E then'.

The National Health/National Insurance Number
In the UK, universal health-care is provided by the state, supported by a tax called National Insurance commonly deducted at source from a person's wages. Britons can choose to take out private health-care insurance on the American system, but they still have to pay National Insurance. Just as all Americans have a Social Security number, all Britons have a National Insurance Number.

Daleks
Trundling, squawking cyborg fascist alien villains from the long-running BBC-TV series *Doctor Who*, the Daleks first appeared in the second *Who* serial in 1963 and were an instant success, spawning a ton of various merchandising. They returned many times to the TV series and appeared in two spin-off theatrical films, *Dr Who and the Daleks* and *Daleks – Invasion Earth: 2150 AD*.

Teddy Bear Coalman
'A story for the very young', written and illustrated by Phoebe and Selby Worthington (1948), common in the 1950s and '60s and in print as recently as 1985. In the Newman household, wicked childish amusement was found in interpreting the hand gesture of the woman who wanted *two* bags of coal as the irreverent two-finger sign equivalent to the American single digit salute.

Upside-Down Gonk's Circus
Gonks were a 1960s toy fad: big Humpty Dumpty-shaped heads with tiny vestigial arms and legs, often caricatures of famous persons or specific types (cowboy, spaceman, schoolgirl, etc). They feature in the film *Gonks Go Beat*. Roughly equivalent to Trolls or Cabbage Patch Dolls. *Upside-Down Gonk's Circus* was the most intriguing-sounding of the slim children's books published to go with the craze, or at least so I thought when I pestered my father to buy it. It has stuck in my memory probably because of the odd disappointment of finding that the cover had been mistakenly bound onto another, less-interesting gonk adventure. The Newman copy of *Teddy Bear Coalman* has survived (my sister recently read it to my nephew), but that doubtless-priceless collector's item misprint gonk book disappeared long long ago.

Little Noddy Goes to Toyland
By Enid Blyton, illustrated by Harmsen van der Beel (1949); the actual title is *Noddy Goes to Toyland*, but I copied an error from David Pringle's *Imaginary People*. First of a series of books featuring a wooden gnome called Noddy, these were amazingly popular for decades but have suffered from a backlash thanks to Blyton's use of racial caricature 'gollywogs' as supporting characters, not to mention elements common to children's books in more innocent times like Noddy and his male best friend Big Ears sleeping together and the hero's tendency to get in trouble with Mr Plod the policeman. The term 'Plod' or 'Mr Plod' is still in use as a demeaning

term for police officer, equivalent to the American 'pig'. The reference is here to prevent the book becoming autobiographical – I found Blyton twee and dull as a child and didn't read her much.

The Lion, the Witch and the Wardrobe
By C.S. Lewis (1950); first of the 'Narnia' series.

Winnie the Pooh
By A.A. Milne, illustrated by E.H. Shepherd (1926). In the 1960s, Winnie hadn't been bought outright by Disney and so retained an English accent.

The Big Book of Riddles
There are several books with this title or something close like *The Mighty Big Book of Riddles*. The 'big red rock-eater' riddle is from the one we had in our house, but the 'Letsbe Avenue' riddle is here as a tribute to Paul J. McAuley, who still laughs when he tells it. 'Why do firemen wear red braces?' is another from the original.

The Buccaneers Annual
The Buccaneers was an ambitious British television series originally broadcast in 1956, starring Robert Shaw as Captain Dan Tempest. Because of the pirate theme that runs through *Life's Lottery*, I invented the annual and its contents – though I later found out that the show spun off at least one such tie-in and saw a copy in the collection of the Museum of the Moving Image. Annuals were (and are) a British form of children's publishing, large-format illustrated hardbacks combining text and comic-strip stories (with factual articles, puzzles and the like), associated with a popular character (Popeye), TV series (*Danger Man*) or weekly comic (the *Beano*).

The Secret of the Unicorn and Red Rackham's Treasure
A single comic strip adventure for Hergé's intrepid reporter hero Tintin, published as two large-format albums.

Doctor Who
Long-running UK television serial, premiered 23 November 1963.

William Hartnell
The first *Doctor Who* (1963–66).

Patrick Troughton
The second *Doctor Who* (1966–69).

Jon Pertwee
The third *Doctor Who* (1970–74).

Tom Baker
The fourth *Doctor Who* (1974–81).

TARDIS

Dr Who's time machine; supposedly able to impersonate anything, its 'chameleon circuit' is broken so it always looks like a blue police telephone box. Even in 1963, these phone boxes were disappearing from the landscape as radio-communication between beat officers and patrol cars became more common (another seminal '60s TV show, *Z Cars*, was even about this new form of policing). Eventually, the BBC bought up copyright on the police box design.

Labour and Tory

The two main political parties in Great Britain. The Labour Party grows out of the Trades Union movement and supposedly represents the interests of working people, while the Conservative (or Tory) Party supposedly represents the interests of the middle and upper classes. The Labour Party eclipsed the Liberal Party in the de facto two-party system of the UK; the Liberal Party, evolved from the nineteenth-century Whigs, were marginalised in the 1960s but joined with elements estranged from Labour in the 1980s to form what is now the Liberal Democrat Party (Lib-Dems), a major force in local government if still perennially in third-place in general elections.

Peter Cook

Comedian, humorous writer and media personality (1937–55). In the UK, best-remembered for innovative stage and television work in partnership with Dudley Moore. Like Moore, he shouldn't be judged on the low quality of the Hollywood films he made (cf: *Supergirl*).

Clement Attlee

Labour Prime Minister; defeated Winston Churchill in the first post-war election and established what became known as the welfare state before the phrase had any negative connotations. Attlee's legacy includes the National Health service.

Wilson

Harold Wilson. Labour Prime Minister in the 1960s, famous for wearing raincoats and smoking a pipe. His speech about 'the white heat of technology' was one of the touchstones for the '60s image of a progressive, exciting Britain as represented by Concorde and cross-channel hovercraft. He resisted pressure from America and refused to commit British troops to Vietnam; no prizes for guessing what Tony Blair would have done under the same circumstances.

Margaret Thatcher

Tory Prime Minister from 1979 and throughout the 1980s – therefore a major figure in this book. See notes on the Falklands War, the Miners' Strike, the Big Bang, Black Monday, etc. Succeeded messily in 1990 by John Major.

James Callaghan
Harold Wilson's successor as Labour Prime Minister after Wilson's resignation in 1976. Defeated by Thatcher in 1979, beginning nearly two decades of Tory rule.

David Steel
Leader of the Liberal Party in 1979; later leader of the Liberal Democrats.

Screaming Lord Sutch
Pop star David Sutch, who cut macabre rockin' numbers in the 1960s ('Jack the Ripper', 'She's Fallen in Love With the Monsterman') along the lines of his obvious idol Screamin' Jay Hawkins and later performers like the Cramps. He was for many years a surreal fixture of general elections, standing for the Monster Raving Loony Party (later the *Official* Monster Raving Loony Party). He committed suicide in 1999.

Sedgwater
Other works set in or near this town include the flashback sections of my novel *The Quorum* and the 'Where the Bodies Are Buried' cycle of stories. It's roughly analagous to the real town of Bridgwater. www.bridgwater.net/ and www.users.globalnet.co.uk/~smedlo/Bridgwater/Bridgwater.htm

Somerset
A county in the West of England, known for King Alfred's defence against the invading Danes, Glastonbury (famous for the Tor, a ruined Abbey, the pop festival and John Cowper Powys's novel *A Glastonbury Romance*), a very strong cider, still-surviving novelty band the Wurzels and the birthplace of Sir Arthur C. Clarke.

Paddington Bear
Hero of Michael Bond's *A Bear Called Paddington* (1958) and sequels.

Stingray
Gerry Anderson-produced puppet TV series (1964–65), a half-hour colour show made between Anderson's *Fireball XL5* and *Thunderbirds*. Set in the future, it follows the adventures of Troy Tempest and his sidekick Phones who crewed the wonderfully-designed super-submarine *Stingray*.

Michael Dixon
See also: *The Quorum*.

'Off-ground touch'
A children's game, a variant on 'tag' in which you couldn't be made 'it' if neither of your feet were on the ground.

Israel Hands
A historical character, better known for his walk-on in *Treasure Island*.

The Man From U.N.C.L.E.
US television series, 1964–68; first seen on UK TV June 24, 1965 – which doesn't quite square with the dates here. Then again, Stephen King blithely lies about the US transmission of *The Prisoner* in *Hearts in Atlantis* and apologises in the end-note and nobody writes him whiny letters about it. If anything, the show was *more* popular in the UK than America, perhaps because one of the leads (David McCallum) was British. The BBC screened two seasons of *Man* and one of *The Girl From U.N.C.L.E.* inside a year and a half.

Napoleon Solo or Illya Kuryakin
My friend David Cross told me that gangs really did ask this question on his school playground and beat up kids who gave the wrong answer (which, for the record, was Napoleon Solo). A more common fight-starter was 'who do you support?', meaning which football team – and not following football was no excuse. The reason I fudge the dates is that David is a year or two older than Keith Marion.

3
THRUSH
The recurring villains on *The Man From U.N.C.L.E.*, a bad guy organisation whose name might have been an acronym for Technological Hierarchy for the Repression of Undesirables and the Subjugation of Humanity. Or it could have been a Cold War way of saying 'Th'Russians'.

Shorts and a cardy
Shorts = short trousers, not underpants. Cardy = a cardigan, the woolly garment named after the Crimean War general.

Doctor Who [as 2]

Daleks [as 2]

Janet and John
The UK equivalents of Dick and Jane in reading primers.

Robert Hackwill
See also: the *Where the Bodies Are Buried* collection, which gives more background on his mundane villainy and monstrous reputation.

P.E.
Physical Education = Gym Class.

Biggles
Created by Captain W.E. Johns, James Bigglesworth – Biggles – first appeared in *The Camels Are Coming* (1932), in which he is a fighter pilot in the First World War. Johns wrote nearly a hundred books in which Biggles and his pals flew into dangers in subsequent conflicts and as peacetime adventurers

in the 'air police'. Biggles also appeared in a brief 1960 TV series and a weak 1986 film, but may now be best-remembered for a Monty Python sketch lampooning the jargon-filled 'banter' of Johns's dialogue. The first science fiction novel I remember reading was *Biggles and the Blue Flame*.

Sergeant Rock
DC Comics character, created by artist Joe Kubert and writer Robert Kanigher in 1959. I've always wondered if Kanigher and Kubert were thinking of the same-named character played by Gene Evans in Samuel Fuller's 1951 film *Fixed Bayonets*.

'White Horses' by Jacky
This was the theme to a children's TV series popular with girls in 1968. It was a girl-and-her-horse show. The hit theme song, sung by Jackie Lee under the name 'Jacky', is breathily evocative.

4
Michael Dixon [as 2]

Dan Dare
British comic strip space hero, created by Frank Hampson, featured in the *Eagle* from 1950 to 1957. A square-jawed, crisp-uniformed 'pilot of the future', he is sort of a sexless Battle of Britain version of Flash Gordon; his arch-enemy is a Venusian tyrant called the Mekon.

Hornet
A British weekly comic; unlike American monthly comic books, British comics were until recently newspaper format, unstapled (a nightmare for collectors), mostly in black and white (with a colour cover feature and maybe centre-page spread) and ran multiple ongoing series or serials. The *Hornet* was a rather staid effort concentrating heavily on sports heroes, war stories and imperial adventures.

Fantastic
One of several British black and white weeklies (Power Comics) that reprinted Marvel material, with individual issues parcelled out in five-page sections. *Fantastic* ran X-Men, the Hulk, the Avengers and Thor.

Dr. Marling's
See also: *The Quorum*.

Reg Jessup
See also: 'Where the Bodies Are Buried'.

5
Dr Cross
See: *Jago*. The character is named after the friend of mine who told me the childhood anecdote that inspired the 'Napoleon or Ilya' choice.

Susan
See: *Jago.*

6

A Jag
A Jaguar. With three syllables.

Thatcher [as 2]

The *Scam*
This London listings/alternative magazine also appears in *Bad Dreams* and *The Quorum*. It's roughly analagous to the real-life 1980s publication *City Limits*, which I worked for.

Anne Nielsen
The heroine of *Bad Dreams*; also appears in *The Quorum*. Those books reveal a lot more about the 'complicated pain' in her background.

Clare
Appears briefly in *Bad Dreams*.

The Bay City Rollers
Early 1970s boy band. Remembered for tartan trousers and unfeasable mullets, they mostly covered standards like 'Be My Baby'. Recruited to fit a pre-decided sound (few of the band performed on their first single), they were a forerunner to today's entirely manufactured pop groups. One member of a later incarnation became the British porn star/director Ben Dover.

The Miners' Strike
In 1984–85, this was a major battle between the Trades Union movement and Margaret Thatcher. The strikers were defeated, after much acrimony, and the government set about dismantling the British mining industry. It forms the backdrop to the successful British movie *Billy Elliot*.

Greenham Common Women's Peace Camp
An anti-nuclear weapons protest around an American air base in Britain. It ran from 1981 to 2000.

The *Belgrano*
Argentine warship, controversially sunk by the Royal Navy during the Falklands conflict, prompting the famously tasteless *Sun* newspaper headline 'Gotcha!'

Lord Carrington
Foreign secretary at the time of the invasion of the Falklands. Admitting that he had misjudged the situation leading up to the conflict, he resigned.

Little Jimmy Osmond
Child star of the early 1970s who had a UK hit with 'Long-Haired Lover From Liverpool'. There wasn't a lad in Britain who wouldn't happily have punched him in the face, but our sisters were big fans.

7
Eleven Plus
Until the early 1970s, the British state education system depended on the Eleven Plus exam, which children took in their last year at primary school (ages 6–11). Those who passed went on to grammar schools and those who failed to secondary modern schools; in theory, the former were more academically-inclined and encouraged pupils to go on to further education while the latter were to prepare children – who would probably leave education at sixteen – for life in the workplace. The Eleven Plus was essentially an IQ test, designed to measure aptitude not knowledge – but, of course, the fact that kids sat mock exams in preparation for the Eleven Plus meant that the format could be learned and mastered. Wealthier parents could (and still can) opt out entirely by sending their children to fee-paying schools. The Eleven Plus was theoretically discontinued in the mid-1970s (it still persists in many parts of the country) and grammar and secondary modern schools were amalgamated into comprehensive schools (roughly the equivalent of American high schools), which practice 'streaming' of pupils with different aptitudes under the same roof, without the stigma of labelling two-thirds of them failures at eleven. It could be argued that I am stretching a point in giving Keith the choice of passing or failing, and that the reader should sit an actual exam to decide the rest of the course of his life, but the unacknowledged fact was that most children could be *taught* to pass the Eleven Plus (and weren't). The issues raised here were debated among kids, many of whom (rightly, to my mind) thought grammar school sounded a lot worse than it needed to be. If you want to play fair, you can download the modern Eleven Plus equivalent from www.elevenplus.com/ and see how you do – though this isn't quite what we had to sit in 1970.

Dr Marling's Grammar School for Boys [as 4]

Rugby
Rugby is a contact sport resembling American football, only British boys don't feel the need to wear all that sissy protective gear when playing it.

Football
Football in Britain = soccer or association football.

Robert Hackwill [as 3]

Prefect
At grammar schools, certain boys or girls in the upper sixth form (the equivalent of seniors in America) were invested with powers as prefects – rather like trusties in prisons or kapos in concentration camps. In the

1970s, outside the private school system, prefects couldn't inflict corporal punishment, though they were entrusted with the power of dishing out other punishments to younger kids.

Tintin
Reporter hero of a series of comic-strip albums by the Belgian cartoonist Hergé.

Jennings
Schoolboy hero of Anthony Buckeridge's novels for children, from *Jennings Goes to School* (1950) onwards. The character debuted on BBC Radio in 1948.

Billy Bunter
Created by author Frank Richards in 1908, Billy Bunter – 'the fat owl of the remove' – was the break-out character of a series of stories published in the periodical *The Magnet* about the fictional Greyfriars School. Part of his appeal was that, unlike the straight-arrow decent sorts who were the heroes of the series (and who seem insufferably priggish), Bunter was gluttonous, cowardly, devious and feckless. Bunter appeared in novels until the mid-60s, and paperback reprints were still read by children well into the 1970s, though the Edwardian public school setting had become bizarrely alien.

Chalet School
A series of girls' school stories written by Eleanor Brent-Dyer, first published between 1925 and 1970. If you think the worlds of Greyfriars and Chalet School, and the numberless other boarding school adventures published in the twentieth century, are gone forever, consider that J.K. Rowling is writing essentially the same stuff. If Keith and Vanda were eleven now, they'd be reading Harry Potter.

10
A Jag [as 6]

Pointing percy at the porcelain
Hackwill is indicating that he needs to urinate.

The bog
The men's room.

The National Lottery
UK institution, a national random-number prize-draw. Government-sponsored, it raises money that is theoretically ploughed into good works.

11
Marie-Laure Quilter
Also appears in *Jago*.

The Bash Street Kids in *The Beano*
Naughty children in a popular comic-strip created by Leo Baxendale. *The Beano* was, and still is, a British weekly comic specialising in irreverent humour.

Bottoms Up!
Spun-off from the 1950s TV series *Whack-O!* which had a brief 1970s revival, this peculiarly British 1959 school comedy did indeed feature an emphasis on corporal punishment jokes.

Jimmy Edwards
Moustachioed British comedian, usually seen as a schoolmaster, RAF officer or other silly-ass, pompous, inept Establishment figure.

The Streak
Less familiar than DC's Batman or Marvel's Doctor Strange, the Streak is the speedster superhero mainstay of comics published by ZC Comics, a company which features in *The Quorum*. My short story 'Coastal City' (www.johnnyalucard.com/coastal.html) is set in the ZC Comics universe.

Denbeigh Gardens
See: 'Where the Bodies Are Buried'.

12
Rugby [as 7]

Top of the Pops
Long-running BBC1 pop music programme (started 1964, still airing), roughly the equivalent of *American Bandstand*.

Softly, Softly: Task Force
A BBC-TV police series (1966–76). It spun off from *Z-Cars* (1962–78) and starred Stratford Johns and Frank Windsor as hard-man superintendent Charlie Barlow and his milder sidekick Watts. Rough American equivalents would be *Kojak* or *The Streets of San Francisco*.

Michael Dixon, Amphlett, Martin, Skelly and Yeo
See *The Quorum* for another account of this period, focusing on these characters.

'Chimp' Quinlan
Also appears in *The Quorum*.

A Levels
Exams taken at seventeen or eighteen. Admission into a university (or, in the 1970s, a polytechnic) usually depends on grades earned in A Levels.

Sindy doll
British equivalent of Barbie. In the earlier version of *Life's Lottery*, I misspelled it Cindy – which is what you get when boys write about such things.

The Glastonbury Festival
Annual event held since 1970 at Mike Eavis's farm near the village of Pilton, near but not in the town of Glastonbury.

Oxford entrance exams
A Level results aren't enough to get into Oxford or Cambridge universities; prospective students have to sit further exams set by those universities, though admission also depends on performance in interview.

14

A Jag [as 6]

General Galtieri
Argentine dictator, invader of the Falkland Islands.

Victoria Cross
Britain's highest military decoration.

Take an early bath
A British sporting expression: in rugby or football, a player sent off the pitch by the referee after foul play is said to take an early bath because he gets to the showers before his team-mates.

Yomp
Royal Marine slang for forced march over rough terrain.

Captain Blood
Pirate hero of the novel by Rafael Sabatini; coincidentally, Dr Peter Blood is transported to the West Indies as a convict for treating men wounded in the Battle of Sedgmoor, the climax of the ill-fated Monmouth Rebellion – which took place very near the locale of this novel.

Seaman Staines
A persistent schoolboy joke has it that the children's TV cartoon *Captain Pugwash* series features characters with *double entendre* names like 'Seaman Staines', 'Master Bates' and 'Roger the Cabin Boy'. This is not the case.

Mr Smee
Captain Hook's mate in J.M. Barrie's *Peter Pan*.

Anne Bonney
Female pirate, glamourised in the film *Anne of the Indies*.

Katie Reed
Katharine, Kate or Katie Reed. A character Bram Stoker intended to put in his novel *Dracula*, she didn't make the final draft but I put her in my novel *Anno Dracula*. She takes a leading role in the follow-ups *The Bloody Red Baron*, *Dracula Cha Cha Cha* (aka Judgment of Tears) and 'Coppola's Dracula', and also appears in the story cycle *Seven Stars*.

Discount Development
A major thread in the plot of my story 'Where the Bodies Are Buried'.

Sutton Mallet
You can find this on a map of Somerset. It also features, in ominous context, in my novels *The Quorum* and *An English Ghost Story*.

15
Captain Scarlet
Captain Scarlet and the Mysterons (1967–68), the last great Gerry Anderson puppet show.

16
'Bobby Moore says "smoking is a mugs' game"'
This slogan ran in ads printed in British children's comics. Bobby Moore was the captain of England's World Cup-winning football team in 1966. He died of bowel cancer in his early fifties.

18
Jason King
A TV detective, famous for his flamboyant dress sense and moustache, Jason King was played by Peter Wyngarde; he was introduced in the series *Department S* (1969–70) and continued his adventures in the spin-off *Jason King* (1971–72). It's possible that his clothes were influenced by the fact that colour television was just becoming popular in the UK, and his shirts were a personal challenge to any slightly-mistuned set.

19
Victoria Conyer
Also appears in *The Quorum*.

O Level
Exams taken in the 1970s by UK grammar school-children at sixteen. Kids who went to a secondary modern took different exams called CSEs. In comprehensive schools, there were O (Ordinary) level and CSE (Certificate of Secondary Education) streams. The inevitable effect of this is that pupils, employers and civilians looked at CSEs as lesser qualifications, though the schools insisted this wasn't the case. A certain number of passes at O level were necessary to qualify to stay on another two years and take A (Advanced) Level exams. Now, the whole system has been amalgamated and British children all take one set of exams

called GCSEs (General Certificate of Secondary Education). It is an often-heard grumble from members of Keith's generation when new record-breaking GCSE and A Level results are announced every year that exams were more difficult back in the 1970s. Then again, the same people claim Mars bars were more chocolatey, pop songs had proper lyrics and all these computers and internet doodads will lead to no good at all.

'The long, hot summer of 1976'
A famous sunstruck spell, leading to drought, hosepipe bans, phew-what-a-scorcher tabloid headlines and Mediterranean sleeping arrangements.

Reading geography
ie: Geography is her Major.

Candy Dixon
Also appears briefly in *The Quorum*.

Wells
A medium-sized town or small city in Somerset. It does have a cathedral, and it's generally assumed that the presence of a cathedral is what separates a city from a town.

Rag Day
A tradition in UK colleges and universities (where it often stretches to Rag Week) in which students do strange things to collect money for charity, often as a license for larkish behaviour. Men dressing up in drag is a tiresomely common feature. A certain amount of anarchy is expected. If it sounds ridiculous and annoying, remember British educational establishments have no tradition of fraternities or sororities, hence no hazing. At least, Rag Day – unlike Hell Night – isn't an excuse to torture other students and contributes something to a good cause.

Penny Gaye
Also appears in *The Quorum*.

21

The assassination attempt on Governor George Wallace
This took place in 1972, and was heavily covered by UK TV news.

10cc's 'Rubber Bullets'
A UK Number One hit in 1973. Though a pastiche of the 'Jailhouse Rock'/'Riot in Cell Block Number 9'-style American prison song, it had a special resonance in Britain thanks to the controversial use of rubber bullets by the security forces in Belfast. In the song, Sergeant Baker breaks up the hop at the local county jail; his line is 'I love to hear these convicts squeal, it's a shame these slugs ain't real'.

The bald coon
Woody Strode as Pompey. Shamefully, this is exactly the sort of language schoolboys in Somerset used in the early 1970s; most of them had never met a black person.

A gasper
UK slang: cigarette

Fags
UK slang: cigarettes

'Bobby Moore says "smoking is a mugs' game"' [as 16]

23
Certificate of Secondary Education
Exams taken in the 1970s by UK secondary modern school-children at sixteen. Kids who went to grammar schools took different exams called O Levels. In comprehensive schools, there were O (Ordinary) Level and CSE (Certificate of Secondary Education) streams. The inevitable effect of this is that pupils, employers and civilians looked at CSEs as lesser qualifications, though the schools insisted this wasn't the case. A certain number of passes at O level were necessary to qualify to stay on another two years and take A (Advanced) Level exams. Now, the whole system has been amalgamated and British children all take one set of exams called GCSEs (General Certificate of Secondary Education). It is an often-heard grumble from members of Keith's generation when new record-breaking GCSE and A Level results are announced every year that exams were more difficult back in the 1970s.

Brinks' Café
Site of an important treaty in *The Quorum*.

Superhero panels drawn by Mickey Yeo
For more on Mickey's comics career, see *The Quorum*.

24
Manchester Poly
Ie: Manchester Polytechnic. In the 1970s, British institutions of higher education came in several forms: universities were considered to be more academic in inclination, while polytechnics were supposedly more practical but also easier to get into. At a stroke, some years later, all polytechnics were turned into universities; which is why many towns now have two or more universities.

The Shape
Mark's magazine features in *The Quorum*.

Poll-tax riot
The Tory government's replacement of a local tax based on property values

with the 'community charge' in the early 1990s was extremely unpopular, triggering a wave of unrest – including protest marches which became unruly and were inevitably tagged 'riots' by the press – that led eventually to Margaret Thatcher's fall from power. The poll tax was quietly scrapped and replaced by a variation on the old rates system.

Marcos
Ferdidand Marcos, dictator. His wife Imelda was famous for the amount of money she spent on shoes.

Live Aid
Organised by rock star Bob Geldof in 1985, this was a huge concert (rather, series of concerts around the world) staged to raise money for African famine relief. It also revived the careers of some fading performers.

25
Slide-rule
plastic calculating aide, rendered obsolete by pocket calculators.

26
Carrie
The 1976 film was very popular with British teenagers, as much for its depiction of the alien rituals of Americans of the same age as the horror stuff.

27
Supplementary benefit
Roughly the equivalent of welfare; now known as 'income support'. Unemployment benefit (the dole) was available only to people who had been in work. Those who had never been employed weren't eligible. The system has changed, and it is now much harder for a school-leaver or recent graduate to get benefits.

Easy Rider
Was reissued in the UK the mid-1970s on a double bill with *Midnight Cowboy*.

Approved school
Old joke: 'the school I went to was so good that it was *approved*. As much a penal as an educational institution, approved schools were for young offenders who needed straightening out. An American kid as uncontrollable as Tony Bennett might get sent to military school.

Dinner tickets
Vouchers, purchased on a weekly basis, for meals in the school cafeteria. Inevitably, also a form of currency among kids. In the 1970s, more schools provided meals than is now the case.

28

Neil Martin
His subsequent misfortunes are extensively covered in *The Quorum*.

Like Morticia Addams gone punk
The term 'goth' wasn't in much use then; my nomination for first-ever goth is Vivian Darkbloom (Marianne Stone) from the Stanley Kubrick film *Lolita*.

Under-age drinking
In Britain, licensed premises are supposed not to sell alcoholic beverages to anyone under eighteen. However, UK citizens are not required to carry identity cards, driving licenses or any other form of identification listing a date of birth, so the matter of whether a drinker is of age is down to the snap judgement of the bar staff. Like the 18 certificate for films (an X certificate in the 1970s), it is generally if unofficially accepted that seventeen or even sixteen-year-olds will pass.

'Wide-Eyed and Legless'
A hit for Andy Fairweather-Low, popular with 1970s drunks.

Theme from *Scooby Doo, Where Are You*
Available on: www.telesearch.org/themesonline/index.htm

Beecham's Powders
A soluble cold medicine.

Bell's
A brand of whisky.

29

Signing on
Claiming supplementary benefit (welfare).

Job Centre
Government-run employment agency.

Sally Army
The Salvation Army, who operate a chain of charity shops.

The long, hot summer of 1976 [as 19]

Giro
Welfare cheque (or check).

Department of Health and Social Security
The DHSS, the government department concerned with health and

welfare. This has now been reorganised, and the relevant initials are DSS for Department of Social Security.

Doctor Who [as 2]

DIY
Do-it-yourself; home improvement handicrafts.

The Beatles' *Double White*
The White Album. It's not true, apparently, that Charles Manson was a big fan; in an interview, he said he was a child of the 1940s and preferred Bing Crosby.

Pissed
Drunk, not angry – in the UK 'pissed off' means what Americans mean by 'pissed'.

30
Neil Martin [as 28]

'Where Do You Go to My Lovely?'
Horrible Peter Sarsted hit from 1969, abused by buskers and entry-level guitar-players almost as often as 'House of the Rising Sun' and 'Streets of London'.

Under-age drinking [as 28]

Rum and black
Rum and blackcurrant juice. Go on, try it, why don't you?

Womble
Troll-like furry creature from the children's TV series *The Wombles*. They had a couple of hit records ('Remember You're a Womble', 'Wombling White Tie and Tails') and a feature film spin-off, *Wombling Free*.

Slag
UK slang: slut, girl of easy virtue.

Tight
UK slang: a girl who refuses to have sex.

Three-piece suites
A sofa and two armchairs; in the 1970s, probably with an eye-abusing orange-yellow pattern fabric cover.

31
'Kites', by Simon Dupree and the Big Sound
A hit in 1967, memorable for the Japanese-language spoken word section.

UB40s
The flimsy card document presented at the DHSS by claimants for Unemployment or Supplementary Benefit. The band UB40 took their name from the thing.

Petrol station
A gas station, garage.

32

Glastonbury Festival [as 12]

Margaret Thatcher [as 2]

Alan Moore
British comics writer: *Watchmen, From Hell*, etc.

Frank Miller Jr.
US comics writer-artist: *Daredevil, The Dark Knight Returns*, etc.

Stan Lee and Jack Kirby
Co-creators of many Marvel Comics characters in the early 1960s.

New Robin
Dick Grayson grew up and became Nightwing, so Batman took on a new Robin, street kid Jason Todd. The character was disliked by many fans and killed off by the Joker after a mildly distasteful phone-poll as to whether he should live or die. DC later brought in yet another new Robin, Tim Drake.

The names of all the Tracy Brothers
From *Thunderbirds*. Scott, Virgil, Alan, Gordon and John.

Hector's House
Children's TV show. Hector was a dog. Originally a French production, entitled *La Maison de Touton*, it was dubbed into English by, among others, Joanna Lumley.

Play School
Children's TV show.

Going 'through the round window'.
A catch-phrase from *Play School*.

Sutton Mallet [as 14]

The three-day week
An emergency measure taken during the oil crisis of 1972–73; it didn't mean shortening the calendar week, but the working week.

The Ulster troubles
From 1969 on, friction between the Catholic and Protestant communities in Northern Ireland, terrorist campaigns on behalf of both factions, and the deployment of troops on the streets of Belfast.

A Mivvi and a Sky Ray lolly
Types of popsicle.

Blue bags of salt
Smith's Crisps (potato chips in the US) used to be sold unsalted, and you had to shake salt into them from a little blue bag.

Mud
Early 1970s British chart band, yobbish glam in character. Hits: 'Tiger Feet', 'The Cat Crept In'.

The Bay City Rollers [as 6]

The Osmonds
Mormon boy-band of the early 1970s. UK hit: 'Crazy Horses'.

Top of the Pops compilations
Not related to the BBC chart music show, but LP collections of soundalike cover versions of recent hits marketed – as specified – with smiling pin-up girls in weird outfits on the sleeve.

Dolly mixture
Licorice-based sweets (candies) which came in several varieties.

Biggles [as 3]

Aurora glow-in-the-dark monster models
Known as 'hobby kits' in America, these representations of the classic Universal monsters (Dracula, the Wolf Man, etc.) mixed with odder characters (the Witch, the Forgotten Prisoner) were commonplace in the UK in the early 1970s. '60s editions were just plastic, but 1970s variants ('frightening lightning strikes!') had luminous heads, hands and accessories.

Dinky toys
Model cars and other vehicles.

Aston Martin
One of the most popular toys of the 1960s, but the gun-pointing minion who could be ejected from the car at a flick of a switch did tend to get lost over the years.

Campaign
A 1970s strategy-based board game with a Napoleonic theme.

Top of the Pops [as 12]

Telegraph
The *Daily Telegraph*, a conservative (and Conservative) newspaper.

Nescafé
A brand of instant coffee.

33
Oxford entrance exams [as 12]

Dave Tamlyn's chunder-up record
Chunder or chunder-up, UK slang = to vomit. Dave Tamlyn is now a book-seller in London; his record was actually set at my twenty-first birthday party, a few years after this scene is set. It remains unbroken.

34
Margaret Thatcher [as 2]

Snowdonia
Mountainous region in Wales.

DIY [as 29]

Sutton Mallet [as 14]

Social Democrat
Breakaway faction formed by right-leaning members of the Labour Party; later amalgamated with the Liberal party to become the Liberal Democrats.

The Grand National
A major horse-race.

36
Scrumpy
A rough, strong cider, associated with Somerset.

'See My Baby Jive'
A 1973 hit for Wizzard.

'Sharing a stick of gum'
This expression comes from a *MAD Magazine* joke.

Sutton Mallet turn-off
For a good reason not to take this, see *The Quorum*.

38
Tipp-ex

A brand of typewriter correction fluid or liquid paper. Now obsolete.

39

'Nights in White Satin'
A 1967 hit for the Moody Blues.

40

Pazuzu
The Assyrian wind demon in *The Exorcist*.

'Nellie the Elephant'
A children's song from the 1950s, recorded by Mandy Miller.

'I Am an Antichrist'
First line of 'Anarchy in the UK' by the Sex Pistols.

Uncle Mac and *Junior Choice*
Uncle Mac (Derek McCullogh) was the host of the children's radio request program *Junior Choice*, a BBC institution for decades. Many of the staples of his playlist are available on the *Hello Children, Everywhere* CD compilations.

'Three Wheels on My Wagon"
A novelty record by the New Christy Minstrels.

'How Much is That Doggy in the Window?'
'Ruff-Ruff, the one with the waggly tail.' A much-covered children's song, the *Junior Choice* favourite version was by Lita Roza.

'She Loves You, Yeah Yeah Yeah'
By The Beatles, who were a popular beat combo of the 1960s, m'lud.

'Satisfaction'
By the Rolling Stones. G.I.s in Vietnam swore Aretha Franklin's version was the superior.

'I'm Not in Love'
By 10cc; maudlin pop hit, often played at the end of school discos in the 1970s.

'Hi-Ho Silver Lining'
By Jeff Beck. The 1970s DJ trick was to turn the sound off for the chorus and have the dancers raucously fill in. Don't you wish you could travel back in time with an Uzi?

41

Braces
Suspenders.

BUPA

A private health insurance firm, like an American HMO; the impression given by their adverts is that BUPA hospitals and doctors are far more efficient, luxurious and personal than the National Health.

42
Pepé le Pew
Ze cartoon skunk formidable.

46
V sign
A reverse 'V for victory' sign, the two-fingered fuck-off salute, equivalent to the American single finger.

'Love is…'
First syndicated in 1970, these little singleton cartoons by Kim Casali – more recently, by the creator's son Stefano – depict a strangely naked child-adult couple, with the sentence completed by some example of everyday devotion and cuteness.

47
Keith Wilson, manager
Vanda is thinking of 'A. Wilson, Manager', a poignant episode of the classic UK sit-com *Dad's Army*.

48
Michael Moorcock paperbacks
Even then, the Moorcock back catalogue was extensive.

Map of Middle Earth
The first drip of an eventual merchandising tidal wave, this modest one-sheet cleared the way for posters, t-shirts, action figures, mugs, tattoo transfers, lunchboxes, etc.

Fabulous Furry Freak Brothers
Underground comix characters lampooning hippies; much-loved by same. Created by Gilbert Shelton.

Rizla
A brand of cigarette papers for roll-your-own enthusiasts. The cardboard packets they come in are more often torn up and used as roach-filters than any other commodity on the planet.

51
'Bobby Moore says "smoking is a mug's game"' [as 16]

Thunderbird 2
Large green, vaguely maternal Thunderbird, piloted by Virgil Tracy. Models of it have pods which are useful for hiding things in.

'Calling International Rescue'
Catch-phrase from the Gerry Anderson show, *Thunderbirds*.

Drongo
Australian slang: idiot.

Light the blue touch paper and retire
The instruction printed on Standard brand fireworks. After decades of jokes at the expense of this somewhat prissily ambiguous warning, the wording has now been updated to 'Light the blue touch paper and stand well back'.

53

Jubilee year
1977 was the twenty-fifth anniversary of the accession of Queen Elizabeth II; in theory, it was celebrated throughout the land with patriotic street parties, but in retrospect the most memorable contributions to the event were the Sex Pistols' 'God Save the Queen' and Derek Jarman's film *Jubilee*. I've still got a Jubilee paperweight in use as a doorstop.

A Levels [as 12]

Wireless
In 1979, not yet an outmoded synonym for radio.

They call themselves the Quorum
For more on this, see *The Quorum* – obviously.

The Interregnum
1649–60; the period between the execution of Charles I and the Restoration of the Monarchy with the accession of Charles II. The English Civil War *was* on the A Level history syllabus in 1977.

They don't know what waits in the shadows.
But they find out in *The Quorum*.

54

Radio Times
The BBC's TV and radio listings magazine; in 1977, it only carried listings for BBC channels, but deregulation means that it now – like its ITV competitor the *TV Times* and several other publications – carries listings for many UK terrestrial and cable-digital-satellite channels. It still publishes a double issue to cover the Christmas-New Year period.

Jim Rockford
James Garner in the TV series *The Rockford Files*. Probably more responsible than anyone else for the popularisation of the telephone-answering machine, though he only ever seemed to get bad news on his.

Imaginary stories
DC calls them 'Elseworlds' now, and Clark and Lois *are* married in current continuity.

Lemsip
A lemon-flavoured cold cure.

UCCA
Universities Central Council on Admissions. Instead of applying individually to multiple universities, English students in the late 1970s filled in a single form which was processed by this body.

55
Judi, Coral, Nina
All appear in *Bad Dreams*.

The Big Bang of 1986
Among the changes to the laws governing the stock market in the UK, the 'Big Bang' included an end to the system of fixed commission for traders, the opening up of stock exchange investments to non-members and the abolition of the Independent Certification System. The changes were a reaction to the increasing globalisation of the money market and the upshot was an influx of new investors, more cutthroat competition and a more extreme boom-and-bust economy.

The City
At once a physical area, the City of London, and a term for London considered as a money and securities market.

Council estates
The rough UK equivalent of American housing projects.

Derek Leech
See: 'The Original Dr Shade', 'SQPR', 'Organ Donors', *The Quorum*, *Seven Stars*, 'Going to Series', 'Where the Bodies Are Buried'.

56
The Lanes
A warren-like area of Brighton; in 1977, full of gift shops and antiques places.

Evening Argus
The Brighton local paper.

The Big Bang of 1986 [as 55]

The City [as 55]

Derek Leech [as 55]

57
Wetland
The Somerset Levels, mostly moorland reclaimed from marshland by drainage schemes.

Glastonbury Tor
A tower atop an artifical hillock; a notable feature of the county.

60
'There are rules'
Cf: James Stewart in *The Philadelphia Story*.

Oxford entrance exam [as 12]

Flash Gordon serial
'Flaming Torture' is Episode Six of *Flash Gordon* (1936).

Spectrum Pursuit Vehicle
From the Gerry Anderson TV series *Captain Scarlet and the Mysterons*. Spectrum, the colour-themed good-guy organisation, had SPVs stashed in hiding all over the world and Captain Scarlet could make use of them if necessary.

61
CND
Campaign for Nuclear Disarmament.

E
Ecstasy.

WPC
Woman Police Constable.

Danegeld
A form of tribute/protection money paid by Saxons to mediaeval Danes in return for not being invaded, raped and pillaged.

DIY [as 29]

63
They call themselves the Quorum [as 53]

64
Derek Leech [as 55]

Heather Wilde
See *The Quorum*, 'Going to Series'.

65

Les Mains sales
A play by Jean-Paul Sartre.

Mademoiselle Quelou

Has a tiny appearance in *Time and Relative*. Not to be confused with the character played by porn star Selen in Asia Argento's autobiographical film *Scarlet Diva*, though I assume we both took the name from French filmmaker Quelou Parente (*Marquis de Slime*).

66

Jobsearch

A peculiarly 1990s bit of newspeak renamed the unemployed 'job-seekers'.

Negative equity

When the worth of your house plunges but you're still having to pay off the inflated price you paid for it.

Work experience

A scheme whereby students spend time in an office or place of employment, not actually having a job but doing menial chores in the hope that the habit of work will rub off on them.

Billy Bunter [as 7]

Postal order

A piece of scrip convertible into cash at a post office; now obsolete. Billy Bunter was always borrowing money and promising to pay it back when his postal order arrived – but it never did.

Sellotape

UK equivalent of Scotch tape.

Take the money, open the box

In the ITV game show *Take Your Pick* (1955–68), contestants eventually had to choose between taking the money they had already won and taking a mystery prize in a box which could be valuable or worthless. The studio audience would compete to shout advice, 'take the money' or 'open the box'. Hosted first by Michael Miles, this was the first UK gameshow to give away cash prizes. You can see why the reference fits into this novel.

The Cob at Lyme Regis

The distinctive stone harbour; it's a key location in the film and book of *The French Lieutenant's Woman*. John Fowles turns up in his own novel towards the end to toss a coin in order to decide which of the endings you read first.

A pound of flesh
Besides referencing *The Merchant of Venice*, this evokes the Vincent Price film *Theater of Blood* to anyone my age, referring to the death of the character played by Harry Andrews. 'It must be Lionheart, only he would have the temerity to rewrite Shakespeare.'

Club Whoopee, Rio de Janiero
A joke from MAD Magazine; Club Whoopee was the name of an early 1980s cabaret band I was in.

The Black Museum
Scotland Yard's collection of gruesome murder weapons and other macabre evidence. See the movie *Horrors of the Black Museum* – the most famous item is the trick binoculars with spikes that plunge into the user's eyes when the focus is adjusted.

Magic Marker
A brand of thick felt-tipped pen.

Patrick McGoohan
Special Guest Murderer on *Columbo* as often as Robert Culp. See the episodes: 'By Dawn's Early Light', 'Identity Crisis', 'Agenda for Murder' and 'Ashes to Ashes'.

Avon and Somerset
At one point, a redrawing of the county boundaries in the west of England created a new administrative entity called Avon in the north of the ancient county of Somerset around the city of Bristol. This was vaguely rescinded later, but the police force of the area remains the Avon and Somerset Constabulary.

67
Biro
Ball-point pen.

J Cloth
A brand of disposable kitchen towel.

Tony Blair
Labour Prime Minister.

Jeffrey Archer
Tory politician and schlock novelist; part of his self-generated myth is that he sank enormously into debt and wrote the best-seller *Not a Penny More Not a Penny Less* in order to escape. A few years after this, he went to jail for perjuring himself in order to win a big-money libel suit.

Reggie Perrin
Created by novelist David Nobbs in *The Death of Reginald Perrin* (1975),

this character became a national institution after Leonard Rossiter played him in the TV series *The Fall and Rise of Reginald Perrin* (1976). Perrin fakes a suicide and starts life over again, rather like Flitcroft in *The Maltese Falcon*. 'Doing a Reggie' became police slang for this scam.

John Stonehouse
A former Labour cabinet minister in the Wilson government, Stonehouse saw a series of businesses collapse in the 1970s and perpetrated several major frauds. In 1974, he left his clothes on a Miami beach to give the impression that he had committed suicide and fled to Australia on a fake passport. He was later arrested, convicted and jailed.

A pound of flesh [as 66]

Sellotape [As 66]

Postman Pat
Created by writer John Cunliffe and developed for television by Ivor Wood, Postman Pat is a British children's character, an idealised version of a Royal Mail delivery person.

'Nellie the Elephant' [as 40]

70
DSS payment
UK equivalent of a welfare cheque.

Sainsbury's
A supermarket chain.

The Teletubbies
Very popular UK TV kids' characters, controversial in America because it was assumed the one with a handbag might be gay.

Crackerjack
Popular BBC-TV children's show of the 1960s; it always begun with the announcement 'It's Friday... it's five o'clock... it's time for *Crackerjack*'. Imagine a more educational *Krusty the Klown*.

Sellotape [as 66]

Magic Markers [as 66]

Thunderbirds
Gerry Anderson puppet series.

Skippy, the Bush Kangaroo
Australian TV series, imported to Britain in the 1960s, well before

Australian soaps (*Neighbours*, *Home and Away*) began to fill in odd, popular hours of British air-time.

Plasticine
UK equivalent of silly putty.

April Dancer
Yes, there was a third choice I forgot to mention earlier. Though Mary Ann Mobley was cast in the role in a *Man From U.N.C.L.E.* episode/backdoor pilot, April Dancer was played by Stefanie Powers in a brief run of *The Girl From U.N.C.L.E.*

71

The Champions
Unsuccessful ITV adventure series (1968–69) about secret agents who gained mild mystic powers in Tibet.

Space Kidettes
A 1966 Hanna-Barbera cartoon series.

Cup-a-Soup
Instant soup product.

74

A Levels [as 12]

The *Herald*
The local paper. See 'Where the Bodies Are Buried 3: Black and White and Red All Over'.

77

Never Mind the Bollocks
By the Sex Pistols.

A Day in Marineville
A tie-in with the Gerry Anderson TV show *Stingray*.

78

NME
The *New Musical Express*; in the 1970s, much more than a pop music paper.

Launderette
UK equivalent of laundromat.

Doesn't compute
Catch-phrase from *Lost in Space*.

Bender

A type of plastic sleeping bag/cocoon, much in use at Greenham Common Women's Peace Camp.

The Exorcism
Perhaps the single most frightening TV hour of the 1970s, this play by Don Taylor was broadcast in a series called *Dead of Night*. Taylor's script was briefly a West End theatre production in 1975, and the four-hander has often been done in little theatre ever since.

Habitat
Terence Conran's chain of upscale furniture and household goods stores.

Betamax
The loser's home video, though many maintain its technical superiority over VHS to this day.

'Super Trouper'
A hit for Abba.

80
Batcave
Under Stately Wayne Manor, the HQ of Batman and Robin.

WPC [as 61]

Sedgwater *Herald* [as 74]

Care-in-the-community
A 1980s scheme whereby patients with mental illness were released from institutions, theoretically to be looked after by relatives or social workers; in effect, a collection of disturbed individuals were thrown onto their own devices.

A Rambo band
A headband, like that worn by Sylvester Stallone in the *Rambo* films. The film director Richard Stanley started wearing hats because he deemed the headband fashion no longer acceptable after it had been usurped by Stallone.

Nescafé [as 32]

The Archers
'An everyday story of country folk'; from 1950 onwards, BBC Radio's longest-running soap opera. The daily instalments are edited together and repeated on a Sunday morning.

Two-Way Family Favourites
Originally *Forces Favourites*, this wartime BBC Radio request music

programme continued into the 1970s. It was specifically for the families of those serving overseas in the armed forces.

Round the Horne
A seminal 1960s BBC Radio comedy show, hosted by Kenneth Horne. Best-remembered for Kenneth Williams and Hugh Paddick's use of gay slang in the 'Julian and Sandy' sketches.

The Clitheroe Kid
A BBC Radio sit-com (1957–72), in which middle-aged but diminutive comedian Jimmy Clitheroe played a naughty schoolboy. In retrospect, vaguely disturbing.

Down Your Way
Long-running and excruciating BBC Radio show (first broadcast in 1946) in which a smug presenter visited a region of Britain, interviewed various locals about their work and played a piece of music they selected. Week after week, we hoped some old lady who made corn dollies in Little Whumpington would request 'Fuck Like a Beast'.

Sing Something Simple
1959–2001. A program of easy listening favourites performed in surreally somnolent style by the Cliff Adams Singers.

Gardeners' Question Time
Originally entitled *How Does Your Garden Grow?*, this was first broadcast in 1947 and continues to this day. Nobody ever asks the team of experts about growing marijuana.

The God slot
Early Sunday evening prime-time on BBC1, usually occupied by *Songs of Praise* or the like.

Mary's little cousin Beth
Appears briefly in *Jago*. In the *Where the Bodies Are Buried* stories, she is revealed to be a serial killer.

Andrew Lloyd-Webber
Composer of long-running musical stage shows; one of those enormously successful people whose output no one will own up to liking.

PG Tips
Brand of tea, long-promoted on television by cheerful chimpanzees.

81
Jubilee [as 53]

85

Survival Kit
See also: 'Organ Donors'.

The *Guardian*
Leftish-leaning daily paper, aka the *Manchester Guardian*.

The *Statesman*
The *New Statesman*. A weekly political periodical with a left-wing slant.

Privatisation
The process, pioneered by the Thatcher government, of selling off state services and industries into private ownership. Caricatured as 'selling off the family silver', this contributed to the bubble economy of the 1980 and, arguably, the lower quality of public services like transport and the utilities.

Poll tax [as 24]

Margaret Thatcher [as 2]

John Smith
Briefly leader of the Labour Party, his death made way for the accession of Tony Blair as party leader and eventually prime minister.

Tony Blair [as 67]

New Labour
Like a detergent, the Labour Party successfully rebranded itself as New Labour in the mid-1990s.

The Spice Girls
Female pop group.

Syreeta
Appears in *Jago*. This is an alternate timeline to that.

Derek Leech [as 55]

Leech's *Comet*
The newspaper features in 'The Original Dr Shade', 'Organ Donors', *The Quorum* and 'Where the Bodies Are Buried 3: Black and White and Red All Over'.

The National Lottery [as 10]

National Lottery Live
The telecast prize draw.

Anthea Turner, Dale Winton, Bob Monkhouse, Carol Smillie
Presenters of the *Lottery* draw on television.

Mystic Meg
'Psychic' whose predictions about the winners are used to pad out the *National Lottery* draw show.

Simon Mayo's Confessions
At the time when this scene is set, the show on before the Lottery draw on BBC1.

87
The *Independent*
Youngest of the UK's daily broadsheet papers.

Great Shades of Elvis!
Perry White's catchphrase on the 1990s show *Lois and Clark: The New Adventures of Superman*.

97
A Levels [as 12]

98
Blood From the Mummy's Tomb
A 1972 Hammer horror film. It features a living, bleeding severed hand and plenty of torn-out throats. Before you do the research, I think I mention it for its associations, not because it actually was on television that evening.

104
Mademoiselle Quelou [as 65]

105
Plasticine [as 70]

Eleven Plus [as 7]

106
Genesis
You *know* he thinks the band sound better with Phil Collins.

107
Tintin [as 7]

108
PE [as 3]

Sedgwater Herald [as 74]

109
NHS
National Health Service.

110
The *Independent* [as 87]

Hello!
Celebrity-focused magazine, obsessed with anodyne gossip. Mild-mannered equivalent of a US supermarket tabloid.

111
Summer of 1976 [as 19]

Amazon Queen
Superheroine staple of the ZC Comics universe. Mickey Yeo kills her in *The Quorum*.

Margaret Thatcher [as 2]

112
Noel's House Party
BBC1 Saturday evening show in the 1990s, hosted by Noel Edmonds, who played purportedly humorous practical jokes on minor celebs and members of the public who then had to pretend to be amused. Spun off the unaccountably-popular pretend children's TV character Mr Blobby. Its popularity was almost certainly a sign of the apocalypse.

Gladiators
The UK version of *American Gladiators*.

EastEnders
The BBC's long-running TV soap.

One Foot in the Grave
Sit-com about a curmudgeonly old git.

The Avengers
The ITV surreal thriller series, not the Marvel Comic.

National Lottery [as 10]

Anthea Turner, Carol Smillie, Dale Winton, Bob Monkhouse [as 85]

Mystic Meg [as 85]

Animated Hand of God
A feature of the initial television ads for the Lottery.

Squirt cider in your ears
See *Guys and Dolls*.

113
Public school
Private, fee-paying.

Nescafé [as 32]

114
Daily Comet [as 85]

Hello! [as 110]

118
Monstrous snarl and glowing red eyes
See 'Where the Bodies Are Buried'.

Wimpy Bar
UK chain of hamburger restaurants, named after the character in the *Popeye* cartoons. Superceded by the arrival of American-style fast food chains in the 1980s. But they're still hanging in there, even if my local Wimpy closed down and was replaced significantly by a Starbuck's.

Shinbone
The town where Liberty Valance was shot.

Jaguar [as 6]

Petrol tank
Gas tank.

Rugby [as 7]

121
Tom Robinson
Wrote the gay pride anthem 'Glad to Be Gay' in 1977. He briefly went through the absurd indignity of being harried by the tabloid press for having a long-term relationship with the woman he later married and had children with. In case the reference here, filtered through an embittered and cynical character, is ambiguous, it should be noted that Robinson strikes me as a genuinely decent, even heroic, public figure.

Poll tax [as 24]

WPC [as 61]

Dixon of Dock Green
In the UK, the BBC-TV series *Dixon of Dock Green* (1955–76) manages to be the equivalent of both *Dragnet* and *The Andy Griffith Show* at once a reassuring police procedural about how crime is swiftly beaten and a family fantasy about the caring, fatherly copper. George Dixon (Jack Warner), who was shot dead in the feature film (*The Blue Lamp*) from which the show spun off but resurrected for a long run, epitomises the image of the bobby on the beat.

'Tomorrow Belongs to Me'
The second most famous Nazi anthem ever written by Jews (after 'Springtime for Hitler'), this John Kander and Fred Ebb number from *Cabaret* was most remembered at the time this scene takes place for a performance on the satirical puppet show *Spitting Image* in which a newly-reelected Thatcher government sang it to an effect more chilling than comic.

Refuseniks
Those who refused to pay the community charge/Poll Tax as a protest.

New Labour [as 54]

126
Reggie Perrin [as 67]

Wetlands [as 57]

127
P.E. [as 3]

Top of the Form
Radio and TV children's quiz show.

Make-your-mind-up-time
Catch-phrase of Hughie Green, host of the long-running ITV 'talent' show *Opportunity Knocks*.

128
Galtieri [as 14]

Goose Green
Site of battle during the retaking of the Falklands in 1982.

129
Black Monday
19 October 1987.

The City [as 55]

Negative equity [as 66]

131
Black Monday [as 29]

132
Mystic Meg [as 85]

Bob Monkhouse
Lottery presenter. Long-time UK-TV (and film and radio) personality, recently a surprise cult figure as the voice of Mr Hell on *Aaaagh! It's the Mr Hell Show*.

134
Postman Pat [as 67]

How to Steal a Diamond in Four Un-Easy Lessons
UK release title of the 1972 caper movie *The Hot Rock*.

The char
Charlady, domestic servant.

Top of the Pops [as 12]

137
CSEs
Certificate of Secondary Education.

Captain Mainwaring
Pompous, inept bank manager/home guard officer played by Arthur Lowe in the sit-com *Dad's Army*.

Make-your-mind-up-time [as 127]

144
Girl Guides
UK equivalent of Girl Scouts.

Bob Monkhouse [as 136]

Abba [as 6]

Mystic Meg [as 85]

145
WPC [as 61]

147
CID
Criminal Investigation Division; the rough equivalent of a Major Crimes Unit.

Deselection
The process whereby a politician holding public office is replaced by his or her party as a candidate at the next election; it's a particularly humiliating way of lame-ducking someone who refuses to resign gracefully.

The *Comet on Sunday*
Derek Leech's Sunday tabloid.

Tony Blair [as 67]

148
Club Whoopee [as 66]

Reggie Perrin [as 67]

150
Char [as 134]

Benefits
Welfare.

DHSS [as 29]

England lost the Cup Final in 1966
See: 'The Germans Won' in my collection *Unforgivable Stories*.

The *Star Trek* episode in which Spock has a beard
'Mirror, Mirror'.

Jeffrey Hunter
Captain Pike in 'The Cage' aka 'The Menagerie'.

Sausage toad
Sausages or sausage-meat cooked in Yorkshire pudding, also known as toad-in-the-hole. No amphibians are actually involved.

152
Arthur Mullard
Gravel-voiced cockney character actor, most often seen as comic criminal dimwits (*Two-Way Stretch*, *The Wrong Arm of the Law*, *Vault of Horror*).

Moose Malloy
The hulking thug in Raymond Chandler's *Farewell, My Lovely* – played by

Ward Bond, Mike Mazurki and Jack O'Hallorann in various films.

WPC [as 61]

CID [as 147]

154
Bob Monkhouse [as 136]

Arthur and Guinevere
Randomising machines used by the National Lottery, which was then operated by a company called Camelot.

157
Snowdonia [as 34]

Match of the Day
A long-time BBC-TV Saturday evening fixture, this show selects several of the many football matches played on Saturday afternoon and screens them with the duller stretches edited out. Struggling these days thanks to live, unedited football matches on many cable sports channels.

159
Shinbone [as 118]

160
Toss off
Masturbate.

162
Crazy-paving
Jigsaw-like arrangement of irregular slates or tiles, used for patios or garden paths.

163
Snowdonia [as 34]

Doc Martens
Boots favoured by fashionable hardnuts.

Bogs
Toilets.

A game of potatoes
You know the drill: one-potato, two-potato, three-potato, four…

Bounty bars
Coconut-filled chocolate.

Sweets
Candy.

165
Council tenant
In the 1980s, the Thatcher government allowed tenants of council-owned houses to buy the properties; one effect of this was a drastic reduction in the availability of affordable public housing.

South-West Gas
In *The Quorum*, Candy is told as a teenager at a séance that she will work for the gas company.

The City [as 55]

WPC [as 61]

Black Monday [as 29]

167
Bob Monkhouse [as 136]

169
Q
Glossy music monthly.

Top of the Pops [as 12]

Daily Telegraph [as 32]

170
Hallam Moseley
Star bowler of the Somerset county cricket side in the late 1970s.

171
Utility belt
Batman's gadget-filled apparel; sometimes, it seemed as if he was likely to keep an autogiro in there.

174
Queen's evidence
UK equivalent of state's evidence.

Rugby scrum
Six blokes interlocked and holding each other's buttocks struggling to control an ovoid ball with their feet.

175
You nut Sean
You head-butt Sean.

Goolies
Testicles.

The nick
Jail.

178
Real Records
A Derek Leech Company.

180
Derek Leech [as 55]

181
Dabs
Fingerprints.

183
TV Times
ITV's listings magazine, far more tabloidy than the BBC's *Radio Times*.

Blu-tack
Putty-like adhesive material used in place of thumbtacks.

185
Crazy-paving [as 162]

186
Holloway
Women's prison.

188
Biro [as 67]

191
Financial Times
Daily national newspaper, printed on distinctive pink paper, with an especial bias towards business and money matters.

Sedgwater Herald [as 74]

192
The Admiral Benbow Inn

Site of the marvellous opening chapter of *Treasure Island*.

201
Anton Diffring
German character actor, typecast as Nazis. He was in *The Colditz Story* and *Where Eagles Dare*.

203
Muttley
Dick Dastardly's sidekick in the TV cartoon show *Wacky Races*; his distinctive grumbling sounds like 'rassin frassin grassin Dick Dastardly!'

206
Twix
Biscuit-chocolate-and-toffee bars, sold in packs of two.

209
Biro [as 67]

217
Daily Comet [as 85]

Sally Rhodes
See: 'Mother Hen', 'Twitch Technicolor', 'Gargantuabots vs the Nice Mice', 'Organ Donors', *The Quorum* and *Seven Stars*.

223
Tossing off [as 160]

235
Yomping [as 14]

Myra Hindley
With Ian Brady, one of the so-called Moors Murderers, among the most despicable of British serial killers. They abducted, tortured and killed children.

238
Lord Lucan
A peer who disappeared in 1974, suspected of the murder of his children's nanny. It is assumed that he either disposed of himself invisibly or became an international fugitive. Legally, he is presumed deceased.

Queen's evidence [as 174]

Comet on Sunday [as 147]

WPC [as 61]

Doc Martens [as 163]

239
Bobby Moore
Captain of the world-cup-winning England football team of 1966.

246
The Man From B.U.N.G.L.E.
Character in the British comic *Smash*.

Porridge
UK slang: time in prison.

247
WPC [as 61]

249
Transhumance
This brand of Swiss crop rotation is seared into my generation's brain by
geography O levels.

251
Lord Lucan [as 238]

Iain Scobie
See 'Where the Bodies Are Buried 3: Black and White and Red All Over'.

252
'Nellie the Elephant' [as 40]

256
GBH
UK police abbreviation: grievous bodily harm.

268
Broadmoor
An institution for the criminally insane.

Iain Scobie [as 251]

Dennis Nilsen and Peter Sutcliffe
UK serial killers; Sutcliffe is known as the Yorkshire Ripper. Apparently,
they really do argue about what television channels to watch.

The God slot [as 80]

Good books
Killing for Company, Brian Masters, about Nilsen; '...*Somebody's Husband,*

Somebody's Son', Gordon Burn, about Sutcliffe.

Michael Eaton
Screenwriter of the underrated *Fellow Traveler* and occasional contributor to *Sight & Sound* magazine. As a writer for television, he does specialise in true crime drama: *The Tragedy of Flight 103* (the Lockerbie crash), *The Flowers of the Forest* (a child abuse panic) and *Shipman* (the serial killer doctor). We can assume that Keith's feelings about *Mountaintop* are coloured by personal involvement, since Eaton's work is remarkably tactful and insightful in a genre rarely distinguished by those qualities.

269
Orienteering
The practice of being dropped in a wilderness and making your way out using only a map; once a common school afternoon-off exercise, a holdover from the days when British boys' schools worked some sort of military training (ROTC – Royal Officer Training Corps) into the syllabus.

274
New Labour [as 54]

276
Treated privately, of course
Outside the National Health Service. Though NHS care is provided for all British citizens, those who can afford it can opt out and pay for supposedly higher-quality medical treatment.

279
The Man From B.U.N.G.L.E. [as 246]

281
Snowdonia [as 34]

294
E-bomb
In this alternate timeline, such things are possible; in our real world, 2001 has come and gone without it. In my defence, Neal Stephenson, who is a lot more clued-up about computers than I am, posited exactly the same thing in his *Cryptonomicon*, which is set *before* 2001.

296
Iain Scobie [as 251]

297
Tony Blair [as 67]

The Spice Girls [as 85]

ACKNOWLEDGEMENTS

Thanks are due to Pete and Dana Atkins, Janies Bacon, Sarah Biggs, Anne Billson, Eugene Byrne, Susan Byrne, Pat Cadigan, Jacquie Clare, John Clute, Loretta Culbert, Julie Davies, Meg Davis, Alex Dunn, Dennis and Kris Etchison, Martin Feeney, Leslie Felperin, Jo Fletcher, Martin Fletcher, Christopher Fowler, Neil Gaiman, Paula Grainger, Charlie Grant, Antony Harwood, Rob Holdstock, Steve Jones, Rodney Jones, Karen Krizanovich, Chris Manby, Dave Mathew, Paul McAuley, Maura McHugh, Silja Muller, Bryan and Julia Newman, Sasha and Jerome Newman, Marcelle Perks, David Pringle, Geoff Ryman, David Schow, Adam Simon, Helen Simpson, Millie Simpson, Dean Skilton, Mandy Slater, Brian Smedley, Michael Marshall Smith, Graham Watkins, Doug Winter.

THE QUORUM

by KIM NEWMAN

In 1961, Derek Leech emerges fully formed from the polluted River Thames, destined to found a global media empire. In 1978, three ambitious young men strike a deal with Leech. They are offered wealth, glamour, and success, but a price must be paid. In 1994, Leech's purpose moves to its conclusion, and as the men struggle, they realize to truth of the ultimate price.

A brand-new edition of the critically acclaimed novel featuring five short stories by the award-winning author.

"'Fans of 'Deal with the Devil' stories ought to be delighted with this fifth novel from British horror writer Newman, which brings a new twist or two to the genre." *Publishers Weekly*

"This well-told tale is peopled with a fascinating array of characters and offers much witty and sage commentary on our materialistic society." *Library Journal*

"Newman's postmodern morality play puts him into the first rank of current horror novelists." *Booklist*

JAGO

by KIM NEWMAN

In the tiny English village of Alder, dreams and nightmares are beginning to come true. Creatures from local legend, science fiction and the dark side of the human mind prowl the town.

Paul, a young academic composing a thesis about the end of the world, and his girlfriend Hazel, a potter, have come to Alder for the summer. Their idea of a rural retreat gradually sours as the laws of nature begin to break down around them. Paul and Hazel are soon drawn into a vortex of fear as violent chaos engulfs the community and the village prepares to reap a harvest of horror.

A brand-new edition of the critically acclaimed novel. This edition also contains the short stories 'Ratting', 'Great Western' and 'The Man on the Clapham Omnibus'.

"A roaring good read." *The Times*

"Newman's prose is sophisticated and his narrative drive irresistible." *Publishers Weekly*

TITANBOOKS.COM

ANNO DRACULA: JOHNNY ALUCARD

by KIM NEWMAN

It is 1976 and Kate Reed is on the set of Francis Ford Coppola's movie *Dracula*. She helps a young vampire boy, Ion Popescu, who leaves Transylvania for America. In the States, Popescu becomes Johnny Pop and attaches himself to Andy Warhol, inventing a new drug which confers vampire powers on its users...

Kim Newman returns to one of the bestselling vampire tales of the modern era in this brand-new novel in his acclaimed *Anno Dracula* series.

THIS LONG-AWAITED SEQUEL SHOULD NOT BE MISSED